I0588065

College life 501;

Post-Grad Management

J.B. Vample

Book Nine

The College Life Series

COLLEGE LIFE 501-Post-Grad Management

Printed in the United States of America

First Printing, 2021

ISBN: 978-1-7374279-19 (eBook edition)
ISBN: 978-1-7374279-0-2 (Paperback edition)

For information contact; email: info@jbvample.com

Website: www.jbvample.com

Book cover design by: Najla Qamber Designs

To my readers.

I can't thank you enough for all of the love that you've shown this series. Thank you for giving my writing a chance, and for taking the journey with these characters.

Even though this series has come to an end, I hope that these characters and their stories will still hold a special place in your heart.

I appreciate you all.

Chapter 1

Sidra Howard took a sip of her seltzer water with lemon as she cradled her cell phone to her ear. "I still can't believe you're getting married," she gushed, a bright smile on her face. "The third one to tie the knot," she chuckled. "I know right? It'll be here before you know it… Like I said before, just tell me what you need me to do and I'll take care of it. No problem." Sidra looked up when someone approached her table. "Sorry, I have to go… I'll call you when I get home… Okay, bye."

Hanging up, she smiled up at the man who had sat down across from her. "Hey."

James Grant smiled back. "Hey," he returned. "How long have you been waiting?"

Sidra glanced at the silver watch on her slender wrist. "Fifteen minutes." Pushing some of her long, brown, softly curled hair behind her ear, she looked back at him, "Should I leave?"

James shrugged. "Eh, give it another few minutes," he advised. "Traffic could've been bad."

"True, the expressway *is* ridiculous at this time," Sidra agreed. "Thanks for agreeing to do this tonight. I know you have a lot going on."

James put a hand up. "It's fine, there are some idiots out here. So, anything I can do to help you weed them out, I'll do," he chortled. "Besides, I wanted to check in on you anyway."

Sidra sipped her beverage. "*For?*" she wondered.

"I wanted to see if you've given anymore thought to the conversation that we had the other day," James replied.

Sidra tilted her head. *I knew he was going to bring this up.* "I *have* given it thought James," she replied. "And as much as I *appreciate* your career advice… I'm fine where I am *now*. I'm fine doing what I'm currently *doing*."

James squinted. "Sidra, you're a paralegal," he pointed out. Sidra rolled her eyes.

"I know that you're an *excellent* one, don't get me wrong." James amended, putting a hand up.

"*I'd* like to think so," Sidra said, confident.

James nodded and continued. "But Sidra, you graduated top of your law class, passed the bar, and even *interned* with my law firm during your last year of law school."

Sidra fiddled with a bracelet on her wrist. "I *know* that—"

"*Yet*, when we offered you a position as a junior associate after you graduated, you turned it down in favor of taking a paralegal position at another firm." James eyed her intently. "To be honest, I still don't get *why*."

Sidra let out a sigh; this was not the first conversation that she'd had with James over her career path. As much as she dreaded it, she knew it would not be the last. Not only was James her friend, he was her mentor. "James—"

James put a hand up. "Listen, this isn't about you working at another firm; if you'd taken a junior associate position *anywhere*, I'd be happy," James corrected. "I see so much potential in you and in my opinion, it's being wasted."

Sidra sighed. "It's not being *wasted*, James" she assured. "I just... I just want to get as much experience as I *can* before moving forward in my career as an attorney."

"Sidra, you're more than qualified. You deserve to advance," James insisted, sincere. "You deserve to be in a *courtroom*."

Sidra stared at him. *Can you just drop this already?* Relief set in when James's phone beeped. While she appreciated him taking such an interest in her career, she wasn't in the mood to discuss it any longer.

James quickly retrieved his phone from his pants pocket and looked at it. "Ah, *speaking* of a courtroom," he mentioned, reading a text. "One of my court appointments has been moved up."

Sidra was deep in thought. So much so, that she'd tuned James out for a moment. "I'm sorry, what did you say?" she asked, snapping out of it.

James chuckled. "It's not important."

Sidra nodded. "From the look on your face, I would've thought that it was Joyce," she said, folding her arms on the tabletop.

James chuckled. "No, I spoke to my lovely wife right before I came in." He returned the phone to his pocket.

Sidra gave a nod. "How is she?"

"Ready for it all to be over," James chortled. "I tell you, we're excited about the baby, but she is *not* a fan of being pregnant."

Sidra giggled a bit. "Sounds like one of my dear friends," she mentioned. "And it's not who you'd *think*."

James laughed; Sidra shook her head in amusement. Though she and James had ended their year and a half relationship over five years ago, they had managed to become great friends. He was the first friendly face that had greeted her when she'd moved to California after graduating Paradise Valley University.

"You know James, I'm really happy for you," Sidra said sincerely. "I told you when you and Joyce first met that you would be perfect together."

James smiled back. "Thank you, I appreciate that." He leaned back in his seat. "I wish the same happiness for *you*."

Sidra waved a dismissive hand at him. "Ah, I'm perfectly fine just dating." Seeing a familiar face walk in, she signaled for James to get up. "Okay, you remember the drill?"

"Yep, pushing hair behind your ear, he's okay and I can leave," he remembered. "Playing with your necklace, get you out of it."

"Appreciate you," Sidra laughed, quickly grabbing a pocket mirror from her handbag. She gave a quick glance to her pretty, brown skinned reflection.

James tapped the table. "You look fine, good luck."

"Thank you," Sidra said at James's departing back. Having decided to jump back into the dating pool after a long drought, Sidra needed all the help that she could get. James often played lookout while she felt out potentials.

The tall, brown skinned, suit clad man took a seat at Sidra's table, unbuttoning his jacket in the process. "You look pretty," he grinned.

Sidra offered a smile back. "Thank you, Rick," she replied, polite. "Was the traffic bad?"

Rick shrugged. "Not really, just got held up in a meeting," he returned, nonchalant. "But that happens when you're as sought after as *I* am." He leaned back in his seat. "Everybody wants my time."

Sidra resisted the urge to roll her eyes at his arrogance. *Not even going to apologize for being late, huh? How nice.* "Uh huh."

"But I told them, 'look, I have a sexy woman waiting for me, so I have to go'," he laughed.

"Uh huh," Sidra repeated, dry. "You actually said that to your bosses?"

"Well...no," he admitted. "But I was *thinking* it, because let's face it. You *are* sexy."

Sidra stared blankly. *Boy, come on with this wack ass interaction.* "I appreciate the compliment."

Rick gazed at her longingly. "You know what?" he prompted.

"What?" Sidra asked, tone dry.

"This place is kind of tired, what do you say we get out of here?"

"*You just* got here," Sidra pointed out, trying her best to remain polite. "And wasn't it *you* who recommended it?"

Rick gave a hard shrug. "I changed my mind." He pushed his seat back. "I know someplace *much* better. A lot fancier, and has the potential to have more excitement."

Sidra folded her arms. "And where would *that* be?"

He winked at her. "*My* place."

Sidra's grey eyes widened as she grabbed the silver chain around her neck. In her haste and irritation, she yanked it, causing it to pop.

"Oh, you broke your necklace," Rick observed.

"Yeah, looks like I *did*," she spat back, observing the broken clasp.

"I can buy you another one."

"No, I can buy my own, thank you," she quickly put out.

Before Rick could say anything else, James darted up to the

table. "Sidra, I'm glad I ran into you, Joyce is in labor," he blurted out in a panic.

"Oh my God, really? Let's go," Sidra quickly replied, grabbing her purse and standing up.

Confusion set in on Rick's face. "You're leaving?"

"Yes," Sidra confirmed. She grabbed some money from her purse and dropped it on the table. "For my seltzer. Bye."

Sidra hurried out of the restaurant with James without looking back. When they got outside, James slowed his pace. "Why are you stopping?" she asked, bewildered. "You need to get to the hospital."

"She's not really in labor," James revealed.

"*Really*? You're using your unborn baby as a 'get-Sidra-out-of-her-date' excuse?" she sneered.

James laughed. "It was the first thing that I thought of." He looked at his watch. "*Speaking* of her, I need to pick up dinner and head home."

Sidra adjusted the purse strap on her shoulder. "Okay, thanks again for your help."

"Anytime. Where's your car?"

"Wherever the valet took it," Sidra joked, handing the valet worker her ticket.

James nodded. "Gotcha, need me to wait with you?"

Sidra shook her head. "I'm fine James, go home to your wife," she urged.

James gave her a soft pat on her arm, then walked off.

Sidra took a deep breath as she felt the gentle warm breeze brush past her. Even though it was evening in early September, the summer weather was still prevalent, typical for the west coast.

As the valet brought the car around, she ran her hand through her hair. *Another complete waste of my time. I would've been better off in bed with a carton of ice cream.*

Sitting at her dining room table, Chasity Adams stared at the laptop in front of her, confusion and agitation on her light brown face. "What in the entire fuck is she *talking* about?" she griped to herself. Grabbing her cell phone from the table, she dialed a number and put it to her ear.

"Hi, it's Chasity...did you see that email from—yeah, *that.* *What* does she *want?*" Chasity pinched the bridge of her nose as she tried to keep the frustration out of her voice. Talking to her manager in even the smallest doses often made her temper rise. "*You* don't know *either*, huh?" Chasity spat. *I knew I shouldn't have opened this goddamn email when I got home.* "I'll call her tomorrow when I get to the office... No, I can*not* do it now, I'll do it *tomorrow.*" Chasity hung up her phone and tossed it back on the table. "I hate these fuckin' people," she complained, putting her face in her hands.

As the lead web designer of a major online development company in Philadelphia, Chasity was often bombarded with the most difficult clients — ones who did not hesitate to email her every single change that they got, with no regard for her after work hours.

Hearing her phone ring, she sighed and picked it up. "Yeah?" she spat.

A deep chuckle came through the phone. "Damn, who pissed you off?"

"My fuckin' job...as usual," she griped, running her hand through her long black hair.

"You're still at work? I thought you said you were gonna try to leave on time this week."

"No, I've been home for a while, but made the mistake of checking my damn emails," Chasity answered.

Jason Adams shook his head, though her tone didn't surprise him. Being with Chasity for seven and a half years, married for four of them, he knew her moods well. "You want to go out to dinner when I get home?" he placated.

"You mean after nine when they finally let you go?" Chasity threw back.

"Touché," Jason chuckled.

"Besides, I had a long day. I'm too mentally drained to go anywhere," she said.

"I hear you baby," Jason sympathized. He too knew the feeling.

Chasity let out a heavy sigh as she ran a hand through her hair again. "I'll just make us something."

"Okay. I really *do* hope to get out of here soon," Jason said, typing on his office computer. "They got me working on this new software project."

"If it's anything like the *last* project you worked on, you'll be there all night."

Jason let out a loud sigh. "I swear to God, I *hope* not," he griped.

Chasity leaned back in her seat. "You want us to drop some dinner off to you later?"

"I appreciate that but no, you relax," he declined. "Love you."

"Love you too."

Hanging up her phone, Chasity turned her laptop off and headed for the refrigerator. She opened it and stared at its contents. Rubbing her eyes, she tried to figure out what to cook, but was too tired. She closed the door. "Fuck it, I'll order a pizza," she muttered to herself.

A knock at the front door pulled her from her dinner plans. Looking through the peep hole, Chasity smiled. It was the first time that she'd smiled since leaving for work that morning. Opening the door, she came face to face with a little girl, held up high by an older gentleman.

"I knew I recognized that little hazel eye," Chasity mused.

"You *should*, it looks just like *yours*," the gentleman chuckled.

Chasity smirked as she held her arms out; she let out a breath when the little girl leapt into her arms. "Girl, I told you about jumping on me," she chortled.

The smiling, dark haired, light-skinned child gave Chasity a big hug. "I missed you Mommy," she spoke.

"Missed you too, mi hija," Chasity returned. She looked at the man standing in the doorway. "Dad, stop standing there looking like a creep. You can come in," she offered.

Derrick Parker let out a laugh. "Was just waiting for the invitation," he replied, walking in and shutting the door.

"How was she?" Chasity asked, adjusting her daughter's weight on her hip. A little hand started playing in her hair; Chasity moved it behind her shoulder and out of reach.

"Perfect, as usual," Derrick gushed. "But I wouldn't expect

anything *less* from my granddaughter."

"Uh huh, what did she con you into buying her *this* time?" Chasity asked.

Derrick shrugged.

"Mommy, look what Pop-Pop got me?" the four-year-old said, grabbing both her mother and grandfather's attention.

Chasity looked at her. "What did Pop-Pop get you?"

"A kitty!" she bellowed, excited.

Chasity glanced down at the little white stuffed kitten, dressed in a pink tutu, in her daughters' hand. She looked at her father, a phony smile on her face. "Oh, you got *another* kitty," she directed at Derrick, who snickered.

"Yes, I'm gonna name her Princess Kitty," she added, excited.

"*And* you're naming her Princess Kitty, like the five *other* Princess Kitty's that you have," Chasity continued, still staring at her father.

Derrick put his hands up. "Her eyes lit up when she saw it," he explained, "You know I can't say 'no' to her."

"You should try it," Chasity jeered. "It's not as hard as you think." She looked back at her daughter, who was busy playing with her new toy. "Kayla, why don't you take Princess Kitty to your room and introduce her to her new friends." Chasity set the little girl down on the floor.

"Okay."

Chasity watched as Kayla took off running for the stairs. "Dad, if you buy her any more of them damn stuffed cats, I'm gonna pack them all up and ship them to *your* house in New York," she warned. "Along with all those damn outfits she has for them."

Derrick laughed. "I was actually thinking about getting her a *real* kitten."

Chasity shot him a warning look. "Don't play with me." She headed for the kitchen, her father trailing after her. "I'll ship *it* to you *too*."

"Listen, thanks for letting me get her for the weekend," Derrick said, leaning against the counter. "I know that I was supposed to bring her back yesterday, but it got late and—"

"Dad, it's fine," Chasity cut in. "Jase and I already said it was okay that she spent the extra night."

"Yeah, but I know that Jason's parents or Trisha usually get her on weekdays while you both work—"

"Do *you* want to get her on weekdays?" Chasity cut in.

"Wish I *could*, but it would be a hell of a commute from New York back here to West Chester every day," her father chortled. "I'll settle for weekends."

"True," Chasity agreed, grabbing a small bottle of juice from the refrigerator.

"Did you at least get to sleep in late yesterday?" Derrick asked.

Chasity gave him a knowing look. "What the hell is *sleep?*" she jeered. "Please, I was up working."

Derrick watched as Chasity sipped her drink. "Job stressing you?"

"Don't wanna talk about it," she shot down, setting the bottle on the counter.

Derrick raised his hands up in surrender. "Okay, subject change to something you'll like," he proposed.

Chasity gestured for him to speak.

He smiled a big smile. "I think Kayla loves New York."

"That wouldn't be surprising," Chasity replied, leaning against the counter. "She likes noise."

Derrick chuckled. "Yeah, I took her through Times Square and—"

"You didn't let anybody from that horde touch my baby, did you?" Chasity spat. She wasn't a fan of New York; it was too crowded for her liking.

"Not at all," Derrick promised, amused. "We went to a movie, out to eat, and I took her on a horse and carriage ride." *Everything that I should've done with you when you were little.*

Chasity stared at him; he was beaming as he spoke of the time spent with his granddaughter. "I'm sure she enjoyed that," she replied, folding her arms. "You heading back tonight?"

Derrick nodded. "Yeah." he glanced at his watch. "Maybe I'll stop by and visit your mother first."

"Yeah, you do that and catch a pan to the face," Chasity joked, earning a laugh from Derrick.

"I guess she's still upset with me over Kayla's birthday

party, huh?" he wondered, amused.

Chasity waved her hand. "Probably, among *other* things. I don't have time to keep up with y'all nonsense."

"Noted," Derrick said, rubbing his chin. "Is she still with that—"

"No time for it," Chasity cut in, having an inkling of what he was trying to ask about.

Derrick put his hands up again. "Do you mind if I get Kayla again in two weeks? I'd love to take her to see a play."

"Dad, that hyper four-year-old will talk *all through* that play...and *loudly*...about *cats*," Chasity replied.

"I'm sure she'll be perfect," he beamed.

"We'll see," Chasity said.

"Fair enough," Derrick resolved, shoving a hand into his pocket. "Okay, I should probably get going," he said.

"See you," she returned. Derrick stood there like he was waiting for something. Chasity caught his gaze. "Yes?"

"Thought I'd be able to get a hug from you today."

Keeping the promise that he'd made to Chasity five years ago when she had revealed that she was pregnant, Derrick had maintained a great relationship with his granddaughter. Being in her life the way that he wasn't for Chasity, growing up. Their relationship seemed to satisfy Chasity, and even forced her to communicate more with him because of Kayla, which he was grateful for. But Derrick still wanted to form a relationship with his *daughter* as well; something that she was still fighting him on.

Chasity just looked at him. Her silence was the answer he didn't want to hear. Resolved, he tapped his hand on the countertop. "Okay then, see you soon."

Chasity followed Derrick's progress out the door, "Yeah," she muttered. Letting out a sigh, she opened a drawer in search of a takeout menu.

"Damn this is some good ass candy," Malajia Simmons-Johnson muttered in between chews. Sitting in her car with a cell phone to her ear, she stuffed the last piece of the candy bar into her mouth. She chewed quickly and loudly, in complete disregard for the person on the other end of the phone.

"Girl, why are you smacking so loud?" The female voice complained.

"I'm tryna eat my candy bar before I go in the house," Malajia explained to her sister. "You know as soon as they see food, they pounce like freakin' animals."

Geri's giggle came through the line. "Understood…we still on for lunch tomorrow?"

"You paying?" Malajia asked, turning her car off and gathering her belongings.

"Um *no*," Geri answered.

"Then *no*, bitch," Malajia barked back. She laughed when her sister's yells started coming through the line. "I'm joking, I'll have to see though." She grabbed a pizza box from the passenger seat and stepped out of the car. "I gotta go, call me later."

"Very well," Geri returned, ending the call.

Malajia adjusted her purse over her shoulder, closing the car door with her hip. "I swear to God, if this damn place is a mess, I'm moving out," she mumbled to herself as she headed up to the front door of her house.

Unlocking the door, she pushed it open only to be greeted by a pillow tossed at the wall. "Seriously?" she spat out.

Twin dark skinned boys darted up to her, yelling incoherently at the same time. Malajia put a hand up. "Hey, hey! I told y'all about talking to me at the same time," she barked.

"Mommy, Marvin hit me with a ratable-taste," one little boy sputtered.

Malajia looked at the other boy, a stern look on her face. "Marvin did you hit your brother with a—" her head snapped back to the other boy, confusion on her face. "Wait Marlon, you said he hit you with a *what*?"

"A ratable-taste," Marlon answered.

Malajia stared at the boy for several seconds. *They're only three years old, don't curse,* she told herself. "Son…*what* is a ratable-taste?" she slowly asked.

Both boys pointed their little fingers at the toy lizard that was laying on the floor. She glanced at the lizard, then back at the boys. Her sons were staring at her, eyes wide.

Malajia pinched the bridge of her nose and let out a sigh. "I can't," she mumbled. "Stop hitting each other with stuff, I told y'all about that." Her tone was stern, "Marvin, tell your brother sorry."

"Sorry," Marvin mumbled.

"Now hug him," Malajia ordered. She shook her head when the brothers embraced.

"Where's Daddy?" They both pointed at the kitchen. "Go put your toys away, the living room is a mess," she ordered.

In the kitchen, Malajia found her husband. His back was turned as he stood in front of the open freezer, oblivious of her presence. She smirked and slammed her hand on the counter. "Hey!"

Mark Johnson spun around, spoon hanging out of his mouth and a carton of ice cream in his hands. "I ain't got nothin'!" he bellowed. He shook his head when Malajia started laughing. "Real funny," he sneered, closing the freezer.

Malajia set the pizza down on the table. "Is this what you're doing now? Eating in the fridge?"

"Yo, those boys are greedy for no *reason*," Mark jeered. "I have to sneak food. If it wasn't for them acting like fools in the living room, they stalkin' asses would've heard me open the freezer and came running."

Malajia leaned over the counter. "Are you *really* surprised that they're greedy?" she asked, pushing her long, curled brown hair over her shoulders. "They're *your* boys."

"Last time I checked, we're *both* greedy, so don't blame their appetite only on *me*," Mark returned, setting the ice cream on the counter.

"Touché," Malajia smirked. "You just getting in from work?"

"Yeah, about ten minutes before you got here." Mark moved around the counter and gave her a kiss. "What did the doctor say about your back?" he wondered.

Malajia gave her lower back a rub. "That I need to stop picking up those heavy boys of ours," she chuckled. "I'm okay though."

Mark shot her a sympathetic look. He had felt a bit panicked when Malajia had called him at work to let him know that she was heading to the doctor because her back was hurting. "I think I need to give you a massage," he offered.

"Or send me to a spa for a *real* one," she threw back. She chucked at the insulted look on his face.

"You got a problem with *my* massages?" he frowned.

"No, but I think the point is for me to *not* end up with dick in me after ten minutes of a rubdown," Malajia countered; Mark snickered.

"Touché," Mark laughed. "Want me to take care of dinner?"

"Already did, behold the pizza box," she said, waving her hand over the pizza box on the counter.

Mark opened the box, taking out a slice.

"So umm…why are your sons calling a toy lizard a ratable-taste?" she asked him as he took a bite of his pizza.

Mark nearly spat out his piece of pizza from laughter. "Yo, they funny as shit," he howled. "They make up their own names for stuff, I swear. The other day I heard them call that owl saltshaker that my grandmother gave us, an Ollie."

"Ollie as in *owl*?!" Malajia belted out. When Mark nodded, she couldn't help but laugh. "Anyway, how was work?"

"Fine actually," he said. "I didn't do much, which I can't complain about."

Malajia played with a piece of paper towel on the counter as she gave a nod. "Oh okay."

Mark stared at her. "You look tired."

"I *am*," she admitted. "I didn't get much sleep last night. and the boys had me running after them all day. Then I had to drive to Geri's house and practically drag that damn babysitter of ours out by her braids so she could watch the kids while I went to my appointment," she vented. "Luckily she was spending the night with Geri, or I would've been mad as shit dragging the boys with me."

"I told you I would've called my mom to come watch them," Mark said.

"And make her drive up here from Delaware?" Malajia pointed out. "Nah, Dana owe me unlimited babysitting jobs *anyway* for all the shit she put me through when we were younger," she yawned.

Mark rubbed her shoulder. "Go relax babe."

Malajia rolled her eyes. "*Can't* relax when the house is a damn mess and the twins are running around throwing lizards at each other," she grunted. "Dana is a damn pushover, she just let them do what the hell they want."

"Yeah, she ran out of here as soon as I stepped foot through the door," he chortled. "I offered to take her back to Geri's—"

"That girl ain't going back over Geri's, she going somewhere to be a hoe," Malajia sneered of her soon to be nineteen-year-old sister.

Mark winced. "*I'll* deal with the boys, and clean up the mess," he offered. "Go and watch that show that we recorded last night."

"Okay." Malajia stretched. "I'm gonna take a bath first. I'll wait for you so we can watch it together. I know you wanted to see it too," she replied, grabbing a slice of pizza.

"That's okay, you can just watch it," Mark quickly declined, looking down at the countertop. "...I'll catch it after I get the boys settled."

Malajia stared at him, narrowing her eyes, "You watched it already without me, *didn't* you?"

Mark put his hands up. "I can explain."

Malajia slapped her hand on the counter. "Damn it Mark, you were supposed to wait for me!"

"I watched it on my phone at work," he explained. "Sorry...it was a good episode too."

Malajia sucked her teeth and walked away.

"Babe, I'm sorry," he called after her, amusement in his voice.

"Yeah? That's why I already saw that movie that you wanted to see," she threw back.

"Damn it!" Mark bellowed, stomping his foot on the floor.

"Ooh, Daddy said a curse word!" one of the boys shouted

from the living room.

"Mind your business son," Mark grunted.

Emily Harris wiped the blackboard clean with an eraser, then stacked some papers on her desk. Seeing a spot, she glanced at it. "How did jelly get on my desk?" she muttered to herself. Grabbing a napkin from a small box, she proceeded to wipe the sticky substance away.

Hearing a soft knock, she glanced up. "Come in," she called. She smiled when she saw who it was. "Hi Anthony," she beamed.

"Hi Miss Emily," the seven-year-old, brown skinned boy smiled back, adjusting his book bag on his shoulder.

Emily signaled for him to come to her. "What can I do for you, sweetie?" she asked, crouching down to meet his height. "You didn't forget your homework assignment, did you?"

Anthony shook his head. "My Dad wants to ask you about my progress," he answered.

Emily giggled. "Oh *does* he?"

Anthony nodded enthusiastically. A few seconds later, the door opened and in walked a tall, dark skinned man.

Emily stood up straight. "Hello, Mr. Palmer," she greeted.

The man smiled as he approached. "Hi Miss Harris," he returned. "I'm here to talk about my son's progress."

Emily shook her head in amusement at his huge smile. "He's progressing just *fine*, Will," she answered. "Is this how you smile at *all* of his teachers?"

Will broke into laughter, moving in and giving Emily a soft kiss on her lips. "No, just you," he promised. "You *are* the *only* future Mrs. Palmer in here."

As a second-grade teacher at Paradise Valley elementary school for the past five years, Emily had all types of fathers come into her classroom to talk about their children. But in her opinion, none of them were as handsome as her fiancé, Will Palmer.

"Dad told me to come in here and say that," Anthony revealed, trying to hop up on Emily's desk.

"Get down," Emily ordered, guiding Anthony away.

"Boy! What have I told you about jumping up on stuff?" Will barked. He pointed to a chair. "Go sit down."

Emily put her hand over her face to keep from laughing out loud.

"I'm about to put him in a sport or something. He needs to burn off that energy," Will griped.

Emily gently touched Will's arm. "He's fine," she placated. "Teacher mode really quickly, Anthony really *is* doing well in class," she said. "He's such a smart child."

"That's because you started working with him back when he was just *two*," Will beamed. "So, I give *you* the credit… He's lucky to have you as a teacher *and* as a mother."

Emily blushed. "Thank you." She waved her hand. "Okay, back to fiancé mode… How was work?" she asked, straightening out the items on her desk.

"Long," Will sighed, setting his jacket on the back of a chair. "The overtime has been kicking my ass."

Emily shot him a sympathetic look. "I know," she said.

"Well, at least the extra money is coming in handy for paying for this wedding," Will replied, rubbing his head.

Emily nodded in agreement. "Yeah…we don't have much left to pay for really," she said. "At least I don't *think* so."

Will chuckled. "Em, use my overtime money to hire a planner," he suggested.

"I don't need a planner, I can handle this," she assured with a wave of her hand. "I'm great at multitasking."

Will shrugged. "Okay, if you say so," he placated. "You want to go to the movies?"

Emily rubbed the back of her neck. "I've had a long week; can we just stay in tonight?" she requested.

"Sure," Will agreed. "My place or yours?"

"Yours… You know I still have the unwanted guest."

Will winced at the bite in Emily's voice. "Your sister still crashing on your couch, huh?"

"Unfortunately," Emily ground out. "I wish I could put her out like everyone *else* has… but—"

"She's your sister," Will finished, understanding.

"*Unfortunately*," Emily grunted.

"She's only there because you have your own place. If you would move in with *me*—"

"And I will, *after* we're married," Emily said. Will put his hands up in surrender. "Anyway, I'm looking forward to my weekend trip up to Jersey in two weeks… I'm gonna tell Mommy all about her lazy, annoying ass daughter."

Will chuckled. "That's a good topic of discussion while you're going over wedding details," he joked.

Emily put her hand over her face. "I am banning wedding talk from my mom when I go up there," she ground out. "That's all she talks about."

"She's just excited." Will placated. "You gonna visit any of the girls while you're up that end?" He glanced at Anthony, who was doing cartwheels around the room. "Hey!"

"I wanted to show you my cool flips," Anthony explained, standing up straight.

Will smacked his palm against his forehead. "Have a *seat*," he drew out, annoyed.

Emily twisted the white gold, half karat circle solitaire diamond engagement ring on her finger. "To answer your question, I *hope* to." She pointed to Anthony, then gestured to a chair. Emily giggled when Anthony obeyed and sat down. "It's been a while since I've seen most of them. I miss them."

Will put his arm around her. "Well, here's hoping that you'll get a moment to catch up." He gave her a kiss on the cheek. "You want me to cook?"

"No, can Miss Emily cook?" Anthony blurted out.

Will stood there with a salty look on his face.

Emily laughed as she signaled Anthony to come to her. He ran over and hugged her. "I thought I told you that we don't talk about your dad's cooking in front of him," she joked, hugging him back.

"But he never uses salt," Anthony complained.

Emily busted out laughing again.

"Hey, you don't *need* salt when you use the right herbs," Will defended.

Emily winced as she turned away from him.

Will let out a loud gasp. "Wow," he muttered, earning a

snicker from his fiancé.

"Sheila, I think that the column should go on page four instead of two," Alexandra Chisolm said to a young woman.

"Yeah?" Sheila replied.

"Yes," Alex confirmed, pointing to an image on her computer monitor. "It'll flow with the other subject in that section, better."

"Okay, I'll get on that," Sheila eagerly promised. "Did the advertisers finalize their payments yet?"

"Sure did," Alex smiled. "All of the final ads have been emailed to marketing. We're almost good to go for this month's print."

Sheila nodded and smiled in return, gathering her folder from Alex's desk. "Thanks for walking me through the process again. I appreciate it."

Alex waved her hand. "Hey, what are bosses for?" she mused. "I know what it's like to be new, so trust me, I don't mind you reaching out for help."

"Thanks," Sheila reiterated. She tapped the folder in her hand. "I'll go work on this, now."

Alex nodded as Sheila scurried out of her office. Sitting back at her desk, she let out a happy sigh. Now the lead editor of a mid-size publishing firm in New York, Alex had come a long way from the broke college student who had worked at diners and pizza shops to get by.

Picking up the phone on her desk, she dialed a number. "Hi, it's Alex over in Editing, how is the website looking? Will the corrections be made before the deadline?" she asked. Alex pinched the bridge of her nose and sighed at the answer she was given. "Okay we really need to have that done... Yes, I appreciate it. Thank you, goodbye."

Hanging up the phone, Alex looked up when she heard a tap on her door. "Yes Laurie?" she said to the receptionist.

"Ms. Chisolm, you have a visitor."

"Oh?"

"Yes, a woman. Sahara?"

Alex's smile could have lit the room. "Oh! Send her in,

please." Alex stood up and made her way around her desk. She practically jumped up and down when her little sister entered, an overnight bag in her hand.

"Heeeey Miss Corporate." Sahara mused, giving Alex a hug.

"Girl, what a nice surprise," Alex beamed, parting from their long embrace. "And why didn't you call me and tell me that you were coming up?"

Sahara dropped her overnight bag on the hardwood floor and flopped down on a cream cushioned chair. "I *planned* on it, but I got back home to Philly and got all excited and distracted," she chuckled.

"Ah yes, it's been a while since you've been back there," Alex realized. "Same for me. I plan on heading back for a visit in two weeks."

"Yeah, sometimes I wonder if I should move back," Sahara pondered. "I mean, don't get me wrong, I love Virginia and I'm glad that I decided to stay after graduating college but…it ain't *Philly*."

Alex chuckled. "Yeah, I know what you mean," she agreed, leaning against her desk. "I *do* love New York though," she mused. "It's so much going on here. So much business… I'm glad that I moved here."

"Yeah 'cause I heard you were commuting on that train for a minute," Sahara teased.

"Girl, a whole damn *year*… Once I got this lead position and that money got better, I grabbed my savings and that new salary and got a damn apartment up here," Alex replied, amusement in her voice.

Sahara played with her shoulder length, brown wavy hair. "So ummm, you have the career, the place…when are you gonna get a *man*?"

Alex rolled her eyes. "You sound like Ma," she sneered.

"Yeah, *and*?" Sahara chortled. "Sis it's been like two years since your breakup with…what was his name? Reggie?"

Alex sighed. "Um hmm."

"And you haven't dated *since*… It's time."

"I'm perfectly fine being single, I tried the dating and relationship thing again and the shit went nowhere," Alex huffed, putting a hand up.

Sahara shot her big sister a sympathetic look.

"That whole Reggie mess was a huge mistake," Alex bit out. The last thing that she wanted to be reminded of was yet another failed relationship. "Anyway," she dismissed, waving her hand. "How long do you plan on staying, exactly?"

Sahara smiled. "At *least* three days," she teased.

Alex shrugged. "I guess I better get the guest room together for you," she said.

"You know I appreciate you," Sahara beamed.

Alex chuckled. "Yeah, yeah," she jeered. She rubbed her stomach. "Ugh, I'm starving. I missed lunch."

Sahara looked at her watch. "Can you get out of here *now*?" she wondered. "We can go get something to eat and have a drink at the restaurant that I saw next door."

Alex moved around to her computer, shutting it off. "Sure." She grabbed her purse. "You're paying though."

"Oh no, you got that New York money," Sahara threw back, standing from her seat. "I'm sure buying dinner and a drink or *five* won't hurt your pockets," she added, heading for the door.

"*Five*?!" Alex exclaimed, amused.

Chapter 2

Josh Hampton pulled a box from the top of a closet; he jerked back when dust flew in his face. "Damn it," he complained, dropping the box to the floor. He fanned his face, coughing in the process.

"You okay JJ?" a female voice called from the other room.

Josh patted his chest, the cough subsiding. "Oh sure, just inhaling years of dust particles," he sarcastically spat. He turned around as his older sister walked into the room, holding a glass of ice water. "When was the last time you were in this closet?" he asked, taking the glass.

"Probably when I moved in here four years ago," Sarah Hampton chortled. She patted Josh's back. "Sorry about that."

Josh drank the water, then cleared his throat. "It's fine," he replied, setting the empty glass on a stand. "I work around engines all day, so it's not like I'm not used to dust and grime."

"I'm *still* shocked that Dad handed over his garage to you," Sarah mused. "I thought he would *never* retire."

"Me neither," Josh chuckled. "I still gotta yell at him about doing those damn pop-up visits."

Sarah laughed. "Yeah, he's a mess," she joked. "But, he's proud of you."

Josh blushed. Ever since his father had handed the car garage over to him two years ago, Josh had hoped that he would be able to do his father proud. With his master's degree in Business, his skills as a mechanic, and his rapport, the old garage had gone from simply getting by to a booming business.

"Thanks sis," he replied. "I always hoped that he would be."

Sarah waved her hand. "You're doing a great job," she smiled. "You were always the *good* child, remember?"

Josh chuckled. "Yeah, I recall." He began pulling more items from the top of the closet.

"So umm... When am I going to gain a sister-in-law?" Sarah blurted out.

Josh shot her a side-glance. "Sarah, concern yourself less with my romantic life, and more with packing this crap."

Sarah shook her head as she sat on her couch and reached for a large roll of bubble wrap. "Look, I'm not saying that you dating all these different women is a problem, but—"

"I'm a grown man, whose fine with just dating," Josh spat. "I'll settle down when I'm ready."

Sarah put her hand up in surrender. "Okay, you're right."

Josh shook head. Hearing a knock at the door, he trotted over to open it. "Hey man, thanks for the boxes," he smiled as Mark stepped in, boxes in hand.

"No problem," Mark returned setting them on the floor. "My dad wasn't using these for shit but storing them dusty ass Christmas ornaments."

"Hey Mark," Sarah waved.

"Hey," Mark waved back. He looked around. "Damn yo, you *still* packing?"

"Unfortunately," Josh grunted. "I worked all damn day and now I'm working *again*."

Mark put his hands up. "I got the perfect solution to your problem."

Josh looked perplexed. "And that is?"

"Watch the twins."

The confusion never left Josh's face. "And that helps me, *how*?"

"Man, *I* don't fuckin' know, just watch them damn twins," Mark snapped, inciting laughter from Josh. "It ain't funny man, I need a sitter so I can take my wife out."

"Man, I told you before, your boys are bad," Josh joked.

"Hey fuck you, don't call my babies bad...they're *energetic*," Mark replied. "They're umm...*curious*, they're—"

"They're you and Malajia *combined*," Josh laughed.

Mark put his hands on his face and pulled down. "God, I knoooow, they bad as *shit*. Just watch them," he pleaded. "You're the Godfather, after all. Do your job."

"I'm the Godfather of *one* of them," Josh pointed out.

"Yeah well, David's in Ohio learning some scientific, medical shit, and *you* decided to marinate here in Delaware and work on cars, so you're it," Mark argued.

Josh folded his arms. "You done?" he challenged, Mark sucked his teeth. "And you aren't too far from Delaware *either.*"

"I'm far *enough,*" Mark jeered. Josh pointed to the door. "Fine," Mark huffed. On his way out the door, he grabbed two of the three boxes that he'd dropped off. "Have fun packing with that one ass box you got left."

Josh tossed his arms up as Mark darted out the door. "Bro, you're twenty-eight still acting like you're eighteen!" he hollered after him. He slammed the door shut as Mark's loud laughter echoed down the apartment complex hallway.

David Summers typed on his laptop with vigor. Leaning back in his seat, he pinched the bridge of his nose, sighing in the process. Hearing the door to the lab open, he turned around.

"You're still in here, David?" the short dark-skinned woman asked, shutting the door behind her.

David smirked. "Where *else* would I be?"

"Oh I don't know, *home* maybe," she countered, amusement in her voice. "Maybe cook some *real* food, or talk to your *friends.*"

David shook his head as he continued to type. "I *do* talk to my friends," he said. "But at eleven at night, I'm sure they're sleep, so it's just me and my labs right now."

The woman cocked her head. "It's *always* you and your labs," she teased. As one of David's lab partners during his PHD program, she was well aware of the time that David spent on his work.

David slowly shook his head. "Which would explain why I'm single," he solemnly replied.

"Yeah, it *would,*" she agreed.

"Thanks Keema," David grunted.

Keema walked over and put her hand on David's shoulder. He looked up at her. "I didn't mean it like that," she placated.

"You know that I'm fully aware of how hectic this program is. Which is why I don't even *bother* with relationships."

David rubbed the back of his neck and sighed.

She gave his shoulder a rub. "But I *do* understand...break up's suck no matter *how* long it's been," she sympathized.

"Thanks, but I'm fine."

Keema smoothed some of her curly hair up into her high bun. "That you are Mr. Summers," she crooned.

David blushed a bit.

Keema smiled at him. "But all seriousness aside, you need to have some fun."

"I *am* having fun," David assured, reaching back for his laptop keys. Keema gave his hand a light tap, causing him to chuckle. "Hey!" he exclaimed, rubbing his hand.

"Look David, you have a brilliant mind, and I admire how dedicated you are to school and your work here, but...you need a life *outside* of here," she observed. "You know how important balance is."

David had to admit that Keema was right. Since he'd moved to Ohio to further his education, David hadn't done a good job of balancing school, work, and personal life. He had to admit that he missed the times when his friends would drag him away from the books to have some fun. "Look," he began. "I appreciate your concern, but I'm here to get this PhD. After that, I can have all the personal life I need."

"You'll be in your thirties before you finish this PHD program...you need a personal life *now*," she insisted. "It's' eleven o'clock at night on a Friday and you're glued to your laptop."

David chuckled again as he watched Keema walk over to a desk and grab several folders. "Are *you* not working this late?"

"Oh this is for *tomorrow*," she informed, patting the folders with a free hand. "I'm going out *tonight*. I need a drink."

"Nice," David chortled as he moved his finger to push his glasses up his nose. They weren't there. He'd been wearing contacts for a few years, yet there were still times that he completely forgot. "Well, enjoy."

Keema headed for the door and paused. "You're really not gonna come out?" she pressed.

David looked at her. "No, I'm good," he declined. "But thanks."

She shrugged. "Suit yourself...go home soon."

"Yes ma'am." he replied as Keema closed the door behind her.

A notification chirped on his phone, he glanced down at the message. It wasn't Keema. Someone had sent a picture of glasses with the words, 'What's good nerd?'.

David couldn't help but laugh. "Still a fool, Mark," he said to himself. Responding to the message, he put his phone down and focused again on work. *Yeah...I gotta see you guys soon.*

Chasity stared at the chrome elevator doors in front of her as she waited for it to reach the designated floor.

"Mommy," Kayla called, prompting Chasity to glance down at her; she resisted the urge to react to the cat-ear headband sitting atop her daughter's head.

"Yes?"

Kayla pointed to the bag in Chasity's hand. "Do you think Daddy's gonna like the cookie I made him?" she asked, eyes beaming.

Chasity smiled. "Of course, he will," she assured. Seeing the door open, Chasity tightened her grip on her daughter's hand and walked off the elevator.

Chasity navigated the space, coming face to face with an older gentleman.

"Hi Chasity, good to see you again," he smiled.

Wish I could say the same. Chasity thought, face lacking pleasantries. "Thanks Patrick," she spoke.

"How's everything?"

Chasity was too tired for small talk. "Busy. Is Jason in his office?"

"As always," Patrick replied.

"Thanks," Chasity replied, holding on to Kayla's hand while the girl was bouncing in place.

"Again, good seeing you," Patrick smiled before heading off.

"Yeah," Chasity muttered, then proceeded to Jason's

office. Opening the door, she smiled as she and Kayla walked in.

Jason, although mentally exhausted, looked up from his computer with a grin. "There's my girls," he beamed, standing from his swivel chair.

"Daddy, I made you a cookie," Kayla announced, running and jumping into his open arms.

"You did?" Jason replied, lifting her up. He leaned over and gave Chasity a kiss.

"Uh huh, it has sprinkles and chocolate chips and peanut butter candy and chocolate candy in it."

"Oh…all that huh?" he chuckled.

"I turned my back for like a second and she mixed it all in there," Chasity cut in, setting the bag that she was carrying on his desk.

"Well, I'm sure I'll love it," Jason said to his daughter. "All the sugar will give me the energy I need."

Chasity reached into her purse. "Kayla, let Daddy eat. Go play your game," she said, handing Kayla a small tablet.

"Okay," Kayla said, taking the tablet from Chasity's hand and skipping off to a corner in the room.

Jason watched Kayla's progress with amusement, then looked back at Chasity. "She still loving that cat-ear headband, huh?" he whispered to her.

"Jase, I swear to God, she had it on ever since I picked her up from your parents. She won't take it the fuck off," Chasity whispered back, earning a laugh from Jason.

Jason shot her a knowing look. "She's stubborn. I wonder who she gets that from."

"Funny," Chasity sneered. "I'm gonna burn them damn ears while she's asleep."

Jason loosened his tie and sat back down in his chair. Chasity took a seat in the chair in front of his desk. "Let her express herself," he said.

"I'm sick of them damn cats everywhere," Chasity griped.

Jason laughed again. "Were you rude to my boss again?" he joked.

Chasity rolled her eyes. "He just doesn't have to talk to me every time I come in here," she griped.

Jason shook his head in amusement. Every time Chasity visited Jason's office, his boss always attempted small talk—something that Chasity found annoying.

"It's bad enough I have to interact with *my* useless manager all day, I *damn* sure don't want to interact with *yours*," Chasity complained. "Anyway, we came by to bring you dinner, since his cheesin' ass got you held captive in here, again."

Jason reached for the bag, pulling out a container. "Thanks babe," he said. "It's freakin' nine 'clock. I should be *home*, having dinner with you two," he sighed.

"I know," Chasity sympathized.

"This project is killing me... I mean, I don't mind the work, I love software development... but it's these late hours," he complained. "And the fact that *I'm* the *only* one working on this."

"They don't pay you enough for this bullshit," Chasity griped.

"Ohhh, Mommy you said a cuss word."

"Cállate," Chasity spat at Kayla.

"Mommy, I thought you said that saying 'shut up' isn't nice," Kayla innocently replied, playing on her tablet.

"*And* she's picking up Spanish fast," Jason chortled. "Wonder where she got *that* from."

Chasity rolled her eyes, but couldn't help but be proud of how smart her child was. "Finish your game, Cupcake."

Jason rubbed his eyes with his hand. "After busting my ass to get my master's degree and being here for three years, I didn't think that I would still be doing all the grunt work," he vented. "When I first came here, they said that after a year they were going to train me for a leadership role, but it doesn't look like that's happening."

"Look, if they don't value you as an employee and as the person who has worked on and launched *several* successful software projects, then maybe you need to find another job, babe."

"I've *looked* Chaz. The job market isn't that great right now. Besides I *do* like working for the company, I just want to *advance*," Jason replied, opening his container. The sight of fried chicken, string beans and baked macaroni and cheese only made his hunger intensify. "Yo, I'm about to tear—"

"Daddy, when are you going to try the cookie?" Kayla interrupted.

"I'm going to try it right now, Cupcake," he promised, removing the large, deformed cookie from its foil covering. He stared at it and took a big bite, maintaining his smile as his daughter watched. "Mmm," he muttered, turning to Chasity. "There's so many sprinkles," he commented in between chews.

"Uh huh," Chasity agreed, trying not to laugh at the tortured look on Jason's face.

He held the bitten cookie out in Chasity's direction. "Here, try it."

"Nah, I'm not eatin' that," Chasity refused, playfully smacking his hand away.

"Mom, I'm just trying to figure out why you ain't cook. You knew I was coming over," Malajia griped, sipping on a mug of tea.

Mrs. Simmons shot her daughter a stern look. "'Cause I didn't *feel* like it," she sneered, reaching for her cup. "Those girls are old enough to fend for themselves sometimes."

Malajia chuckled. "Dana and Taina *yes*, but Melissa is only eleven."

"*And?*" Mrs. Simmons scowled. "There are pizzas in the freezer. She better get to thawing."

Malajia laughed; her mother soon joined in laughter. "No, I'm kidding, we're going out to eat a little later," Mrs. Simmons admitted.

"That has nothing to do with *my* plate," Malajia pointed out.

"Aren't you cooking at *your* house?"

"Sure...*nuggets*," Malajia joked, earning a playful tap to her arm from her mother. As Malajia had gotten older, especially after giving birth to her sons, she'd grown to enjoy spending quality time with her mother. This visit, even just sitting at the kitchen table talking, was no different.

"Anyway—" A loud noise interrupted her. Malajia jerked around in her seat, glaring into the living room. "Hey! Boys, I know that was you!"

Hearing jumbled excuses come from their little voices, Malajia rolled her eyes. "I can't understand what y'all are saying, just sit down and shut up." She looked over at her mother, who was laughing with her hand over her face. "Mom, it's not funny."

"Oh it *is*," Mrs. Simmons contradicted. "Now you know how *I* felt…hell, *still* feel."

"They're terrible," Malajia jeered. Hearing another noise, followed by yelling, Malajia let out a loud huff. "And they're about to get their behinds TORE UP!"

"Sorry Mommy," the twins sputtered in unison.

Malajia shook her head.

"Don't be popping my grandbabies," Mrs. Simmons teased, sipping her tea.

Malajia shot her a challenging look. "You better leave me alone," she threw back. "Or *you* can take them."

"Oh nooooo," Mrs. Simmons sang. "You got it baby. You're doing *such* a great job."

"Yeah well, I guess," Malajia muttered. "I have to admit, it's…tiring… *Overwhelming* at times."

"Well sweetie, they're going through their terrible three's, and there's *two* of them… And they're *boys*…who act like *Mark*—"

Malajia couldn't help but chuckle.

"But, I meant it when I said that you're doing a great job raising them. *Both* of you are," Mrs. Simmons gushed, patting Malajia's arm. "Motherhood isn't easy, trust me… I had *seven* of you crazy asses."

"I guess I just need to do more stuff outside of the house," Malajia complained. "Sometimes I wish I wasn't doing this 'stay at home mom' thing… I mean, I *did* agree to stay home for the first year with them, then one year turned into *two* and…I'm *still* doing it."

"Did you talk to Mark about it? About going back to work?"

Malajia sighed. "No," she admitted. "When the twins were born, Mark said that he'd rather be the one to work and take care of everything and let me stay home—and I get it, after what happened, but—"

"Sweetie, you *did* scare him...*all* of us actually," Mrs. Simmons placated. "So, I can understand why he feels like the stress of the workplace should fall only on *his* shoulders—"

"Mom, it's been three years, I'm fine," Malajia spat. "I *been* fine."

Mrs. Simmons put her hand up. "I'm not disagreeing with you, Malajia," she replied, tone soothing. "I'm just giving you both sides."

"I know," Malajia sighed, folding her arms on the tabletop. "I guess I can't complain. He's doing a great job at taking care of all the bills and everything... We don't want for anything."

"Just like your father did for *us*."

Malajia rolled her eyes. "Please don't mention your husband," she sneered.

"Malajia," Mrs. Simmons warned.

"What?" Malajia bit out. "Is he not your husband?"

Mrs. Simmons flagged her daughter with her hand. "I really wish that you two would stop butting heads," she sighed.

"I wish that he would stop acting like a jerk towards *my* husband," Malajia threw back. "Bad enough he still acts like a butthole after all these years, but he actually had the nerve to try to talk me out of marrying Mark the night before my damn wedding," Malajia hissed.

Mrs. Simmons let out a sigh. "And trust me, he got cussed out," she promised. "I let him know that he was wrong for that," she assured. "His excuse is that he wanted what was best for you... I told him that he was full of it."

Malajia tipped her cup in her mother's direction. "Thank you." Malajia chucked. "And thank you for making him pay for the wedding venue."

"Child please, I don't care *how* much he didn't approve of the wedding, he was going to pay for that place regardless." She took another sip of her tea. "That *and* walk you down the aisle. He had no choice."

Malajia shook her head as she recalled her wedding day. "His face was tight the *entire* time too."

Both women looked into the living room at the sound of the door opening, followed by the twins excited yelling.

"Hey Geri," Mrs. Simmons called out.

"Hey Mom—there's auntie's babies, let me sit my bags down," Geri said, amusement in her voice. After some commotion, Geri walked into the kitchen with a boy holding on to each leg. "Malajia, your boys have fused themselves to me again," she joked.

Malajia stared at her, unfazed. "I don't know what you telling *me* for. Tell them to get off you," she suggested. "Be an aunt."

Geri flagged Malajia with her hand, before bending down and giving her a kiss on her cheek. "Hey sis."

"Eww," Malajia jeered, wiping her face.

Geri moved around the table to give her mother a kiss. "I had some free time today, so I figured I'd come over to see what you cooked."

Malajia laughed. "You hungry as shit driving from Philly to Baltimore looking for a plate." Geri chuckled. "*And* salty, 'cause she ain't cook a damn thing."

Geri threw her head back and groaned. "Mom, you slippin'."

"Hey, y'all better leave me the hell alone, before I put you *both* out," Mrs. Simmons ground out. "I don't need this nonsense."

"Shiiiit, I'll leave if I can leave the boys here," Malajia joked.

"I'll get them next weekend," Mrs. Simmons grunted.

"Yesssss!" Malajia rejoiced. "Just for that, I'm gonna cook *you* dinner."

Mrs. Simmons smiled. "Aww sweetie—"

"Sike!" Malajia cut in, earning laughter from Geri.

Mrs. Simmons pointed a warning finger at Malajia, "Keep it up, hear?"

Malajia laughed.

"Geraldine," Marvin called. "Can you get us a snack?"

Geri looked down at her nephew, confused. "Baby, what did you call me?"

"Geraldine," he repeated.

Geri slowly looked up at Malajia, glaring. Malajia avoided eye contact. "Malajia, why are they *still* calling me Geraldine?" she hissed. "I want you to tell these boys that my name is Geri...*Aunt Gi Gi* to them."

"They're three, they'll remember when they're ready," Malajia defended. She signaled for the boys to come to her.

"No, *you* started them on that," Geri griped. "I *still* don't know where you even *got* Geraldine from. My name isn't short for anything."

Malajia leaned down where the twins stood in front of her. "Remember, we only call Aunt Gi Gi, Geraldine behind her *back*," Malajia joked.

"Mom, I'm about to smack her," Geri ranted, pointing at Malajia, who pulled her boys close to her.

"Don't threaten me in front of my babies," Malajia threw back, fighting to keep a straight face. "I'll make them spit on you."

Mrs. Simmons sipped her tea. "I can't with you two."

Alex took a sip of her red wine, closing her eyes to try and savor it. "Ugh, this isn't working," she muttered, setting the half empty glass on the end table next to her. Leaning over in her seat, she tapped the keys of her laptop.

Bringing work home wasn't foreign to Alex, especially when there was a deadline to be met. Normally Alex looked forward to her job, but her mind just wasn't into it. Running her hands over her thick wavy hair, which had grown past her shoulders, Alex scratched her scalp and let out a sigh.

Grabbing her phone from the arm of the chair, she dialed a number. She smiled into the camera when the video call picked up. "Hey Em," she beamed.

Emily's bright face beamed back on the screen. "Hey Alex, how's it going?" she asked.

Alex let out a long sigh. "Girl, busy."

"I hear you, trust me," Emily chuckled. "Teaching these babies keeps me pretty busy on this end too."

"How is it going? Do you still love it?"

"Of *course* I do. It's my dream job," Emily assured. She then started mumbling something incoherently.

"You okay?" Alex asked, concerned at the annoyed look on her friend's face.

"Sure," Emily grunted.

Alex wasn't convinced. "You're not a good liar, you know that."

Emily sighed. "Yeah, I know," she agreed. "Sorry, I don't mean to bring our conversation down, but I'm just tired of picking up after this girl."

Alex shook her head. "Em, your sister is a grown woman, you—"

"Trust me Alex, I already know," Emily cut in, frustrated.

Alex sighed. She was well aware of Emily's frustration with Jazmine, especially now that the girl was staying with her.

"I should've just ignored that phone call," Emily vented.

"You only tried to help," Alex placated.

"And those two weeks that she needed to 'crash until her place was ready' turned into a whole year," Emily sulked. "It serves me right for being an idiot."

"Em, stop beating yourself up," Alex placated. "If *my* sister needed a place to stay, I'd definitely let her stay with me."

"*Your* sister doesn't treat you like crap," Emily reminded. "Anyway, Jazmine has occupied enough of my day, let's not talk about her anymore, please?"

Alex nodded in agreement. "Okay," she granted. "Are you still coming up this end soon?"

"You mean Jersey?"

Alex chuckled. "Yeah…it's close enough."

"Yes, I still plan on making a visit," Emily assured. "I want to see you girls while I'm up there… I miss everybody. It's been forever."

"I know, for me too," Alex agreed. "Chaz and Mel don't live far, so we four can try to link up… I know they're busy with their families, but I'm sure we can tear them away for a few hours."

"Yes, I hope so," Emily beamed. "It's a shame that Sidra lives so far."

Alex leaned back in her seat, grabbing her glass. "I know, but we'll get to see her soon enough with the wedding and everything."

"Yeah," Emily said. "End of January...in Virginia. It's going to be *freezing*."

Alex giggled. "It might not be that bad," she said. "It'll be indoors anyway. Besides you said it yourself, weddings are cheaper in the winter."

"Yeah," Emily repeated. "Which is necessary since we're paying for this wedding ourselves."

"I thought your parents said they were going to pitch in," Alex recalled.

"They did, but Will and I really wanted to do this on our own," Emily replied. "Besides, as much as I love my mother, her investing any money in this wedding will mean that she thinks she can have control, and that's *not* happening."

"Smart woman," Alex chortled.

"She is already giving me grief over my dress, among other things," Emily vented.

"Try not to let her stress you sis."

"I'll try," Emily promised.

"Do you need me to do anything?" Alex asked. "I know you're doing a lot of DIY projects, so if you need to send stuff to me, I'll do it and send it back. Or I'll come down there—"

"Alex, you don't need to come all the way down from New York to help me make a boutonniere," Emily chortled. "I'm fine, I can handle my projects."

"Okay sweetie, just know that your bridesmaids are here to help you."

"I know. Listen. I have to go okay," Emily said. "I'll call you tomorrow."

Alex smiled to hide her disappointment. Anytime she spoke to one of her friends, she felt like the conversations weren't long enough. She missed the days when she could have a long conversation, like they used to when they were in college.

"Sure," Alex said. "Talk to you tomorrow."

Hanging up the phone, Alex let out a sigh and looked around her furnished apartment. The first home of her own, the place she had spent months decorating just the way that she wanted. Though she loved it, in that moment she didn't want to be sitting in there.

"Time to put the work away and get some food," she said to herself. She closed the laptop and made her way to her shoes, near the door. She slipped them on, grabbed her purse from a nearby table and headed out.

Her journey took her to a restaurant a block down from her complex. Electing to sit at the bar instead of waiting for a table, Alex was getting ready to indulge in some fattening food while enjoying a glass of wine. As soon as she had placed her order, she heard someone call her name.

Curious, Alex spun around in her seat. Her curiosity turned to annoyance. "Ugh," she grunted.

The tall, light skinned man chuckled as he sat down next to her. "Is that how you talk to your ex-lover?" he grinned.

Alex made a face as her wine was placed in front of her. "Please Reggie, don't make me relive those less than stellar moments," she snarled.

The last person she expected or *wanted* to see in that moment was her ex-boyfriend, whom she'd deemed a waste of her time to her sister more than a week ago. Still, she wasn't surprised to run into him. Reggie lived not far from her; they used to frequent the restaurant together when they had dated.

Reggie made a face at her in retaliation. "Yeah, you weren't saying that when you—"

"Why did you come over here?" she cut in, annoyed. "You're ruining my appetite."

He shook his head. "I just wanted to say hello to an old friend, that's all," he reasoned.

Alex waved her hand at him dismissively. "I'm neither old *nor* your friend," she spat, taking a sip of her drink. "I made that clear when I left you for being too *friendly* with other women."

"I made mistakes in our relationship, I admit," he explained, putting a hand on his chest.

Humph, you are a mistake, she thought, but decided against saying it. Alex had given him more than enough attention for the day. "Please save the excuses, it doesn't matter," she cut in. "We've been over, and I wish you well." It was the truth. She might have gotten hurt, but unlike her first relationship, she was not going to allow bitter resentment to take hold of her.

"Let me buy the drink at least," he offered, smiling.

Alex shook her head. "I can pay for my own drink," she ground out.

He shrugged. "Okay then," he said, standing up. "Good seeing you again, Alexandra."

She rolled her eyes. "Bye *Reginald*," she grunted at his departing back and sipped on her wine. *Unbelievable*, she thought, still annoyed.

Emily reached for a notepad, then sat back on her couch. As she started jotting items down, Will handed her a glass of juice.

She smiled up at him. "Thank you."

"Of course," he replied, taking a seat next to her. He glanced over at her book. "What are you doing?"

"Just going over this wedding to-do list."

Will took a sip of his own juice. "Is there a lot left to do?"

Emily let out a sigh. "Kind of," she answered, honest. "I still have to make the favors, boutonnieres, bouquets, decorations—"

"I thought that the venue already had decorations," Will cut in.

"I mean yeah, they do, but it's standard things like the lighting, and tablecloths... I still want our own stuff you know," Emily explained. She rubbed her forehead. "Anyway, I have to get someone to do the addresses on the invitations—"

"*I* can do that," Will beamed.

Emily shot him a skeptical glance. "Umm...as much as I love your handwriting," she pacified. "I'd rather people be able to *understand* what they're reading,"

Will snickered. "Damn, it's that bad huh?"

Emily giggled and gave his arm a rub. "It's cute," she placated. She looked back at her list. "Anyway, there's still—"

Will gently grabbed the notepad from her. "Okay, time to put this down and focus on something else," he said. It was clear that wedding planning was beginning to stress her out.

Emily put her hands up. "Okay, what do you have in mind?"

"Let's go see that movie that everyone says is terrible," he suggested.

Emily looked confused. "Why would you want to see a movie that's bad?"

"So we can laugh at it," he shrugged. "We *both* need a good laugh after this week."

"Yeah, these parents are irritating me with all their complaining about the supply list," Emily sighed. "School started back *three weeks* ago and some of these children *still* don't have the stuff that they need," she vented, leaning back in her seat. "I swear, I just want to say forget it and get the stuff myself."

"No, that's not your job," Will pointed out. "You already go above and beyond for your students. Their cheap parents need to get it together."

Emily chuckled, "Thanks." She threw her legs over Will's legs. "Can we just make dinner and watch a movie on TV?" she asked.

"*Or*, we can go *out* to dinner and come back to watch a movie on TV," he countered. Emily shook her head in amusement. "Come on, we need to get out for a bit."

Emily gave a nod. "Okay, you won me over," she agreed "Is Anthony spending the night at your parents tonight?"

"Yep," Will answered. "I told Mom that I would come pick him up, but she cussed me out and told me to stop calling."

Emily giggled. "You know Ms. Wanda adores her grandson."

"Yes, I know," Will chuckled. "I've been replaced in my mother's heart by my son."

Emily laughed as she touched Will's arm. "Don't be silly," she said. Hearing a key jiggle in her door, the humor left her face. She rolled her eyes. "Great," she muttered.

The door swung open. "Oh, didn't expect y'all to be here," Jazmine commented, walking into the living room.

"Why wouldn't you? I *do* live here," Emily muttered.

Jazmine rolled her eyes and made her way to the kitchen. "You have a whole man that lives upstairs from you," she mentioned, removing a food container from a paper bag. "Instead you're down here on my nerves."

Emily rolled her eyes. *If I was up there with him all the time, there would be no need for me to have this place, leaving your raggedy butt out on the street.* As much as Emily wanted to say that, she decided against it.

Will shook his head. "Come on Emily, let's go to dinner," he calmly said, standing from the couch. Jazmine had always rubbed him the wrong way. It would be best if both he and Emily left, before he said something out of line.

Emily looked at him. "Can you give me a few minutes, please?" she requested. When he held a skeptical look, she gave a nod. "It's okay, I'll meet you at the car."

Will let out a sigh. "Okay, see you in a bit."

Emily waited for Will to walk out of her apartment before she headed into the kitchen. Glancing at the food container, Emily folded her arms. "You bought that?" she asked.

Jazmine frowned. "No, I hoe'd myself for a chicken platter," she spat, sarcastic. "What are you all in my business for?"

Emily narrowed her eyes. "That was unnecessary," she threw back. "I asked you because it's apparent that you have money."

Jazmine shrugged in annoyance. "A few bucks for a damn platter."

"It doesn't matter, it's still *money* and you have *yet* to give me *any* for bills since you've *been* here," Emily argued, fighting to remain calm.

"Don't start this shit again," Jazmine spat, moving around Emily to get to the living room.

Emily sighed, putting her face in her hands. "Jaz, the electric bill is through the roof," she called to her. "You being here all day, *every* day with the TV on, the lights on...it's ridiculous."

"Fine, I'll keep the lights off," Jazmine grunted, flopping on the couch.

"Well, that would be good," Emily ground out. "But also helping me *pay* the bill would be *better*... Did you happen to look for a job today?"

Jazmine let out a loud huff. "There are a few stores that are hiring. I'm going to apply tomorrow," she answered, tone filled with disdain.

"You've been saying that for *months* now," Emily muttered. "Ever since you got fired from your *last* one."

"Look, just because you have the same job that you were *lucky* enough to get right out of college, doesn't mean you can look down your nose at me," Jazmine hurled.

Emily looked confused. "I'm not looking down my nose at you," she promised. "And me getting that teaching job wasn't *luck*," she stressed. "I worked hard during my student teaching internship and made a good name for myself. I busted my behind to get my GPA back on track after being on academic probation, and *keeping* that GPA until I graduated. I also studied hard for and passed my teaching boards, so I *earned* that job."

Jazmine once again rolled her eyes. "Did *not* care to hear all of that," she scoffed.

Emily let out a sigh; Jazmine had made it a habit to downplay her accomplishments. "Whatever Jazmine," she muttered, heading for the door. "See you later." *A few more months and I won't have to be bothered with her anymore.*

Jazmine ignored Emily as the door shut behind her.

Chapter 3

"Sidra, I swear to God, if you ask me about that damn dress one more time, I'm showing up to the wedding in just my drawls," Malajia barked into the phone. She was in front of a door, key in the doorknob. "...I get it and I *told* you I would take care of it... Girl, why are you more concerned about this wedding than Emily? ...*She's* not even bugging us about the dresses. You're doin' too damn much as *usual*—" She pinched the bridge of her nose. "Look, drink some tea or something to calm your ass down—No! No more damn coffee... I'll talk to you later." Malajia hung up the phone. "All the way in California and she's *still* on my damn nerves," she muttered to herself.

Pushing the front door open, Malajia stood in the doorway, striking a pose. "Hey boo!" she bellowed.

Chasity looked up from her laptop at the kitchen table. "God," she muttered. "Mel, how many times have I told you that I gave you that spare key for *emergency purposes only*."

Malajia shut the door and walked over. "It *is* an emergency," she affirmed. "I'm hungry, what you cook?"

Chasity rolled her eyes. "Girl, get the fuck out my damn house," she spat.

"Nah, I think I'll stay and bug you," Malajia teased, leaning over the counter. "Haven't seen you in a minute."

Chasity looked confused. "It's been like three days."

"*And?*" Malajia barked. "Bitch, I missed you, so shut up and entertain me."

Chasity couldn't help but let a chuckle come through. She didn't know why she even bothered arguing with Malajia; her best friend of eight years was still going to make it her mission to annoy her to the best of her abilities.

"I swear, I regret telling you when that house around the corner became available." Chasity huffed, closing her laptop.

"*I* don't," Malajia giggled. "I told you before I graduated that I was gonna live near you. You didn't believe me."

When Malajia became pregnant with her twins, she and Mark had been desperate to find a place bigger than the one-bedroom apartment they'd shared. Chasity and Jason, having moved into their West Chester house a year prior, had learned of a vacant three-bedroom home for rent around the corner from them and passed the listing along. Mark and Malajia had jumped at the opportunity.

Chasity ran her hands through her hair. "Did the neurotic self-proclaimed, wedding planner call you today?" she asked.

"Girl, I just got off the phone with her ass," Malajia griped, playing with a candle on the counter. "She's getting on my nerves about these damn dresses and tuxes."

"I told her that we already got fitted for the damn dresses," Chasity sneered. "Jason got fitted for his tux already. I told her to leave me the hell alone."

"Wait, Jase got fitted for his tux already?" Malajia zoned in.

"Yeah," Chasity drew out slowly. "Did Mr. 'Waits till the last minute' not do his fitting?"

Malajia smacked her palm against her forehead. "No, why would he do *anything* that I told his ass to do last month?" she complained. "See, now I gotta go home and cuss his black ass out."

"What *else* is new?" Chasity teased.

Malajia ran a hand through her hair. "Fuck that tux," she said. "Emily don't give a damn *what* we wear, as long as we show up," she chuckled.

"Yeah, I know, and *because* of that, we're gonna wear what she *asks* us to," Chasity insisted.

Malajia nodded in agreement. "Yeah, she definitely doesn't ask for much...which is weird because when *we* got married, we were bothering our bridesmaids for every little thing."

"No, that was *you* when *you* got married," Chasity recalled. "*I* didn't ask y'all to do shit but have your dresses, keep pink out of my bridal shower decorations and no stripper..." She narrowed her eyes at Malajia. "That *last* request was just completely *ignored.*"

Malajia laughed. "You damn *right* I ignored that shit," she boasted. "You lost all that baby weight, there was no way I wasn't gonna have a big, sexy black stripper pick your ass up." She folded her arms. "Yeah, I remember. Your rich ass mom hired that planner that had everything on point...Your wedding was easy as shit to be a part of...which is crazy because you're normally a bitch."

Chasity couldn't help but chuckle. "Y'all can thank Kayla for that," she joked. "Having a six-month-old kept me busy enough."

"How did your grandmom feel about you waiting until *after* you had the baby to get married?" Malajia wondered.

Chasity looked confused. "She didn't feel *any* way. She was just happy that I was *getting* married." She shook her head. "I think everyone in my family originally thought that I would die alone and bitter."

Malajia laughed a little. "Proved all they asses wrong." She shook her head as memories of her own wedding flooded back. "Shit when it came to *my* wedding, *I had* to badger my bridesmaids," she defended. "You, Alex, Sid and Em were on point, but my *sisters*... You remember how lazy those heffas were."

"Maria still mad at you for making Geri and I your maid and matron of honor?" Chasity asked.

"*Please*, Maria lucky her ass was *in* the wedding after she tried to suggest that nasty ass wedding cake." Malajia flung some hair over her shoulder. "Didn't nobody want no damn banana pound cake."

Chasity scrunched her face in disgust. "Ugh."

Malajia tossed her hands up. "Well, enough about our weddings, as fun as they were," she said. "I'm so happy for Em... You think Sidra's ass will *make* it to the wedding? You know she don't like to come home and shit."

"Don't be petty," Chasity chided. "You know she wouldn't miss it."

"Her ass ain't been back on this end since them bad ass twins was pulled from my uterus," Malajia grumbled. "Three damn years ago."

"Your ass hasn't been down *there* to see *her either* in those three years," Chasity pointed out.

"Explain to me when I have time to take a week off from being a parent to go see her," Malajia fussed. "Shit, I had to lie to Dana about my back hurting two weeks ago so she would watch them boys for a few minutes."

"Oh, you mean that day you spent like four hours at the movies?" Chasity recalled.

"Yup," Malajia confirmed without a qualm. "Was tearing that dry ass popcorn up while watching those matinees."

Chasity just shook her head. "*Anyway,* Sidra has a life like the rest of us. She can't fly back to the East Coast every five minutes, and you know that," she defended. "You just miss her so you're being dramatic."

"Yeah well...so what," Malajia pouted, folding her arms in a huff. "She can still visit every once in a while...and watch these kids." She watched as Chasity went to the refrigerator and took some items out. "Whatchu' about to make?" she wondered, eyeing the thawed pack of ground beef, onion, green pepper, box of pasta and spaghetti sauce on the counter.

"Spaghetti," Chasity blandly replied.

"How you gonna make spaghetti when my Goddaughter don't like it?" Malajia griped.

"*First* off all, Kayla don't run *shit* in this house," Chasity hissed, pointing at Malajia.

"You're full of shit, and you *know* it," Malajia laughed. "That's how she got all them damn toy cats."

"Fuck them cats," Chasity threw back. Malajia laughed again. "Second...she's at Jason's parents' house, so she'll eat dinner there."

Malajia giggled. "Uh huh." She scratched her head. "You think they'll take the twins?"

"Fuck no."

Malajia slapped her hand on the countertop. "Damn it," she grimaced, then scratched her head again.

Chasity frowned, watching Malajia go from scratching to patting her head. "You wanna stop smacking your goddamn tracks all around my counter?" she scoffed.

"Fuck you, this shit itches," Malajia complained, smacking her head again. "It's time to get this sew-in washed and redone." She caught Chasity's judgmental gaze. "Don't look at me like that, you don't know what I'm going through."

Chasity smirked. "No, no, I don't."

Malajia made a face. "Screw you and your locks... *My* hair don't grow like that, so I'll stick to my cute ass weaves."

"I told you to lay off the perms," Chasity shrugged.

"Shut the hell up," Malajia snapped, flinging her hand in Chasity's direction.

Chasity laughed a little, then proceeded to rinse her utensils.

Malajia shook her head. "*Anyway*...you making enough for *me* to get a plate?"

"No greedy!" Chasity snapped. "You always over here looking for food."

Malajia shrugged. "And your point isssss, what?" she slowly drew out.

"Go home and eat what the hell *you* made."

"I don't want that bullshit!" Malajia barked. "I made a damn casserole... I don't even remember what I put in it."

Chasity rolled her eyes as she reached under a cabinet to grab a pan. "It's probably all dry and shit."

"Very," Malajia jeered. "The carrots was coughin' and shit."

Chasity snickered. "You actually put *carrots* in something?"

"It was my mom's dry ass recipe," Malajia replied. "You know she put carrots in *everything*."

"Well, run the shit under some water or something," Chasity ground out, placing the pan on the stove. "Just go home and eat it."

"So, you really not gonna feed me?"

Chasity eyed her intensely. "Get. Out."

Malajia stared at Chasity for several seconds; she nodded slowly. "Okay, that's fine...I'll leave, rude ass," she agreed, twisting the white gold wedding band on her finger. She moved around the counter. "Let's see how you make your spaghetti without your ground beef!" she quickly spat, grabbing the pack off the counter and darting for the door.

"You play too fuckin' much!" Chasity yelled, running after her with a wooden spoon in her hand.

Malajia glanced behind her, then let out a scream. "You ain't gotta run up on me like that!" she panicked, holding the meat pack up.

Chasity snatched the pack. "Get your slow running ass out," she ordered.

Malajia let out a loud huff. "Very well," she relented, snatching the spoon from Chasity. "I need this to scoop my casserole."

Chasity grabbed the collar of Malajia's shirt, halting her progress out the door. She snatched the spoon back and gave her a shove. "Out."

"After all these years, your ass is still stingy," Malajia jeered, walking out the door. "I'll call you later, love you cranky."

"Yeah, yeah. Love you too, moron." Chasity punctuated her response by closing the door.

Jason knocked on the door to his parents' house and waited. He managed a smile when the door opened. "Hey Mom," he said.

Mrs. Adams smiled back and gave her eldest son a hug, moving aside so he could come in. "What are you doing here?"

Jason chuckled. "What, you're not happy to see me?"

His mom waved a dismissive hand. "Oh stop it, you know I love when you visit," she returned. "I just thought that Chasity was picking Kayla up."

"She was going to, but I told her I'd do it," he replied. "Figured she could use a few minutes to herself."

Mrs. Adams folded her arms. "Honey, you look exhausted."

Jason ran a hand over the back of his head, sighing in the process. "I'm fine," he said. His work day had been practically nonstop; he couldn't wait to get home and get some much-needed sleep.

Mrs. Adams pointed to the couch. "Sit down for a minute," she ordered; Jason complied. "Now I told you, you work too hard."

"Yeah well, I don't have much of a choice right now," Jason replied, rubbing his eyes.

Mrs. Adams sighed. "I understand, but the late nights, the weekends...I know it's taking its toll," she said.

Jason offered his mother a tired smile. "I'm fine," he said. "Is the little ball of energy ready?"

Mrs. Adams chuckled. "I'll get her. I took her to the zoo today and she did a lot of walking, so she should be good and tired," she said, heading for the stairs. "Oh, she mentioned that she wants a real kitten."

"Yeah, that's not gonna happen," Jason chortled. "She's just going to try to dress it up in tutu's and Chaz would probably throw it out."

Mrs. Adams pointed a warning finger at her son. "Y'all better get my grandbaby a kitten," she said, heading upstairs.

Jason shook his head, letting out a sigh as he let his head rest on the back of the couch. He closed his eyes for a second, only to jerk them open at the sound of a deep voice.

"Long day, huh?" Mr. Adams wondered, sitting down in an accent chair across from his son.

"As always," Jason replied. He studied his father's appearance. "You look like you had a long day too."

"Yeah well, your daughter has a lot of energy," Mr. Adams joked.

Jason smirked. "Yeah."

"Reminds me of you and Kyle when y'all were little," he reminisced fondly. "Always active."

"When was the last time that you spoke to Kyle?" Jason asked.

"A few days ago," Mrs. Adams answered. "You?"

"Same," Jason replied.

"Yeah, you know your brother. He's probably riding that damn motorcycle somewhere." Mr. Adams shook his head. "Dropped out of college to ride a damn motorcycle around."

Jason ran his hand over his head. "He didn't drop out to ride a motorcycle," Jason calmly stated. "He left to explore other options."

"Bottom line, he left school," Mr. Adams grunted.

"Well, we knew after his first year that he wasn't going to stay," Jason pointed out. "His attention span just wasn't there.. I'm sure he'll go back eventually."

"Yeah well, if he does, he's on his own financially," Mr. Adams spat. "Two years wasted."

"It wasn't wasted," Jason argued. "He still has the experience and the knowledge. Besides, college isn't for everybody."

When his twenty-three year old brother had informed the family of his decision to take time off from college, Jason's reaction was far more understanding than that of his parents. Jason knew that as much as Kyle wanted to be like him, he wasn't. "He'll be fine."

Mr. Adams let out a sigh. "Yeah... So, how's the job?" he asked, changing the subject. "They still treating you like you're still entry level, even though you have a master's degree?"

Jason rolled his eyes. He knew his father was still a bit disappointed that he hadn't entered the pro-football draft after graduating college. "Thanks Dad," he griped.

"I didn't mean it like that."

Jason was going to respond, then decided against it when he saw Kayla run downstairs with her book bag in hand. Jason stood up and took hold of Kayla's hand. "See you later," he bit out, heading for the door.

Mr. Adams sighed as Jason walked out.

"Mama, is Daddy sure he can't fly down with you?" Sidra let out a sigh. "That sucks but I understand... Okay, I'll see you in a few weeks... Bye."

Sidra placed her cell phone on her desk and clicked on her laptop. Tapping the keys, she heard her office phone ring. Picking it up, she put it to her ear. "Taylor and Shaw Law, Sidra Howard speaking."

"Miss Howard, I do believe that I am in need of a lawyer," a male voice on the other end said.

Sidra giggled. "David, you've never done *anything* for you

to need a lawyer. You're one of the most law abiding people that I know."

David laughed into the line. "True," he agreed.

"And you know I'm not actually a *lawyer*, so you definitely called the wrong line," she chortled.

"You *will* be," David stated, confident.

Sidra let out a sigh. "Right," she muttered. "Anyway, why did you call my work phone when you could've called my cell, silly?"

"I wanted to see if your work voice still sounds like your normal voice," David joked. "As always, no difference."

Sidra laughed a little. "Yep, my bougie voice never takes a break," she joked. "But speaking of needing a lawyer, you might need a *trademark* lawyer one day. After you patent your disease cures."

"Yeah well, until I finish this program, I won't be patenting much of *anything.*"

"How *is* school going?" Sidra wondered, twirling a pen around on her desk.

"It's a lot of work, long hours, scientific jargon and petri dishes, but it's great," David beamed. "You'd think that I'd be tired of school by now."

"I know." Sidra chuckled. "You went from bachelors, to masters and now you're on your way to your PhD... *How* many more years until you're finished?"

"*Too* many," David mentioned, amusement filling his voice.

"I hear you." She adjusted the phone in her hand. "When are you going back home to visit?"

"Umm, I don't know... I want to soon though," David answered. "When are *you* heading back for a visit?"

"I don't know...things are so busy, I just—" She took a deep breath. "I will eventually."

"Cool, well hopefully we'll see each other sooner than later," David hoped. "I have to head back to work. I'll call you again soon."

"Okay, miss you."

"Miss you too," David returned. "Talk to you later."

Sidra smiled as she hung up. She'd barely gotten a chance

to look back at her laptop screen when her office door opened. "Sidra, did you finish going over those contracts?" A woman questioned. "Mr. Shaw needs them."

Sidra resisted the urge to roll her eyes. *This damn girl still doesn't know how to knock when the door is closed.* She put on her best professional smile. "Yes Carlie, I *did*. I finished the review and amendment of the contracts. I've also finished the legal research that Renee needs and prepared the affidavits that Douglas needs." She patted a stack of folders on her desk. "I'm getting ready to walk everything over now."

"Great," Carlie breathed, walking over and taking the seat across from Sidra.

Sidra eyed her fellow paralegal, raising an eyebrow. "Unless, *you* would like to take them."

Carlie put a hand up. "Girl no, those attorneys had me running all morning, I need a minute," she declined.

Sidra shook her head. "Very well," she sighed, typing something on her laptop.

Carlie watched her. "You were here late last night."

"Had to get this these tasks completed," Sidra replied, eyes not leaving the screen. "Not a big deal, I'm used to it. I used to stay up late while I was in law school—"

Carlie leaned forward, surprise registered on her face. "Wait, you actually went to law school?"

Sidra looked at her. "Yes."

"Oh…well, that explains why they give you all the more detailed tasks," Carlie chortled. "Don't get me wrong, I'm fine with it because it takes work off of *my* plate."

Yes, lazy, I know, Sidra thought, though her expression remained neutral. Carlie Weston was a coworker that Sidra tried her best to avoid. The woman did half the work, lacked professionalism, kept her nose in office gossip, and talked way too much for Sidra's liking.

Carlie stared at Sidra, bewildered. "So *why* aren't you a lawyer, by the way?"

"Because I like *this* job, is there something else that I can do for you?" Sidra quickly put out, a hint of agitation in her voice. She rubbed her face with her hands.

"No, I'm good," Carlie answered, shrugging slightly.

"Okay so, if you don't mind, I have a few more things to do, including handing these files off." She eyed Carlie with intensity. *Take the hint and get out.*

Carlie waved a dismissive hand. "Fine Ms. Law school, I'll leave you be," she jeered, standing up. "So uptight all the time. Maybe you should go have a drink after work tonight, to take the edge off."

"Have a good day Carlie," Sidra threw back, feigning politeness. She rolled her eyes as Carlie finally left.

Mark took a sip of his drink and set it on the edge of the pool table. "Damn that's strong," he griped of the rum and cola. Gabbing a pool stick from a rack, he turned around when he heard his name called.

"What up?" he beamed, giving Josh a handshake.

"Man, I'm tired," Josh chuckled.

"Work?" Mark asked, reaching for his drink.

"Yeah, since six this morning," Josh answered, taking it upon himself to rack the pool balls on the table.

Mark shook his head as Josh yawned. "Why didn't your yawnin' ass stay home?"

Josh almost coughed as his yawn subsided. "Well, I didn't want to pass up an opportunity to see my brothers." He glanced around. "Where's Jase?"

After settling his sons, Mark had decided to call Josh and Jason to meet up for a few drinks and a game of pool. "On his way," Mark answered. A moment later, Jason walked into the pool hall.

"Hey guys," Jason tiredly greeted, exchanging handshakes.

"You hype as shit coming up in here with a tie on," Mark chortled.

"I came right from work, fool," Jason threw back, loosening the tie. "You know what, let me go get a drink before I even try to deal with your nonsense."

"Yeah whatever," Mark grunted. "Aye yo, did you tell Chaz that you were coming here?"

Jason stopped on his way to the bar; he turned around, confused. "Am I twelve?"

"Stop bullshittin'. It's almost nine thirty, you know you'll get cussed out for coming straight here after working all those hours," Mark goaded. "I don't need her cussing me out 'cause I invited you."

"No, *you* would get cussed out, by *your* wife," Jason threw back, pointing. "You know Malajia has those reigns tight." Mark let out a phony laugh; Jason flagged him with his hand. "Anyway, I already talked to her. She's cool with it," he threw out on his way to the bar.

Josh laughed at the banter as he chalked his pool cue.

"Man, quit chuckling and just shoot," Mark demanded. He glanced down and saw his phone light up on the edge of the table.

Josh looked confused when Mark ignored it. "Bro, your phone."

"No it's not," Mark denied, getting ready to make a shot.

Josh pointed to the phone. "It's flashing… It says that Malajia's calling."

"Nah man, I don't know what you're talking about," Mark dismissed.

"Mark, yes it does, it—"

"Yo man, get your hype ass away from my phone!" Mark snapped. "Damn, Jason talked her up and shit."

Josh laughed. "You're foul man."

"Them boys probably woke up and are pissing her off and shit," Mark replied.

After a few rounds of pool and drinks, the guys were relaxed. "Yo, we really need to hang out more often," Mark said. "I mean, I know we all have lives and shit, but that's no excuse for not having our chill time."

"Yeah I agree, but it's hard," Josh said. "David is in Ohio, Jason works all the time and has to spend his *free* time with his family. *You* work and have a family, and my life is—"

"Josh, your life is cars and women," Mark cut in, jokingly. "Stop tryna act like shit is tough."

Josh made a face at Mark. "Funny," he said. "But it *is* tough. I'm running a *business*, and dating isn't necessarily that damn easy."

"Josh grew some facial hair and think he a pimp now and shit," Mark teased, looking at Jason.

Jason snickered.

"Shut up," Josh grunted at Mark. "Facial hair has nothing to do with it, I dated women in college."

"One Josh, *one* woman you dated in college," Mark jeered. "December."

"No, she was my *girlfriend* at one point, but after her, I dated a *few* women," Josh argued.

"Eating wing dings in the cafeteria with them does not mean you were *dating* them," Mark threw back.

Josh rolled his eyes. "Whatever," he spat.

"Josh's goatee is laced with confidence and shit," Mark teased.

Jason busted out laughing. "Leave the man alone, Mark."

"You're laughing *too* Jase, you know I'm right," Mark laughed back. Taking notice of the stern look on Josh's face, Mark put his hands up. "My bad."

Josh shook his head and sighed. "All I gotta say is be lucky that you have what you have."

"Trust me, I am," Jason agreed. "Wouldn't trade my family for anything."

"I hear that," Mark agreed; he chuckled. "Bad ass boys and Malajia's ignorant mouth and *all*."

Josh shook his head in amusement, running a hand over his hair. "Truth be told, dating is getting *tiring*," he sighed.

"That's 'cause you not *built* for that life," Mark pointed out, taking another shot with his pool stick. "You're that 'propose to a girl after six months' type of dude."

Josh shook his head again.

"And you *know* it, that's why you haven't committed to anybody yet," Mark added.

"Mark, chill," Jason cut in, humor in his voice as he took his shot. "We said we'd let him figure that out on his own."

"Figure *what* out?" Josh wondered, looking back and forth between Jason and Mark. "You two been talking about me?"

"No, of course not," Jason denied. His eyes shifted.

Mark shook his head. "Jason, you *know* you can't lie right when you drink," he ground out, earning another laugh from Jason.

"Subject change." Josh grunted.

Mark downed the rest of his drink and set the glass back on the edge of the table. "Okay fine. I have an idea," he began. The two guys stared at him in anticipation. "We should go to homecoming this year. *All* of us."

Jason frowned in confusion. "You mean Paradise Valley University's homecoming?"

Mark narrowed his eyes. "What *other* college did we *all* graduate from?" he barked. "Don't you drink another fuckin' thing."

"I just had this *one* drink," Jason threw back. "I'm *tired.*"

"I actually think that's a good idea," Josh cut in. "I mean, when's the last time any of us have been back?"

"Not since we graduated, as far as I know," Jason shrugged.

"Then it's settled, we out," Mark nodded. "I'm gonna start checking out hotels."

"We didn't even check with the girls to see if they agree," Jason pointed out, rubbing his eyes.

"They ain't got a damn *choice*," Mark stood firm. "All the shit they make *us* do? They better shut up and flow with it."

"You think David and Sidra will come?" Jason wondered.

"*Sidra* probably won't," Josh commented, taking another shot with his pool stick.

"When was the last time you two talked?" Jason asked.

Josh shrugged. "A few months maybe."

"Oh shit, foreal?" Mark replied. "*I* just talked to her like two days ago... I thought y'all were closer than that."

"So did *I*," Josh mumbled.

"Well, I have to make sure that I can get off work that weekend, but if I can, Chaz and I will be there." Jason cut in, hoping to diffuse the tension from Josh. Jason stretched. "Look, I gotta get out of here. I wanna read my baby a bedtime story."

"It ain't gonna be about nothing but *cats* anyway," Mark laughed. Josh joined in, and Jason was not amused.

"Hey, you leave Kayla and her cats alone," Jason barked. "She can like whatever the hell she *wants*."

Mark pointed to Jason, while looking at Josh. "He got a house full of kitties and shit," he goaded.

Josh laughed harder. Catching Jason's angered stare, Josh put his hands up. "My bad Jase, but you know Mark is a fool."

Jason grabbed his wallet off the pool table and shoved it in his back pocket. "At least my child likes *real* animals and not *made up* ones like *your* boys."

Mark slammed his hand on the table. "Hey! A ratable-taste *is* a real animal," he argued.

"A *what*?" Josh asked, confused.

Mark let out a quick sigh. "Look, they make up names for shit...don't worry about it. My boys got imagination, so fuck you, cat boy," he hurled at Jason.

"Yeah okay, fuck that ollie in your kitchen," Jason threw over his shoulder as he walked out. "And call your wife back so she can stop calling *mine*."

"I'll call Malajia back when I *feel* like it!" he hollered at Jason's departing back. He picked up the phone from the table. "And I feel like doing it *now*," he muttered. As Mark dialed his home number, he glanced up and caught Josh staring at him. "What?"

"What the hell is an ollie?" Josh asked.

Mark flipped him the finger as he put the phone to his ear.

Chapter 4

Emily knocked on the door and patiently waited for someone to answer. Her eyes lit up when the door opened. "Hi Mommy," she beamed, giving her a hug.

"My baby," Ms. Harris gushed, holding on to Emily for what felt like dear life.

Emily giggled as her mother held her. "Mommy, you have to let go so I can come inside," she teased.

Ms. Harris released Emily with a laugh. "Sorry, sorry," she said, grabbing Emily's hand and pulling her into the house. "I thought you were coming *tomorrow*."

"Well I had some extra days, so I took off a little early," Emily replied, setting her small suitcase by the door. Her planned weekend back to Jersey had finally arrived; Emily had been looking forward to it for some time. "It actually feels weird not sitting in my classroom on a Thursday."

"Well, you deserve an extra day off," Ms. Harris smiled, heading into the kitchen; Emily followed. "I'm so glad that you decided to stay here with me, instead of going to a hotel," she began, moving a plate of cake from the counter to the kitchen table.

Emily smiled. "Yeah, me too," she said, peering at the table. "Is that lemon pound cake?" she asked, pointing to the plate.

"Of course," Ms. Harris smiled, sitting down.

Emily clasped her hands together; it was her favorite dessert. Truth be told, she was glad to be spending the weekend with her mother. Despite the tension of her mother's smothering ways during Emily's college years, the two women had come to an understanding about their mother/daughter relationship and had been on good terms since.

"So, how was work this week?" Ms. Harris asked.

Emily washed her hands in the sink, then sat down at the kitchen table. "It was good."

Ms. Harris nodded. "I know those children love you."

"Yeah, I love them too," Emily smiled. "And I get to give them back after eight hours, so that's perfect," she joked. "Except for Anthony, I'm happy to keep *him*."

"Well I know that boy loves you too."

"Yeah," Emily agreed.

"Is he excited for the wedding?" Ms. Harris asked.

Emily cringed on the inside. *Please don't bring up the wedding now.* She grabbed a piece of cake and set it on a napkin, shrugging in the process. "I don't think that he thinks much of it, he's seven after all," she explained.

"I guess I mean, is he excited about you becoming his stepmother?" she clarified. "How does he feel about that?"

"From what I can tell, he's fine with it," Emily replied.

Ms. Harris nodded. "Does he remember his mother at all?" she wondered.

"I don't think so," Emily answered honestly. "He was only two when she died—Will does talk to him about her."

Ms. Harris nodded. "How do you feel about that?"

Emily looked skeptical. "How do I feel about Anthony knowing about his *mother*?" she questioned. "I feel good about it, he *should* know about her."

Ms. Harris gave a slight shrug, her tell that she wanted to say something less appropriate.

"Are you implying that I should feel *angry* about it? Because I *don't*." Emily added, defensively. "I *know* that I'm not his mother, and I'm not trying to replace her."

"No sweetie, that's not what I am implying," Ms. Harris assured.

Emily folded her arms as she sat back. She knew that her mother liked Will and Anthony, but she suspected that her own mother wasn't too fond of Emily being a stepmother.

"Can we talk about something else, please?" Emily requested.

Ms. Harris put a hand up. "Sure," she agreed. She took a piece of cake from the plate and set it on a napkin in front of her. "Are you going to make Jazmine a bridesmaid?"

Emily rolled her eyes; this was why she did not want to talk about the wedding with her mother. She knew that it was going to turn into a conversation about Jazmine, and that was the last person that she wanted to talk about. "I came here to *relax*, Mom, not to be stressed," she sighed.

"I'm not stressing you," Ms. Harris said.

"Bringing up *Jaz* is stressing me," Emily threw back.

"Emily, all I'm saying is that she's your sister. Your *only* sister."

"And that same *sister* told me when I got engaged that I'm too boring to have a wedding and that I should just elope," Emily recalled. She had told her family over a Thanksgiving dinner that she was engaged, Jazmine's attitude had gone sour over the news. The comments had been so bad, she'd put a damper on Emily's whole visit. "That same *sister* asked Will if he was sure that he actually wanted to marry me. And has been criticizing everything about my wedding," Emily vented. "She's lucky that she's even *invited* to it after everything that she's put me through."

"Okay okay," Ms. Harris placated.

Emily took a deep breath.

"Have things gotten better with her staying—"

"Mom, I don't want to talk about her at *all*," Emily stressed, putting her hand on her head in exasperation. She was beginning to regret agreeing to stay there.

Ms. Harris let out a sigh. *God, I just wish that they could get along.* "So, what do you plan on doing while you're up this end?" she asked, finally changing the subject.

Emily took a bite from her piece of cake. "I hope to be able to see some of the girls for one," she said between chews. "As a matter of fact, I have to call Alex — she's supposed to be in Philly this weekend."

"Oh…" Ms. Harris muttered. "That sounds like fun."

Yeah, fun is what I need, Emily thought, finishing her cake.

Alex tapped on her laptop at the kitchen table in her family home. "This is not coming together like I wanted," she muttered to herself.

Mrs. Chisolm walked into the kitchen. "You still working baby?"

Alex sighed. "*Trying* to anyway."

"Oh, I'll be out of your way—"

Alex let out a laugh. "No Ma, that's not what I meant," noticing the apologetic look on her mother's face. "I mean that I can't seem to get focused."

Mrs. Chisolm giggled. "Okay." She headed to the stove to check on the food. "You've been working on that thing since you got here this morning," she observed. "You need to take a break."

"I know, I will," Alex promised, looking back at the laptop. "Just trying to tie up some loose ends first...deadlines and all."

"I understand," Mrs. Chisolm said, grabbing seasonings from the cabinet. "Your sister just left to head back to Virginia the other day."

"Yeah, I know, she told me," Alex replied, amusement in her voice. "She said she figured that she'd bugged you and Dad enough... It would be nice to see Semaj while I'm here," she said of her seventeen-year-old brother.

"Child, that boy is always somewhere," Mrs. Chisolm laughed. "He's probably at work."

"Yeah, that wouldn't surprise me; he loves having money," Alex replied, closing her laptop. "I told him that I would send him some money if he needs it. He needs to focus on school."

"Alexandra, your brother is like your father and *you*...stubborn," Mrs. Chisolm chuckled. "He wants to make his own."

"I know, I know," Alex said, sitting back in her seat.

"*Speaking* of money," Mrs. Chisolm began, fixing a gaze on Alex. "Stop sending *us* money."

Alex's eyes widened. "Ma—"

"Stop sending it," Mrs. Chisolm repeated, stern. "Now we appreciate what you're trying to do, but we're good over here... You keep your money for yourself. You earned every last penny."

Alex put her hands up in surrender. She knew it was only a matter of time before her mother reprimanded her for sending them money every month. She couldn't help it. Now that Alex was financially secure, she felt the need to take care of her family. "Okay fine, Ma," she relented. "I hope you know that I wasn't doing it to insult you."

"Oh, we know that," Mrs. Chisolm assured, walking over to Alex and putting her arms around her. "But like I said, we're good over here."

"At least let me get you a new laptop," Alex offered. "That one that dad bought second hand is hanging on by tape."

"Which is fine by us because we don't use the thing anyway," Mrs. Chisolm joked, moving back over to the stove. "We're not into all that technology."

"It's so *convenient* though," Alex harped. "You can pay your bills online and everything."

"Mailing the payments has worked just fine for us over the years," Mrs. Chisolm maintained. "Your father mails them off one month, I send it off the next."

Alex stared at her for a moment. "Okay Ma, whatever you say," she relented. "What smells so good?"

Mrs. Chisolm smiled. "Bar B Q chicken, yellow rice, and cabbage."

Alex put a hand over her chest. "Good, I miss your cooking," she breathed.

"I'll make sure to send you back with plenty," her mother promised. "Don't want you missing any meals being so busy and all."

Alex pointed to her ample behind. "Does this booty *look* like I've missed any meals?" she joked.

"Not a one," Mrs. Chisolm laughed.

"Ma!" Alex bellowed, amused.

"I just got to my mom's," Chasity spoke into her phone as she knocked on her mother's front door. "...Lunch isn't for like another hour, why are you sweating me... Girl—shut up and feed your damn kids before they jump you... Bye."

Hanging up the phone, Chasity sucked her teeth. "Lady, answer the damn door," she grunted, knocking again. When the door opened, she regarded her mother with an annoyed look.

"And the attitude is *for*?" Trisha Duvall ground out,

placing a hand on her hip.

"You took all long, it's hot as hell out here," Chasity ground out, moving around Trisha to walk inside.

Trisha shook her head as she shut the door behind Chasity. "Why didn't you just use your key?"

"No thank you, not after I almost walked in on you and your boyfriend being grown on the couch that one time," Chasity admonished, recalling an incident just a few months ago.

Trisha put her hand over her face in embarrassment. "God, don't remind me... I almost traumatized my grandbaby."

Chasity shook her head. "No she was fine, she just wanted to know why that man jumped off of Mom-Mom."

Trisha walked over and playfully tapped Chasity's arm. "Stop it...thank God we were still clothed."

Chasity set her purse on the chair. "Um hmm," she muttered, folding her arms. "How *is* my future stepdaddy anyway?" she teased.

"Girl, I'm about to throw his ass out with the trash," Trisha grunted.

Chasity laughed. "*Again?*"

Trisha made a face. "Shut up."

"What did he do? Bring you red wine instead of white?"

"I said, shut up," Trisha barked.

Chasity was amused. She had been a listening ear on several occasions when her mother vented about the little disagreements between herself and her boyfriend of three years. Her mother could overreact over small things at times. "Leave that man alone Trisha, I actually *like* him for you," she warned.

Trisha flagged Chasity with her hand. "Whatever."

"Stop being petty," Chasity shot back. Hearing a noise from the den, she frowned. "Eww Mom, he's not here is he?"

"No, it's just Aja," Trisha clarified. Chasity rolled her eyes and Trisha shot her a warning look. "Chasity be nice, that's your cousin."

Chasity's eyes widened in shock. "I didn't even *say* anything."

"You didn't *have* to, your face tells everything," Trisha chuckled.

"Besides, that's *your* cousin," Chasity spat, turning her lip up.

"My first, your second, go say hi evil," Trisha demanded, pointing to the den.

Chasity stomped her foot on the floor and let out a whine. "She keeps calling me 'cousin', I hate that shit. I have a name."

"Go," Trisha commanded, stern.

Chasity complied, though she was not happy about it. She headed to the den and stood in the doorway. "Hi Aja," she greeted, unenthused.

The dark-skinned young woman looked up from her laptop and smiled bright at her. "Cousin," she beamed.

"Ugh," Chasity grunted.

Aja giggled. "Come on, don't be like that," she teased.

It wasn't that Chasity didn't like Aja. Her second cousin on grandfather's side—whom she'd only officially met a year ago when the girl had moved from her own mother's home in Atlanta to attend college in the city—seemed nice enough. But the twenty-four-year-old was too chipper for Chasity's liking. Aja seemed to always want to be up under her whenever she was around.

"Ooh, what are you doing later? We should hang out," Aja proposed.

"I already have plans," Chasity rebuffed, looking at her watch.

"Well, how about I come *with* you and we can hang out afterwards?" she pressed.

Chasity stared at her in disbelief. *The fuck?* "How about no?" she sneered.

Aja just laughed; for some reason she didn't take Chasity's attitude seriously. "It's fine, we'll hang out one of these days."

"Great," Chasity muttered, examining her nails.

"Can you at least help me with my coding assignment?" Aja asked. "This summer class has been killing me."

"No," Chasity refused.

"Come on, *please*?" Aja pleaded, clasping her hands together. Ever since she'd learned that Chasity had graduated college with a degree in computer science, she never hesitated to ask for her cousin's help with her assignments.

"Aja, you *suck*," Chasity mocked. "I've seen your work, you need to find a new major sweetie." As she turned to walk away, she nearly bumped into Trisha. Her mother spun her back around to face Aja.

"Chasity, help the girl," Trisha ordered; she'd heard everything.

"There aren't enough hours in the goddamn day," Chasity threw back.

"She's getting better," Trisha argued.

"Hey Cousin Trish, did you ever get around to thinking about letting me intern for you?" Aja cut in.

Chasity folded her arms and shot Trisha an amused look. Trisha on the other hand looked horrified. "I'm sorry?" Trisha questioned.

"Remember I asked if I could intern a few weeks ago?" Aja reminded. "You know to get some experience."

"Experience with *what* exactly?" Chasity wondered.

"Web design," Aja answered. She focused her sight on Trisha. "You told me that Chasity used to do your pages while she was in school. Figured I could do the same thing."

Trisha held the same horrified look; Aja was nowhere *near* as good as Chasity was back in school.

Chasity was amused as she glanced over at Trisha. "I think I like that idea," she teased. Trisha cut her eye at her. "You said it yourself, she's getting better, right?"

"Um…" Trisha hesitated. She didn't want to hurt Aja's feelings, but she wasn't about to let her website suffer. "How about you pass your class first and we'll revisit it," she pacified.

"Fair enough," Aja smiled, closing her laptop.

Chasity leaned close to Trisha. "She's gonna fuck up your site," she muttered.

"Hush," Trisha said, poking Chasity on the arm. Chasity laughed and retreated to the living room.

Aja stood from her seat and gathered her belongings. "I have to head to class, thanks for letting me crash here while my apartment is being repainted."

"No problem," Trisha replied. "You're welcome anytime."

Aja smiled as she made her way to the front door. She waved to Chasity. "See you later cousin."

"*Chasity*, but yeah, see you later," Chasity scoffed.

Once the door closed, Trisha shook her head and chuckled. "Your evil ass was *meant* to be an only child," she joked.

Chasity rolled her eyes. "Anyway, you called me over here. What's up?"

"Oh, I wanted to give you the stuff that I bought Kayla," Trisha beamed, heading over to a closet. Chasity watched as Trisha dragged several large bags out. "I found the cutest tea party set, and—"

Chasity sucked her teeth. "Mom, come on, I told you to stop buying her all that stuff," she admonished. "The girl is already spoiled."

"You can't blame that all on *me*," Trisha argued.

"True, there's also *Dad*, Jason's *parents*, *Grandmom*—"

"Don't forget Jason's *grandparents*," Trisha cut in. "*You* and *Jason* too."

"On no, *you guys* take it *overboard*," Chasity argued back.

Trisha waved her hand dismissively. "I will not apologize, nor will I stop buying things for my grandchild," she stated, defiant. "It's my money and I can do what I want with it."

"Yeah, well my house won't fit all this shit in there," Chasity pointed out. "Half of her stuff is already in the basement."

"Chasity, I have already said that I would either give you one of my bigger properties, or give you the *money* for a bigger house."

"And *I* already said no," Chasity refused. "We're fine renting the house we have for now. I like the house. Besides, I could always sell the condo in Miami or the house in Tucson if we really wanted to *buy* one."

"I really don't want you to sell those properties," Trisha said.

"They're *my* properties and I can do what I *want* with them," Chasity threw back.

Trisha let out a sigh. She had the money at her disposal, and she wished that Chasity would just take it, but Trisha admired that her daughter didn't want it or need it. "Fine, but I'm still getting whatever I want for Kayla," she maintained.

"Just like I wanted to get her that bounce house for her birthday party."

"You still mad that Dad got the bounce house for her?" Chasity asked, trying to hold in her laughter.

"Yes, I said that *I* was getting the bounce house," Trisha snapped, stomping her foot on the floor.

Chasity's eyes widened at the outburst. "Okay petty," she teased. She glanced at her watch. "Look, I don't feel like loading this stuff now, I'll get it later," she said. "I have to go anyway."

"Oh that's right, you're having lunch with the girls today," Trisha recalled. "Did Sidra come down?"

Chasity shook her head.

"Well, I hope you have fun. It's been a while since you've been out."

"Yeah, I know," Chasity sighed.

Trisha reached out and rubbed Chasity's arm. "I know it's hard. You and Jason both working demanding jobs, then your free time is spent with baby girl," she sympathized.

"I don't even mind that," Chasity said. "Spending my free time with my baby, that is," she amended. "And it's not like I can't go out when I really *want* to, I've just been...too irritated to do anything."

"Why? What's going on?" Trisha asked, concerned.

Chasity took a deep breath. She wanted more than anything to vent her frustrations about her job, but she already knew what her mother would say—Chasity wasn't in the mood nor had the time for it. "Jason has been on another project at work and I barely see him." That was a partial truth; she hated his projects as much as he did.

"I don't get it. Jason is the best developer that they have, they should be *catering* to him," Trisha frowned. "Why do they keep putting so much on him?"

"Because that's what the hell they do to people who are good at their damn job," Chasity ground out. *I should know.*

Trisha shook her head. "Yeah well, hopefully Jason will get a job somewhere better."

"He won't," Chasity said. "He's still hoping that they'll promote him."

"Well…hopefully they'll do *that* and cut his damn hours back to a normal timeframe."

"Yeah, me too," Chasity put out, giving Trisha a hug. "I'll see you later."

"Okay, bring Kayla with you when you come get this stuff," Trisha waved.

"You want her overnight?" Chasity asked.

"Of course!" Trisha squealed, clapping her hands together.

Chasity shook her head in amusement. "All right, I'll bring her," she promised, heading out the door.

Chapter 5

Alex scrolled through her phone as she sat at a Mexican restaurant in downtown Philadelphia. She reached for her glass on the table and took a sip of water.

Someone grabbed her shoulder, startling her.

"Hey!" the person barked, causing Alex to almost spit out her water. She spun around in her seat to see Chasity, standing there laughing.

"If I wasn't so happy to see you, I'd throw this water on you," Alex chuckled, standing up from her seat. She wrapped her arms around Chasity, who hugged her in return. "It's so good to see you," she gushed.

"You too," Chasity replied as the women parted.

"I ordered everybody a drink," Alex smiled, sitting back down.

"You *did?*" Chasity chuckled as she too sat. "Is it invisible? 'Cause I don't see it."

"Hush up, they haven't brought it yet," Alex threw back, putting her phone in her purse. "Still a smart ass."

"Always," Chasity agreed.

"Malajia came with you?" Alex asked, taking a sip of water.

"Yeah, she should be walking in any minute," Chasity answered, pushing hair over her shoulder.

"Didn't you ride here together?" Alex wondered. Chasity nodded. "Then why didn't she just come in *with* you?"

"Oh, I smacked her phone out of her hand and it fell down the side of my car seat. She's probably still trying to get it out."

Alex chuckled at Chasity's nonchalant answer. "Dare I ask *why* you did that?"

"She put her hand in my face and she knows not to do that," Chasity replied with the same nonchalance.

Alex shook her head in amusement. "You two… Still at it, after all these years, huh?"

Chasity chuckled. "Yeah."

Before Alex could utter another word, Malajia stormed into the restaurant. Alex stood up and held her arms out for a hug.

"Chasity it never should've taken that long for me to figure out how to move your seat back," Malajia huffed, pointing her phone at Chasity, who just laughed. She then looked at Alex, who was still standing there, arms outstretched. Malajia frowned her face up. "What?" she scoffed. "Girl ain't nobody hugging you."

Alex's mouth fell open. "Seriously?!" she exclaimed. "I haven't seen you in—" her rant was interrupted by Malajia throwing her arms around her.

"I'm just playing, my favorite mop," Malajia gushed. "You know I missed you."

Alex couldn't help but laugh. "Missed you too, crazy." The girls parted and sat down.

"Alex ordered us invisible drinks, and shit," Chasity joked.

Malajia sucked her teeth. "Alex, you better have ordered a real drink. Ain't nobody playing around with you, you got money now," she hurled.

Alex narrowed her eyes at Malajia.

"Besides, you owe us for all that cheap ass food you used to buy back at school," Malajia continued.

"Keep talking smack hear? You won't get a damn *sip*," Alex fussed.

"Oh, I'm *gonna* get a damn sip," Malajia mumbled, folding her arms on the table. "Got me chopped."

Alex just shook her head as the waiter approached and placed her ordered drinks on the table.

"Are you ladies ready to order?" the young man asked, holding a notepad.

"Not yet, we're still waiting on one more person," Alex answered.

"Okay, no problem, I'll check back in a few."

Malajia followed the guy's progress as he walked off. "He's a cutie," she mentioned.

"Girl, you better stop staring at him before I tell Mark,"

Alex teased.

Malajia waved her hand. "I can *look*," she argued. "I'm married, not *blind*... Shit *you* should be looking. Ol' single ass," she directed to Alex.

Alex rolled her eyes. "Whatever, there is nothing wrong with being single," she argued. "I plan on *staying* that way for now." She took a sip of her drink. "I forgot to tell y'all, I saw Reggie not too long ago."

"Eww, his arrogant ass is still alive?" Chasity sneered.

"Probably still flirting his way through New York and shit," Malajia chimed in.

"I never liked his ass," Chasity added.

Alex looked shocked. "You never told me that," she hurled at Chasity.

"The hell I *didn't*," Chasity threw back. "The day we met him when you brought him to my birthday dinner, I *told* you that. I told you I felt like he was trying to flirt with me."

Malajia raised her hand. "Yup, I remember," she chimed in. Alex's mouth fell open. "*I* told you that I didn't like how close his breath was to my damn face when he said 'good to meet you' and you told me to stop being ignorant."

Chasity snickered hard.

"Malajia, because you *were* being ignorant," Alex pointed out.

"I just didn't like that suit he had on. Nobody else had a suit on at her birthday dinner, he was trying too hard," Malajia snapped, waving her hand in Alex's face. "You dodged a bullet with Mr. Hot Breathed Suit Man."

Alex couldn't help but laugh. "Yeah, I suppose I *did*." She let out a sigh. "I guess I kind of knew, which is why I wasn't surprised when I found those messages he was sending to those other women."

"Fuck him," Malajia grunted. "*And* he wasn't even cute. Girl, please."

Chasity shook her head at Malajia, then put her hand on Alex's wrist. "Sorry you got hurt," she said sincerely. She remembered how excited Alex had been when she'd first started dating in New York. Chasity knew from many a phone call how much Alex wanted companionship.

"Thanks, but I'm okay," Alex assured, patting Chasity's hand. "I know there are good men out there, so I'm not worrying."

"True," Malajia agreed, tipping her glass to Alex.

A few minutes passed and Alex took another sip of her mojito. "It feels so good to be back down this end. I love New York, but I miss Philly."

Chasity ran her hand through her hair. "Alex, I would love to participate in further conversation, but I'm fuckin' starving," she complained.

"God, let me call Emily to see where she is," Alex quickly said, reaching into her purse for her phone. "I know how cranky you get when you're hungry...or tired...or just woke up...or—"

"Funny," Chasity grunted; Malajia giggled.

Emily hurried through the door before Alex could dial. "I'm so sorry I'm late," Emily panted.

Malajia glanced down her length. "You sweatin' hard as shit," she laughed at Emily's glistening face.

"It's *hot* outside," Emily complained, reaching for a napkin. "It's *September*, where's the *breeze*?" She waved a dismissive hand. "Forget it, hi girls," she beamed, giving everybody hugs.

"God Em, you just got sweat all over my arm," Chasity jeered as Emily parted from their embrace.

"I'm sorry!" Emily laughed as Chasity wiped her forearm on her jeans. Emily grabbed more napkins from the table as she sat down. "Ooh, what drinks are these?" she asked, patting her face.

"Mojitos," Alex smiled. "I figured it's nice and refreshing to go with lunch, don't you think?"

"It tastes like grass," Chasity spat.

"Yeah, Alex I wasn't gonna say nothing, but it *does* taste like somebody threw lawn shavings in there," Malajia added.

Emily busted out laughing at the annoyed look on Alex's face.

"You better drink it," Alex fussed, pointing.

An hour later with full stomachs, the girls sipped their

drinks and caught up. "Anybody talk to Sidra today?" Emily asked, leaning back in her seat.

"No, I talked to her *yesterday* though," Alex said. "I wish she was here. It feels weird not having all five of us together."

"Well, maybe if she takes the sand out of her ass to make a damn trip *home* once in a while, we can see her," Malajia grunted.

Emily looked confused. "Why would she have sand in her—"

"'Cause California got all those beaches," Malajia defended, folding her arms.

"Maybe we can all go down *there* to visit," Alex suggested. "I've never been to California, it could be fun."

"I'm gonna go down there next year," Chasity said.

Malajia looked at Chasity. "You mean *we're* going down there next year."

"Bitch I speak Spanish, not French, I said *I*," Chasity threw back.

Malajia sucked her teeth and Emily snickered.

"Anyway, I guess I'll get my ass down there *eventually*," Malajia ground out. "Having the twins, it's hard to get away for more than a few hours."

"Y'all parents won't take them?" Alex asked, looking at a dessert menu.

"Yeah, for a few *hours*," Malajia reiterated. "They're a lot to handle."

"They're not that bad," Chasity argued.

"*You* wanna take them for the weekend, *Godmother?*" Malajia quickly threw out.

"Nope," Chasity threw back.

"A damn shame," Malajia grunted.

"Oh bitch cut it the fuck out, I barely have time for my *own* child on the weekends, with all this work I have," Chasity argued.

"Yeah, yeah," Malajia dismissed. "*Speaking* of which, I gotta find out who's watching these kids for the week of your wedding, Em."

Alex looked confused. "But we'll only be in Virginia for the weekend."

"Yeah, it's just five hours away. I would never have you guys take off the whole week," Emily put in.

"Don't nobody need to know all that," Malajia barked.

"*That's* why your ass can't get a sitter, 'cause you're always trying to get over," Chasity sneered.

"That's not even true." Malajia rolled her eyes then looked at Chasity. "Who's watching Kayla for that weekend?"

"My dad," Chasity replied. "He's taking her to New York."

"You think he'll take the boys?" Malajia asked, hopeful.

Chasity frowned at Malajia, "*No!*"

Malajia sucked her teeth. "Well then fuck it, I'm sending them with Geri," she resolved.

Emily laughed. "Just bring the boys *with* you," she suggested. "I won't mind."

"It ain't about what you *mind*," Malajia jeered, earning a snicker from Emily. "It's about what I'm *not doing*… Nah, Geri got em."

"That's a damn shame," Alex laughed. She then clasped her hands together. "Ooh, let me see some recent pictures of your babies, I know you have some."

Chasity reached for her phone as she smiled. "I have the cutest video of Kayla—"

"Chasity, nobody wants to see that video of Cupcake picking that one ass apple off that dry ass tree in your backyard," Malajia cut in.

"Hey!" Chasity barked, slapping her hand on the table and earning laughter from Alex and Emily. "My baby picked that apple all by herself and she was excited about it. So, you're gonna watch the fuckin' video and enjoy it!"

Malajia sat there staring at Chasity, wide-eyed.

Alex held her hand out for Chasity's phone. "Aww, Marra, *I'll* watch it," she placated.

"Oh, I know *you* will, but Malajia's gonna watch it *first*, just for being a smart-ass bitch," Chasity barked, pushing the phone in Malajia's face.

"I *saw* it already," Malajia complained,

"Watch it again," Chasity insisted, angry.

Malajia let out a huff and snatched the phone from Chasity. "Why you always gotta yell at me?" she ground out, looking at the video. "Aww, how cute," she threw out, sarcastic. Chasity snatched her phone from Malajia and handed it to Alex, who eagerly began watching.

Malajia looked over at Emily, who had tears running down her face from laughing. "You laughing kinda hard over there, Emily," Malajia observed.

It took several tries for Emily to compose herself long enough to speak. "Oh my God, I missed you two so much," she said, wiping a tear from her eye.

Alex's smile was bright as she watched the video. "Oh my God, Chasity she's beautiful."

"Thank you," Chasity replied.

"And she got so big," Alex gushed; she placed a hand over her chest. "Aww, look at her little pink tutu."

"She's four Alex, she's *supposed* to grow," Chasity chuckled. "And fuck that tutu, I hate those things."

Alex giggled.

"Yeah, she's adorbs and all, but you wanna see something *really* cute?" Malajia cut in, grabbing her phone from her purse. "Take a look at this video of my boys playing basketball with their daddy."

Malajia smiled as she handed Emily her phone. Alex and Emily leaned in to watch it.

"They're so cute," Emily squealed.

"I know right," Malajia approved, proud. "Look at how good they're playing."

Emily stared at the screen. "Umm, Malajia I don't think they're playing," she observed. "One of the twins just got the ball snatched by the other one and he fell on the ground."

"But he fell like a G though," Malajia defended, putting a hand up.

"Uh, he just started kicking and screaming, and Mark just told him to shut the hell up," Alex informed.

Malajia sucked her teeth; she snatched her phone back and shoved it in her purse. "Fuck y'all," she grunted.

"What did we do?" Emily laughed.

"Y'all ain't even have to point that shit out, *I* know what's on the damn video," Malajia threw back, shaking her hand in their direction.

"I told you to stop showing people that shit," Chasity teased.

"Shut the fuck up, Chasity," Malajia barked.

Chasity snickered.

"Malajia, temper tantrums or not, your boys are adorable," Alex gushed.

"Yeah thanks," Malajia grunted, folding her arms on the table. "They be embarrassing me just like Mark," she joked. "*Speaking* of Mark, he had an idea."

"What's that?" Alex wondered.

"He said that we should all go to homecoming this year," she informed. "Josh is already in and David said he's going to try to make it too."

"Yeah, Jase told me about that," Chasity said.

"Really?" Emily smiled. "Y'all are really going to come?"

"I don't have an issue with it," Chasity shrugged.

"I'm down for going," Malajia added. "I think it'll be good for everyone to hang out as a group again, you know."

"I love it, I'm in," Alex beamed, tapping the table with her hand. "Anybody ask Sidra?"

"Not yet," Malajia answered.

"Let's call her now," Alex suggested, grabbing her phone from her purse.

"Aww shit, Alex done got herself a new phone!" Malajia bellowed. Remembering Alex's outdated flip phone from college, she was impressed by the sleek grey touch screen in Alex's hand.

Alex made a face at Malajia as she dialed Sidra's number, moving her seat around so that all the girls could see her phone. She smiled when Sidra's face popped up on the screen.

"*And* she got video call," Malajia added, excited.

"Malajia," Alex warned.

Malajia put her hand up as she giggled. "My bad."

"Oh my God, y'all are together?" Sidra pouted. "I wish I was there."

"Yeah, we wish you were here too," Emily consoled, pushing her hair behind her ears.

"Yeah, yeah, miss you, blah blah, real quick—

Homecoming this year, we're all going," Malajia quickly cut in. "So bring your ass to Virginia."

Sidra glanced at something off to the side. "*When* is it?"

"In October," Malajia informed. "Just like it is *every* year."

"Nice," Sidra scoffed of Malajia's sarcasm. She then let out a sigh. "I don't think I can make it."

"Why *not*?" Alex asked, disappointed. "I think it'll be so much fun."

"I know, but my work to-do list is sky high… I don't think that I'll be able to take off," Sidra returned.

"Sid, it's like a month from now and we *know* you have vacation days saved up, so stop playing," Malajia said. "Somebody *else* can file those papers. You'll only need a Friday and maybe a Monday off."

Sidra scratched her head. "I *do* have the time, but— Can we just go *next* year?"

"No, no, *we're* going to homecoming *this* year," Chasity cut in, earning a snicker from Malajia. "You wanna sit this out that's on *you*. But the *rest* of us won't."

"Took them ignorant ass words right out of my mouth," Malajia goaded.

Sidra ran her hands through her hair, letting out another sigh. "So is…*everybody* going?"

"Bitch are you coming or *not*? Don't be asking no questions," Malajia barked.

Sidra shook her head. "Malajia, your whole vibe is just utterly unnecessary," she ground out.

"Yeah? Unnecessarily tired of your *shit* is what I am," Malajia threw back.

Alex shot Malajia a confused look.

"Made no sense, retract it," Chasity commented of Malajia's sorry comeback.

"Too late. It's already out there, and I'm standing by it," Malajia maintained, unfazed.

"Anyway, I'll think about it," Sidra relented after a moment. "But look, I have to get to this meeting, so I'll talk back later. Love you girls."

"Love you too, Sid," Alex said, before ending the call.

"Well, hopefully she shows up." She signaled for the waiter. They'd taken up space in the restaurant long enough. "Do you girls want to do something else since we're already out?" she asked. "Maybe we can go catch a movie? Go get dessert somewhere else, maybe? I'm not ready to part from y'all just yet."

"Whatever you want to do, I'm down for it. Mark is stuck with the kids today, I'm taking full advantage," Malajia said.

"Perfect," Alex beamed, reaching for her purse. "Let's start with brownie sundaes from the cookie shop next door."

Malajia nodded in agreement. As the waiter set the check on the table, she grabbed her purse. "Last one at the table, pays the bill!" she blurted out, jumping up along with a laughing Emily.

Malajia and Emily ran for the door, and Chasity jumped up right as Alex did. She pushed her chair in front of Alex to block her, before she ran out after the other girls.

"Y'all play too much!" Alex hollered after them. She grabbed the bill. "This bill is ninety-seven bucks!"

Malajia stuck her head back in. "You got it. You owe Chaz money for all those times she paid for your shit back in school anyway."

Alex's mouth fell open. "And I paid her *back*."

"You *didn't*, but I'm not trippin'," Chasity chortled from outside.

"Whatever, I got you Chasity and Emily, but none of that has nothing to do with *you*, Malajia," Alex hurled at Malajia.

"It does, 'cause *I* ain't got it," Malajia laughed and pulled her head back outside.

Resolved, Alex let out a huff. As she whipped out her wallet, she looked up and saw Malajia jog back inside. Alex stared, annoyed as Malajia snatched her container of leftovers from the table.

"Forgot this," Malajia said. "Hurry up and pay so we can get going," she threw over her shoulder as she ran back out the door.

"You're paying for the brownies!" Alex called after her.

"*Emily* is," Malajia threw over her shoulder.

"Huh?!" Emily exclaimed.

Sidra retrieved a folder from her nightstand. She pulled out its contents and spread them across her bed. Folding her legs up, she stared at the papers strewn across her comforter.

Reaching for her mug of tea, she heard a knock on her bedroom door. "Come in," she called.

Mrs. Howard opened the door and stuck her head inside. "Sweetie, do you want another refill on your tea?" she asked.

Sidra managed a smile. "No I'm okay, thanks though."

Mrs. Howard nodded as she walked in the room. "Brought work home, huh?"

"Yeah," Sidra sighed. "This deadline for these contracts to be revised has been moved up, so I just want to get a head start for tomorrow."

"Makes sense, I guess." Mrs. Howard folded her arms. "Have you given any thought to—"

"Mama, if you're going to bring up me being a lawyer again, I'd like to request that it wait until I've had a glass of wine," Sidra requested, looking up at her mother. "I'd prefer to be a little inebriated before I listen to you tell me how I wasted you and Daddy's money on a law degree."

Mrs. Howard's mouth fell open in shock. "Princess, I'd *never* say that," she assured. "And I'd never *think* that, don't be silly."

Sidra let out a sigh. "Sorry… I just…" *Great, I'm projecting my own thoughts onto my mother.*

"I mean, I *was* going to ask about your future goals, but I'd *never* say that you wasted your education," Mrs. Howard added, hurt in her voice.

"I know you wouldn't Mama. I'm sorry, forget I said that. I'm just tired and a little frustrated," She took a few sips of her warm tea. "Anyway, what time are you flying back tomorrow?" she asked, setting her mug back in place.

"Plane leaves at eleven," Mrs. Howard answered, sitting on Sidra's bed. "I'll be back soon enough," she added, noticing the somber look on Sidra's face. "I'll see if I can bring Gabrielle with me."

Sidra smiled bright at the idea of seeing her five-year-old niece. "Well tell Marcus to make room in Gabby's closet, because I plan on buying her everything that she wants," she beamed. Sidra enjoyed her mother's visits to California. Mrs. Howard had made it a point to fly out every few months to spend time with her only daughter. Though she stayed for a few days at a time, Sidra always grew sad when it was time for her mother to leave again.

Mrs. Howard laughed. "You know how your brother feels about people spoiling her."

"I don't care *what* he says, I'm doing it," Sidra returned.

"I'm sure he's looking forward to you telling him that to his *face* when you see him over Thanksgiving," Mrs. Howard said.

"Yeah..."

Sidra's trailing off was not missed by Mrs. Howard. "You're still coming back for Thanksgiving, right?" she asked. "You've missed the last three."

"I know I have and yes, I still plan on coming," Sidra assured, then let out a sigh. "It's just that... I might be heading back East sooner than that."

Mrs. Howard raised an eyebrow. "Oh?" she pondered. "For what occasion? You friend's wedding isn't until January, right?"

"Yes...and you don't have to make it seem like I only come home for certain events," Sidra sneered.

"*Don't* you?" Mrs. Howard threw back. "Then you run right back."

Sidra made a slight face; she knew her mother was right. "Well...I talked to the girls the other day," she began. "They're going to Paradise Valley's homecoming next month...actually the whole *group* plans on going, so of course they want *me* to come."

"And you still haven't fully decided yet?" Mrs. Howard questioned, picking up on Sidra's hesitation.

"I mean, I *want* to go... I miss the girls, and I know I'll have fun... God *knows* I could use some," Sidra answered.

"What's keeping you from making the decision?"

Sidra glanced down at her hands.

Mrs. Howard tilted her head. "The same reason why you don't come home more often," she concluded. "You're worried about running into Josh."

Sidra rubbed her face with her hand, nodding. "Except this time I wouldn't *run into* him," she clarified. "I'll be forced to be in his presence the *entire* weekend."

"Sidra—"

"I know Mama, I *know*, you don't have to say it," Sidra cut in. "I'm being stupid."

"You're not stupid," Mrs. Howard placated, patting Sidra's hand.

"Thank you."

"A bit silly, maybe...unreasonable, *definitely*," Mrs. Howard said. Sidra let out a loud sigh. "Sweetie, seeing him can't be *that* bad. I mean, you two still talk, don't you?"

"Well yeah, *occasionally*. But of course *seeing* him is different." Sidra let out a huff. "I mean, what if he brings whoever he's dating now to homecoming? I don't want to see some heffa with her hands all on him."

Mrs. Howard squeezed Sidra's hand. "And if he does, you don't have the right to have an attitude about it."

Sidra rolled her eyes. *Yes, I know that but I can still have one.*

"Sidra, *you* made the decision five years ago not to tell Josh how you felt about him," Mrs. Howard bluntly stated. "You wanted him to move on and he *did*... Now either you live with that, or you finally fess up."

"If it was too late for me *then*, it's *definitely* too late for me *now*," Sidra said, a twinge of annoyance in her voice. She checked her attitude. "But you're right. *I* made the decision and I'll live with it... I've *been* living with it."

"So, you think that avoiding Delaware, burying yourself in work and occasionally going on a date with some pompous, stuffy businessman is you *living* with it?" Mrs. Howard sneered.

Sidra was taken aback. "Just smack me in the face with my life why don't you?" she bit back.

"And I won't apologize for it," Mrs. Howard countered. She stood up from the bed. "I'll let you get back to your work."

"Appreciate it," Sidra mumbled, then sighed once her mother left the room. She went to pick up a piece of paper, only to toss it back down. Her mind was too preoccupied for work. She leaned her head back against her padded headboard. "Damn it," she hissed to herself.

After a moment of pondering her conversation with her mother, Sidra grabbed her phone from her nightstand. Dialing a number, she sat back and placed the phone to her ear.

"Hey Mel," she said when the person picked up.

"Sidra, just because it's still early there, don't mean it's early *here*," Malajia barked into the line. "I was in bed."

Sidra frowned in confusion. "Since *when* are you in bed before *nine*?"

"Since—I'm lying, I'm sitting out on my front step eating fruit snacks."

Sidra laughed. "Why?"

"Because I don't want the boys to see me eating them. They gonna want some and I ain't sharing," Malajia replied, mouth full. "Look, I already told you not to call me unless you decided to go to homecoming... I'm tired of you."

Sidra shook her head. "Yes, I remember and I'm *calling* you, aren't I?" She took a deep breath as she pinched the bridge of her nose. "I'm going to come."

"Yeah well, you should've led with that," Malajia replied. She let a smile come through. "It'll be good to see you, I miss you."

"I miss you too," Sidra smiled. "Even though you talk to me crazy all the time."

"That shit ain't new and neither is you being dramatic about it," Malajia jeered.

Sidra shook her head, giggling slightly. "This is true," she agreed. "Well, I'll let you go. I'm sure you're enjoying the quiet."

"Damn it, I *was*. They saw me," Malajia chuckled. "Let me go put them to bed."

"Kiss them for me."

"I ain't doing that bullshit," Malajia joked; Sidra laughed. "Call me tomorrow."

"I will."

Chapter 6

Chasity stared at her laptop, frowning. Feeling a headache forming, she rolled her eyes and rubbed her temples with her fingers. "I swear to God, I'm about to go the fuck off," she seethed to herself.

Chasity had been on edge since she'd woken up that morning. She'd barely slept the night before due to stress—typical for a Sunday evening. She knew when she sat down at her kitchen table Monday morning and opened her laptop, she would be hit with a ton of work emails. What she didn't expect was to see an email from her boss, telling her that the web page design and configuration that she finished on Friday for one of her most difficult clients, had to be scrapped.

Chasity was so angry she felt like crying. It didn't help that her daughter was jumping up and down next to her, tapping her arm. "What, girl?" Chasity grunted.

"Mommy, you wanna see the dress that I put on Princess Kitty?" Kayla asked, brimming with excitement.

Chasity rolled her eyes. "No, I *don't*. Go get your book bag so you can get dropped off at Mom-Mom's house."

"But Mom—"

"And I mean *now*," Chasity snapped, slamming her hand on the table, startling Kayla.

Jason walked downstairs just as Kayla was scurrying up the stairs. "Everything okay down here?" he wondered, noticing the annoyance on Chasity's face.

Chasity glanced up at him. "Not really."

Jason grabbed a bag of bagels out of the cabinet. "What's wrong?"

"Doesn't matter," she blandly returned.

"Okay," Jason mumbled, untying the bag. "Did you eat breakfast?"

"Was trying to, then I lost my appetite," Chasity spat, standing from the seat and closing her laptop. "I gotta get to work, are you dropping her off at my mom's or you want *me* to?"

Jason glanced at her. "*I* can," he returned. He placed two bagel slices into the toaster and turned it on.

"Okay, I'll pick her up then; I should be leaving work before you." Chasity slung her purse and laptop bag over her shoulder and headed for the door. "Have a good day at work," she muttered.

"Thanks, you too," Jason replied. Hesitant, he spun around to face her. "Umm babe, speaking of work…"

Chasity looked at him, skeptical. "What is it Jase? I gotta go."

"I just found out yesterday that I have to fly out to Phoenix for a week."

Chasity raised an arched eyebrow. "I'm sorry, what?" she ground out.

Jason sat down at the table. "I have to fly to Phoenix for a week," he repeated, tone sullen. He too was stressed the night before. There had been an email from work that was sent to him Friday after he'd left the office, telling him of his mandatory upcoming business trip. It had him a little on edge. He'd never been away from his family that long, and he had no idea how Chasity would take the news. "*Next* week actually… I leave on Sunday."

"As in *Arizona*?" she snarled. Jason nodded. "For *what*? And why didn't you tell me *yesterday*?"

"The company is opening a new office there and they want me to go and start getting things in order," Jason answered. "And I didn't tell you *last night* because you seemed upset… Thought today would be different, but…"

Chasity rolled her eyes. "I'm annoyed, shit has been on my nerves," she barked.

Jason looked down at the table. "I can sense that," he sympathized. "Tell me what's wrong."

"Doesn't even matter," she hissed. "And why do *you* have to go to Arizona anyway?" she argued. "That's a manager's job and *you're* not a damn manager."

Jason frowned. "Yes, I *know* that. Thanks for throwing that in my damn face," he threw back.

"That's not what the fuck I meant, and you *know* that, so stop it."

Jason pinched the bridge of his nose with his fingertips. "Look...apparently they think I'm the best person to go," he explained. "To be honest, I don't even *want* to go, but I *have* to and you giving me attitude about it isn't going to change that."

Chasity shot him a glare. "Whatever yo," she threw out on her way to the door.

Jason followed her progress with a frown. "So, you're really gonna walk out of this house pissed at me?" he hurled at her departing back.

She turned and looked at him. "Your goddamn bagel is burning."

Jason jumped up from the table, groaning in the process. When he got over to the toaster, the blackened slices popped up. "Son of a bitch," he complained, snatching the slices from the appliance.

"Burnt it, *didn't* you?" Chasity sneered.

"I *like* 'em this dark," Jason lied, snatching a paper towel from the holder.

"Yeah okay," Chasity grunted, walking out the door.

Jason rolled his eyes. "Bye! Love you," he spat as the door closed.

She pushed the door back open. "*Bye*," she barked, then slammed it back.

Jason shook his head and let out a loud huff as Kayla ran back down the steps.

"Daddy, do you want to see the dress I put on Princess Kitty?" she smiled.

Jason fought to keep his frustration in check. After all, he wasn't irritated with his daughter, but he was in no mood to talk about toys either. "Later. Go put your shoes on," he ordered.

Malajia walked through the hallway of her home, gathering strewn toys and clothing from the floor. "I'm about to throw *all* this shit in the trash," she mumbled, heading into the boys' room. She placed them in the toy box, before tossing the clothes in the laundry basket.

"Boys, I keep telling you to keep your toys out of the hallway," she scolded.

The boys sat on the floor, staring at her, quiet. She tilted her head, staring back at them. They were *too* quiet, which was rare. "What did y'all do?" she calmly asked. When they didn't answer, she scanned the room with her eyes.

Anger and annoyance set in when her eyes laid on the wall near their closet. The white wall was defaced with colorful crayon. "The hell?!" she erupted, storming over. "All that paper on the floor and you write on my *wall*?!" She looked back at them.

"Sorry Mommy," they pouted.

"I'm not tryna hear that right now!" she boomed.

Running her hand through her hair, she stormed out of the room and headed for the bathroom in search of cleaning supplies. *They're on my goddamn nerves!* Retrieving the items, she marched back to the room and attempted to clean the wall. When the colors smeared, she gave up.

"Fuck it, Mark's ass is repainting this whole damn wall," she grunted to herself. She stood up and held her hand out. "Give me the crayons…*all* of them," she demanded. Once the twins gathered and placed the broken crayons in her hand, she grabbed the cleaning supplies and left the room. "Take a nap," she threw over her shoulder. When one of the boys started crying, she spun around. "Shut up and get in the bed!" she yelled.

Malajia rolled her eyes as she leaned her back against the wall in the hallway. A deep sigh escaped her; she was tired. Ever since Mark had left for work earlier that morning, she'd been running after the boys, bathing them, getting them fed and dressed, taking them with her to run errands, then returning home to clean up, plan dinner—she needed a moment to herself.

She went to her room, not bothering to shut her door. Tossing the cleaning products on a chair, she grabbed the tablet off her nightstand. She sat on her bed and began scrolling through the job site she was looking at the night before. "Corporate marketing specialist," she read aloud. She scanned over the requirements with her eyes. "I could do that...hell I *did* that," she said aloud. Holding her finger over the 'apply' button, she took a deep breath.

She closed the page instead.

Loud banging and screaming abruptly broke the momentary peace. Malajia jumped up and darted out of her bedroom. Sticking her head in her sons' bedroom, she found them tussling on the bed. "I thought I told y'all to take a nap!" she hollered, startling the boys. "Why don't you two listen?!"

The boys flopped down on the bed. "I'm hungry," Marvin whined.

Malajia glanced at her watch. *Damn, it is their snack time.* Letting out a huff, she signaled for the boys to come with her. "Come on."

Malajia headed downstairs, her sons following close behind. While walking into the kitchen, the boys laughed and grabbed onto her legs. "Get off my legs, I'm not playing right now," she demanded, causing them to let go. She opened the refrigerator and pulled out some yogurt.

"Can we have cookies?" Marvin asked.

Malajia let out a sigh. "You're not getting any cookies right now," she grunted. "You can have some fruit and yogurt. Cookies are for after dinner." When the boys started crying, she slammed her hand on the counter. "Then you must not be hungry. Get out my face and go take that nap."

I'm about to pull my fuckin' hair out, she thought as the boys scurried out of the kitchen. Malajia pulled a chair from the kitchen table and sat down. Putting her face in her hands, she took several deep breaths in an effort to relax herself. After a moment, she grabbed her cell phone from her jeans pocket and dialed a number.

While she waited for the person to pick up, she began to wonder if the feelings that she had were normal. The feeling of being both overwhelmed and underwhelmed at the same time.

"Hey Mom," Malajia tiredly said once the line picked up.

"Hi sweetie, what's up?" Mrs. Simmons eagerly greeted.

"Nothing much..." Malajia played with a cloth napkin on the table. "Can I ask you a question?"

"Sure."

Malajia hesitated for a moment. "Um…when you first—When we were little—" She rubbed her face with her hand.

"When you kids were little, *what*?" Mrs. Simmons wondered, concerned by Malajia's lackluster tone.

Malajia shook her head, deciding to keep the real reason for calling to herself. "Um…did we have any food allergies when we were little?" she asked instead.

"No," Mrs. Simmons chuckled. "Well, we thought that *you* were allergic to Brussel sprouts, but the doctor confirmed that you were just putting red dots on your arm with a marker to get out of eating them."

Malajia couldn't help but snicker. "Yeah, that definitely *sounds* like me," she replied.

Mrs. Simmons laughed. "Your father and I were so mad, we spent money at the doctor just for them to wipe your arm with an alcohol pad to remove the marker."

Malajia put her hand over face and shook her head. "Yeah, I'd be pissed too."

Once Mrs. Simmons's laughter at the memory subsided, she let out a sigh. "That's part of parenthood, dealing with silly and often *expensive* behavior from your children."

Malajia sighed. "Yeah."

"Malajia, are you okay? You sound tired."

"I am." *In more ways than one.* "But it's fine."

"No, it's not fine that you're tired. You need to get some rest," Mrs. Simmons pressed.

"Not gonna happen right now," Malajia huffed. "I gotta get started on dinner, I'll talk to you later." She ended the call and stood from her seat.

Jason adjusted his tie as he clicked open his email list. Opening the first one, he read a few words before letting out a groan, pinching the bridge of his nose. "Come on, *another* one?" he griped to his empty office. "I'm sick of this shit." Just as he was about to take a sip from his cup of coffee, his office door opened.

"Jason, glad I caught you before you started working," Patrick smiled.

Jason fought the urge to roll his eyes. *When am I not working?* "What's up?" he wondered.

"I'm sure you saw the email about the new project that we acquired."

"I did just now, yeah," Jason replied in his best calm voice. On the inside, he was screaming. He'd just finished a project a few days ago, was preparing to fly out of state for a week, just to have to come back and begin working on a new project. "How long is this one going to take?"

"A few weeks probably," Patrick replied, nonchalant.

Which means another few weeks of late hours... Chasity is gonna kill me, he thought. "Okay. Well, I guess I'll start preparing *now* then—"

"We want to try something different this time."

Jason frowned slightly at the interruption. "Um...o-kay," he slowly put out, skeptical.

"Instead of having you do all the work this time...which by the way, you always do an amazing job," Patrick began. "We're bringing in some new people and we want you to *oversee* the project."

"You mean *train* them?" Jason corrected. "As in...train them to do *my* job?"

"Well, not in those exact words, but yes. You'll be training them," Patrick confirmed. "This is a *good* thing," he added, sensing Jason's apprehension.

Jason looked confused. "O-kay," he repeated. "Not that I'm complaining about not having to do all of the work but...is there *another* reason why you're bringing in other people?"

"What do you mean?"

Are you trying to replace me? he thought, but neglected to say. "Nothing," Jason dismissed. "When do they come in?"

"You'll actually meet them in Phoenix when you go," he revealed. "They'll be flying back with you. They'll train here first then—"

"Then what?" Jason cut in.

Patrick smiled. "I'll go over the entire plan at a later date, I promise," he said. "I'll let you get back to work."

"Great," Jason muttered as Patrick headed out of the office. He sat back in his seat, astonished.

All this time, all this work and these fuckin' bastards are trying to replace me? he fumed. "I should send a damn virus through this system," Jason muttered to himself. Seeing an alert pop up on his computer, he sucked his teeth and grabbed some papers from his desk. "They got the nerve to have a damn meeting right now," he griped.

Chasity sat at her desk with her head in her hands, vigorously tapping her high-heel-covered foot on the floor as she read through emails. Each word made her want to explode.

Hearing a tap on her desk, she glanced up, not bothering to hide the annoyance in her eyes.

"Chasity, can you come to my office for a moment?" The middle-aged woman asked.

Chasity didn't bother responding—she just stood up and followed her manager to the office. Chasity walked in and took a seat as the woman closed the door.

"I know that you saw the emails," she began, sitting down at her desk.

"Uh huh," Chasity muttered, folding her arms.

"And I assume that you're a little bothered."

"Bothered?" Chasity questioned, trying to keep her voice calm. "You think I'm *bothered?*"

"Well, *aren't* you?"

Chasity took a deep breath as she stretched her neck from side to side. "Pamela, after weeks of back and forth emails, meetings, confirmations, revisions, work, *more* revisions, and *more* work," she spat. "I *finally* finish everything by the deadline just for that b—" Chasity put her hand up to stop herself from letting the profane word fly out of her mouth. "For that *woman* to just say scratch everything and start over... *Start over?* Is she crazy?"

"Chasity—"

"Do you *know* how much this project has stressed me out? How much of a migraine it gave me?" Chasity vented. "Not to *mention*, that you threw four *other* start up site projects on me that I had to work on along *with* this one, and *now* you're telling me all that work was for *nothing?*"

Pamela put her hands up. "Chasity, I understand. I *truly* do."

No, the fuck you don't bitch, 'cause you don't do shit but forward everything to me to do!

Pamela kept talking. "But the bottom line is that it's our job to make our clients happy—"

"You mean *my* job," Chasity cut in.

Pamela clasped her hands together. "—And if that *means* developing her website all over again from scratch…" she took a deep breath as Chasity's angry hazel eyes burrowed through her like a laser. "Then that is what we're going to do."

"You mean *me*," Chasity spat.

"If you want to put it that way Chasity, then yes, *you*," Pamela sneered.

Chasity shook her head. "Pamela, I can't go through this for a third time with this client," she refused. "She isn't satisfied with anything that I've done."

"That's not true, she actually does value your work Chasity."

"No, she does *not*," Chasity insisted.

"Listen, like I said—"

"You *have* to give this to someone *else*," Chasity demanded. "Lest you forget, I have the other sites to work on with tight deadlines."

"I didn't forget, *I'm* the one who gave those projects to you," Pamela stated, haughty.

Chasity narrowed her eyes; she couldn't stand her boss. "Like I *said*," she ground out. "Give the client to someone else, *please*."

"I'm not going to do that," Pamela stood firm, folding her arms. "You're our senior developer, you can handle this."

Chasity ran her hands through her hair and tried to keep her temper in check. "I'm not doing it," she refused.

Pamela stared at Chasity. "You don't have a *choice*, Mrs. Adams," she spat. "It's your *job* and you're being paid a high salary to *do* your job…so you're going to *do* it."

Pamela kept talking, but the words turned to muffled sounds in Chasity's ears. She felt her blood run cold, frustration bubbling over. To have to sit there and take what she felt was wrong, wasn't something that Chasity was used to. She didn't know how much longer she could stand it without letting her full-on angry side out.

Fearing that she would say or do something that she *and* Pamela would regret, Chasity slowly stood from her seat. "I need a minute," she muttered, heading for the office door.

"Chasity, we're not finished—"

"Please, I just need a minute!" Chasity snapped, startling Pamela.

Pamela put a hand up. "Okay fine, take your minute," she granted. "Then we have to get ready for a meeting."

Chasity gave a half nod before walking out of the office. Ignoring the chatter of her coworkers, she made a swift beeline for the bathroom. Shutting the door, and locking it, her anger rose to a head. She paced back and forth, breathing heavily. She wanted to scream. She wanted to hit something, better yet some*one*. She raised her fist to punch the wall, then decided against it. Not knowing what to do with her hands, she ran them through her hair and covered her face, sobbing quietly.

Don't walk out, don't walk out, she told herself. Wiping the tears from her face, Chasity stared in the mirror at herself. "Fuckin' eyes are red now…great," she muttered to herself, snatching a piece of paper towel from the holder.

"The links aren't working *again*?" Alex griped, clicking the mouse vigorously.

"I'm afraid not," Sheila confirmed, regrettably.

Alex clicked again. "Oh wait, now they're—" she closed her eyes; what she hoped was working, still wasn't. "Damn it," she huffed.

She pushed her chair away from her desk and stood up, running her hands over her hair. Alex's week was rough enough. Finding out the company's website was malfunctioning, just before a subscription launch, was pushing her over the edge. "How many times is this going to *happen*? What is up with our web content group? These kinks are getting ridiculous."

"I wish I had an answer for you," Sheila shrugged.

Alex pinched the bridge of her nose. Letting out a sigh, she stood from her seat.

"You want me to get them on the phone for you?" Sheila offered.

"Yes, please." Alex sighed once again as Sheila hurried out of Alex's office. Just as the young woman headed out, a distinguished, older light-brown skinned woman stepped into Alex's office.

"Alex, the links aren't working on the website and this month's subscription of the e-magazine is due tomorrow."

"I know Marlene, I don't know why we keep having these issues. Sheila is getting the tech department on the phone now," Alex returned. "I wish I knew technical stuff, I'd fix it *myself.*"

"While I admire your initiative, just stick to editing," Marlene chuckled.

Although Alex appreciated her boss's attempt at making a joke, Alex was in no laughing mood. The website bugs were making her look bad, and she didn't like it. "If this doesn't get fixed...we might have to push the release date back."

"I'd hate to do that," Marlene said.

"Trust me, *I* would too," Alex agreed. "But after the influx of complaints from customers about things online not working *last* month, I'd rather be safe than sorry."

Marlene rubbed her chin. "You do have a point."

Alex took a deep breath. "Did they have a lay off or something over in the tech department?"

"Yes."

"Did they let all the *smart* people go?" Alex grunted. She clicked a button on her phone. "Sheila were you able to get them on the phone?" she asked when the line picked up.

"Yes, they said that they are trying to figure out what went wrong," she answered. "They said they will get back to me ASAP."

"Okay thank you," Alex returned, sullen, releasing a button. She ran her hands over the back of her neck.

"If this keeps up, we're cutting ties with the in-house techs and moving to outsource," Marlene said.

"Wish we could do it *now*," Alex muttered.

Marlene gave Alex's shoulder a quick tap. "You're doing a great job handling everything. Kinks and all," she praised. "Don't forget to take your lunch break soon."

Alex giggled. "You sound like my mother," she quipped.

"Well, she's a smart woman I'm sure."

"Yes, very," Alex agreed.

Alex sat down at her desk and reached for her phone as soon as Marlene left. Dialing, she let out a sigh and brought the phone to her ear. "Hey Sid, it's Alex, calling to wish you a happy birthday," she began when the voicemail prompted. "…I hope your day is going better than *mine*. See you in a few weeks." Alex hung up the phone and let out another sigh.

Yet another call to one of the girls going to voicemail. What she wouldn't give to walk across the hall to one of her friends' rooms for a good laugh right about now.

Looking at her computer, Alex vigorously clicked a few links. They still weren't working; she nearly tossed her mouse across the room.

"Where's a freakin' computer whiz when I need one?" she muttered to herself. After a moment of sulking, she had a thought. Ignoring the work line, Alex grabbed her personal cell phone. She vigorously typed out a message and sent it. Tapping her fingers on her desk, she waited.

Not more than a minute later, her cell vibrated. Picking it up, she gave the message a quick read. Then she picked up her work phone.

"Hi, it's Alex over in— Yes well, I know you're still trying to figure out why the links aren't working on the web site…." She stared at the text message as the tech rep on the other line spoke. "Okay, well did you check to make sure that the spelling and capitalization in the file name on the server matches the link code in your page? …Can you check that please? …Yes, I'll hold." Alex tapped her fingers in a steady rhythm while she waited. Moments passed, then she straightened up in her seat when she heard the voice again.

"Yes…you want me to try it right now? …Okay hold on." Alex clicked her mouse a few times then let out a squeal of delight. "It works, thank you."

Hanging up the phone, she smiled. "My girl," Alex mused to herself, leaning back in her seat.

"Em, do you know what your mom's favorite dessert is?" Will asked, glancing at his phone.

Emily was so preoccupied with grabbing small glass jars from the store shelf, that she didn't hear him.

"Em," Will called again. Still not getting a response, he touched her shoulder, startling her. Will laughed a little as she flinched. "Sorry, but you were tuning me out."

Emily looked at him, wide-eyed. "I was?" she asked. Will nodded. "I'm sorry." She put the jars back and grabbed a bag of seashells from the shelf. "I'll be better off ordering these jars in bulk," she muttered. "What were you saying?"

"Was just asking what kind of cake your mom likes."

"Pound cake," Emily answered, then cleared her throat. "Why?"

"My mom wanted to know," Will answered. "I think she wants to make desserts for the rehearsal dinner."

"She doesn't have to do that," Emily said, clearing her throat again.

"She *wants* to. Are you okay?" Will asked, concerned when Emily touched her throat.

She looked at him. "I'm okay, just getting a little sore throat."

"That means that you're coming down with a cold," Will observed, touching her forehead with his hand.

Emily moved his hand away. "I wouldn't go that far," she denied.

"I'm gonna make you my special tea when we get back." Will watched as she moved around the aisle, placing items in her shopping cart. "What are you getting from here anyway?"

Emily counted items off in her head. "The supplies for the favors, bouquets and boutonnieres," she answered. "I wanted to make bouquets with faux flowers, and the favors that I want, I can't find, so I'm gonna make those too."

Will scratched his head. "You sure you can handle all that yourself? It seems like a lot."

"It'll be fine," she assured. "I like arts and crafts remember? I do them with my students."

"Yeah, making cardboard nests is a little different than making bouquets for a whole wedding party *and* favors, not to mention—"

"Will, I said I can handle it," Emily cut in, trying her best not to get annoyed. While she appreciated his concern, she wished that he and everybody else would stop doubting her capability.

Will put his hands up in surrender. "Okay."

Emily maneuvered around the store with Will in tow. Having a thought, she looked at him. "My mother asked how Anthony felt about me becoming his stepmom," she brought up.

Will smiled. "He's thrilled about it," he stated, confident.

"Really?" Emily wondered.

"Of *course*," Will promised. Noticing Emily's look of uncertainty, he frowned in concern. "Why do you look like you don't believe me?"

Emily shrugged. "It's not that," she replied. "I guess I just wonder if he feels like I'm trying to replace his real mom."

Will stood in front of Emily and put his hands on her shoulders. "Babe, you *are* his real mom," he insisted. "You might not have birthed him, but you've been in his life since he was spitting cereal at people for laughs—"

Emily couldn't help but giggle.

"That hyperactive boy *adores* you," Will smiled. "He *knows* of his mother, she was a good woman and I'm sure on some level, he misses her even though he doesn't remember her. But to him, you are *also* his mother."

Emily didn't even know why she brought up the subject; she'd never felt insecure about her relationship with Anthony before. "Okay," she said after a minute. Will gave her a hug, rubbing her back tenderly.

"*Speaking* of the boy, you almost finished in here?" he asked, breaking their embrace. "We need to pick him up from my parents'."

"Oh sure," Emily said, counting the items in her cart. "I just need sand."

Will looked perplexed. "Sand?"

"Yeah, for the sand jars," Emily replied, an innocent look on her face.

Will scratched his head. "We're gonna have sand jars for a winter wedding?"

Emily laughed. "Yes, they'll be the favors." She adjusted the purse strap on her shoulder. "Maybe it'll make everyone forget how cold it's going to be in January."

Will nodded in agreement.

Emily stuck her key in her door, adjusting a bag she was carrying in the process. After she and Will had picked up Anthony, the three of them had gone to the movies, then grabbed a bite to eat. Emily left them to head to her apartment in hopes of getting started on some work that she'd brought home. She wasn't pleased to find that the door was already unlocked.

Emily let out a sigh as she pushed it open. "Jaz, how many times have I told you to lock the door?" she grunted.

Jazmine rolled her eyes as she flipped through the TV channels. "Mom called for you."

"Thanks for ignoring what I just said," Emily muttered, trying to get past Jazmine, whose feet were up on the coffee table. She let out a long sigh. "Do you mind?"

"God, can you just go back to where you came from?" Jazmine sneered, removing her feet from the table and plopping them on the floor. "You just bought the mood all the way down in here."

Emily set her bags on the kitchen table. "I'm tired," she grumbled.

"*And?*" Jazmine huffed.

"I worked all day, then had to deal with wedding stuff, I'm *probably* getting sick, and *now* I have to grade a bunch of tests before tomorrow, so excuse me if I'm not a ball of sunshine for you," Emily threw back, not hiding her disdain. "*Then*, I come home to find my door unlocked. What if somebody who *wasn't* me, walked in?"

"Emily, you don't have to worry about anybody trying to steal this wack shit that you have up in this apartment," Jazmine spat.

It's more than you have. "That's nice Jazmine," Emily bit out.

Jazmine sucked her teeth and took a sip of soda. "It was a joke."

"It *wasn't*," Emily said, tired. "What did Mommy want?"

"First, for you to answer your cell phone," Jazmine ground out.

Emily rubbed her forehead. "I left it—doesn't matter, what else did she say?"

"Something about some stupid dress fitting appointment," Jazmine hissed.

Emily's eyes widened. She darted for her planner, which sat on an end table. "Crap, that's this week," she panicked. "I totally forgot."

Jazmine scoffed. "Don't even know why you're bothering with all that shit, you need to elope."

Emily rolled her eyes. "I'm not eloping," she hissed, annoyed. "I'm *bothering* because this is going to be the most important day of my life and I want it to be perfect."

"Please," Jazmine grunted.

Frustrated, Emily slammed the planner back on the table. "God, why can't you just be happy for me for *once*?" she snapped.

"First of all it's *your* day, not *mine*, so I really don't have to be *anything*," Jazmine threw back. "You're lucky I'm even *coming*."

Emily frowned. "You know what—" She put her hand up. There was no point in arguing about her wedding; she refused to be stressed. "I need money for bills this month," she threw out.

"I won't have it," Jazmine dismissed.

"Well, you need to *get* it," Emily stood firm. "What happened with that interview that you went on last week?"

"*Obviously* I didn't get the job," Jazmine fussed.

Not surprised. "Sorry to hear that," Emily replied, tone unenthused. "But you need to keep looking because I can't handle the bills by myself anymore."

Jazmine looked at her.

"And that's not just for this month," Emily clarified. "As long as you're staying here, I'm going to need you to pull your weight," she maintained. Seeing that Jazmine had nothing else to say, Emily grabbed a bottle of water from the refrigerator and headed for her bedroom. *The free ride stops now.*

Chapter 7

Sidra cut a piece of cake with her fork and put it in her mouth. She closed her eyes, relishing the rich flavors of the chocolate cake, layered with chocolate icing and topped with chocolate chips and sprinkles. "Oh my God, this is orgasmic," she mused to herself. After a moment, she shook her head. "This is just *sad*," she spoke to the empty room. "The most excitement that I've had in months is because of *cake*."

Dismissing her thoughts, she took another bite then grabbed her phone. Sidra smiled, laughing to herself as she read all the sincere and, in some cases, over-the-top silly birthday messages from her family and friends. Her face fell when she realized that she'd received birthday wishes from everyone except for one person…Josh.

Sighing, she tossed the phone on the plush sofa cushion beside her and reached back for her plate. A knock at the door paused her eating.

Sidra glanced over at the door. Raising an eyebrow, she stood up and headed for it. Peering out of the peephole, she chuckled slightly, then pulled the door open. "Hi Robin. What a pleasant surprise," Sidra greeted the pretty, dark skinned visitor.

Robin Bellevue smiled a bright smile. Sidra knew the woman from work; she was the firm's receptionist. She and Sidra had hung out on a few occasions; Sidra always thought that Robin was sweet. "Happy birthday," Robin gushed, throwing her arms out.

Sidra chuckled. "Thank you," she replied, running a hand through her hair. "What brings you by?"

Robin, dressed in a pink sparkly tank top, dark blue skinny jeans and pink high-heeled sandals, shot Sidra a knowing look. "Girl, we're here to take you *out*."

Sidra looked confused. "We?" she zoned in, holding her hand on the door.

Robin smiled, then signaled for someone who was out of sight.

Sidra successfully hid her displeasure seeing Carlie saunter up to her door. *Ugh, perfect.* "Hello Carlie," she greeted, hoping that her tone did not express how annoyed she was.

"No time for pleasantries, you need to get dressed," Carlie dismissed, moving around Sidra to enter her apartment with Robin in tow. She spun around, a box in hand. "I was shocked that you *actually* took off work today."

"I refused to work on my birthday this year," Sidra replied, tone dry.

"Sidra, we're serious, go get ready. We're taking you out," Robin pressed.

Sidra ran a hand through her hair yet again. "Listen ladies, as flattered as I am that you want to hang out, I'm really not in the partying mood."

"Oh honey, you don't have a *choice*," Carlie insisted with a wave of her hand. "Come on, you don't have to be so stuck up *all* the time."

Sidra frowned. "*Excuse* me?" she spat, offended.

Robin stepped forward. "What she *means* is, you deserve to have some fun tonight," she amended.

Sidra looked past Robin and focused her piercing gaze on Carlie. "Carlie, don't call me stuck up again," she demanded. It wasn't that Sidra wasn't used to being called stuck-up—she'd taken the dig from her friends for years—but it hit differently coming from a coworker that she didn't necessarily care for.

Carlie rolled her eyes. "Fine, I apologize Sidra," she huffed. "It was just a *joke*."

Sidra narrowed her eyes.

Robin stepped in front of Sidra. "We came over to pre-game and take you out to a club," she jumped in, hoping to diffuse the tension.

"Yeah and to get some numbers or something," Carlie added, excited.

Sidra shook her head. "I don't *want* any numbers," she griped.

"Well, *I do*, so let's get going," Carlie insisted, flopping on Sidra's couch.

"Yeah, come on Sidra, go get all fancy like you do. Let's sip this wine, then hit the town," Robin smiled, pointing to the box of wine in Carlie's hand.

Sidra stared at it, raising an eyebrow. "You...you want *me* to drink *that*?" she scoffed.

Robin looked at it. "Yes. You like wine, right?"

Sidra still held her gaze. "Not from a *box*."

"Oh God, it all tastes the same girl," Carlie teased.

"No, it *doesn't*," Sidra threw back, folding her arms.

"Well, you don't have to drink it, I'll drink it for you. Can you please just go get ready?" Carlie threw back.

Robin clasped her hands together. "Please? It'll be fun," she pleaded.

Sidra rolled her eyes. She'd much rather prefer to stay in, alone. Yet in spite of the fact that Robin had ambushed her with Carlie, Sidra would feel bad turning Robin away, after the woman had come out of her way to take Sidra out for her birthday. "Fine," Sidra sighed, grabbing her cell phone from the couch. "Give me like thirty minutes."

Leaving the chatty girls in the living room, Sidra retreated for her bedroom. Searching her closet for party attire, she let out another sigh. "I don't *feel* like this mess tonight," she huffed to herself. Her phone rang, and she answered without looking at the caller ID.

"Hello," Sidra spoke.

"Happy birthday, you old ass bitch!" Malajia bellowed into the line.

Sidra frowned. "Well *damn* Mel," she grunted. "Not *only* did you text me that *same thing* earlier, you just had to scream it in my ear too?"

"Oh shut up you old ass, bougie hag," Malajia threw back.

Sidra couldn't help but laugh. "You are so irritating," she said. "Anyway, thank you crazy."

Malajia laughed. "What are you doing tonight? I wish we were there to party with you."

"Yeah me too," Sidra pouted. "My birthdays haven't been the same without you guys."

"You're probably sitting in your room, eating cake, looking all dry," Malajia teased.

Sidra giggled. "Yeah well, the *cake* part you're right about, but I'm actually about to go out," she revealed. She pulled out a top and stared at it, before shaking her head and hanging it back up. "I'm being dragged out by my coworkers," she continued. "They want to take me out for a birthday, girls' night thing."

There was silence on the line for a few seconds.

"Hello?" Sidra questioned, confused.

"Who are these *new* bitches?!" Malajia barked.

Sidra smacked her forehead with the palm of her hand. "Jesus Christ, Malajia," she grimaced.

"Nah fuck that. I had to threaten Chasity before graduation, and I see I should have done the same to *you*," Malajia argued. "Ain't no new friends."

"Well, if you guys were here *with* me, I wouldn't *need* to hang out with anybody else," Sidra threw back, humor in her voice.

"Not *my* fault that you and your ponytail skipped town," Malajia countered.

Sidra shook her head.

"Fine, go ahead and hang out with your little raggedy associates," Malajia relented. "But you *better* not bring them around me."

"Wouldn't *dream* of it," Sidra chuckled. "I don't even half *like* one of them."

Malajia giggled. "Ahh, there's that petty side I miss," she joked.

"Yeah, yeah," Sidra replied, waving a hand. "Listen, I have to get ready before they get drunk on that box wine they brought. Then I won't be able to get rid of them."

"See, who the hell drinks *box* wine?! Uncultured heffas," Malajia sneered.

"Says the girl who drinks vodka straight from the *bottle*," Sidra threw back.

"I did that *once*," Malajia argued.

"*Twice*," Sidra corrected, holding up two fingers. "And *both* times were at your wedding."

"That is just irrelevant," Malajia sneered. "All right, have fun."

"I'll try, bye." Sidra hung up the phone. Before she could go back to finding something to put on, it rang again. Sidra immediately answered.

"Malajia, if you call me old or a bitch *one* more time—"

"Happy birthday Sidra," a male voice cut in.

Sidra felt her heart skip a beat. "Josh?" she stammered.

A chuckle came through the line "Yeah, it's me."

Sidra put her hand on her chest; she missed the sound of his voice. "Thank you."

"Sure," Josh returned. "I was going to call earlier but—"

"You were busy. I understand," she cut in, walking over and sitting on her bed.

"No, I just wanted to make sure that it was after work hours so that I could talk to you," he corrected. "Didn't want to get the machine. After all, it's been a while since we've talked."

Sidra closed her eyes and let out a long sigh. "I know," she agreed. "I'm sorry… I've been—"

"Busy, I know," Josh finished.

You have no idea how much this is killing me, she thought. "Umm…are you going to homecoming?" she asked, hoping to change the subject.

"Of course. Wouldn't miss it," he raved. "Looking forward to some nostalgia."

Sidra giggled a bit. "Yeah, I know what you mean." She paused for a moment. "I guess…I'll see you there."

"You're actually going?"

"Yeah," Sidra confirmed, smile heavy in her voice.

"Oh okay… It'll be good to see you," he said after a moment.

Sidra held her smile, but didn't say anything.

"Well, I won't keep you. I'm sure you have plans."

I'd much rather talk to you than go to some funky club. "Yeah, I'm sure your date will be pretty mad if you stay on the phone with me," she said with a nervous chuckle. *You fuckin' idiot!*

"I guess you're right," Josh replied. "I'll talk to you later."

"Bye Josh." Sidra waited for Josh to hang up, before staring at her phone, bewildered. "Why the hell would— God what is *wrong* with me?" she snapped out loud before flopping back on the bed and stomping her feet on the floor repeatedly. "'Yeah, I'm sure your date will be pretty mad if you stay on the phone with me,'" she mocked of herself in a silly voice. "You stupid, old dumbass."

Sidra was startled when her room door swung open. She bolted up right and laid eyes on Carlie and Robin, who were staring at her.

"Girl, why are you in here talking to yourself?" Carlie asked.

Sidra opened her mouth to respond, but was distracted by Carlie's slurred voice. Zoning in on both girls' half lidded eyes, she frowned. "Are you drunk?"

"*I'm* not, *she* is," Robin said, gesturing to Carlie.

"I'm not drunk…I'm *tipsy*," Carlie corrected. "That wine can't get anybody drunk."

Sidra stared at them wide-eyed. "Don't throw up *anywhere* in my place."

Carlie flagged her. "Girl please, I can hold my liquor." She clapped her hands. "Hurry up so I can call this cab… I hope that we find some sexy men," she said in an aside to Robin as they walked out the room, closing the door behind them.

Sidra stared at the closed door. "I never should've let them in."

Mark clicked his controller with vigor, an intense look on his face. "Come on man!" he bellowed, slamming his controller on the couch.

"Bro, why do you *always* have to be loud?" Josh grunted, clicking his controller.

"Why do *you* always ask stupid ass questions?" Mark threw back. He looked at his sons, who were tearing up paper and throwing it on the floor. "Hey, my dudes, stop messing up Uncle Josh's house before I drop kick you."

The boys looked at Mark and laughed; Mark just shook his head.

Josh reached for his cup of soda, laughing along with them. "Mark, those boys haven't listened to you all night."

"Shut the f—just shut up," Mark barked at him.

Josh laughed harder, and they went back to playing their game.

"Yo, why you lie to Sidra and make it seem like you had a girl here, when in reality ain't nobody here but me and these kids, eating up your food and shit?" Mark asked.

Josh shot Mark a confused look. "You were listening to my conversation?"

"You were sitting right here *next* to me," Mark defended. "*And* your phone was up loud as shit."

Josh narrowed his eyes at him. Mark had stopped over with the boys for a session with Josh's new gaming system. Mark was already annoyed that Josh had stopped in the middle of the game just to talk to Sidra, but he hadn't expected Mark to eavesdrop on his conversation. Josh flagged him with his hand. "Whatever."

"Punk ass," Mark muttered. "This is pre-junior year all over again."

"What the hell are you talking about?" Josh wondered, fiddling with his controller.

"Before you finally told Sidra how you felt," Mark explained. "You doing that same, awkward, 'you think it's subtle, but it ain't,' bullshit."

"Look, I don't know what you *think* you know, but I'm over my feelings for Sidra okay," Josh argued. "Have been for *years.*"

Mark rolled his eyes. "*And* you're lying about it. *Just* like before."

"Worry less about *me* and more about your boys, who are pouring water on my carpet," Josh threw back, gesturing to the boys who were in fact spilling water on the floor.

"Hey, hey!" Mark yelped, slapping his hand on the arm of the couch. "My mans, I'mma need y'all to clean that water up before I pour the rest of it on you."

Josh shook his head as the boys started laughing again. "Bro, they don't *listen* to you," he said, amused. Growing up, he couldn't imagine Mark being a father. Seeing him with his boys now, even if they *were* cutting up, was both heartwarming and hilarious.

"They do *so*," Mark snapped, before bolting up from the couch. "HEY!" he boomed, startling them. "Clean that water up *now!*" He watched with satisfaction as the boys began pulling tissue from a small box and proceeded to soak up the water from the floor. Mark sat back down. "See, they know when I'm not messing around," he boasted. "They got that water up."

Josh nodded. "Yeah, that's true," he agreed. "*Now* they're tearing the wet paper up."

Mark put his hand up in Josh's face. "Don't go bringing up new shit," he jeered. "Focus on the water dawg."

Josh smacked Mark's hand out of his face.

Alex picked up a large slice of cheese pizza from her plate and took a big bite. "Ooh, ooh, hot, hot," she complained in between careful chews.

"I don't know *why* you didn't blow it. You *know* they gave it to us right out of the oven," Stacey Adison chuckled, fanning the steam from her slice with her free hand.

Alex swallowed her food and reached for her can of soda. "Girl, you know my big ass is greedy," she joked, taking a sip. "I'm glad you were in town. After the week I've had, it's good to hang out with one of my besties." Alex didn't get to see her friends often, including her oldest friend Stacey; she treasured their visits. Even if it *was* as simple as sitting outside in the park on a breezy fall day, eating pizza.

Stacey leaned her head on Alex's shoulder. "Aww, you had a bad week?"

Alex let out a loud sigh. "Stace, between the website crap earlier this week, the ten thousand meetings the other day, and an advertiser wanting to change his ad at the last minute *today*…I'm ready to scream," she vented.

"I bet a ten-page paper sounds like heaven right now, huh?" Stacey teased.

"Girl, writing a ten-page—no, a *twenty*-page paper would be *cake* compared to this job this week," Alex agreed. "Ooh, *speaking* of cake, we should stop and get some on the way back to my place."

Stacey tilted her head at her best friend. "You're sure eating a lot today, sis," she observed, squinting. "Are you about to be somebody's mama?"

Alex's head jerked back. "Girl—the only way I would be pregnant is through Immaculate Conception," she said, laughter in her voice. "I've been handling my *own* business for over two years now." She giggled when Stacey shook her head.

"Don't you think it's about time you started dating again?" Stacey asked, taking a sip of her soda.

"No," Alex spat. "Don't *you* think it's time you married that man you're shacking up with?" she threw back.

Stacey's eyes widened. "*No*," she spat back.

"Uh huh, don't like it, do you?" Alex chortled. "Listen, I know everybody is concerned about my dating life. But I'll date again when I'm *ready*. Just like *you* will take your relationship to the next level, when *you're* ready."

"Point taken," Stacey resolved.

Alex chuckled again as she pulled her phone out. Stacey watched as Alex's fingers moved across the screen.

"Are you seriously *working* when you're supposed to be hanging out with me?" Stacey asked, feigning offense.

"No sweetie, I'm not working," Alex promised.

Stacey moved some of her curly, shoulder length hair out of her face. "Then what has you concentrating so hard?"

"I'm paying some bills," Alex answered.

"Oh okay," Stacey chortled. "Yeah, I just paid mine the other day too." She took another bite of her pizza. "It pains me to part with that much money."

Alex laughed a little. "I hear you on that," she said. "I paid *mine* two weeks ago."

Stacey looked confused. "But you *just* said—"

"I'm paying my parents' bills," Alex revealed. She caught Stacey's shocked expression. "What?"

"Alex, you know your parents are going to *kill* you if they find out you're doing this," Stacey warned.

"Well they won't accept my cash gifts anymore, so I'm finding another way to give back to them," Alex explained.

Stacey squinted her eyes. "They won't accept your money because they don't *want* it."

Alex rolled her eyes. "Look Stace, I know my parents okay. I'm doing what's best," she reasoned. "And they *won't* find out."

"How do you figure?" Stacey asked, skeptical.

Alex looked up from her phone. "I'm doing this all online. My parents don't do *anything* online, they won't even get a new laptop," she explained. "They rely on paper bills, and since I pay the bills after the current cycle, they don't see the credit right away. And when the next bill comes, my mom will think my dad paid it and vice versa. As long as the bills are paid, they don't question each other."

Stacey was still skeptical, but decided to drop it. Who was she to tell Alex what she should or shouldn't do for her parents? "Are you going to homecoming this year?" she asked, changing the subject.

Alex smiled. "Yes and I'm really excited," she beamed. "I don't think I've been this excited to go to campus since my freshman year." She placed her phone in her purse. "Are *you*?"

Stacey shook her head. "No, me and that man of mine are going to New Orleans that week."

"Nice!" Alex praised, giving a light pat to Stacey's arm. "Have fun girl, I'll catch you at homecoming another time."

"You could've caught me at homecoming the last few *years,* had you *come*," Stacey teased.

"Okay, okay, no need to rub in the fact that I'm a bad alum," Alex jeered, giving the giggling Stacey a light backhand to her arm.

Chapter 8

Malajia squinted at her tablet as she twirled an oven mitt around in her hand. "Mark, did you book the hotel for homecoming yet?!" she hollered in the other room.

"Huh?!" he yelled back.

"Did you book the hotel yet?" Malajia repeated.

There was a pause. "What?!"

Annoyed, Malajia stomped her foot on the floor. "Boy—Just come here," she barked. She held an angered gaze when Mark walked into the kitchen laughing. "You play too damn much."

"This you already know, Sugar face," he teased, leaning over the table.

"Yeah, yeah," she grunted. "Did you book—"

"Not yet, but I *will*," he cut in, smiling.

Malajia rolled her eyes. "Fuckin' around with your procrastinating ass, we'll be sleeping in the car."

Mark shrugged. "At least it's a *nice* car."

Malajia wasn't amused. "*I'll* just book the room now," she ground out.

"Suit yourself, I *said* I'll take care of it," Mark insisted.

Malajia shook her head and concentrated on her tablet.

"You know, PVU built a hotel behind campus like three years ago… We could stay *there*," he proposed.

Malajia's head jerked up. "Boy ain't nobody staying in that nut ass hotel they built," she scoffed, earning laughter from Mark. "What's their room service menu gonna be? Caf wing dings and shit?" She set her tablet down and walked over to the oven.

"Either *that* or that dry ass lasagna they used to have," Mark joked.

"Right, nobody wants that bullshit," Malajia agreed. "Oh,

speaking of shit that you have *yet* to do, did you get your tux for this damn wedding?"

Mark put his hand over his face.

"Mark, I'm serious, *do* it," she demanded. "I'm sick of Sidra's ass calling me about it."

Mark chuckled. "She's calling *you* 'cause *I* stopped answering her."

Malajia glared at him.

"Chill babe, I already got fitted for it."

"Mark, I'm not playing with you, you *better* had done it," she fussed. "Don't make me divorce you."

"I *did*," Mark promised. "Damn, you gonna divorce me over a suit and shit?"

"Yup," she mocked. "I *almost* filed papers when you ate the last of that cake the other day," she added, opening the oven.

"It was good cake," he joked, watching her. "Whatchu' make?" he asked, changing the subject.

"Lasagna," she replied, pulling the pan from the oven.

"I hope it ain't dry like the caf's," Mark mocked.

"Keep fuckin' with me and I will throw it on you. Hot ass cheese and all," Malajia spat back, placing the hot pan on the counter.

Mark put his hands up in surrender. "I'm just messing with you." He leaned over and grabbed Malajia's tablet, looking at the hotel site. "I'm looking forward to homecoming."

"Me too."

"It's gonna be cool, all of us staying in the same hotel too," he mused as Malajia grabbed some plates from the cabinet.

"I know, we can go bug the others like we used to do when we lived in the dorms...and in the clusters...and in the Wyngate homes," Malajia chortled.

"Exactly," Mark agreed, scrolling through the page. Zoning in on an open tab, he frowned in confusion. "Um, babe," he called.

"Yeah?" Malajia answered, grabbing utensils.

"You looking for a job or something?" he asked.

Malajia spun around, looking at him. "Huh?"

Mark showed her the tablet. "Your resume is open...and so

is a job search site."

Malajia's eyes got wide. Mark had no idea that she was thinking about going back to work, let alone actually *looking* for work. "Why are you going through my web browser, dawg?" she barked.

Mark knew her deflection techniques well. "Mel, come on now."

Malajia shrugged hard. "There's nothing wrong with updating my resume," she said, frustration filling her voice.

"I didn't say there was anything *wrong* with it," he returned. "I just… Do you want to go back to work? I thought we agreed—"

"Mark, I'm not going back to work. I just want to update my resume okay."

"And the job search?" he pressed.

"Is there something wrong with keeping up with the job market?" she hissed. "I watch cartoons all damn day, sometimes I just want to know what's going on in the world *outside* of 'Puppy Pete and the Rescue Barks'," she argued.

Mark stared at her; he didn't believe a word of it. "Malajia…am I not doing a good job taking care of things? Of *you*?" he asked, somber. "Are the boys too much? Do you need help when I'm not here?"

Malajia spotted the defeat in Mark's face and tone easily; the last thing she wanted was for him to feel like he wasn't doing a good job of taking care of his family. That she felt like she *had* to work because he was lacking somewhere. When in reality, she *wanted* to work for her *own* fulfilment. But she didn't know how to express that to him without insulting him, or hurting his feelings.

Malajia walked over to him. "Mark…you're doing a *great* job taking care of our family," she reassured him.

"You sure?" he asked.

Malajia smiled and nodded. "Yes." She wrapped her arms around his waist. "Now fix your face."

Mark smiled and gave her a quick kiss on the lips. "Let's let that food cool for a minute," he suggested, gesturing to the pan. "Might as well start that movie we fell asleep on last night."

Mark walked out of the kitchen, leaving Malajia to glance at her tablet, letting out a sigh. She walked into the living room and flopped down on the couch next to him.

Mark flipped on the TV. "Do we have any liquor?" he asked her.

"Nope, I finished it when you went to sleep last night," Malajia answered, examining her nails. Mark jerked his head in her direction, and she met his gaze with a defiant one of her own. "You bet not say *shit*. Remember that damn cake."

Mark shook his head. "We need to go *out* for a drink," he said.

"No damn babysitter," Malajia grunted as Mark flipped through the TV recordings. "Dana is out with her ho ass friends, and Geri said she won't watch them until I stop making them call her Geraldine."

Mark laughed. "Yo, stop doing that shit. You fuckin up our options."

"No, her name is Geraldine and she'll just have to deal with it," Malajia joked. "Anyway, so I guess it's lasagna and TV."

Mark opened his mouth to speak, but his cell phone rang instead. He pulled it out of his pocket and eyed the caller ID. "It's Mom," he said.

"Tell her I said 'hi'," Malajia said, taking the remote and leaning back against Mark.

Mark put the phone to his ear. "Hey Mom, what's up? ...Nothing, me and Mel are just relaxing...the boys? They're in their room probably writing on the walls... Wait what?"

Malajia's ears perked; Mark's tone sounded like he was confused.

"You mean now? ...Like *right* now?" Mark vigorously tapped Malajia's shoulder, getting her to glance up at him. "I'm on my way... Nah, an hour drive ain't nothing... I'll bring whatever you need... See you soon. Bye." Mark jumped up as he ended the call.

"Boy, what the hell are you so hype for?" Malajia answered, annoyed that her cushion had moved.

"Yo, Mom just said that she wants the twins for a few days," Mark informed, excited.

Malajia's eyes widened. "Don't lie to me Mark or I'll file those papers."

"No bullshit, she said she misses them and wants me to bring them over tonight," Mark confirmed.

Malajia jumped up. "Fuck this movie." She headed for the steps. "I'mma get the boys ready."

"Babe, just grab whatever they ain't write on, and let's go before she calls back and changes her mind," Mark urged.

"Don't you answer that goddamn phone if she calls back," Malajia hurled, running up the steps. "Boys! You're going to Nana's house!"

Mark snickered at the sounds of his sons excited screaming.

"Hey! Save your screams for *her*!" Malajia yelled.

Mark was about to run to the kitchen, but a thought stopped him. "Mel! Want me to pack up half of this lasagna?" he called up the steps.

"Mark, if you don't throw that whole dry ass lasagna in the damn car!"

Jason stepped out of the driver's seat of his car, then walked around and opened the door for Kayla. He smiled tiredly, watching her jump out the car and skip up the walkway to their home. She bounced up and down, waiting for him to open the door. "Calm down a little bit," he chuckled, pushing the door open.

Chasity looked up from the couch, where she was working on her laptop. "Hey you two," she greeted, tone dry.

"Hey," Jason returned, shutting the door. Kayla ran over to Chasity and tried to jump on her lap.

Chasity gently nudged her way. "Stop it, Mommy is working," she said, stern.

"But...I want to tell you what I did today," Kayla pouted.

Chasity tried her best to remain calm. Just because she was having a bad week, she didn't want to take it out on her child, but her stress was making that task nearly impossible. She ran her hand over her hair. "Later, okay," Chasity promised.

"But—"

"I *said* later," Chasity barked, startling her.

Jason walked over and sat on the couch next to Chasity. "Kayla, go play. She'll come up when she finishes, and you can tell her all about your day, okay?"

Chasity glanced down at the laptop as Kayla nodded at Jason, clutching her toy kitty to her chest. Chasity felt horrible; her child only wanted to talk to her, and she was snapping.

As Kayla went to run for the stairs, Chasity reached out and gently grabbed her arm to stop her. "Give me a hug, Cupcake?" Chasity asked. Kayla smiled and jumped into her mother's arms, hugging her.

Jason watched Kayla skip up the steps, then turned to Chasity, who had resumed working. "You're actually working later than *I* am," he observed.

"Yeah, I know," she returned, eyes fixed on her screen.

Jason watched her as her fingers moved swiftly across the keyboard, not so much as glancing up at him. They had made it to the end of the week and it seemed that her irritation over Jason's work trip had not yet subsided.

"So, I'm leave Sunday evening," he said to her. She didn't answer him, so he tapped the top of her laptop. "Chaz?"

She frowned up at him. "Huh?"

"I leave Sunday night."

"Yes, I know," Chasity replied. She was too stressed about meeting her new deadlines to think much about her husband leaving for a week.

"You going to be okay while I'm gone?" he asked.

Chasity looked confused. "Am I five?" she asked, smartly. Jason rolled his eyes. "I think the kid and I can manage being by ourselves for five days."

"Attitude is still present I see," he mumbled.

"What?" she questioned, not sure if she'd heard him correctly.

"Nothing," he sniped back. He sighed as Chasity went back to typing.

Truth was, Chasity wasn't the only one stressed out; Jason was still dealing with stress of his own. No matter how many times he'd been told otherwise from his boss, Jason still felt that he was about to be fired. Still, he didn't want to be at odds with his wife. "Chaz," he called again.

"Yes, Jase?" she answered, still typing, not bothering to glance up at him.

"Look...I'm sorry okay," he apologized.

Chasity stopped typing and looked at him. "Sorry for what?" she asked, confused; Jason hadn't done anything to be sorry for.

"You just seem like you're still mad at me," he pointed out. Chasity held her stare. "I mean... I know I should've told you about my trip sooner. I know that my work schedule keeps me from spending more time with you—"

"Jase, I'm not mad at you," she cut in.

"You sure?"

"Yes," she assured. "I know your job is demanding. I know how much you wish you could be around here more... And I might not *want* you to go next week, but I know you *have* to." She pushed some hair behind her ears, "...If I made you feel like I was mad at you, *I'm* sorry."

Jason held his gaze on her. "Well, if you're not mad at *me*...what are you mad at?"

Chasity looked down at her laptop. Her work stress was carrying over into her home life. She was snapping at her family, and that was the last thing that she wanted to do. "I'm not mad, I'm just...stressed."

"What's stressing you?" Jason asked, concerned. "What's going on?"

Chasity closed her laptop and slowly set it on the floor. "I hate my job, Jason," she answered after a moment.

Jason shot her a sympathetic look. "Really?"

Chasity slowly nodded. "I've hated it for a while now," she vented. "I'm getting all of these projects thrown on me, with these ridiculous deadlines, and this bitch of a client keeps changing shit after I work *weeks* on a project for her. They act like I'm the *only* person in that company who can do any-fuckin-thing, so I get *no* help and—" she took a deep breath as she ran her hands along the back of her neck. "I just hate it... I mean, I still *love* web design but...I *hate* my *job.*"

Jason reached out and grabbed her hand. "Baby, why didn't you tell me this before?" he asked. "I ask you how work is all the time and you always say that it's fine."

"I know," Chasity admitted.

"If you're unhappy about something you need to *tell* me."

"I *get* that, but like I can't help *you* with *your* stressful job, you can't help me with *mine*," she said. "So, I was just trying to keep work at *work*...but I realize that I'm bringing it home *with* me, *literary*."

Jason let out a sigh. "Chaz, if the job is stressing you that much... I think you should quit."

Chasity frowned. "You're crazy," she threw back. "We have bills, and a *child*, and *bills*... I *can't* quit."

"You can go back to freelancing,"

"We can't *afford* that," Chasity argued. "Freelance work can be sporadic... I'm not trying to blow through our savings on bullshit."

"It wouldn't *be* bullshit, babe," Jason countered. "If I have to pick up extra hours to—"

"*Hell* no, you work *enough* hours," Chasity shot down.

Jason ran his hand over the top of his head. "Babe—"

"No, if I *do* leave, it wouldn't be before I have another job lined up," she threw back.

Jason held an intense gaze on her. "Chasity, the truth is you shouldn't be working for anybody other than *yourself*," he pointed out. "That's what you've *always* wanted. You were *happy* doing freelance after you graduated college."

Chasity thought for moment. He was right, but she didn't say anything.

Jason glanced down at his hands. "Had I just gone ahead and went into the pro football draft...we could've been set up, and you could have the luxury of sticking to your freelance work... You could've even started your own company by now."

Chasity stared at him, tilting her head. "Do you really feel that way?"

Jason shrugged. "I think about it sometimes," he admitted. "I think about how easy our lives could be if I had gone through with it."

"*I* don't," she said. "It wasn't what you wanted."

"Yeah, well, I *did* what I *wanted* and a lot of good *that* did," he grumbled.

Chasity sighed. "Look, I still stand by my feelings about that draft," she said. "You weren't *going*. It was *my* decision to take that job when I got pregnant, so you don't have to feel bad about that."

"I get it, but—"

Chasity patted Jason's leg. "Stop," she urged. "I'll be fine… Maybe once I get through these damn projects, I'll feel better."

"You *won't*," Jason contradicted. "You won't feel better until you quit."

Chasity rolled her eyes. "Well I'm *not*, so…"

"Want me to drop it?" he asked, picking up on her tense body language and stern tone.

"Please?" she confirmed.

"Okay," he complied, squeezing her hand. He took a long pause. "Since we're venting about jobs," he began finally. "…*I* might be the one blowing through our savings."

"Why?" Chasity asked, confused.

"I think they're going to fire me," he revealed.

"The fuck?" Chasity barked. "Are they stupid?"

Jason nodded. "Apparently so," he spat. "They're acting funny. I'm supposed to be training this new team and they want me to be hands off for the upcoming software project…talking about the new team is going to be helping me. No, it sounds like I'll be training them to take my job… I'm actually supposed to meet them in Phoenix next week."

Chasity was livid. Jason worked hard for that company. "I'm sorry babe," she sympathized, touching his face. "But hopefully that won't be the case."

"Yeah…thanks," he sulked.

"But if they really *are* that fuckin' stupid and fire you, I'll send a virus through all their shit," she hissed.

Jason laughed. "I'll be right there *with* you," he joked. "Take their shit down from the inside." He took a deep breath. "I guess I better start looking for a new job *myself*."

Chasity shook her head. "They're idiots."

"Yeah." He looked at her. "But *whatever* happens, we'll be fine," he promised.

She nodded; he leaned in and gave her a kiss.

"How about we go out to eat?" he suggested.

"I don't really feel like going out," she declined, leaning her head on the back of the couch.

"That's fine," Jason shrugged. "I'll make dinner then."

"Don't bother—I know you don't feel like it," Chasity said. "Just order some take out and call it a night."

"Thank God," Jason breathed, earning a laugh from Chasity. "You order us some cheese steaks, *I'll* go make us a drink."

"Just bring me the whole damn bottle," she said.

"You got it." As Jason moved to get up from the couch, his phone rang. Seeing who it was, he put the phone on speaker. "What's up Mark?"

"Yo bro!" Mark bellowed into the phone. "What y'all doing?"

"Chillin', why what's up?" Jason asked, as Chasity rolled her eyes.

"You got any drinks over there?" Mark asked.

Jason opened his mouth to answer, but Chasity cut in. "*Why* boy?" she bit out.

Mark paused. "Chaz?"

"Who *else* does it sound like?" Chasity spat.

"Yo Jase, you got me on speaker?" Mark questioned, shocked.

Jason chuckled. "Yeah."

"Yo man, you can't be doing that shit and not telling me," Mark barked.

"What are you *mad* for? You trying to hide something?" Chasity threw back.

Jason laughed. "Babe chill," he said to Chasity.

"Man, ain't nobody—"

"Yeah why *are* you mad about being on speaker?" Malajia's voice cut in on the line, cutting Mark off in the process. "What the fuck do y'all be talking about?"

"Mel, why you arguing with me right now?" Mark threw back. "I'm tryna get us to the drinks."

"'Cause ain't nobody fuckin' around with you," Malajia hissed back.

Jason put his hand over his face and shook his head.

"Hi Malajia," Chasity said flatly.

"Hey boo boo," Malajia squealed.

"Oh yeah, hey sis," Mark said to Chasity.

"Fuck you," Chasity sneered.

Jason snickered. "Look, Chaz and I had a long week. We're really trying to relax, what do y'all want?" Jason cut in.

"We ain't got the kids so we're coming over," Mark blurted out. "So get that stashed bottle out from under the sink and break out the shot glasses."

Chasity and Jason shot each other horrified glances. Entertaining their loud friends wasn't on their to-do list that evening.

Chasity vigorously shook her head at Jason, who stammered. "Umm, not tonight guys."

"Come on bee!" Mark bellowed. "I just *said* we ain't got the kids. We want to drink."

"So go *out* and drink," Chasity pointed out, agitated.

"We wanna come over *there*," Malajia insisted. "Stop being assholes and open the damn door."

"Look *you* might have a sitter, but *we don't*," Jason pointed out.

"What that got to do with *us*?" Mark asked after a moment of silence. "*Your* kid ain't bad. She'll stay in her room while we chill."

"God, you have the house to yourself," Chasity barked. "Just fuck each other and leave us alone."

"Oh, we plan on doing that *still*," Mark said, as Malajia laughed. "In *y'all* basement after we get drunk on y'all liquor stash."

"Jason hang up on them, *now*," Chasity ordered to a laughing Jason.

"Bye guys," Jason said. He hung up the phone before Mark could get whatever loud protest he was in middle of out. "Something is wrong with those two," he said to Chasity.

Chasity shook her head as she folded her arms. "You're *just now* realizing that?" she scoffed.

As they stood up from the couch, they heard their doorbell ring. The couple paused and looked at each other. "*Can't* be," Jason said. He pinched the bridge of his nose at the sound of several erratic knocks on the door.

"Fuuuuuck," Chasity groaned, rubbing her face with her hand.

Jason walked to the door and opened it. Just as he suspected, Mark and Malajia were standing there, dancing in place with big smiles on their faces. "Guys, I *said* not tonight," Jason grunted.

"Oh yeah?" Mark quipped. "Well *we* heard, 'sure, come on over and share our bottle my good friends'."

Chasity narrowed her eyes, as Jason moved aside and let Mark and Malajia in. "You got that lying ass invitation from 'not tonight?'" she sneered, folding her arms.

Malajia walked over to her. "Sure did," she teased, planting a quick, hard kiss on Chasity's cheek.

Disgusted, Chasity smacked Malajia on the back of her head. "Eww," she scoffed.

Malajia laughed, "We were already walking over here when we called," she confessed, heading for the steps. "Where's my goddaughter?"

"Malajia, don't go up there making all that damn noise. You're only going to rile her up," Chasity hissed, pointing at Malajia, who was still inching her way towards the steps.

"Kayla! Your mommy is tryna stop our fun!" Malajia bellowed, running up the steps; Chasity tore after her.

Hearing the ensuing commotion upstairs, Jason shook his head. He laughed when he heard Malajia scream, followed by his daughter's giggle.

"God, she's probably getting her ass beat," Mark joked, putting his hand over his face. "You gotta bob and weave Mel!" he shouted up the steps.

"Jason, your wife is childish!" Malajia hollered back. "She just tripped me."

Jason headed for the kitchen as the noise died down, grabbing a bottle of vodka from the cabinet. "I know this is what you came for—go ahead and get the shot glasses," he directed at Mark, who eagerly rubbed his hands together.

"You ain't gotta tell me twice, brother," Mark grinned, fetching them from another cabinet. Mark watched as Jason filled them to the rim. He noticed the change in Jason's demeanor; he locked sullen. "You cool man?" Mark asked.

"Yeah, why?" Jason replied, grabbing a bottle of juice from the refrigerator.

"You look all gloomy and shit," Mark observed.

Jason rubbed his eyes as he set the bottle on the table. "Like I said on the phone, I had a long week."

"Oh...you want us to leave?" Mark asked. "I mean, if you're really serious—"

Jason stared at him. "Really? You'll *actually* leave?" he asked, tone even.

"Nah." Mark laughed at Jason's eye roll. "No seriously, if you want us to leave, we'll go."

"Forget it, you're already here—"

"Thank God," Mark breathed, cutting Jason off. He downed his shot. "Whooo, this is the *good* shit," he rejoiced, picking up the bottle and examining it. "This is what that computer money can buy, huh?"

Jason shook his head. "Look, since you're here drinking up my liquor and will probably be eating my damn food—"

"Ooh, what y'all cooking? Or are y'all ordering out?"

Jason stared at Mark, a stern look on his face. "Anyway," he began after a few seconds. "I have to go out of town for work next week."

Mark poured himself another shot. "Oh yeah?"

"Yeah," Jason confirmed as Mark downed the shot. "If you could just check in on my girls while I'm gone, I'd appreciate it. Even if you just drive by the house to make sure things look okay."

"Sure, I got you," Mark promised, smiling.

"Thanks," Jason replied, rubbing the back of his neck. He watched as Mark poured yet another shot, his third in only a few minutes. "Are you going to save us *any*?"

"Nah," Mark chuckled.

Chapter 9

Emily picked up a sparkly tiara, examining it.

"Do you like that?" Ms. Harris asked.

Emily put it back on the shelf, shaking her head in the process. "No, the princess look is more Sidra's thing," she chuckled to herself.

"What did you say honey?" Ms. Harris wondered, eyeing other accessories in the bridal shop.

"Oh, I was just saying that it's not my style," Emily amended, before letting out a cough. With a few days off from work due to her sore throat turning into a full on cold, Emily had taken the opportunity to take a trip back to Jersey to make her nearly forgotten bridal shop appointment. She was checking on her dress and figured she'd run around with her mother on other wedding duties while she was there.

Ms. Harris frowned in concern when Emily let out another cough. "Are you okay? That cold sounds terrible, you sure you shouldn't be in bed?"

"I'm okay," Emily insisted, rubbing her forehead with her hand. "I just want to get this stuff done."

"I understand... But the bright side is that I get to see you." Ms. Harris then smiled a small smile. "*And* take care of you. Do you want me to make you some soup when we get back?"

"Sure," Emily smiled back.

"I'll even make you my special cough drop tea," Ms. Harris beamed. "And I'll make some cake."

"Mommy, you don't have to do all of that," Emily protested.

"Nonsense, it's no trouble," she insisted, putting a hand up. "I'll make enough cake for you and your brothers. They'll be stopping over a little later."

"Good, then I can ask them in person if they've gotten fitted for their tuxes yet," Emily chuckled. "Your sons have been avoiding my texts."

"Don't you worry about them, *I'll* get them in line," Ms. Harris promised.

Emily glanced at her phone, responding to a text. "Thanks." She looked back at her mother. "So…I talked to Daddy the other day and—"

"He's not bringing that little girlfriend of his, *is* he?" Ms. Harris sniped, adjusting her purse on her shoulder.

Emily rolled her eyes to the ceiling. Ever since her mother had learned of her father's serious relationship, the woman did not hesitate to make snide comments. "Mommy, please don't be like that," Emily chided. "You and Daddy have been divorced since I was little. I'm sure you knew that he would date *eventually*."

Ms. Harris flagged Emily with her hand. "Oh please," she huffed.

"Come on. Claire is really nice."

Ms. Harris folded her arms.

Emily shook her head in amusement. Her mother was letting her childish behavior surface. She placed her arm on her mother's shoulder. "Listen, to answer your question, I *did* extend a plus one to Daddy for her."

"Fine," Ms. Harris grumbled. "I'll just put her in the back when I do the table arrangements."

"Mommy, Will and *I* are doing the table arrangements," Emily informed, sitting down on a plush white ottoman.

Ms. Harris looked shocked. "You're putting her at the parent's table?"

Emily pinched the bridge of her nose as she felt a cough come up. *God please give me the strength to get through the rest of this wedding planning.* "Please don't make this difficult," Emily begged, tone calm. "If *you* were bringing a date, I'd sit him with *you too*… When *are* you going to date anyway?"

Ms. Harris put her hand up. "When I'm good and ready."

Emily stared at her, blinking slowly. "Okay then," she relented. As far as she was concerned, the topic could be dropped.

Ms. Harris craned her neck for the bridal shop attendee. "I can't wait to see what the dress looks like with the buttons taken out," she said. "Even though I *still* think that you could have just altered *my* old wedding dress and worn it." Ms. Harris shot Emily a hopeful glance. "It's not too late for you to do that, you know."

Emily stared at her mother with wide eyes. This wasn't the first time that her old wedding dress had been brought up. And each time, Emily tried to find a way to let her mother down easy. "Ummm, it's okay. I already put a deposit on *this* dress so..."

"Well I'm sure if it's something that you wanted, I could give you your money—"

"No, no need to bother," Emily quickly cut in. "Did you pick out your jewelry yet?"

"Of course," Ms. Harris beamed, "I actually got the both of us matching sets."

Emily answered another text. "You did?"

"Yes, a crystal and light rose quartz set."

Emily resisted the urge to wince at the description. Sure, she liked crystal, but rose quartz, not so much. But her mother seemed excited about it, and if it got the woman's mind off trying to get Emily to wear her old, outdated wedding dress, she would pretend to be intrigued. "Oh...that's sounds nice," she placated.

"It's *beautiful*," Ms. Harris gushed, clasping her hands together. "It's going to look great on you. I know the light will pick up the sparkle."

"Okay," Emily commented. "I'm sure it'll look nice in pictures."

"I'm so excited for this wedding, baby girl," Ms. Harris harped, earning a smile from Emily. "I *especially* can't wait to walk you down that aisle."

Emily's smile vanished. "I'm sorry, *what*?" she asked, confused.

"I can't wait to walk you down the aisle," Ms. Harris repeated, confident.

Emily was horrified; she had no idea that her mother was

expecting to be the one to carry out that task. "Umm…you know that *Daddy* is walking me down, right?" Emily carefully put out.

Ms. Harris frowned. "Excuse me?"

"Yes… He's my father, and it's tradition," Emily pointed out.

"Who cares about *tradition*?" Ms. Harris sniped. "People do what they *want*. You told me that your friends' *mother* walked *her* down the aisle for her wedding."

"Yes, but Chasity didn't have a *relationship* with her father, *I do*," Emily countered, placing a hand on her chest. She completely understood Chasity's reasoning for letting Trisha walk her down the aisle, instead of her father. Chasity's father wasn't the best, but *Emily's was,* and she wasn't about to deny him that honor simply because her mother felt entitled.

Ms. Harris was livid. "I can't believe— *I* raised you—"

"He didn't *want* it that way—that was *your choice,* remember?" Emily corrected. Ms. Harris's jaw tightened. "Bottom line is that he was and still *is* a big part of my life." Emily's tone was stern. "He's walking me down."

Ms. Harris's face fell as she adjusted the purse strap on her shoulder once more. "All I've done for you and *this* is how you repay me?"

Emily frowned. "I'm *sorry*?" she questioned, annoyed.

Ms. Harris put her hand up. "I've stood by and watched as you made those girls your bridesmaids over your sister—"

"You mean my *friends*?" Emily ground out. "The girls who are more like sisters to me than my *actual* sister?"

"You had your reasons for it and while I did not *agree*, I stood by it," Ms. Harris harped. "You *insist* on getting married in some random hotel in Virginia, instead of a church here in Jersey. You're not having real flowers in your bouquets. Your bridesmaids' dresses aren't appropriate—"

"You mean they're not big, puffy and ugly?" Emily cut in, angry. "You really have a problem with *every* decision that I've made, and that's sad."

"Bottom line is that I've *supported* every one of the *questionable* decisions, but I cannot and *will* not support a decision that strips me of the honor that I deserve."

Emily's mouth dropped open in shock. "I can't believe that you're acting like this," she argued. "I can't believe that you're *saying* this to me right now. You're hurting me *again*, I hope you know that."

"Yeah well, you're hurting *me* and I feel disrespected," Ms. Harris hissed.

"*Disrespected?*" Emily spat.

Ms. Harris pointed at Emily. "Yes, *disrespected*. And to be honest, the way that I feel, I don't even think I want to come to the wedding," she ground out.

Emily was furious; she could not believe the turn that this visit to the bridal store had taken. After all this time, her mother was reverting right back to her guilt trips and temper tantrums. Emily stood from the ottoman, and tightened the purse on her shoulder. "Then *don't come*," she spat. She turned on her heel and stormed out of the shop, leaving her mother standing there.

Hastily walking around the corner to a coffee shop, Emily's head was pounding as she tried to keep herself from busting out in a fit of tears. Not only did she have to reschedule her dress appointment because she'd walked out, her train back to Virginia didn't leave for two more days. With her plans to stay with her mother shot, Emily had to figure out a new place to stay.

Emily cradled her cup of ginger and lemon tea in her hands as she waited. She'd been at the café for an hour. A text came in on her phone. She looked down at it, then glanced outside. A familiar minivan had pulled up in front of the shop. Grabbing her to-go cup, she stood up and walked out. Approaching the rolled down passenger side window, she offered a slight smile.

"Hey light skin, you cute. You need a ride?" Malajia teased from the driver's seat.

Emily sighed. "You *know* I do."

"Well hop your ass on in here," Malajia replied, gesturing for Emily to get in.

Emily opened the door and got herself situated. After she

put her seat belt on, she turned to the back seat and smiled at Malajia's sons. "Hi little guys."

They waved, but didn't answer; Malajia shot them a stern look through the rearview mirror. "Hey, Aunt Emily don't want those raggedy waves, you *speak* to her," she scolded.

"Hi Aunt Emmy," they said in unison.

Emily giggled as she turned back around in her seat. She looked at Malajia, chuckling at the annoyed expression on her face. "What's wrong?"

"I said *Emily*, not Emmy," Malajia grunted.

"Well, I think it's cute that they call me that," Emily approved.

"Don't nobody care what you like, they irkin'." Malajia snarled, pulling off.

Emily leaned her head back again the headrest. "Thank you for coming to get me," she said, grateful.

"Oh girl please, I wasn't doing shit but cleaning anyway," Malajia dismissed with a wave of her hand. "But you're welcome... I can't believe that your mom showed her ass like that."

Emily sighed. "Yeah," she sulked. "I thought she was beyond doing stuff like that, but I guess I gave her too much credit."

Malajia glanced over at Emily while she waited at a red light. She couldn't get the sound of Emily's trembling voice out of her mind when she had called nearly an hour earlier. Emily had sent a group text to the girls while ordering her tea, and Malajia had called Emily almost immediately after. After hearing about the argument and learning that Emily was sulking alone in a coffee shop, Malajia did not hesitate to pack up her children and drive to Jersey to pick her up.

"Em, don't let her and that petty shit she said ruin your wedding planning," Malajia advised, sincere.

"I don't even want to *talk* about the wedding right now," Emily dismissed. "Everything *about* it is stressing me out right now."

"I understand that, trust me," Malajia sympathized. "Well, despite that nonsense...I'm glad you're back in town."

Emily offered a small smile. "Yeah, I guess the bright side

is that I can spend the next two days hanging out with you guys… When you're not busy, that is."

Malajia frowned when Emily coughed. "Hell no girl, you're about to get out with those germs."

Emily managed a laugh. "Don't be mean, I'm sick and depressed."

"Ain't nobody tryna hear that," Malajia threw back, shaking her hand in Emily's direction. Her hand was so close to Emily's face that when Emily turned her head, she got poked in the eye.

"Ow Malajia! You just poked me in the eye!" Emily shrieked, frantically rubbing at it.

Malajia couldn't get her apology out; she was too busy laughing. "I'm about to pee on myself!" Malajia screamed as Emily stared at her, one eye closed. Malajia caught Emily's stare and forced herself to cut her cackling short. "My bad," she apologized.

Emily shook her head, opening her eye to examine it in the visor's mirror.

"Foreal, my fault."

"I *know* it's your fault," Emily barked, still annoyed. "I can see why Chaz is always smacking you, your hands are always in her face."

Malajia frowned. "Nobody told you to turn around that hype," she countered. "And you don't know *what* Chaz does, so stay out our business."

Emily made a face in retaliation.

Malajia made a face back. After a few seconds of silence, she sucked her teeth. "You want me to buy you some ice cream?"

Emily glanced at her, still rubbing her eye. "Yes."

"Fine," Malajia sighed.

"Can we have ice cream too?!" The twins bellowed.

"No! Ice cream is for people who *didn't* throw spaghetti at each other earlier," Malajia barked.

Emily snickered.

"I'm not gonna lie, I forgot they were back there for a second," Malajia joked after a moment.

"You're still buying them ice cream, aren't you?" Emily

assumed, amused.

Malajia let out a quick sigh. "Yeah man."

Sidra gathered her work folders and her cup of coffee, and headed out of her office with Carlie in tow.

"Ugh, the last place I want to be is hot Arizona," Carlie griped, smoothing a few strands of hair back into her bun.

Sidra took a sip of her coffee as she shot Carlie a glance. "You *do* know that California is *just* as hot, right?" she sniped.

"Yeah well, I'm used to *that* heat," Carlie grunted, rolling her eyes.

Sidra shook her head. Even though Carlie's complaining was wearing thin, Sidra had to admit, having to travel to Phoenix with her law firm for the next few days wasn't exactly what she wanted to do either. The traveling, paired with the fact that she had been up late going over important paperwork multiple times for one of the attorney's cases, had her on edge. "Anyway," Sidra sighed. She set her coffee down on a nearby desk, and opened a folder in her hand. "You looked over these files for the case, right?"

Carlie tilted her head. "You mean all the stuff that's being presented into evidence?" she asked; Sidra nodded. "I mean *yeah*, the whole *team* had to."

"Yes, I know," Sidra replied, ignoring Carlie's snide tone. "Curious, on the lease…did you notice how some of the line items were worded?"

Carlie looked confused. "No, everything seemed pretty straight forward. The team feels that it's an airtight case."

"But, what if it's not? I mean from what I read—"

Carlie folded her arms. "Look Sidra, if there was anything off, the attorneys would have figured it out," she pointed out." And unless you want to actually put that fancy law degree to use and *become* an attorney, you need to not question what they say."

Sidra narrowed her eyes at Carlie. Though she didn't appreciate the attitude, Sidra knew that Carlie was right. What if by opening her mouth, she'd open a can of worms that could cost the team the case? "Fine," Sidra relented. She closed the folder, staring at it for only a moment more, then finished her coffee. "We need to get to this meeting."

Carlie let out a groan, and Sidra rolled her eyes.

Both ladies headed across the room. As they prepared to turn a corner, Sidra spotted a familiar figure through the glass doors, just in the building's hallway.

"Is that who I think it is?" she said to herself, staring.

Carlie sidled up next to her. "What are you stopping for?" she asked, curious.

Sidra ignored her and headed for the door. "Oh my God," she beamed, tossing her empty paper coffee cup in a nearby trash bin.

"Sidra, where are you going?" Carlie called after her.

"I see a friend, I'll be right back," Sidra threw over her shoulder. She pushed open the doors and darted out just as the person was beginning to walk away. "Jason!" she called.

Jason, food container in his hand, stopped walking and turned around. He smiled. "Oh, hey Sidra."

Sidra bolted over to him and the two friends embraced. "It's so good to see you," she squealed as they parted. It had been so long since she'd seen any of her friends; this was the highlight of her day. "What are you doing here?"

"I'm here for the week," Jason answered. "My tech company is opening an office in this building, and I've been sent here to oversee some stuff and train a new team."

"That's great," Sidra replied, shifting the folders in her hands. "Doing big things, I see."

Jason smirked. "Yeah, not really," he joked. "Anyway, what are *you* doing here?"

"I had to travel here with my firm," Sidra answered. "Case stuff, and they wanted their favorite paralegal to tag along."

Jason chuckled. "Favorite?"

"Most *competent*," Sidra amended, voice laced with humor. "Anyway, I'll be here for the next three days."

"Same here," Jason said. "Been here since Sunday."

"Did Chasity come with you?" she asked, hopeful.

Jason shook his head. "No," he sulked. "Wish that she could've." Sure, his time out in Phoenix wasn't as bad as he thought it was going to be, but he missed his family. Jason caught a glimpse of his watch. "Damn, as much as I would love to catch up, I need to scarf this food down so I can get back to work."

Sidra's eyes widened as she too glanced at her watch. "Shit, I need to go too," she said. "Hey, would you be opposed to joining me for dinner some time before you head back to the East coast?"

"No, not at all." Jason smiled.

"Okay, we can do dinner tomorrow," Sidra proposed, waving to him. "I'll call you."

"Sounds good," he returned, heading for the elevator. "Talk to you later."

Sidra waved as the elevator doors closed. "Well, how about that," she mused to herself. After a moment, she walked back through her company's doors, and was immediately greeted by a smiling Carlie.

"Giiiiirl, who was *that*?" Carlie charged, practically drooling.

Sidra rolled her eyes.

"He was *too* damn fine," Carlie went on.

Sidra shook her head. "That's my friend Jason, from college."

"Where does he work? 'Cause I need to go see about that after I get off," Carlie prodded, reaching for the lip-gloss in her blazer pocket. "He'd make the *perfect* addition to my hotel room tonight."

Sidra frowned. "He's off limits," she said, stern.

Carlie glanced up at Sidra. "Ooh, my fault. Are *you* working on him? Is he a prospect?"

"Not at *all*," Sidra confirmed. "Not *only* is he like a brother to me, he's *married*."

Carlie snickered, waving a dismissive hand at Sidra. "Girl, I'm not worried about that."

Annoyed and disgusted with Carlie's blatant disrespect, Sidra stepped in front of Carlie as the woman moved towards the door. "I don't think you *heard* me," Sidra reiterated, voice filled with disdain. "He's *married*...to one of my *best friends*." Sidra stared Carlie square in her eyes, grey eyes flashing with warning. "He's. Off. Limits— Understand?"

Carlie's gaze shifted; she followed up with a nervous laugh. "Come on Sidra, I was just joking."

Sidra's gaze did not waiver. "Uh huh," she spat out.

"I don't mess with married men," Carlie back peddled. "We have to get to this meeting, right?"

Sidra followed Carlie's progress towards the conference room with a glare. *Disgusting heffa.*

Chapter 10

Hearing a knock at the door, Chasity got up to answer it. She peered through the peephole, and smiled when she opened it. "Hey Em." She extended her arms for a hug.

Then Emily coughed.

Chasity quickly backed away and proceeded to shut her door. "Fuck no," she ground out.

Emily busted out laughing as the door shut in her face. "Oh come on Chasity!" she pleaded, knocking on the door.

"I can't get sick Emily," Chasity hurled through the door.

Emily knocked again. "But I miss you and I love you," she pouted. "I'll cough into a towel or something. I had a bad day, please open the door." Emily grinned as the door opened back up.

"Very well." Chasity relented, stepping aside. "Come in."

Emily practically skipped inside. Malajia walked up after her, and was greeted by Chasity shutting the door in her face.

"Bitch, *I* ain't got no cold," Malajia barked, pushing it open.

Chasity snickered.

"Rude ass," Malajia grunted, shutting the door behind her. She had hung out with Emily most of the afternoon, dropping her sons off with Mark as soon as he was home from work. That way, they could wait for Chasity to get home from work to crash her place with Emily.

Chasity made her way over to the kitchen. "Em, does your sick ass want some tea?" she offered.

Emily giggled. "You're sweet in your own way Chaz, yes," she replied, grateful. Removing her jacket and purse, she settled into an accent chair.

Malajia walked over to the kitchen. "You never offer *me* any tea," she spat, folding her arms.

"Girl—I *have* when you were sick, so shut your lying ass the fuck up," Chasity barked, removing a box of tea bags from the cabinet. "I had a long day, don't piss me off."

"And there goes the *sweetness*," Malajia grunted, ignoring Chasity's warning.

Chasity sucked her teeth. "Whatever," she ground out, filling a tea kettle with water. "Oh, and tell Mark that he isn't slick riding past here every day all slow and shit," she directed at Malajia, setting the kettle on the stove to boil.

Malajia lowered her head and shook it. "I *told* his stalking ass to just knock on the door to check on you," she griped. "He always gotta do some dramatic shit."

"Yesterday he stopped and stared at me for like a minute while I was on the front step," Chasity spat out, earning a loud laugh from Malajia. "Then gave me the peace sign and pulled off like a damn fool."

"He's so stupid," Malajia concluded, laughter subsiding.

Emily looked confused. "*Why* is Mark riding by the house every day?"

"Jason is out of town for the week and he asked Mark to check on Chaz," Malajia explained.

"Oh." Emily looked around. "Wow, it's nice in here Chasity."

"Thanks, you've seen it before," Chasity replied.

"It's been a while, I forgot what it looked like," Emily chortled.

Malajia glanced over and observed the food on the counter. "What did you make for dinner?" she asked.

"Nothing, I picked something up on the way home," Chasity answered, dry. "I'm too mentally drained to cook."

"Well, *what* did you pick up?" Malajia pressed.

"*Why*?" Chasity snapped.

"'Cause me and Em are hungry!" Malajia snapped back.

Emily put her hands up in surrender as Chasity looked over at her. "I didn't say anything about being hungry," she denied. "Malajia, please don't get me yelled at."

Chasity folded her arms. "I have extra if you want some Emily," she said. Malajia's mouth fell open. "It's just tacos."

"Tacos sound great, thanks," Emily beamed.

"So, you're really not gonna offer *me* any?" Malajia fussed. When Chasity didn't bother responding to her, Malajia turned to Emily. "Don't smile too damn hard. She only had extra because she forgot for a hot second that Jason wasn't here, and bought food for three people," she spat.

"Doesn't matter, I still get to eat though," Emily threw back, causing Chasity to snicker. Malajia made a face at Emily in retaliation. Emily giggled, then hearing a child's laughter coming from upstairs, she pointed up the steps. "Can I go up and say hi to Kayla?"

Chasity looked at her like she was crazy. "You don't have to *ask* Emily. You're her aunt, just take your ass upstairs," she said.

While Chasity was known to be overprotective when it came to people being around her child, it didn't apply to the people she trusted—namely her friends.

Emily practically skipped towards the staircase; Chasity looked at her. "Just don't cough on her," she called after her.

Emily laughed. "I promise, I won't," she assured, heading upstairs.

Malajia looked over at Chasity as Chasity began prepping Emily's tea. "So, I really can't have any tacos?" she asked. She turned away when Chasity shot her a piercing glare.

"I can't believe that your mother is acting like that Emily." Sidra's voice was loud and angry through the speaker.

"Tell me about it," Emily replied, adjusting a throw blanket around her midsection. "She had the nerve to send me text messages like an hour ago, trying to justify how she'd acted."

"She can't be serious," Alex said through the line. "This is *your* wedding and she's being ridiculous."

Emily ran a hand through her hair. "I don't even know why I'm surprised," she sulked. "She really feels like I'm disrespecting her."

"She's an idiot," Chasity griped. "Sorry but *not* sorry."

"I agree, and I say you kick her ass out of the wedding," Malajia followed up, reaching for a bowl of popcorn on the coffee table in front of her.

It was later that evening after dinner. Malajia, Chasity, and Emily were relaxing in Chasity's living room, discussing Emily's argument with her mother. The girls had decided that this needed to be a group conversation, so they'd phoned Sidra and Alex on speaker.

"Well, she already told me that she didn't want to come *anyway*," Emily grumbled. She sighed. "I'm so disappointed in her."

"God, why can't she act *right* for once?" Sidra vented. "I'm tired of her and your dusty sister making everything about *them*."

Malajia chuckled. "She said 'dusty'."

Emily shook her head and played with the blanket fabric. "I was just hoping that for *once* everything could be perfect."

"Your wedding will be," Chasity promised.

"Right, we're not going to let you give up on that dream because of a few rotten apples...or I should say rotten *people*," Alex commented.

Malajia reached out and rubbed Emily's shoulder. "Everything will be perfect, don't worry about it," she consoled.

Emily gave a slight nod, but didn't say anything.

"Tell us what you need us to do, sis," Malajia said.

"Yeah, anything Em, were serious," Sidra chimed in.

Emily put a hand up. "I'm fine. I have everything under control," she insisted. "I'm just having a moment."

"Come on Em, surely we can help you with *something*," Alex pressed.

"Just make sure the guys have their suits," Emily deflected.

"That's a given," Malajia assured. "I'll beat Mark's ass."

Emily giggled, grabbing some popcorn from the bowl.

Malajia playfully smacked Emily's hand away. "Nah, this is my bowl," Malajia barked. "You ate yours."

Emily sat up in her seat. "*You* ate all of mine!" she exclaimed, then reached back for the bowl. "So share *yours*."

Malajia and Emily tussled with the bowl, and Chasity pinched the bridge of her nose. "Y'all are giving me a headache," she griped. If her agitation with the girls horsing around wasn't enough, Malajia accidentally knocking the bowl over, spilling popcorn all over them, took it to a new level.

"Get the fuck out Malajia!" Chasity erupted, pushing popcorn from her lap.

"Why I gotta—"

"'Cause you always starting shit!" Chasity yelled, interrupting Malajia. "We were chillin' and here *you* go with the dumb shit."

"Okay, calm down. I'll get it up before I leave," Malajia replied, sitting back in her seat. She looked over at Emily, who had her hand over her mouth, trying not to laugh out loud. Malajia rolled her eyes.

"Are y'all finished acting like children over there?" Alex asked, humor in her voice. "Do I need to take a trip?"

"*Please* do, and take Malajia's ass back *with* you," Chasity huffed.

Malajia shot Chasity a side-glance.

"Back to the situation at hand," Sidra interjected. "Em, other than keeping the guys in line, what *else* do you need from us?"

"Nothing Sidra, I *promise* I'm fine," Emily assured.

"Damn it!" Alex bellowed into the line.

"Alex, what's wrong?" Emily charged, concerned.

"Sorry for the outburst, the document that I was writing just closed before I had a chance to save it," Alex panicked. "Oh my God, that's the mockup for next month's magazine. What am I gonna do?"

"Just relax," Chasity calmly said.

"Chasity I *can't* relax, I just lost all of my work!" Alex exclaimed.

"First, stop yelling at me," Chasity shot back. "Second, just recover the file."

"How? I didn't *save* it," Alex bellowed, hysterical.

"I *know* that," Chasity bit out, rubbing her eyes. "Calm your ass down and go to your recent documents, search for the name of your file, then click recover unsaved documents."

It was silent for a moment on Alex's end, except for a few huffs here and there. After another moment, she let out a squeal of delight. "It worked, I love you!"

Chasity rolled her eyes. "I know and I *know*."

"Let me get off this phone and concentrate before I lose

something else," Alex breathed, relieved. "Love y'all, see you soon."

"I guess I should get going too," Sidra yawned as Alex hung up. "I need to finish pulling these records before I turn in."

"Sidra, you still content with being a file girl?" Malajia joked. "You bored as shit over there."

Chasity pinched the bridge of her nose. "Malajia, come on," she chided.

Malajia put her arms up. "What?"

"*First* of all," Sidra jumped in, upset. "Paralegals do *way* more than file papers. Our job is highly important, so don't you dare disrespect the profession."

Emily winced, while Chasity smirked at the stunned look on Malajia's face.

"Look girl, I'm not disrespecting *paralegals*, okay," Malajia argued. "I'm sure you and everyone *else* in the field work harder than *I* did when I was working."

"So, what's your *point* Malajia?" Sidra challenged.

Malajia grabbed the cell phone from Chasity and pulled it close to her face. "My *point* is that *your* ass is supposed to be a goddamn *lawyer*. I mean, you *did* carry your ass all the way out there to go to that top-notch law school, *didn't* you? Wasn't that your *goal*?"

"Mel, drop the shit and leave her alone," Chasity calmly urged.

"No, fuck that. I don't like her attitude," Malajia threw back, pointing her finger at Chasity. "I was *joking* and she wanna take the shit *left*."

"Malajia, how about you mind the business that pays you," Sidra spat out.

Malajia turned her attention back to the phone. "Well bitch, I'm not *working*," she jeered. "So since no *other* business is paying me, I'll keep minding *yours*."

"Whatever Malajia," Sidra dismissed. "Chasity, Emily, goodnight."

"Night Sid," Emily said.

"Later," Chasity followed up.

Malajia narrowed her eyes. "So, you really just excluded me like that?" she sneered.

Sidra sucked her teeth right before the line went dead.

Malajia glanced down at the phone; seeing that Sidra had hung up, she sucked her teeth right back. "Rude ass. I hope Jason stand her ass up for their little 'friend' dinner tomorrow."

Chasity chuckled. "He won't, he's happy to have a familiar face out there and you deserved that shit; she told you before about bringing up her job. You know how defensive she gets."

Malajia just flagged her. "Whatever," she grumbled.

Emily stretched. "I appreciate you letting me stay here for the next few days Chaz," she said, changing the subject.

"It's no problem," Chasity replied, rubbing her eyes. "If *you* don't mind hearing a four-year-old talk your ear off about cats, then I'm fine."

Emily laughed. "Aww, I love to hear about her interests," she said. "I can watch her for you tomorrow if you want. I'm not doing anything."

Chasity looked at her. "No Em, you don't have to—"

"No, I *want* to. That way you don't have to worry about getting her up and everything," Emily insisted. "I don't mind spending the day with her. I can put on my teacher hat and we can do some fun learning stuff… I'm great with kids."

Chasity stared at Emily's smiling face. She knew she had to be at her office earlier than normal, and she didn't feel like dealing with the hassle of getting Kayla up, ready, fed and dropped off at her in-laws. "Okay… Thanks, I appreciate it."

"You don't have to thank me, it's really no problem," Emily returned with a wave of her hand. Spending time with her niece surely would take her mind off the conversation that she needed to have with her mother *and* Will about her behavior.

Malajia leaned forward. "Does this mean you're gonna watch the twins *too*?" she asked, hopeful.

Emily looked at her. "Well, I guess—"

"You'll be watching them at *her* house," Chasity cut in.

"That defeats the purpose," Malajia argued. "And what problem you got with my babies coming over here, witch?"

"They're bad!" Chasity snapped, laughter in her voice. "When I'm *here*, its one thing, 'cause they know *I* don't play. But they will run all over Emily, *literally*."

Emily shook her head in amusement. "Another time

Malajia," she promised.

Malajia sucked her teeth. "I don't need your pity offer," she scoffed.

"Well, Malajia if I had stayed at *your* house, I would've certainly watched them for you," Emily pointed out.

Malajia had a thought. "Hey, you can take the couch at *my*—"

"No thank you," Emily cut in, politely.

Chasity busted out laughing at the salty look on Malajia's face. "Girl, nobody wants to sleep on that hard ass couch you got," she teased.

Malajia flipped Chasity off. "Whatever, I'll watch my *own* bad ass kids… Not like I got shit *else* to do anyway," she muttered.

Josh had been tinkering with the parts underneath this client's car long enough to develop a diagnosis. Making a final adjustment, he slid out from under the car with a sigh.

"Sarah," he called.

"Yeah JJ?" Sarah replied, walking out of the office.

"Can you call Dad back and tell him that his friend's car needs to be scrapped?" he griped. The woman's car that he was working on—as a favor for his father—was at least twenty years old and in bad shape.

Sarah shook her head. "I *told* Dad to tell Ms. Bernadette that it was time for a new car."

"He thinks that every car can be salvaged," Josh grunted, standing from the floor. "I told him before, sometimes the money that has to be put out to fix a car this old isn't worth it."

Sarah handed Josh a towel to wipe the grease from his hands. "Are you going to fix it?"

"Yeah, I'll fix it," Josh said. "I'm just saying."

Sarah giggled. "You want some water or something before I get back to doing this inventory?" she offered.

"No, I'm okay," Josh declined. "You can get going actually. We don't have any more clients scheduled for the day."

"Nope, I'll leave when *you* leave," Sarah insisted, putting her hand up.

"Okay," Josh shrugged, "Since you're staying, can you do me a favor?"

Sarah tilted her head. "What's that?"

"Look over those locations that I picked out," he replied. "They're in the folder titled 'expansion', on the computer."

Sarah frowned. "Expansion?"

"Yeah…I'm thinking of opening a new location," he clarified. "This shop is doing really well, it's only right that I open a second garage."

Sarah nodded in agreement. "I can't argue with that," she approved. "Is the new shop going to be here in Delaware?"

Josh chuckled. "Go check out the locations that I'm considering," he ordered, pointing to the office.

Sarah playfully backhanded him in the ribs. "As you wish, boss," she teased, walking away.

Josh tossed the soiled towel on a nearby counter. He had to admit, ever since he'd hired his sister as the shops' office manager over a year ago, the appointment records, office maintenance, and over all work environment had improved. Sure, the other mechanics that worked for him did an okay job before Sarah came on board, but there was nothing like having his sister be a part of the family business.

As Josh got ready to continue his work on the car, Sarah walked back in. "I almost forgot to tell you," she began.

Josh looked at her. "You almost forgot to tell me what?" he wondered.

"I talked to Sidra the other day," she beamed.

Josh hoped his face did not reflect the flutter that he felt in his stomach just at the mention of her name. He hadn't spoken to Sidra since her birthday. In those past two weeks, he couldn't stop thinking of her. "Oh yeah?"

"Yeah," Sarah confirmed. "We talked for a while too. I hear she's doing great—"

"Did she call you?" Josh asked.

Sarah frowned at his tone. "No, I called *her*." She folded her arms. "Is something wrong? Was I not supposed to call her?"

Josh ran his hand over his face. "No Sarah, nothing is wrong," he said.

Sarah tilted her head. "I promise there was no ulterior motive to me talking to her JJ," she explained.

"You don't have to apologize," he cut in. "You didn't do anything wrong. I'm sorry for making it seem like you did."

Sarah stared at him. "I just miss her."

Josh let out a sigh. *Yeah, I miss her too.* "I know," he said, instead. "It's cool. I'm glad y'all got to talk."

"Are you going to see her when you go to homecoming?"

"I'm pretty sure," he answered. "If she still decides to show up."

"You don't think she will?" Sarah pressed.

Josh shrugged. "I don't know… She seems to be really good at staying away." He looked at his watch. "I think I should just go ahead and close up."

"Good idea," she agreed. "You going on any dates tonight?"

Josh shook his head. "No, just going to chill at home." Truth was, ever since he'd last spoken to Sidra, he hadn't been on any dates. He just couldn't bring himself to go on any.

Damn, one conversation and my head is messed up all over again. This shit has to stop.

Chapter 11

"Ma, you need to stop worrying about it," Alex reassured her mother, taking a cookie out of a jar in her parents' kitchen.

Mrs. Chisolm looked perplexed, eyeing the piece of paper in her hand. "You don't think it's weird that our electric bill has a zero balance for the month?" she asked.

Having her back to her mother successfully hid the panicked look on Alex's face.

She'd made a stop at her family's home in Philadelphia and had expected to spend a few moments with her mother, before continuing the journey to Paradise Valley, Virginia for her university's homecoming. What she didn't expect was for her mother to be frazzled over the house's utility bills, or lack thereof.

Alex fixed her face and turned to face her mother. "Ma, I'm sure it's nothing to worry about," she placated. "The meter was probably off when they came to read it." Alex didn't know much about how meter reading worked, but she hoped that would convince her mother. "They'll probably adjust it next month."

"Yeah maybe," Mrs. Chisolm resolved, putting the bill on the table.

Note to self, leave a small balance next time, Alex told herself. "Ummm, curious Ma— what made you question the balance?" she wondered. "Did Dad say he didn't pay it?"

"I *know* he didn't pay it because *I* was supposed to handle the bill payments this month," Mrs. Chisolm answered. "I felt it would be more organized for *me* to make sure they're paid going forward, instead of us taking turns." She folded her arms on the table. "Your father couldn't seem to remember when he'd made payments on the water bill, even though the balance was zero. He just said 'it's paid ain't it?'"

"Well…he has a *point*," Alex slowly drug out.

"No, he *doesn't*," Mrs. Chisolm argued. "We need to keep records of these things."

Alex ran a hand along the back of her neck. She wanted to get off this topic as soon as possible. "I have to get to the corner store to pick up more snacks for my drive. Do you need anything?" she quickly put out.

"I'm actually surprised that you're heading down there this early," Mrs. Chisolm said, ignoring Alex's question. "I thought you were leaving tomorrow."

"Yeah, well, I figured I'd use some of this banked up PTO and head down there a day early," Alex answered, scratching her head. "I want to take some time and visit my old professors, maybe go to an alumni meeting… I want to find out how I can donate to the school."

Mrs. Chisolm smiled. "That's sweet of you."

"Yeah, I like to give back," Alex said, staring at her mother with intensity. "You know…to repay for what was given to *me*."

"Yeah well, you can stop looking at me like that, 'cause you're not giving *us* any of your money," Mrs. Chisolm said, standing from the table.

Alex let out a sigh. "Ma, what do you need from the store?" she reiterated.

"Nothing love."

"Okay." Alex shrugged, quickly heading for the door.

The brisk walk out of the house was just what Alex needed at that moment. "God, will she just relax? Like Dad said, the balance is zero, so just chill," she mumbled to herself as she headed off her block. Standing at the corner, waiting for the traffic to clear so that she could cross the street, Alex glanced up at the trees. The leaves had turned. Fall was officially here, and she couldn't wait to get to Virginia. From what she could remember, it was always pretty during this time of the year.

"Come on, when did this light become so long?" she huffed, annoyed with waiting.

"Since when did you take up talking to yourself?" A male

voice asked.

Startled, Alex spun around. "Excuse me?" When she saw who it was, her eyes widened. *Well look what the breeze rolled in,* she thought.

Paul smiled at her. "How are you Alex?" he asked.

Alex composed herself. "I've been good," she replied. She was surprised that she could actually look at, let alone *talk* to, her former boyfriend. Especially after he'd cheated on her with her then best friend Victoria, during her freshman year at college. Usually she only wanted to curse him out, or punch him.

"I've heard," Paul replied. "How is New York?"

Alex frowned.

"Oh, you know this neighborhood talks," Paul added, picking up on Alex's perplexed look.

"How could I forget," she mumbled, pushing some of her hair over her shoulder. "But New York is great."

"Good, I'm glad," Paul said. "It's good to hear that you're doing great. You deserve it."

Alex nodded. "I *am* and *do* thanks." She glanced at her watch as Paul fidgeted with his hands.

"So, I'm still in the military," he continued. When Alex just stared at him, he cleared his throat. "You hadn't heard that I joined the military five years ago?"

Alex shook her head, though she did in fact know; Stacey had told her during her senior year. "The neighborhood always failed to let me know about things that *you* were doing," she replied.

Paul glanced down momentarily in shame. "Yeah," he muttered. "Anyway, it keeps me away a lot, but at least I get to see Tamara when I'm home...my daughter."

"That's good." Alex was trying to remain as polite as possible. She might not have hated Paul anymore, but she certainly did not want to waste the time that she had talking to him. She was not interested in his life, or what he was doing *with* it. That chapter in hers was closed.

"Yeah, that's the *one* good thing that Victoria does," he added. "She doesn't keep her from me, though she tried when we broke up—"

"Paul, I'm sorry but I have to get to this store and get back," Alex cut in. "I'm leaving for Virginia in like another hour or so, so I want to relax a little bit."

Paul looked disappointed, "Oh—oh sure, yeah do what you gotta do," he said. "Didn't mean to keep you. I just got excited when I saw you, that's all."

"Good luck to you, Paul," she said, before walking off. As she made her way across the street to her destination, she shook her head and chuckled to herself. "Wait till I tell the girls this mess," she mused.

Sidra slung her purse on her shoulder and shut her computer off. "And that is *it* for the next four days," she said to herself.

As she hurried out of her office door, she was stopped by her boss. "Sidra," he called.

Sidra spun around. "Hi Mr. Shaw," she greeted.

"I see that you're heading out, I won't keep you," he replied, walking over to her.

"Okay." Sidra folded her arms. "What do you need?"

"We've taken on a new case, so I wanted to prepare you," Mr. Shaw informed. "This one is a bit more involved than the Windon case—"

"I feel terrible that you lost the case," Sidra cut in, sincere. "I know that he's losing millions of dollars." That case had kept her at the office late on many days, and was the reason she had to travel to Arizona weeks ago. She felt as terrible about losing it then as she did now.

Mr. Shaw nodded his head. "You win some, you lose some," he pointed out. "Despite the loss, you did an excellent job with all of your research."

Sidra smiled slightly. "Thank you, sir."

Mr. Shaw smiled back. "So enjoy your time off, and be prepared for the influx of work when you get back."

Sidra held her smile, even though on the inside she was rolling her eyes. *You really could've saved this conversation until Monday.* "Okay." She watched her boss walk off. But as she went to continue on her way, she stopped. "Mr. Shaw?" she called.

He stopped walking and spun around. "Yes?"

"I know this isn't exactly my place to ask, but I'm curious, what happened?" Sidra wondered. "Everyone said that the case was airtight."

Mr. Shaw shoved his hands into his pants pockets. "A flaw was found in a business contract," he replied.

Sidra's eyes widened slightly.

"The wording was—the detail was so small, that we're surprised anyone was able to use it against us, but they did." He smiled slightly. "Again, you win some, you lose some."

Sidra let out a sigh as her boss walked off yet again. "I was right," she muttered to herself. "I was right."

"Mom, we're here!" Malajia yelled into the house, carrying one of the sleeping twins in her arms. Mark walked in after her, carrying the other one.

"Babe, why you gotta be all loud? You want to wake them up?" Mark chuckled, closing the door behind him.

"I don't give a damn, they're my *parents'* problem for the next few days," Malajia joked, laying her son on the couch. As she removed his sneakers, Mark sat the other one down, along with the overnight bag that he was carrying.

"Mark, did you grab that damn *ratable-taste* out of their toy box?" Malajia asked, looking up at Mark; he was removing the other child's jacket and sneakers.

Mark snickered.

"Seriously, *did* you? 'Cause my mom will ship them to us if they start screaming about that damn toy," Malajia added.

"Yeah, I got it," Mark assured. "It's in the bag."

Malajia shook her head. "I swear, I still don't know why they call it that," she muttered. "It's a damn orange lizard with yellow spots on it."

Mark laughed a bit, watching his sleeping sons. "They're so cute when they're asleep," he mused.

"Yeah, I know," Malajia smiled. She was about to say something else, when she heard a male voice from upstairs. She let out a loud huff.

"I didn't hear a knock," Mr. Simmons said, walking down the stairs.

"I used my key," Malajia replied as she and Mark stood up. "Where's Mom?"

"She's in the backyard," Mr. Simmons answered. He held his arms out. "You going to give your father a hug?"

Malajia made a face, then walked over and gave him a hug. "Hi Dad."

"Try that with less attitude," Mr. Simmons returned, glancing over at his sleeping grandchildren.

Malajia mocked him behind his back.

Mark smiled and extended his hand for his father-in-law to shake. "We appreciate you watching the boys for us this weekend."

Mr. Simmons gave Mark a halfhearted shake. "I always enjoy spending time with my grandchildren," he said. "Malajia, when I was fishing with Jordan and Shad—"

Malajia frowned. "When did you go fishing with Jordan and Shad?" she interrupted.

"The other day," Mr. Simmons answered.

Malajia slowly folded her arms as she stared at her father, agitation written all over her face.

Mark tapped her shoulder. "I'm gonna wait in the car," he said to her. He gave a slight wave to Mr. Simmons, "Good seeing you sir." His departing greeting to Mr. Simmons was ignored; Mark let out a sigh and saw himself out.

Malajia followed Mark's progress out of the house. When her husband shut the door, she snapped her head in her father's direction. "Really Dad?" she charged.

"What?" he wondered, folding his arms.

"Soooo you go fishing with *Maria's fiancé* and *Tanya's husband*, but you didn't invite *mine*?" she hissed. Mr. Simmons pinched the bridge of his nose and let out a sigh. "That's rude Dad."

"How is that rude?"

Malajia looked confused. "You invited your other sons-in-law's and you left one *out*," she barked.

"I figured he was working," her father defended.

Malajia shook her head. "You didn't even call to *ask* him," she hissed.

Mr. Simmons couldn't say anything; she was right.

Malajia held her disappointed gaze on him. "After *all* this time, you *still* treat him like shit."

"Now look—"

"What are you two arguing about *now*?" Mrs. Simmons interrupted, stepping foot into the living room.

"Your husband purposely left Mark out of his little father/son fishing trip the other day," Malajia bit out.

"If you think you're going to disrespect me, you can let that door hit you right in your ass on your way out," Mr. Simmons snarled, pointing to the door.

"Richard, come on, that's unnecessary," Mrs. Simmons cut in, shooting her husband a glance.

"It's fine Mom," Malajia said, putting her hand up. "I was leaving *anyway*." She walked over to her sleeping sons and gave them both a kiss on their cheek, before heading for the door. "I'll call you when we get to Virginia, *Mom*."

Mr. Simmons rolled his eyes as Malajia walked out the house, shutting the door behind her.

Mrs. Simmons shot her husband a stern look. "You need to stop being an ass," she sniped at him.

Mr. Simmons tossed his arms in the air as his wife stormed away from him.

Malajia got into the passenger's seat, looking over at Mark as she put her seatbelt on. He was staring down at his phone. "You okay?" she asked him.

Mark just nodded, plugging the aux cord into his phone. He sighed and pulled it out, handing it to her instead. "You can control the music if you want," he said.

Malajia looked down at her hands. They always playfully argued over whose music playlist to use during car rides together. The fact that he was giving her control without a fight, meant he was feeling more than a little down. This had been happening often after encounters between her husband and her father.

"Mark," she called.

"Yeah," he answered.

"You okay?"

Mark fiddled with his phone. "Yeah, why?"

His tone was unconvincing. Malajia rubbed his shoulder. "Don't pay my dad any mind," she said. "He's an asshole."

Mark shook his head. "It's cool Mel," he returned. "At least he's being *cordial* and not calling me stupid or idiot like he *used* to."

Malajia rubbed her forehead. She was getting pissed off, remembering her father's treatment of Mark earlier in their marriage. *He's such an asshole!*

"I guess that's all I can ask for from him," Mark added.

Malajia took her hand and ran it along Mark's freshly cut hair. "You want me to trip him for you?" she joked.

Mark let out a slight laugh.

"I could do it while he's holding one of those nasty beers he likes to drink," Malajia added.

Mark's laughter subsided. "I appreciate the thought, but naw."

"Well, let me know if you change your mind," she continued, touching his face. "You know his knees are bad, so it wouldn't take much for him to go down."

Mark laughed again, leaning over and giving her a kiss on her cheek. "Seriously I'm fine," he promised. "I have a father who I have a great relationship with, so I'm not really lookin' for another one… But I just hope that your father at *least respects* me."

Malajia let out a sigh. She hated watching Mark go out of his way to try to gain her father's acceptance, only to be rejected time and time again.

"I know," was all that she could say to him. "Let's get out of here."

Mark smiled at her before pulling out of the driveway.

"Yes, I corrected it already," Chasity said into her cell phone. She rolled her eyes as the person on the other end droned on. "Yes, I did *that too*, I'm on schedule with *all* of my projects... I'm off today, you remember that right?"

Jason walked back into the house and looked at Chasity, taking in her tense demeanor and the angered look on her face. *Must be her job,* he thought.

Chasity caught his gaze. He tapped his watch and she gave him a slight nod. "I'm sorry? ...She wants me to *what*?" On the verge of going off on her boss, Chasity took a deep, quick breath. "We'll go over it Monday... Fine... Uh huh." Chasity quickly hung up the phone and raised it to throw it across the room. "I fuckin' *hate* that bitch!" she erupted.

Jason quickly crossed the room to his wife and took the phone from her hand. "I know, but what have I told you about breaking up your stuff in anger?" he placated.

Chasity faced him and buried her face in his chest. "I know, I know," she groaned as he wrapped his arms around her.

"Forget about that place for now," he said, gently rubbing her back.

"I'll try," she muttered.

"I mean it," her husband insisted. "Let's go have some fun."

"Okay," she agreed, finally.

Jason released her and trotted over to the counter, grabbing a packed bag of snacks. "Car is all packed, Kay is all set with your mom, let's be out." Before he could get to the door, the house phone rang.

Chasity jumped. "I forgot we even *had* that damn thing," she chuckled. "Everybody is always calling our cell phones."

Jason laughed as he grabbed the cordless phone from an end table. "Hello? ...Hey Mom," he greeted. "My cell phone is in the car, Chaz and I are getting ready to leave... Wait what? ...Is—Okay, I'll be over in a few."

Chasity fixed her gaze on Jason as he ended the call. "Everything okay?"

"Yeah," he replied. "You mind if we stop at my parents' house for a few before we get on the road?"

"No, that's fine," she replied. "You *sure* everything is okay?"

"I'm sure it is," he amended. "Kyle is home and Mom

seems pissed with him about something. Which isn't surprising, he's always doing something stupid."

Chasity shook her head.

Jason stepped out of the car and stood in shock. There was broken glass all over the front step. "What the fuck?" he reacted, as Chasity stepped out the car and looked for herself.

"Ooooohhhh," Chasity gasped, placing a hand over her mouth.

Jason glanced over at a familiar motorcycle, parked on the grass. He pinched the bridge of his nose and approached the house. "Kyle," he sighed.

Chasity just shook her head as Jason opened the door for her.

"Watch the glass babe," he said to Chasity.

"I see it," she said, carefully stepped over the pile of glass shards as Jason followed her in the house.

They walked in to see Mrs. Adams in a fit of rage, hollering at Kyle. Kyle was merely sitting on the couch, trying and failing to get a word in.

"Hey, hey!" Jason hollered over the noise.

Both his mother and brother looked at him. "Jason, cuss his behind out please," Mrs. Adams huffed. She walked over and gave both Jason and Chasity a hug.

"What happened?" Jason wondered.

"This fool broke my damn storm door with his damn motorcycle!" Mrs. Adams raged.

"He hit the door with his motorcycle?" Chasity asked, confused.

"*No*," Kyle blurted out, jumping up. "I was trying to park the bike and a rock got caught under the wheel while it was moving, and the wheel kind of launched it at the door."

Jason was bewildered and it showed on his face. He stared for several seconds. "*What?*"

"I *told* him that damn bike was nothing but trouble," Mrs. Adams huffed.

"But it was a *rock* and it was an *accident*," Kyle defended.

"We just *got* that door and now we have to replace it," Mrs.

Adams ranted. "We don't have money for that right now, and God knows *you* don't since you blew all of our money that we saved for your education on bullshit, *including* that damn *bike*!"

Kyle sucked his teeth.

"Okay, everybody just calm down," Jason cut in, stepping forward. "Mom, it was an accident and as annoying as it *is*..." he shot his brother a stern glance. "And it *is*," he reiterated. "But it *was* an accident." He should have been on the road with Chasity bound for Virginia and instead, he was playing referee for another family argument with his brother.

"Kyle, you might want to get to cleaning up that glass homie," Chasity suggested.

Kyle let out a sigh. "I'm on it," he said, before giving Chasity a hug. "Good to see you sis. You get prettier every time I see you."

"Stop flirting with my wife and get to that damn broom," Jason goaded, earning a chuckle from Kyle; he gave his brother a firm hug. "Good to see you," Jason said.

"You too," Kyle replied, heading to the kitchen.

Jason looked over at his mother, who was still clearly upset. "Mom, calm down," he urged.

"That boy is *always* doing some irresponsible shit," she vented.

"It wasn't intentional."

"Jason, I *get* that but I'm not trying to hear that right now," Mrs. Adams spat.

"Maybe I should go wait in the car," Chasity cut in.

"No, it's fine sweetie," Mrs. Adams said to her, offering a smile. She let out a sigh. "It seems like money keeps flying out the door," she explained. "Your father was forced to retire ever since he had his heart attack. We're still dealing with bills from the surgery, on *top* of other checks ups... We try to do stuff with the house and things keep breaking... Then Kyle is always asking to borrow—"

"Borrow for *what*?" Jason frowned.

Mrs. Adams waved her hand. "It doesn't matter," she said.

Chasity stepped forward. "Ms. Nancy, why don't you let us pay you when you watch Kayla?"

Mrs. Adams shot her a hurt look. "Chasity, how many times have I said that you can call me Mom?" she said, offended. "'Ms. Nancy' is so…*formal*. It reminds me of when we weren't getting along, and I don't like to be reminded of that time."

Chasity shook her head. She was amazed at how far their relationship had come, considering how her now mother-in-law hadn't been fond of her when she had first started dating Jason. Though she hadn't gotten in the habit of calling her Mom, Chasity was grateful for their relationship. "Fine *Mom*, why don't you let us pay you when you watch Kayla?" she repeated.

"I told you, I will not accept money to watch my own grandchild," Mrs. Adams refused, waving her hand.

"But you're not just *watching* her, you're helping take care of her while Chasity and I work," Jason added. "If she was in a daycare—"

"Y'all better not put her in no damn daycare. All these grandparents she has," Mrs. Adams hissed.

"The point *is* Mom, if we *were* to put her in daycare, we would be *paying* them," Jason pressed. "I just feel—"

"I *said* no."

"At least let me pay for the door," Jason offered.

Mrs. Adams put her hand up. "No, *Kyle* is going to pay for the door."

"With *what, air?*" Chasity muttered, folding her arms.

Jason snickered. "Mom, *I'll* pay for the door… It's fine," Jason insisted. He glanced at Chasity. "You okay with that?"

"Of course," Chasity assured.

Jason nodded, then looked back to his mother. "Kyle will just pay me back. Don't worry."

Mrs. Adams let out a sigh. "Okay… You know we appreciate you."

"Don't worry about it." Jason looked around. "Where's Dad? I would think that he would've had Kyle gripped up by his neck."

"Yeah, he *would've*, but he's at a doctor's appointment."

"Is everything okay?" Jason asked.

"He was having some chest pains—"

"Wait what? *When?*" Jason cut in.

"Last week," Mrs. Adams answered. "Don't worry. I took him to the emergency room and everything is okay, turns out it was heartburn...but he's just there for a follow up."

"Mom, you have to *tell* me about stuff like that."

"It was no need worrying you," Mrs. Adams returned. "I just said that he's okay."

Jason looked perplexed. "You call me about a *door*, but you can't tell me that Dad was in the *emergency room*?" he fumed.

"Jase," Chasity called. He looked at her and she shook her head no. She didn't want him to end up arguing with his mother too.

Jason calmed down. "You said it was nothing to worry about, so I'll take your word for it," he said to his mother. "I'm going to see what's taking Kyle so damn long with that broom."

Chasity followed his progress out of the living room.

"Chasity, tell your mother I feel some kind of way that she hasn't returned my phone call this week," Mrs. Adams said to her.

"Don't take it personal," Chasity replied. "She's not arguing with her man this week and she don't know how to act."

Mrs. Adams chuckled.

Chapter 12

Alex opened her hotel room door and walked in, dragging her suitcase behind her. She left it standing by the bed, flopping down on the king-sized mattress.

"This is nice," she mused. It had been a long day. What was supposed to be a four-hour drive, had turned into almost six. Between the route that she'd taken, the traffic jams, and having to make multiple gas stops due to her rental car being a gas guzzler, Alex had nearly reached her breaking point. It wasn't until she saw the sign "Welcome to Paradise Valley" that she was able to calm down.

After a few moments, she heard a tap on her door. Excited, she jumped up and darted for it. Snatching the door open, she let out a happy squeal. "Hi Em," she beamed, embracing her. "You got here quick."

Emily walked into the room. "As soon as I got your call saying that you were in town, I rushed over," she explained, sitting on the bed. "That, and I live like ten minutes from here."

Alex sat down next to her. "Have you heard from the others?"

Emily shook her head. "Not yet. I think you're the first one to arrive."

"Well, you want to take me to *your* place?" Alex smiled. "I can help with some of the wedding projects."

"*Jazmine* is at my place," Emily sulked.

Alex chuckled. "Em, I'm not Chasity or Malajia, I can be cordial to your sister."

"I don't care about that. *I* don't even want to be cordial to her." Emily returned. "No, I meant that I don't want to bring you around that negative energy. You shouldn't have to deal with that."

"Neither should *you*," Alex pointed out.

Emily let out a sigh. "You sound like Will." She shook her head. "You know what, let's not talk about weddings *or* idiot family members."

Alex nodded.

"I just want to have a good time with you guys," Emily added.

"I agree," Alex replied, reaching for the room phone. "Why don't we do some damage to room service before the others get here?"

Emily rubbed her hands together. "Yes, I'm starving."

Two hours later, Emily and Alex sat on the bed, eating their order of cheeseburgers and fries, catching up in the process.

"I don't know what it is about these room service burgers, but I swear they taste better than any burger that I've had," Emily commented, wiping the ketchup from her mouth with one hand, while holding the rest of her sandwich in the other.

"As much money as this cost, it *better* be the best burger," Alex jeered, taking a bite of a few fries.

Emily giggled. Hearing a knock at the door, she glanced at it, smiling. "Wonder which one it is?"

"I texted them all my room number when I got here, so who knows," Alex replied, standing from her bed. She walked over to the door and peered through the peephole. She squealed with excitement as she opened the door. "Sidra!"

A smiling Sidra threw her arms around Alex. Emily jumped up from the bed as Alex and Sidra embraced for what seemed like forever. Parting from Alex, Sidra hugged Emily just as long. "I swear I'm about to cry," Sidra gushed, parting from Emily. "It's been so long."

"I know, haven't seen you face to face since Malajia's babies were born," Alex recalled, sitting back on her bed.

Sidra ran her hand over her hair. "I know," she sighed. She looked at Emily. "Em, do you need—"

Emily put her hand up. "No, no wedding stuff," she cut in.

Alex chuckled. "Yeah, she got on me about that too."

Sidra nodded, sitting on the bed beside them. "Okay," she said. "I couldn't get out of that airport fast enough."

"Rough flight?" Alex wondered.

"Not so much the flight. It was the damn crowds in the airport," Sidra grunted. "You know people irritate me when they move too damn slow." She adjusted a bracelet on her wrist. "Anyway, as soon as I checked in to my room, I washed that airport filth off me and made my way here."

"What floor are you on?" Alex asked.

"Third," Sidra replied, adjusting the earring in her ear. "It's cool that we're all staying here." She let out a happy sigh. "I texted the other two, are they here?"

Before anybody could answer, several loud knocks in a rhythmic beat sounded on the door.

"I already know who *that* is," Alex laughed.

Sidra jumped up from the bed and sprinted for the door. Pulling it open, she let out a giggle. "I knew it was your extra behind," she mused. Malajia danced in front of her with Chasity standing next to her, shaking her head.

Sidra hugged Malajia, then reached her arm out to bring Chasity in too, but Chasity moved around her.

"Nah, I don't hug strangers," Chasity joked, moving into the room.

Malajia pulled away from Sidra. "Oh yeah," she chimed in, waving her hand in Sidra's face. "She done got some sand under her feet and forgot all about us."

"Oh come on!" Sidra exclaimed, holding her arms out. She walked over to Chasity. "You better *give* me a damn hug girl."

Chasity laughed. "Hi Sidra," she said, hugging her.

Sidra parted and wiped her eye. "Now I really *am* crying," she pouted. "We're all together again."

Malajia rolled her eyes. "Here she go with that fussy bus shit," she griped.

Sidra flagged her with her hand. She didn't care what Malajia had to say, she was excited to be back in the presence of her girls again.

"When did you two get in?" Alex wondered as Malajia reached for her plate, taking the rest of her burger. "Hey!" Alex yelped, trying to grab for it.

Malajia moved it out of Alex's reach. "You already knew I was coming, you should've ordered more food," she protested, taking a bite. "This is mine now."

Alex shook her head. "Still greedy *and* skinny after all these years," she muttered.

"Girl this skinny ain't nothing but stress. Them bad-ass kids run me ragged," Malajia joked. She ate another piece of the burger. "I got here like three hours ago."

Alex's mouth fell open. "I texted you."

"I *saw* it," Malajia countered.

"Why didn't you *answer*?" Alex shot back, folding her arms Malajia shot her a knowing look. Alex laughed. "You freak."

"Oh what, you don't expect us to take advantage of being kid free? Girl, you lucky my ass is in here *now*," Malajia replied, unfazed. She pointed at Chasity, who was spinning herself around in a swivel chair. "*She* got here like fifteen minutes after *I* did."

Chasity stopped spinning and regarded Malajia with a frown. "You dumb raggedy bitch," she barked. "Always gotta drag me into your shit."

Emily nearly choked on her soda from laughter.

"Ask her why *she* ain't answer your texts," Malajia pressed, unfazed by Chasity's name calling.

"I was *asleep*," Chasity replied, before Alex could get her question out.

"You were *not asleep* all that damn time, you liar. You were getting it in *too*, I *heard* y'all," Malajia argued, grabbing fries from Alex's plate. "My room is right next to yours."

Chasity flipped Malajia off. "It is *not*, you lying snitch."

"Maybe not, but you didn't deny it, *did* you?" Malajia countered, amusement in her voice.

Unable to argue any further, Chasity just spun around in her seat. Malajia laughed at her.

"*How* old are you two again?" Alex cut in, putting her hands up.

"As old as these fries' taste," Malajia muttered.

"You know what, I actually missed this," Sidra mused, sitting down.

"Are Josh and David here?" Emily asked, wiping her hands on a napkin.

"*Josh* is," Chasity informed.

Sidra felt her heart skip a beat at the mere mention of Josh's name, but she didn't let it show. At least, she hoped it didn't.

"Yeah, he was checking in when we were on our way out," Malajia chimed in. Then her eyes widened when Chasity shot her a look.

"Wait, on your way out *where*?!" Alex exclaimed, putting her hands on her hips. "I thought y'all were—"

Malajia pointed at Chasity. "Chasity's hungry ass wanted tacos, so she made me go with her to a taco place a block from here," she told.

Chasity stomped her foot on the floor. "I swear to fuckin'— *You* wanted those nasty ass tacos, not *me*," she fumed.

Malajia thought for a moment. "Oh yeah."

"So, you two knew that Emily and I were here, and instead of coming to hang with *us*, you two were gallivanting at some taco place," Alex fussed, folding her arms. "You could've *invited* us at least."

"Shut the fuck up, Alex," Chasity scoffed, over the nonsense.

"Yeah, those tacos were nasty anyway," Malajia added.

"*You* shut the fuck up *too*," Chasity hurled at Malajia, directing a glare at her.

Malajia's mouth dropped open. "Childish," she muttered. "You shouldn't cuss like that you know. You're a mother." She laughed again when Chasity made a face at her.

Sidra took the end of a rattail comb and adjusted the middle part in her hair. Satisfied, she then smoothed her straight hair with her hands. Setting the comb down on the bathroom sink, she donned her sapphire stud earrings with care. Giving herself a once over in the mirror, she smiled. "Ready...*finally*," she spoke to herself.

After spending a few hours catching up with the girls, everyone had retreated to their rooms to get ready for a planned group dinner at the hotel restaurant.

Her phone beeped; she walked out of the bathroom and over to her bed. Grabbing the phone, she read a text message. *"Hurry your ass up."* Sidra shook her head in amusement. "Can never just send a normal text, huh Mel?" she mused to herself.

Grabbing her purse, Sidra tossed the phone into it, checked to make sure she had her room keycard, then left the room. Heading for the elevator, she passed by another room just as the door was opening. Hearing a familiar voice, Sidra stopped and turned around. She froze in place at the sight of Josh, walking out of the room with his cell phone to his ear.

Spotting her, Josh ended his phone call. He smiled slightly. "Hi."

Sidra didn't mean to, but she stared at him. Sure, she'd seen Josh through occasional video calls, but standing in his presence again, she found herself in awe of how handsome he was. "Hi," she returned after a few awkward seconds.

Josh closed his room door. He stood still before her for a few moments, before extending his arms for a hug.

Hesitating initially, Sidra embraced him. "So, you're staying on this floor?" Sidra asked as they parted. She shook her head when Josh looked at the room door that he had just walked out of. "Stupid question," she chuckled.

He chuckled himself. "It's okay, but yes," he confirmed.

"Me too," Sidra replied. She pointed down the hall. "I'm a few doors down."

Josh nodded. "Cool."

Sidra rubbed her hand down her other arm as she stood there. It was awkward, and she hated it. They'd been friends since they were practically in diapers; now in their late twenties, they were standing before one another acting like they barely knew each other.

"I take it you're on your way to dinner with the others," Josh stammered after a moment. He hadn't been in her presence in so long. Now that he was, feelings that he thought were behind him were beginning to surface. *Come on man, don't start this again*, he thought.

"Yeah," she replied, then chuckled. "I just got a 'hurry your ass up', text from Malajia."

"That sounds almost like my 'stop brushing your goddamn beard and come the fuck on,' phone call that I got from Mark as I was walking out," he said.

Sidra laughed. "God, those two. Can you believe they're

married, with *children*?'"

"Sometimes, I *can't*," Josh said, amusement in his voice. "But…they're perfect for one another… Must be nice."

Sidra glanced down at her shoes. "Yeah, yeah it must *be*."

"So," Josh took a deep breath. "Shall we get going?"

"Yeah," Sidra agreed, heading for the elevator.

"Let me get a sip of that," Mark said to Malajia, reaching for her drink.

Malajia picked her margarita up and moved it out of his reach. "Boy, you'll be sleeping in the lobby tonight," she hissed, taking a sip.

Mark stared at her. "A damn shame," he ground out. Malajia just shrugged.

"You two still at it, huh?" Alex chuckled.

Most of the gang had made it down to the hotel restaurant on time. However, with other alums in town and staying at the same hotel, the tables were packed, making the wait long. So they had decided to sit at the bar.

"Always," Malajia confirmed, taking another sip of her margarita.

Mark shook his head as he sipped his own drink.

"Jason and Chasity, how does it feel to be living around the corner from those two?" Alex asked, amusement in her voice.

"We hate it," Chasity spat out; Jason almost choked on his drink, trying to hold in a laugh.

Malajia cut her eye at Chasity. "They always frontin'," she ground out.

"Alex, you making a lot of smart ass comments about us," Mark pointed out.

Malajia put her hand on Mark's shoulder. "Babe, she just mad 'cause she still haven't lost that freshman thirty-five yet," she goaded, earning laughter from the group.

Mark erupted with laughter. "Damn!"

Alex's mouth fell open. "Really Malajia?!" she shrieked. "That was rude."

Malajia shrugged, taking another sip of her drink.

Alex looked at Chasity, who was cracking up laughing. "It

wasn't that damn funny, Chasity," she hissed.

Chasity frowned up at Alex, laughter subsiding. "And just like *always*, you catch attitude with *me,* when *Malajia* played the shit out of you," she threw back.

Alex rolled her eyes. "*You* probably said that mess to her behind my back at some point," she grunted. "We *both* know she's not that clever."

Chasity sucked her teeth.

"Hey fuck off," Malajia barked. "You mad 'cause you gained the freshman thirty-five."

"You *said* that already," Alex sneered. "And it's the freshman *fifteen.*"

"Not in *your* case," Chasity sneered.

Malajia busted out laughing, as Alex glared daggers at Chasity.

"See how I just said that to your face?" Chasity goaded, grabbing a chip from her plate. Alex made a face at her.

"Whatever, I look *damn* good," Alex boasted, fluffing her hair. "Big ass and *all.*"

"We know, Alex," Chasity pacified.

"Right, these are just *jokes*," Malajia chortled. "You fine as shit and everyone sees it... Still so sensitive."

Alex waved a dismissive hand at them both.

"Hey guys," Sidra greeted, walking up to the bar with Josh in tow.

"'Bout *time*," Mark commented as Sidra gave him a hug.

"Hush," Sidra chided, giving hugs to the others. She sat down in an empty seat next to Chasity. "You know how long it takes me to get ready."

Mark watched as Josh walked over to an empty seat next to Alex and sat down. "Yo Josh, why you ain't sit over there next to Sidra?" he blurted out.

Sidra looked down at the counter as Josh cut his eye at Mark. She'd noticed that as well. "Mark, don't start. That seat is closer to the bathroom," she reasoned.

Her explanation was met with confusion.

"*Huh* Sidra?" Chasity questioned.

"Nothing," she huffed, snatching Chasity's cherry vodka and soda from her hand. "Gimme."

She then took a big gulp.

Chasity watched as Sidra made a face, trying to swallow the mouth full of strong liquid, little by little. Annoyed that Sidra had swiped her drink in the first place, Chasity slapped Sidra on the back, hard. "You need help with that?" she mocked.

The slap startled Sidra, causing her to swallow all the liquid at once. She put her hand on her chest and began coughing hysterically. Satisfied, Chasity grabbed her drink back, smiling slyly.

"You a'ight down there?" Mark wondered, peering down the bar.

"Sure," Sidra lied, between coughs.

"What the hell just happened?" Malajia laughed.

"*Chasity* is what happened," Sidra grunted, coughs subsiding.

"Keep your hands off my shit," Chasity threw back.

Emily folded her arms on the countertop. "Has anybody heard from David?" she wondered.

"I spoke to him earlier, he said that he was trying to make it," Jason answered, signaling for the bartender.

"So, he's not sure if he's coming?" Alex asked, confused.

"That's...that's what *try* means," Chasity jeered, before Jason had a chance to respond.

Alex narrowed her eyes as her friends snickered. "Let's just order," she grunted.

"Em, is Will gonna join us for any of the homecoming festivities?" Mark asked, taking a bite of one of his loaded quesadillas. "He got his degree from here too, right?"

Emily took a sip of her punch. "He did, but he's not going to attend anything," she answered. "He decided to pick up some extra hours this weekend."

Mark nodded. "I can respect that," he praised.

"I've been wondering Em, how does Will feel about the guys being groomsmen?" Alex brought up, grabbing her burger from her plate. "I know that normally the groom chooses people from *his* side."

Emily dipped a tortilla chip in spinach dip. "He knows how I feel about *all* of my brothers," she clarified. "He's perfectly fine with it. He only had two people to put on his side anyway. He doesn't have a big family."

"That's good," Alex smiled.

"Yo, *speaking* of sides, who these two new bitches on the girls' side Em?" Malajia sneered, shaking her hand in Emily's direction.

Sidra put her head in her hands. "Malajia, really?" she chided.

"They're my cousins," Emily chuckled.

"You're disrespectful, you know that?" Sidra scolded, pointing at Malajia.

"Yup. I don't like new people," Malajia defended. She pointed to Chasity, who was shaking her head emphatically. "*She* don't *either*, look at her face."

"I don't have to talk to them, do I?" Chasity asked, sipping her drink.

Emily nodded. "Yes, yes you do," she answered, amusement in her voice.

"Ugh," Chasity scoffed, rolling her eyes.

"I'm sorry, but I've gotten pretty close with them over the past few years," Emily explained. "I'd feel bad if they weren't a part of my wedding."

Sidra put her hand up. "Em, it's your wedding, you don't have to explain anything to us," she said.

"*Sure* she does," Malajia contradicted.

"No, she *doesn't*," Sidra insisted, fixing an angry gaze upon Malajia. She turned her attention back to Emily. "Sweetie, don't worry about anything. We will openly communicate with your other bridesmaids on everything," she promised, then paused. "Except the shower and the bachelorette party."

Alex snickered. "I knew it," she chortled.

Sidra laughed. "Sorry Em, but *we've* got this," she said, gesturing to the other girls.

Emily put her hands up. "Fine by me."

"Ooh! Can we take Will to a strip club?" Mark blurted out, grabbing some fries from Malajia's plate.

Jason and Josh eyed Mark with wide eyes when the girls

College Life 501; Post-Grad Management

fell silent.

"What?" Mark asked, looking around.

"You bring that up in front of the girls?" Josh pointed out.

Mark sucked his teeth. "Josh, who you answering to, dawg?" he threw back. "I'm sure those random chicks you eatin' greasy chicken wings at the car shop with don't care *what* you do. So why you bitchin'?"

Josh flagged Mark with his hand. "Whatever," he grunted.

Sidra hoped nobody noticed her eyeroll; she didn't care to know of Josh's little dates. She just quietly sipped her seltzer water with lemon.

"Why are *you* so damn hype?" Malajia sneered, glaring at Mark.

"Look, Will cool but he kinda corny—no offense Em," Mark defended. Emily just shook her head in amusement. "So, I know that his *best man* is corny, resulting in a corny ass bachelor party. I'm just tryna look out for the cookout."

"No, you're just tryna see *ass*," Malajia hissed, tossing a balled-up napkin at him.

"Look, I don't mind, just make sure he has a good time," Emily shrugged.

"Yes!" Mark rejoiced.

"*You* ain't *going*," Malajia barked, smacking him on the back of the head.

Mark grabbed the back of his head as he tried not to laugh. His friends made no attempt to hide their laughter.

"You yesin' hard as shit for no reason," she added, grabbing a quesadilla from Mark's plate.

Jason looked over at Chasity, who was staring back at him. He smiled a hopeful smile at her; she narrowed her eyes. "Now babe, you know there's nobody I'd rather have strip for me other than *you*—"

"Save it boy, you can go," Chasity bristled, rolling her eyes at him.

Jason laughed, giving her a kiss on the cheek.

"Yeah, yeah, stop pushin' up on me," Chasity jeered in return.

Alex was shocked and it showed on her face. "Jason, not to cause trouble but—"

"Then *don't*," Jason muttered through clenched teeth.

Alex put her hand up, "Chasity, *you're* okay with Jason going to a *strip club*?" she pressed, ignoring Jason.

Chasity looked at Alex, then Sidra, who was staring at her with wide eyes. "Why is that so shocking?"

"Because it's *you*," Sidra bluntly stated.

"*Exactly*," Alex followed up.

Chasity shrugged. "I'm secure in my shit," she explained. "And I trust *him*, so..." she gestured to Jason, who smiled back at her. "*And* he knows that I have *no* problem dragging a bitch ''

Jason put his hand over his face and shook his head.

"*There* she is," Alex joked, laughing.

Mark looked at Malajia. "Come on babe, everybody *else* is going?" he pouted.

"*So*?" Malajia maintained; Mark let out a loud huff. Malajia sucked her teeth. "*Fine* Mark, you can go," she relented. Mark started dancing in his seat. "Oh but best believe when it comes to the bachelorette party for *Em*, we're gonna make sure we have *plenty* of dicks swingin'."

Emily spat out her drink.

"Yeeessss!" Alex rejoiced, reaching over and giving Malajia a high five. "One in every shade of brown, honey."

"Wait a minute," Jason protested when Chasity started celebrating with the girls. "You cheerin' kinda hard over there Chasity."

"Were *you* not just cheerin' a minute ago?" Chasity reminded, picking up her drink. "Oh, it's a problem for you?" she mocked when he frowned at her.

"Yeah well...they better not touch you," Jason mumbled, reaching for his glass.

"Nah, Malajia, I'm not having it," Mark protested. "You be takin' shit overboard."

"Too late, it's already in the works," Malajia threw back.

Emily shook her hand in Malajia's direction. "Um...I'm not really into strippers—"

"This right here ain't about you baby girl, sorry," Malajia cut in, earning a snicker from Alex.

Chapter 13

Sidra rolled over in her bed and stretched as her alarm sounded. She grabbed her cell phone and turned the annoying alarm off. *Why am I up so early on my day off?* she thought, eyeing the 7am time. After hanging out until the wee hours of the morning with the group the night before, Sidra had returned to her hotel room and crashed. As tired as she still was, she couldn't bring herself to fall back to sleep.

Sitting up in bed, she started scrolling through her messages. After a few moments of reading boring work emails, she decided to make a phone call.

She played with the fabric of the comforter while waiting for the line to pick up.

"Hey," Josh answered.

"Hey," Sidra returned.

"You're up early," he chuckled.

"Yeah," she replied, clutching the fabric in a firm grip. "Um… Do you want to maybe grab some breakfast from downstairs? They have free breakfast until like ten or eleven."

"Well, I'm about to go jogging right now—"

"That sounds cool," she cut in, trying not to sound too disappointed.

"You…you wanna go jogging *with* me?" Josh asked.

Sidra's eyes widened. She hated jogging; she hated working out *period* unless it was by way of DVD in her apartment. Luckily for her, she never really had to. But she wanted to get some alone time in with Josh. "Sure," she hesitantly agreed.

There was a pause on the line. "*Really?*"

"Yes," Sidra chuckled. "Let me get myself together and I'll meet you at your room. Say in about twenty?"

"Sounds good," he agreed. "We can grab something to eat

afterwards."

"Cool." Sidra hung up the phone and put her face in her hands. "What the hell did I just agree to?"

"I miss you," Kayla said through Chasity's phone screen.

"Awww," Chasity pouted. "We miss you too."

"We'll be home in a few days," Jason replied, touching the phone screen. Chasity and Jason were lounging in bed eating breakfast, and had called Trisha to talk to their daughter.

"Are you being a good girl for Mom-Mom?" Chasity asked.

"Yes," Kayla smiled. "Mom-Mom said that she was gonna get me a kitty."

Jason buried his face on Chasity's shoulder, as Chasity fought to maintain her smile. "Oh? Okay," Chasity replied. "Do me a favor, put *Mom-Mom* on the phone."

"Okay," Kayla granted.

"Love you," Jason said to her.

"Love you too," Kayla replied, dropping the phone and running off.

Jason reached for a piece of turkey bacon on the tray in front of him. "Wouldn't it be funny if we went to pick her up and she had a real cat?" he laughed.

"No. No, it would *not* be funny," Chasity bristled. When Trisha picked up the phone, Chasity stared at her image. "Is Kayla near you?"

"Not at the moment," Trisha answered.

"Mom, don't you get her no goddamn cat," Chasity snapped. Trisha busted out laughing. "I'm not playing with you."

"You are not the boss of me, I can do what I want," Trisha threw back. "My baby wants a kitty—"

"She's *my* baby and she's not *getting* no damn cat," Chasity argued.

Trisha flagged Chasity with her hand. "Hi Jason," she deflected.

"Hi Mom," Jason greeted, amused.

"Please tell your wife to calm her ass down," Trisha said.

Jason looked to Chasity. "Calm—"

"I will choke you in your sleep," Chasity threatened.

Jason laughed once again. "We'll see you Sunday," he said to Trisha.

Trisha waved to them, ending the call.

"If Mom buys her a cat, I'm buying a bird and I'm releasing it in her fuckin' house," Chasity hissed, taking a sip of her orange juice.

"Why?" Jason chuckled, looking at her.

"She's scared of birds," Chasity shrugged.

Jason shook his head. Hearing his phone make a noise, he rolled over and grabbed it from the nightstand. Reading an email from his job, he sucked his teeth. "What the hell?"

"What's wrong?" Chasity wondered.

"It looks like I have to go back to Phoenix next week," he sighed.

"For *what*?"

Jason shook his head, annoyed as he continued to read the email. "Some bullshit about wanting me to monitor the team while they work on their first software project out of the new office... I leave on fuckin' Tuesday."

Chasity rolled her eyes but knew that she couldn't get upset, because *he* was already upset. She rubbed his shoulder. "Okay," she placated.

"Shit," he huffed. The last thing he wanted to do was leave his family for another week. Especially for a job that he was sure was about to replace him.

"It's okay, you gotta do what you gotta do," she said to him. "God only knows what's waiting for me in *my* work emails."

Jason set his phone back on the nightstand. "Don't check them, Chasity," he stressed.

"I'm not," she promised. Hearing a knock on the door, she got out of bed, and walked over and checked the peephole. "What the hell do *you* want?" Chasity barked through the door, eyeing the person standing in the hallway.

"Come on Chasity, please open the door," Sidra begged.

Chasity opened the door and stared at Sidra, who was staring back. "What girl?"

Sidra put her hands up. "Okay this is a weird question but…do you have any workout clothes?" she asked.

Chasity frowned in confusion. "What?" she questioned.

Sidra pushed some behind her ears. "I'm going jogging with Josh and I have nothing workout related in my wardrobe."

Chasity held the same confused look. "*What*?"

"No, Alex, nobody is going to that damn alumni brunch," Malajia griped, running her hand through her disheveled hair.

"Come on, the school is putting forth some effort to make alumni feel welcome, I think we should go," Alex pressed, adjusting a button on her pajama shirt.

Malajia rolled her eyes. After ignoring Alex's phone calls a half hour ago, Malajia was shocked when Alex had showed up at her room door. "It's too early for your shit," Malajia huffed, pointing to the door. "Get out."

"No," Alex refused, folding her arms. "It's too early, yet *you're* up."

"We have twin three-year-old, badass boys, we're *used* to being up," Malajia grunted.

Alex giggled, then tugged on the belt to Malajia's robe. "Come on, it'll be fun," she said.

Malajia smacked Alex's hand away. "Stop pulling that before you see some shit you don't wanna see," she bit out. "I ain't got a damn piece of clothing on under here."

Alex sucked her teeth as she hopped up from the bed. "Oh come on, I didn't need to know all that!"

Malajia shrugged nonchalantly. "Go bother somebody else and you wouldn't have to hear about my nakedness."

Alex ran a hand over her hair. "Sidra is out jogging—"

"Wait Sidra is out doing *what*?" Malajia questioned, putting her hand up.

"Jogging," Alex repeated.

Malajia busted out laughing. "Where is her bougie ass jogging to?" she wondered.

"I have no idea, but she went with Josh."

Malajia raised an eyebrow. "Uh *huh*," she muttered. *Damn girl is probably miserable right now trying to be up under Josh,* she thought amused.

"Anyway," Alex began again. Malajia let out a groan and smashed her head into her pillow. "I was thinking after the brunch, we could go to the—"

"Alex, I said we not going to that shit!" Malajia fussed, slamming her hand on the bed repeatedly.

Alex put her hands on her hips and regarded Malajia with a frown.

"Babe," Mark called from the bathroom.

"Yeah?" Malajia answered, looking at the closed door.

"Is she still here?" Mark asked.

Alex sucked her teeth.

"*Yes*, her ass is still here, getting on my fuckin' nerves," Malajia griped.

"A'ight, let me know when she leave and shit," Mark replied. He'd ran into the bathroom as soon as Malajia had opened the door to let Alex in.

Malajia snickered at the annoyed look on Alex's face. Hearing her phone ring, Malajia grabbed it, looked at the caller ID, and answered. "Yeah Mom, everything okay? ...You *what?*" Malajia frowned. "Evelyn, you better *find* that damn ratable-taste!" she barked.

"What happened to the ratable-taste?!" Mark yelled from the bathroom.

Malajia looked at the bathroom door. "Mom talking about she lost it."

"Damn it!" Mark belted out.

"It's okay babe, they're staying with her until she finds it," Malajia said to Mark. Malajia went back to talking on the phone. "Mom—Why are you hollering at me? ...I *told* you they would start screaming if they don't have that stupid lizard... Well, I won't be home until Sunday... Mom, you had seven kids, stop acting like a punk." Malajia put her hand over her mouth to cover her laughter, as her mother's loud voice came through the phone. "I love you Mommy, here's Alex."

"Huh?" Alex looked at her wide-eyed as Malajia quickly tossed her the phone.

Malajia then darted for the bathroom and opened the door.

"Yo!" Mark barked.

"Shut up, you act like I didn't just see it like forty-five minutes ago," Malajia barked back, walking in and closing the door behind her.

Alex was baffled as she stood there, holding the phone. She slowly put it to her ear. "Hi Mrs. Simmons," she sputtered into the line.

Josh chuckled at Sidra as he sat across from her at an outdoor breakfast bistro. After a five-mile jog, they had finally stopped for something to eat. The fall breeze felt good after the sweaty run.

"What's so funny?" Sidra hissed, her head resting on the table.

"You look tired," he observed amused.

She lifted her head up. "I just ran five freakin' miles!" she exclaimed. "*Yes* I'm tired, and *hot* and I will probably feel every *part* of that run tomorrow."

Josh reached for his orange juice while she continued to vent.

"I haven't worked out in like a *year*… I hate running," she fussed.

"Then why did you *come*?" Josh wondered.

"Because I'm an idiot," Sidra muttered, reaching for her breakfast sandwich. "I didn't even bring any workout clothes. I borrowed these from *Chasity*."

Josh shook his head in amusement.

"But to honestly answer your question, I guess I just wanted to spend some time with you," she admitted. "It's been a while."

Josh smiled. "Well…your complaining aside, it was fun running with you."

Sidra returned his smile with one of her own. "I'm not running back," she put out. Josh busted out laughing. "I'll pay for a cab."

Josh put his hand up in surrender. "Okay," he agreed, voice filled with amusement.

For the next forty-five minutes, Sidra and Josh were both, unbeknownst to one another, the happiest that they've been in a while. Just sitting in front of each other talking was one of the many things they had missed.

"I can't believe James is married with a kid now," Josh began, learning of the news.

Sidra sipped her orange juice. "I know," she agreed, chuckling. "He was a nervous mess, both when he was about to get married and when his wife was in labor."

Josh folded his arms on the table. "Not to dampen the mood or anything but…how do you feel seeing your ex move on like that?"

Sidra set her cup down. "The mood isn't dampened," she assured him. She then shrugged. "In all honesty…it's no big deal for me."

"Really?" he questioned.

Sidra nodded. "James and I broke up *years* ago, and when it happened—even though *he* was the one who ended the relationship…we *both* knew that we just weren't meant for each other."

Josh stared at her while she spoke.

"Truth is…I'm really happy for him," she said.

Josh took another sip of his drink. "So, you consider him just a friend?"

Sidra nodded. "Strictly," she assured. "It's been that way ever since I moved to California. Nothing more."

Josh nodded after a moment. "I think that's cool," he said.

"Yeah?" Sidra asked, curious. Considering how Josh had felt about James while she was dating him, she was a little shocked.

"Yeah," he confirmed. He noticed the questionable look on her face, and chuckled a bit. "Why are you looking at me like you want to call me a liar?"

Sidra glanced down at the table. "I guess I'm just a bit surprised, considering…"

"Sidra, come on, give me a little credit on my maturity over the past five years," Josh said.

"You're right," she agreed. "I'm sorry."

"It's okay," he replied, grabbing his sandwich.

Sidra watched him eat for a bit. She was wondering if she should even ask the question that was on her mind. "So…are you friends with any of *your* exes?"

Josh thought for a moment. "Can't say that I am really."

"Really? Not one?"

Josh shrugged. "Honestly Sidra, I haven't had too many girlfriends," he admitted. "I mean, yeah I've dated quite a few women, but as far as *relationships* go, there hasn't been many. And my last serious relationship didn't end too well, so we're not friends."

Sidra folded her arms on the table. "How long ago was *that*?"

"Senior year."

Sidra's eyes widened. "Wait...you're telling me that your last *serious relationship* was with *December*?"

Josh nodded.

"So...you haven't...*been* with anyone since her?"

"I didn't say that," Josh answered.

Sidra bit her bottom lip; she didn't want to think about Josh's casual sexual conquests. "Oh okay." She looked around at the outside scenery, hoping to find something to change the subject to. Finding nothing, she looked back at him. "You wanna jog back?"

Josh looked confused. "*Now*?"

Sidra nodded.

"But I thought—"

"I got my second wind," she lied, standing up. Josh shrugged and followed suit. Throwing their trash in a nearby trash can, Josh started the jog with Sidra following.

Mark picked up his burger and paused. "I can't believe I'm about to eat a 'caf' burger," he mused, then took a big bite.

"And it still tastes the same," Chasity chuckled, reaching for a curly fry.

Mark nodded in agreement as he chewed.

Alex smiled as she reached for her cup of soda. She wasn't successful in getting the group to go to the alumni brunch, but she succeeded in getting them to have lunch in the cafeteria. They'd even managed to sit in their old booth. It was truly nostalgic for her.

"So, guess what I have," Alex beamed, pulling a flyer from her jeans pocket.

Malajia looked over at her. "Don't tell me that's one of those homecoming event flyers," she said.

"Yep, and like old times, I'm about to read it to y'all," Alex replied, excited. She cleared her throat as groans sounded around the booth. "Like always, I don't care about the complaints." She looked at the flyer. "So, today they had the alumni brunch—" she eyed the group sternly. "Which we *missed* by the way."

"Whatchu' mad for? They're serving the leftover food now for lunch," Malajia joked, earning snickers from the table.

Alex rolled her eyes. "Anyway… Ooh, they have a bowling tournament—"

Mark sent a text message, then looked up at Alex. "Alex, that tournament is about to be ass," he jeered. "The Art department probably made the pins out of foil and shit."

Malajia snickered.

"So, we're crossing that off too, huh?" Alex sulked.

"We can go bowling off campus before we all head back on Sunday," Josh suggested. "It's been a long time since we all went together… Maybe we can go tomorrow night, then go out to dinner afterwards."

"Josh getting sentimental and shit," Mark teased.

"Well, *I* think it's a great idea Josh," Sidra praised, giving Josh's shoulder a rub. Josh smiled at her.

"I bet you *do*," Chasity muttered, earning a kick to her ankle from Malajia under the table.
"Ouch!" Angry, Chasity kicked her back.

"Damn it Chasity, that was right on my fuckin' shin!" Malajia shrieked, reaching down and grabbing her leg.

"What is going *on*?" Alex wondered confused.

"Malajia is about to get fucked up, is what's going on," Chasity barked, fixing an angry gaze on Malajia, who just made a face back as she continued to rub her leg.

Mark and Jason just shook their heads; they were used to this behavior from their wives. "Anyway, I think that'll be cool," Jason agreed.

"Well, it's not a *campus* activity, but I'm for it," Alex

shrugged, looking back at the flyer. "They have a game—"

"Next," Malajia cut in, unimpressed.

"Girl, shut up and listen," Alex threw back, frowning. "They have something called 'alumni find the flag' in the field behind the Agriculture building later today."

Mark's ears perked. "Word?"

Malajia put her hand over her face. "God," she griped. If Mark was interested, she knew that she would be dragged into it.

Mark sat up in his seat. "Oh, we on that," he boasted.

Sidra eyed him in confusion. "You don't even know what the game *consists* of," she pointed out, picking up her cup of juice.

"I know that it'll consist of Team *Ninja Strike* being back in affect," Mark threw back, grabbing a few fries from his plate.

"Dude, can we come up with another name?" Josh pleaded.

"No, and don't ask me another stupid ass question," Mark threw back. Josh shook his head in agitation.

Alex was brimming with excitement. Finally, a campus event that her friends would do. "Great! I'll sign us up." She kept reading. "They're having a 'welcome home party'. I think we should go to that."

"Is there a party where we *don't* have to be surrounded by teenagers and them old ass professors?" Chasity asked.

"We can hit up a lounge off campus," Jason answered.

"Very well," Alex relented. "Tomorrow is the homecoming tailgate, then the big game—"

"Yo, can we cook out at the tailgate?" Mark cut in.

"Yeah, I think so," Sidra answered. "I remember seeing something about that. They're providing a few grills, but its first come, first serve."

"Cool, I'mma go hide one later tonight so we can make sure we have one," Mark volunteered.

Alex looked perplexed. "Wait, why would—"

"'Cause I'm lookin' out for the cookout *literally*," Mark interrupted, shaking his hand in Alex's direction. "We alumni now, we can get away with shit."

Perplexity masked Alex's face. "No, we *can't*," she argued.

"Fellas, we on that grill," Mark said, ignoring Alex, who

just waved her hand at him dismissively.

"Well, prepare for some burnt ass hot dogs," Malajia grunted.

Mark side-eyed her. "My grilling is on *point*," he flashed back.

"No, not talking about yours," Malajia clarified; she pointed to Jason. "*His.*"

Jason looked shocked. "Hold up—"

"Shhh, don't argue baby," Chasity placated, putting her hand on Jason's arm.

Jason looked at Chasity, stern. "Wait, you're saying that I burn my hotdogs on the grill?" he asked as Chasity snickered.

"It was just that one batch," Chasity teased.

"Chasity, the last *five* cookouts we had at your house, them dogs were burnt," Malajia contradicted, as laughter erupted around her. "You ain't gotta lie just because that's your husband."

Jason stared at Chasity as she continued to laugh at his expense. "Really Chasity?"

"Look, I *told* you that nobody likes them that damn dark, now swing your attitude somewhere else," Chasity threw back.

Jason reached for his cup of soda as he nodded. "You know what, I'm not going out like that. I'm on the grill too."

"Naw bro, you—"

"Shut up," Jason demanded, cutting Mark off.

Mark snickered. "Jason tryna prove himself and shit," he teased. Jason flipped him the finger in retaliation.

"Okay, soooo I guess we can go to the store in the morning to pick up the food," Alex beamed after a moment.

"Sidra gotta make the potato salad!" Malajia blurted out as Sidra opened her mouth to speak.

Sidra looked confused. "Make it *where* exactly? In the hotel room?" she sneered.

"Yup," Malajia maintained.

Sidra rolled her eyes. "That's gross and it's *not* happening," she refused.

Malajia sucked her teeth.

Alex stared at the flyer in her hand. "Okay sooo Sunday… Ooh alumni breakfast—"

"Alex, NO!" Malajia snapped, slamming her hand on the table.

Sidra nearly spat her juice out trying to hold in her laugh.

"What is *with* you people and not wanting to attend these damn food events?" Alex huffed.

"They *corny*," Mark hurled. "Nobody wants to see Mr. Bradley's fat ass eating cheese eggs—"

Chasity busted out laughing.

"Wait, what?" Jason laughed at Mark's comment.

Mark too laughed. "No foreal, I saw him across campus earlier," he told. "He don't look like he be eatin' a dozen eggs with a blanket of cheese every day?"

Malajia playfully slapped Mark's arm. "Oh my God, shut up," she laughed.

"That's a damn shame," Alex condemned. "Talking about that man's weight like that."

Mark rolled his eyes. "Next time we come back here, I say we leave fun-killer Alex back in New York," he grunted.

"I agree with you babe," Malajia praised. "Just for your good idea, you get to put it where you want it tonight."

"You promise?" Mark returned, grinning at her.

"Oh wow," Josh commented, amusement in his voice.

Sidra put her hand over her face in embarrassment. "Eww!" she scoffed, loud. "Keep your freaky bedroom talk to yourself."

Malajia flagged her. "Maybe *you* should take it up there once, it'll loosen you up," she jeered to Sidra.

"Malajia!" Sidra exclaimed mortified. "God that was so *unnecessary*."

"It really doesn't," Chasity muttered. Jason put his hand over his face, and shook his head.

"Chasity!" Sidra belted out, eyes widened. She put her hands up. "This conversation has gotten too vulgar for me."

Alex sat there intrigued. "Not for *me*," she said, leaning forward, "So Chaz and Mel, you two have actually—"

"No Alex, no," Sidra cut in, flustered, causing Alex to laugh. "Talk 'nasty talk' with them when I'm not around."

Josh was about to say something, but movement from the cafeteria entrance caught his attention. "Is that who I think it is?" he smiled, seeing someone walk through the door. Everyone looked over, pleasantly surprised to see David walk in.

David smiled bright as he walked up to the booth while his friends cheered. "Aww, come on guys," he blushed.

"Oh snaaaap, David don't have the glasses on," Mark quipped as David greeted everyone at the table with hugs.

David looked at Mark confused. "You *been* knew that I no longer wear glasses," he pointed out. Mark snickered. "I video chatted you just *yesterday*."

"I know man, but what kind of reunion would this be if I didn't mention the glasses?" Mark chortled.

David shook his head in amusement as he sat down in the booth. "Wow…it's so good to see everybody," he smiled, folding his arms on the tabletop. He looked around. "Where's Em?"

"Oh, she had to work today," Alex informed. "But she's gonna meet us later."

David nodded, craning his neck to look around the cafeteria. "Damn, it hasn't changed a bit," he chuckled.

"And neither has the food," Sidra giggled.

"Perfect," he replied, amused. "I could use some nostalgia." He stood up from the table and pulled something from his wallet. "I even have my old student ID." He smiled. "I'll be right back."

Once David walked away from the table, Chasity looked at the others. "You think we should tell him that that old ass ID of his isn't gonna work?" she asked.

Malajia snickered as Sidra's eyes widened.

"Wait, nobody told him that he needs a voucher from the alumni committee to eat in the cafeteria this weekend?" Sidra questioned, shocked.

"Nah, if he had gotten here yesterday like everybody *else*, he would've *known*," Mark answered, trying not to laugh.

Jason shook his head. "That's fucked up," he chortled.

All eyes were on David as he handed his card to the cafeteria worker. When she handed the card back to him, he regarded the group with a salty look. They couldn't help but laugh.

"He salty!" Malajia screamed with laugher.

"Ahhh, just like old times," Mark joked, taking a sip of his soda.

Chapter 14

"Aww, the building still looks the same," Sidra cooed, standing on the steps of Torrence Hall with Chasity. "I'm about to cry."

Chasity side-eyed Sidra, watching her put her hand over her chest. "Girl, it's only been five years, don't be corny," she bristled.

"Let me be sentimental you damn demon," Sidra grunted. After spending time in the cafeteria, the group paired off for a bit, wanting to visit different parts of campus before meeting back up later. Chasity and Sidra's journey had taken them to their freshman dorm.

Chasity laughed at the bass in Sidra's voice. "Damn, you felt that, didn't you?" she teased.

"Yes," Sidra confirmed. "Now hush and let's go see our old room."

Chasity frowned in confusion as Sidra walked to the entrance. "What are we gonna do, knock on the door and say 'hey, I used to live here nine years ago, can I come in?'"

Sidra thought for a moment, then looked back at Chasity. "Yup." She walked over and grabbed Chasity's wrist. "Come on."

Chasity rolled her eyes as she allowed herself to be pulled into the building. Stepping inside, the girls looked around. The lounge area was crowded, which wasn't surprising.

"I wonder if they still have that small kitchen that everybody has to share," Sidra mused, pushing hair behind her ears.

"Wouldn't be surprising if they did," Chasity replied, unenthused.

"You remember, I almost got into a fight over leftovers?" Sidra giggled, looking at Chasity.

Chasity nodded as Sidra broke into laughter. "I do. All because your dramatic ass was stressed over finals," she remembered. "Almost got your ass jumped over Chinese food."

"Oh my God, I know," Sidra recalled. "In my defense, I really wanted that food." Chasity just shook her head in amusement. "If you hadn't showed up, they might've tried it." She tapped Chasity on the shoulder. "Your evil ass had my back and I love you for it."

"I didn't think your bougie ass could fight back then," Chasity joked.

Sidra regarded her with a frown. "Just say 'I love you' back."

"I love you back," Chasity chuckled, earning a playful backhand to her arm.

As they headed for the stairs leading to their old floor, they heard someone calling their names. They stopped and turned around.

Seeing the smiling woman approach, Sidra smiled. "Wait a minute...Drea?" she asked.

"Yeah, it's me," Drea confirmed, excited.

Chasity stared at her former freshman year resident advisor; she never cared for her.

"Wow," Sidra gushed. "You don't still work here, do you?"

Drea waved her hand dismissively. "Girl no, I'm just here for homecoming. My cousin goes here though," she replied. "And, get this, she stays in my old room. Can you believe it?" she added, overly enthused.

"No, no I can't," Chasity replied, feigning enthusiasm.

Sidra fought to keep from snickering at Chasity; she gave her a slight pinch on her side.

Drea looked at Chasity. "Hello Chasity. You still mad that I accidentally scratched you that one time?"

"Think about it every single day," Chasity returned, sarcastic.

"Okay, come on now," Sidra cut in, amused. "Drea, it was good to see you. We're about to go check out our old room."

"Okay, are you going to the game tomorrow?" Drea asked.

"Of *course*," Sidra beamed. "I hope they win like they *used* to when we were here."

"Me too, but let's face it, they don't have Jason Adams anymore," Drea replied; she let out a light sigh. "God, not *only* was he a great athlete, he was *so* damn fine."

"Still *is*," Chasity goaded.

Drea looked at her, raising an eyebrow. "You two are actually *still dating* after all these years?"

"No," Chasity answered.

Drea looked smug as she folded her arms. "Oh really? Aww, I'm sorry to hear that."

Chasity smirked at her. "*Don't* be, we're married."

Drea's mouth fell open. "Wait, you and Jason Adams are *married*?"

Chasity nodded. "*And* we're parents."

Sidra grabbed Chasity's arm. "Time to go Chaz," she urged, looking back at Drea. "It really *was* good seeing you again." They walked off, leaving Drea standing there shocked. As they walked up the steps, Sidra looked at Chasity. "You are so petty," she chided.

"So what, I just don't like her face," Chasity spat.

Approaching the floor, Sidra practically skipped to her old room. She put her hand on the door and smiled. "Awww."

"God, just knock already," Chasity huffed, folding her arms.

Sidra flagged Chasity with her hand, before giving the door a soft tap. They stood waiting for someone to answer. When the door opened, Sidra greeted the young woman with a bright smile.

"Hi," the girl said.

"Hi," Sidra greeted in return. "So umm...do you live in this room?" she asked after a moment of hesitation. Sidra had to admit, asking a teenager to allow strangers into her room didn't seem like such a good idea anymore.

Chasity smacked her forehead with her hand. "Jesus," she muttered. She looked at the girl, who shot Sidra a confused look. "I apologize for my friend's weirdness," she said. "We graduated from here five years ago and we used to live in this room our freshman year, so we were just wondering if you'd be so kind as to let us come in and see our old room for a minute."

Sidra shot Chasity a shocked look; her speaking voice had gone high, and overly polite.

"Oh," the girl beamed. "Sure, let me tell my roommate to move her mess." she said, going back into the room. "Just a sec."

"Where the hell did *that* voice come from?" Sidra asked Chasity when the girl was out of earshot.

"That's my 'work' voice," Chasity answered, tone back to normal.

"That is *hilarious*," Sidra replied, voice laced with laughter. "I need to start calling you while you're at work."

"I promise I won't answer," Chasity returned.

The girl returned to the door and signaled for the girls to come in. Sidra stepped in and looked around. "I'm Sidra by the way. And this is Chasity."

Chasity gave a wave. "Hi."

"Hi, I'm Brooke and this is Gabi," Brooke answered, pointing to her roommate who was sitting on a bed.

"I used to sleep over there," Sidra smiled. Chasity shook her head in amusement.

"You two were roommates?" Gabi asked, intrigued.

Sidra nodded, looping her arm through Chasity's. "Yep, met freshman year and are still friends to this day."

"Oh, that's cool," Brooke beamed. "You two must've hit it off right away."

"Uh...no," Sidra chuckled, while Chasity vigorously shook her head. She pointed to Chasity. "The first thing this heffa said when she walked in freshman year was 'who are you and what are you doing here?'...No 'hi' or anything."

"You gotta let that hurt go sweetie," Chasity jeered, earning a back hand to her arm. The hit stung. Annoyed, Chasity smacked her back on the arm.

"Ow!" Sidra shrieked, grabbing her arm as Brooke and Gabi busted out laughing. "That hit was *so* much harder than mine."

"You've been pinching and smacking me all damn day, you're lucky I didn't punch you in the goddamn face," Chasity threw back, examining her own arm.

"I hope *your* roommate isn't as rude as *mine* was," Sidra griped to the girls as she rubbed her arm.

Chasity narrowed her eyes at Sidra. "Would you rather live with someone who's rude, or a stuck-up bitch who wears ponytails every-damn-day?" Chasity threw back.

The teens glanced at each other for a moment. "Ponytails *everyday*?" Gabi asked in disbelief. "That's...weird."

Chasity snickered hard, then busted out in full on laughter at the annoyed look on Sidra's face. Sidra slowly glanced over at Chasity, folding her arms in the process as Chasity continued to laugh.

Alex stopped in front of a building as Malajia kept walking. "Malajia, where are you going?" Alex called as Malajia kept her pace.

Malajia stopped and turned around, shooting Alex a confused look. "You said you wanted to go see our old dorm."

"I know," Alex confirmed.

Malajia held her arms out, still confused. "So, we should meet Sid and Chaz at Torrence so we can walk over to Paradise Terrace."

Alex shook her head. "And we *will*, but I meant our *first* dorm," she clarified, pointing to the sign on the building she was standing in front of.

Malajia glanced up and frowned at the Wilson Hall sign. She sucked her teeth. "Alex, ain't nobody tryna go in that hot ass dorm!" she exclaimed.

Alex laughed. "It's *October*, I'm sure they turned the heat off by now," she said. "Come on."

"No Alex, I don't need to relive my days on that raggedy bunk bed," Malajia refused.

"Just come *on*," Alex insisted, stomping her foot on the ground. "Chasity and Sidra are visiting *their* first room, it's only right that we visit *ours*."

"If *my* old room was in the newer freshman dorm like *theirs* was, I'd go visit it too," Malajia grumbled, walking over to Alex. "*We* had to live in this outdated ass dorm in a smedium ass triple room."

"Well, I *enjoyed* living in our *smedium* room," Alex countered, folding her arms.

Malajia folded her arms right back. "Not surprised, it was a step up from that shoebox room you had back in Philly," she mumbled. She looked up and caught Alex's glare. "What?"

"I should punch you. Right in the mouth," Alex hissed.

"*What*? It was a *joke*," Malajia insisted.

"And like *always*, it's not *funny*."

"Of course it's not funny to y*ou*, the joke is at *your* expense," Malajia threw back, then pointed to her head. "Duh."

Alex rolled her eyes.

"Come on, your apartment in New York is fancier than my whole damn *house*, so just let me have this," Malajia teased.

Alex shook her head, sending a text message. "Whatever, let's just go up," she demanded.

Malajia sucked her teeth. "Fine," she huffed. "But I'm telling Emily that we did this without her… She salty she had to go into work today."

"It was only for a half day," Alex corrected, glancing out in front of her. "Speaking of Em, she's walking up *now*."

Malajia watched Emily approach, rolling her eyes. "Ugh," she griped.

Emily giggled. "Nice to see your rude self *too*," she said, standing next to Alex.

"Girl, you know I'm happy to see you, but ain't nobody got time for this dorm," Malajia complained.

"Still complaining, huh?" Emily teased in an aside to Alex.

"*Always*," Alex returned.

Malajia looked back and forth between the two, a frown on her face. She grabbed her cell phone from her purse. "Fuck this," she muttered.

"Who are you calling?" Emily asked.

"I'm calling Chasity, y'all got me fucked up," Malajia ground out, putting the phone to her ear.

Emily and Alex shot each other confused looks.

"Bitch, where are you?" Malajia spat into the phone. "Oh, well bring your ass to Wilson Hall, Alex and Emily are out here tag teaming me and shit."

Emily busted out laughing, while Alex looked annoyed.

"Because we mentioned your *complaining*?!" Alex exclaimed, holding her arms out. "You're *beyond* dramatic."

Malajia put her finger up at Alex as she continued to talk on the phone. "Naw 'cause—hello? Hello?!"

"She hung up on your whining ass, *didn't* she?" Alex asked.

Malajia tossed the phone back into her purse. "Mind your goddamn business," she barked.

Emily looped one arm through Alex's and one through Malajia's. "Come on, it'll be nice to see our old room," she grinned.

"Says *who*?" Malajia grunted, looking at Emily.

Emily eyed her back. "Malajia, be nice or I'm gonna make you wear a hot pink bridesmaids dress."

"Eww!" Malajia blurted out; Emily busted out laughing. "Okay, okay," she relented, putting her hand up. "It's bad enough we have to wear pink *anyway*, but *hot* pink is just hideous."

"Oh come on, the shade that I picked is light," Emily chortled. "I wore red for *yours* and black for *Chasity's*... You can wear pink for *mine*."

"You tell her Em," Alex beamed.

"Shut up, what color bridesmaid dresses are we gonna wear for *your* dry ass wedding?" Malajia hissed, glaring at Alex. "Mustard yellow? *Brown*?"

Alex shot a glower Malajia's way. "Your smart ass won't be wearing *any* color dress because you won't be *in* it."

"Bet money I will," Malajia threw back.

"Wait, did you say mustard yellow?" Emily directed at Malajia, laughing.

Malajia nodded. "You remember those ugly ass colored shirts she used to wear and shit?" she laughed back. "All baggy and shit."

"Hey!" Alex interrupted, clapping her hands in an effort to halt Emily and Malajia's laughter. "Let's just go."

Malajia snickered as she followed both girls inside the building. They walked in and up the steps to get to their old floor.

"They *still* ain't got no elevator in this bitch?" Malajia griped, face scrunched up.

"Oh my God, will you shut the hell *up*?" Alex barked, exasperated. "I'm *so* glad that I don't share a room with you anymore."

Malajia shot her a shocked look. "What? Screw you, at least *I* smelled good!"

Emily suppressed a laugh as she quickly stood in front of Alex, who looked like she wanted to smack Malajia. "All right, stop it now," Emily cut in, she looked at Alex. "She was joking Alex. You never smelled bad."

"Shiiiit," Malajia joked.

"Malajia, cut it out," Emily urged.

Malajia looked at the angry Alex and snickered. "Alex, you know I'm playing with you, stop bitchin'," she dismissed with a wave of her hand. When Alex's face didn't change, Malajia held her arms out. "You still mad?"

"You get on my nerves," Alex bristled.

"But you love me," Malajia smiled, moving closer to her. "Come on, let me grab your boob since you haven't been touched in a while."

Alex sucked her teeth and moved around Malajia to head to their old room, leaving a laughing Malajia to walk down the hall with Emily.

"You need to stop," Emily chuckled to Malajia.

"I can't, it's still too easy," Malajia laughed.

Approaching the door, Alex knocked. She folded her arms while she waited, shooting Malajia a glare in the process.

"Look, would you rather have 'complaining Malajia' or 'annoying Malajia'?" Malajia asked, pointing to herself.

"I'd rather have *quiet* Malajia," Alex hissed.

"Well, you ain't *getting* her so shut the hell up," Malajia threw back.

Alex let out a loud huff and knocked again.

"That's why nobody's home," Malajia muttered, amused. "You walked your happy ass up all those hot ass, rickety steps for nothing."

Fed up, Alex let out a huff and stomped off.

"Alex, we can try back later!" Emily called after her.

"*I'm* not coming back over here later," Malajia refused.

Emily stomped her foot on the floor. "That's it! Hot pink for you," she hurled, walking off.

"Emily, I'll rip that dress the fuck up with my bare hands and put the shreds on your wedding cake," Malajia promised, following her.

Jason walked into the athletic building and looked around; the building was nearly desolate. With students attending homecoming activities outside, he wasn't surprised that hardly anyone was in the building.

He slowly walked down the hall, recalling all the time he'd spent in there. Continuing his journey, he came to a large glass trophy case and scanned the numerous awards. He smiled when he saw the ones that his team won. Pride filled him when he saw a picture of himself in his uniform, next to a plaque bearing his name and the caption, 'Most valuable player'. *Good times*, he thought fondly.

His thoughts were interrupted by a male voice.

"You're Jason Adams, right?"

Jason turned around to see a young man standing before him, cradling a football under his arm. "Yes," he replied.

The brown skinned teen's hand jerked out with enthusiasm. "Drake Morris," he introduced, grinning from ear to ear.

"Nice to meet you Drake," Jason smiled back, shaking the young man's hand in a firm grip.

"Man, I've heard so much about you," Drake gushed, shifting his football from one hand to the other.

Jason folded his arms. "Oh yeah?"

"Yeah, my high school coach used to show us videos of you and the team playing," Drake beamed. "He's an alum and he always bragged about the team."

"You play football too?" Jason asked, intrigued.

"Yes, I'm the starting quarterback this season...just came in as a freshman," Drake replied, enthused. "Just like *you* did."

Jason smiled and nodded. Drake seemed like he was star stuck; Jason was flattered, but he was way too humble to let his campus legacy go to his head. "Well, congratulations," Jason said. "This is a great school to play for."

"Yeah, I heard," Drake returned. "Can't lie, I'm kind of nervous."

Jason tilted his head. "Why is that?"

Drake shrugged. "It seems like a lot of pressure...being the main focus on the team...the one that's responsible for carrying it."

Jason nodded slowly. He remembered his bouts of nervousness, the pressure while being on the team. "I get it. I felt that way myself. *Especially* my junior year," he remembered.

Drake was quiet as he listened to his football idol speak.

"Trying to play well and keep up with my grades...it started to drain me at one point," Jason added. "So much so, that I got hurt and had to sit out for a season."

Drake's eyes widened. "Oh wow, really?" he probed. "Coach didn't mention that."

Jason chuckled. "I'd highly doubt he *would*." The humor left his face. "I didn't tell you that to scare you. I was just sharing part of my story."

Drake put his hand up. "Oh I appreciate it, trust me," he breathed. "Do you...have any *advice*?"

Jason thought for a moment. "While playing football is the purpose...don't let that be your *only* purpose," he advised. "Make sure you keep your grades up. You always need something to fall back on."

Drake nodded. "Trust me, I understand that," he agreed. "I mean, it's my dream to go pro, but I also know how important school is."

"Good," Jason praised. "Oh, and always remember that you're part of a *team*. When you're a good player, the school will make it all about *you*... It's *not*. You can't do it without your whole team."

Drake, stuck his hand out one more time. "Thank you. I appreciate you talking to me."

"No problem," Jason replied, shaking his hand yet again. "Good luck to you."

"Thank you," Drake said as Jason walked away. "Hey, how

come *you* didn't go pro?" he asked at Jason's departing back.

Jason stopped and turned around. "That wasn't *my* dream," he answered, honest. He gave Drake one last nod before continuing on his way. Walking towards the exit, he pondered his own words. Playing pro was never his dream, but with the overwhelming thoughts of 'what ifs' swirling in his head regarding his *dream* career, Jason wondered if his decision *not* to play was the right one.

Mark scanned the aisles of the Mega-Mart. "Damn, they moved *all* the shit around in here," he muttered to David and Josh.

"Yeah, it *does* look different in here," David chuckled, scratching his head. "*Why are* we here anyway?"

"Yeah, I thought we were going to the liquor store," Josh chimed in.

"We *are*, but I wanted to pick up some black t-shirts," Mark informed.

"What are you buying *t-shirts* for?" Josh asked, perplexed.

"The game later," Mark answered. "We gotta be in sync with our outfits so…black tee's it is."

David raised an eyebrow. "Are those mandatory?"

"Yes," Mark shot back, folding his arms.

"By the *school*?" Josh questioned.

The constant questions were working Mark's nerves, and it showed on his face. "Look damn it! We are Team Ninja Strike and Team *Ninja Strike* is known for wearing black!" he snapped.

"We played *one* game as Team Ninja Strike… Paintballing," David argued. "I in *no* way see how that makes us *known* for something."

Mark stared at him in anger, while Josh snickered at the look on Mark's face. "*You* got disqualified before we even *played*, so *technically your* scientific ass ain't even *part* of the team," Mark threw back.

David's eyes widened. "That was *your* fault!" he hurled, pointing.

Josh put his hands up. "Guys, come on, we're almost thirty. We don't need to be arguing over stupid shit that happened like seven years ago," he cut in.

"Yeah, yeah, good point," Mark agreed, "So David stop bringing old shit up."

David sucked his teeth.

"Oh, I also gotta get snacks," Mark added, searching the aisle. "Mel and I ate all the ones we brought when we were chillin' in the room last night."

"You two are *still* greedy," Josh joked.

"Boooooo," Mark jeered in dramatic fashion.

Josh flagged Mark with his hand.

"I take it those chicks you be dating don't go out with you because of your sense of humor," Mark goaded. "Dry ass digs and shit."

"Man, shut up," Josh barked. "And my dates find me *quite* funny, thank *you* very much."

"All lies. Y'all dates be serious as shit," Mark laughed.

"Come on Mark," David laughed. "Josh can be funny at times."

Josh shot David a questionable look. "What do you mean *at times*?"

David's eyes widened. "Hey, don't take it as a *bad* thing. *I'm* not funny *at all*," he chuckled, putting his hands up in surrender.

Mark sucked his teeth. "David, man, that's not true," he said.

David had a hopeful smile. "Yeah? You think I have a sense of humor?"

"Nah, neither *one* of y'all asses are funny," Mark concluded without a qualm. Josh rolled his eyes, and David shook his head in amusement. "The only person who found you funny, Josh, was *Sidra*."

"How the hell did this even become a topic of conversation?" Josh hissed.

"'Cause you was tryna buss on me and my baby's eating habits," Mark threw back.

"Come on guys," David cut in. "Chill out." He couldn't help but find the banter amusing. He didn't realize how much he'd missed being around his friends. Bickering and all.

"All jokes aside," Mark began after a pause and more walking around. "Josh, how is it seeing Sidra again after all this time?"

Josh looked perplexed. "*That* was out of nowhere."

"Nah, it wasn't," Mark contradicted. "Been meaning to ask you since we got here."

Josh shrugged. "It's perfectly fine," he replied, nonchalant. "How *should* it be?"

Mark shot Josh a knowing look and twisted his lips to the side. "Never mind." He had no patience to deal with Josh and his vagueness when it came to the topic of Sidra.

David heard his cell phone beep. "I wonder who *this* is," he muttered, reaching into his pocket for his phone.

"Tell them Bunsen burners to chill, you'll be back Sunday," Mark joked, earning a snicker from Josh and an eye roll from David.

Not bothering to respond, David just looked at the text message. "Funny, funny," he laughed after a moment.

Josh looked over as David responded to his message. "Who was that?" he wondered.

David shoved the phone back into his jacket pocket. "My lab partner—" he paused briefly. "A friend of mine was just trash talking our football team."

"Oh *really*?" Josh questioned, amused.

David nodded. "Her homecoming was last weekend, and now her alma mater is playing *our* team tomorrow and she *actually* thinks they're going to win," he said, amused. "She went to Prime State."

Mark ran a hand over the back of his neck. "Kinda figured that when you said that her school was playing ours tomorrow… We already know we're playing wack ass Prime State," he jeered, putting his arms up in exasperation. "Yo, where's the fuckin' *shirts*!" he snapped. "We've been walking around here for like an hour."

Ignoring Mark, Josh focused on David. "Are you dating her?" he asked.

Mark snapped his head towards David. "Aww shit, David's about to get some when he go back to Ohio," he teased.

"We're not dating," David clarified.

"I noticed that you avoided the 'getting some' part," Mark commented.

David stared at him, "We are not *dating*," he stressed.

Mark smirked. "Understood."

David shrugged. "We're *friends*," he said. "Truth is, I haven't dated anybody since Nicole. Been too busy... Which is the *exact* reason Nicole used when she ended our relationship...not that I blame her."

Mark gave David a hard pat on his back. "Don't beat yourself up. You're busy for a good reason, tryna find cures and antidotes and shit," he placated. "You and Nicole had a good run for three years—"

"Three and a *half*," David corrected.

Mark put his hands up. "My bad," he said. "But like I said, y'all made it work as long as you could."

David rubbed his back as he craned his neck to examine it. "Thanks, but did you have to slap me that hard?" he grunted.

"Stop bitchin'," Mark mocked.

Josh shook his head at Mark, then looked at David. David had taken it hard when Nicole had ended their relationship; he knew how much David loved her. "David, everything will work out the way it's supposed to," he said, sincere.

Mark sucked his teeth. "Josh, nobody who's going through stuff wants to hear that bullshit," he ground out.

Josh frowned at him. "Whatever, Mark."

Ignoring Josh, Mark looked off to a section in the store. "*There* they are," he said of the shirts, walking over.

As Mark began rummaging through rows of colored shirts, his phone rang. Grabbing the phone from his jeans pocket, he glanced at it and put it to his ear. "Yeah babe?" he said to Malajia. "Yeah, I'm about to grab snacks and then we're gonna head to the liquor store... You want me to pick up some *what*?" Mark frowned. "A *crab leg* platter? ...From *where*? This ain't Maryland."

Josh chuckled at the annoyed look on Mark's face.

"Yo, you greedy as shit Malajia, you just ate not too long ago... Aye! Let me tell you one goddamn thing— You know what, just for talking to me like that, I ain't buying you *shit*."

David looked at Mark as he abruptly ended the call. "Damn, what did she *say*?" he laughed.

Mark shook his head. "She's disrespectful," he jeered. He hesitated for a moment, then scratched his head. "So uh, we gonna hit a seafood spot on the way back so I can get me some crab legs and shit."

Josh busted out laughing. "You're full of shit," he teased. "You don't even *eat* crab legs."

Mark hung his head in shame and shook it. "What do you want from me?" he shrugged, amusement in his voice. "I watched her give birth to my kids and shit, I gotta give her what she wants."

David gave Mark a pat on his shoulder. "Good man," he commended.

Chapter 15

"I swear to God, I don't know *why* I allowed you to sign me up for this," Sidra griped, adjusting her ponytail.

"Sidra, stop whining," Mark jeered as he stretched. "You on the winning team."

Sidra shook her head and tugged on her t-shirt.

Later that afternoon, Sidra, along with Mark, Alex, and David were standing in the crowded agriculture field waiting for the others. Like every other game, Sidra was dreading being talked into participating in the first place.

"Come on Sidra, it'll be fun," Alex mused, giving Sidra's arm a light tap.

"So you say about *every* game that I end up either falling, or getting dirty from," Sidra muttered, adjusting her shirt yet again. "Why is this thing so big?" she complained.

Before Mark could open his mouth to speak, he was joined by others in the group: Jason, Chasity and Malajia. "Where are y'all shirts?" he barked, pointing at the girls.

"I just wasn't wearing that baggy ass shirt," Chasity threw back, smoothing her fitted black t-shirt down. "It was like three sizes too big."

"You know four out of five of us don't wear no extra-large shirt," Malajia grunted, adjusting the strap on her black tank top. She looked at Alex, who was staring back at her.

"Say what you want, but *I* am quite *comfortable* in my shirt," Alex boasted, placing her hands on her hips. "I'd rather have it a little baggy, than extra damn tight."

Malajia narrowed her eyes. "Explain to me where it's baggy on you," she mocked.

Alex glared. "Definitely not in the *breast* area, which is more than I can say for *yours*." She smirked. "You might want to go for a push up bra next time."

Malajia's mouth fell open in shock, she placed her hands over her chest. "Fuck you, my boobs are perfectly sized, you— you *mammoth*."

Alex flagged Malajia with her hand, dismissing the comment. Alex had struck a nerve with her dig; she was satisfied.

Malajia made a face in Alex's direction, then looked at Mark. "This whole conversation is *your* fault for buying these dumb ass shirts," she hurled, annoyed.

Mark sucked his teeth. "Look. Those were the only size girl shirts that I could find," he explained.

Josh raised an eyebrow. "You didn't even bother *looking* for other sizes," he contradicted. "And those aren't even girl sizes. You grabbed that pack from the *guy* side."

"Mind your goddamn business Joshua," Mark barked back.

"So wait a minute, you mean I could've put on something other than *this* baggy thing?!" Sidra exclaimed, pulling on her shirt. "Yeah, I was just trying to be thoughtful since he spent his money, but hell, *I* don't want to wear this *either*."

"And I want that money *back*," Mark hurled.

"Boy shut the fuck up, that shit wasn't nothing but five dollars," Chasity spat, pushing her hair over her shoulder.

"*I* ain't giving you shit," Malajia hissed at him. She pulled a black top out of a plastic bag, "Here Sid, I knew you would want to change," she chortled.

Sidra smiled, accepting the short-sleeved shirt from Malajia. "Thank you, I'll be right back." She took off sprinting for some privacy.

Mark sucked his teeth yet again as Emily walked on to the field and headed over to them.
"Where's the black shirt I got you?" he charged.

Emily looked down at her pink t-shirt. "Wait, we really had to *wear* that?"

Jason snickered at the salty look on Mark's face. "Relax bro, we all appreciate the gesture."

"Nah, fuck that. You need to pay me back for your wife's shirt," Mark hurled at Jason, pointing.

The humor left Jason's face. "How about you pay *me* back for all the goddamn food and liquor you consume whenever you come to our damn *house?*" he countered. "Yeah, shut up," he added when Mark went to speak.

Mark was quiet for a moment. "Why you always gotta bring up shit that ain't got nothing to do with the issue at hand?" he spat.

Jason just turned away from him.

Sidra walked back over to the group a few moments later, old t-shirt in hand.

"Sidra, give your shirt to Em," Alex suggested. Sidra complied, and Emily pulled the shirt over top of her pink one.

"You look crazy and bulky," Malajia teased.

Emily just shrugged.

Mark clapped his hands together. "All right, we're ready," he beamed. As other teams poured onto the field, they noticed a familiar face.

"Oh *hell* no, *Carl?*" Malajia called, amusement in her voice.

Jason's former football teammate and Will's cousin Carl walked over. "About time y'all made it to homecoming," he grinned. He gave Emily a hug. "Hey cousin," he smiled, looking at her shirt. "Why you got that big ass shirt on?"

Emily tossed her hands up in the air in amusement. "I'm just trying to be a team player."

Carl approached Jason and gave him a firm handshake. "What's up bro?" he was excited; Jason had always been his favorite teammate.

As Jason and Carl proceeded to catch up, David glanced off to the side and noticed another familiar face. One that he was not at all prepared to see.

"Nicole," he mumbled. Seeing his ex-girlfriend made David want to sit the game out, leave the field, and flee campus all together. *Is she playing in these games too?*

Alex noticed the troubled look on David's face; she patted his shoulder. "Are you okay sweetie?" she asked, cutting into his thoughts.

David sighed. "Yeah, yeah I'm fine," he lied.

Mark leaned in. "Get your shit together Summers," he hissed.

David looked down at the ground, sighing in the process.

"*She* used to call me Summers."

"Hey, hey! Save the sentimental bullshit until *after* we win," Mark demanded, pointing his finger in David's face. "Don't make me take you out before we even *start...again*."

"Leave him alone you jerk," Alex snarled at Mark. "He has a right to feel how he feels about his ex."

Mark put his hand close to Alex's face; she smacked it right down. "Childish," Mark ground out, grabbing his hand.

Alex shook her head and returned her attention back to David; he ran a hand over top of his head, letting out a heavy sigh. "You want to leave?" Alex asked him.

David shook his head after a moment. "No, I can play," he assured.

Mark clapped his hands together. "Good," he commended, giving David a hard smack on his back.

"Ow!" David howled, trying to rub his back.

Mr. Bradley made his way to a podium and grabbed a microphone. "Okay everybody, first I'd like to say welcome to all of the alumni who decided to participate in this game today," he began, enthused. Once he had the attention of the entire field of spectators and participants, he continued. "The rules to 'find the flag' are simple. We have hidden flags of different colors scattered along the field. Hiding places include tree branches, barrels, hollow logs, under fake rocks, etcetera..."

"Guys, I think I forgot to put on deodorant after I showered," Alex quietly alerted, lifting her arm. Her announcement earned her sucked teeth and huffs. Alex sniffed her arm, then smiled. "Oh wait, never mind."

Malajia looked at Alex confused. "You should've figured that out before you even said anything," she griped. "Just want to hear yourself talk."

"Hush," Alex returned, waving her hand at Malajia.

"Each color is worth a number of points," Mr. Bradley continued. "White flags are worth one point. Orange flags are worth three points, pink flags are worth five points, green seven points, purple nine points, and the black flags are worth a whopping twenty-one points."

Malajia scrunched her face up. "How the number skip from nine to twenty-one?" she questioned, confused.

"The more important question is, did his corny ass just say 'whopping'?" Mark followed up.

"Oh my God, will you both shut up?" Alex fussed at them.

"Your team will have one hour to find as many flags as you can," Mr. Bradley continued. "Once the hour is up, you will bring your flags to this table over here." He pointed to a six-foot table off to the side. "And our flag counters will count the flags, tally up the points and declare a winner... We have four teams playing. So, get with your team and strategize."

"This shit is fuckin' stupid," Chasity spat, folding her arms.

"Yeah, it *does* seem like they just threw this shit together," Jason agreed, amusement in his voice.

"Like that extreme Easter egg hunt they did junior year," Sidra chortled.

"*That* was actually fun," Alex recalled, adjusting her wild ponytail.

"Says the person who won the damn prize money," Malajia griped.

"Look, can we just strategize like he said and get this over with?" David asked, watching the other groups huddle together.

"Man, we ain't gotta strategize a *goddamn* thing," Mark boasted to the group. "When they say go, we mow them bastards down."

"I actually think we should split up," Alex suggested. "The more we spread out, the more ground we cover and the more ground we cover, the more flags we can get."

"Good idea, glad I thought of it," Mark joked; Alex sucked her teeth.

"Oh, there is one more part of this game," Mr. Bradley announced excited, cutting the chatter short.

"God, don't he have a steak to inhale or something?" Mark grumbled, earning a few snickers.

"There are four large bags stationed over there," Mr. Bradley said, pointing to the bags in question. "They are filled with water balloons, which you can use to deter your opponents from the flags."

The teams stood there in stunned silence.

"Oh *this* just got real," Jason said after a moment.

"Wait," Sidra protested, putting a hand up. "You mean I have to get *wet*?" she fussed. "I didn't sign on for all that."

"Girl shut up, you act like you've never been moist before," Malajia teased, earning a hard snicker from Chasity.

Sidra was not amused. "Shut *up* Malajia," she barked.

Emily laughed. "Wait, did she just say *moist*?"

The loud buzzer rang out, and Mark bolted in the direction of the bags. "Let's be out!" he shouted. "Grab as many balloons as y'all can!"

The teams took off running. Some headed straight for the field, while others, including Team Ninja Strike, sprinted for the balloons. As David grabbed a balloon, one flew past his head. Startled, he dropped his balloon and took off running for the field.

"Where the hell are you going?!" Mark yelled after him.

"I'm going to start grabbing flags!" David yelled back, continuing on his way.

Annoyed, Mark, arms full of balloons, headed for the field. "I'm fuckin' his scared ass *up* with one of these balloons," he seethed.

"Mark, don't you waste them damn balloons on David's ass. Save them for our enemies!" Malajia called after him, running.

As the group ran for the grove of trees, hordes of balloons were hurled at them.

"The fuck?! How many goddamn balloons *are* there?" Chasity snapped, throwing one of her balloons, connecting with an opponent's neck.

"Run Chaz, I'll cover you," Jason urged, tossing several balloons while running behind his wife.

Sidra screamed as a balloon splashed on her shoulder. "Too close to the damn face!" she shrieked, pausing mid-run.

"No stopping," Josh said, grabbing her arm and pulling her along with him.

Throwing and dodging balloons in a flurry of movement and swears, the group made it to the center of the field. They tried to compose themselves and catch their breath.

"Damn, it's like the other teams ganged up on us," Alex

panted, examining her wet shirt. She ran a hand over her damp hair. "Yeah, this is gonna be fun to tackle later," she grunted.

"Look, we may be soggy as shit right now, but we got some hits in," Mark boasted.

Malajia sucked her teeth. "Us grabbing like three balloons each was stupid as shit," she ground out, pulling her damp hair to the side. "They had like fifty."

"Emily grabbed *one* lonely ass balloon," Chasity told, fanning herself with her hand.

Emily's mouth fell open. "Well…at least I *hit* somebody with it," she reasoned. "Sidra didn't grab *any*."

"Look, when I went to grab some, I got smacked on the damn arm with one," Sidra argued. "Besides, I wasn't gonna be able to carry but so many anyway."

"Yeah, we definitely didn't think this through," Jason admitted, running a hand along the back of his neck. "We should've grabbed a bag of them."

"Who was gonna *drag* that shit?" Mark wondered. "Naw it's all good. This water ain't stoppin' no show. We're still gonna get the most flags and shit."

"*Speaking* of flags, we should probably get a move on and start grabbing some," Josh put in. He looked around. "Where's David by the way?"

"Fuck him, he took off running like a bitch," Mark grunted. He tossed a balloon in the air and caught it. "I still got one balloon left. When the time comes, I'll use it as a distraction."

"Let's split up," Alex advised.

Mark put a hand out. "All right Team Ninja Strike, all in together," he beamed.

"We some moist ass ninjas," Malajia muttered, putting her hand on top of his.

"Stop saying that word!" Sidra snapped, stomping her foot on the ground. Malajia busted out laughing.

"Hey, shut up and put your damn hands in," Mark demanded. As all hands came together, Mark closed his eyes and bowed his head. "God, help us beat these other sorry teams, and let it be known that the person on *this* team with the least number of flags gotta buy everybody drinks tonight."

"Amen," the group chimed in, amusement in their voices.

As they got ready to split up, they saw David jogging towards them, smiling. "Guys, I found like ten flags already," he bragged. His celebration was short-lived when a balloon hit him in the head. "Damn it Mark!" he yelled, stumbling back.

"You threw our last damn balloon," Malajia barked, backhanding Mark on the arm. "What happened to 'distractions'?"

"I *was* distracted when David's dry ass came over here all jolly and shit after leaving us to fend off the attack," Mark threw back.

"You are such a butthole," Alex fumed.

"How many flags do we have?" Sidra asked, fanning herself.

Alex looked down at the flags in her hand. "We have fifteen."

Sidra shook her head. They were only twenty minutes into the flag hunt, and she was already over it. "Okay, I say we grab a few more and head back," she suggested.

"No, we're gonna keep searching until the end of the damn game," Malajia demanded. "Stop tryna quit."

"I'm hot, wet, and I broke a damn nail," Sidra whined, examining them. "I just got these done the other day."

Malajia held a hand up. "I broke *two*, what *else* you got?" she threw back.

Alex craned her neck, zoning in on a flag stuck behind a bush. "Ooh, I see one," she announced.

Chasity frowned in confusion as Alex just stood there. "Well *get* it," she ordered.

Alex vigorously shook her head. "Oh hell no," she refused. "The last time I grabbed one, I got hit in the face with a balloon. Which was *your* fault by the way," she hurled at Chasity.

Chasity pointed to herself. "How the fuck was that *my* fault?" she barked. "*I* didn't throw it."

Alex pointed at her. "*You* were supposed to be on the lookout."

"Girl—nobody looked out when *I* took balloons to the back, getting the last *five* flags, so get out my goddamn face," Chasity argued.

"God, let's just finish this damn game okay?" Sidra cut in, annoyed. "*I'll* get the damn thing." She walked over to the bush and as she reached for it, a balloon broke on her chest. "Goddamn it!" she screamed.

While Sidra was busy cursing and wiping water from her face, an opponent was making their way to the flag that Sidra was going for. Seeing the girl, Malajia grabbed a twig from the ground.

"Distractions!" Malajia yelled, throwing the twig. It completely missed the target. "Shit." Her attempt was met with skeptical looks.

Chasity shook her head. "Fuckin' stupid," she hurled. Grabbing a handful of leaves, she charged for the girl.

"That's right Chasity! Blind that bitch with them crunchy ass leaves," Malajia rejoiced.

Chasity threw the leaves at the startled girl, who took off running, as Alex ran over and scooped up the flag.

Malajia started clapping. "Yeeessss, great teamwork ladies."

"Malajia, I'm pretty sure throwing sticks at people is against the rules," Alex chastised, walking over and standing next to Chasity. "What if you had hit her?"

"Shut your sweaty ass up," Malajia bit out. "We got the flag, *didn't* we?"

Alex shook her head as Chasity pushed some of her hair behind her shoulder. Overheated, Alex grabbed the collar of her shirt and quickly moved it in and out, fanning herself.

Chasity glanced over as the air that Alex was generating made its way to her. Chasity frowned. "Alex, I love you," she said after a moment.

Alex paused her fanning and looked at her, smiling. "I love you too sis," she gushed, tapping Chasity's arm. "Awww, did us working together just now make you sentimental?"

"*Fuck* no, I just wanted to soften you up before I told you that you smell like onions," Chasity said.

Malajia tossed her head back as Alex's eyes widened in shock. "*Thank* you! Somebody *finally* said it," Malajia belted out.

"That's a lie!" Alex exclaimed, lifting an arm.

"Please don't do that," Chasity urged, earning a laugh from Malajia.

Alex sucked her teeth. "Whatever Chasity, it's not *me* who smells like that," she denied. She looked at Sidra. "Sid, come on, confirm for me."

Sidra took a step back. "Umm, no...sensitive nose." she hesitantly put out. "You said *yourself* that you forgot your deodorant earlier," she added when Alex narrowed her eyes.

Arm still up, Alex shook her head. "No, but then I realized that I *didn't*." She looked at Emily. "Em, can *you* vouch for me?"

"Alex, stop tryna get people to smell that hoagie you got in a headlock," Malajia teased, Chasity snickered.

Giggling, Emily walked over. "I'm sure you're fine Alex," she assured. She leaned her face close to Alex's arm and inhaled. "Ooh!" she blurted out, backing away.

Alex's face fell. "Em?"

Emily held her hand to her nose. "Ummm...I love you Alex," she placated.

"You *stink* Alex," Malajia threw in. Alex frowned as she put her arm down. "Making all that money and you still buying that cheap ass deodorant."

Embarrassed, Alex stomped off without saying a word.

"Come back Alex, we can use you as a deterrent!" Malajia laughed after her.

"*Spell* deterrent!" Alex yelled back.

"'A-l-e-x-a-n-d-r-a's a-r-m-p-i-t-s!'" Malajia spelled out.

Sidra shook her head. "Malajia, you're terrible," she chastised. Malajia just shrugged.

"And *you*," Sidra directed at Chasity. Chasity raised an eyebrow. "Did you *have* to blurt it out like that?"

"I couldn't fuckin' *take* it anymore," Chasity reasoned, annoyed. "She kept coming near me."

"She *was* running near Chaz extra hype," Malajia put in.

"Sweating hard as shit."

"Stop it," Emily ordered, trying to keep her laughter in.

The girls walked a bit more, before coming to a hollow log. Malajia squatted down and peered inside.

"Yo, there's three flags in there," she announced, standing back up. "We need those."

Sidra looked at her. "*You* found them, go get them," she demanded.

Malajia put her hand up. "I can't crawl—I got weak back muscles from carrying twins," she explained.

Sidra squinted at her. "I want to call you a liar, but I feel like I *can't*," she slowly drew out.

"I *am* lying," Malajia admitted. "I just don't want to go in there."

Sidra sucked her teeth, flagging her with her hand. "Chasity?" Sidra proposed.

"No," Chasity refused.

Malajia looked at Emily. "Em, you haven't gotten any flags yet, go grab those for the cause," she commanded, pointing.

Emily's eyes widened. "I'm not going in there! There's a bug like *right* there." She pointed to the crawling critter at the entrance.

Malajia lost her patience. "Emily, get your bright ass in there!" she erupted, stomping her foot on the ground.

"*No*, Malajia," Emily calmly refused, scratching her arm.

Malajia sucked her teeth and placed her hands on her hips. Looking around, she saw something on the ground nearby. She darted for it. "Yeessss," she cheered, picking up a water balloon. "Somebody salty as shit they dropped this."

"How is *that* going to get those flags out of that bug infested log?" Sidra wondered.

Chasity, spotting someone lurking in the distance, signaled for the girls to come closer. "I think I have an idea," she said.

"You think, or you *know*?" Malajia quipped. Chasity shot her a lethal glance. Catching the look, Malajia gave a nervous chuckle. "Carry on."

After a few moments, the lurker crept up to the log and carefully maneuvered inside to retrieve the three flags. As the guy began to celebrate his find, he heard something hit the log.

"Distractions!" Malajia yelled as she and Chasity began tossing leaves in his direction.

As the guy began moving away from the log, Malajia yelled. "*Now* Sidra!"

Before their opponent knew what happened, he was hit with a water balloon in his face. "Damn it! That got in my eyes!" he bellowed, dropping his flags on the ground as he frantically wiped at his face.

Seizing the opportunity, Emily darted out from behind a tree. Recognizing the victim, she winced. "Sorry Carl," she blurted out, scooping up the flags. "I'll give you an extra piece of cake at the wedding," she promised, running away.

"No apologizing to the enemy," Malajia barked, running behind Emily and Chasity. "Sidra, move it."

"I'm coming!" Sidra wailed, trotting after them.

Chapter 16

"We only have like fifteen more minutes before they stop this game," David pointed out, glancing at his watch. "Let's just go back now."

"Stop bitchin," Mark threw back, reaching for a black flag that was stuck to a tree. "I'm tryna win."

"I wonder how the girls are doing," Josh wondered, searching through a bush.

"Stop worrying about the girls and worry about doing *your* part," Mark ground out, stretching his arm up.

Jason stared at him. "Mark, you've been reaching for that damn flag for the past ten minutes," he argued.

"I just gotta stretch a little more," Mark grunted.

"Unless you grow another *foot*, you're not getting it," Jason said.

Mark let out a huff as he tossed his arms up. Having a thought, he kneeled down and put his hands out. "Come on, I'll give somebody a boost," he proposed.

Jason scowled. "Fuck no," he refused.

"Why not?" Mark frowned, offended.

"The last time you tried to give somebody a boost, you did it too hard and the person lost their balance and fell," David reminded.

Mark rolled his eyes. "That was like a year ago and you don't even remember who it was."

David's eyes widened in agitation. "It was *twenty minutes* ago and it was *me*!" he barked, arms in the air.

Mark snickered. "My bad yo. But I said I was lifting you on three."

"I fell on a bunch of twigs," David mumbled, rubbing his

back.

"You always crying about some shit," Mark jeered. "You fell, so the hell what? My *three-year-old's* fall harder than that and take it like a G."

"I'm sure that's a lie, considering how many times they've fallen out kicking and screaming over something as simple as a cookie," David threw back.

"Yeah?" Mark bristled. "I'mma tell them you clowning them, beaker boy, and they gonna sneeze on you when they see you."

David flagged him with his hand.

"Whatever man…" Mark huffed. He then sucked his teeth. "Fine, give *me* a boost."

Jason pointed at him. "No, you do too damn much," he said.

"You jumped on my hand hard as shit last time," Josh hurled, rubbing his hand.

"I was trying to get my footing," Mark explained. When his response was met with frowns, Mark stood up. "Fuck it, I'm doing this another way."

The guys watched as Mark backed away from the tree.

"Mark…I know you're not about—"

"Chill Joshua, I got this," Mark assured, putting his hand up.

Jason didn't say anything; he just folded his arms and leaned against another tree, waiting.

Mark took several deep breaths before taking off running. Reaching the tree, he jumped, put his foot on the trunk, and tried to boost himself up. Losing his footing, he slipped and fell. With a loud, profane ridden outburst, Mark tumbled to the ground.

"Yep, saw that coming," Jason said, laughter in his voice.

"Fuck you Jason!" Mark grunted, angry. "When I find out whoever stuck that fuckin' flag up there, I'm kicking their ass!" He struggled to get up, groaning in the process.

Josh shook his head as he walked over, extending his hand out for Mark to grab. "Let it go Mark," he urged, helping Mark stand.

Mark placed a hand on his back. "Good idea," he winced.

"I fell on some twigs."

"Hurts, *doesn't* it?" David jeered.

Mark ignored him and dusted himself off. "Fuck that flag," he spat. "Let's get the hell back."

"Good, I'm starving," Josh commented. As they walked away from the tree, a few balloons flew across the field, hitting them. "Come *on*!" Josh yelled.

"Damn, these muthafucka's *still* got balloons?" Mark fumed, looking around in every direction. "Y'all corny as shit holding on to them."

A few male opponents approached; Jason signaled to the other guys. "Guys, we gotta go," he belted out.

"Protect the flags!" Mark yelled. He took off running along with the other guys, while balloons were hurled at their retreating backs.

David took a balloon to the back of the head, sending him falling to the ground.

Josh turned around. "David, you cool?" he asked, trying to keep from laughing.

David picked himself up and continued running. "Man, I'm glad that I don't wear glasses anymore, they would have broken," he panted.

"*Still* talking about those glasses," Mark mocked.

They came to a clearing, and stopped to catch their breath.

"All right, we made it," Jason said, wiping his forehead with his hand. "I'm thirsty as shit, let's get these flags counted."

"You should've drank some of that water out of one of those balloons," Mark joked.

Jason frowned; he was not amused. "I'm too tired to even respond to that stupid ass suggestion," Jason returned, annoyed.

"You *just* responded though," Mark mumbled.

"What?" Jason challenged, shooting him a glare. Mark snickered.

Josh reached into his pocket. "Here's my flags," he said, offering up his eight flags.

Mark looked at him. "How you only find eight?" he bristled.

"Just take the goddamn flags!" Josh snapped, pushing the flags into Mark's hand. He was over it.

Mark eyed the flags that Jason pulled from his pockets. "Yes Jase, twenty flags for the cause!" he rejoiced. He put his hand up for a high five. "Up top."

"Get away from me," Jason grunted. He was over this too.

Mark flagged Jason with his hand as he counted their flags along with his own. "Okay so we have forty flags so far—"

"How are you talking trash and you only got four more flags than *I* did?" Josh threw in, frowning.

"Point *is* that I *got four* more flags than *you* did," Mark spat back. Josh rolled his eyes. "And it would've been *five* had somebody given me a damn boost to get the one from the tree."

"Let that shit *go*," Jason bit out. "David, how many do you have?"

David cleared his throat as he searched his pockets. He frowned in confusion when he realized his flags were missing. "Uh—"

"Uh?" Mark charged. "The fuck you mean *uh*? Where's the damn flags?"

David squeezed his pockets and searched again. "They're not here," he hesitantly put out. His revelation was met with stern looks. "I must've dropped them when I fell."

Jason pinched the bridge of his nose with two fingers and let out a long sigh; Josh shook his head and turned away.

Mark pointed his finger at David. "See this is why— How you drop the goddamn flags?!" he erupted. "How you fall from a damn water balloon?!"

"Look, they fell out of my damn pockets!" David yelled back. "I didn't realize it."

"What's up with your shallow ass pockets and shit?!" Mark hurled.

Josh stepped in between David and Mark, putting his arms out. "Okay, chill out. We can still win with what we already have. I'm sure the girls did well."

"Nah fuck that, we're getting those flags back," Mark insisted.

"Mark, they're probably gone by now," Josh pointed out.

"Right, somebody probably picked them up already," David added.

Mark stared at his friends intensely. "Then we *taking* them from whoever *got* 'em," he said, tone menacing.

David busted out laughing. "Yeah okay," he dismissed. When he saw that the other guys weren't laughing, the humor left him. "You guys aren't *serious*, are you?"

"I'm actually not opposed to it," Jason said. "I didn't go through all that just to lose."

Mark nodded his head in approval. "*That's* why you my brother from another mother," he praised, pointing at Jason.

"I guess—"

"Shut your ass up, 'eight flags'!" Mark hurled at Josh before he could finish.

"Go to hell with all that, all right!" Josh threw back. "I was about to say that I'm in."

Mark laughed. "My bad bruh," he said. "I thought you were about to punk out."

"Just shut up," Josh spat, much to Mark's amusement.

"David, you ain't got no choice but to go back in there with us," Mark added. David ran a hand over his head. "This is *your* damn fault anyway."

"Yeah, yeah," David muttered. "Question though. I had all white flags. If we see someone with white flags, how are we gonna know that they're *mine*?"

"Doesn't even matter. The first person we roll up on, getting they flags confiscated," Mark promised. David shook his head while Mark clapped his hands together in anticipation. "Let's do this one last time Team Ninja Strike."

As the guys were about to head back into the grove of trees, they heard the buzzer, signaling the end of the game.

"Goddamn it!" Mark ranted.

"Well, so much for that," Jason chucked. "Let's go, we have like five minutes to get to the counting table."

Defeated, Mark let out a sigh. Getting ready to head back, Mark spotted a few people emerging from the tree line. Eyeing the flags in the hand of one opponent in particular, he had an idea. "Yo David," he called.

Facing Mark, David looked perplexed. "Yeah?"

Mark hesitated until the person came closer. "Turn around right quick," he prompted.

Confused yet curious, David turned around. "What is this

all ab—" The rest of the words got caught in his throat as he came face to face with *her*.

"Hi David," Nicole Elliot smiled.

David tried to speak, but the words wouldn't come out. Seeing her from a distance was one thing—having her standing in front of him was another.

Nicole chuckled. "Now come on Summers, I know you're learning all those fancy medical words in Ohio, but don't tell me you forgot the word 'hello'," she teased.

As David went to finally speak, Mark blurted out, "Distractions!" snatching the cluster of flags from Nicole's hand.

"Really Mark?!" Nicole shrieked.

"Mark! Why do you have to be such an asshole?!" David yelled at him.

"For Team Ninja Strike!" Mark belted out, running off with a laughing Jason running alongside him.

Josh waved to Nicole. "Good to see you again," he said, running off to catch up to them.

Nicole shook her head. "I see some things never change," she muttered, placing her hands on her hips. She looked back at David, who was staring at her.

"Sorry about that," he said.

Nicole just shrugged. In that moment, she didn't care about flags, or the game for that matter.

"Anyway… Hi," David smiled.

She smiled back.

"What took y'all so damn long?" Chasity asked, opening a bottle of water.

"Right," Malajia chimed in, eating chips from a small bag. "We been here for like a half hour."

After dropping their flags off at the counting table, the guys had joined the girls at the refreshment table.

"It hasn't even been that long," Mark grunted, reaching for a bottle of water.

Sidra looked around. "Where's David?" she asked.

"Back there talking to Nicole," Josh answered, removing

his damp t-shirt.

Sidra stared at his bare, toned chest while he wiped the sweat from his face with the shirt.

Malajia catching the exchange, tapped Chasity's arm, signaling for her to look. Chasity caught a glimpse. "Josh, look at Sidra right quick," Chasity blurted out.

Snapping out of her lustful trance, Sidra quickly turned away as Josh looked at her confused. Josh then looked at Chasity. "What happened?" he asked.

"Never mind," Chasity smirked; Malajia had her hand over her mouth, trying to hold her laughter in.

Sidra narrowed her eyes at them, shaking her head.

Alex walked over, arms folded tight. "I hope Nicole is being nice to him," she put in. "There's nothing like running into an ex and have it be tense."

Mark looked at her as he drank his water. "Why you standing there looking all uncomfortable?" he wondered.

"Oh, her deodorant quit on her," Malajia answered before Alex had a chance to speak.

"Damn is *that* what that smell was when we were all huddled together after the first attack?" Mark laughed. "Alex, you too old for that."

Alex rolled her eyes as laughter erupted around her. "Shut up," she hissed. "Look, I tried this new 'natural' deodorant and…apparently it doesn't work in active situations. Lesson learned."

"Ain't nobody tryna hear that," Malajia grunted. "You try new shit when you're not around *us*. Subjecting us to odors and shit."

Emily gave Alex a sympathetic pat on her shoulder.

Alex couldn't help but chuckle. "I'm not going to be able to live this one down, am I?"

Emily shook her head in amusement. "Sorry."

The group stopped talking as Mr. Bradley stepped up to the podium. "The flags have been counted," he announced, grabbing everyone's attention. Looking at a card in his hand, he cleared his throat. "And the winner is…Team Ninja Strike."

"Yeeeeesssss!" Mark rejoiced as cheers and claps rang out around them.

"Way to go everybody," Alex cheered, clapping.

"Alex, just stop fuckin moving. You're making my stomach hurt," Chasity barked at her.

Alex glared at her. Annoyed, she raised her arm and moved near Chasity. "Come here," she hissed through clenched teeth.

"Eww!" Chasity shrieked, ducking behind Malajia and pushing her in front. As Alex came closer, Malajia screamed at the top of her lungs.

"God, is all that *necessary*?" Sidra complained, covering her ears. "I swear, you can shatter *windows* with that pitch."

"Sidra, for that corny joke, you buying a round of drinks tonight," Mark said.

Sidra snickered. "Fine."

A young student with a camera stood in front of them. "Can I take your picture since you're the winners?" he asked.

"Ugh, I look a mess," Sidra muttered, putting a hand on her head.

"Just shut up and smile," Mark mocked, earning a swift backhand to the arm from Sidra.

Emily pointed to David, who was jogging up. "Wait for David."

"Y'all were gonna take a picture without me?" David asked, stopping next to Alex. As the group posed for the picture, David scrunched up his face. "Did somebody just eat a hoagie?"

Alex rolled her eyes and laughter erupted just as the camera flashed.

Sidra retrieved her debit card from the bartender, returning it to her wallet. Grabbing her drink, she took a quick sip. "This is good," she smiled, nodding at the woman.

The lounge that the group had picked for the evening was packed. Music videos played on monitors throughout the lounge, blaring their songs through the speaker system and sending patrons to the dance floor. Some of the group however, had decided to congregate at the bar. Sidra was one of them.

As Sidra sipped her drink, Josh approached her. She smiled at him. "I saw you dancing out there," she teased.

"Nah, it was more of a stiff two-step," he chuckled, signaling for the bartender.

Sidra giggled. "No, you looked good," she placated.

Josh placed his drink order. "I know you're lying, but I appreciate it," he joked. Once he paid for and received his drink, he took a sip.

Sidra took another sip of hers. "So...tomorrow is our last night here," she mentioned. "Ready to get back to reality?"

Josh chuckled a bit. "Not really." He took another sip. "No, reality isn't bad. I can't complain," he amended. "It's not like I hate my job or anything."

Sidra nodded. "Yeah, I hear you," she said. Her voice was somber.

"I take it *you're* not ready to go back," he observed.

"I'm not saying that exactly," she replied. "I just..." she dipped her straw repeatedly in her glass. "...I have to go back to being far away, you know?"

Josh nodded.

"I mean, California is okay. But...being out there by myself—" She let out a sigh. "Me being here with you guys made me realize how much I miss you all."

"Yeah...that's the funny thing about college," he said. "You don't appreciate the experience until you're not living it anymore."

Sidra sighed. "Yeah, tell me about it," she agreed. "I went from seeing everybody every day to seeing some like once every other *year*."

Josh looked at her. "You know it doesn't have to *be* that way, right?" he mentioned, stern.

"What do you mean?"

"You can see us more often," he clarified. "But...that's impossible when you hardly ever come home."

Sidra was taken aback by the tone of his voice. "Excuse me?" she ground out. "So...us not seeing each other is *my* fault?"

Josh let out a sigh. "That's not what I meant."

"No, clearly it *is* what you meant," Sidra scowled. "Look, like *I* can get on a plane to come home to Delaware, *you* can get on one to come to California."

"So, this is about *me* not coming out there?" Josh zoned in.

"I've been out there for five years and yes, while I've only come home a handful of times, at least *I came* back," she threw back. "*You* haven't been out to see me *once*. Hell at least *some* of the group came to see me the first year I was out there."

"I was in graduate school and was taking finals, Sidra," Josh explained. "I *told* you I couldn't come then,"

"And *after?*" she pressed. Josh sighed once again. "You're my best friend and we don't even make an attempt to see each other."

Josh frowned at her. "*Am* I?"

She looked confused. "Are you *what?*"

"Am I still your best friend?" Josh clarified.

Sidra was shocked. "Of *course* you are," she insisted.

"You sure? Because I don't feel like that's the case," Josh bit out. "We barely talk anymore. Hell, half the time I call you your phone goes to voicemail."

"Josh you know that my career is demanding." Sidra knew that was a silly excuse; she made time to talk to others, but she didn't want to let *him* know that. It would hurt him more than he already was.

"*So* demanding that you can't spare *five minutes* to talk to me?" He threw back. Sidra looked at her shoes. "You want to know why I haven't been out there to see you?" he asked.

She looked up, but didn't say anything.

"It's not because I don't have time or because I *can't*," he said. "It's because I'm not even sure if you would *want* me there."

Sidra turned away from him. "Josh...that's not true," she denied, looking back at him. "I can't believe you would think that—"

"Face it Sidra, things between us changed before you left," Josh interrupted. "I mean I know things were sorta off since Junior year, but I thought we were getting past that."

"We *were* past that," she promised. "We *are*."

Josh slowly shook his head. "No...something—I don't know what happened. I don't know what changed."

My feelings for you did, she thought. Sidra felt horrible. In running from her true feelings, she was purposely shutting him out, making Josh feel that she didn't want to be around him. She knew that she needed to say something, but couldn't bring herself to do it. "Josh...how did this argument even start?" she said instead.

Josh shrugged. "I don't know." His tone was short. "But I guess I'll take the blame for it." He set his glass on the bar counter. "Well, at least our time *earlier* was pleasant," he sneered. "I'm gonna go find the others."

Sidra didn't get a chance to respond before he walked off. She lowered her head and let out a long sigh. "Shit," she hissed to herself.

"Everything okay?" Alex asked, walking up.

Sidra looked at her. "Yeah, I'm just a little worn down from all that running earlier," she lied. "I'm gonna head back to the hotel and get some sleep."

Alex looked disappointed. "You sure sweetie?"

Sidra forced a faint smile. "Yeah, I'm sure." She moved hair behind her shoulder. "I'll grab a cab."

"I'll let the others know," Alex said as Sidra walked off. "Breakfast tomorrow?"

"Of course," Sidra threw over her shoulder.

"Chaz, why don't you buy your brother a shot," Mark proposed, dipping a buffalo wing into some blue cheese dressing.

"Lest you forget, I'm an only child," Chasity scoffed. With Jason off to the bathroom and Malajia dancing, Chasity and Mark were left alone at the bar.

Mark chuckled. "Nah, you my sister, you don't need no damn blood." He took a big bite of his wing.

Chasity scrunched her face up. "You hype as shit eating that nasty ass blue cheese." Although she didn't say it, she appreciated his words.

Mark nearly choked on his food. "You don't know what you're missing, bee," he said, wiping his mouth.

"That shit smells and *tastes* like some bullshit," Chasity ground out, reaching for her drink.

"I put that shit on everything, including Malajia," Mark

joked, earning a backhand to his arm.

"I just ate, you nasty fuck," Chasity sneered.

Mark laughed, eyeing the drink next to him. "Jase better hurry his ass back from the bathroom before I drink his damn drink."

"Go ahead and make him punch you," Chasity warned.

While Mark resumed eating his food, Chasity went back to sipping on her drink. She was bobbing to the music when someone tapped her shoulder. She looked over and a woman was standing there.

Chasity shot the woman a skeptical glance. "Yes?"

"Hi, can I ask you a question?" the woman asked.

Chasity frowned. "Do I know you?"

The woman let out a small laugh. "No," she answered. Chasity had no traces of amusement on her face; she just stared at her. "I just wanted to ask you if that man is with you."

"*What* man?" Chasity questioned, annoyed.

The woman pointed to Mark. Chasity looked at him; he was oblivious as he bobbed his head to the music, devouring his wings.

Chasity looked back at her. "*Him*?" she scoffed. The woman nodded. "He's my best friend's *husband*, what the hell do you want?"

"Oh, nothing disrespectful," she assured. "I was just picking up on his aura, and I wanted to ask him if he was looking to change jobs because I see him changing positions."

Chasity stared at the woman as if she was crazy. "You said you picked up on his *aura*?" she slowly drew out. The woman nodded eagerly. "Girl, step off," she dismissed, turning away from her.

Malajia and Jason walked up as the woman walked away. Malajia looked at Chasity, who was mumbling something to herself. "What's wrong with you?" Malajia wondered.

Chasity looked at her; Malajia's eyes were glazed over. "You drunk?" she asked, handing Jason his drink.

"Very *tipsy*," Malajia clarified, laughter in her voice. "Why you over here talking to yourself light bright?"

Chasity rolled her eyes. "'Cause these hoes stay coming up with new shit," she ground out.

Malajia reached across Chasity and grabbed the drink in front of Mark. "What do you mean?"

"Some weird bitch came over here talking about she sees Mark's aura," Chasity sneered, pushing hair over her shoulder. "Talking about seeing him in a different position or some bullshit."

Malajia didn't say anything. She stood there, face void of expression. Then she slammed the glass down, walked over to Mark and poked him on the side of his head, startling him.

"What's wrong babe?" Mark asked, confused.

"The fuck you *mean* what's wrong?" she snapped. "I go away for five minutes and you over here acting like you ain't fuckin' *married*."

"Huh?!" Mark responded, shocked. "I'm over here eating these hard ass *wings*, what are you *talking* about?"

"Malajia, what the fuck?" Chasity wondered, just as confused.

"Yo, y'all cool?" Jason chimed in.

Malajia smacked the bitten wing from Mark's hand, sending it falling on the counter. "You over here showing bitches your *aura*?!" she yelled.

Chasity put her hand over her face and shook her head. "Oh my God," she muttered.

Mark put a hand up. "Malajia, what—"

"No, Chasity said you showing bitches your aura!"

Mark looked at Chasity, eyes wide. "Yo Chaz, what did you say to her?"

Chasity put her hand up. "Your wife is fuckin' simple *and* drunk, I didn't say that you showed anybody *anything*."

"Boy, don't blame my bestie, at least *she's* looking out for me," Malajia ranted, waving her hand in Mark's face. "You out here showing these nasty hoes shit that *I* haven't even seen! You never showed *me* your goddamn aura and I'm your fuckin' *wife*!"

Mark was totally confused. "Woman…you trippin'," he said of Malajia.

"Oh, I'm trippin'?" Malajia challenged. "How about I go back on the dance floor and show them twenty-one-year-old dudes *my* aura? Would you like *that*?"

Mark stood up. "You ain't showing nobody *shit*," he threw back, pointing at her. "That's *my* damn aura."

Jason shook his head. "I can't believe that either of them have degrees," he commented in an aside to Chasity.

"Who you tellin'?" Chasity agreed, standing from her seat. "And we can't seem to get rid of them."

Jason snickered. "Awe shit, she's about to throw that dressing right at his face. It's time to go," he said. Jason walked over to Mark and gave him a pat on his shoulder. "Come on man, let's take a walk," he urged.

"I ain't even *do* nothin', Jase," Mark explained. "I was just eating wings."

"I know man." Jason was trying hard not to laugh. "Let's go."

As the guys left the bar, Chasity stood in front of Malajia, eyeing her sternly. Malajia put her hand on Chasity's cheek. "Thanks for telling me boo. You're my rock."

Chasity smacked her hand down. "Get your stupid ass off me," she barked. "Let's go."

Malajia sucked her teeth as Alex approached. "Alex, I'm about to be single like *your* ass. I'm divorcing Mark," Malajia said to her.

Alex held a blank stare. She then glanced at Chasity.

"Don't even ask," Chasity warned.

Alex looked back at Malajia. "Why?" she hesitantly asked.

"This bastard out here showing chicks his aura and shit," Malajia griped. "He got me fucked up."

Alex's face held the same blank stare. "Umm…" she looked back at Chasity.

Chasity pointed at her. "Don't look over here, I *told* you not to ask," she ground out, gripping Malajia's arm. "Come on crazy."

Alex let out a sigh as Chasity pulled the fuming Malajia along. "I'll go get Josh," Alex said, heading off in search of him.

Chapter 17

Sidra buttoned her jeans, then reached for her maroon and grey school sweatshirt. She couldn't remember the last time she'd worn her school shirt…if she ever had. Sweats were never really her thing.

Hearing her phone beep, she grabbed it from the bed. She read the text message and rolled her eyes. "I already told that girl that I'm not making no damn potato salad," she muttered. Sidra had barely gotten any sleep the night before. Following her spat with Josh, she'd retreated to her bed at the hotel room, but sleep just didn't happen.

She walked over to the mirror and began fussing with her hair. Hearing her phone ring, she loudly sucked her teeth. Snatching it up and putting it to her ear, she huffed. "You better not be calling me to ask me about that goddamn potato salad."

There was a pause on the line. "Umm, I *wasn't*," the stern female voice on the other end answered.

Sidra put her hand over her mouth in shock; she hadn't bothered to look at the caller ID. "Mama—I am *so* sorry," she sputtered, running a hand through her hair. "I thought you were Malajia."

Mrs. Howard chuckled; Sidra was relieved. "Malajia still loves potato salad, huh?"

"Yeah," Sidra replied, flopping on the bed.

"I won't keep you long, I just wanted to check in to see how things were going," Mrs. Howard said. "How's homecoming?"

Sidra sighed. "It was fine—"

"Was?" Mrs. Howard cut in. "What do you mean *was*?

What happened?"

Sidra shrugged slightly. "Josh and I got into this stupid thing last night," she alluded. "An argument."

"About what?"

Sidra rolled her eyes. She didn't even know why she'd brought it up; she had no desire to talk about it. "It was something stupid, and I kinda don't want to get into it right now."

Mrs. Howard sighed. "Well, okay if that's what you want."

"It is," Sidra assured. "I have to go to this tailgate. I'll call you later." Once her mother said her goodbye, Sidra ended the call. Hearing a knock at the door, she went and opened it.

"How you just gonna ignore my text?" Malajia charged.

"Girl, I'm not in the mood for...*you* right now," Sidra spat, folding her arms.

Malajia flagged her with her hand. "Whatever, I don't want your funky potato salad anyway," she spat. "You done been in California too damn long; you probably put raisins in it now and shit."

Sidra sucked her teeth. She grabbed her purse from a chaise lounge and headed out the door. "Let's just go."

"Wait," Malajia said, halting Sidra's progress. "You got any liquor in your room?"

"No, and you already knew that, let's go," Sidra huffed, closing the door behind her.

"I ain't liking your attitude right about now," Malajia ground out as they walked down the hallway.

"Well, get used to it because I'm cranky today," Sidra muttered.

"You know what I think we should do later? Just us girls?" Alex brought up to Emily, who was standing next to her.

"What's that?" Emily asked, opening a can of soda.

"We should have a girls' night in my hotel room," Alex beamed. "I can order a bunch of room service, get some wine and we can just relax and talk...like we used to when we all lived together."

Emily took a sip of her soda, pondering the suggestion.

"Will won't mind if we steal you away tonight, will he?" Alex chuckled. "I know since we've been here, we've taken up a lot of your time."

"Oh please, he's fine with it," Emily assured. "He's been working late anyway, and the less I see of Jazmine's lazy face, the better."

Alex decided not to press Emily on the issue of her freeloading sister; she wanted to keep the topic happy. The weather was perfect that Saturday morning for the tailgate; the clear skies allowed the sun to add a little warmth to the crisp autumn air. Students, faculty, and alumni congregated in the parking lot outside of the football stadium. The air was filled with the mouthwatering smell of Bar B Q food as people manned grills. Some elected just to eat concession stand food, while listening to the music blasting from the DJ table.

Alex put her arm around Emily. "Well, hopefully tonight will take your mind off of her," she said. "It's our last night here, and I just want to spend it with my girls."

"Sounds like a plan," Emily smiled, sipping her drink. "I'm in."

"Jase, I told you I got this," Mark said, flipping a burger on the grill.

Jason frowned as he tried to place some hot sausages on the grill. "I'm not gonna burn the goddamn things," he fussed. "This is a big ass grill—it's enough room for more than one person to man it."

Mark turned around and pointed his spatula in Jason's face. "Put the damn sausages down and step away from the grill," he slowly warned.

Jason frowned at Mark. He slowly turned his head towards Chasity, who was standing off to the side snickering. "You really find this funny?"

Chasity busted out laughing. "I do," she said.

Mark snatched the box of sausages from Jason when he wasn't looking. "Move, you slowing me down."

Annoyed, Jason smacked the spatula from Mark's hand. "Fuck you," he hissed. "With those flat ass burgers you brought."

Mark grabbed the spatula from the ground as Jason walked away. "That was petty bro," he spat. Tossing the utensil off to the side, he grabbed a pair of tongs. "And this box of burgers cost me eighteen bucks—y'all gonna *eat* these damn things."

Chasity held her arms out for Jason. "Aww, you're great at everything *else*," she teased, hugging him.

Jason couldn't help but chuckle. "Yeah, yeah," he said. "Bet he can't beat me in an *inside* cooking contest."

"Nah, you got his ass beat with that," Chasity said as they parted.

Jason busted out laughing.

"Malajia said that he burns rice every time he tries to make it," Chasity told.

Jason shook his head as Chasity reached for her phone. He watched as she studied the screen with a frown. "What's wrong?" he wondered. "Is Kayla okay?"

"She's fine, this isn't about her," Chasity answered, eyes still scrolling across the screen.

"Then what *is* it?" Chasity didn't answer. "Chasity," he called.

Chasity let out a sigh. "It's a text from my boss," she revealed.

Jason frowned. "I thought I told you not to check any work messages this weekend," he sternly said.

Chasity shot him a challenging look. "You act like I fuckin' *meant* to," she sniped. Jason ran a hand over his head. "She usually emails me, I didn't think she would *text* me. I thought it was my mom."

"Okay, okay sorry," Jason placated. It was clear that Chasity was upset, and him arguing with her wasn't going to make things any better. "Well…what is she saying?"

"Talking about pushing my project completion deadline up a week," Chasity fumed, clutching her phone tight in her hand. "That stupid bitch could've waited to piss me off when I got back to the office Monday."

Jason gently grabbed Chasity's hand and took the phone from her, shoving it into his pocket. "Yeah, she's a real piece of work," he agreed.

"If I could have five minutes with her ass outside that damn job, I would fuck her up," Chasity ranted.

"I know," Jason said, taking her hand. "Come on, let's go for a walk."

"I just walked *over* here," Chasity ground out.

"Please don't fight me on this," he urged, gently. He needed his wife to calm down, and her going for a walk usually did that.

Chasity rolled her eyes, letting out a frustrated sigh in the process. Not saying a word, she just gave a slight nod, allowing Jason to lead her away.

"Where y'all going?" Mark bellowed, spinning around as Jason and Chasity walked by him. He held a burger out in Chasity's direction. "Chaz, taste this burger to see if it's done all the way."

Chasity snapped her head towards him. "Get the fuck out of my face!" she snapped, making Mark flinch. The sound of Mark's voice was not what she wanted to hear at that moment.

Jason put his hand up as Mark's mouth fell open in shock. "Mark, not the time man," Jason warned, calm.

Mark just shook his head as they walked away. "She can still scare the shit outta people," he murmured.

Josh walked up carrying a box of sodas. "You *still* flipping those burgers?" he commented.

"Make me flip *yours* on the ground," Mark threw back.

Josh shook his head in amusement. Folding his arms, he leaned against a table. "Where's everybody else?"

Mark glanced at him. "You really care about everybody else, or are you asking about one person in particular?"

"Mark, don't start your shit today," Josh bit back. "It's our last day here, let's try to get through it without me punching you."

"Ha!" Mark bellowed. "Come on man, I'm grilling, don't make me laugh. I might spit on
these burgers."

Josh rolled his eyes. "Whatever," he mumbled.

David sent a message on his phone; Sidra and Malajia were hovering over him.

"Who you texting David?" Malajia wondered, flinging her hair over her shoulder.

David looked up from his phone. "Oh…just a friend of mine," he answered.

Sidra was curious. "*What* friend?"

"You don't know her," David assured.

"That doesn't mean that we don't want to know who she *is*," Malajia chimed in. "Stop acting like you don't know us."

David chuckled. "Right," he said, shoving the phone in his pocket. Sidra handed him back his can of soda. "My lab partner Keema. She's cool."

Sidra was intrigued. "Should we be meeting her?"

David chuckled. "No, she's not my girlfriend."

"David, stop lying," Malajia jumped in. "Just let us talk to her, we won't embarrass you…*that* much"

"Really ladies, there is no relationship between us," he assured. "I don't *want* another one right now *anyway*."

Sidra rubbed David's arm. "You still miss Nicole?"

David looked at her, nodding slightly. "Silly right?"

"Not at all," Sidra promised, sympathetic. "There is no law that says that you have to get over someone right away." *Or ever.*

David sighed. "I *thought* I was getting over her, but seeing her yesterday just brought up some old feelings."

Sidra looked off to the side. *I know how you feel, brother.*

David took a long sip of his drink.

Malajia folded her arms in a huff. "You know what, fuck that short bitch," she ground out.

David nearly choked on his soda. Sidra scowled at Malajia, shaking her head.

"Nah, she hurt my brother's feelings and I don't like that shit," Malajia continued to rant.

"In her defense, I didn't have time for her anymore, Malajia," David reasoned. "She deserves all the time in the world."

"I don't give—" Malajia stopped when she heard Mark call her name from a few feet away. "*Yes* Mark?" she huffed.

"Come over here and taste this rib," Mark said. "I wanna see if it's done."

Malajia looked over at him; he was holding up a sauce covered rib with tongs. She stared at him. "And if it's *not* done are you gonna put it the fuck back on the grill?" she spat. "Or better yet, take me to the damn hospital to be treated for food poisoning?"

Mark stared back at her, then smiled.

Malajia shook her head at him. Even when he annoyed her, Malajia still couldn't resist Mark's smile. "Boy put that damn rib down and fix me one of those burgers."

"Bet," Mark agreed, putting the rib in a pan. "You can eat this burger now and I'll give you the sausage later."

"Oh God, can you two stop being nasty for one day?" Sidra grunted.

Malajia busted out laughing. "Nope," she refused, walking away.

Sidra let out a huff. "I'm going to get some food, you want anything?" she asked David.

"No thanks," David answered.

Sidra made her way over to the pans of food laid out on a small table next to the grill. As she examined the meat, she glanced over at Mark, who was putting the finishing touches on Malajia's burger.

"Mark, did you have to put sauce on *everything*?" she wondered. "I mean, all the meat is drenched."

Mark stared at her for a moment. "And you will *eat* it," he demanded through clenched teeth.

Sidra put a hand up. "Fine Mark," he huffed. Arguing with Mark over something as petty as meat wasn't on Sidra's to do list, especially when she wasn't in the best of moods anyway. As she proceeded to make herself a hamburger, someone walked up beside her. Glancing up, her breath got caught in her throat; Josh was standing there. "Hey Josh," she spoke.

He looked at her. "Hey." His tone was dry. He turned away from her, grabbing a bag of rolls from the table.

It was silence, *awkward* silence. They'd barely said two words to each other since the night before. "Josh," she called.

Josh looked over at her.

"Umm… I'm sorry about last night," she said, setting her completed burger on a paper plate.

Josh pulled a burger roll from the bag, blinking slowly. "Okay," he replied. "Me too."

Sidra stared at him. His words seemed empty. "I just don't want things to be awkward," she continued. "It's our last night and I want—"

"Not awkward, it's fine," Josh cut in.

Sidra frowned. She knew that tone; he was brushing her off. "Josh—" she hesitated for a moment as he prepared his food. "Do you think we could go somewhere and talk?"

Josh let out a quick sigh. "Sidra, not now, okay," he sneered. "I'm just trying to enjoy myself."

Sidra frowned. "So, you're *okay* with us leaving here with this animosity between us?" she scoffed. "Knowing that this could be the last time we see each other for a while?"

"Wouldn't be anything new," Josh grunted.

Sidra was taken aback. "Are you ser—"

"Josh?" a female voice interrupted.

Sidra frowned as she and Josh turned in the direction of the voice. They were both shocked to see December Harley approaching.

You've got to be kidding me, Sidra thought.

"Is that you?" December smiled as Josh stared at her.

"Yeah…it's me," Josh replied, setting his food back on the table. He smiled back. "Hi."

"Hi," December returned. "Long time no see. How have you been?"

"Yeah, it has… I've been good," he answered.

Sidra stood there seething. She didn't know what was more annoying, the fact that December was there in the first place, or the fact that both of them were acting like *she* was invisible. She cleared her throat, halting the catch-up session.

December glanced over. "Hello Sidra."

Sidra resisted the urge to roll her eyes at December's flat tone; she narrowed them a bit instead. "Hello December."

December gave a nod, turning her sights back on Josh. "I'm sorry, was I interrupting something?" she asked.

"No, you weren't," Josh answered, much too quickly for Sidra's liking.

Sidra glanced over at him, yet he paid her no mind. Appetite gone, Sidra left her food on the table and walked away.

December followed Sidra's progress for a moment. "Are you sure I wasn't interrupting something?" she asked.

"No, we were just getting something to eat," he promised. "Do you want something?"

December chuckled a bit. "Yes…a hug."

Josh looked skeptical. "Seriously?"

December shrugged. "I mean, yeah," she answered. "I know it's been a while and we didn't exactly leave off on good terms, but…I'll admit it, I'm happy to see you."

Josh smiled and gave December her requested hug.

"Feel better now?" Jason asked Chasity as they ambled along a path through campus.

"Not better, calmer," Chasity replied, pushing hair over her shoulders. It was the truth. The twenty-minute walk did in fact calm her down a bit. However, she was still agitated.

"Well, I'll take that," he said, glancing at her. "Let's just try to enjoy our last night."

"I will," she promised, walking. "I didn't mean to snap at you."

"I know that," Jason assured, putting his arm around her. "I just hate to see you stressed."

"I know," she returned. Chasity looked around as her stride continued. "I don't remember how many walks I took around this campus whenever something pissed me off."

Jason chuckled. "I wouldn't even try to figure that number out," he joked.

She chuckled a bit. "I remember taking about *five* of them the first day I got here freshman year."

"Yeah, I remember how *tense* you were then," Jason recalled, amusement in his voice.

"Is that your way of saying that I was evil?"

"Yes," he joked.

Chasity giggled. "Yeah well... I had a lot going on."

As they walked a bit more, letting the breeze blow past them, Jason relished this moment alone. Aside from being in their hotel room, they hadn't gotten much of it since coming back to campus.

Passing by the gates across from the practice field, Jason stopped. "Chaz," he called.

She stopped walking and faced him. "Yeah?"

"Does this look familiar?" he asked her, gesturing to the gate.

Chasity glanced over, looking perplexed. "The gate?"

"No, the *spot*," he clarified.

Chasity scratched her head. "Umm, every inch of this *campus* looks familiar," she said.

Jason pointed to the spot across the field. "I was standing right over there, when I first saw you," he said.

Chasity looked to where he was pointing, then smiled. "Oh yeah, that's right," she recalled.

"I was practicing football when I saw you walking pass," he reminisced. "Then you stopped."

"And you were staring at me...like a stalker," she teased.

Jason laughed. "Yeah well, I hadn't seen a woman as beautiful as you before, I was mesmerized to say the least," he defended. She stood there smiling. "*You* stared at *me too*."

"Only because *you* were," Chasity laughed.

Jason shot her a knowing look. "Babe, we're married with a child. You can stop lying to yourself now."

"Yeah, I guess you're right," she chuckled. "I thought that you were cute."

"Just *cute*, huh?" He smiled.

"No, I thought you were *more* than that, but your cockiness outshined your looks," she teased.

Jason put his hand over his face and laughed. "Gonna throw that up in my face, huh?"

"Oh absolutely," she flashed back, folding her arms.

Jason put his hand up in surrender. "Okay, you're right."

"But I *will* say that you changed that very quickly," she smiled, touching his arm.

"Not quick enough for my nuts," he joked.

Chasity busted out laughing.

Jason shook his head in amusement. It was nice reminiscing about their first encounters. It made him appreciate how far they'd come as a couple. His smile faded after a moment. "Can I ask you something?"

"Sure," she replied.

"Do you have any regrets?" he asked.

Chasity was taken aback by his question. "Regrets about *what* Jason?"

"I mean with us? Being with me?"

Chasity didn't understand where this was coming from. "Why would you ask me that?" she wondered. "Do *you*?"

"Not one," he confirmed. "I knew what I wanted the moment I saw you. Even through our rough times, I never once regretted being with you… You and Kayla are my everything. Always *will* be."

Chasity stared at him.

"I just wonder if…you ever felt like you missed out by marrying the first man you ever…well did *everything* with."

Chasity took a step forward, standing close to him. "No, I don't," she assured.

"You sure?" he questioned. "I mean, some people would say that you miss out when you—"

"*Some* people spend years of their lives looking for that one that is meant for them," she cut in. "I was lucky enough to find *my* one at eighteen years old, standing on the other side of this gate."

Jason smiled at her, adoration in his eyes for the woman who had stolen his heart in their first semester of college. "I love you."

"Love you too," she returned, touching his face.

He leaned in closer, planting a kiss on her lips. "You wanna ditch the game and go back to the hotel?" her husband crooned.

Chasity chuckled. "Yes, but we're not *going* to," she said. "Keep it in your pants until later."

"Fine," Jason relented, putting his arms around her to pull her into a hug.

Parting, she grabbed his hand. "I feel better now, let's get back," she smiled.

Jason squeezed her hand as they started walking the way they'd came.

Chapter 18

"Yo, if we lose this game I'm giving my degree back," Mark grunted, taking a sip of his soda.

"Boy, shut up," Malajia ground out, adjusting herself in her seat. She grabbed his soda from his hand and took a sip.

Mark shot her a side-glance. "You just gonna take mine after you sat here and drank all *yours*, huh?"

"Yup," she threw back without a qualm.

Tailgate over, the crowd had gathered to the football field in anticipation of the big game. Luckily, the group was able to get seats close to one another. Just like old times.

Mark glanced in the row behind him, looking at Emily who was scarfing down a hot dog. "Em, you get that from the concession stand?" he asked.

Emily swallowed her food. "Yes."

"What for?" he barked. "After all those hot dogs I grilled earlier?"

Emily looked at him wide-eyed. "They were burnt," she carefully replied.

Jason, who was sitting a few seats over, busted out laughing. Mark regarded him with a salty look. "*Now* what jokes do you have?" Jason taunted.

"That was Alex's damn fault," Mark blamed. He pointed to Alex, who was sitting beside Emily.

"Wait, *how* is that my fault?!" Alex exclaimed.

"You kept coming over to the damn grill asking for ribs and shit," Mark fussed. "Distracting me."

Alex looked dumbfounded. "The hotdogs weren't even on the *grill* when I was asking about the ribs," she threw back. "You're always lying."

Not having anything else to say, Mark turned around in his seat with a huff. He looked at Malajia, who was busy sipping his drink. "Babe—"

"Mark, I love you, but I'm not defending those charred ass dogs," Malajia immediately cut in. "You got too damn hype after clowning Jason and you fucked up."

Mark stared at her, eyes narrowed. "Gimme my goddamn drink back," he spat, teeth clenched as he snatched the cup from her.

Malajia nearly spat out what was in her mouth from laughter.

"Em, would you mind going to the store with me after the game?" Alex asked, pushing some of her hair out of her face. "I wanted to grab a few snacks for our girls' night."

"Sure," Emily agreed.

"Thanks," Alex smiled, adjusting herself in her seat.

As she concentrated on the game starting on the field, some guy near her spoke. "So how much do you think we'll win by?" the voice asked.

Alex shrugged, not looking up at first. "I don't even care as long as we—" she glanced up and the rest of her words were caught in her throat.

"I think the word that you meant to say was 'win'," he chortled.

Alex stared, her mouth falling open, still speechless.

"Hi Alex."

"Hi Eric," Alex finally replied. She couldn't believe that it was really him. Eric Wendell, the first man that she'd had feelings for after Paul. The man who she'd had a casual sexual relationship with during her junior year. The man who had rejected her when she finally asked to be exclusive, telling her to find herself instead.

Hearing the name Eric, some of the group turned around. "Aye, what's up Eric?" Mark beamed, extending his hand.

Eric shook it. "What's going on man? ...Hey everybody." Eric hadn't seen Alex's friends since before they'd graduated. He always found them to be a fun bunch.

Alex tried to keep her composure as the group exchanged pleasantries. Eric was just as handsome as she'd remembered.

"Hey FB," Chasity teased, earning a nudge from Jason. Chasity snickered. "Sorry, couldn't help it."

Alex wasn't amused, "How about I smack you? Would that make you 'help it'?" she fumed.

Chasity smirked. "Yeah okay."

Alex shook her head, then looked back up at Eric. "Umm, you want to sit?"

"I *would*, but there doesn't seem to be much room—"

"You can have my seat," Emily offered, standing up.

Alex shot her a grateful look.

"Thank you Emily," Eric said. "But are you sure?"

"Positive," Emily assured, stepping down to the next row. "Malajia, can you scoot over some?"

"Nah, you ain't getting in this row. You ain't eat my hotdogs," Mark jeered, as Malajia went to move over.

"If you don't move over, you can't take Will to a strip club for his bachelor party," Emily said, folding her arms.

Mark sucked his teeth. "We'll go *without* him," he mumbled.

"No the fuck you *won't*, now shut up and move your ass down," Malajia huffed, nudging him with her arm.

Not saying another word, Mark complied. Emily sat down next to him and smiled. "Thank you."

"Yeah yeah," Mark grunted. "You ain't have to threaten our good time."

Emily laughed.

Alex shifted in her seat as Eric sat next to her. "So…it's been a while," she began, looking at him.

"I know," he agreed. "You look great."

Alex blushed. "Thank you. So do you."

"Ahh, you're just saying that," he joked.

Alex giggled. "I'm serious…" as she went to say something else, the crowd began cheering. She glanced at the field.

"Touchdown baby!" Mark bellowed, reaching over to give a proud Jason a high five.

Alex cheered, then turned her attention back to Eric, who was still clapping.

"Man, I miss these games," he said.

"Yeah…I miss them too," Alex agreed. *Among other*

things, she thought.

Eric looked at her, "I know it's crazy loud right now."

"Yeah, not exactly a great time or place to play catch up," she agreed. "Do you umm...do you wanna call me later?" She ran a hand along the back of her neck. "I can give you my new number."

"I wish you had done that when you first changed it," Eric said.

"I know...I'm sorry, I *meant* to but when I switched phones, I lost a lot of my contacts," Alex revealed, apologetic. "Trust me, I wish I hadn't."

Eric nodded. "No harm done, just three years of not hearing from you," he chuckled. "But to answer your question, yes I'd love to have your new number."

Without hesitation, Alex retrieved her phone from the pocket of her sweat jacket. After giving her number to Eric and saving his, she held the phone in her hand. "Umm do you want to talk for a little bit after the game?" she asked, hopeful. "I'm hanging with my girls after, but that won't be till later."

"I wish I *could* but I'm leaving after the game to head back home," Eric replied. Alex didn't hide her disappointment. "I have to work tomorrow."

"On a *Sunday*?" she questioned.

Eric shrugged. "Projects don't have a nine to five schedule," he chortled.

Alex too shrugged. "True." She knew all too well how work could spill over into the weekend. Deciding not to try to talk over the noise any longer, Alex turned back around to focus on the game.

Alex poured some red wine into a glass and took a sip. "Ooh, this is good," she nodded in approval, taking a seat on her bed.

"It's a'ight," Malajia downplayed, picking up a cluster of cheese fries from a plate. "Stop showing off 'cause you paid more than eight dollars for it," she teased.

Alex made a face at Malajia as she took another sip. Malajia giggled, devouring her food.

Emily picked up a cupcake from a tray and peeled the paper back. "You went all out with the food Alex," she mused.

It was later that evening, and Alex had made good on her promise to hold a girls' night in her hotel room. She'd ordered dinner for them via room service. The desserts, snacks and wine, she had picked up after the game.

"Well, I know we always get hungry when we have girl talk, so I figured I'd stock up," Alex reasoned, adjusting her position on her bed.

Chasity looked up from examining her nails, perplexed. "No, we don't," she contradicted.

Alex thought for a moment. "Maybe that's just me," she giggled. She glanced over at Sidra; she was sitting on a chair, holding a pillow to her chest, glancing out the window. "You okay Sid?"

Sidra looked over, snapped out of a daze. "Yeah, I'm fine,' she said, tone unconvincing.

"You sure?" Alex pressed. "You disappeared after the tailgate."

Sidra let out a sigh. After the tense exchange with Josh, paired with December popping up, Sidra's anxiety was on high. So much so that she'd decided to skip the game and head back to her hotel room. If it wasn't for Alex calling to tell her about girls' night, she would've stayed in her room the rest of the evening. "Yes, I'm fine," Sidra repeated, this time forcing a smile. "I was just tired."

"Okay," Alex relented, taking another sip of wine. After a moment, she looked around at her friends, who were busy eating. "So, let's get to it," Alex began.

"Get to what?" Malajia asked, looking up from her plate.

"*Talking*," Alex answered. "I mean, I know that we talk on the phone but there's nothing like catching up in person, you know?"

"True," Emily agreed, eating her cupcake.

"Emily, are you sure that you don't want us to do anything wedding related?" Sidra asked. Crafts and lists would be a perfect distraction as far as Sidra was concerned.

"Nope, I have it all under control," Emily said. "I already started some of the favors and stuff."

"By yourself?" Sidra charged. Emily nodded proudly. "Em, you shouldn't be doing *any* of that, that's what *we're* for."

"Sidra come up off it," Chasity cut in, reaching for her drink. "The girl *likes* doing stuff like that. Not everybody has to follow your bridal rules."

Sidra rolled her eyes. "Clearly *you* didn't when I said that black wasn't a wedding color," she snarled.

"Why do y'all keep saying the damn dresses were black? They were *eggplant*," Chasity stressed, annoyed.

"They were *dark*," Sidra maintained.

"*And*? You fuckin' wore it *didn't* you?" Chasity threw back.

"I *did*, and it was absolutely beautiful," Sidra quickly returned, smiling.

Chasity chuckled. "Uh huh."

Emily put her hand up. "Okay, okay. Let's not argue over something that we shouldn't even be *talking* about right now," she chimed in.

"You're right Em," Sidra agreed, standing from her seat. "Are there any brownies on that dessert tray over there?"

Alex pointed to said tray. "Yup, have at it," she smiled. Sidra grabbed a brownie and took a bite, flopping down on Alex's bed; Alex glanced around the room. "Today's game was awesome," she began. "The first time being back to this place in five years, and Paradise Valley kicks Prime State's ass."

"Chasity, Jason jumped out of his seat like five times," Malajia laughed. "He was cussing the refs out."

Chasity shook her head. "You should see him when he's watching the damn games at *home*," she said.

Emily grabbed a nacho from a nearby plate. "Does he miss playing football?" she asked Chasity.

"He still plays," Chasity replied, twirling hair around her finger.

Sidra looked surprised. "Really?"

"Not *professional* of course, but he plays with Mark and Josh from time to time," Chasity clarified.

Malajia sucked her teeth. "No, he just plays with *Josh*," she jeered. "Mark gets sent to the bench, 'cause he can't catch for shit." She shook her head when the girls busted out laughing. "I don't get it. My man is *great* at basketball, but when it comes to any *other* sport…"

"You remember how much he lost all those other games we played back in college," Alex teased, sipping her wine. "Always challenging us to something then lost."

"I can't even argue with that," Malajia laughed, eating more cheese fries. "Alex, I'm surprised you actually *noticed* that the team won."

"What do you mean?" Alex wondered.

"Girl please, you were all up on Eric the entire game," Chasity chimed in. "Looking all horny and shit."

Alex nearly spat out her wine. "He's *still* fine, girl," she crooned, fanning herself.

"Is he going to call you?" Sidra asked.

"I don't care whether he is or isn't, *I'm* calling *him* as soon as I get back home," Alex promised. "That's crazy, I didn't expect to see him. Hell, I didn't expect to run into *Paul* a few days ago either."

Sidra turned her lip up. "Ugh, what the hell is *he* doing with his life?" she scoffed.

Alex shrugged. "He was talking about—"

"Next," Chasity cut in, rolling her eyes.

"Yeah, we don't care nothing about him," Malajia chortled.

Alex busted out laughing. "That's fine with me, 'cause neither do *I*."

Sidra brought her legs up on the bed. "I *do* have to ask you though," she directed at Alex. "Do you really not feel anything for him anymore? …Paul, I mean."

"Not a thing," Alex confirmed, shaking her head. "I am completely over Paul and everything that he did."

"So, you *can* get over someone you used to sleep with," Sidra pondered.

Malajia stared at Sidra. "Umm, Sid, you got something you want to share sis?" she asked. "Have you gotten some from one of those bougie dudes named Biff?"

Sidra looked confused. "Biff?"

"I don't even know where that name came from. It was corny and I am asking you to forget that I said it," Malajia quickly threw out.

Sidra just shook her head. "Anyway, no I haven't slept with *anybody*," she assured. "I was just thinking out loud."

"*Still* holding on to that virginity, huh?" Malajia teased.

Sidra made a face at her. "Yes."

"Malajia, come on," Emily chided.

"I'm just messing with her," Malajia assured, waving her hand. "She know I love her dry ass."

"I'm *far* from dry, okay," Sidra spat out. "And can we not talk about my lady parts or the lack of action that they've gotten?"

"Still can't say vagina, huh?" Malajia teased, earning a pillow thrown at her by Sidra.

"Sid, you knocked over my fries," Malajia barked, picking up the fallen fries. "This hotel is gonna charge Alex an arm and two legs to get that cheese up."

Alex jerked her head in Malajia's direction. "Oh no they're *not* because you're gonna clean that mess up," she demanded.

"No, *Sidra*'s gonna clean this mess up," Malajia threw back, tossing her food in the trash. "You wait on *me* and you won't get that hundred dollars a night holding fee back." She held her hand out. "Now hand me another glass of that nasty wine."

"Pour it your*self*," Alex sneered, flagging Malajia with her hand.

Emily fiddled with her hands. "Okay since we're on the topic of umm...sex," she began. "I want to ask you something."

The girls looked at her in anticipation. "Don't tell me Will is into that freaky bondage stuff," Malajia charged. "He likes to tie you up and smack you in the face with a wet noodle while shoving gummi bears up your ass?"

Alex and Emily eyed Malajia with confusion. Chasity was more annoyed than confused. "What in the entire *fuck*?" Chasity drew out.

Sidra was disgusted. "Malajia—I can't." She threw her hands up in surrender.

Malajia looked around, shocked by the responses. "What? I was *asking*?"

"What kind of shit do *you* do, to even *concoct* some bullshit like that?" Chasity snapped.

Malajia smiled. "Well—"

Alex put her hand up. "No! God, please don't answer that, I don't even want to know," she protested. "You and Mark are on some *other* stuff."

Malajia chuckled, then looked at Emily. "Well Em? *Does* he?" she pressed.

"*No,*" Emily answered, disgusted. She quickly shook her head. "Anyway so…you know that Will and I are waiting until we get married to have sex—"

"You have no idea how much I commend you for it," Malajia chuckled. "To be all up under that fine ass man and not get any… Hell, even held off *living* with him."

"I know," Emily agreed. "I mean, even before we started dating I'd think about it… I fantasized about doing it but as time went on, I just realized that waiting until marriage was something that I wanted to do, but…" she let out a quick sigh. "Do you think it's *weird* for me to have him wait when I'm not a virgin?"

"Absolutely *not,*" Alex charged. "Virgin or *not,* you have that right. And like Malajia said, it's commendable."

Sidra tilted her head. "Em, did he say something?" she asked. "Is it an issue for him?"

Emily put a hand up. "Oh no nothing like that," she stressed. "No, Will is…he's great. He completely understands and is perfectly fine with waiting… I guess *I'm* just questioning my decision because like I said, I'm not a virgin."

"So what?" Chasity said. "People decide to be born again virgins more often than you think."

"Facts," Malajia confirmed, nodding.

Emily let out a sigh. "Yeah well, in all honesty, I wish I didn't have to be a *born again* one," she vented. "If I wasn't so stupid when I was younger, I would've been an *actual* one."

Alex, who was sitting close to Emily, put her hand on her shoulder to comfort her. She didn't realize that Emily was harboring this guilt for a mistake that she'd made when she was fifteen years old.

"Speaking from experience of a first-time mistake…you can't hold on to that sweetie, because you can't change what happened," Malajia chimed in.

Emily ran a hand through her hair. "Yeah, I know," she said. "Still doesn't stop me from thinking about it though."

"Have you told Will how you feel?" Alex asked.

Emily nodded. "Yes," she confirmed. "He pretty much said what *you* girls are saying… I guess, I just needed to hear it from you too."

Alex rubbed Emily's shoulder. "Em it's great that you have someone who is so understanding," she gushed.

"Hell, he came into the relationship with a whole *child*, he *better* be understanding," Malajia commented.

Emily couldn't help but chuckle.

Alex sipped more of her wine as she looked on with pride. Her girls' night was a success so far. Between eating, sipping wine, talking, and playing games for the past three hours, it felt like old times back on campus.

Sidra looked at her watch, and Alex took notice. "Ready to go already?" she chuckled.

Sidra glanced up; she shook her head, but didn't say anything. It was a lie, she was ready to go. She was tired and felt that her bad mood would surface. She thought she'd done a good job of concealing it throughout the evening, but Sidra didn't know how much longer that would last.

"We should try to get together and do this more often," Alex suggested. "We really shouldn't go this long again without all of us getting together."

"I agree with you Alex, but it's hard you know," Sidra said, tone dry.

"Hard for *you*," Malajia chortled.

Sidra shot her a glare, but Malajia didn't catch it.

"Are all the desserts gone?" Malajia asked Alex.

"Yes, greedy," Alex sighed.

Malajia scrunched her face up. "Well, call room service and get some *more*," she demanded. "Put that credit card to work, Ms. Editor."

Alex rolled her eyes. "Girl, hush up," she dismissed.

Emily stretched, then glanced at her watch. "It *is* getting late," she observed. "I should probably get going."

"Aww, you're not gonna spend the night?" Alex pouted.

"I didn't know it was supposed to be an overnight thing," Emily said.

"Well, I mean—"

"I'm not spending the night in here with you," Chasity scoffed at Alex, interrupting her.

"I know right. That nasty ass wine I've been drinking is about to make me horny, so I doubt y'all are gonna wanna be in the room with me much longer," Malajia joked.

Emily snickered, while the other girls either muttered something under their breaths or rolled their eyes.

"Gross Malajia," Alex condemned. "Anyway, I know we all need to get back to our lives, but how about we make an agreement that for Thanksgiving, we try getting together," she proposed.

"I'm cool with that," Malajia shrugged. "It'll be like we did back in school."

"Right," Alex beamed, "I figure since we'll all be back on the East Coast, or close to it during that time, it'll be perfect."

"I'll try," Emily said. "With me and my mother not speaking at the moment, I don't know if I'll be in Jersey or *here* for the holiday."

"Understandable Em, at least you're considering it," Alex smiled.

Emily offered a smile in return and gave a nod.

Alex looked at Chasity, who was rubbing her eyes. "You tired too, huh?" she asked.

"Yup," Chasity answered.

"You in for getting together then too? Maybe that Friday?" Alex pressed.

"Yup," Chasity repeated.

"Cool," Alex replied, then looked at Sidra, who seemed to be staring off into space. "Sid, you're still going to be in Delaware for Thanksgiving, right?"

Sidra looked over at Alex, tired. "I don't think so," she answered, even toned.

Malajia looked at her, confused. "What do you mean?"

"That I don't think I'm coming back for Thanksgiving,'" Sidra ground out.

"Why *not*?" Malajia pressed. "You said you were going home this year."

"Well now I'm *not*," Sidra threw back, annoyed.

Malajia jerked her head back. "First off, *eww*," she commented of both Sidra's reply and her nasty tone.

Sidra narrowed her eyes at Malajia.

"*Second*, why did you change your mind?" Malajia harped.

Sidra ran a hand through her hair. "Malajia, I really don't have to explain my decisions to you," she sniped.

Malajia frowned. "What is your problem Sidra?" she hurled. "You trippin'."

"My *problem* is that I don't understand what the big deal is," Sidra fussed. "I'm *entitled* to change my mind about things, including not wanting to go back to *Delaware* if I don't *want* to."

"Nobody said that you *weren't*," Malajia threw back. "But, *I'm* entitled to *my* opinion about you changing your mind, and my *opinion* is that you *trippin'*."

"Whatever," Sidra spat.

Alex put a hand up. "Okay, let's not argue," she calmly put in.

"It's no argument," Sidra said, flustered. "I just wonder why *I'm* always getting cussed out about not visiting."

"Girl, nobody cussed at you," Malajia grunted. "Stop being dramatic."

"I'm not *being* dramatic," Sidra argued. "It's always 'Sidra, why won't you come visit?', 'Sidra, when are you coming down?'— It's like everybody always wants *me* to get on a plane for them."

"No Sidra don't do that," Chasity cut in, putting her hand up. "That's not even true, I don't ask you to visit because I *know* that's far to travel. I grew up in Arizona, I *get* it."

"Chasity, *you've* asked me," Sidra threw back.

Chasity looked confused. "I asked you *twice* in *five years* to fly down," she said. "Once was when I had Kayla, and second was my damn wedding."

"Right, nobody expects you to come home every five minutes," Malajia added. "So cut that shit out."

"Really? I can't tell," Sidra huffed, folding her arms.

"Ladies," Alex clapped her hands to grab their attention. "I mean it, we're not doing this. We had a good night."

Sidra didn't know if the conversation was as big a deal as she was making it, but in that moment, she was fuming. "No, I'm tired of this. When was the last time any of you came to visit *me*?" Sidra charged, pointing at each girl.

Emily looked shocked, pointing to herself. "Huh? I didn't even say anything," she said. "Why am I getting dragged in?"

"Sweetie, I'd love to come out there," Alex placated. "The other girls and I were just talking about taking a vacation out there to see you."

"Was anybody gonna fill *me* in on that conversation?" Sidra sneered. "Y'all always seem to make plans that don't include me."

"Sidra, what is the point of making plans with you if you're not planning on being a *part* of them?" Malajia jumped in. "Hell, I had to damn near cuss your ass out to get you to come to *homecoming*."

"I figured I might as *well* come, I was tired of hearing you whine about it," Sidra snarled to Malajia.

"Yeah a'ight," Malajia dismissed, waving her hand.

Alex rose to her feet, holding her hands up. "Okay listen. Sid, we're sorry if you feel left out sweetie," she said, trying to diffuse the tension. "I admit that I need to do a better job of spending time with *all* of you."

Chasity let out a huff. She wasn't in the mood for arguing, or Sidra's unwarranted pity party. She stood up.

"Uh uh bitch, where are you going?" Malajia charged.

"This night has turned into some bullshit, I'm over it," Chasity huffed.

Sidra glared at Chasity. "What's *bullshit* exactly?" she questioned.

"Your whining," Chasity threw back.

"I'm not *whining*, I'm just expressing my disappointment in how I've been treated ever since I moved away," Sidra argued. "Is it too much for *Satan* to understand that?"

Chasity narrowed her eyes at Sidra. She thought about responding, but the headache forming in the back of her head meant that she should table this argument for another time.

"And on that note, I'm leaving."

"Chasity just sit back down," Malajia ordered.

"Nope, good night," Chasity threw over her shoulder, heading for the door.

Sidra smirked. "Just like old times, Chasity's running away when the conversation gets rough."

Chasity spun around; she'd had enough of this. "Oh bitch I *know* you're not talking about nobody *running*," she threw back.

Malajia's eyes widened as she hopped up from her seat. "Uh okay, sis, you might be right, we need to go," she said to Chasity, grabbing her arm.

"What exactly are you trying to say, Chasity?" Sidra frowned.

"She's not trying to say anything," Malajia nervously cut in as Chasity went to speak. Malajia nudged Chasity to the door. "Let's go."

Sidra jumped up from the bed. "Malajia, the girl has an ignorant ass mouth of her *own*, she can answer," she challenged.

Chasity moved the pleading Malajia behind her. "Nah, she's right, I can answer," she snarled.

"God," Malajia muttered, turning away.

"*First* of all, I'm not running anywhere," Chasity fumed, pointing at Sidra. "I am voluntarily removing myself from a situation that might result in me punching you in the goddamn face."

"Very mature," Sidra snarled, folding her arms.

"Yeah? So is carrying your ass halfway across the United States just to avoid *one* person," Chasity hurled. "No, that's *stupid*. My fault."

Sidra's mouth fell open in shock. "*Excuse* me?!"

Shit! Malajia thought. She jumped in front of Chasity and put her arms out. "Whoa, whoa, whoa…whoa…whoa." She turned to Chasity. "You got anymore liquor in your room? Mark and I drank all ours."

Chasity glared at her. "No bitch!" she snapped; Malajia flinched.

"Malajia, shut up," Sidra fumed. "I want to know what the

hell Chasity is talking about."

"Girl stop," Chasity spat. "You know *exactly* what I'm talking about."

"Damn it, Chasity," Malajia muttered, pinching the bridge of her nose.

Sidra was still confused as to what Chasity *thought* she knew. "I have no idea—"

"Sidra, she *knows* okay," Malajia cut in, aggravated. "I told her."

"Wait, what's going on?" Alex asked. Emily, who had stood from her seat, was just as confused as she was.

Sidra looked at Malajia with shock. "You *what*?" she fumed. "You promised me that you wouldn't say anything to anybody."

"Look, you should've known that to be a lie. I told everybody's business back in school," Malajia threw back in a sad attempt to defend her betrayal.

"*Malajia*!" Sidra exclaimed.

"Sidra, I'm sorry. I only told Chasity. I can't *not* tell her shit," Malajia explained, poking Chasity's arm and glaring at her in the process. "You were supposed to keep that a damn secret."

"Oh fuck you, she pushed me," Chasity sneered, folding her arms.

"Hold up, what is going *on*?" Alex put in. "Sidra, what are they talking about?"

Sidra looked like she wanted to cry; Malajia and Chasity stood there silent. Eventually, Malajia tossed her arms in the air. "Fuck it, I might as well finish the job," she said, letting out a huff. "Sidra didn't move to California because of that law school," she revealed.

"What?" Emily charged, shooting a perplexed look Sidra's way.

"Sid, you told us that was why you were going," Alex added. "Why would you lie?"

Sidra didn't respond; she just stood there.

"She used that as an excuse," Malajia continued. "The truth was, she moved to get away from Josh…because she's in love with him and she couldn't tell him."

"Whoa!" Emily exclaimed, putting her hands on her head. *"Seriously?"*

"Sidra—what?" Alex followed up, just as shocked. "Malajia, are you lying again?"

Chasity shook her head, confirming.

"What do you mean *again*?" Malajia asked Alex, offended. She pointed to Sidra; her face was streaked with tears. "Look at her face Alex... Does it *look* like that's a lie?"

"Oh...my...God," Alex slowly drew out, running a hand over her hair. "So— Hold up, When— Did you realize that when he told you—"

"How could you do this to me Malajia?" Sidra sniffled. "You betrayed me."

"Sid, I'm sorry, I really am," Malajia apologized. "But you know what, it needed to get out. You're *miserable* because you're too scared to face him. You're cutting yourself off from *all* of us, because you're afraid that you might hear from one of us about him dating someone. You're dating guys who you *know* aren't good enough for you, because the one guy who *is* good for you, doesn't know how you *feel*."

Sidra couldn't focus on the truth that Malajia was speaking. She was too angry, too embarrassed. Without saying another word, Sidra grabbed her purse and stormed out of the room, slamming the door behind her.

Everything fell silent for a few moments as the other girls tried to wrap their heads around what had just happened.

"Nice girls' night Alex," Malajia muttered.

"Wait, what?!" Alex exclaimed.

Chapter 19

Jason walked into his office with his cell phone in one hand and a folder in another, trying to referee another family spat. "Kyle, I already told you to stop pissing Mom off," he said into the line, heading over to his desk. "Well, you sitting around all day is what's pissing her off... You better get your ass out that house..." Jason tossed the folder on his desk as he sat down. "Look, I have to go, I'll talk to you when I get back in town in a few days... Later."

Ending the call, Jason set his phone on his desk and began typing on his laptop. He'd been back in Phoenix for four days, and was trying to finish up some work before lunch. Glancing over at a picture of his wife and daughter that he had sitting on his desk, he smiled, then sighed... He missed them.

A knock on the door made him look up.

"Jason, how's it going?" Patrick asked, walking in the office.

"Things are good," Jason replied, adjusting himself in his seat. Why his boss had decided to do a pop up at the Phoenix office was beyond him.

Patrick walked over to Jason's desk, smiling. "I was just checking in with the team and they are doing great," he beamed, "You're doing a great job managing them."

Yeah, that would mean something if I was a manager, Jason thought, annoyed. Nevertheless, he contained his true feelings and just nodded. "Thank you," he said. "They picked up really fast and are nearly finished the implementation process...should have the software up and running in a few days."

"Excellent," Patrick raved. "We'll be acquiring some new projects soon and this team will be handling a lot of them."

Jason stared at him. "Oh okay," he replied, going back to typing.

"Hey, have you had lunch yet?"

Jason looked up at him again. "Not yet," he answered. "I plan on going after I finish up."

Patrick waved his hand. "Ah, that can wait. Why don't we head out now?" he proposed.

God, just get the fuck out! Jason once again concealed his annoyance. "Uh…" The last thing Jason felt like doing was sitting through lunch with his boss. He just wanted to finish what he was doing so that he could leave the office on time. Nevertheless, he relented. "Okay," he agreed, standing up.

"Phoenix is a great city and still growing," Patrick gushed, eyeing the scenery out of the car window.

Jason rubbed his eyes as he clutched his bag of leftovers in his hand. Having grabbed lunch at a restaurant that his boss suggested, they were now on their way back to the office. "Yeah, it's nice," he agreed.

"It's a great place to raise a family too," Patrick said.

Jason looked confused. "Do you have a family that nobody knows about?" he joked, knowing Patrick's bachelor status.

Patrick belted out a laugh; Jason looked perplexed. His laugh was loud and obnoxious…and unnecessary.

It was not that funny, Jason thought.

"Nope, not at all," Patrick laughed. "Not exactly ready to settle down yet."

"Uh huh," Jason muttered.

As the driver turned a corner, passing a residential area, Patrick scanned the area with his eyes. "These are some nice houses, don't you think?" he asked.

Jason peered out the window at the two-story single homes on the palm tree lined street. "Yeah, they're *really* nice," he agreed. "You can see the mountains from here…hell you can see them no matter *where* you are."

Patrick nodded. "Yeah. There are plenty of neighborhoods with nice homes in this area," he mentioned. He looked at Jason. "You said your wife grew up here, right?"

"Tucson," Jason clarified, raising an eyebrow at him. Why he was bringing up Chasity was beyond him. "Why?"

"Just asking," Patrick deflected.

"Why?" Jason pressed.

"Making conversation," Patrick insisted. "Anyway, I know that I said this before, but you're doing a great job. You've gotten everything up and running smoothly out here and we all appreciate it, trust me."

"Sure," Jason replied, even toned. As the ride continued, Jason sat in silence. As far as he was concerned, the praise meant nothing.

Chasity typed away on her laptop, eyes fixed on the screen. Pamela walked up and stood right by her desk, something that always irritated Chasity.

Chasity halted her typing and let out a sigh. "Yes Pamela?" she asked, traces of agitation in her voice.

"How's it going with the site?" Pamela asked.

Chasity slowly turned and looked at her, narrowing her eyes slightly. "It's fine, I gave you an update like ten minutes ago," she answered.

"Oh I know, I saw it."

Then why the fuck are you at my desk?! Chasity stared at her. "O-kay," she replied. "Is there something else?"

"Just wanted to make sure that you'll be finished by the end of the day," Pamela pressed.

Chasity's eyes borrowed through her. "That is what I said in my *update*.. that I emailed you *ten minutes* ago," she slowly put out.

Pamela nodded. Chasity had worked there long enough for Pamela to sense when she was at her boiling point. And even though she was Chasity's boss, she still wanted to keep her distance when she got to that point. "Great. Keep up the good work," Pamela said, then hurried off.

"Fuck you, bitch," Chasity muttered under her breath as she went back to typing. Hearing her work phone ring, she placed the headset on her head and picked up without looking at the caller ID.

"This is Chasity," she answered, eyes still focused on her screen. When she didn't hear anything, she frowned. "Hello?" Still not hearing anything, she glanced at the caller ID. Recognizing the number, she stopped typing. "Sidra?" she asked finally.

"Yeah, it's me," Sidra answered. "Hi, Chasity."

"Hi," Chasity replied. She and Sidra hadn't spoken to each other since their last night at homecoming, five days ago. After their argument, Sidra had retreated to her hotel room, and left for the airport early the next morning. "Did you need something?" Chasity asked after a moment.

Sidra took a deep breath. "Yes...I need to say that I'm sorry," she replied.

Chasity sighed. "Okay...I'm sorry too." She was over the tension; she had enough of it at work, she didn't want it in her friendships too.

Sidra let out a sigh of relief. "To be honest Chasity, I don't even know how we ended up arguing."

"You were being a nagging bitch," Chasity bluntly stated.

Sidra chuckled. "Oh wow... Well, yeah, that sounds about right," she agreed. "Seems that I have been doing a lot of that lately... I was wrong for poking at you...I admit that my mood wasn't the best that day."

"Yeah well, be that as it may, I shouldn't have put your business out there like that," Chasity admitted, running a hand through her hair. "It wasn't mine to tell... That was very *Malajia* of me and I'm sorry."

"I appreciate that Chaz," Sidra said, sincere. "And I forgive you and to be honest, I'm glad that the rest of you girls know. It's a bit of a relief."

"*Is* it?" Chasity wondered.

"Yeah," Sidra confirmed. "At least I can complain about my stupidity over this entire situation to more than one person."

Chasity shook her head. "Yeah, I'll save my opinion about it until I'm in front of a drink," she said.

"You promise?" Sidra chortled.

"Yeah."

"I look forward to it," Sidra was silent for a moment. "I meant to call you *before* now," she said. "I know we did that 'argue, then not talk for a week' stuff when we were teenagers—"

"*Teenagers?*" Chasity scoffed.

"Okay, in our early twenties too," Sidra amended. "The point is, I don't want to do that anymore... It's bad enough we don't talk as much as we would like because of our lives. I don't want one of the reasons to be because we're mad at each other, you know?" Sidra didn't hear Chasity say anything. "Chaz, you know what I mean?"

"I mean, it was a little long winded," Chasity teased.

"Wench," Sidra ground out.

Chasity laughed. "But I agree with you." She glanced at her watch. "Look Sid, I gotta finish this work, I have a lot of it. '

"Oh sure, I'll call you later," Sidra said. "Or *you* call *me* once you get settled... I have no life, or no man, so I'll answer whenever."

"You sure about that?" Chasity asked.

"Yes...about the answer whenever *and* the no life or man part," Sidra replied.

"Opinion saved about the latter until later," Chasity reiterated, causing Sidra to giggle.

"Noted," Sidra said. "Bye sis."

"Later."

"Oh wait!" Sidra shrieked as Chasity was about to hang up.

"What?" Chasity wondered, perplexed.

"What happened to your 'work voice'?" she chuckled. "That's what I wanted to hear when I called that phone."

"I literally don't care how mean I sound at this place anymore," Chasity replied. "Now get your ass off my phone."

Sidra laughed. "Very well."

Chasity ended her call, then went back to working on her laptop. Glancing at her watch again, she let out a sigh.

Malajia darted to her door and opened it. "Hey Josh," she greeted, moving aside to let him in.

"Hey," he returned, removing his wet jacket.

"Thanks for doing this, I didn't want to take them out in this rain," Malajia said, grabbing her jacket and umbrella out of the closet.

Josh walked over to the twins, who were sitting on the couch, watching TV. "Hey boys," he beamed.

"Uncle Josh!" Marvin shrieked, while Marlon busted out laughing.

Malajia shook her head; Josh laughed. "They're umm, very animated," Josh joked.

"You can say *loud*," Malajia grunted, putting her jacket on. "Anyway, I should be back in like an hour and a half to two hours. My appointment shouldn't take too much time."

Josh grabbed a snack cake out of a box on the coffee table. "I'm happy to watch them, it was slow at the shop today anyway." His mind had been in a bit of a haze since homecoming. Sidra had been on his mind heavily, so much that he couldn't focus on much else. He was relieved when Mark had called him to ask if he could watch the boys for a few hours, while Malajia went to her appointment. Babysitting two three-year-olds was sure to distract him.

"Yeah, we'll see if you still feel the same in an hour," Malajia jeered. "I'll be back boys," she said to her children, who were singing songs along with the cartoon on the screen.

"Bye Mommy," they said in unison.

"Damn, they're talking in sync already, huh?" Josh chuckled. He then looked at Malajia, who was checking in her purse for her car keys. "You're a little overdressed for a doctor's appointment, don't you think?" he observed.

Malajia paused, then glanced down at her black dress pants, red blouse and black heels. She then glanced back up at Josh. "What, are you the fashion guru?" she sniped. "I've been in my pajamas all damn morning, maybe I just want to be cute in case I run into people."

Josh stood there stunned at her attitude.

"Is that okay with you?" Malajia ground out.

Josh put his hands up in surrender. "I was just making an observation," he placated.

Malajia slung her purse over her shoulder after retrieving her keys. "Yeah well, observe your bad ass nephews," she spat.

"I *will*," Josh threw back.

"Well *good*," Malajia returned.

"Fine," Josh added.

"*Great*," she snarled.

Josh chuckled after a moment. "Yeah, that was childish," he admitted amused. Malajia couldn't help but giggle. "Hey, before you go, can I ask you something really quick?"

"Yeah, what's up?"

"Have you talked to Sidra?" he asked, rubbing his arm.

Malajia nodded. "Yeah, she called to yell at me the other day," she informed.

"Yell at you about what?" Josh wondered.

Malajia hesitated. Sidra had indeed called her two days after getting back to California and yelled at her about spilling her secret about Josh to Chasity, to which Malajia was unfazed. But Malajia didn't want to make that same mistake with Josh. "Umm, nothing. Just some girl stuff," she alluded. "Why? *You* haven't?"

Josh shook his head. "No, we kinda had a little...argument or whatever that was called, before we left homecoming."

Malajia stood there. She already knew about it; Sidra had told her after they'd made up, that and about December showing up. "Oh, well that sucks," she said, glancing at her watch, "You should call her."

"Yeah, I will," he assured. "I just... I don't know what to say to her anymore, you know?"

Malajia held a sympathetic gaze on Josh. Clearly, he was missing his best friend, and as far as she was concerned, it was Sidra's fault for distancing herself. "I'm sorry Josh, I know that things between you and Sid have been a little awkward for a long time now."

Josh flopped down on the couch. "I just don't get what happened," he vented, "I mean, I thought the weirdness that was between us after my whole 'I'm in love with you' fiasco was behind us."

"I think that it *was*, Josh," Malajia carefully said. "I honestly don't feel that it was anything that *you* had done...or *felt*."

Josh shrugged, then let out a sigh. "Maybe...maybe I still make her uncomfortable."

"Not in the way that you think," Malajia muttered under

her breath.

"Sorry, did you say something?"

"Nope," Malajia quickly lied.

Josh sighed again. "I guess she didn't really mean it when she told me that she loved me before she got on the plane to leave for the first time," he sulked.

Malajia's eyes widened. That was the first she'd heard that. "She *what*?"

"Yeah," Josh confirmed. "She said it right before the elevator door closed."

Malajia was dumbfounded. If Sidra confessed it to him, then why were they not together? Why didn't he go after her? Why was Sidra still running? "Josh—what—why didn't you go after her?"

"Go after her for *what*?" Josh asked, confused. "Nobody could stop her from going. You know that."

"*You* could've," Malajia argued.

"*How*?" Josh was still confused.

"Because she told you that she *loved* you!" Malajia exclaimed, tossing her arms up. "That was your chance to go *get* her ass."

"Mommy's yelling," Marvin chortled.

"Hush little boy," Malajia chided, then turned her attention back to Josh. "Josh, what the hell man?"

"Malajia…she loves me like a *brother*," he said. "You know that, hell *everybody* knows that. It's nothing new."

Malajia's eyes widened; she pinched the bridge of her nose with two fingers. *He totally misunderstood! Damn it Sidra!*

"But clearly *that* changed too," Josh vented. "I just wish I knew what I did… I miss her."

Malajia tilted her head as she had a thought. "Josh maybe…maybe you should go visit her."

"You think so?"

"Oh absolutely," Malajia assured. "Maybe if you're face to face you can talk out your issues…whatever those may be."

Josh thought for a moment. He did want to go; he'd *been wanting* to go. "I guess I'll bring up the idea when I call her—"

"No no, I think you should *surprise* her," Malajia jumped in.

Josh looked perplexed. "Nah, I don't think that's a good idea," he disagreed. "I can't just pop up on her, she has a life."

Malajia waved her hand dismissively. "Boy, she ain't got no damn life," she scoffed. "No, I think you surprising her is *just* what the hell her ass needs." *She can't make excuses or run if she doesn't know you're coming.* "I'll talk to her and see what her work schedule is looking like, and I'll let you know when to buy your plane ticket."

Josh smiled. "Okay…thanks, I guess," he chuckled. "Should I at least talk to her beforehand?"

"Nope, save it *all* until you get there," Malajia advised. She looked at her watch yet again. "Okay, I really have to go."

"Oh sure, take your time. I've got everything under control here, don't worry," Josh smiled.

"Trust me, I'm not worried," Malajia replied, walking out the door. Once she made it to her car, she retrieved her cell phone from her purse and made a call. "Chaz, I know you're working but I'm about to do some sneaky shit. You wanna hear about it?" Malajia sucked her teeth. "No, I *haven't* learned my lesson… Bitch, do you want to hear it or not?..." Malajia smiled at Chasity's response. "Good."

Emily dipped a tater tot into some ketchup and popped it into her mouth. "I'm starving. I haven't eaten all day," she muttered in between chews.

Will, sitting in a small chair across from her desk, chuckled. "Yeah, I can tell," he teased. "You're tearing those tater tots and chicken nuggets up."

Emily laughed. "Well, that's all they had in the cafeteria." She grabbed a nugget. "I have to prepare these tests for tomorrow, and I don't want to take work home with me."

Will adjusted his position in his chair, nodding in the process. Having finished work, he'd gone to Emily's job to wait for her so they could go home together.

Emily looked up when she heard the chair squeak. Amusement showed on her face; Will looked uncomfortable. "Will…you know you don't have to sit in the children's chair, right?"

"I was trying to live out my teacher fantasy," he joked.

"In a *baby* chair?" she questioned, wiping her mouth with a napkin.

Will thought for a moment. "Yeah, I sound *and* look stupid, don't I?"

Emily laughed in lieu of answering him. Will laughed right along with her, simple and easy as they had always been.

"Let me get my stupid ass up," he said, standing from the seat.

Emily wiped a tear from her eye as her laughter subsided. She was grateful for Will's silliness. Her day had been long and tiring; she needed the laugh.

Will walked over to her and grabbed a chicken nugget from Emily's plate. "I got a call from the venue today," he announced.

Emily rubbed the corner of her eyes with two fingers. "God, what is it *now*?" she complained. Realizing that she had gotten the crumbs from her fingers in her eyes, she sucked her teeth. "Damn it!"

"You okay?" Will asked, handing her a tissue.

"Yeah," Emily answered after a moment, rubbing her eyes. "What did they want?"

"Just wanted to go over décor and other planning stuff," Will shrugged. "I umm... I told them that wasn't my department," he chuckled.

"No, no it's not," Emily agreed, tired. "To be honest, my mind hasn't been on any of this wedding stuff. "

"Stressed?"

"You could say that," Emily replied. Between work, and her issues with her sister and her mother, Emily hadn't had much time for wedding planning. She leaned back in her seat and sighed.

Will stared at her. "Can I make a suggestion?"

"Kick my sister out?" Emily answered for him.

"Well...*yeah*," Will replied. "But forget her for now...talk to your mom."

Emily rolled her eyes. "Please, after she threw that damn tantrum?" she grunted, folding her arms. "No."

Will shook his head. "Em, as much as your mother was wrong, you don't need any more added stress… Babe, your mom being mad at you is just adding to it."

"Well, lucky for me, I've learned to manage my stress a lot better than I did my sophomore year of college," she ground out.

Will let out a sigh. He was well aware of Emily's bout with alcohol abuse in the past. "Yeah, I know," he said.

Emily looked at him. "Look, I appreciate your concern, but I *refuse* to call her," she stood firm.

Will held a sympathetic gaze.

"No, people can't just hurt me and expect me to—" her voice cracked. "Can we go get something to eat?" she quickly said. She felt herself beginning to tear up, and she didn't feel like crying. "These nuggets and tots aren't working."
Will touched her face and nodded. "Okay. We'll go to dinner," he agreed.

Chapter 20

Alex snatched her jacket from her chair with such force that it sent the chair spinning in a circle. "Damn it," she huffed, stopping it with her hand. Glancing at her watch, she let out a groan; it was seven o'clock. Much too late for her to be leaving the office. "Stupid IT and their bullshit," she ranted to herself. As she headed for the door, it opened.

"Alex—"

Alex put her hand up. "Marlene, I swear, we *have* to do something about that IT department," she cut in, flustered. "It doesn't make any sense that things aren't being fixed. Forget fixed, set *up* right."

Marlene rubbed the back of her neck. "I agree," she said. "The constant issues are causing us to work overtime in order to make up for time lost."

Alex sighed. "Listen, you know that I don't mind staying to make sure things get done," she said, calmer. "I want things to be perfect. But this is getting ridiculous."

"Trust me, I know."

Alex ran a hand over her hair. "We're about to completely take over the online managing of our author's web pages and e-books, and we can't be having these webpage problems," she vented.

"I know," Marlene repeated. "It's time to let some people go."

Alex sighed once again. "I'd hate for someone to lose their job but—"

"It's necessary," Marlene cut in.

"Yeah," Alex agreed.

Marlene smiled. "Go home and get some rest. We'll deal with this on Monday."

"You sure you don't need me tomorrow?" Alex asked. As grateful as she was to not have to work on a Saturday, it wasn't like she hated her job. Working a few extra hours from home on her day off wouldn't be an issue.

"No, I'll handle it," Marlene insisted with a wave of her hand.

Alex smiled gratefully; she couldn't have asked for a better boss. "Okay then. See you Monday," she said, walking out of the door. As Alex made the journey out of the building, her phone rang.

Retrieving it from her bag, she put it to her ear. "Hello?"

"Hi Alex," the man answered.

Alex paused mid-walk and smiled bright. "Hey Eric." She'd called Eric and left him a message the night before. She wasn't expecting him to call back so soon; hearing his voice was a nice surprise. "What's going on?"

"Two things," he began. "Sorry that I missed your call yesterday, I was tied up with a few things."

"That's okay," Alex said, continuing her walk out of the building. "I figured you were busy."

"No excuse, I should have called back," he insisted. "We seem to be playing a lot of phone tag."

Alex put her hand over her face. "Yeah, sorry about last week." In the few weeks since homecoming, Alex and Eric had in fact been playing a game of phone tag, resorting to voice messages as a method of communicating.

"It's okay," Eric assured. "I know you're busy as well. Which brings me to my second reason for calling…now that I finally got you."

Alex listened, full of anticipation.

"If you're *not* busy one of these days, I'd like to take you out for a drink…and food of course."

Alex's eyes widened.

"Just a friendly outing," he chuckled, sensing what he thought to be apprehension on her part. "To catch up."

"I'd love that," she replied. The smile was heavy in her voice. "But how soon are you talking with you living in

Virginia?"

"Who said I was still living in Virginia?"

Alex looked confused. "Well, the last time we talked—"

"Was like three years ago," Eric jumped in. "I live in *Connecticut* now, but I'm in New York often. It's nothing for me to drive there."

Alex pulled the phone away from her ear and started jumping up and down with excitement. Not only had she reconnected with Eric, but he was living close enough so seeing him wouldn't be difficult at all. She would take the two-hour train ride in a minute if he asked. Alex stopped celebrating when she started receiving weird looks from passersby. *Don't get ahead of yourself, crazy,* she thought of herself.

"Hello?"

She quickly put the phone back to her ear. "Sorry, I'm here," she sputtered. "Umm, that—that sounds great... Are you in New York *now?*"

"I am, actually," he confirmed.

Alex twisted some hair around her finger. "Then how about *tonight?*"

Eric smiled. "You sure?"

Hell yes I'm sure you sexy chocolate man! "Yes, I'm sure." she downplayed, running a hand over her hair. "I just left work, but it won't take me long to get home. I can drop my stuff off, then we can meet at this nice little restaurant not too far from my place."

"Okay, sounds like a plan."

After giving Eric the directions to her apartment complex, Alex ended the call. She let out a squeal of delight before hurrying off.

Adjusting her gold hoop earrings in her ears, Alex lingered at the floor length mirror in her living room. She'd pushed her and Eric's meeting time back so that she could do a complete overhaul of her look. This was their first outing in years; she didn't want to meet him in the work clothes that she had been in all day.

She showered and changed into a pair of brown wide

legged dress pants, paring it with a cream long-sleeved blouse and a pair of brown stiletto ankle boots. She fluffed up her natural curls, and even made her face up—something that she rarely did. Eyeliner, lip-gloss and a minimum amount of powder to keep the shine off, was her go to make-up routine. A full face was something that she didn't do. She was so unskilled at it, that she had to call for some help. Reaching for her phone, she dialed a number and put it on speaker.

"Malajia, these lashes feel really weird," she said, once Malajia picked up.

"Why are y'all jumping on my couch?! Sitcho' little behinds DOWN!" Malajia hollered in the background.

"Hello?" Alex chuckled.

"Sorry, your nephews are driving me crazy," Malajia explained, voice calmer. "And yes, they feel weird because they aren't yours. Did you get the kind with adhesive already on there?"

Alex fussed with the addition to her eyelid. "Yeah, though I'm thinking that maybe I should've opted for the other because this adhesive doesn't seem to be sticking too well," she said, uncertain. "I don't get why you suggested that I get these in the *first* place."

"'Cause your lashes are short as shit," Malajia ground out. "So you— Hey!— Mark, get your sons!"

"On it, babe," Mark's voice was heard in the background. "SIT DOWN!"

"Boy—I could've yelled that myself," Malajia barked at Mark.

"They sat down, didn't they?"

"Do I need to call back?" Alex asked, interrupting the side conversation.

"You'll just hear this same shit later. For this is my life now," Malajia huffed. "Alex, you got bald ass lashes and you sweat too damn much, so mascara would just run."

Alex sucked her teeth. "I sweated bad that *one* time—you know what, never mind, these things just better stay on."

"They will," Malajia promised. "Now get off my phone so I can go eat this ice cream in my children's faces."

Alex laughed.

"Have fun on your date."

"It's not a da—"

"Get some penis sis, bye!" Malajia blurted out before hanging up in Alex's ear.

Alex looked at the phone in shock, then shook her head. "That girl," she muttered.

Hearing a knock at the door, her heart dropped down to her stomach. Running to answer it, her heel got caught in a frayed piece of her throw rug, tripping her up and sending her tumbling to the hardwood floor. "Goddamn it!" Alex yelled.

"You okay in there?" Eric's muffled voice asked.

Alex slowly picked herself up from the floor. She rubbed her ankle, then gingerly limped to the door. She winced as she opened it. Eric was standing there; Alex forced a smile. "Heeey," she drew out.

Eric eyed her skeptically as she hobbled aside to let him in. "You okay?"

Alex closed the door and faced him, shifting her weight from her hurt ankle to the other. She thought about making up a lie, but she was in pain, and pretty sure that she had knocked an eyelash loose in the fall. "I umm... tripped on my rug and busted my ass on the floor," she admitted. Eric just stood there. "I think that I may have twisted my ankle."

Eric was silent. He folded both lips into his mouth.

Alex stood there for a moment before waving her hand in his direction. "Go head and laugh."

Eric couldn't hold it any longer; loud laughter erupted from him. Alex giggled at the sight. "Awww, poor baby," Eric placated, laughter subsiding.

"Trust me, I've taken worse spills," Alex admitted. "I'm always tripping over something."

Eric chuckled.

Alex, tiring of the heaviness over her eyes, pulled her lashes off. "You've seen me naked before, *surely* you don't mind seeing me pull these tarantulas off my face," she said when Eric looked shocked.

Eric put his hands up. "I just wasn't expecting that, but I'm not bothered by it," he assured.

"Yeah well, I was trying to be extra cute I guess," she

muttered, balling the lashes up in her hand.

"You don't need to do anything extra," Eric smiled. He reached for her arm. "Well, we surely can't go out with your ankle hurting."

"No, no I can walk," she promised, putting her weight down on her ankle. The pain made her wince. "Never mind."

Eric helped her over to her couch, guiding her down. He helped her remove her shoe and held her foot in his hand, examining her ankle. It was starting to swell a bit. "You need some ice," he said.

Alex let out a loud sigh, putting her face in her hand. "I'm so sorry," she pouted.

"It's cool," Eric consoled, removing his blazer. "If you don't mind the company, we can order in."

"I have wine," Alex smiled.

"Cool." Eric stood up. "I'll go get you some ice for your ankle," he said.

She pointed in the direction of the kitchen, "Thank you," she said, grateful. "You can bring that wine out with you too."

Eric smiled at her as he headed for the kitchen. "Let me find out you're trying to get me drunk to take advantage of me," he teased.

Alex's eyes widened slightly. Though she was sure that it wasn't intentional on Eric's part; that comment sent a tingle through her body. She'd realized just how long it had been since she'd had sex. But Eric was someone that meant something to her, even after all this time; she didn't want to create a casual moment. "No, it's not that," she chuckled. "Figured it wouldn't hurt to numb myself right now."

"I'm just messing with you," he said. "Where are your menus?"

"Third drawer from the fridge," she directed, running a hand over her hair.

Eric stared at her.

"What?" she asked, curious.

He pointed to the front of her hair, which had something stuck to it. "I umm…I think one of your tarantulas have nested on your hair," he teased.

Alex quickly moved her hand over her hair and pulled the stuck lashes from it. She was mortified; she'd totally forgotten that they were in her hand. Alex flung them on the coffee table. "Damn it," she fussed.

Eric shook his head in amusement. "Let me go get that ice," he said.

Alex put her hand over her face and busted out laughing as Eric disappeared into the kitchen.

Sidra rolled her eyes, cradling her cell phone with her shoulder while closing her container of grilled chicken salad in the process. "Mama, you can't yell at me, I'm at work…" Sidra sighed. "I really don't have time for this right now… I get that you're upset about me changing my mind about Thanksgiving, but can this *wait*?"

Sidra was frustrated, and regretting returning her mother's phone call after just ten minutes on the phone. Hearing a beep come from her work phone, she glanced at it. "I have to go. I'll call you later." Sidra didn't give her mother a chance to respond; she abruptly ended the call. She pushed the button on her work phone for the next call. "Yes Robin?" she answered.

"Ms. Howard, you have a visitor," Robin replied.

Sidra rubbed the back of her neck. "Thank you, who is it?"

"A Mr. James Grant."

Sidra raised an eyebrow. "Oh okay," she said. "You can send him up." The last time she had heard from James was a few days after his wife had given birth; he'd called to let her know of the baby's arrival. She was curious as to why he'd popped up.

After a few moments, she heard a knock on the door. "Come in." Sidra stood up as the door opened, then put her hands over her mouth in shock. "Oh my God," she squealed, seeing James standing there holding his infant.

"Hi," James smiled. "It's okay that I stopped by, isn't it?"

"Sure, it is," Sidra assured.

James let out a relieved sigh. "Okay cool." he stepped inside. "Sidra, meet my son, James Grant Jr.," he beamed with pride.

"He is so adorable," Sidra cooed, walking over. "Can I hold him?"

"Of course," James replied, handing the squirming baby out for Sidra.

Sidra darted to her desk and grabbed the hand sanitizer. "One second," she said, squirting some into her hands.

James chuckled. "You women and that hand sanitizer," he teased.

"Hush, he's too little for germs," Sidra threw back. She held her arms out and James placed the child into her arms. She smiled as she cradled him. "James, he really is adorable."

"Thank you," James beamed.

"Hey you," she cooed to the boy. "You are going to be a little heartbreaker, aren't you?" His little eyes were wide and bright as he made gurgling noises.

"You're a natural," James smiled.

"Really?" she questioned, looking up at him. "Because I *swear* I'm nervous as hell right now."

"Why?"

"Because I'm always afraid that I'm going to break little babies when I hold them," she admitted. "They're so fragile. It took me *forever* to hold my niece for the first time."

"You're doing fine," James assured, placing the receiving blanket on Sidra's shoulder.

Sidra bobbed the little boy in her arms. After a moment, she looked back at James. "Can I ask you something?"

"Of course."

She hesitated for a moment. "When you first started working in the law field...did you ever—" Sidra glanced down at the baby as he began to fuss.

James held his arms out for his son; Sidra handed him to James. "Looks like he's getting cranky. I better get him home," he said.

"Okay," Sidra replied. In a way, she was grateful for the interruption. She didn't know why she even brought up the topic of work with James; she knew it would result in him trying to talk her into leaving her job again. She handed the receiving blanket back to him. "It was good seeing you and congratulations again. To you *both*."

"Thank you," James smiled, adjusting his son in his arms. "What was your question by the way?"

Sidra waved her hand. "Nothing important. I'll see you around."

James offered a smile before walking out of the office.

Once the door shut, Sidra stood there and let out a sigh. She didn't want to admit it to herself, but seeing James with his son had made her think about what she could have had with Josh, had she been honest with him all those years ago. She wondered how different her life could've been.

Her phone beeped again, snapping Sidra out of her depressing thoughts.

Sidra pushed the button. "Yes Robin?"

"You must be popular today," Robin chortled through the speaker.

Sidra frowned. "What do you mean?"

"You have another visitor."

"Who is it *this* time?" Sidra wondered.

"He says he's a friend."

"*He?*" Sidra questioned. She didn't have any male friends in California, except for James, and he'd just left. "Do you recognize him?"

"No, but he's cute," Robin mentioned.

Sidra rolled her eyes. "Yeah big help," she scoffed. "I'll be out." Rather than chastise Robin for not getting proper information from the visitor, she figured she would just get the meeting over with.

She headed out of her office, making her way down the hall and out to the reception area. She walked over to Robin's desk. "Where is the guy?" she asked.

Without saying a word, Robin pointed to a figure standing off to the side. Annoyed, Sidra spun around. Her breath was caught in her throat; her eyes widened as she came face to face with him. "J—Josh!" she exclaimed.

Josh smiled at her as he walked over. "Hi."

Sidra was shocked to say the least. "Hi—wait hold up— what are you *doing* here? When did you *get* here? How long are you here *for*? Why didn't you call me and tell me you were coming?"

Josh stared at her as she fired off her questions. "Any other questions?" he chortled once she finished.

"Start with *those*," she demanded, folding her arms.

"Okay," Josh relented. "I came here to see you, I got here this morning, I'm here until Tuesday morning, and I didn't tell you I was coming because I wanted to surprise you," he answered in one breath. "I was told that I should."

"Should *what*?" Sidra snapped.

"Surprise you," he answered.

Sidra frowned. "By *who*?"

"Malajia," Josh answered.

Sidra's eyes nearly popped out of her head, they had gotten so big. "Mala—I'm gonna smack the *shit* out of her when I see her," she fumed through clenched teeth.

Josh's face fell. *Well damn*, he thought. He didn't know what he expected Sidra's reaction to be, but he didn't expect it to be *this* bad. "I take it you're not happy to see me."

Sidra relaxed her frown. "That's not it—"

"Look, I know I should've called and talked to you first. *Especially* after how we left things at homecoming," he cut in calmly. "I don't know why I listened to Mel, I guess I was just excited… I'll never do *that* shit again."

Feeling terrible for how she'd reacted, Sidra reached out and touched Josh's arm. It wasn't that she didn't want to see Josh; she just wished she'd had the time to prepare herself mentally and emotionally. "I'm happy to see you," she said to him.

"You sure?" Josh wondered.

"Yes," she promised. "It's just that if I would have known…I could have made plans or reservations or something."

Josh waved his hand at her. "Nah, the best things are left unplanned," he smiled.

Sidra eyed him skeptically. "If you say so," she chuckled, then glanced at her watch. "Ugh, I still have three more hours of work—"

"Don't worry about it, I'll do some sightseeing before heading back to my hotel," he said. "Maybe we can hang out later?"

"Of course."

"Cool." Josh was about to move in for a hug, but paused. "Is it okay if I hug you?"

"Of course," Sidra repeated.

Josh moved in and enveloped her in a warm embrace. And just like that, he headed for the exit.

Sidra watched him walk out of the door, fanning herself with her hand. Turning around to head back to her office, she saw Robin and Carlie had come out at some point earlier. The two women were staring at her, smiling.

"What?" Sidra ground out.

"Like I said, he's cute," Robin smiled. "Who is he?"

"I'm aware, and he's my friend." Sidra's tone was sharp. Robin, she didn't have an issue with, but Carlie standing there practically drooling, annoyed her.

"Is he single?" Carlie asked.

Bitch I'll cut you. "Ms. Taylor needs the notes from the witness interviews that you conducted yesterday," Sidra hissed, ignoring Carlie's question. "You might want to get them to her." She punctured her response by sauntering away.

Robin giggled as Carlie made a face at Sidra's departing back.

Alex folded her arms, her eyes narrowing in the process. The laughter that was taking place in front of her was irritating. "Seriously?" she spat.

Malajia and Chasity, seated across from her at the small table, continued laughing. "Wait, wait," Malajia panted between laughs. "Tell me again how you busted your ass running for the door." She slapped her hand on the table repeatedly.

"No, I'm not telling y'all anything else," Alex huffed. "And it's *not* that damn funny."

"Wait, so not *only* did you fall all stupid, but your lashes got stuck in your hair?" Chasity said, still laughing. "You goofy as shit, yo."

Alex rolled her eyes. She'd decided to take an impromptu trip to Philadelphia that Saturday to not only see her family, but to hang out with Chasity and Malajia. Happy that both girls were free for a few hours, and taking advantage of the mild weather that fall afternoon, Alex had met them for lunch at an outdoor bistro downtown.

After telling both girls all about her awkward date with Eric a week ago, they'd erupted with laughter, making Alex regret saying a word. "You know, you two are disrespectful," she grunted.

Chasity grabbed a napkin and wiped the tears from her eyes as her laughter subsided. "That's what you get for trying to be something you're not," she said.

"What is *that* supposed to mean?" Alex frowned. "Malajia, come on!" she barked, smacking her hand on the table as tears rolled down Malajia's face; she had yet to stop laughing.

"You know *damn* well you don't wear stilettos *or* fake lashes," Chasity pointed out, amusement in her voice. "You tried to be extra and fucked up your ankle, you dumbass."

Malajia screamed with laughter, gaining the attention of other patrons.

"Bitch that was *right* by my ear," Chasity ground out, shooting Malajia a glare.

Malajia gained her composure. "Oh my God, I can't breathe," she panted, fanning her face. "That laugh was everything."

"Are you finished?" Alex hissed.

"For now," Malajia countered, reaching for her drink.

"Anyway, I guess you have a point," Alex admitted, putting a hand up. "I learned my lesson. I'm sticking with my thick heels and natural lashes from now on. I always say comfort rules anyway."

"Yeah, yeah," Malajia dismissed. "Did y'all get it in or *not*? And why are we *just* hearing these details?"

"First off, *no*," Alex spat. "*Second*, because I knew you two would do *exactly* what you did."

"Hurtful," Chasity mocked, reaching for a piece of cantaloupe from Malajia's fruit bowl.

Malajia glanced at her, watching her eat it with confusion.

Chasity, noticing Malajia's weird stare, looked at her. "What, weirdo?"

"Nothing," Malajia quickly dismissed, then turned her attention back to Alex. "So, your clumsiness and lack of penis aside, did y'all have a good time?"

"*I* did," Alex answered. "I can only hope that *he* did *too*. I mean, even though all we did was talk, I enjoyed myself... I always liked talking to him."

"As much as you liked fucking him?" Chasity asked, earning a snicker from Malajia.

"Two totally different things, potty mouth," Alex replied, grabbing the sandwich from her plate. "The good thing is that he lives close to New York, so we can have a date do over."

"I thought he said it wasn't a *date*," Malajia recalled.

Alex waved her hand as she swallowed the food in her mouth. "I'm convinced that he only said that because he thinks that I didn't *want* it to be considered a date," she stated, confident.

"You sure about that?" Chasity asked, reaching for her water.

"Nope," Alex chuckled. "But instead of getting my face cracked *twice*, that's what I'm telling myself." She wiped her mouth with her napkin.

"If he *did* want to date you, are you really in a place to do that?" Malajia asked.

"Yes," Alex immediately replied. "Without a doubt. I made a huge mistake not dating him when we were in college. So much time wasted."

Chasity shrugged. "Not necessarily," she contradicted. "You needed to see what else was out there first and now that you *have*...which is a bunch of *nothing*—"

Alex snickered.

"You know what you want now," Chasity finished.

"This is true," Alex agreed, smiling. "Hopefully I won't ruin it this time... I really want this...*him*. I can see our future already." She stared at the girls intensely. "Is that crazy?"

"Yes," Chasity mocked.

Alex couldn't help but giggle; she flagged Chasity with her hand. "Whatever."

Malajia tapped the table. "Hey, before you start making us

get fitted for brown ass bridesmaid dresses, go on a *real* date with him first," she chimed in.

Alex made a face at Malajia.

Malajia's cell phone rang and she grabbed it from the table. Eyeing the caller ID, she smirked. "Ooh, this is Sidra," she announced. "I ignored her call yesterday." She put the phone to her ear. "Hey sunshine," she crooned into the phone. "…Wow, your vulgarity is *astounding*," she teased as an irate Sidra ranted in her ear.

Chasity and Alex shook their heads.

Malajia jerked her head back from the phone as Sidra's loud voice pierced through.

"Ooh, I heard *that* one," Chasity chortled.

"Sidra—sweetie you're breaking up… Uh huh, I know that I'm a sneaky heffa, I love you too… Tell Josh 'hi' for me… Okay byeeeeee." Malajia laughed as she hung up.

"She's pissed," Chasity concluded.

"Malajia, you know you're wrong for setting Sidra up like that," Alex scolded.

"Oh boo hoo," Malajia mocked. "I'm sick of *both* they asses. Josh running around dating these weird bitches, knowing he still has feelings for Sidra, and Sidra out here being a scared idiot, holding her feelings in. They both looked awkward as shit at homecoming." She folded her arms. "No, they need to sort this shit out like *now*… She's lucky I didn't pull a 'Chasity' and spill the beans to Josh my-*damn*-self."

"It was *one* time!" Chasity exclaimed. "And that's a *you* thing and you know it."

"Whatever," Malajia muttered.

Chasity glanced at her watch and sucked her teeth.

"Trying to leave already?" Alex charged.

"I don't *want* to, but I have to finish this project by Monday morning," Chasity grunted. "I'm creating five different fuckin' websites at once and of *course* they're all due this week… I'm sick of this shit."

"Girl, be lucky you have projects that don't involve finger paint and crayons," Malajia said, then sipped her drink. "I wish *I* knew how to create a web page *and* run it."

Chasity let out a loud sigh. "No, you *don't*," she spat.

Malajia nearly choked on her drink laughing. "I don't," she admitted. "You got that tech shit, I'm good."

Alex had a thought. "Chasity," she called.

Chasity grabbed her purse and slung it over her shoulder. "What?"

"If I gave you the outline for what I wanted on a website...you could build it and maintain it?" Alex asked.

Chasity held a blank stare on Alex; Malajia shot Alex a confused look. "Did you *not* know what she did for a living all this time?" Malajia asked.

"Shut up Malajia," Alex bit out, then turned her attention back to Chasity. "*Could* you?"

"Yes, Alex," Chasity answered, traces of frustration in her voice.

"Well...could you create a mock site for *me*?" Alex pressed. "It's for a side thing that I'm doing."

"You want me to do it right *now*, while I'm sitting here?" Chasity mocked.

Alex narrowed her eyes. "*No* cranky. I'll email you the details...but would you mind doing that for me?"

"You paying her?" Malajia jumped in.

Chasity put her hand up before Alex could respond. "Not necessary. Send me your raggedy information and I'll see what I can do," she assured, standing up.

Alex smiled, clasping her hands together. "Thank you, I love you."

"Ugh," Chasity scoffed, earning a snicker from Alex. "See y'all later...and Malajia that doesn't mean bring your ass to my house after you leave this restaurant either."

"I'll do what I damn well please," Malajia hurled at Chasity's departing back.

Alex giggled. "You better stop messing with her," she advised.

"She don't scare me," Malajia replied, unfazed. She folded her arms on the table. "By the way, her job *is* out of pocket," Malajia mentioned after a moment. "They put a lot on her."

"Well...when you're as good at your job as *she* is, unfortunately that's what happens," Alex resolved.

Malajia made a face. "That's not a good excuse at *all*," she argued. "*I* was good at *my* job and my bosses didn't do that to *me*."

"Maybe you weren't as good as you *thought*," Alex joked.

Malajia's mouth fell open. "I made more than *you*, you clumsy ragdoll," she threw back.

"Well, you don't *now*, you—"

"Nope! You slow *and* corny," Malajia interrupted, pointing at an annoyed Alex.

Alex flipped her the finger.

"Yeah, shove that right up your ass," Malajia sniped.

Chapter 21

Sidra carefully sliced up some cheese and placed the slices on a china plate next to an arrangement of crackers, olives, and grapes. She glanced at her watch and took a deep breath; Josh was on his way over to her apartment.

After running errands all day, Sidra had called Josh and invited him over. Though she was nervous, she had no choice but to suck it up and face him. After all, he'd flown six hours to see her.

She grabbed the plate from her kitchen counter and walked into the living room just in time to hear a knock on the door. Quickly setting the plate on her coffee table, she rushed to open it.

"Hi," she smiled.

"Hi," Josh returned, walking in once Sidra signaled for him. As she shut the door behind him, Josh glanced around the living area. "Wow," he said, eyeing the décor. "This is *exactly* how I pictured your apartment."

Sidra tilted her head. "Yeah?"

"Yes," he confirmed. "A lot of cream, blue and *glass*."

She giggled at the amusement in his voice. "Yeah well, it's spotless too," she added.

"Never doubted it," Josh said, stuffing his hands in his jeans pocket. "It's nice."

"Thanks, but before you make that conclusion, let me show you the rest of it," she smiled, leading the way through the rest of the place. Sidra took Josh through her two-bedroom apartment, showing him every nook and cranny. He was the first of her friends back home to see her place. When a few of the gang had visited a few years ago, Sidra was still in a modest one-bedroom apartment close to her law school.

They paused as they entered her bedroom. "Sidra, this looks better than my hotel room," he mused, glancing around.

Sidra spun around and looked at him. "I mean...you *could stay* here," she offered after a moment. Josh looked at her. "The guest room, I mean."

Josh chuckled. "Where *else* would I sleep?"

Don't even, Sidra, she thought, trying to keep her mind off *those* thoughts. "Right... Seriously though, I have plenty of room as you can see." She tucked some hair behind her ear. "I'm sure your hotel room is nice—"

"Eh," Josh shrugged. "No, it's cool. You know me, I don't need anything fancy."

"I know," Sidra replied, folding her arms. "But...come on Josh, I don't mind you staying here." She swallowed hard. "With me...for a few days."

Josh tilted his head. "Are you sure?"

Sidra nodded. "Of course," she assured. "Had you told me you were *coming*," she added, giving his arm a light tap. "You wouldn't have had to waste money on the hotel in the *first* place."

Josh ran his hand over the back of his head, giving a nervous chuckle. "Uh, right," he said. "Bad move, huh?"

"Not all the way...I really *am* glad to see you," she said. Josh smiled. "But yeah, when dealing with Malajia, you should know by now to do the *opposite* of what she says."

"Noted," Josh replied, amusement in his voice. "And thank you."

Sidra just nodded, then led the way back to the living room. "I put snacks out," she announced, pointing to the tray on the table.

Josh grabbed a few cheese slices and some grapes as he sat down next to her. "So, what's fun to do around here?" he asked, stuffing his face with the food.

Sidra stared at him. "Umm, there's a few lounges around here...some restaurants..." she shook her head. "To be honest, I don't hang out much."

"*That's* not surprising either," Josh chuckled.

"Look, I'm sorry that I didn't get to hang out with you yesterday. I got in from work really late and figured you'd be sleep," she said, apologetic.

"I wasn't sleep, but that's okay," he returned, grabbing a few crackers. "I know that I just popped up on you, so I didn't expect for you to drop what you were doing."

Sidra lowered her head. She lied; she hadn't gotten in late from work, she was just trying to gather her thoughts and her nerves. She'd needed the night to process the fact that it would just be she and Josh alone in the same city for *days*. No friends to buffer. "Yeah well, I still feel bad," she said. "So, I figured I'd make it up to you by making you dinner."

"You sure you wanna mess up your pristine kitchen?" Josh teased, earning a playful tap to his arm.

"Hush," she giggled. "But seriously, I went to the store and got all the stuff to make stuffed shells."

"Okay sounds good," he replied. "...You what, how about *I* make them?" he offered after a moment.

Sidra's face took on a blank expression. "Umm..."

Josh looked hurt. "Wait, you think I can't cook?"

Sidra scratched her head. "I mean...you *did* make that soup that one time."

Josh laughed. "That was senior year and it was my first attempt at making soup from scratch," he threw back. "And you said it wasn't that bad."

Sidra shot him a sympathetic look. "Sweetie, I lied."

Josh put his hand over his face and shook his head. "I've gotten better, I promise," he insisted, standing up. "I'll even make dessert."

Sidra watched him as he headed to the kitchen. "Joshua, I don't want you burning my kitchen down," she called after him.

"Sidra, *you* hush and come show me where your stuff is," he threw back, stern.

Resolved, Sidra stood up and headed for the kitchen, but not before grabbing some cheese and crackers from the tray. "This might be the only thing that I get to eat tonight," she muttered to herself.

Sidra sat at her kitchen table and watched in awe while Josh maneuvered about the kitchen for the past hour and a half.

He had prepared the cheese and spinach filled pasta shells, fresh sautéed string beans, garlic bread, and even a coconut cream pie. Though the pie was still in the oven, everything else was ready.

"Oh my God," she breathed, amazed when Josh sat a plate of food in front of her. She leaned forward and smelled it as Josh sat his own plate down, taking the seat across from her.

"You have to *taste* it first," he laughed at her reaction.

"If it tastes anywhere as good as it *smells*, you have succeeded in proving me wrong," she said, grabbing her fork and digging in. Josh watched Sidra in anticipation as she cut into one of the large shells, then took a bite. Sidra's eyes closed, savoring the flavors. "And I have been proven wrong."

Josh clapped his hands together. "Yes," he rejoiced, digging into his own food.

"This is *really* good, Josh," she praised, devouring her food.

"Thank you," he replied, eating.

"When did you start cooking like this?"

"When I moved into my apartment," he answered. Then thought for a moment. "Well…not when I *first* moved. I started spending way too much money on takeout, and burned way too many pots and pans, before I decided that I needed some help."

Sidra giggled. "You took cooking classes?"

"No, I went to my mother…and Sarah…and Chasity…and Malajia—I needed a *lot* of help," he replied, laughter in his voice.

"Awww," Sidra sympathized.

"My mother and sister were patient with me," he continued. "Chasity yelled at me a lot." Sidra busted out laughing. "It was justified though—I almost caused a fire in her kitchen while I was trying to fry fish…oil was too hot."

Sidra's eyes widened. "Oh my God!" she exclaimed.

"Yeah, luckily it didn't happen… I burned the hell out of the pan though," he finished.

Sidra shook her head in amusement.

Josh took another bite of his food. "And when I over boiled pasta at *Malajia's* house, she threw a few of the noodles at me." Sidra laughed yet again. "They stuck to my face… It didn't help that Mark and their boys were laughing at me."

Sidra patted her chest and took a sip of her juice. Laughter subsiding, she reached for her fork again. "That's a shame," she commiserated. "*I* wouldn't have yelled at you."

"Yeah, you would've," he assured.

Sidra giggled, then the humor left her face as realization set in. *Damn, I missed out on a lot.*

"Hey," Josh began after a few moments of silence.

Sidra looked over at him. "Yeah?"

"I'm sorry about how we left things at homecoming," he began. "I shouldn't have caught an attitude with you."

Sidra put her hand up. "No Josh, *I'm* sorry," she replied. "If I hadn't given you attitude *first*, you wouldn't have had to throw one back."

Josh nodded. "I appreciate that," he said. "I guess we were *both* acting a bit weird, huh?"

"Yeah, we *were*," she agreed.

"I just…I don't want it to be that way between us anymore, you know?" Josh added. "I'm tired of it… I miss you."

Sidra looked down at her plate. "I miss you too."

Sidra didn't know why, but she felt like this was the right time to say the other thing that she was feeling. The real reason why things were weird between them. The reason *she* was making it weird. They were alone, no distractions, no excuses. *Just tell him! It's now or never.* Sidra set her fork down and clasped her hands together. "Josh."

"Yeah?" he replied, staring intently.

She hesitated. "Does…does December know you're out here visiting me?" she asked.

Josh was taken aback. "I'm sorry?"

"I mean…does she *know* that you're out here…with *me*?" she stressed.

Josh frowned. "No, she *doesn't*," he answered. "The real question is why she would *need* to?"

Sidra raised an eyebrow. "I just figured that you two—"

"Aren't a thing," Josh finished. He sat back in his seat. "Wait, you thought because we ran into each other at homecoming that we're back together?"

"You act like stuff like that doesn't happen," Sidra argued.

"It didn't with *us*. There is nothing between December and I, hasn't been since we broke up," Josh clarified. "*And* she's *married*."

"Oh…" Sidra looked down at her hands. "Well, how do you feel about that?"

Josh shrugged. "I'm happy for her," he answered.

"That's good," she muttered. Sidra hadn't meant to, but she let out a long sigh of relief. She didn't know what made her assume that Josh and December would ever get back together. Maybe it was her own fear and insecurities. But now that the situation was clarified, Sidra started to regain her courage.

"Well…" she began, adjusting her position on her seat. "Okay, there's something that I need to say to you."

Concern masked Josh's face. "Is everything okay?"

Sidra opened her mouth to speak, but the words got stuck. "Umm… I umm…."

Josh's mind was racing as he tried to anticipate what else Sidra was about to say to him. Whatever it was, it seemed serious and he was nervous.

Sidra felt her stomach do flips as she stared at Josh. *What am I about to do? Do I really want to do this? Will he be happy? Will he be mad? Does he still feel the same about me? What if he doesn't? Am I about to make a fool out of myself? Oh my God, is this how he felt when he told me?*

"Sidra, please just say it," Josh urged.

"Okay," she said, gathering her courage. "I—" Her words were interrupted by a noise from Josh's phone.

"Ignore that," Josh insisted.

Sidra tried, but another beep came through. "Maybe—"

"It's just text messages, I'll look at them later," Josh interrupted.

Another one came through; Sidra pointed to his pocket. "Look at your phone, it could be important."

Sighing, Josh did as she asked. Sidra sat there patiently while Josh thumbed through his phone. She figured that she'd waited all this time to tell him how she felt, what's a few more minutes? "It's Sarah, it's about the shop," he announced. "I'm gonna call her really quick, be right back."

"Sure, tell her I said hi," Sidra said as Josh walked out of the kitchen.

"I will," he returned.

Sidra looked down at her hands; they were trembling. She didn't remember the last time that she felt so nervous. Before she knew it, she began to feel hot; her stomach was in knots. As she fanned herself with her hands, her thoughts began screaming in her head. *He doesn't feel the same way anymore. What the hell is the point of telling him that I love him if it's not going to go anywhere? I'll just make things more awkward.* "I can't do this," she whispered to herself.

"Sorry about that," Josh said, walking back into the kitchen, startling her. "Sarah said that the owner of a location that I was looking at, was calling and she wanted to know what to say to them."

Sidra put her hands on her lap, hoping to stop the shakes. "Location? Location for what?"

Josh sat back down and put his phone on the table. "I plan on opening another car shop."

Sidra smiled. "Really?" Josh nodded. "That's great Josh...I'm proud of you."

Josh smiled back. "Thank you," he returned. "So...what did you need to tell me?"

Sidra held a long gaze on him. Her nerve was gone. "Umm, I just wanted to say that I can't get off Monday like I originally thought," she said, disappointment in her voice. "I know that Monday is your last full day here, and I wanted to take off, so we could hang out some more. But we got a new case in, and I have to start doing the prep for it."

Josh nodded slightly. "Oh...I understand. I didn't except you to take off, but I appreciate the thought." Josh was a little confused; Sidra had made it seem she had something way more serious to say than that. Sidra just looked sad. "Hey, don't worry about it," he stressed. "I'm a grown man, I can entertain myself while you're at work."

Sidra, you're an idiot, she thought. "I know but—"

"I was actually thinking that I could stay an extra day...maybe two," he put out.

Sidra smiled. "You sure?" she asked, resting an elbow on the table.

"Yeah, Sarah can look after the shop for a few extra days," he said. "I mean, if that's cool with you."

Sidra nodded. "It's cool."

"Cool," he smiled back. Smelling the pie, Josh stood up. "I think the pie is done."

Sidra just forced a smile, then sighed as she went back to eating her food.

"Will, can I take this blindfold off?" Emily asked, touching the pink fabric covering her eyes.

Will pulled into a parking spot. "Not yet," he said.

Emily was excited. After a long day of prepping for work for the week, cleaning, and working on wedding projects, while trying to deal with Jazmine's everlasting bad mood, Will had surprised her by stating that he was taking her on this outing. As she sat blindfolded, she anticipated what it could be, where they were going.

"Okay," she agreed, putting her hand down. Hearing the driver's side door open, she turned her head in that direction. "Will?"

"Hang on, I'm coming around to get you," he promised. Within a moment, he opened Emily's door, taking hold of her hand to guide her out of the car.

"Step this way," he urged, holding on to her.

Emily gripped his arm. "Wait, I need to take this off, I'm gonna fall," she panicked, taking a step.

Will chuckled. "You're not gonna fall, I got you," he promised.

"Okay. But if I *do* fall, I'm going to be really mad at you."

Will laughed a little, guiding her through the glass door of a restaurant. He walked her over to a table and sat her down in a seat.

Hearing him sit down across from her, she reached her hand out. "Can I take this off now, please?" she asked.

"Yes," he granted. "But first," Will blurted out as Emily's hand moved to remove the blindfold.

"What?" she asked.

"Before you take that off, I just want to say that I love you and I did this because I felt like it would help you," he explained.

Emily smiled. "You're so sweet," she gushed. "I love you too." She sat there as Will removed her blindfold. Her excitement turned to confusion when she laid eyes on who was really sitting in front of her at the restaurant. "Mommy?" she blurted out.

Ms. Harris sat across from Emily, a stern expression on her face.

Emily frowned. "What—what are you *doing* here?" she questioned. She completely ignored the fact that Will was standing right next to her.

As Ms. Harris went to open her mouth, a male voice cut in. "She's here to apologize to you."

Emily knew that voice, and her head snapped in the direction it had come from. "*Daddy?*" she reacted, stunned as her father made his way over to the table.

Emily looked up at Will with questioning eyes as her father sat down at the table. "What did you do? And *why?*" she ground out.

Will looked nervous. "Umm...remember what I said to you before—"

Emily glared at him. "Space, I need it," she fumed.

Taking that as a warning, Will decided it was best if he obliged. It wasn't often that Emily had gotten angry with him, but when she did, he made it a point to not make things worse by being in her presence.

Emily followed his progress as Will made his way to another seat, several tables down. Her angry gaze lingered for a long moment, until she decided to focus on her *own* table. She glanced at her mother, who just looked away. Sucking her teeth, Emily turned to her father.

"Daddy, what is this all about?" she asked. "I thought you were away working on a new building project in Jersey."

"I was, but this matter is more important," Mr. Harris replied, shooting Ms. Harris a glance. "I hear from my future son-in-law that my ex-wife is acting a fool."

Ms. Harris snapped her head at her ex-husband. "Excuse me?" she hissed.

Emily put her hand over her face. She knew from experience how bad an argument between her parents could get "Daddy, don't worry about it," she interjected. "I'm sorry he called you."

"*I'm* not," Mr. Harris replied, his focus still on his ex. When he'd received the call from Will, expressing concern for Emily's feelings and asking him for help in getting her and her mother together for a resolution, Mr. Harris had jumped at the opportunity. "I can't believe you're acting like this. Not talking to our daughter over a decision that she made for *her* wedding."

Ms. Harris glared daggers at him. "You might want to save that attitude for your little *girlfriend*," she barked.

Emily closed her eyes as she tried to imagine being anywhere else.

"And there it goes," Mr. Harris scoffed. "Kelly, knock it off and apologize to Emily for your behavior. This cold shoulder you're giving her is ridiculous."

"You do not dictate how I handle my daughter," Ms. Harris snarled.

Emily frowned at her. "*Handle* me?" she ground out.

"Emily—"

"So this is you *handling* me?" Emily fumed, interrupting her mother. "I can't believe you're acting like this. I can't believe you're treating me like this, *again*."

"I think you should calm down," Ms. Harris grunted.

"No, I think *you* should *leave*," Emily barked. "If you're not going to apologize, which is *all* I want to hear from you at this moment, then you're wasting my time."

Ms. Harris grabbed her purse and bolted from her seat.

"Kelly, just stop. Come sit back down," Mr. Harris called after her.

"I'll see you in the car," Ms. Harris spat, heading for the exit.

Emily placed her face in her hands and let out a long sigh. "I'm sorry you traveled all this way," she muttered after a moment.

Mr. Harris reached out and touched her hand. "I'll never be sorry for being here for you," he said.

Emily looked up at him. "Thank you…at least I have *one*

thoughtful parent."

Mr. Harris shook his head. "If it's one thing I know for sure, I know how much she loves you and not talking to you will eat at her."

"I don't even care at this point, Daddy," Emily vented. "I'm just over everything…I'm tired."

Mr. Harris sighed. "If you want to keep the peace…maybe just let her walk you down, I don't mind."

Emily looked at him like he was crazy. "*I* mind," she argued. "No, I will not be manipulated by her. She'll get over it, or she can stay home with her other daughter."

"You plan on uninviting Jazmine?"

"I doubt I'll *have* to, it's not like she'll show up anyway," Emily grunted. "She's had nothing but negative stuff to say about it… Then again that's not new."

"You let me know if you need me to get her together," Mr. Harris said. "That girl needs to get a damn grip on her life and stop taking advantage of you."

"If her mother can't get her to act right, *you* definitely can't," Emily replied.

"I don't care *how* Jazmine feels about *me*. The way she's treating *you*, needs to stop," he vented. "I try not to intervene because you're grown but—"

"No, I get it and I appreciate it," Emily sighed. "And you're right… She takes advantage of me and it's because I *let* her…and I need to put a stop to it. I know that."

"As long as you know," Mr. Harris approved. He looked at his watch. "Should I make your mother wait while you and I have some lunch?"

Emily giggled. "That would be what she deserves," she said. "But no, you should get back before traffic gets too bad."

"Rain check on lunch then?" he smiled.

"Of course," she smiled in return.

Mr. Harris leaned over and gave Emily a kiss on her cheek, before gesturing to Will, who was still sitting at the other table. "Don't be too hard on him, he was just trying to do what he thought was right."

"Yeah, I know," Emily agreed. She waved to her father. Once he was out the door, she signaled Will to come over.

Her fiancé approached with caution. Slowly sitting across from her, he wasn't sure what she would say. "So…am I in trouble?" he wondered.

After a moment, Emily shook her head no. "I appreciate what you tried to do but, forced make up sessions…they don't work."

"I get it and I'm sorry," Will replied, sincere. "I just want everything to be perfect for you, you deserve it."

Emily forced out a small smile.

"But I will stay out of *this* part of your life as long as you want me to," he assured.

Emily reached over and grabbed his hand. "I don't want to talk about this anymore," she said. "I want to go to Essex Orchard and pick pumpkins. Get cider and pumpkin donuts. Then I want to go back to your place and carve pumpkins with you and Anthony… Can we do that?"

Will smiled. "Sure can," he beamed, standing from his seat. "Let's go."

Chapter 22

"Mom, thanks for watching the boys for me while I handle some business," Malajia said, guiding the twins towards the kitchen to her mother.

"Of course, sweetie," Mrs. Simmons smiled, watching the boys run around her into the kitchen. "Boys, we're going to bake some cookies a little later, okay?"

"Okay!" they squealed with excitement.

Malajia shook her head as her mother chuckled. "Mom, if you overload them with sugar, they're spending the night with you," she groused.

"Oh stop, I never gave *y'all* a bunch of sugar," Mrs. Simmons dismissed with a wave of her hand. "Y'all were just hyper on your own."

"Yeah, and I'm paying for that now," Malajia muttered. "Anyway, I'll be back in a few hours."

"Okay," Mrs. Simmons said, studying Malajia. "You running some fancy errands?"

Malajia looked perplexed. "Huh?"

"You look like you're dressed for an interview."

Malajia ran a hand over the back of her neck. "Mom, you remember how I used to get *dressed* dressed just to go to the store when I was younger," she reminded. "I still do the same thing, just minus the miniskirts and bra tops."

Mrs. Simmons frowned as she slowly folded her arms. "You never went out of this house in a bra top."

Malajia's eyes shifted. "Oh yeah, maybe I changed into that *after* I left the house," she recalled. Catching her mother's angered stare, Malajia sucked her teeth. "Mom, I'm twenty-eight now, you gonna smack me with your slipper over something I did when I was eighteen… Seventeen…six— fifteen."

"Keep tempting me," her mother grunted, turning to head into the kitchen.

Malajia chuckled. "I love you. You're the best mother in the world," she called after her mother, amusement in her voice.

"Yeah, yeah, carry your sneaky behind on somewhere," Mrs. Simmons jeered from the kitchen.

Malajia's mouth fell open. "That was rude, Evelyn," she threw back. As she got ready to head out of the door, she heard her father's voice calling her as he walked down the steps. "Ugh," she grunted.

"You look nice," Mr. Simmons commented, standing at the bottom of the staircase.

Malajia looked at him. "Thanks, see you."

"Hey, wait a minute," he called, halting her hasty departure out of the door.

Malajia let out a sigh and spun around to face him. Her face was void of any pleasantries.

Mr. Simmons approached her. "You still insist on keeping up with this teenaged attitude, huh?"

"Still insist on treating my husband like trash, huh?" Malajia threw back, folding her arms.

Mr. Simmons rolled his eyes. "I'm very civil to him."

"You're *condescending* to him," Malajia spat. "That's not being civil."

"Look Malajia, I have accepted Mark okay. You married him and had kids with him, I have no choice *but* to," he explained.

Malajia shook her head. "Dad, you show more respect to the stray cat that keeps digging up Mom's herbs," she snarled. "Hell, *Dana*'s ugly boyfriend probably gets more respect."

Mr. Simmons stared at Malajia. "Dana has a boyfriend?"

Malajia sucked her teeth. "Focus Richard, *God*," she huffed, opening the door. "Oh, and she has *two* of them," she told, walking out and shutting the door behind her.

Sidra grabbed her folders and stood from her seat. The staff meeting had gone on for longer than she'd anticipated. "Ugh, I'm so behind," she muttered to herself, glancing at her watch.

"Talking to yourself again, huh?" Carlie commented, reaching for her bottle of water.

"Yeah," Sidra curtly replied, walking to the door.

"Hey, are you working late tonight or are you hanging out with your cute friend?"

Back facing Carlie, Sidra rolled her eyes. "Working late," she threw over her shoulder before walking out. Sidra made the journey down the hall to her office. Walking in, she put her folders down and sat at her desk. Her phone showed a missed call; Sidra immediately hit the redial button.

"Hey Em, you called?" Sidra said once Emily picked up.

"Yeah, sorry to bother you, but I have a wedding question," Emily replied.

"You're not bothering me, what's up?" Sidra wondered.

"If people don't RSVP by the noted date on the invitation, do I cross them off the list or leave them on?" Emily asked.

Sidra frowned. "If it were *me*, I'd cross them off," she said. "You gave people over two months to RSVP."

Emily sighed. "I know, but I'll be crossing off a lot of my family."

Sidra shook her head. "Yeah, they *would* be the ones to not listen," she ground out. "Tell you what, give me their numbers, and I'll call to follow up with them."

"No that's okay, I'll do it," Emily insisted. "I should've *been* followed up with them."

"You shouldn't *have* to, let me handle it for you," Sidra pressed.

"I got it, but thank you," Emily replied. "I'll call you later."

Sidra sighed. She didn't understand why Emily kept refusing to allow the girls to help. "Okay Em. Talk to you later."

Ending the call, Sidra turned her attention to her laptop. As she began typing, she heard a tap on the door. "Come in," she called, glancing up. She smiled when Josh opened the door. "Hey you."

"Hey," Josh replied, walking in and shutting the door behind him. "Robin said I could come on up."

Sidra adjusted her position in her seat. Josh had been in town for four days and she was enjoying his company. She was dreading the day that he would head back to Delaware. "What brings you by?"

"Well, I know that you said you couldn't get off today, but I was hoping that maybe we could grab some lunch," he proposed.

Sidra let out a sigh. "I'm sorry sweetie, I'd love to but I'm behind on some work that I need to do for this case, so I'm just going to work through lunch today."

Josh successfully hid his disappointment. "Oh, that's no problem, I understand," he said. He had made good on his promise and delayed his flight for two more days; Josh just wanted to spend as much time with Sidra as he could. "I've worked through plenty of lunches."

Sidra chuckled. "You're the boss, you can take a lunch break whenever you want."

Josh thought for a moment. "This is true," he shrugged. "Okay, well, I'll leave you to your work. I'll just see you later… We can hang out then if you're not too tired."

"I'll be working a bit late tonight, but I won't be too tired. I'll see you when I get home."

Josh nodded. "Sounds like a plan."

"What are you going to do until then?" Sidra asked as he reached for the doorknob.

"Probably check out this car show that's going on today," he answered.

"Of *course* you are," Sidra giggled. "Have fun."

"Thanks."

Sidra watched as Josh walked out of the office. "Damn it," she hissed to herself, vigorously typing on her laptop.

Josh exited the glass doors of the office space and headed for the elevator, until he heard someone calling his name. He spun around, confused. "Did you just call me?" he asked Carlie, who was heading for the elevator herself.

Carlie smiled a seductive smile. "Yes," she confirmed.

Josh held the same confused look. "Sorry…do I know you?"

Carlie shook her head. "No, not *yet*," she crooned. "I work with Sidra."

Josh relaxed his frown and smiled. "Oh okay." Sidra had only introduced him to one coworker, and that was Robin.

"I overheard her mention your name...that's how I knew what it was," she clarified.

Josh nodded. "And *your* name is?"

"Carlie." Carlie stuck her hand out. As Josh shook it, she put her other hand over top of his. "Came to visit Sidra, huh?"

"Yeah, I wanted to see if she could have lunch with me but she's busy."

"Yes, she's the firm's Miss Worker Bee," Carlie chortled, releasing Josh's hand from her grip. "It's a shame that you came all the way down here just to eat lunch alone."

The way that she was staring at him wasn't missed by Josh. "It's fine," he returned. He gave a slight wave. "It was nice meeting you Carlie."

"You too," Carlie said. "Hey, hold on," she called as he went to walk away. Josh turned around. "I know I'm not Sidra, but *I'm* free for lunch if you want some company," she proposed.

Josh stared at her. No she *wasn't* Sidra, but Josh had to admit that Carlie was an attractive woman. "Well..."

"I know this nice little restaurant around the corner," she added.

Josh hesitated for a moment. He didn't know if Sidra would appreciate him going out to lunch with her coworker. Then again, it wasn't like they were in a relationship. *She doesn't care what I do, anyway.* "Okay," he agreed finally.

Carlie gave him a wink. "Great... Shall we?"

Josh gestured for her to walk ahead of him as they headed for the elevator.

Chasity picked up her cup of coffee and took a sip. She made a face at the bitter taste, then put it back down. Seated at a small table in a coffee shop downtown, she alternated between taking bites of her sandwich and typing on her laptop. Working while on her lunch break had become routine for Chasity over the past few weeks.

Her phone rang. She glanced at it, then glanced at her watch before answering the call. "Yeah Dad?" her tone was unenthusiastic. She put her head in her hand as he began to speak. "You're *where*?" she pinched the bridge of her nose. "I'm working right now— Yes, through lunch… Okay, that's fine. I'm at the coffee shop at the end of the block."

"Great," she muttered to herself once she disconnected the call. She went back to work on her laptop, but the sound of someone calling her name distracted her. Looking up, Chasity saw her father walk into the shop, holding her daughter's hand.

Despite her bad mood, Chasity feigned a smile as they walked up to her table.

"Hi Mommy," Kayla cooed, reaching up for her. Chasity bent down and hugged her.

"Hi," Chasity returned. She picked Kayla up and sat her on her lap, as her father took a seat across from her.

"You look tired," he commented.

Chasity narrowed her eyes. "Thanks," she sneered.

"I didn't mean it in a bad way," he amended, apologetic.

"Doesn't matter," Chasity replied. She wasn't surprised that she looked tired, because she *was* tired—*exhausted* even—and the coffee wasn't helping.

Derrick tapped his hands on the tabletop. "Well, the play was great," he mentioned, enthused.

"That's good," Chasity returned, tone dry.

"Kayla really enjoyed herself. Even said that she wanted to write a play when she grows up."

"It'll probably be about cats," Chasity commented, earning a giggle from Kayla and a chuckle from Derrick.

Chasity was so preoccupied with work that week that she'd almost forgotten that her father had asked to take Kayla to a play that day.

"I'm actually glad that the one in New York was sold out and we had to go to the one here in Philadelphia," he continued. "I've never been to the venue down here. It's nice."

Chasity was half-listening as she typed on her laptop with one hand, while Kayla played with the bracelets on her other.

"You know your mother almost bit my head off when I went to her house to pick Kayla up," he chortled. "She's so territorial."

"I know, she's crazy," Chasity mumbled, still focused on her screen.

Derrick looked at Chasity for a few moments; she stared at her laptop screen with laser like focus. "Chasity," he called.

"What?" she answered, still typing.

"Chasity," he called again, voice stern.

She looked up, annoyed. "*What?*"

Derrick folded his arms. "Are you going to engage in this conversation?"

"I *spoke*, what more do you want from me?" she snarled.

"For you to actually *engage*," he calmly returned.

Chasity frowned. "You don't see that I'm working?" she threw back. "I told you when you *called* me that I was working. What are you *doing* here anyway?"

Derrick sat back in his seat and let out a sigh. "The play was over and since we were downtown, I figured that we would pay you a visit before I dropped her back off at your mother's house," he answered. "Kayla wanted to see you."

Chasity rolled her eyes. "Doubt it," she grunted.

Derrick put his hands up. "Okay, *I* wanted to see you," he admitted. "I would've felt bad, being within minutes of you, and not stopping by."

"Wouldn't be anything new," Chasity muttered under her breath.

Derrick leaned forward. "I didn't hear you."

Chasity put Kayla down; her squirming was getting on Chasity's nerves. "I said take her to Mom's, I have to finish what I'm doing," she deflected.

"Aww, I want to stay with *you*," Kayla whined.

Chasity put her hand over her face and let out a forced laugh; she was two seconds from snapping. "Little girl, *please* don't get on my nerves," she warned. "Go with your granddad. I'll see you later."

Pouting, Kayla walked over and grabbed Derrick's hand as he stood from his seat.

"If you want, I can hang out with her until you get off, and just drop her off at your house," he offered. "That way, both you and Jason can go straight home."

"Dad, you can hang out with her as long as you *want*," Chasity ground out. "Just go *do* it."

Derrick gave a nod as Chasity went back to her laptop. "I guess that means 'leave me alone', huh?"

Chasity glared up at him. "You *really* want to keep annoying me right now?"

Derrick shook his head. "No…that's the last thing I want to do," he muttered. "See you Chasity." He looked down at Kayla and smiled, even though he didn't feel like it. This visit hadn't gone as he had hoped. "Let's go little one."

Chasity watched them head for the door, zoning in on her daughter. Guilt hit her like a ton of bricks. Chasity knew that she'd just hurt her daughter's feelings. Kayla had just wanted to stay with her, and she was pushed away. Like a tidal wave, Chasity's own childhood sadness flooded back to her. *Oh my God, what am I doing to my baby?* Tearing up, Chasity moved her laptop aside. "Wait," she called.

Both her daughter and father turned around. Chasity signaled for Kayla to come to her. Kayla walked over and stood in front of her; she looked down at her shoes.

Chasity put her finger under Kayla's chin, lifting it gently. "I'm sorry," Chasity apologized, sincere. She touched her little face. "I—I didn't mean to snap at you. I'm not mad at you."

"It's okay, Mommy," Kayla replied, fiddling with her little bracelet.

A tear spilled down Chasity's cheek. "No, it's *not*," she stressed, wiping the wetness from her face. "It's *never* okay. You didn't do anything wrong, baby." She pulled Kayla into a hug. "I'm so sorry. I love you."

"I love you too," the little girl spoke.

Derrick put a hand on Chasity's shoulder. "Chasity, she's okay," he soothed. "She understands that you're busy and she knows that you love her."

While Chasity appreciated her father's words, she didn't believe them; she felt like a terrible mother. Releasing Kayla from her embrace, she smoothed a few wayward strands back into her ponytails. "Go finish having fun with Pop-pop. I'll see you later okay?"

Kayla nodded, smiling.

Chasity watched them leave, before letting out a deep sigh. Wiping the remaining tears from her eyes, she pulled her laptop back in front of her.

Sidra stuck her key in her door and pushed it open. "Josh," she called. "I'm back, sorry I'm so late." She hung her jacket on her coat rack and set her purse and keys on a nearby end table. Removing her heels, she looked around. "Josh," she called again. Hearing no answer, she looked confused.

Josh had taken Sidra up on her offer to stay at her place, so she'd given him her spare key. She figured he'd be there when she got home; it was almost eight in the evening and they were supposed to hang out. She reached for her phone but didn't get a chance to dial; the key jiggled in the door. She watched as Josh pushed it open.

"Hey," Josh smiled.

"Hey," she returned, setting her phone down.

Josh walked over and flopped on the couch. "How was work?"

Sidra sat down next to him. "Productive, I guess."

Josh nodded.

"Are you hungry?" she asked. "You want me to make some dinner? Or do you want to go out to eat?"

"You just got home from work," he pointed out. "I know you're tired, your eyes are half-closed."

Sidra giggled. "They're not that bad, Josh."

"You look drunk," he teased, earning a light backhand to his arm.

"Stop it," she pouted.

"Hey, don't worry about it. Even half-lidded, your eyes are beautiful," he complimented.

Sidra turned her head so he couldn't see her blush. "Thanks." She tapped his leg as she faced him. "But seriously, I may be a little sleepy, but it's not like it's the first time I've done things while tired. We can go out, I just have to freshen up."

Josh sat up as Sidra rose from the couch. "Um, Sid—"

"Give me like fifteen minutes."

"Sidra—"

Sidra tapped her finger to her chin. "Make it twenty."

"Sidra stop," Josh called, halting her progress.

Perplexity masked Sidra's face. "What's the matter?"

Josh stood up. "I mean it, you should rest for the night," he insisted.

The confusion had yet to wane from Sidra's face.

"We can do something after you get off work tomorrow."

"I said I'm *fine*," she insisted, folding her arms.

Josh let out a sigh. "Look, to be completely honest… I already made plans to do something else tonight," he broke to her.

Sidra scrunched her face. "What *kind* of plans?" she charged. "And why does it seem like whatever it is, you don't want *me* to go."

Josh rubbed the back of his head. "Because, it'll be a little weird for you to be sitting at a table with me and a date," he answered.

Sidra's arms dropped to her side. She didn't know if she heard him correctly. "I'm sorry, what?"

Josh shrugged. "I have a date tonight."

Sidra's eyes widened. "A date with *whom*?" she barked, upset. "Who do you *know* out here besides me? You just *got* here."

"So?" Josh threw back.

"*So*, you're supposed to be out here spending time with *me*," she fussed, pointing to herself.

"Is that not what I've been *doing* for the past few days?" Josh argued. "I lost money on my hotel just so I can spend as much time with you as possible."

"Oh, sorry that it's *such* an inconvenience for you Josh," she spat. "I'll give you the money back for your hotel."

Josh frowned. "Stop trying to play me, Sidra," he chastised.

"I'm not, *Joshua*," she countered, voice laced with agitation. "You can't blame me for being upset."

"The hell I *can't*," he argued.

She put her hands up. "Josh, you're leaving on Wednesday," she stressed. "Who knows *how* long it'll be before we see each other again."

"I *told* you that I will make it a point to visit more," he huffed.

"That is not the *point*," she harped. "The point is that instead of hanging out with *me*, you're wasting time with some random chick who you'll never see again."

"How do *you* know I'll never see her again?" Josh spat, folding his arms. Sidra rolled her eyes. "And she's not that random, you know the girl."

Sidra stared at him. "Excuse me?"

"You know the girl I'm going out with," he reiterated. Sidra held her stare; she was totally lost. "Your coworker...Carlie."

Sidra's mouth dropped open. Her blood ran cold. "Are you freakin' serious?!" she erupted.

"Are *you* serious?" Josh hurled back. "I can't believe you're acting like this."

"Well, *believe* it," Sidra flashed back.

Josh frowned at her.

"Josh, are you out of your damn *mind*? You can't date my *co-worker*," she ranted, pointing at him. "Especially one that I don't even *like*."

Josh stood up as he shook his head in disappointment at Sidra's ranting. "You not liking someone isn't my problem," Josh barked. "I'm a grown ass man, I make my own decisions."

"She goes after married men," Sidra told. "She was going to try to go after Jason when she saw him in Arizona. I had to practically threaten her ass."

Josh stared at Sidra, frowning. That certainly made him think twice about his date. However, he was still annoyed with Sidra's judgmental behavior. He wasn't about to give her the satisfaction of cancelling his plans. "Well," he began, eerily calm. "It's a good thing that I'm not married, isn't it?"

Sidra's lip curled in disgust. "Oh *really*?" she challenged. "*That's* what you're into these days? Homewrecking hoes?"

"Who I'm into is none of your goddamn business," Josh ground out.

Sidra jerked her head back. "You—Josh you're *not* going out with her."

Josh raised an eyebrow. "I know you're not trying to *forbid* me."

"You're damn *right* I'm forbidding you!" she erupted.

Josh smirked. "Yeah okay," he dismissed, walking towards the door.

"Where are you going?!" Sidra yelled at him. Josh ignored her. "Josh! Are you planning on sleeping with her?"

Josh spun around. "Whether I do or *don't*, is *again none of* your damn business!" he hollered back.

Sidra put her hands on her head. She felt her stomach churn, her breathing quickened; panic was setting in as Josh headed for the door. She knew that if he left, the way that he was feeling, he might sleep with Carlie just to spite her. Sidra couldn't handle the thought of any other woman having him, least of all Carlie. "Josh," she called, voice calmer.

"*What,* Sidra?" he huffed.

She took a deep breath, trying to fight the tears from forming. "Don't go out with her…*please*," she pleaded.

Josh let out a quick sigh and turned back around. "Sidra, you don't control what I do or who I see," he bit out.

Sidra looked at the floor. "I promise you, I'm not trying to."

"You *are*," he insisted, upset. "And I don't understand *why*."

Sidra shook her head. "You can do better."

Josh rolled his eyes. "Sidra, you're doing that judgmental shit again," he hissed. "I don't judge the men *you* date."

"I don't *date* anybody," she said, fixing a desperate gaze on him. "I don't want—" She put her hands out. "Josh you… You deserve better than *her*…better than *any* of these girls that you've been dealing with."

Josh folded his arms. "Yeah?" he taunted. "Since you are the expert in my relationship choices, tell me, who is better for me? Who is the perfect woman for me? Who should I date? *Please* enlighten me on your expertise."

Sidra hesitated; she couldn't hold the tears back anymore. They filled her eyes, glassing them over. "Me," she answered finally.

Josh made a face. "Come again?"

Sidra took a deep breath. She started, now she had to

finish. "Josh—"

"You said 'you', I did hear that correctly, right?" he cut in.

Sidra nodded. "Yes...um... The reason why I don't want you dating anybody else is because...I want you to date *me*."

Josh stared at her in disbelief.

"I want you to be with *me*," she finished.

Josh held his gaze. "Are you joking?"

"No, I'm dead serious," she promised, a tear spilling down her face. "I've been wanting that for a while now."

"How long is a *while*?" he asked, still not believing what he was hearing.

Sidra swallowed hard. "Like umm...five years."

Josh's eyes widened. "Five years?!" he erupted.

Sidra flinched at the bass in his voice. "A little longer, to be honest," she corrected, nervously fiddling with her hands. "I realized how I felt about you..." she sniffled, "before we graduated."

Josh stared at her for a long moment, trying to process what he'd just heard. "You've got to be out of your goddamn mind," he barked finally. "Over five years?! You knew that your feelings changed for me *that* long ago and you didn't *tell* me?" Josh was livid. "How could you *do* that to me knowing how I felt about you?!"

More tears streamed down her face. "I thought you had moved on from me."

"You know damn *well* I *never* moved on from how I felt about you!" he yelled. "Every relationship that I've had, I let *fail* because of the feelings that I had for *you*. And you just *left*, knowing—why did you *do* that?"

Sidra sucked in a breath. "I'm sorry... I didn't know how to tell you," her voice quivered.

"Bullshit!"

Sidra hid behind her hand as she fought to keep from sobbing out loud.

"I *knew* shit was weird with you, I *knew* shit had changed with you and you let me walk around thinking that it was my fault," he ranted.

"I'm sorry," she cried.

Josh shook his head. Sidra had gotten on that plane five

years ago without telling him the truth, and it *hurt*. She knew that he had still loved her, had watched him tear up when she'd headed for the elevator. If she had just told him the truth, Josh knew they could have been together. Instead, five years had been wasted on empty relationships, and unnecessary distance. "You're fuckin' selfish for that shit," he spat, snatching open the door.

"Josh, I'm sorry. I love you," she sniffled as he stormed out the door. "Please don't leave!" she hollered after him. He slammed the door behind him, and Sidra collapsed in a heap on the floor and cried out loud.

Chapter 23

"What time are you leaving work later?" Chasity asked into her headset while typing on her laptop.

"On time," Jason chortled. "And so are *you*."

"Oh, I *am*," Chasity assured. "I worked through my damn lunch *again* so I could leave here on time. I'm over it."

"Trust me, I hear you," Jason replied. "You know, it looks like I'll be leaving on time for a while, now that the big projects are being sent to the Phoenix team to handle."

Jason's sullen tone wasn't missed by Chasity. "Still think they're going to fire you after everything you've done to get that team up and running?" she asked.

"Who knows," Jason sulked. "They have yet to have a meeting about my future here, but in the meantime, I'm not giving this place anymore of my time after the eight hours that I signed on for."

"I don't blame you," Chasity said, looking through her emails. "I've said it before, they don't appreciate you there."

"I feel the same way about *your* job," Jason returned. "All that overtime you worked last week was ridiculous."

Chasity sighed. "I know. I *hate* it, but I needed to get those other projects done."

"*And* you did it while you were sick," Jason added. "You feeling any better today?"

Chasity shrugged, forgetting for a moment that he couldn't see her. "I wasn't sick, I was just feeling run down," she answered. "And no, I'm not feeling any better."

"You need more sleep."

"Maybe," she returned.

"Not *maybe*, you *do* stubborn ass," Jason insisted. "I'll take care of Kay and dinner. I want you to go to bed early. You need the rest."

There was a pause on the line. "Fine," Chasity replied after a moment.

Jason chuckled. "Were you trying to ignore me just now?"

"No, sorry, I just got called into by boss's office," she informed, staring at an email.

"Oh. Everything okay?"

"Who *knows* with this bitch," she muttered. "I gotta go, I'll see you later."

"See you," Jason replied.

Chasity ended the call and rose from her seat. Letting out a huff, she made her way to her boss's office.

"Hi Chasity, have a seat please," Pamela requested, pointing to the empty chair.

Chasity sat down, crossed her legs, and folded her arms. She was in full defense mode. Every time she was called into this office, she left more agitated than when she'd went in.

"First, I have to let you know that you need to stay until seven today," Pamela began.

Chasity's eyes widened. "Excuse me?" she challenged.

"Yes, we have an important meeting at six. I need you here for it."

Chasity tried her best to keep calm. "I can't work overtime today," she argued. "I worked it the last week and a half."

"Sorry but it's mandatory that you stay for it," Pamela stood firm.

Unfolding her arms, Chasity took several deep breaths. She grabbed the chair handles and gripped them tight. She could've choked Pamela with her bare hands. "Is that all?" she asked through clenched teeth.

Pamela clasped her hands together. "No, it isn't."

God, just kill me now, Chasity thought as she sat there trying not to jump across the desk.

"I also want to say that you've done an excellent job with those projects," Pamela praised.

Chasity's face had no traces of a smile. *So the fuck what?* She elected not to respond.

"Our clients are very happy."

Chasity stared at her. "Okay, nice to know... Is *that* all?"

Pamela tapped her hand on her desk, grinning. "I have

some great news," she began.

Chasity's eyes burrowed through Pamela. "Okay," she managed to get out through her tight jaws.

"Word of mouth has traveled about how well our company is handling our clients and because of the excellent reviews, we have signed on five new clients."

Chasity fought the urge to roll her eyes. *I promise, I don't give a fuck.* "Congratulations." Her tone was dry.

Pamela nodded. "And of *course* they are expecting the same type of service that the other clients have been raving about." She took a deep breath. "Therefor, we...*I* feel that the best way to meet their expectations is to give them to...you."

Chasity frowned. "What?" she hissed.

Pamela put her hand up. "Listen—"

"Are you taking the other clients that I *currently* have away from me and giving them to somebody *else*?" Chasity questioned, angry. "Because that is the *only* way that I'm going to be able to handle five new ones."

"We are adding them."

Chasity wasn't hiding her anger any longer. "Have you lost your mind?" she snapped. "You can't keep *doing* this to me, you *have* to give some of this work to someone else."

"They don't want to *work* with anyone else."

"I don't care *what* these damn people want," Chasity argued. "It's not my fault that you won't hire people who know what the hell they're doing."

Pamela let out a long sigh as Chasity ranted.

"This is too much for one person to handle," Chasity continued. "You *know* it, that's why *you* won't do it."

"I'm the manager," Pamela bit out. "I *manage*. I don't have to do what you do."

Chasity was taken aback. "The only thing you've *managed* to do is make my life here a living hell," she flashed back.

"Is that so?" Pamela challenged. "Chasity, I've put up with more from you than any other person here. I've tolerated your attitude for years—"

"What about what *I've* tolerated?" Chasity threw back, pointing to herself. "And I'm not the type of person who *tolerates anything.*"

"Listen Chasity, I'm not going to go back and forth with you, it's done. You're getting these new clients and one of them is coming in for this mandatory meeting, so just be prepared."

Chasity sat there for a moment, not saying anything. She tried her best to calm herself down, but for the life of her, it wasn't working. Feeling herself once again reaching her breaking point, she got up from her seat and stormed out of the office. Hastily walking past her desk, she grabbed her cell phone and retreated to the bathroom. Locking the door, she paced back and forth, just as she had done so many days before. And like those days, angry tears spilled down her cheeks. This time, they didn't stop. They kept coming. Chasity felt like she couldn't breathe.

Dialing a number, she put the phone to her ear and kept pacing.

"Hey babe," Jason greeted.

"Jason, I can't do this anymore," she cried, between labored breaths.

"Whoa, baby what's wrong?" Jason asked, voice filled with concern. "Are you crying? What happened?"

Chasity stopped pacing and leaned her back against the wall. "I…I can't take this job anymore," she sobbed. "I can't."

Jason let out a deep sigh. He hated to hear her upset. If he could fly down to her job and curse everybody out for her, he would. "You know what you need to do, Chasity," he said.

Chasity closed her eyes. Her mind was racing—how could she walk out of her job? A well-*paying* job? What if Jason lost *his* job? What would they do? Sure, they had some savings. Sure, she still had her Miami condo and her childhood home in Tucson that she could sell if need be. But why even put her family in that situation?

Jason could sense her hesitation, and he knew her fears. "Chasity," he called.

"Yeah," she answered, still trying to calm herself down.

"Do what you need to do," he insisted. "We'll be okay. I promise you."

"Jason—"

"I *promise* you," he insisted. He didn't care if he had to

work *three* jobs, Jason was not going to allow Chasity to suffer anymore. He was tired of it, just like she was.

"Okay," she said finally. "I gotta go."

"I love you."

"Love you too." Hanging up, she stared at her phone and took a deep breath. Chasity wiped the tears from her face, and walked out of the bathroom. She went to her desk, grabbed her purse out of her drawer, and shoved the one picture that she had of her family inside of it. She shut down her laptop and grabbed her jacket from the back of the chair.

Pamela walked over to her. "Chasity, I need to see you back in my office," she said. "The client sent us some samples of what they want, and we need to get a presentation together of how we're going to implement it."

Chasity glanced at her, fire in her eyes. "Do it your fuckin' self, *manager*," she hissed.

"*Excuse* me?" Pamela barked, shocked.

"You *heard* me. I quit."

Pamela spun around to face Chasity's departing back. "You *can't* quit. Are you out of your—"

Chasity turned around and fixed a glare that would have killed her boss if looks had the ability; it was enough to shut Pamela up. Without uttering another word, Chasity walked away, leaving Pamela and her coworkers stunned.

Alex sipped her sangria. "Oh my God, this thing is so good," she mused.

Eric chuckled. "Finally came to the dark side with the liquor, huh?" he teased. "First wine, now this. I remember you hardly ever drank."

"Yeah well, it's amazing how a glass of wine or a frozen drink can destress you after a long day," Alex joked in return. After barely talking to each other due to busy work schedules, Eric and Alex had finally met up for another date. Sitting in a steak restaurant overlooking Times Square, Alex was excited. "This is nice," she smiled.

Eric stuck his fork in his salad. "Yeah, it is," he agreed. "I can't believe that I finally got you to go out with me."

Alex giggled. "I know right," she teased. "No, but I do feel bad for how things were between us when we were back in college."

"Oh?"

"Yeah," she nodded. "I gave you a lot of mixed signals... A lot of attitude and bitterness—"

"Come on, let's not relive that," Eric cut in, sincere. "We were both young and both had growing to do."

Alex shrugged, but she still felt bad.

"Who knows," Eric continued. "If we would have been together then, we might not be where we are now, you know?"

Alex sighed. "I guess you're right," she agreed. "I might not have moved out here had I been in a relationship."

"Sure, you would've," Eric contradicted. "You're not the type of woman who would put her dreams on the back burner for a man." Alex's mouth fell open. "Trust me, I don't mean that in a bad way."

"So, you're telling me you like ambitious women?" Alex asked.

"Absolutely," Eric confirmed, confident. "It's an attractive quality."

Alex smiled as she reached for her fork. "Well…that's good to know."

As the two ate their starter salads, the server returned with their entrees and another round of drinks.

Eric leaned forward and took a whiff of his ribeye steak. "This smells so good," he breathed. He took a bite. "And tastes even better."

Alex ate some of her food. "This is actually the place that I wanted to bring you the last time you came down here," she said. "But unfortunately…well you know how that turned out."

Eric chuckled. "Yeah, I remember," he teased. "How's your ankle by the way?"

"Very sturdy," Alex threw back, amused. "I'm just glad that you didn't *see* me fall."

Eric laughed. "I'm glad that you didn't see *me* trip down that last step outside your building."

Alex busted out laughing. "Wait *what*?"

Eric nodded as he cut into his steak. "Yeah, my head jerked

back all hard. I dropped my car keys," Alex laughed some more. "Somebody had to stop and ask me if I was okay."

"Wait, stop I can't breathe," Alex panted, putting her hand up as she tried to control her laughter.

"I felt stupid, I can only imagine how I *looked*," he chortled.

Alex fanned herself as her laughter finally subsided. "Wow…you poor thing," she sympathized. "But thank you for telling me that. You made me feel so much better about *my* spill."

"No problem," Eric smiled.

Alex sipped her drink once again. "So…I know we talked but didn't really go into depth… How have the last few years been for you?"

Eric sipped his own drink. "They've been good," he replied. "I finished grad school, started my career—"

"Dated?" Alex questioned.

"Well, of course," he answered. "Been in a *few* relationships actually."

Alex fidgeted in her seat. She'd brought up the topic; she knew they had to talk about past relationships. Especially if they were going to move forward in the way she hoped. They were both adults with a past, so she was ready to handle it.

"I know that *you* have as well," Eric added when Alex didn't respond.

She shrugged slightly. "Yeah…I have," she confirmed. "I actually didn't even go on a date until like a year after I graduated…"

"Oh yeah?"

"Yeah, I went on a few random dates," Alex answered. "Then ended up in a relationship with some guy that I met at a holiday party."

Eric listened. "And?"

"*And* he turned out to be a piece of shit," she said. "A year's worth of wasted time." She folded her arms on the table. "After I broke up with him, I just decided to chill on the dating for a while."

Eric nodded. "Not every relationship is meant to last, you know," he said. "I mean it sucks when they end, but in some cases you're just meant to take something from them. To *learn* something…then you move on."

"Yeah well, the only thing I learned, was what I *don't* want," Alex replied. She looked at Eric as he ate more of his food. "*Speaking* of which…I *know* that I want to give *us* a chance."

Eric looked up at her.

"Truth be told, I've been thinking about you a lot and I know what I want now so…I'm willing to at least *try*." She stared at him, hopeful. "If that's what you want too." When Eric looked away briefly, Alex was mortified. "Oh my God…that's *not* what you want," she concluded.

Eric looked back at her. "No, no, Alex—"

"God, I'm so sorry," she cut in, completely embarrassed. "There I go, forcing my wants on to people."

"Alex—"

"Eric, you don't have to feel bad about it," Alex assured him, putting her hands up. "I was just being overzealous—"

"Alex, will you stop?" Eric cut in, holding out his hand for one of hers. "Calm down," he soothed. Alex gave him her hand. "That *is* what I want."

Alex smiled. "Yeah?"

Eric nodded. "Of course," he confirmed. "You and your crazy self have held a piece of my heart for a long time."

Alex chuckled. She couldn't believe it; finally she would have everything she wanted and needed. A great career, family, friends, and a relationship with someone just as ambitious as she was. Someone who she could build a life with, travel with, marry and one day have children with, when she was ready. Which was certainly not now, but the possibility still excited her.

"But—"

"Huh?" Alex snapped out of her mental bliss. "But what?"

"Before we go down this road…I need to tell you something," he began.

Alex looked nervous. "What's that?" When Eric hesitated, Alex fought the urge to panic. Alex withdrew her hand. "Oh God, you're not married are you?"

Eric looked insulted. "*No.* Why would I be here with you if

I was married?" he bristled. "Don't lump me into some—"

"I'm not Eric, I just figured I'd ask," she cut in.

"Alex, I am absolutely a hundred percent *single*," he assured.

"Okay…" she thought for a moment. "Are you sick or something?"

Eric chuckled. "I am absolutely, a hundred percent *healthy*."

"Okay…have you been to jail?" she wondered.

Eric shook his head; she was clearly grasping at straws. "No. My record is clean… It's not a bad thing, I assure you," he said.

Alex couldn't take the suspense anymore. "Okay Eric…what is it?" she pressed. "Whatever it is, I can handle it… *We* can handle it together."

Eric rubbed his hands together as he tried to gather his words. "So, you remember I said that I had relationships within the last few years?"

"Yeah."

"Well… One of those relationships resulted in a child," he revealed.

Shock overtook Alex's face. "Oh," was all that she could get out.

"Yeah…I'm a father," he said. "My daughter is two… Her name is Zoe."

"Oh…" Alex was still in shock. "Are you and umm…the mother…"

"We co-parent, that's *all*," he assured. "There are no feelings there, I promise."

Alex put her hands on her head. "Oh…"

Eric tilted his head. "Are you okay?" he asked her.

Alex grabbed her drink and took a sip. "Um hmm," she muttered as she sipped again.

"Look, I'm sorry that I didn't tell you before," he began as Alex sat in silence. "I wasn't sure where this thing between you and I was going, but now that I know, I needed to tell you, so that you could have the option to decide if you wanted to continue on or not."

Alex just sat there as Eric spoke. It wasn't that she didn't like children; she *loved* them. It wasn't that she didn't want children. She *did*, just not yet. And when that time came, she always dreamed that her first child would also be her husband's first child. She didn't know how to handle this information. The man that she wanted was sitting in front of her, willing to move forward with her, and she just couldn't wrap her head around being a stepmom too.

"Alex," Eric called when she didn't say anything. Alex stared at him. "Are you sure you're okay?"

Alex held her gaze on him. She knew what she felt, but didn't have the heart to say it. "Umm...yeah," she said after a moment.

Chapter 24

"Mom, I already told you I'm not cooking for Thanksgiving," Malajia bristled, placing items in her cart as she pushed it through the grocery store aisle.

"Malajia, *you* have a house *too*. You can cook one Thanksgiving dinner," Mrs. Simmons argued. "Hell, give me a damn break."

Malajia rolled her eyes. "Mom, you already know you make the best food, so just embrace it and make your greedy family dinner," she pressed.

Mrs. Simmons flagged Malajia with her hand. "Girl—"

Malajia giggled, making a face at her sister Maria when she walked up to them in the aisle. "Eww, I knew I smelled cheese."

Maria frowned at Malajia, then shot her mother a side-glance when Mrs. Simmons snickered. "Really Mom?"

"Maria I'm sorry but you know your sister is a fool," Mrs. Simmons laughed.

Maria rolled her eyes. "*That*, she is," she agreed.

Malajia giggled again. She was elated when Mrs. Simmons had popped up for a surprise visit, even with Maria in tow. She even had them both tag along with her while she went grocery shopping.

"Sike naw," Malajia dismissed, holding out a pack of candy. "Here, put this in your cart."

"No," Maria barked. "Every time I shop with you, I always end up paying for half of your stuff."

"Not my fault you let me guilt you into buying me things since you used to be mean to me when we were younger," Malajia threw back, shrugging.

Maria narrowed her eyes at Malajia. "Remind me why I stopped."

Malajia laughed. "Because I'm an awesome sister and you love me."

"Yeah, yeah, I do," Maria relented, snatching the candy from her sister. She placed it into her hand-held basket. "Are you still coming over my house this weekend?"

Malajia looked perplexed. "Was I *supposed* to?"

Maria sucked her teeth. "Malajia, you said you would bring the boys over."

"Girl don't nobody wanna come over your house," Malajia ground out. "You never have good snacks. Everything is wheat and *grains*."

"Wheat *is* a grain, stupid," Maria threw back.

"And nobody *wants* that," Malajia hurled back, shaking her hand in Maria's face. Malajia looked at her mother. "Mom, don't let her bring anything to Thanksgiving."

"First of all, my bread pudding is awesome," Maria argued, pointing to herself.

"Is it made with *wheat* bread?" Malajia teased, earning a laugh from her mother and a flipped middle finger from Maria.

"Hey now," Mrs. Simmons chided, pointing at Maria. "Malajia, be nice to your sister."

"I love her, I just don't like her food choices," Malajia maintained; she glanced back at her sister. "We'll be over one of these days, but this Saturday I'm going to some pumpkin patch, apple farm with Chasity... We're taking the kids."

Maria raised an eyebrow. "Pumpkin patch, apple farm?" she questioned.

"That's what her daughter calls it," Malajia chortled. Passing by another aisle, Malajia gasped. "Ooh, they have the pumpkin cookies! Maria, buy me these," she demanded, placing several packs of the cookies in Maria's basket.

"Malajia, no! You're going overboard," Maria barked, placing the cookies back on the shelf.

Malajia sucked her teeth and stomped her foot on the floor. She then turned her charms on her mother, smiling.

Mrs. Simmons caught her stare. She raised an eyebrow. "*What* girl?"

"Mommy," Malajia cooed. "You buy the best cookies."

Mrs. Simmons tried to hold her stern face, but couldn't help breaking into laughter. "Give me the damn cookies," she demanded. "You're lucky my grandbabies like cookies," she added as Malajia placed two packs of cookies in her mother's outstretched hand.

"They ain't getting none of these," Malajia muttered.

"What did you say?" Mrs. Simmons challenged.

"Nothing," Malajia quickly lied. She looked up as a man walked over to them.

"Hi Malajia," he greeted, polite.

Malajia smiled at him. "Hey Brenden," she said.

"I was picking up a few things when I saw you over here, figured I'd come over and say hi."

Malajia nodded. "Okay...*hi*."

Brenden chuckled. "Well, I'll be on my way, but since I'm here, I figured I'd ask if you considered—"

"No, not yet," Malajia quickly put out, cutting him off. "But I'll let you know if I do."

"Okay great," he beamed. "Talk to you later then."

"Yup," Malajia said as he walked off. Malajia scratched her head, avoiding the gazes of her mother and sister.

"Umm, who was *that*?" Maria charged.

"Someone who obviously knows me," Malajia ground out.

"*Clearly*," Maria replied. "What was he asking you to consider?"

"Mind your business wheat germ," Malajia spat.

Maria sucked her teeth. "I'll be at check out," she bit out, walking off and leaving their mother to continue her questioning.

"Malajia..."

"What? You never had anybody say hi to you in a store before?" Malajia huffed, examining items on a shelf.

"Oh of *course* I have," Mrs. Simmons assured. "But I never looked guilty when they *did*." Malajia shot her mother a side-glance. "What's going on with you Malajia?"

Malajia rolled her eyes. "Mom, I can tell you've been watching those suspense movies on cable again," she bit out.

Mrs. Simmons couldn't help but chuckle. "Those movies are so good."

"I'm sure they *are* but they make you act all suspicious," Malajia pointed out. "Change the subject, talk about what you're gonna be making for Thanksgiving. It's like two weeks away, you need to plan accordingly."

Mrs. Simmons shook her head. "Fine."

"Thank you," Malajia grunted. "But seriously, don't let Maria bring that nasty bread pudding. I'd rather eat carrots."

Mrs. Simmons just continued shaking her head.

"Alex, you have to suck it in," Emily said, holding the fabric of Alex's bridesmaid dress while trying to fasten it at the back.

"I *am* sucking it in!" Alex exclaimed.

Emily let out a huff as she tried to attach the clasp. "Come on," she gritted through clenched teeth. As one of her fingers slipped from the clasp, another got caught in the fabric. Emily jerked her hand, and her nail snapped. "Ouch! Damn it!"

Alex spun around, covering her mouth with her hand. "Are you okay?"

Emily clutched her finger, feeling the pain radiate through. She winced. "Sure, my nail just split to the middle of my finger, but I'm fine," she grunted.

Alex grabbed Emily's hand and examined it; it was starting to bleed. "I'm sorry sweetie," she replied, sincere. "I'll get the clippers and cut it down."

"Thanks." Emily sighed, sitting down on Alex's couch. Having gone to Jersey for another wedding dress alteration, Emily had decided to make the rest of the journey by train to see Alex. While she was there, Alex was excited to show Emily that she had her bridesmaid dress ready to go. What Alex wasn't expecting was to not be able to fit into it.

Alex returned from her bathroom with nail clippers, peroxide, and a bandage. She adjusted her dress, then sat down next to Emily. "Here, give me your hand," she prompted, holding her own hand out. "I'm about to perform surgery."

Emily stared at her. "Can you numb me first?" she asked,

then winced when Alex held the clippers to her damaged nail.

"I'll be gentle, I promise," Alex replied then carefully began to clip Emily's nail. "I swear, the dress fit just fine a month ago."

"I don't doubt that," Emily replied, keeping her eye on her hand.

"Yeah well, I guess I've been eating a little too much," Alex muttered.

"Well—" Emily winced as she felt her nail pull.

"Sorry," Alex said, still cutting.

"You look good no matter what you weigh, Alex," Emily tried to console. "So don't beat yourself up about it."

Alex chuckled. "Thanks, you just made my fat ass feel a bit better." Emily giggled a little. "I'll lose these extra pounds, don't worry."

"I'm not worried. It's not a big deal, you can just get the dress altered," Emily proposed.

"Oh hell no I'm *not*," Alex refused. "That is unnecessary money when I can just cut down on the tacos and tiramisu to lose these extra pounds."

Emily raised an eyebrow at her. "You eat those two things together?"

Alex stared back at her. "Sometimes."

Emily giggled. "Well suit yourself." After Alex finished cutting Emily's nail, she swabbed it with peroxide and carefully wrapped it in the bandage.

"Better?" Alex smiled.

"A little," Emily replied, examining her finger. "Oh, I almost forgot to tell you—" she began. The sound of Alex's phone ringing interrupted her.

Alex reached for it and glanced at the ID. "It's Malajia," she announced, putting the call on speaker. "Hey—"

"Yeah, yeah, no time for pleasantries, I have Chasity on the line," Malajia curtly interrupted.

"Is everything okay?" Emily asked.

"No, hold on. That was rude Malajia," Alex hissed.

"So was Emily coming up this end and not coming to visit me," Malajia threw back.

Emily's mouth fell open. "Malajia, I'm only up here for a

few —"

"God, will you come on with the purpose of this phone call? I have shit to do," Chasity ground out through the line.

"Girl, you can play kitty tea party later, this is important," Malajia barked back.

Chasity sucked her teeth. "I will fuckin' hang up and you know it."

Alex chuckled. "Wait, Chasity you're really playing kitty tea party?"

"No!" Chasity yelled; she huffed. "*Maybe*, just come the fuck on."

"Anyway," Malajia interjected. "Have any of you spoken to Sidra?"

Emily shook her head. "No, not since that phone call she made to us after she and Josh had that blow up."

"Yeah, I haven't either," Alex chimed in. "I keep calling her, but she's sending me to voicemail. I tried her job phone too; she seems to be forwarding personal calls to the receptionist."

"Same here," Chasity added.

"Okay, then it's not just me," Malajia said. "This is pissing me off. I know she's upset but damn, she's just blowing us all off."

"I agree," Alex commented. "I hate that she lives so far, because you know I'll pop up on her butt."

"Hell yeah, we'd *all* be sitting right outside her apartment until she opens the door," Malajia added.

"This is true," Emily agreed. "But I guess we should just give her space. She'll talk when she's ready."

"Normally I would agree with that Em, but she was pretty damn distraught over Josh's reaction," Chasity said. "I'm not gonna lie, I'm a little worried about her."

"I'm right there with you Chaz." Alex scratched her head. "So, what are we going to do?"

"I'm gonna keep blowing her goddamn phone up until she answers," Malajia said. "I'm not playing with her ass."

"Look, I really have to go, but I think I know what to do," Chasity alluded.

"You wanna tell us what that *is*?" Malajia asked.

"I will once I figure some stuff out," Chasity answered. "Malajia, give me Ms. Vanessa's number."

"Sending it now," Malajia said.

"Cool, I'll call y'all later."

Malajia let out a sigh as Chasity hung up. "Y'all bitches stress me out," she huffed.

"Malajia—"

"Later," Malajia stopped Alex's would be scolding by hanging up.

Alex frowned at her phone. "That girl—" she shook her head. "I feel bad for Sidra… I kind of know what she's going through. I remember telling Eric that I wanted to be with him before graduation, and how horrible I felt when he shot me down."

Emily reached out and gave Alex a sympathetic pat on her shoulder. "Speaking of Eric," she began. "I have space for him at the wedding. So, if you want to bring him as your plus one, you're more than welcome."

Alex let out a sigh. She was annoyed at herself for even mentioning Eric; now she had to deal with her conflicting feelings for him. "Thanks sweetie, but don't waste your money."

Emily looked confused. "It's not *wasting* money," she said. "If you two are together now, why *wouldn't* I invite him? Besides, I already counted for a certain number of people and I'm still missing RSVP's of people who I'm sure won't come *anyway*, so the space is his."

Alex clasped her hands together as she pondered her next words. "So…*about* that," she began, looking at her. "Eric, I mean."

"What's wrong?" Emily asked, taking notice of Alex's tone.

"I don't know if Eric and I are really together or not," Alex alluded. "I mean…I haven't talked to him in like a week."

Surprise registered on Emily's face. "Why?"

Alex shrugged. "Things are just a little complicated right now." She waved her hand in Emily's direction. "You know what, never mind."

"No, no 'never mind'," Emily insisted. "Obviously you

want to say something, so go ahead."

"No Em, I don't want to bother you with my issues," Alex said.

"*Please* bother me, I need a distraction," Emily begged.

Alex rubbed Emily's shoulder. "Is your family still—"

"We're talking about *you*, what's going on with you and Eric?" Emily cut in, adjusting her position on the couch. "I thought you were moving towards a relationship with him. Did he change his mind or something?"

Alex too adjusted her position in her seat. "It's just that…I'm starting to wonder if a relationship with him is…in the cards for me right now."

Emily tilted her head. "Alex…what's the matter?" she asked point-blank.

Alex put her hands up. "Okay… I found out that he has a child."

Emily stared at her. "*And*?" she asked, giving her head a slight shake. Alex had made it seem like it was something awful.

"*And* I don't know if it's something that I want to deal with right now," Alex added.

"Alex, a child shouldn't be looked at as something that you *deal* with," Emily pointed out.

"But Em…it *is*," Alex insisted. "I mean, what if I want to go on a date and he can't get a sitter?"

Emily shrugged. "Then you go over his place and do something *there*."

"Okay well, what if I want to take a trip and he can't go because he can't get a sitter… Or the child is sick or—"

"Alex, these are all things that you will need to consider when you have your *own* child," Emily pointed out.

Alex tossed her hand in the air. "Yeah, when I'm *ready* for a child," she huffed. "I don't mean to sound rude, but…I never saw myself with someone who already had a child. My ideal situation would be…not *this*."

Emily stared at her wide-eyed. "You *do* know that things don't always work out how you want right?" she asked. "They sometimes work out how they're *supposed* to."

"Come on Em," Alex returned. "Who would *really* find

that situation ideal? I mean come on, nobody really *wants* to be a stepparent."

Emily frowned slightly. "Hello," she said, waving her hands. "Did you forget that *I* am a stepmother?"

Alex looked apologetic. "Em, I know that, and I don't mean—"

"To sound ignorant?" Emily finished. "You definitely do."

Alex's head jerked back. "Well…damn."

"Yeah," Emily confirmed, her voice stern. "You're entitled to feel how you want, but the way that you said all that stuff just now…" she shook her head. "I hope you don't come off that way to him."

Alex folded her arms and sat back in her seat.

Emily let out a sigh. "Look Alex, his situation might not be ideal for you and that's fine," she said. "Being a parent to someone else's child isn't necessarily an easy thing for everyone—"

"How do *you* handle it?" Alex cut in, looking at her.

"Easy, I love Anthony like he was my own," Emily reasoned. "I've been in his life since he was two years old."

Alex reached out and patted Emily's knee. "You're a good woman, sweetie."

"Thanks…and you are too when you're not being ignorant," Emily joked, giving Alex's hand a light tap. Alex chuckled. "But seriously, if it's not something you want, you *do* need to tell him, just in a better way."

Alex sucked her teeth and repeatedly stomped her feet on the floor, whining like a child. "But I *do* want him," she pouted.

"Then you have to accept the fact that he has a *child*, Alex," Emily urged, amused by Alex's temper tantrum.

"I know, I know." Alex sat back up. "I have some thinking to do." She stood up. "What time does your train head back to jersey?"

"In like three hours," Emily answered, watching Alex stretch.

"Good, I still have more time with you," Alex smiled. "Let me get out of this dress and fix us something to eat…something *healthy* I guess."

Emily nodded as Alex made her way to the hallway.

As Alex took another step, she tripped over the long dress and stumbled into the wall. "Oh my God!" Alex shrieked, holding onto the wall. "I think I *do* need to get this thing altered. It's too long." She turned around to find Emily doubled over with laughter. Alex pushed herself up and slowly put her hands on her hips. Emily could barely breathe. "Really Em?"

"How did that even *happen*?" Emily laughed.

Alex flagged her, lifting the bottom of her dress up and stomping down the hall.

Chapter 25

"I'm trying to figure out why everything is so damn expensive," Malajia griped, folding her arms.

"*You're* the one who ordered the most expensive shit on that menu," Chasity replied, handing pink cotton candy to her daughter.

"You damn right, this caramel popcorn is good as shit," Malajia chuckled, shoveling a handful of popcorn into her mouth. She held the bag out in Chasity's direction. "You want some, or are you gonna eat that dry ass lemon with a candy stick in it?"

Chasity side-eyed her. "You know I'm pissed about this shit, right?"

Malajia laughed. "You swore that a 'lemon stick' was something fancy. You paid three dollars for a half of lemon with a candy stick stuck inside."

"Shut up," Chasity griped. She and Malajia had made the two-hour drive with their children to the Pennsylvania farms, as promised. "I would've thrown this damn thing at that girl, but I have to set a good example for my daughter…I guess."

"Shit, my boys would've thrown it at her *for* you," Malajia joked. "With they bad asses." She looked down at the twins, who were arguing over their shared cotton candy. "Aye, stop fighting or I'mma eat the damn candy in your face."

Chasity laughed. "Why didn't you just get them their own?" she asked, as they made their way from the crowded concession stand.

"Easy for *you* to say, you have *one* child," Malajia threw back. "Nope, they better share and love it."

Chasity looked at her lemon stick and rolled her eyes. "I don't even *want* this shit."

"Can I have it?" Kayla asked, holding her little hand out.

Chasity handed it to her. "Knock yourself out kid," she said, taking some of the cotton candy.

Malajia held out her bag of popcorn again in offering. "*Sure* you don't want some?"

"I don't," Chasity answered, eating the cotton candy.

Malajia shrugged and went back to eating. As they continued walking, she pointed to a sign in the distance. "Ooh, let's go get some pumpkins." Walking through the opening, they headed into the back, towards the hordes of pumpkins and people.

The children immediately ran over to the box filled with little pumpkins and began rummaging through it. "So y'all just gonna touch all the pumpkins with your sticky little hands, huh?" Malajia asked the smiling children.

"Yes," they answered.

"Right on." Malajia returned, eating more popcorn as Chasity snickered. Malajia nudged Chasity. "You gonna get a big pumpkin?"

"For *what*? It's just gonna sit on the counter," Chasity ground out.

"Whatchu' mean? You're not gonna carve it? Or make a pie?" Malajia asked, surprised.

"Nope."

Malajia flagged her with her hand as she watched her sons pick out their pumpkins. "You corny."

"Where's *your* damn pumpkin?" Chasity griped. "You over here up *my* ass about me not getting one, and you haven't walked *your* cheap ass over there to get one."

"Oh no, I don't need to get a big one because little do these boys know, I'm giving them little ones they're picking out to my mom to make a pie with," Malajia said without a qualm. She gestured to her boys. "That's right boys, pick out as many as you want."

Chasity shook her head. "That's a damn shame."

"Trust me, they won't care," Malajia dismissed.

Fifteen minutes later, the group meandered through the crowds to the face painting area. "Can we stop at the car so I can drop these damn pumpkins off, first?" Malajia complained, adjusting the large bag of little pumpkins that she had purchased.

"Nope, you must pay for your stupid choices," Chasity refused, a small bag with Kayla's two little pumpkins in hand. "You should've known that they were going to go overboard picking those things. They're *your* kids after all."

"Nobody asked you for your opinion, Chasity," Malajia snarled. She looked down at Kayla, who was bouncing happily, watching other children getting their faces painted. Her long ponytails bounced with her. "Cupcake, you wanna hold these for Auntie Lajia?" she asked, holding the bag out.

"Make me smack them goddamn pumpkins on the ground and step on them," Chasity threatened, giving Malajia a hard nudge.

"Some good example, witch," Malajia spat. She sucked her teeth and adjusted the bag once again. They approached the sign. "Okay, so they have face painting and temporary tattoos," Malajia read. "Which one do y'all want?"

"Face paint," Kayla beamed, tossing a hand in the air.

"And let me guess which one you want," Chasity said. "Kitty."

"And I guessed right," Chasity chuckled. "Pink right?" Kayla nodded. "Glitter too, right?" Kayla once again nodded. "Yeah…you know that's getting washed off before you go to bed later, right?"

"She can sleep in it for a night," Malajia cut in before Kayla could respond.

"Shut up," Chasity spat at Malajia. She handed some money to the cashier, while Kayla told the lady what she wanted.

Malajia looked at her sons. "Okay, what do y'all want?"

"Tattoo," Marvin answered.

Malajia rolled her eyes to the sky. "They *would* pick the more expensive ones," she muttered to herself. She pointed to the pictures. "Look, they have a bunch of nice ones. Pick one out."

The twins spent about a minute staring at the poster.

"Anytime now, boys," Malajia urged.

"Umm...I want the star," Marvin answered.

"I want the star too," Marlon chimed in, excited.

Malajia frowned. "Foreal?" she asked. "You want that star?" the boys nodded. "My dudes, it's all little. Why don't you get something else?"

"Star," Marvin smiled, tossing his arms up.

"Nah bruh look, they have a dog one. Y'all like dogs remember?" Malajia insisted. "And it's big too. You can put it on your shoulder."

"We don't like the dog," Marlon pouted.

Malajia looked down at her boys; she was not amused or sympathetic. "Really? All of a sudden y'all don't like dogs?" she grunted. "Y'all be barking all day long at that stupid dog cartoon on the television, rolling around the damn house, playing fetch with cookies, and now that you have an opportunity to get a dog tattoo, that will last you a few days, you decide to get this little minuscule *star?* ...Y'all are *really* gonna make Mommy pay twelve dollars *apiece* for a tiny star?"

The boys looked at each other, then looked back at Malajia. "But the star is for twin power," Marlon said.

"Twin—*twin* power?!" Malajia smacked her face with her hand and pulled it down. "Twin power," she muttered to herself. "I'm about to twin *they* damn power." As she pulled money from her purse, Malajia glanced over at Chasity, who was cracking up laughing at her. "Shut *up*, Chasity," she barked.

Chasity was practically in tears.

Kayla tugged on Chasity's arm. "What's so funny Mommy?" she asked.

"Auntie Lajia is salty," Chasity laughed. Kayla looked at Malajia, whose eyes were narrowed, and busted out laughing too.

"You don't even know what you're laughing at Kitty face," Malajia hissed at Kayla.

Chasity moved Kayla behind her. "Get out my baby's face," she barked.

Malajia threw her head back and let out a loud groan. "Yo, I *can't* with these kids, sis," Malajia complained, handing the cashier her money. "Two stupid stars, please."

"Yay, twin power," the boys rejoiced.

"Shut up! Just shut up," Malajia snapped.

Chasity busted out laughing again.

After the children finished up with their tattoos and face painting, they went back to the car to place their bags in the trunk, then headed to a grassy area with a bench. Chasity and Malajia sat down, while the children played in the grass ahead of them.

"I'm so damn tired," Chasity complained.

"We've only been out here for like two hours," Malajia pointed out.

"I also drove the two hours to *get* here," Chasity argued. "You're driving back by the way."

"Fine," Malajia agreed, adjusting the lightweight scarf around her neck. "Thanks for inviting us to come with y'all today though… This was cute."

"Sure," Chasity replied, examining her nails.

"Even though I spent like a hundred dollars on popcorn, pumpkins and twin-power tattoos and shit," she griped. Chasity snickered. "I'm glad that's funny to you."

"It is," Chasity chortled.

Malajia stared out at the children playing in front of her. "They're so cute," she cooed.

Chasity sighed. "Yeah, they are," she agreed. "They make you do shit you normally don't do… I don't like no damn farms." This time, Malajia snickered. "But Kayla wanted to come."

"I'm surprised you even agreed to it," Malajia said, "This seems like something your mom or Jason's parents would do with her."

"My mom and Jason's parents aren't *her* mom," Chasity pointed out. "*I'm* the one who should be doing this stuff with her."

Malajia looked at her. "You're not feeling guilty, are you?" she asked, crossing her legs.

Chasity shrugged slightly. "Work had me tied up a lot," she vented. "It was getting to the point where she was hesitant to ask me to do things with her anymore because my answer was always 'no', or 'later'… It makes me feel like shit."

Malajia held her gaze. "Chasity, you *can't* beat yourself up about that," she consoled. "She knows that you and Jason love her, and she also knows that you both work and that you spend time with her when you *can*." She gave Chasity's arm a rub. "Stop it, you're a great mom."

Chasity looked at her. "Even when I snap at her because I had a bad day?" she questioned.

"Yes," Malajia confirmed.

Chasity sighed, shaking her head slightly. "I don't know how true that is, but thanks for saying it."

"It *is* true," Malajia insisted, stern. She gave Chasity's arm a slight squeeze. "Okay?"

"Okay," Chasity answered, despite how she really felt.

Malajia glanced out ahead of her to check on the children. "*Speaking* of your work, you seem to be home more often," Malajia added.

"I know," Chasity replied.

"What, they're letting you work from home now or something?"

Chasity looked out in front of her. "No, I quit."

Malajia's head snapped towards Chasity, her mouth falling open. "Wait, what?"

"I quit my job," Chasity confirmed.

Malajia was still in shock. "What? *When*?"

"A week ago."

Malajia jerked her head back. "And why am I *just* now hearing about this?!"

"Quitting a job isn't something that you run and tell someone," Chasity pointed out.

"Bitch, I'm not just *someone*," Malajia fussed; Chasity rolled her eyes. "We tell each other *everything*… I even tell you what color *drawls* I have on."

"I wish you would stop *doing* that shit, too," Chasity threw back, annoyed.

"*No*, and I have on black ones today," Malajia threw back. Chasity flagged her with her hand. "Well…how are you feeling about it?"

Chasity shrugged. "I don't know," she admitted. "I mean, on one hand, it's nice not to go to bed dreading what'll be waiting for me at work the next day… But on the other hand…I quit a *job*. A high-paying job at that."

"And you'll find *another* one," Malajia cut in. "As good as you are at what you do? Please, you can work anywhere. Those people at that company treated you like shit. They didn't appreciate you, and I hope all of their clients leave them."

Chasity chuckled. "Hell they just *might*. *None* of those idiots that still work there, know anything."

"Well, good for 'em," Malajia said. "Seriously though…you'll find something else."

"I don't even know if I *want* to find something else," Chasity said. "I'm not cut out to work for anybody."

"Then *don't*," Malajia said. "Go back to freelance like you did when you graduated...but not right away if you can help it… You deserve a break for a while."

"Yeah, that's what Jason says," Chasity said. "It's crazy, I'm a stressed out, worried mess and he's just like 'we'll be fine'."

"You don't believe him?" Malajia wondered.

"Not saying that, just overthinking shit as usual."

Malajia sighed after a moment. "Well, *I* seem to be having the *opposite* issue," she alluded.

"Meaning what?"

"That I think I've had *enough* of a break from the work world," Malajia clarified.

Chasity looked at her.

Malajia let out another sigh. "Chaz as much as I love being a wife and mother…*just* being that isn't for me anymore," she confessed, glancing down at her hands. "I miss working…so much so that I've been sneaking around, going on job interviews."

"Who sneaks to go on a job interview?" Chasity wondered, perplexed.

"I know right?" Malajia agreed. "People sneak around doing all *kinds* of shit and *I* lie about going to appointments when they're really job interviews," she snickered. "I'm sure my mother thinks I'm cheating on Mark… She was looking at me sideways when one of my old coworkers came up to me in the grocery store." She adjusted her scarf again. "He emailed me a while ago about a position at my old company becoming available and went to ask me if I was considering applying for it, but I cut him off before he could ask me… Evelyn runs her mouth too much."

Chasity shook her head. "You know that's crazy right?"

"Who you tellin'?" Malajia agreed. "She knows I'm not cheating on Mark. And *especially* not with a dude who wears pinstriped pants to a grocery store."

"No crazy, that's not what I mean," Chasity said, shaking her hand in Malajia's direction. Malajia looked at her. "Why are you hiding the fact that you're going on interviews?"

Malajia let out a sigh. "Because Mark has feelings about me working," she said.

"And what feelings are *those*?"

"He doesn't *want* me to," Malajia bluntly stated.

Chasity frowned. "That's very…1950s'ish," she commented.

Malajia chuckled as she nodded slightly. "Yeah, I know," she said. "But I know that's not because he feels like he wants to control anything… Let's face it, he don't run a damn thing." She pushed some of her hair over one shoulder. "I think he just feels that if I have to work, that means that he's lacking and I don't want him to feel like that, because he's *not*."

"Malajia, I get that you want to protect his feelings, but what about *yours*?" Chasity pointed out.

"I know," Malajia sulked. "I know. I also think that he feels like me working while I was pregnant caused my pressure to go up the way it did… I think it scared him."

"Did you tell him that that had nothing to do with it?" Chasity asked. "Your pressure went up because of you being *pregnant*, not because of you working."

"I know, my job wasn't stressful at *all*," Malajia remembered. "I *told* him that and he didn't believe me… He felt like shit and begged me not to go back to work right away…and now it's almost four years later and I—" she took a deep breath. "Do I sound like a shitty person? I mean, I'm sitting here complaining about having the ability to be with my children all day…about not *having* to work… I feel like I sound ungrateful."

"Come on, cut that shit out," Chasity chastised. "There's nothing wrong with wanting change. Being a stay-at-home mom isn't for everybody and a lot of times it's more stressful than actually *being* at work."

"This is true, at least in *my* case," Malajia agreed.

"Besides, you didn't go through four years of getting on everybody's nerves trying to pass those damn classes to get your degree to not *use* it," Chasity added.

Malajia looked at her. "I got on your nerves?"

"You *still* do," Chasity teased. Malajia giggled. "Talk to him, Mel."

Malajia glanced back down at her hands. "Yeah…I will eventually," she said. "See…*this* is why I tell you everything."

Chasity didn't respond; something behind Malajia had her words frozen in her throat.

Malajia looked up at her, frowning at the horrified look on Chasity's face. "What's the matter with you?"

"I umm…I think there's a possum over there by that tree," Chasity slowly drew out, trying not to raise her voice.

Malajia stared at her. "Bitch don't play," she hissed. "Don't scare me like that, I fuckin' hate possums. One was sitting in the bottom of my garbage can last week…scared the shit out of Mark when he went to throw the trash out."

"I swear to God, I'm not playing," Chasity promised, slowly moving up in her seat.

Malajia slowly turned around, and looked behind her. "Eww! Oh my God," she shrieked, snapping her head back. "Ewww," she whined, shaking her hands out in front of her. "It's over there walking all ugly what do we do?"

Chasity slowly stood up. "Let's just get the kids without alarming them and get the fuck out of here."

"Okay, okay," Malajia agreed, trying to calm herself down. She stood up. "Okay…calm, cool and collected. We got this."

"Right," Chasity said, looking at the children. "Kayla ven aqui, we gotta go now!" she hollered, causing Kayla to take off running for her.

"Don't show off because you and your baby can speak

Spanish!" Malajia hurled at Chasity as Kayla jumped into Chasity's outstretched arms.

"Get your damn kids!" Chasity hollered back at her.

"Boys, we out! Run over here like you ran from your baths last night!" Malajia yelled, holding her arms out.

The boys took off running, then suddenly stopped and looked over at the possum.

"Hey! Why are y'all stopping?" Malajia hollered.

"Ooh, a puppy," Marvin beamed.

"That is not a puppy!" Malajia erupted, clapping her hands with each word. "Get *over* here," she demanded through clenched teeth, hurrying over to them and grabbing them by the hands. "It is *not* the time to act like your Daddy."

Chasity laughed as they ran for the car.

"Shut up, Chasity!" Malajia barked.

Chapter 26

"Guess who's coming home for Thanksgiving?" David spoke through video chat.

"Bro, we're too old to do this with you," Mark bristled, earning a snicker from Jason, who was sitting next to him at a bar.

David sucked his teeth, "Fine, it's me."

"No shit," Mark chuckled. While the women and children were still out, Mark and Jason had decided to go out for a drink.

"Always have to be a jackass," David grunted, fussing with something off screen. "Have you talked to Josh recently?"

Mark rolled his eyes. "No, not since he called me screaming in my goddamn ear that day on his way to the airport," he said. "He's trippin', *you* need to talk to him."

"Trust me, I've *tried*. He won't answer the phone," David told them. "It's not surprising though. You know how he gets."

"Yeah well, he better get his shit together before Thanksgiving," Mark grumbled. "Ain't nobody tryna see Josh cryin' while I'm eating my turkey and shit."

Jason shot Mark a confused look. "What does one even have to do with the other?"

"I don't even know," Mark chuckled, sipping his drink.

"Seriously, I can't even wrap my head *around* this thing," David said. "I mean, after all this time Sidra and Josh might *actually* end up together."

"Judging by how pissed Josh was, I doubt it," Mark ground out. "Man, Sidra was trippin' holding on to that information all that time."

"Yeah," Jason agreed. "I don't get the point in that."

"I'm sure she has her reasons," David placated. "Though I wouldn't know what those reasons *are*...she won't answer my phone calls either."

"It's cool, the girls will handle her ass," Mark commented.

"I guess *we're* handling Josh?" Jason assumed.

"Oh *we* ain't handling *shit*. He's David's problem now," Mark joked.

"Wait, what?" David laughed.

"David, you know you got that patience shit that nobody else has," Mark explained. David shook his head. "Nah, *I* don't have it in me to deal with this 'Josh and Sidra' mess anymore."

"Well, I'd love to stay on and talk about all the stuff you're lying about now, but I have work to do," David said to Mark. "We *both* know if Josh called you today to vent about Sidra, you'd listen."

"Yeah...but I wouldn't *like* it," Mark muttered. "Aye David, before I hang up on you, are you finally gonna tell us if you banged that girl you mix formulas with?"

David sucked his teeth before hanging up to the sound of Mark's laughter.

"He swear 'cause he don't wear glasses anymore that he can talk shit," Mark jeered.

Jason shook his head, reaching for a nacho on his plate. "I don't even know why I'm eating this," he said. "I gotta go home and cook."

Mark reached for one of his potato skins. "Okay Mrs. Adams," he teased.

"Hey fuck you," Jason grunted. "There is nothing wrong with cooking for your family...bitch."

Mark nearly choked on his food as he laughed. "Nah, I'm fuckin' with you," he said. "I take care of dinner sometimes too." He rubbed the crumbs from his hand. "I know Mel gets stressed looking after the boys by herself a lot. I try to take some of the burden off of her you know? ...Like today, she's farming it up with the boys, so I'mma take care of dinner... Pizza and cheese steaks on deck."

Jason chuckled. "Sounds like it'll be a night full of clogged arteries," he joked.

"Yup," Mark agreed without a qualm.

The amusement left Jason's face as he took a sip of his drink, pondering his next words for a moment. Jason wasn't sure if he even wanted to say them. "Hey umm, this question will be out of nowhere, but… Is your company hiring?"

Mark looked at him. "I don't think so, why?"

Jason shrugged slightly. "I guess I'm just trying to be proactive."

"For what?" Mark wondered. "Don't tell me you lost your job."

Jason shook his head. "No…at least not yet," he explained. "So, like I said, I'm just trying to be proactive."

"Damn," Mark said, sympathetic. "I hope that doesn't actually *happen.*"

"Me too," Jason agreed, somber.

"But honestly bro, I don't think my company will be hiring anybody for a while," Mark added. "They had layoffs last week."

"Oh shit," Jason reacted.

"Yeah, it sucks. The holidays are coming up and shit," Mark sympathized.

"Good thing *your* department wasn't affected," Jason said.

"Right?" Mark breathed. "I was scared as shit all day that day. They said they had one more round of layoffs, but my manager highly doubts that my department will be affected."

Jason nodded. "Good."

Mark glanced back at Jason; he looked troubled. "You really worried about losing your job?"

Jason nodded slowly. "Yeah…the amount of work that I'm doing has been cut significantly … Not to mention they had me train a whole team to do the job that *I* used to do—" he sighed. "Nobody has said anything to me, but I just have the feeling. I've applied to some companies, but haven't gotten any interviews yet."

"Shit, why *not?*" Mark griped. "You would think that a damn software engineer would have plenty of options."

"Nah, 'cause other companies who have software engineers aren't stupid enough to let them go, thus not creating an opening for *me* to get in," Jason complained. "It's cool, I'll figure something out…even if I have to work in another field."

"Doing *what?*" Mark wondered. "Unlike *me*, who hated accounting and was happy to switch careers, you *like* doing what you're doing."

"Sometimes you gotta do what you have to do to support your family," Jason pointed out.

"You talk to Chaz about this?" Mark asked.

"Of *course*, but I haven't brought it up lately because I don't want to stress her out," Jason answered, picking up another chip. "*Especially* since I talked her into quitting *her* job last week."

"What?!" Mark exclaimed.

Jason glared at him. "Was that necessary?" he grunted.

Mark put his hands up. "Sorry, you know I'm loud when I'm shocked," he defended.

"*Just* when you're shocked?" Jason quipped.

Mark shrugged; Jason shook his head. "Damn," Mark continued. "Quit huh?"

"Yeah. They were fucking her over, she *needed* to," Jason explained.

"Hey, I'm all for the Mrs. being stress free," Mark approved. "That's why I don't want Mel to work… I feel like that stress needs to be on me, not her."

Jason just sat there. "Yeah." He glanced at his watch. "Shit, I gotta go. I have to swing by my parents' house on my way home."

"Something wrong?" Mark asked as Jason stood up and put his coat on.

"Not really, I just have to drop something off to them," Jason replied, tossing some money on the bar counter. "I said that I would pay to get their storm door fixed. My damn brother broke the shit last month."

Mark picked Jason's money up and handed it to him. "Can y'all afford to do that in your situation?" Mark asked.

Jason set the money back down on the counter. "Yes," Jason curtly answered. "See you later."

"Later," Mark said to Jason's departing back. "Oh!"

Jason spun around. "Yo, you *gotta* find a goddamn indoor voice and *use* it bruh," he ground out.

Mark laughed. "Noted," he said. "Do y'all want to get together the day after Thanksgiving? All of us…I mean, whoever is in town?"

Jason shrugged. "I'm cool with it." He looked at Mark,

who was staring at him. "You're referring to everybody getting together at *my* house, aren't you?"

Mark shrugged. "I mean…you *do* have the biggest house… Not unless you wanna meet in Josh's apartment—he uses his spare room to store car parts and shit, but hey, we can make room," he joked.

Jason fought the urge to laugh. "Whatever, let me see what Chaz says."

"Her mean ass gonna say no and shit," Mark dismissed.

"She just *might*," Jason laughed, leaving Mark at the bar to finish his food.

Emily stared at the photo on her laptop. "I wonder if the girls will like these," she said to herself, simultaneously arranging packs of colored sand, a funnel, small mason jars, ribbon, markers and name tags on her kitchen table.

Jazmine passed by Emily, a plate of food in hand, eyeing the earrings on the screen. "Those are ugly," she spat.

Emily rolled her eyes and immediately closed the browser screen, shutting her laptop for good measure. "Thanks Jaz," she spat back, sarcastic.

"What? I'm just saying," Jazmine shrugged. "You weren't planning on *buying* those, were you?"

"Not anymore," Emily muttered, setting her laptop on the floor next to her.

"Well…*whoever* you were going to get them for, tell them to thank me because they would've been pissed." She laughed, "*I* wouldn't even wear those."

Emily looked up at Jazmine, who had taken the liberty of sitting across from Emily. "Is there something that you want Jazmine?" she asked.

"What, I can't sit here?" Jazmine ground out. "I'm about to eat and you're always bitching about me eating in the living room. Now that I'm about to eat in the kitchen, you have an issue."

"You know—" Emily clasped her hands together in an effort to calm herself down. She took a deep breath. "I don't feel like going back and forth with you right now," she said, tone calmer. "I need the table space," Emily gestured to the items. "I have stuff to do for the wedding."

Jazmine hopped up from the table, rolling her eyes in the process. "Whatever," she grumbled.

"Listen," Emily began, eyes on Jazmine as she headed for the living room, "I need your bill money on the first."

"Emily, I don't *have* it."

"I don't really *care* Jaz, you're gonna have to find some way to *get* it," Emily maintained. "I can't keep supporting you."

Jazmine let out a huff. "Sure Emily, I'll just go sell my ass then," she jeered.

"Well then *do* that," Emily flashed back. She was in no mood for Jazmine's pity party. Everybody was right; if she wanted Jazmine to respect her, she needed to make her. "I need it and I'm not playing this time."

Jazmine held an icy glare on Emily. "I would suggest that *you* sell some ass to get better items for your cheap ass *wedding*."

Emily pushed herself back from the table and stood up. Jazmine had just sucked the air out of the room, along with Emily's desire to work on her crafts. "Screw you," she barked, heading for the door.

"Maybe if you let that man of yours do that to *you*, you wouldn't be so fuckin' annoying," Jazmine hissed.

Emily spun around. "All the screwing *you're* doing hasn't made *you* any less annoying, so your argument is stupid," she threw back. "Oh, and find your own damn way back to Jersey for Thanksgiving because you're not riding with me."

"Wouldn't want to *anyway*," Jazmine hurled at Emily's back.

"Good, 'cause you're *not*!" Emily countered, storming out of the apartment.

Too worked up to wait for the elevator, Emily stomped up the flight of stairs and headed for Will's apartment. She knocked on the door.

Will opened it and smiled. "Hey my sunshine." Noticing the anger on Emily's face, his smile faded. "Oooh…she on your nerves again?" he assumed as Emily walked in.

"Yep."

"Why don't you sleep here tonight," he insisted, closing the door behind her. "I'm about to make some sundaes, and we can watch movies."

Emily let out a sigh, running a hand over the back of her neck. "Thanks, but I don't have an appetite."

"Okay...no sundaes then...for you," he joked.

Emily wanted to laugh, but couldn't. She let out another deep sigh instead. "I told her that she needed to have the bill money on the first." She flopped down on his couch. "She tried that 'I don't have it' mess again."

Will sat down next to her. "Don't back down this time babe," he said. "She *needs* to pay up."

"I know," Emily sighed. "I was about to make the wedding favors and now the mood is gone... It was supposed to relax me."

"It's weird how doing work relaxes you," Will chuckled.

Emily shrugged. "Only arts and crafts can do that."

"Gotcha." Will reached for the remote and turned the TV on.

Emily looked around. "Where's Anthony?"

"At my parents," he replied, running a hand over his head. "Mom insisted on him staying for dinner. I'll pick him up when he's ready."

Emily nodded, leaning her head on Will's shoulder.

Will put his arm around her and planted a kiss on her cheek. "Hey, you know what we could do, since we have the place to ourselves for a few hours?" Will asked.

"What's that?" she asked, somber.

"We could crack open that game system and test drive it."

Emily's eyes widened; she lifted her head. "You mean the game you bought Anthony for Christmas? The one that I already gift wrapped?"

Will nodded. "Yep."

"That's terrible," she chided, somewhat amused. "How are you gonna open his gift before *he* does...and *play* it?"

"Look, his hyperactive behind is lucky he's getting it in the *first* place," Will replied, laughter in his voice. "With this wedding and trying to get us a new car, I'm tapped out."

"Well, he's a good kid, he deserves it," she said. "Especially if it's *unopened*."

"Nah, we're cracking it open," Will maintained, jumping up from the couch and running in the back room.

Emily shook her head as she watched him step back into the living room, holding the intricately wrapped box in his eager hands. "Will don't, I spent so much time wrapping that," she pouted.

Will sat back down next to her and gave her a quick kiss on the lips. "And you did a great job," he smiled. "I'll be careful not to rip the paper."

Emily sat upright in her seat. "Have you *seen* the way you rip open mail? And chip bags?!" she exclaimed. Will laughed. "Please, you're gonna tear my work to shreds."

"Then I'll wrap it back."

"Eww, please," Emily huffed, folding her arms.

Will shrugged and slowly began to pull the tape from the paper. Hearing a small rip, he winced. "Shit."

Emily just shook her head. Keys jingled in the door, and she frowned slightly. "Do you hear that?"

Will paused and listened. They heard it again, accompanied by two familiar voices on the other side. Will's eyes widened. "Ooh! That's right, Anthony has a key," he panicked, grabbing the box and jumping up. "Damn it, I thought that he was gonna call me to come get him."

Before Emily could say anything, the door opened. Just as Anthony and Will's mother walked in, Will slid the box in his room and slammed the door shut.

"Hi," Anthony smiled.

"Hi little man," Emily smiled, holding her arms out.

Anthony ran over and gave her a hug, holding a bag in his hand. "Grandma made us cookies," he announced.

"Thank you Miss Wanda," Emily said, grateful.

"Yeah, thanks Mom," Will added.

"Oh stop it, no need to thank me," Wanda Palmer said with a wave of her hand.

Anthony looked at his father. Will was standing by his room door, a guilty look on his face. "Dad, what did you break?"

Emily busted out laughing; Will put his hand over his face and shook his head.

Chapter 27

Sidra adjusted the white fluffy robe around her shoulders, flipping through the channels on her fifty-seven inch flat screen television. Annoyed that nothing worth watching was on, she turned the TV off and tossed the remote to the floor. She'd used enough force that the back fell off, sending the batteries flying out.

"To hell with it," she muttered, adjusting her position on the couch. That cream sofa had been Sidra's solace for the past few weeks. After leaving work, she'd come straight home, change into her robe, grab food from her kitchen, flop down on the couch, and sulk. On weekends, she hardly left it. This Sunday was no different.

Sidra hadn't heard from Josh since he'd stormed out of her apartment. When he didn't return to her place or return her calls, Sidra knew that he'd taken the first available flight back to Delaware.

She'd told the girls what had happened, then refused to answer any more phone calls. Sidra was sure that she was worrying people, but at that point, she didn't care. Reaching for a plate on her coffee table, she grabbed a fork full of pie and stuffed it into her mouth, flopping her head back on her pillow.

She'd closed her eyes, hoping to sleep away her thoughts, but Sidra was disturbed by a knock on her door. She opened her eyes, but didn't get up. *The hell? I'm not expecting any company.* She closed her eyes again, only to hear another knock. "God, go away!" she barked at the door.

The knock turned into a loud rhythmic beat; Sidra jumped up from the couch in frustration, tied her robe closed and stomped to the door. Snatching it open, she snapped, "What?!" A look of shock immediately fell upon her face when she saw who was standing there. "*Chasity*?!"

"Hi sunshine," Chasity replied with exaggerated enthusiasm.

"What the hell are you *doing* here?" Sidra was stunned.

Chasity frowned. "Nice to see you *too*, Sidra," she ground out, moving past Sidra to get into her apartment. She rolled her carry-on suitcase near an accent chair, and turned back to Sidra.

Sidra closed the door. "Sorry." She held her arms out. "Hi," she greeted as Chasity hugged her.

"Sidra, this robe feels crusty," Chasity complained, parting from her.

"Shut up, it does not," Sidra spat. She ran her hand down the front, feeling something hard. "Ohhh, *there's* that candy that fell out of my mouth," she observed, pulling a piece of red candy from her robe.

Chasity scrunched her face up in disgust. "Ugh."

Sidra sucked her teeth as she walked over and laid back down on her couch, tossing the sticky candy on the coffee table.

Chasity sat on an accent chair and folded her arms. "You look disgusting," she ground out.

Sidra flipped her off, then bolted up straight. "Hold up," she began, putting a hand up. "My initial question was warranted. What are you *doing* here?"

Chasity examined her black nail polish. "Well, the last time we were together you were bitchin' about nobody coming to see you, so I figured I'd come visit for a few days," she said, nonchalant.

Sidra stared at her, blinking slowly. "Seriously?"

Chasity nodded.

"So..." Sidra pinched the bridge of her nose. "You fly across the United States to do a *pop-up* visit on me?"

Chasity nodded again.

"That doesn't sound crazy to you?"

"It does, but we all know that I'm a little bit crazy," Chasity dismissed. During the last group conversation with the other girls, Chasity had decided that instead of continuing to try to reach Sidra by phone, she would be the one to visit in person.

Sidra couldn't believe how Chasity was acting. "A *little* bit?" she bit out. "How did you even know I'd *be* here? You didn't even *check*."

"If you turn your goddamn *phone* on, you'd see that I and everybody the fuck *else* called you *several* times," Chasity bit out, fixing Sidra with a stern gaze.

Sidra reached for her phone without saying a word, quietly turning it on.

"Yeah go ahead and check," Chasity taunted.

"Whatever," Sidra muttered, tossing the phone on the table. "Still doesn't answer the question as to how you knew that I would be home."

"Where *else* would you be? You *have* no life," Chasity sneered, folding her arms.

Sidra narrowed her eyes.

"And I talked to your mother. She told me that you'd be home," Chasity revealed. She tilted her head. "Nice to know that at least you're talking to *her*."

Sidra glanced away momentarily, trying to avoid Chasity's laser like stare. "Look Chasity—"

"Save it," Chasity interrupted.

Sidra let out a huff. "I can't believe you actually called my mother," she bit out.

"Am I not allowed to talk to her?" Chasity questioned.

Sidra folded her arms across her chest, staring out in front of her. "Not saying that," she muttered. "So, you came all this way to yell at me?"

"Yes…but mostly to check on you," Chasity answered honestly. "You're worrying people."

Sidra tossed her head back, letting out a loud sigh. "I'm *fine*," she hissed.

"Judging by this messy ass living room, your uncombed hair, your ashy ass face, and that nasty ass robe you got on, I'd say that's a *lie*," Chasity argued.

Sidra frowned at Chasity. "So, they send the *evil* one to come check on me, huh?"

Chasity smirked. "Well, I'm out of work right now, so I'm the only one who has time to deal with your shit."

Sidra's mouth fell open. "Hold up, you're out of work?" she asked, surprised. "You got fired?"

"Please," Chasity scoffed.

"So…you *quit*?" Sidra corrected. Chasity nodded.

"Sweetie, why? What happened—"

"Didn't come here to talk about that," Chasity quickly cut in, moving from the chair to the couch. She pushed a throw blanket and a throw pillow to the floor, then sat down.

"Did you just throw my stuff on the floor?" Sidra asked, angry.

"Bitch, you got everything *else* on the floor," Chasity snapped, gesturing to the mess of papers and food crumbs on the floor. "Don't get on my damn nerves."

Sidra flagged Chasity, then ran a hand through her hair. She sucked her teeth when her fingers became tangled in the mess of uncombed tresses. "Eww," she mumbled.

Chasity stared at Sidra for a moment. "You wanna talk about it?"

"No," Sidra sulked.

Chasity sighed. "Well…you don't have to do it *now*, but you'll get tired of me being in your face asking you, so…"

"You check into your hotel yet?" Sidra deflected, looking at her.

Chasity smiled at her. "No."

Sidra took a deep breath as she came to a realization. "You're staying here with *me*, *aren't* you?"

Chasity's smile grew brighter, relishing Sidra's annoyance. She wrapped her arms around Sidra and pulled her in with force. "We're gonna have *so* much fun," she teased. "It'll be just like freshman year."

"Ugh," Sidra grumbled, much to Chasity's amusement. "I'd rather *have* 'freshman year Chasity' right now."

Chasity chuckled, releasing Sidra from her grip. She stood up. "Come on, get your sad ass up and do something with yourself."

"Why?" Sidra whined.

"Because you're showing me around," Chasity insisted.

"You've *been* to California before," Sidra ground out.

"You really wanna do this with me right now?" Chasity questioned, shooting Sidra a challenging look.

"I *would* but I don't have the energy for it," Sidra mumbled.

"Good, now get up," Chasity ordered, turning to head for

the kitchen. "I'll make you something to eat while you go wash your depression off."

"I already ate," Sidra called after her, stopping Chasity in her tracks.

Chasity spun around and stood there as Sidra reached for her plate of half eaten pie. She frowned when Sidra placed a fork full into her mouth, chewing slowly. "The fuck are you eating?"

"Pie," Sidra muttered between chews. "Coconut cream pie."

Chasity frowned her face up. "Eww."

"It's not *eww*, you insensitive demon," Sidra barked. "*Josh* made it."

Chasity stared at her. "Sidra, Josh made that pie almost *three weeks* ago."

"*So?*" Sidra barked, taking another forkful.

Chasity felt like she wanted to throw up. "How the fuck did I get stuck doing this?" she mumbled to herself. Taking a step forward, she held her hand out. "Sidra, give me the pie."

"No," Sidra spat, eyeing Chasity defiantly.

"I'm not gonna ask you nicely again," Chasity warned. "*Give* it to me."

Sidra held her gaze. "Screw you," she hurled.

Chasity narrowed her eyes at Sidra. Then she darted over to the couch and jumped on top of Sidra. "Fuckin' *give* it to me!"

"Noooo! Leave me alone, I wanna eat it," Sidra screamed, trying to hold the plate out of Chasity's reach. "This is all I have left of him!"

"You're acting like a fuckin' brat. Stop it," Chasity yelled, grabbing the plate. When Sidra tried to bite her hand, Chasity punched her on the arm.

"Ouch!" Sidra released the plate, grabbing her injured arm as Chasity got off of her. "That was *so* uncalled for," Sidra fumed.

"So is eating *this*," Chasity threw back, tossing the plate on the coffee table. "This *looks* old and you're sitting here inhaling it." Sidra didn't say anything as she rubbed her sore arm. "Now this isn't you, stop it."

"I *can't*," Sidra blurted out. "I'm depressed." She sat up in her seat. "Josh hates me and it's my fault."

Chasity rolled her eyes as she sat down next to Sidra. "It *is* your fault, but he doesn't hate you," she said. "And even if he *did*, that doesn't give you the excuse to just sit here and be pathetic."

Sidra let out a sigh and leaned her head back on the cushion. Her emotions were bubbling up, and she couldn't hold them back anymore. "Chasity…I messed up," she sniffled, tears spilling down her face.

Chasity softened. "You *did*," she stated bluntly. "But do you think that hiding from him—from *everybody* is going to fix it?"

Sidra wiped the tears away with her sleeve.

"Come on Sid, you know better than that."

"I just don't know how to handle this," Sidra admitted. "I don't know what to say to him. I don't know how to *face* him… He's right, I was selfish—"

"Sidra, I love you, but you look way too ugly for me to feel sympathetic, sweetie."

Sidra tossed her hand in the air. "*Again*, they sent *you* here to check up on me?" she hissed.

Chasity couldn't help but chuckle as she reached out and wiped a lone tear from Sidra's face.

"Thanks," Sidra said, grateful. "How long are you staying?"

"Until Wednesday," Chasity replied.

"The day before Thanksgiving?" Sidra questioned.

Chasity stared at her. "Thanksgiving is *Thursday* right?" she jeered.

Sidra narrowed her eyes at her. "Oh, I'm gonna miss you when you leave."

"You won't *have* to because you're coming *with* me," Chasity informed.

"Chasity, I already told everybody that I'm not coming home for Thanksgiving," she fussed. "Nobody listens to me."

"No, no we don't," Chasity confirmed. "So, like I said, you're coming back with me. Your mother wants you to bring her sweater that she left."

"Mama has ten thousand other sweaters, she won't miss

that one," Sidra bit out, eyeing the chipped polish on her nails. "I'm not going."

Chasity was silent for a moment. "Okay," she replied, calm. She glanced down at a purse Sidra had left on the floor. "That's a cute bag," she complimented.

Sidra looked down at her blue leather satchel. "Thank you." She picked it up. "It came with a matching wallet."

"Really? Let me see," Chasity demanded, holding her hand out.

Sidra eagerly retrieved the wallet from her purse and handed it to Chasity. She smiled while Chasity opened and examined it. "Maybe when I stop being miserable, we can go to the place where I got it. I'm sure they have it in black."

"Sounds good. Do me a favor, can you get me something to drink? Wrestling with your ass made me thirsty," Chasity requested.

"Sure," Sidra said, getting up from the couch. She walked into the kitchen and grabbed a glass from her cabinet. After rinsing it out, she poured some apple juice into it and walked back out. She handed the glass to Chasity. "Here."

Chasity was busy looking through her phone. "Thanks, you can set it down."

Sidra sighed as she sat the glass on the table in front of Chasity, then flopped back down on the couch. After a few moments, she glanced over at Chasity. "What are you doing?"

"I'm on the airline's website," Chasity nonchalantly answered.

"Oh." Sidra put her hands on top of her head. "Checking your flight time?"

"Nah, I just bought your plane ticket," Chasity announced.

Sidra bolted up and faced Chasity. "You did *what*?!"

Chasity showed Sidra her phone; Sidra squinted to read it. Surely enough, it was the confirmation of a flight to the Philadelphia airport, with her name on it. "Chasity what the hell? I said I wasn't *going*," she hurled, upset.

"Well, *now* you are," Chasity confirmed.

Sidra slammed her hand on the couch; she was livid. "I can't believe you just bought me a plane ticket against my will."

"Oh, *I* didn't buy it." Chasity clarified. "I'm out of work, I have to save my money."

Sidra looked confused. "Then how—" she paused when she eyed her open wallet on the coffee table. In Chasity's other hand was a card. Sidra pointed, "Is...is that my credit card?"

Chasity nodded. "*One* of them."

Sidra lost it. "You— You bought a plane ticket to Philadelphia on my credit card?!" she erupted. "On a fuckin' holiday week? Last minute? Are you crazy?!"

"Sidra we've already established that I *am*, there is no need to yell," Chasity calmly taunted.

Sidra's eyes and mouth both went wide. "Do you have *any* idea how expensive that is?"

"Yeah, it's like seven hundred dollars," Chasity revealed.

"Oh my God!" Sidra screamed, "How did you even know that I *had* the money?"

"You have it," Chasity stated, confident.

Sidra tried to grab the phone from Chasity's hand. "Give me the damn phone! I have two hours to cancel it."

"No," Chasity refused. Sidra jumped up and grabbed for it again. This time, Chasity stood up and held her hand out. "Hey! I haven't fucked anybody up in a *long* time, but I will *gladly* come out of retirement for *you*," she barked.

Sidra was breathing heavily. She was so upset, she didn't know what to do with herself. "I can't believe you just did that Chasity. I hate you so much."

"Stop, you don't mean that," Chasity dismissed, walking towards the hallway.

Accepting defeat, Sidra let out a sigh. She smoothed her disheveled hair from her face. "Are you flying first class?"

"Of course," Chasity confirmed.

"Did you at least get *me* a first-class ticket?" Sidra asked.

Chasity spun around. "Oh no honey, they were all sold out." She wanted to bust out laughing at the look on Sidra's face. "You have the last seat in the back. Last minute and all."

Sidra held a fiery gaze on Chasity. She could have ripped her hair out.

Chasity was unfazed. "So, you gonna take me shopping or

what?" she asked.

Sidra just continued to stare, not saying anything.

Malajia ran her fingers through a few curls on her head, waiting for the elevator door to open. She rolled her eyes when the door opened, and Mark stepped out, smiling.

He chuckled. "Why do you look so mad?"

"'Cause your smile was extra big for no damn reason," she grumbled, shaking her hand in his direction.

"I'm happy to see you, *damn*," Mark quipped, walking over to her. Despite her attitude, he gave her a kiss on the lips Mark had called Malajia earlier and asked her to meet him at his job for lunch, which she reluctantly accepted. "You still pissed at me from last night?"

"Yes," Malajia spat, moving hair over her shoulder.

"Babe, I'm sorry that I ate your crab legs," Mark apologized, putting his hand on his chest. "I didn't know that you wanted it."

Malajia narrowed her eyes at him. "You didn't think that I wanted my platter that I had just *bought*?" she questioned, annoyed.

Mark stood there with a silly look on his face.

"You don't even *eat* them," she barked.

"I do *now*," he argued. "My bad, I saw that butter and seasoning and I just wanted to try them...so I *did*... And before I knew it, the platter was gone."

Malajia shook her head. "I really hate you sometimes."

Mark lowered his head and laughed a little. "That's not shocking. Come on, let's get out of here," he said, gently nudging her along.

Even though they were enjoying lunch at a cafe, Mark could sense that something was wrong. Mark knew how Malajia felt about her food, but this was something else. He knew this level of irritation from Malajia, and it stemmed from somewhere else.

"What's up Mel?" Mark asked as Malajia took a bite of her

sandwich.

She covered her mouth, trying to quickly chew her food, using a sip of her soda to push it down. "You *would* ask me a question once I put food in my mouth," she ground out.

"Sorry, you know my timing is bad," he replied, taking a bite of his own sandwich.

"Yes I know, that's how I ended up pregnant with the boys," Malajia threw back.

Mark nearly choked on his food as he tried not to laugh. "Funny, real funny," he replied, wiping his mouth with a napkin. "Come on, what's up? You seem stressed out."

Malajia sat back in her seat, letting out a sigh. "Your children embarrassed me today," she began, agitated.

Mark frowned. "What do you mean?"

"While we were in the doctor's office waiting for them to get their checkups, they saw a lady sitting across from them with these...moles or something on her face," Malajia explained. "And Marvin's little smart ass looks at me and says, 'Mommy, why does she have spots on her face?'"

Mark sat there trying his hardest not to bust out laughing.

Malajia stared at him. "Then *Marlon* starts singing 'spot face, spot face' very, very *loudly*."

Mark put his hand over his face.

"Then the bitch looks at *me* sideways, like I *told* them to do that shit," Malajia fussed, folding her arms on the tabletop. Mark couldn't help it anymore, he busted out laughing. "That's funny?" she hissed.

"Yes," Mark laughed. Malajia rolled her eyes. "I mean, not about the fact that the lady had a skin condition, that's really...unfortunate."

"There isn't one ounce of sincerity in your voice," Malajia pointed out.

"Come on babe, they don't know what's inappropriate or not, just yet," Mark placated. "Shit, I embarrassed my parents doing way more stuff, than *that*."

"Me too," Malajia chuckled. "They're gonna be a hot mess when they become teenagers."

"Maybe we should have a little girl to mellow them out," Mark suggested, reaching for his food again.

"I'll beat the shit out of you if you suggest another baby to me again," Malajia bit out. Mark chuckled. "I told you, I'm done. Pregnancy was hard enough the first time around."

The humor left Mark's face. "I understand," he said. "I'm content with the two that we have now." He sighed. "I umm...I wish I could've made things easier on you while you were pregnant."

"Mark, I *told* you, it was nothing that you could've done to change what happened," she said, sincere.

"You were stressed."

"My pressure went up *yes*, but I told you that it wasn't stress," Malajia insisted. "It's something that happens to pregnant women sometimes... It just *does*."

Mark heard what she was saying, but just couldn't shake the guilt. "You almost died...and so did *they*."

Malajia tilted her head. "But, we *didn't*," she pointed out. "We're still here getting on your nerves," she added, trying to add humor to the situation.

Mark smiled slightly. "Yeah," he said, he let out a sigh. "Did you know your dad blamed me?"

Malajia's eyes widened. "He *what*?" she barked. This was the first that she'd heard that. "What the hell did he *say*?"

Mark rubbed his arm. "In so many words, he accused me of stressing you out."

Malajia frowned. "*Fuck* him, *he* stresses everybody he comes in *contact with* out," she grunted.

Mark just shook his head.

Malajia reached out and grabbed his hand. "Seriously, Mark, none of that was your fault," she stressed. "You were absolutely perfect the entire time. I promise."

Mark squeezed her hand. "Okay... Thank you."

"Of course," Malajia replied. She held onto his hand; she didn't know why, but she felt like this was the time to say what was on her mind—what had been on her mind for months now. "Look...I need to tell you something."

"What's that?" Mark wondered.

"I want to..." she hesitated for a moment. "I feel like it's time for me to umm..."

"Time for what, babe?" he asked, concerned. "What's up,

what do you need?"

Malajia glanced up at the ceiling. They could talk about everything with no problem, yet she was hesitant on telling him this one thing. She looked back at him. "I need a spa day," she answered.

"Oh, is *that* all?" he replied. "I gotchu'. Just let me know when you want to go."

"Okay," Malajia sighed. "And take my car to get an oil change too, while you're being generous."

"I'll do you one better. Once raises kick in, I'll get you a *new* car," Mark proposed.

"I *just* need an oil change babe," she chuckled. Mark shrugged. She leaned forward and gave him a kiss. "But thanks for the offer."

"Sure," he smiled. "I told you, I got you."

Malajia smiled back. Sitting back in her seat, she had a thought. "You normally would've gotten your raise by now."

"I know, but with the layoffs that just happened, I guess they want to redo the company budget first," Mark replied.

Malajia frowned. "They had layoffs?" Mark nodded. "Damn...that's fucked up."

"It happens."

"I know, but still," she said.

"Yeah...so I'm sure I'll get it soon." Malajia just nodded. Mark looked at her, a knowing look on his face.

Catching his gaze, Malajia raised an eyebrow. "*What* boy?"

"You wanna head back to my car for a quickie?" he proposed, eager.

Malajia squinted at him. "You're so nasty," she condemned.

"Is that a yes?" Mark chortled.

"Yup," Malajia confirmed.

Mark quickly wrapped his sandwich up. "Last one to the car gotta do foreplay," he challenged.

"Fuck that," Malajia uttered, grabbing Mark's sandwich from his hand and tossing it on the floor. "Ooh, he made a mess!" she yelled, jumping from the table.

"You disrespectful— I ain't doing *shit*!" Mark hurled at her departing back, bending down to retrieve the trash from the floor.

"Then you ain't *getting* shit," Malajia threw back, running out the door.

"Damn it... I *want* it," Mark muttered, throwing the trash away. He laughed to himself as he hurried out the door.

Chapter 28

Josh reached for his cup of coffee and took a sip, flipping through pages in a folder. He eyed the content intently, rubbing his eyes when the words began to run together. "I need to make a damn decision," he muttered to himself.

"Talking to yourself again?" Sarah asked, walking into his office.

"As always," he returned, leaning back in his seat.

Sarah stood in front of his desk. "You still going over those shop locations?" she asked, peering at the paperwork.

"Yeah," he answered, running a hand over his head. "Never thought it would be this hard to make a decision."

"Well, maybe because there're not really too many good locations here where we live," Sarah shrugged. "You ever think about opening one out of state?"

Josh thought. "No, not really," he answered honestly.

"Think about it," Sarah suggested. "It'll get our name out there more, you know?" Josh just sat there, pondering. "Anyway," Sarah began, sitting down in the seat across from him. "Before I get back to inventory, I wanted to let you know that you ordered the wrong part for Don's car."

Josh frowned. "I did?"

Sarah nodded, handing him the order sheet. "Yeah."

Josh took the sheet and looked at it. "Shit," he hissed. "Okay I'll umm, I'll order the right one and I'll install it at a discount to make up for the extra wait."

Sarah took the sheet back. "Okay. You want me to call and tell him?"

Josh shook his head. "No, it was my mistake, *I'll* do it."

"Okay…you want me to return the part?"

"Nah, we can keep it," Josh answered. "Might need it for someone else's car. I'll cover the cost of the extra part."

Sarah nodded. "Very well." She sat back in her seat, folding her arms. "So, you wanna tell me what's got you unfocused?"

Josh looked up at her. "Huh?"

Sarah shot him a knowing look. "Come on JJ, you know I can tell when something is off with you," she said. "Call it sister's intuition."

Josh rolled his eyes.

Sarah gestured for him to come forward. "Now come on, tell me what's going on."

Josh didn't want to talk about it, but felt that he *needed* to. After all, his thoughts were getting in the way of his work. He couldn't risk making any mistakes while working on people's vehicles. He took a deep breath. "Okay...you remember when I went to California a few weeks ago?"

Sarah nodded. "Yeah, to see Sidra."

"Right."

Sarah smiled. "I miss her face, how is she?" she asked. "You didn't tell me how the trip went."

Josh stared at her, perplexed. "You miss her *face*?"

"What? You know I love Sidra, and her face is pretty," she chuckled. "Now stop deflecting."

Josh shifted in his seat. "Anyway...things were good when I got there," he began. "We spent a lot of time together. We talked and...it felt good... It felt like I was getting my best friend back."

"Well that's great," Sarah beamed. "That doesn't explain why you've been zoned out lately, though."

"Sarah...she told me that she has feelings for me," he revealed after a moment.

"What feelings?" Sarah asked, confused.

"The feelings that I have for *her*, feelings," he clarified.

Sarah's eyes nearly popped out of her head. "Are you *serious*?"

"Very."

"Oh My G—*Finally*."

Josh rolled his eyes. "Sarah," he warned.

"*What*?" Sarah shrugged, bewildered. "This is great. This is what you've been wanting since you were like *thirteen*."

Josh rolled his eyes again. "Stop pretending like you knew how I felt back then."

"Come on Josh, I might have been high through most of your teen years, but even *I* could see how much you cared for that girl," Sarah threw back.

"Whatever," Josh ground out. "I mean, I know that I always hoped that she would feel the same way that I felt about her, but—"

"But *what*, Josh?" Sarah pressed.

"She started feeling this way before we graduated *college*," he argued. "Meaning over *five years* ago and she *just* said something to me *three weeks* ago."

Sarah's mouth formed an O. "Oh," she winced.

"Right," Josh fussed. "She had the ability to...to change my *life* and she just left and didn't *say* shit."

Sarah shot him a sympathetic look. "Well...what was her reason for keeping that to herself?"

"I don't know," Josh muttered, looking off to the side. "I was so hung up on what she did, that I just left... I haven't spoken to her since."

"You don't think that's a bit childish?" she chastised.

"Nope," Josh maintained.

Sarah leaned forward. "Come on now."

Josh let out a quick sigh. "Fine, I *have* been childish by not answering her phone calls," he admitted. "Funny, I did this when I told her that I loved her, and she rejected me... Now she loves me *back* and I'm doing the same thing."

"Well, in *both* cases your feelings were hurt," she placated. "Sidra *did* keep this from you, and she *shouldn't* have...and she owes you an *explanation* for why she did that."

"Yeah," Josh sulked.

"But...she can't give you that if you don't talk to her," Sarah concluded. "I know you know that."

Josh nodded. "I do," he agreed. "And, I will."

Sarah smiled. "Good...so make it quick so I can plan y'all wedding and get me a niece or nephew out the deal."

Josh shook his head. "Worry about that grocery store run you gotta take with Mom later so she can do her Thanksgiving shopping."

"No, she said *you* were taking her," Sarah refuted.

Josh pulled out his phone and read a message from his mother. "'Josh, tell Sarah to pick me up around six to go to the store, I want to get in and out'," he read.

Sarah let out a whine. "My God, she's *never* in and out," she complained. "We'll be in there all night."

Josh looked at his watch. "It's almost six, you better get going," he teased. "It's a good thing she moved back to Delaware huh? Or you would've been driving to Jersey."

Sarah made a face at him.

"Ma, I'll be home tomorrow, you need me to go to the store with you?" Alex asked into her cell phone.

"Girl, I already went yesterday, you know I don't have time to wait until the last minute," Mrs. Chisolm chortled.

Alex smiled. She couldn't wait to get back to Philly. Thanksgiving was one of her favorite holidays, and she loved being back home for it. "I'm glad that I get to come down a day early. It would've been hell coming down *on* Thanksgiving."

"Well, I can't wait to have all three of you in my kitchen helping me."

Alex's eyes widened. "Wait, you're letting Semaj help cook?" she grimaced. "That boy can't cook rice."

"Hey, you leave my baby alone," Mrs. Chisolm demanded, laughter in her voice. "He invited his girlfriend over, and he wants to impress her by making something."

"Lord," Alex muttered. "Well, I'll be there to watch him like a hawk," she joked. She looked up at her office door when someone knocked. "Hold on Ma," she said. "Come in."

The door opened. "Ms. Chisolm, you have a visitor," the receptionist said. "Eric Wendell?"

Shit, Alex thought, looking at her watch; it was five-thirty. She'd totally forgot that they had arranged to go out to dinner that evening. "Okay you can send him in." She put her ear back to the phone once her door closed again. "Ma, I have to go."

"Okay...Eric, huh?" Mrs. Chisolm cooed into the phone. "I overheard."

"Ma, stop."

"What? You used to talk about him all the time,"

"Yes, I remember, but look I have to go," Alex quickly dismissed.

"Are you bringing him home for Thanksgiving?"

"Doubt it, love you. See you tomorrow," Alex spoke, ending the call. She wanted to get off before her mother tried to probe any further.

Running her hands over her hair, Alex let out a long sigh. There was another knock; she grabbed the mirror on her desk and gave herself a onceover. Satisfied, Alex looked up at the door. "Come in." She smiled when Eric walked in. "Hi," she greeted, typing on her laptop.

"Hey," Eric replied, shutting the door behind him. "Working hard?"

"Eh, not really," Alex answered truthfully. "Just paying some bills for my parents."

Eric looked bewildered as he stood in front of Alex's desk. "I thought you said they didn't want you to," he said, recalling something mentioned in one of their previous conversations.

"Well, what they don't know won't hurt them," Alex quickly dismissed.

Eric shrugged. "Well, are you ready to go?" he asked.

Alex looked up from her laptop. "Umm…" she felt terrible. Though she did start calling Eric again after her conversation with Emily, she still hadn't told him how she felt, nor shaken the feeling off. "Eric, I really don't feel like going out tonight," she revealed finally. "I'm going back to Philly for the holiday tomorrow and I have to pack."

Eric looked disappointed. "Oh… Wish I had known before I drove down here."

Alex put her hand over her face. "God, I'm so sorry," she said. "I feel terrible."

"It's fine," Eric replied. "I mean…we *could* just hang out at your place instead for a bit."

Alex pondered the thought. She might have been unsure of her future with Eric, but one thing *was* for sure: her hormones were raging. She needed a release. Her head was so cloudy after Eric had broken the news about his child, that she wasn't in the mood to sleep with him the night that they had decided to move forward in their relationship. Though he'd tried, as much as she was turned on, she just couldn't get out of her funk. Alex had been kicking herself over it ever since.

"That's fine," she agreed.

"Great." He thought for a moment. "I don't have to pick up Zoe from her mother until later on so— "

Alex's smile faded. *And there goes my libido,* she thought. "Whenever you need to leave is fine, Eric," she said, hoping that her tone did not reflect her displeasure. "Do what you need to do."

Eric nodded as Alex began gathering her belongings. "So...going back to Philly for Thanksgiving huh?" he asked after a moment.

"Yeah," she replied, grabbing her coat. "Can't wait... What are *you* doing?"

"Going to my parents' house in Maryland," he answered, adjusting the scarf around his neck. "What are you doing Friday?"

Alex put her coat on. "Uh, I'm supposed to be meeting up at my friends' house...Chasity and Jason's house," she informed. "We're all getting together for a game night."

"That sounds like fun," Eric beamed. "You know...I'm free Friday."

"Won't you have your daughter?" Alex asked.

"Well *yeah*, but I'm sure my parents won't mind looking after her for a few hours," Eric stated, confident. "Hell, they've been *begging* me to bring her down."

"So, her *mother* is okay with spending the holiday apart from her child?" Alex wondered. She hoped she didn't sound bitter, though she felt it.

Eric raised an eyebrow at her. "We have an arrangement, everything is good," he assured. "You good? You sound funny."

"Just tired, I want to get out of here," Alex quickly returned.

"Okay," he replied. "Let's go then."

Alex pushed her hair from her face as Eric headed for the door. Her attitude had the potential to push him away, and she didn't want that. Despite how she felt, she didn't want him to slip through her fingers. "Eric umm... If you want to come with me on Friday, I'm sure they won't mind."

Eric looked back at her and smiled. "Cool. I'll pick up a bottle."

Alex smiled back. "Oh, give me like two minutes, okay," she requested, putting two fingers up. Eric nodded and walked out the door, closing it behind him. Alex quickly grabbed her cell phone from her purse and dialed a number. "Hey Chasity," she said, once the line picked up.

"Hey, what's up?"

"Before I ask you what I need to ask you, how is 'Operation Sidra' going?"

"I'm getting on her nerves, what's up?" Chasity replied.

"Umm... Okay, so I just invited Eric to come with me to your house Friday for game night. Is that okay with you?"

"Girl, don't nobody care if you bring Eric," Chasity barked. "Stop asking me stupid ass questions and get off my damn phone."

Alex laughed. "Thanks love."

"You're welcome."

"Oh!" Alex exclaimed.

"*What*, girl?" Chasity sneered.

"Did you have a chance to look at the email that I sent you the other day?" Alex asked.

"Yes, and I will work on it this weekend, don't rush me. Bye."

"Bye," Alex chortled, hanging up. She shoved the phone back in her purse and walked out the office, turning the light off behind her.

Alex had no idea how she managed to get her key in her apartment door and open it while making out heavily with Eric. But, she did. Tossing both keys and purse to the floor, the two of them snatched off their coats. Alex kicked them to the side, practically jumping back in his arms. Making out again, they made their way to her couch and fell on it.

On their way back to Alex's apartment, Eric had talked her into stopping for a drink. One drink had turned into two for Eric and four for Alex. Eric kissed her as soon as they got in the car—that was all that Alex needed to send her hormones into overdrive. Luckily, the bar was less than ten minutes from her building.

Now she was laying on her couch, relishing Eric's touch. Alex tried to unbutton her blouse, but it was tedious, and she was feeling impatient. "Come on, come on," she grunted, trying to unfasten the tiny buttons. Frustrated and wanting, she let out a huff. "To hell with it. Rip it," she told Eric.

Eric complied, grabbing her shirt and yanking it open, popping her buttons. She jerked out of it and helped Eric pull his sweater over his head. She was tipsy, she was horny and in that moment, she didn't care *what* Eric had going on—she was going to have him right there on her couch.

Eric kissed her lips, moving to her neck and slowly kissing down her frame. She closed her eyes and grabbed on to the arm of the couch as he began to unbutton her pants. The memories of her past sexual experiences with Eric flooded back, and she couldn't wait to experience it again. Just as Eric's hand gripped the fabric of her underwear, his cell phone went off.

They both let out a groan. "Perfect timing," he jeered.

God no! No, no, no! Not now! Alex thought. "Ignore it," she breathed.

Eric reached into his pants pocket. "Sorry, I can't. It might be important," he said.

Alex folded her arms in a huff as Eric looked at his phone screen.

"It's Zoe's mother," he announced. "Give me a sec," he said to Alex as he moved off of her.

Alex rolled her eyes behind Eric's back. *Great*, she thought, laying there while he spoke on the phone.

"Yeah, I'll be leaving in about—Oh you're not going? ...Okay, do you still want me to get her tonight? ...That's fine. I'll just pick her up after I leave work tomorrow... Yeah...I'm heading straight to Maryland once I leave your house... You can pack it, but I have stuff at my place too, so we'll figure it out... Okay, see you tomorrow... Later." Eric hung up and set the phone on the floor. "Looks like I don't have to drive back tonight *after* all," he beamed, reclaiming his position over Alex.

"You mind if I stay over?"

"No, I don't mind," Alex replied, unenthused.

Eric ignored her tone and went back to kissing her neck. Alex tried to get back in the mood, but she couldn't. "Umm...Eric," she called.

"Yeah?" he asked, face still buried in her neck.

"I'm not in the mood anymore," she said.

Eric lifted his head up, confused. "Why? What's wrong?"

Alex bit her bottom lip. "My umm...I think my period just came on," she revealed.

Eric stared at her. "Ooooh," he replied.

"Yeeeaahh," she slowly drew out.

Eric sat up. "You umm...you want me to rub your back or something?"

Alex chuckled. "No, I'm fine." She stood up from the couch and buttoned her pants. "You might as well order us some food and find a movie for us to watch."

Eric nodded. "Okay...what do you want to eat?"

"Whatever you get is fine," she said, heading for the hallway.

"Hey Alex," Eric called; Alex spun around. "You know...I'd have *no* problem running the red light if you know what I mean."

Alex made a face. "No," she shot down, tone laced with amusement. "I'm down for a lot of stuff, but *that*, I'm not into."

Eric stared at her. "What stuff *are* you into?" he crooned.

Alex pointed at him. "Order the food," she demanded. She shook her head at him, then headed for the bathroom. Once inside, she shut the door, closed the toilet seat, and sat on top of it. She put her face in her hands and sighed. She was lying, her period was weeks away. She just didn't know how to explain to Eric why her mood had changed once he'd gotten on the phone with his daughter's mother. And she didn't know how she would continue to handle this situation.

"Shit," Alex muttered.

Sidra enjoyed the breeze whipping past her face as she chewed on a loaded nacho. Across from her, Chasity was bundling her jacket up to her neck. "Will you stop it?" Sidra chortled. "It's *not* that cold."

"Fuck you, it's freezing," Chasity griped, tugging on her zipper.

Sidra shook her head. "Anemia strikes again," she said. "Chasity, the zipper isn't going to go up anymore, sweetie."

"I know," Chasity replied, resolved. She reached for a nacho.

Sidra took another bite and chewed. Chasity had been in town since Sunday. It was now Wednesday, and Sidra had finally gotten her mood together enough to hang out with her. So much so that Sidra had taken time off from work just to spend the day out with Chasity. Luckily, she had time; their flight back didn't leave until the evening. They were sitting at an outdoor restaurant, enjoying some nachos and drinks.

"You barely touched your sangria," Sidra observed, pointing to Chasity's drink.

Chasity shook her head. "It tastes like dirty berries," she ground out, eating her nacho.

Sidra let out a laugh. "I can't stand you," she joked. "Give it here, I'll finish it." She reached for her drink, taking a sip. "It's good, crazy."

Chasity just shrugged as she watched Sidra sip on it. "So…you still have the urge to punch me in the face?" she joked.

Sidra cut her eye at her. "Well, not *today*," she muttered, smiling when Chasity snickered. "No, but…despite how I've been acting, I'm *really* glad you came," she said sincerely. "I appreciate you taking care of me these past few days… Well, putting *up* with me."

"It's cool," Chasity replied, nonchalant.

"No, I mean it." Sidra insisted. "Thank you."

Chasity smiled. Reaching over, she patted Sidra's hand. "You're welcome," she said. "To be honest, I didn't really know what to expect when I got here. I just knew I needed to see for myself how you were."

"I know…and I know that I was wrong for ignoring everybody," Sidra admitted. "I handled it wrong…just like I handle *everything* wrong."

"That's not true," Chasity placated.

Sidra shrugged slightly, "I'm not so sure about that." She looked up at Chasity. "Chasity, how bad was what I did?"

Chasity let out a sigh.

"I mean...keeping what I felt from Josh, I know it was wrong but... How badly did I mess up?"

"I can't answer that question Sidra," Chasity replied. "I can't tell you how bad you messed up with Josh because I'm not *Josh*."

Sidra looked down at the table.

"But, if you want my opinion from the outside looking in...it was pretty bad," Chasity added. Sidra just slowly nodded in agreement. "You held that for over five years Sid... That's a long time. Especially since you *knew* how he felt about you."

Sidra just held her gaze on the table; she felt horrible.

"I'm not gonna ask you why you did that," Chasity promised. "Because it's up to you to tell *him* that."

Sidra looked at her. "Malajia already told you why I decided to do that, didn't she?"

"Yeah," Chasity immediately replied.

Sidra couldn't help but snicker. "Yeah, I figured." She reached for another nacho and held it in her hand. "Can I ask you a personal question?"

Chasity gave a nod. "Sure."

"After you realized how you *truly* felt about Jason back in school," she began. "What made you decide to just throw caution aside and...*tell* him...not knowing if he still felt the same about you after time passed."

Chasity thought for a moment. "I didn't want to lose him," she answered finally. "I knew that despite how he felt about me...that he wouldn't wait around for me forever. So, it was either stop being scared and tell him the truth, or watch him end up with someone else." Chasity folded her arms across her chest as a breeze blew past. "I knew that I couldn't handle it if that happened."

"Yeah," Sidra sulked. "And because I didn't have the courage that *you* did, I let all this time go by... Let him sleep with all those...*girls*."

Chasity chuckled. "Josh wasn't sleeping with as many hoes

as you think."

Sidra put her hands up. "I didn't call them hoes."

"Oh, but you *wanted* to," Chasity threw back.

Sidra laughed slightly, "I mean..." The humor left her face. "Anyway. It might not have been many, but I'm sure there were *some*," she spat out.

Chasity shrugged. "Well, he's technically a single man so..."

Sidra let out a deep sigh. "I can't allow that to happen anymore Chaz," she said. "I *have* to get him...or at least *try*... I love him so much."

"I know you do," Chasity sympathized. "You gotta talk to him... It starts with that."

"I know, and I guess I'll get the opportunity to do it face to face whether he likes it or *not*," Sidra said, shooting Chasity a glance. "Since I'm being dragged home tonight against my *will* and all... You sneaky hussy."

Chasity laughed. "I will give you your money back for your plane ticket," she offered. "I'll admit, I shouldn't have done that."

"No, you *shouldn't* have, heffa," Sidra agreed. She waved a hand in Chasity's direction. "But you don't have to give it back."

"Good, 'cause I don't have it," Chasity chortled, looking away briefly.

Sidra laughed. "Yes, you *do*," she contradicted. "If it's one thing you've *never* been, is broke."

"Neither have *you*," Chasity countered.

"This is true," Sidra agreed. "So you're right, I have the money and in all honesty, I really *did* want to go back for Thanksgiving." She folded her arms. "So, thanks again...I guess." She took another sip of Chasity's drink. "I have to send a few emails to my bosses before we head to the airport."

"Do what you need to," Chasity said. She watched as Sidra took a few more sips of her drink. She didn't know if it was a good time to bring up what was on her mind, but Chasity felt that she needed to. "Sid, now that you've brought up work...can I ask you something?"

Sidra dipped her straw in and out of the half empty glass of sangria. "Sure."

"Your job...do you really like it?" Chasity asked. "I mean, are you really satisfied with what you're doing?"

Sidra jerked her head back a bit. "That was out of nowhere."

"You gonna answer?" Chasity challenged.

Sidra folded her arms on the tabletop. "I mean—yeah."

Chasity squinted her eyes slightly. "You know, you can tell everyone *else* that lie, but it's not going to work on me," she said. "It never *did*."

Sidra frowned slightly. "Chasity...what are you trying to get at?"

"Sid, ever since I've known you, you've expressed how much you wanted to become a lawyer," Chasity explained. "You busted your ass in all of your Criminal Justice classes, you went to one of the best law schools, graduated top of your class, and was offered attorney positions from *four* different firms when you graduated and yet...you didn't take *any* of them. That doesn't make any sense."

Sidra looked down at the table, letting out a sigh. She'd been trying to avoid facing her career decisions, but she was finding it harder to do so. "I know," she admitted, somber. She tapped her nails on the table. "...I knew that I wanted to become a lawyer ever since I was seven years old... I used to watch this one law show with my mom, and I was so fascinated by it." She smiled as the memories flooded back. "The more I studied it, the more excited I became about making it my career choice... I just knew that I was going to be this high-power attorney who could start her own firm one day."

"So, what changed?" Chasity asked.

Sidra shrugged slightly. "I guess somewhere along the way...I lost my confidence," she admitted. "Yeah, I did well in *school*. But school isn't *real life*. If I'm wrong, or *miss* something, it can cost people their freedom, money, their family—" she sighed again. "I question myself all the time, even while doing the job that I have *now*... It's gotten to a point where I'm not sure about anything... I found something that could have helped win a case for my team and because I questioned myself, I didn't say anything."

Chasity tilted her head. "Sidra...I get it. You're nervous, and that's okay—"

"Chasity—you are the best at what you do," Sidra cut in. "Emily is an *amazing* teacher. Alex is killing it in her career, Malajia—the girl went from wanting to design *clothes* to being a marketing *powerhouse* and I just—" she sat back in her seat. "What if *I'm* not as good as I think I am? What if being a lawyer isn't what I'm meant to be? What if I'm just meant to be in the background?"

Chasity pondered Sidra's words for a moment. "Can I be honest?" she began.

"Please do," Sidra prompted.

"You're running from your career like you ran from Josh."

Sidra looked like the wind had been knocked out of her. The reality that she had avoided for so long hit her like a ton of bricks. She let out a breath, as if the words had gotten caught in her throat. "I—"

"You're better than you think you are, Sid," Chasity said, sincere. "Like you found the courage to tell Josh the truth, find the courage to be what you're destined to be." Chasity leaned forward. "Just don't take five years to do it."

Sidra took a deep breath; "Wow." She let a small smile come through and nodded. "Thank you," she spoke after a moment.

Chasity gave a nod. "Anytime." She glanced up at the sky. "Now let's get the hell out of here, these damn birds are circling."

Sidra giggled. "Yeah," she agreed, gathering her trash.

Chapter 29

"Semaj, that's it! Get out of my kitchen," Mrs. Chisolm barked, pointing her spoon towards the entryway. "You done burnt my damn gravy."

"Ma, you just told me to watch it," Semaj explained, dumbfounded.

"Boy! Watch it doesn't mean just stand there and look at it *burn*!" she hollered.

Alex put her hand over her face and shook her head, but Sahara made no attempt to hide her amusement. Just like every other Thanksgiving morning, Alex was in the kitchen with her mother and sister, helping to prepare dinner for the rest of the family, who would be coming over later that afternoon. Alex couldn't wait for the house to be full of people; it would be a perfect distraction from her thoughts on Eric.

"Well...Ma you *did* just say *watch* it," Sahara reasoned.

"*See*?" Semaj said to his mother.

His mother was *not* in the mood for her children's foolishness. "Sahara, shut up, and finish snapping those beans," Mrs. Chisolm barked. Sahara snickered loudly. Mrs. Chisolm then pointed to Semaj. "Get out and go make sure your room is clean."

Semaj shook his head and let out a sigh. "Okay," he sulked.

Alex glanced at her mother once her brother was out of earshot. "Aww, he was only trying to help," she said, laughter in her voice. "And it doesn't smell too burnt. It can still be salvaged."

Mrs. Chisolm held a stern gaze on Alex, but didn't say anything.

Alex quickly wiped the smile off and swallowed hard.

Though she was a grown woman, Alex knew when her mother was not playing. Alex grabbed a chair and sat down at the kitchen table next to Sahara.

"She's making that face, Alex," Sahara observed.

"I know. Give me some of those green beans to snap before she smacks me," Alex panicked, grabbing for the bowl.

Mrs. Chisolm shook her head and went back to tending to her food. "Sahara, are you inviting anybody over for dinner?" she asked.

"Nope," Sahara immediately replied.

"Really?" Alex questioned, snapping a green bean in half and placing it in another bowl. "Not even Mustafa?"

"Girl, I don't like him no more," Sahara ground out; Alex let out a laugh.

"Child, you go through more *friends* than a little bit," Mrs. Chisolm commented.

"Hey, when they get on my nerves, they gotta go," Sahara quipped. "Besides, it's not like I'm giving my *goodies* away to them all… Some of them don't get past the first *date*."

"Well, at least you're testing the waters," Alex commented, still working on the green beans. "You're young, you don't have to settle down any time soon."

"*Speaking* of settling down, how's Eric?" Mrs. Chisolm asked, glancing over at Alex, smiling. "I was hoping that you'd invite him to dinner."

Glancing down at the bowl of green beans, Alex pushed her hair over her shoulder, avoiding her mother's gaze. "He's…he's good," she replied. "He's with his parents in Maryland for Thanksgiving."

"Oh, well that's understandable," Mrs. Chisolm shrugged. "Maybe next year."

"Yeah, maybe." Alex muttered. "Do you have any wine, Ma?"

"No, but your aunts are bringing some later."

Yeah, I can't wait that long, Alex thought, standing from the table. "I'm gonna go to grab some now."

Sahara frowned. "Alex, it's Thanksgiving, no liquor stores are open."

"They sell wine at the grocery store now," Alex informed. "Saw it yesterday. Need anything while I'm out?"

"Yes, a new damn turkey neck so I can redo this ruined gravy," Mrs. Chisolm bit out.

"I was trying to help," Semaj belted out from the living room.

"I said clean your room!" Mrs. Chisolm shouted.

Alex giggled, then headed out of the kitchen. Mrs. Chisolm glanced over.

"Oh Alex, sometime before you head back to New York, can you help me set up accounts on the bill pay sites?"

Alex spun around, her eyes wide. "Ma'am?"

Her mother chuckled. "Why do you look like I'm about to yell at you?" she asked, amused.

"No reason," Alex lied.

"Okay then, can you do that for me?"

Alex ran a hand over her hair. "Umm, I thought you didn't like paying bills online," she sputtered. "And umm, not to mention that your laptop is on the fritz."

"Semaj fixed the laptop for me," Mrs. Chisolm beamed. "Taught himself how to do it, can you believe that?"

Alex stood there. "No, no I can't believe it," she muttered.

"Besides, I think it's time for me to update my way of doing things," Mrs. Chisolm replied. "I think doing it that way will be better for me to track payments."

Alex stood there, quietly panicking on the inside. If her mother gained access to the bill sites, she'd be able to see that the bills had been paid by Alex, which her parents had explicitly told Alex *not* to do. This wouldn't end well.

"Umm..." Alex glanced at Sahara, who glanced away. She had told Sahara not too long ago what she had been doing; Sahara had promised to keep it a secret. "Yeah Ma... I'll umm..." Alex scratched her head. "Sure."

Mrs. Chisolm smiled. "Thanks... The turkey neck, please."

"Oh, sure thing," Alex said, nervous. She made a face at Sahara, who shook her head in a taunting manner.

"Liar," Sahara mouthed.

Alex quickly put two fingers in front of her lips, quietly

telling her little sister to "zip it", before hurrying out of the house.

"Mom, we were there for Thanksgiving *last* year," Jason said into his car speaker system. "You know that we rotate between your house and Chaz's mom's house."

"Jason, you don't have to remind me, I *know* that," Mrs. Adams spat into the line. "That doesn't mean that I don't still feel some kind of way that I won't see my grandbaby today."

Jason rolled his eyes as he maneuvered the car through Chasity's old neighborhood. The Adams's were making their way to Trisha's house for Thanksgiving dinner. In order to give each of their families equal time with them during the holidays, they had decided once they were married to rotate holidays. But just as it happened each time before, their parents did not want to abide by the arrangement.

"Mom, we were just over there *yesterday*," Jason ground out, putting a hand up. "I *promise* Kayla hasn't changed since yesterday."

Chasity snickered.

"Chasity, are you laughing at me?" Mrs. Adams asked.

Chasity couldn't contain the laughter in her voice. "No," she lied.

"Umm hmm," Mrs. Adams muttered, which made Chasity laugh.

"Mom, stop acting spoiled," Jason chided.

"At least send me a picture of her in her cute little Thanksgiving outfit," Mrs. Adams begged.

Jason let out a groan. "We *will*."

"Hey, how about we just stop by after we leave my mom's?" Chasity proposed. "That way you don't give my husband an aneurysm."

Jason chuckled as he glanced at Chasity. He rolled his eyes at the exaggerated squeal that erupted from his mother.

"Ooh, we'd love that," she said.

"Great, see you later," Jason said. "Love you, bye." He pushed the end call button on the dashboard. "Babe—"

"I know, we go through this every year," Chasity finished.

Jason shook his head. "They trippin'." He pulled into the driveway of Trisha's home. Once parked, they stepped out of the car.

Chasity took hold of Kayla's hand, while Jason grabbed a bag from the backseat of the car. As Jason walked around the front of the car, he looked over at Chasity; she'd put her head in her hand.

Kayla looked up at her. "Mommy what's wrong—"

"Shhhh," Chasity hissed, closing her eyes.

Jason frowned in concern, touching Chasity's shoulder. "You okay?"

Chasity lifted her head up, blinking a few times. "I'm fine. I think I just got out of the car too fast," she reasoned, moving hair over her shoulder. "Got dizzy."

Jason rubbed her arm. "Take it easy," he advised.

They walked up to the door and gave it a knock. Jason glanced over at her. "Yo, what if Melina brings that casserole like she did last year?"

"I'm not eating that shit," Chasity grimaced, earning a laugh from Jason.

"That…was an interesting dish," Jason commented, still laughing.

"*Nasty* is the word you need to use," Chasity spat. "I don't know *why* she thought that would be a good idea."

Jason's laughter subsided as the front door opened.

"Hi," Trisha beamed, greeting them with hugs. "What's in the bag?" she asked, looking at Jason's hand.

"Just a few pies," Jason answered, moving aside to let Chasity and Kayla walk in first. He stepped in and they removed their coats.

"I told you, you didn't have to bring anything," Trisha said, watching Kayla take off for the den.

"She's going for those toys," Chasity mentioned, gesturing to the den.

"As she *should*," Trisha chortled.

"Bringing some dessert was no problem," Jason smiled, bringing the subject back. On his way to the dining room with Chasity, he heard his name being called. Glancing, he saw Chasity's grandmother sitting on an accent chair.

"Jason, come over here and give me a hug," Grandmother Duvall beamed, holding her arms out.

Chasity narrowed her eyes at her grandmother. "Grandmom, how are you gonna give him a hug before you give *me* one?" she pouted.

Jason let out a laugh as Grandmother Duvall playfully flagged Chasity with her hand. "Don't be jealous," Jason teased.

Chasity shot him a glare as he embraced her smiling grandmother. "Don't get cocky brotha, she just wants to feel your muscles," she jeered.

"Chasity, will you leave this man alone," Grandmother Duvall chuckled.

"Yeah, yeah, don't be feeling up my husband, Grandmom," Chasity joked, taking the bag from Jason's hand. Hearing her grandmother's boisterous laugh at her joke, Chasity couldn't help but laugh herself.

Walking into the dining room, Chasity set the desserts on the massive table, laden with food. Instead of heading back into the living room with the rest of her family—both immediate and extended—Chasity leaned against the doorway, watching people interact. Years ago, she had dreaded the holidays. But now, especially after having a child, she'd come to appreciate them.

Chasity observed as her daughter roamed the living room, playing with a toy that she had retrieved from the den. Kayla walked over to a shelf, which contained a shrine to Brenda. Kayla touched Brenda's picture, then smiled and waved her little hand before skipping away.

Kayla knew of Brenda; the late great-aunt that she never got to meet. Lacking any good memories of Brenda herself, Chasity had left the telling of her aunt's good qualities to her mother and grandmother. Chasity had only told Kayla that she'd lived with Brenda until she was eighteen, leaving off the details about her childhood. Kayla was too young to understand.

Chasity was staring so much that she startled when someone spoke to her.

"Girl, put a bell around your neck or something," Chasity spat, spinning around.

Melina Duvall made a face. "I called your name like five

times," she threw back, setting a foil covered pan on the table. "It's not *my* fault you've mastered the art of zoning out."

"Yeah, yeah," Chasity dismissed, flagging her.

Melina chuckled. "Girl, give me a hug," she demanded, moving in for a hug. "Happy Thanksgiving."

"Same to you," Chasity returned as they parted. The two cousins had come a long way. Melina and Chasity had spent most of their lives hating each other. But now, they had learned to be civil.

Melina removed foil from her pan. "I can't *wait* to dig into this," she beamed.

Chasity turned her nose up. "Oh my God," she muttered, putting a hand over her nose. "The fuck is *that*?"

Melina frowned. "My casserole."

Chasity felt like dry heaving. "Did something *die* in it?" she grunted. "It smells worse than *last* time."

Melina made a face at her as she put the foil back on. "Funny," she sneered.

"There is not *one* trace of humor in my voice or on my face," Chasity threw back.

Melina flagged her. "Whatever. My food is good."

"It's really *not*," Chasity stated bluntly.

Melina sucked her teeth. "Screw you," she ground out, walking away. "Hi Jason," she greeted as Jason passed her on his way into the kitchen.

Jason waved back. "You okay?" he asked Chasity, noticing the annoyed look on her face.

Chasity pointed to Melina's dish, but didn't say anything.

Jason walked over, lifted the foil, and winced. "God," he grunted, earning a snicker from Chasity. "Should we hide it?" he joked.

Chasity thought for a moment. "No, we should *trash* that shit."

Jason let out a laugh.

Sidra tried to pry her mother's cheek from hers, but to no avail.

"I'm so happy my Princess is home," Mrs. Howard gushed,

holding onto Sidra with a vice grip. Ever since Sidra had arrived back at her parents' home in Delaware the previous evening, her mother had been doting on her to no end.

"Mama please, you're messing up my makeup," Sidra protested, gently nudging her. She glanced up as her father walked down the steps. "Daddy, she's doing it again."

"Vanessa, let the girl go," Mr. Howard chuckled, heading into the kitchen.

Sidra giggled when her mother sucked her teeth at him.

Mrs. Howard let go. "Okay fine," she relented, smoothing her hands down her dress. "People should start arriving soon. Everybody is looking forward to seeing you."

"Yeah," Sidra replied, somber.

Mrs. Howard tapped Sidra's arm. "You feeling any better?" she asked.

Sidra looked at her mother and poked her bottom lip out. Mrs. Howard held a sympathetic glance. "No, I'm—I'm okay,' Sidra promised, waving her hand.

"You sure?"

Sidra nodded. "But if I sulk some more, will you let me cut into that chocolate cream pie now?" she smiled, clasping her hands together in hope.

"No," Mrs. Howard denied. She chuckled when Sidra let out a huff. "No Sidra, you'll ruin your appetite."

"Fine," Sidra relented, putting her hands up. The doorbell sent her mother darting to answer it. Sidra's smile was bright as her brother Marcus walked in, holding his daughter. "Gabby!" Sidra shrieked, running over and practically snatching the five-year-old from her father.

"Damn Sid, no hug for your big brother?" Marcus laughed, watching Sidra spin the laughing little girl around in her arms.

Sidra looked over at him, then looked at Gabby. "What do you say Princess? Should I give your daddy a hug?"

"Oh really?" Marcus chuckled.

Gabby nodded and Sidra giggled, walking over and giving Marcus a big hug. "It's good to see you."

"You too," he said, parting from their embrace.

She helped Gabby take her coat off. "Oh my God, she's wearing the dress that I bought her," Sidra gushed, placing a hand on her chest.

"I had no *choice*; she had it sitting on her chair since last week," he replied, hanging the coats up.

Sidra bent down in front of Gabby. "What do you say tomorrow, we go shopping?" she cooed.

"Can we get nail polish too?" Gabby asked, smiling.

"Of *course*, we can," Sidra answered.

"Sidra, *please* don't buy her anything else," Marcus pleaded.

Sidra put her hand up at him. "Shut up, shut up, we're having girlie time," she dismissed.

Spotting Mrs. Howard in the other room, Gabby went running for her. Sidra followed her progress, grinning.

"She's so cute," Sidra commented to Marcus. "Glad she takes after *our* side of the family and not after—"

"Stop it," Marcus cut in, giving her a playful tap on the arm. "India and I aren't together, but she's still the mother of my child, so be respectful." Sidra raised her eyebrow at him. "Please?" he added.

"I'll be respectful," Sidra promised, folding her arms. Marcus looked shocked; he knew how much Sidra hated his ex. "I won't call her a raggedy bitch to her face... Ooh look, she's not here, *is* she?"

Marcus put his hand over his face, shaking his head.

"Our brothers should be here soon," Sidra informed, looking at her watch.

"I thought they would've beaten me here," Marcus said, scratching his head.

"You know traffic is crazy," she said. "Remember, they're coming from DC."

Marcus nodded. "Right. You know what, let me go put a to-go plate up now before they get here."

"How are you going to put up a to-go plate when we haven't even started *eating* yet?" Sidra hurled at Marcus's departing figure.

"'Cause I'm *me*," Marcus boasted, heading for the kitchen.

"Marcus! Don't you touch that food yet!" Mrs. Howard barked from the dining room.

"Yes ma'am," Marcus sputtered, earning a laugh from

Sidra.

"Gammy, can I have a cookie?" Gabby asked.

"Of *course* baby," Mrs. Howard gushed

"Mom! Really?!" Marcus exclaimed.

Sidra snickered. "It's good to be home," she said to herself.

The doorbell rang again; Sidra watched as her father opened the door, warmly greeting more family members. She was looking forward to the evening, but before she could fully enjoy it, she had to make a phone call.

Grabbing her cell phone from an end table, she retreated upstairs to her old bedroom. Her parents had yet to convert it into something else. Sidra was grateful; she didn't realize that she'd missed sleeping in her old room. Sitting on the canopy bed, Sidra dialed a number and put the phone to her ear. She let out a sigh when the call went to voicemail.

She cleared her throat. "Hi...it's me..." she spoke. "I just wanted to say Happy Thanksgiving and umm... I'm going to Chasity and Jason's tomorrow for game night...was wondering if you were going too... I just..." She let out a deep sigh. "Happy Thanksgiving Josh."

Sidra hung up the phone, staring at the blank screen. Tears began to prick her eyes, but she quickly dabbed them with her fingers. "Nope, cry tomorrow," she told herself.

Chapter 30

Malajia rubbed her hands in anticipation. "I'm on that last deviled egg," she said. But upon entering the kitchen, she found Dana stuffing it in her mouth. Malajia threw her hand up. "Dana, I *know* you ain't just eat that egg."

Dana looked at her. "Yup," she boasted, mouth full.

"You knew I wanted it," Malajia fussed, clapping her hands with each word.

Dana swallowed, then wiped her mouth. "I didn't know *anything*, and you had like four at dinner," she threw back.

Thanksgiving dinner in the Simmons's household had been served earlier, but the house was still full of family and friends who had already packed up most of the remaining food. Scavenging for remnants was nearly impossible.

"My *kids* ate them," Malajia argued.

Dana shrugged as she headed for the fridge. "Not my problem."

Malajia narrowed her eyes at her nineteen-year-old sister. "I know you got more in that plate you put up," she assumed. "Give me one before I snatch them plaits out your head."

Dana snapped her head towards her. "No," she refused, flinging her long braids over her shoulders. "I'm not ten anymore, you can't just demand stuff from me."

Malajia sucked her teeth. "Yeah, a'ight," she muttered, storming over to the refrigerator just as Dana opened it. "Which one's yours?"

Dana tried to nudge her away. "Get your greedy ass away from here!"

"I know you, you hid that shit in the—got it," Malajia rejoiced, pulling a foil-covered plate from the vegetable crisper. "You hide your shit in the same spot every year."

Furious, Dana tried to grab the plate from Malajia. "Malajia, stop playing. Give me my damn plate," she demanded.

Malajia smacked Dana's hand away, then peeled back the foil. "Ooh, found one!" She quickly grabbed the deviled egg, then set the plate on the counter.

"I'm not fuckin' around with you Malajia!" Dana erupted, grabbing hold of Malajia's hand as she tried to put the egg in her mouth.

Malajia raised her arm, keeping the egg out of Dana's reach. "I'm telling Mom you up in her house cussing," Malajia flashed back as they struggled. "Mom! Dana in here being grown and selfish."

"Mommy! Malajia's stealing my food!"

Mark, hearing commotion and looking for more sweet potato pie, walked into the kitchen. Malajia was holding her arm up, while Dana desperately tried to pry her hand open. He folded his arms and stood by the entryway, trying not to laugh when Malajia and Dana began slapping each other's arms.

"Ouch! Dana, when did you get so heavy handed?" Malajia barked, taking another slap to the arm. She slapped Dana back.

"Give me my goddamn egg!" Dana screamed, squeezing Malajia's hand, crushing the egg in the process.

Angry, Malajia flung the crumbled bits in the sink. "See what your hype ass did?" she fumed.

Dana went to grab a paper towel. "I'm satisfied with the outcome. At least *your* ass didn't get it," she taunted, wiping the egg pieces from her hand.

Malajia stared daggers at her while washing her hands in the sink. She eyed the rest of the food on Dana's plate, then without warning pushed the whole plate in the sink, sending food splattering.

Dana stood there, eyes wide in shock. "I hate you!"

"You gonna be hungry as shit tomorrow with no leftovers," Malajia mocked, drying her hands with a paper towel. She walked away from her fuming sister, leaving the kitchen to find Mark standing there. Her husband held his hand over his face, laughter erupting from him. "You saw all of that?" she asked.

Mark removed his hand, still laughing. "Yo Malajia...you silly as shit. You really in here fighting over a deviled egg?"

"She's disrespectful," Dana grunted, cleaning the mess.

"All she had to do was share, and this could have all been avoided," Malajia argued, in an animated fashion.

Laughter subsiding, Mark shook his head.

Malajia shrugged, then walked past him to the living room, where her father and two sisters Tanya and Geri were talking.

"What are y'all in here running your mouths about?" Malajia charged, sitting on the arm of the couch.

"Nothing I'm interested in," Geri jeered, earning a snicker from Malajia.

"Geri's just mad because we're talking about relationships. Something she hasn't yet mastered," Tanya taunted, earning a middle finger from Geri.

"Hey, I'm still in the room," Mr. Simmons commented, grabbing his drink from an end table. "Keep the middle fingers to yourselves."

Mark walked out of the kitchen, shoving a piece of pie into his mouth.

"I hope you saved some for the *rest* of us," Mr. Simmons commented, eyeing Mark sternly. Mark slowed down his chewing as he looked off to the side.

"Dad, leave him alone," Malajia snapped back. She gave Mark's back a rub as her father focused his attention back to his own drink.

"You know what, Malajia?" Tanya began.

"What?" Malajia wondered, unenthused. He father annoyed her; he'd been passive aggressively picking on Mark all night long. Mark was trying his best to ignore it, but Malajia couldn't.

"Being around your little boys, makes me want to have more children."

"Hell, you want *them*?" Malajia joked.

Geri snickered as Tanya giggled. "I'm *serious*," Tanya insisted. "I mean, Caleb is going on six now and I think I want to give him a sibling."

Malajia put her hand up. "Knock yourself out, sister."

"You ever think about having *more* children?" Tanya asked.

"*Hell* no," Malajia immediately blurted out.

Tanya's mouth fell open. "Come on now, you could have *one* more," she urged.

"I could punch you in the throat, is what I *could* do," Malajia spat back. Mark shook his head in amusement. "No, this uterus is closed to babies," Malajia added, gesturing to her midsection.

Tanya rolled her eyes at Malajia, then looked to Mark. "How do *you* feel about that Mark?"

"He ain't got a *choice*," Malajia cut in, pointing to him.

Mark chuckled. "I'm good with it," he cosigned, giving Malajia's shoulder a rub. "We're perfectly happy with the two that we have."

"I wish y'all would stop pressuring her to have more children," Geri cut in, traces of agitation in her voice. "She *said* she's done, so she's done."

"*Thank* you, Geraldine," Malajia praised, patting her chest twice then pointing at Geri. "That's why you my fave."

Geri stared at her. "Call me Geraldine again," she warned, earning a laugh from Malajia.

"I *do* hear you though, Malajia," Tanya relented, putting her hands up. "It's hard with *one*, so I can only *imagine* two at the same time… At least you get to stay home and raise them."

Malajia held a blank stare. "Uh huh," she muttered.

"Mark, that's great that you take care of everything so that she gets to be a stay-at-home mom," Tanya added. "I'm sure more women wish they could do that."

"Doubt it," Malajia muttered, low enough that only she could hear.

"Do you ever get stressed being the one handling all of the bills?" Tanya pressed.

Malajia frowned. "Why is this the *topic* right now?" she ground out. "Go back to Geri's nonexistent relationships."

Geri sucked her teeth as Tanya shrugged. "Just curious," Tanya explained.

"*My* question is, why are you praising him for doing something that he's *supposed* to do?" Mr. Simmons jumped in

Mark's jaw clenched as he pinched the bridge of his nose.

Malajia fixed an angry gaze upon her father. "Really Dad?"

Mr. Simmons shrugged. "What? I'm just saying," he defended. "He's *supposed* to work to take care of his family. That's his *job* as the man of the house. So, saying that he's doing a good job at doing that is like praising *you* for being a good parent. It's something that you're *supposed* to do. You don't get a cookie for it."

"I'm gonna go find cookies," Mark commented, walking away.

Malajia tried to take hold of his arm; Mark didn't notice and continued his journey to the kitchen. "Dad, you *do* know that men aren't the only ones who have to work now, right?" she bit out. "*Both* parents can work and *both* can equally contribute to raising the children."

"Your mother didn't work," he argued.

"Mom had *seven* of your big-headed kids and didn't *want* to work!" Malajia exclaimed, then thought. "Six, she had *six* big-headed kids... *My* head is perfect."

"Not when you were little," Geri muttered, amusement in her voice. "Lest we forget the deformed nose, *Buttons*."

Malajia put her hand up at Geri, making a face in the process. "Y'all done irked my face," she grunted, standing up. She walked into the kitchen. Mark was standing by the counter by himself, eating another slice of pie. "Hey," she said.

"Hey," he solemnly uttered.

She stood next to him and rubbed his arm. "You okay?"

Mark glanced at her and nodded.

Malajia sighed. "Babe, I know that my Dad has been an asshole all night," she began.

"Mel, it's cool," Mark dismissed, wiping his hand on a napkin. "I'm used to it."

"You shouldn't *have* to be used to it," she pouted. "He's ridiculous and I'm sick of it."

Mark forced a small smile. "Don't worry about it."

Malajia let out a deep sigh, then gently grabbed his face with both hands. "You wanna get out of here?"

"Nah, it's okay. I know you still wanna hang with your family."

"*Fuck* them," Malajia grunted, removing her hands. "*You're* my family. So we can go… You wanna go see your parents?"

Mark chuckled. "You wanna drive to Delaware *now*?"

Malajia shrugged, "Why not? You *know* they're still up." She folded her arms. "They're probably trying to figure out whose gonna take your drunk grandmom home."

Mark busted out laughing. "Granny can still drink everybody under the table."

Malajia too laughed, "She put *both* our asses to shame last year." Laughter subsiding, she tapped his arm. "Seriously, we can head down there if you want… Or, we can pack up the rest of these pies, and go home."

Mark thought for a moment. "Let's go home."

Malajia tapped the counter. "Cool, *you* grab the rest of the pies on the counter, and *I'll* go get that apple one that my dad tried to hide," she directed, moving towards the refrigerator.

"Bet," Mark replied, grabbing the pies.

Malajia pointed to a tray. "Grab that tray of cookies too. The twins like those, and I'mma grab a couple of these to-go plates and we out."

"Wait, you're about to steal people's plates?" Mark laughed.

"You damn right. I'm not cooking for the rest of the week," she said, rummaging through the refrigerator's contents.

Mark stared at her for a moment. "I fuckin' love you."

"Love you too, now hurry up and run that shit to the car," Malajia threw back, pulling plates out.

Sitting on the side of the bathtub in the bathroom, Emily scrolled through her phone. Hearing a knock on the door, she rolled her eyes.

"I'm coming out, I just need a minute," she huffed, looking up at the closed door.

"Em, you've been in there for *thirty* minutes," a male voice said.

Emily looked back at her phone. "It's really been that long?"

"Yes. Time to come out now. Dinner is getting cold."

Emily sighed as she stood up. She went to the door and opened it; she was greeted with a smile from her oldest brother Dru Harris.

"I know you're hungry," he teased.

Emily resisted the urge to crack a smile; she shook her head instead. Despite the current state of her and their mother's relationship, Dru had convinced Emily to come to New Jersey for Thanksgiving. It was the first time that he was hosting it in his new house.

"Truth is, I'm *not* hungry actually," Emily ground out, running a hand through her hair. "It's funny how sitting across from a petty mother and a miserable sister can ruin your appetite."

Dru let out a sigh. "I'm sorry that Mom is being…well *Mom*."

Emily couldn't help but let out a slight chuckle.

"She's acting ridiculous, but I couldn't *not* invite her—"

"No Dru, I wouldn't expect you not to," Emily cut in. "I just appreciate you giving me the heads up that she was going to be here."

"Of course," he said. "And hey, at least she spoke to you and gave you a hug."

"If you can *call* that a hug," Emily spat. "It's okay though. Not like I expected anything more than that."

Dru put a hand on Emily's shoulder and gave it a rub. "Try not to let them get to you today," he urged. "I want us to have a good time."

Emily let out a sigh, then gave a slight nod.

Dru, taking this as an agreement, grabbed Emily's hand and pulled her out of the bathroom.

"Look whose back," Dru announced, walking back into the dining room with Emily close behind.

Will looked up from the table and smiled at her. Although he didn't say anything, Emily found his presence comforting. She made her way to the table and sat down.

"I remember how you used to hide in the bathroom when you were a teenager," Ms. Harris dryly mentioned, scooping food onto her plate. "I used to always wonder what you did in there."

"Even back *then.* I needed a minute," Emily muttered.

Will reached under the table and took Emily's hand.

As the family prepared their plates, Emily's other brother Brad Harris decided to break through the silence. "So Will, are you excited about the wedding?" he asked, scooping mashed potatoes onto his plate.

Will took a sip of his drink. "Of course," he beamed, looking at Emily. "Who wouldn't be excited to marry her?"

Emily looked down at the table, smiling and blushing.

"Awww," Brad teased, looking at Emily.

Emily giggled. "Stop it."

"Are you still planning on having your brothers in the wedding?" Ms. Harris cut in, spearing a piece of turkey with her fork.

Emily shot her mother a stern look. "Why *wouldn't* I, Mom?"

"I was just making sure," Ms. Harris shrugged. "After all, your *sister's* not in it, *I'm* not in it…was just asking."

Dru put his hand up as Emily opened her mouth to speak. "Brad and I are still groomsmen, stop starting Mom," he ground out.

Ms. Harris looked at him wide-eyed. "I'm not starting anything," she lied. "It was a question. Are we not allowed to have a conversation?"

"Not when it comes at the expense of my *sister*, you can'–," Dru argued.

"Play nice everybody," Brad cut in.

His pleas were ignored.

Jazmine leaned forward. "Oh please," she spat at Dru. "She used to annoy you *just* like everybody else, now you wanna be her *savior*?"

"Thanks Jazmine," Emily spat. "I always appreciate you bringing up how annoying I am."

"You're not annoying," Will said to Emily, squeezing her hand.

Dru shot Jazmine a glare. "Just because *you* can't seem to get over whatever *your* damn issue is with Emily after all these years, doesn't mean that *I* haven't," he argued back. "And if you want my opinion, which I know you *don't,* but I couldn't care less about what you want. It's *pathetic* how you still treat her."

Emily just sat there staring at her food as the argument continued around her. If she knew that she would have been the sole topic of conversation at this so-called "happy" dinner, she would have stayed in Virginia.

"You're right, I *don't* care about your opinion," Jazmine spat.

Dru frowned at Jazmine. "What are you so miserable for?" he asked. "Are you mad because you had to take the train here?"

Jazmine glared at him. "Nope," she hissed. "I *preferred* it, at least I didn't have to listen to Emily's whining the whole way here."

Emily let out a loud huff. "Jazmine, I'm not bothering you, so stop taking digs at me," she threw out. She had made good on her promise of not letting Jazmine ride back to Jersey with her, and it was clear that Jazmine was bitter about it, among other things.

"Please," Jazmine ground out.

"Just leave me alone," Emily threw back.

Dru put a finger up. "Oh no, I know why you're miserable," he added, still focused on Jazmine. "It's because you've been kicked out of every family member's house *except* for the sister you keep *shitting* on."

"Screw you boy," Jazmine fumed, slamming her hand on the table.

"Okay, stop," Ms. Harris cut in. "That's enough with the arguing."

"Is it *also* enough of the petty behavior from you Mom?" Dru hurled, annoyed.

"Excuse me?" Ms. Harris spat, shooting her oldest child a challenging look. "How dare—"

"You know what Dru, I appreciate you trying, but don't waste your breath on *either* of them," Emily bit out, pushing herself back from the table.

Will stood up as Emily rose from her seat. He followed her

out of the dining room as the rest of the table sat in silence.

Will gently grabbed Emily's arm before she tried to dart up the steps. "Hey," he said.

Emily turned around, eyes glistening with built up tears. She was irritated and tired.

Will touched her face. "You want to get out of here?"

Emily stared at him and sighed. She did want to leave, but she would only feel bad that Will had driven all this way, and wouldn't even be able to finish his meal.

Wiping her eyes with the sleeve of her shirt, Emily shook her head. "I just... I just need a minute," she put out, heading up the stairs.

Will followed her progress up, sighing in the process. It was going to be a long night.

Chapter 31

Malajia leaned over Chasity's counter and dipped a tortilla chip into a bowl of salsa. She took a bite. "Yo, you ever want to drop kick the bullshit outta somebody?" she asked, between chews.

Chasity picked up a chip. "You forget who you're asking," she replied, before taking a bite.

"Oh right," Malajia chortled, reaching for her glass of rum and cola.

"Who do you want to drop kick?" Chasity asked, finishing her chip.

Malajia sucked her teeth. "My stupid dad," she vented. "He pissed me the hell off yesterday. I'm sick of him being a smart ass to my husband."

Chasity looked at her as she opened a bottle of water. "He's *still* doing that bullshit?"

"Yes, and I wanna kick him in the kneecaps," Malajia huffed.

It was Friday evening, and as planned, the group had begun migrating to Jason and Chasity's home for game night. Not surprisingly, Mark and Malajia were the first guests to arrive.

"Well...you can't exactly kick your father in the kneecaps," Chasity said, trying not to laugh. "You know they're bad... I heard one of 'em crack one time."

Malajia busted out laughing. "And he *swears* nobody hear that shit," she said. "But seriously, he better leave Mark alone." She grabbed another chip. "That's why I found that pie he tried to hide in the deep freezer *and* took the plate he put up...among *others*."

"Are you serious?" Chasity asked, laughter in her voice.

Malajia nodded. "Yup." She took a quick sip of her drink. "Mom called me last night and said people was mad as shit they couldn't find their plates… Me and Mark were sitting on the couch watching Christmas movies, fuckin' that food up."

Chasity busted out laughed. "You stupid, yo."

Malajia gave a slight bow and tipped her glass towards Chasity. "So how was *your* Thanksgiving?"

Chasity shrugged. "Nobody argued, so I'll say it was good." She thought for a second. "Oh wait… There was one."

Malajia narrowed her eyes at Chasity. "Who did your mean ass argue with?" she accused, knowing her best friend all too well.

"Melina," Chasity answered, nonchalant. "Turns out that throwing someone's casserole in the trash in front of them is pretty disrespectful."

Malajia sat there for a moment before erupting with laughter. "I can't stand you."

Chasity ran a hand through her hair. "So what? The smell of it made me throw up; the shit had to go," she defended.

Malajia wiped a tear from her eye as she calmed down. "I would've *loved* to see that shit. You know I *still* don't like her ass." She took another sip of her drink. "Was that other cousin of yours there too? That hype chick that's *way* too happy that she's related to you?"

Chasity chuckled. "Now, now petty," she teased.

"No, she don't know you like that, she need to step off," Malajia grunted. "I said no new friends, but I see that I should have extended that to *family* too… She better calm her little ass down."

Chasity shook her head in amusement.

Malajia muttered something else, then looked around. "The guys still outside tossing that damn football around?"

"Yup," Chasity jeered. "Probably tearing their old asses up diving on that grass."

Malajia lowered her head. "God," she huffed. "I just *know* I'm gonna have to massage Mark's rickety ass ankle later."

Chasity snickered until it turned into full-on laughter. Malajia couldn't help but laugh herself. The door opening caught both of their attention.

"Look who I found," Mark announced, holding the door open for Alex, who walked inside.

Alex looked back at him, bewildered. "How did you find me when I clearly *came* here?" she bit out.

"Shut up," he shot back, closing the door.

Alex sucked her teeth and took off her coat. She looked over at the girls. "Heeeeey," she beamed, bolting over to them. She hugged them both. "God, I *so* needed this get together," she said, sitting on a stool at the counter. She eyed the different alcoholic and non-alcoholic beverages sitting on the counter. "Ooh, wine," she rejoiced.

Chasity handed her an empty wine glass. "*You* look good and stressed," she observed.

Alex waved a hand at her, pouring herself a glass. "Girl, between those tech problems at work and...*other* stuff, my stress has been through the roof." She took a sip. "I'm just glad to be here with my girls."

"*Speaking* of tech stuff, I finished what you asked me to," Chasity revealed, walking over to a shelf in the living room. She removed a flash drive, and handed it to Alex.

Alex smiled. "You're amazing, thank you so much."

"Yeah, yeah," Chasity jeered, waving her hand at her.

Alex pocketed the drive and reached for a cookie on a tray.

"You might want to grab that celery stick," Malajia commented. "I heard you can't fit into your bridesmaid's dress."

Alex paused mid-grab and shot Malajia a glare. "I *know* you heard it because *I'm* the one who *told* you," she sneered.

"Whatever bitch, just eat a vegetable before you fuck up our pictures and shit," Malajia snapped, causing Chasity to spit out the water she was drinking as she busted out laughing.

Alex let out a shriek as water droplets hit her face. "Come on Chasity!" She quickly grabbed a napkin. "Learn how to hold your laugh in until you swallow," she ranted, wiping her face.

Chasity coughed as she tried to compose herself.

Malajia reached over and patted Chasity's back as her coughing subsided. "Oh, shut up," Malajia hurled at Alex.

Alex flagged Malajia with her hand.

Malajia headed over to the radio and turned the music up. "Ayyeeee, this is my song!" she bellowed as a popular track blared through the speaker. "Chaz, I like this speaker, let me have it."

"Malajia, don't make me put your ass out," Chasity sneered, wiping the counter off with a cloth.

Malajia just giggled and glanced as the front door opened. "Hey Miss Bride-to-be," she sang, seeing Emily walk in.

Emily smiled. "Hi," she greeted, closing the door behind her. She removed her coat and held it up for Chasity to see.

"Just set it over there on the bench with the rest of them," Chasity directed, pointing to a cushioned bench by the wall.

Emily did as she was told, then gave Malajia a hug, heading for the kitchen. She greeted Chasity and Alex with hugs, before fixing her eyes on the spread. "Ooh, you have snacks, perfect," she breathed, grabbing a few cookies. "I'm starving."

Malajia adjusted the volume of the music before joining the others back at the kitchen.

"You didn't fill up on leftovers?" Alex asked, grabbing a handful of chips from a bowl.

Emily shook her head as she chewed the chocolate chip cookie. "I didn't take any leftovers," she answered finally.

Malajia jerked her head back. "Girl—you crazy. I'm not cooking dinner for a *week*, I took so much."

Chasity chuckled; she was the only one who knew Malajia wasn't exaggerating for once.

Emily sat down on one of the barstools. "Dinner as a whole was just...*wrong*," she alluded. "Ruined my whole night... I didn't even regain my appetite until we left the hotel to come *here*."

"What happened?" Alex wondered, concerned.

Emily let out a sigh. "My mother's attitude and my sister's *everything* happened," she grunted. "I don't know how I'm going to get through my wedding day if they keep this mess up."

Alex gave Emily a sympathetic rub on her back. "Everything will work itself out," she soothed.

Emily offered a faint smile to Alex. "Thanks Alex, but I'm not that naïve little girl anymore," she said. "I know that's not possible."

"Oh it *is* possible, because *we're* going to *make* it possible," Malajia chimed in, gesturing to herself Alex and Chasity. "We got your back, nobody is going to ruin your day."

"You want me to tell your sister she can't come to the wedding?" Chasity offered. "I'll make sure to be as disrespectful as possible."

Emily chuckled.

"And that's not hard for her to do," Malajia added, gesturing to Chasity.

Alex gestured for them to stop.

"No Chaz, but I appreciate it though," Emily said. She put her hands up. "Let's change this dreary subject."

"Done, where's Will?" Malajia asked.

"Oh, he got persuaded by Mark to play football with him and Jason," Emily chortled.

"Your man's gonna get tackled like shit," Chasity teased.

"I know," Emily agreed, amused. "Poor thing, he's *so* not the athletic type."

Malajia waved a dismissive hand at Emily. "That's okay, you can just rub his balls later," she said, earning disgusted looks from Chasity and Alex.

Emily's mouth fell open. "Oh wow."

"Oh that's right, you're waiting until your wedding night," Malajia amended, "Well hey, you can do that *then*." She pointed to her head. "See? Ideas."

Emily stared at Malajia for several seconds, before turning to Alex. "So Alex, is Eric coming tonight?"

Malajia tossed her hands in the air at the blatant dismissal. "What did I say wrong?"

"Just shut up," Chasity spat, waving her hand at Malajia.

Malajia shook her head, turning to Alex. "Anyway, on to you. You invited Eric?" she pressed.

Alex gave a nonchalant shrug. "I mean, yeah," she answered. "I didn't know that it would be this big of a deal."

"It's a big deal because you're actually letting him hang out with us," Malajia replied, amusement in her voice. "I remember how you used to keep him at a distance."

"That's because you all were *ignorant*," Alex spat.

"We *still are*, what's your point?" Malajia threw back.

"So…is he *coming*?" Emily repeated.

Alex let out a quick sigh. "I mean I *guess*," she answered, agitated. "He seems like he really wants to be here so…"

Chasity frowned slightly. "You want to sound less like a *bitch* about it?"

Alex took a sip of her drink, rolling her eyes in the process. "*What*? Am I supposed to do a backflip or something?"

Malajia rolled her eyes. "You drying around Alex," she spat. "I say we take some shots to loosen up."

"No," Chasity refused.

"Bitch—get the damn shot glasses Chasity," Malajia demanded. "I'm not fuckin' around with you tonight." When Chasity didn't budge, Malajia went into the cabinet and grabbed the shot glasses herself, setting one in front of each girl.

Chasity made a face as she watched Malajia pour vodka into each glass. Feeling queasy, she grabbed her stomach. "I'm not drinking that, I don't feel good," she protested.

"Shut up," Malajia threw back. She sat a glass in front of Emily. "You doing this or no, baby girl?"

"How come *she* gets a damn choice?" Chasity barked. Malajia flagged her with her hand.

Emily thought for a moment. "Yeah, I'll do one," she agreed.

"*Really*?" Alex asked, surprised. Emily hadn't drank hard liquor since sophomore year of college, sticking mostly with wine or wine coolers.

Emily nodded. "Yep."

"Alex, stay out her business and take *your* shot," Malajia demanded.

Alex grabbed hers. "Hell, why not?" she muttered before downing it. "Oh God!" she belted out, putting her hand over her face. "What the— *Why* does it have to be that damn *nasty*?"

"'Cause it's *cheap*. And guess who bought it?" Chasity said, gesturing to Malajia.

Malajia sucked her teeth. "Oh stop bitchin' it's not that bad," she denied. She downed her shot, then pinched the bridge of her nose as the strong liquid poured down her throat. She leaned her head on the counter. "Dear God in heaven," she admonished. "That shit is *horrible*… I apologize for this."

Chasity pushed her glass aside. "Yeah, I'm not drinking that shit."

"Yeah, I'll pass too," Emily declined, putting hers down. "Chasity, can you pass me a wine cooler?"

"Pass me one too, I need a chaser," Malajia panted, holding her hand out.

"No, you deal with it," Chasity refused. "You need to learn to stop doing this shit."

"Come *on*! It's burning my goddamn esophagus," Malajia barked, slamming her hand on the table.

Alex slapped her hand on the counter several times. "I'm gonna be tasting that all night," she grunted. "Malajia—you're too old to still be buying cheap shit like this. Mark has a good job. Do better!"

Malajia laughed.

"Throw the ball in my neighbor's yard one more time, hear?" Jason warned, running to retrieve the football from his neighbor's yard.

Mark tossed his arms in the air. "Not my fault your ass can't catch anymore Mr. Former Quarterback," he mocked.

Jason stopped in his tracks, shooting Mark a glare. "How the *fuck* am I supposed to catch a ball that you threw *behind* you?" he fumed. "Dickhead."

"My hand slipped, *damn*," Mark barked back.

Will was too busy laughing at the banter to chime in.

The guys had been playing football outside for nearly an hour. That was thirty minutes too long as far as Jason was concerned; Mark had no knack for football.

Jason rolled his eyes as he grabbed the football.

Mark glanced over as a familiar car parked in front of the house. "Yo!" Mark belted out, waving.

Josh turned his car off and stepped out; David stepped out of the passenger's side. "Yo, yo," Josh returned, shoving his car keys into his pocket. "How was everybody's Thanksgiving?"

"Pretty good," Jason replied, jogging over.

"Oh snaps, David made it over to hang with the group," Mark commented in dramatic fashion. "Nice surprise, Ohio boy."

David stared at him. "You already *knew* I was coming," he ground out. "I told y'all I was coming back for Thanksgiving and I *talked* to everybody yesterday *and* confirmed my attendance."

Mark chuckled. "Why you so mad though?"

"'Cause you always state the obvious," David fussed, adjusting his scarf.

"How long have y'all been out here playing?" Josh asked, eyeing the football. "What are the girls doing?"

"In there doing girl shit," Mark replied. "Dancing and running their mouths about shit that they'll force us to listen to later."

Will chuckled. "Aww, I love listening to Emily talk about stuff."

"Yeah, give it time," Mark joked.

Jason snickered at Mark. "Anyway Josh, we've been playing for about an hour," he answered. "About to call it quits and go get a drink... Unless *you two* wanna play."

"I can play for a bit," Josh shrugged.

David opened his mouth to respond, but didn't get the chance because Mark tackled him, sending them both falling into a pile of leaves.

"The hell?" Josh frowned while Jason stood there, looking confused.

"Mark, what the fuck, man?!" David yelled, glaring at Mark, who had fallen over him. "What did you do that for?"

"My bad, I thought we were playing football," Mark answered.

David's eyes were wide with anger. "Did I *say* that I wanted to play?!"

Mark stared at him, a silly look on his face. "I guess I misjudged."

Jason turned away, attempting to hold his laughter in.

"Misjudge— Man get the hell off me!" David nudged Mark off him. "You still play too damn much," he fussed, picking himself up off the ground.

Mark laughed as he rose to his feet. "Totally worth it," he commented, dusting leaves from his jeans.

Jason tucked the football under his arm. "Yeah, I think it's time to go in," he concluded. He walked into the house, followed by the others.

"Heeey. Newcomers have to take a shot," Malajia announced, pouring liquor into shot glasses.

Josh shrugged as Malajia handed him one of the glasses. He downed his shot at the same time that David did. "Oh my God," Josh complained of the taste. "It tastes like battery acid."

David immediately started coughing, spitting liquor on the floor in the process.

"Dude, you just spit on my damn floor," Chasity barked to him.

David put a hand up. "I'm sorry, that stuff was so disgusting," he sputtered between coughs.
"I thought that my pallet was strong, but I guess not."

Mark laughed. "Baby, you still giving people that nasty ass vodka?" he asked Malajia.

"Of course. *Somebody* has to drink it," Malajia threw back. "The rule is last person to arrive has to take two shots. So Sidra better beat Eric here."

Alex grabbed a pencil from the coffee table. "Eric probably won't drink," she said. "He's gotta get back to Maryland tonight."

"Really?" Malajia questioned, pulling a container of food from the refrigerator. "I would think that he'd spend the night with *you*."

"Nope," Alex grunted. "He has to get back *tonight*."

Chasity looked over at Malajia. "Get out my damn fridge!"

"How you holdin' out on the mac and cheese?" Malajia accused, ignoring Chasity's demand. "Y'all feeding us pizza and wings and you got leftovers in here."

"Ooh, you got baked mac and cheese?" Mark belted out, running over.

"Jason!" Chasity called.

"Hey, get y'all greedy asses out of the goddamn refrigerator," Jason barked, pointing at them. "The leftovers are *ours*."

Malajia sucked her teeth as she pushed the container back on the shelf. "Selfish bitch," she grunted.

Will laughed as Emily handed him a small plate of chicken wings. "Oh wow," he commented.

"This is normal," Emily dismissed, waving her hand.

"Let's get a game started," Alex suggested, sitting up in her seat. "Do you guys want to play charades?"

"Hold on, we have to wait for Sidra," Emily cut in, opening a bottle of water.

Josh ran a hand over his head and sighed. As much as he wanted to see Sidra, he was relieved that she wasn't there yet. He needed to get his mind together before laying eyes on her again.

Malajia glanced at him. "You need another shot there, Josh?" she asked, noticing his uneasiness.

Josh looked back at her. "Yes, but not of that poison you brought."

Malajia giggled as Josh made his way to the kitchen. "Yo Sidra got ten more minutes then we're starting without her," she proclaimed, glancing at her watch. "Don't nobody got time for her shit."

"It's cool," Mark cut in, making himself a drink. "We can use the time waiting on Sid, finding out if David smashed that girl he fills beakers with yet."

David ran a hand down his face. "God," he muttered. "Shut *up*, will you?"

Mark laughed.

David shook his head. "Keema is just my *friend*," he stressed. His phone vibrated in his jeans pocket; David immediately checked it.

"Yeah, like none of us ever smashed someone who was just a *friend* before." Mark drawled, sarcastic.

David stared at his phone for a moment, reading a text message. "Please, like *who*?" he challenged Mark.

The group pointed to Alex, who in turn tossed her hands up and sucked her teeth. "Nice," Alex jeered.

Jason slowly raised his hand, simultaneously pointing to Chasity.

Chasity narrowed her eyes at him. "Really?" she sneered.

"Well…it's *true*," Jason laughed. Chasity just made a face at him.

"Oh yeah, y'all *did* bang before you became a couple," Mark recalled.

Chasity held her glare on Jason. "You see what you started?"

"Yeah, I regret that now," Jason chortled, reaching for a slice of pizza from an open box.

"Mark, *you* did too," Josh recalled. "You *stayed* in some *friend's* dorm room freshman year."

Mark shook his head. "Nah, them chicks weren't friends," he denied.

Malajia stared daggers at him. "You gonna keep reminiscing about them hoes you used to mess with?" she sneered.

Mark caught her glare, then pointed at David. "Damn David, you see what you started?" he hurled.

David looked up from his phone, shocked. "Wait, *what?*"

Chapter 32

Sidra checked her appearance in the rearview mirror. She smoothed her straight hair down and took a deep breath. Procrastinating long enough to endure several threatening messages from Malajia, Sidra had finally made it to Chasity and Jason's house. Grabbing a large fruit arrangement from the passenger's seat, she stepped out of the car.

She walked up to the door and knocked. Hearing commotion from inside, she knocked again. "Guys, come on," she huffed. She twisted the knob, and found the door unlocked. She walked in to the sounds of arguing and laughing.

"A platypus?! Really?" Malajia hurled at Mark. "You got that from an oval with lines in it?!"

Mark put his hands on his face and pulled down. "It was a *guess*!" he barked.

"It was a *stupid* guess," Malajia threw back, tossing the pencil on the table.

David eyed the drawing on the paper. "Malajia, what was it *supposed* to be?" he asked, tilting his head.

Malajia folded her arms in a huff. "A raisin."

Mark jumped up. "That doesn't even *look* like a fuckin' raisin!"

"Oh, but it looks like a *platypus*?" Malajia shot back. "I want a divorce."

Mark flagged her with his hand as he sat back down.

"Hello," Sidra cut in, waving a hand. "You didn't hear me knocking?"

"Sorry, you know their voices carry," Jason chortled, walking over and grabbing the fruit basket from her. He gave her a hug.

Sidra removed her coat and set it on top of the others, as Jason took the basket to the kitchen. "Sorry I'm late," she said, heading over and hugging everyone else. She looked around. "You're playing charades?"

"Not any*more*," Chasity muttered, walking into the kitchen. "I've had enough of those two non-drawing asses, arguing."

Sidra followed Chasity to the kitchen; she looked around.

Chasity watched Sidra scan the space with her eyes. "Josh is in the bathroom Sidra," she said.

Sidra's eyes widened; she put a hand over her face in embarrassment. "Am I that obvious?"

"Yes," Chasity confirmed.

Sidra shook her head. "God, I'm pathetic," she muttered.

Chasity chuckled. "No, you're not."

"Anyway...do you like the fruit basket?" Sidra asked, changing the subject. "It's made to look like a flower bouquet."

"Sidra, *why* did you bring that bullshit?" Malajia hurled from the living room. "Your bougie ass *gotta* be the one to bring some damn fruit. You ever heard of a *bottle*?"

"Leave me alone Malajia," Sidra spat at her.

"Thanks Sidra, the fruit is fine. I'll eat it," Chasity cut in, removing the cellophane wrapping.

Sidra glanced in the living room. "See? My gift *is appreciated*," she hissed at Malajia. She looked back at Chasity. Seeing her eat a piece of fruit, she frowned in confusion.

Catching her stare, Chasity frowned back. "What?"

"Nothing," Sidra dismissed, reaching for a glass. "It's just that, I thought you hated cantaloupe."

Chasity made a face. "I *do*."

Sidra pointed to Chasity's hand, which held a bitten off piece. "Then why are you *eating* it?" she asked, laughter in her voice.

Chasity looked down at the fruit. "The fuck?" she mumbled to herself, tossing it down on the counter. She held a confused look for a moment, then closed her eyes as she had a thought. *Oooooh shit.*

"You okay?" Sidra wondered, noticing the distant look on Chasity's face.

"I'm fine," she assured, handing Sidra a shot glass full of vodka. "Here, drink this."

Sidra rolled her eyes. "Fine," she huffed, taking the glass. "Just one won't hurt."

"It will," Chasity contradicted, grabbing a bottle of water from the counter.

Sidra watched as Chasity headed out of the kitchen. "Wait, aren't you gonna take one *with* me?"

"Nope," Chasity declined, continuing on her way.

Shrugging, Sidra downed the shot, then immediately started coughing. "What in the high hell *is* this?!"

"Ha, got another one," Malajia laughed, pointing.

Sidra slammed the glass on the counter and grabbed a bottle of water. She twisted the top off and started downing it Fanning her face with her hand, she wished that the burning in her chest would just stop. "Never am I taking another shot from *any* of you," she fussed.

She briefly forgot about the pain in her chest when she saw Josh walk down the steps. Their eyes met as he made his way to the kitchen.

"Hi," Sidra sputtered.

"Hi," Josh replied, pouring himself a glass of soda.

Sidra fiddled with the bracelet on her wrist while Josh sipped his beverage. "So…how was your Thanksgiving?" she asked finally.

"It was fine," he answered. "Yours?"

Sidra pushed hair behind her ears. "It was fine," she replied. "Umm…did you get my message? ...*Messages*?"

Josh took another sip, nodding in the process. "Yes, I did."

Sidra frowned slightly. "You didn't think that you should *return* them?"

"Yes, I did," he repeated. "Just *didn't*."

Sidra let out a sigh. "Look Josh…we need to talk—"

"We *do* and we *will*, just not tonight," Josh cut in. "Come over to my place tomorrow and we'll do it then."

"But I think that we should do it while we're here *now*," she insisted.

"Tonight is about us having fun," Josh said, stern. "And I don't want to dampen the mood right now."

Sidra let out a huff. "Josh—"

"Sidra you waited five years to tell me the truth, *surely* you can wait another day to tell me *why*," Josh spat, fixing a stern gaze on her.

Sidra's mouth fell open. She certainly wasn't expecting that response. Not wanting to press the issue, she just put her hands up in surrender. "Fine," she said finally. "It's fine...whatever you want."

"Good." Glass in one hand, he grabbed a bowl of chips with the other. "You look pretty by the way," he said, walking back into the living room.

"Thanks," Sidra muttered after a moment.

"Alex, where the hell is Eric?" Malajia asked, impatient.

Alex took a sip of her wine. "He said he's on his way." As if on cue, there was a knock on the door.

"Yes, another man... I'm sick of y'all women out numbering us," Mark rejoiced, putting his arms up.

Malajia looked perplexed. "What the—just shut up," she ground out, flagging him with her hand. "Before Eric showed up, it was even, fool."

Jason opened the door and greeted Eric as he walked in. "Sorry I'm late everybody," Eric said, handing Jason a bag. "Traffic was a mess."

"Whatchu' bring bee?" Mark asked, peering over at the bag in Jason's hand.

"Oh, just some tequila," Eric replied, removing his coat.

"Yes Eric, at least *somebody* knows what to bring to a party," Malajia praised, then shot Sidra a side-eye.

Sidra just rolled her eyes, but refused to respond. There was enough on her mind, and arguing with Malajia over a fruit basket wasn't worth it.

Eric walked over to Alex, who was reaching for a brownie from a tray. He leaned in for a kiss. "Hey," he greeted, smiling.

Alex tilted her face, causing him to kiss her cheek instead of his intended target, her lips. "Hey," she dryly returned.

Eric looked at her; the lackluster response didn't go unnoticed. "You okay?"

"Um hmm," Alex muttered, stuffing her mouth full of brownie.

Jason handed Eric a glass. "You want some of this tequila, man?"

"Yeah, just a little," Eric smiled.

"You sure you should be drinking?" Alex asked, looking at him. Eric looked confused. "Don't you have to get back to Maryland?"

"You're kicking me out or something?" he asked her.

Alex shook her head slightly "No, that's not—"

"What are we playing now? 'Cause charades ain't hittin'," Malajia spat out, cutting through the side conversation. "Let's play 'never have I ever'."

"No, you freak," Sidra commented.

"Oh yeah, you'll just be sober when it's all said and done," Malajia threw back. Sidra made a face at Malajia in retaliation.

"Still want that drink Eric?" Jason asked.

Eric put his hand up. "No thanks, I'm cool," he politely declined. "Apparently I'm driving back to Maryland tonight." He side-glanced Alex, who just avoided his gaze.

Emily looked at Alex. "Aww, why can't he spend the—"

"I'm staying in my parents' house and that'll be a little inappropriate, don't you think?" Alex abruptly bristled. She rubbed her hands together to remove the brownie crumbs. "Chaz, is there any more wine?"

Chasity stared at Alex from the accent chair in which she sat, narrowing her eyes. "No, I think you've had enough," she commented. Alex's attitude wasn't missed by Chasity, and she was pretty sure it was picked up by others, including Eric.

Alex put her hands up. "Fine, give me a shot."

Malajia grabbed a bottle. "Yeeeessss."

Chasity signaled for Malajia, who looked over at her. Chasity shook both her head and her hand no. Malajia quietly set the bottle back down.

"Eric, if you're coming to the wedding, will you be hanging out with us at the bachelor party too?" Will asked, between bites of his food.

Eric looked perplexed. "Umm, I didn't know that I was *invited*," he slowly put out.

Emily shot Alex a questionable look; Alex just shrugged slightly and looked away. "Sorry Eric, I forgot to tell Alex that she could bring you as her plus one," Emily lied.

"Oh," Eric replied. "Well, that's nice of you. If Alex is

okay with it, I'd love to come." He looked over at Alex, who was twisting a bracelet around her wrist. "Alex," he called.

She looked at him. "Huh?"

"Do you have an issue with me coming to Emily and Will's wedding?" he asked.

"Umm, no, no I don't," Alex quickly answered. "But it's in Virginia and everybody plans on staying down there for like three days."

"So?" Eric questioned.

"*So*, are you sure that you'll have things *situated* to be able to be away for three days?" Alex asked, tone lowered.

Eric frowned at her. "It shouldn't be a problem."

Alex shrugged. "Then fine."

Sidra stared at Alex, tilting her head; Alex wasn't her normal bubbly self, and Sidra was becoming concerned. "Alex, are you all right?"

"Yes, I'm fine. Everything is good," Alex threw out, putting a hand up. "Are we gonna play another game or *what*?"

The other girls exchanged questionable glances with one another.

Mark put his hand up. "I say we play strip poker," he suggested.

Sidra looked at him. "Do you even *know how* to play poker?"

"Nope," Mark laughed.

"Alex, why don't *you* suggest something?" Malajia challenged, pointing at Alex. "Since you so hype about these damn games."

"Isn't this a game night?" Alex spat.

"Umm, not really," Jason chuckled. "It's just a get together where you guys drink up all our shit and eat up our food."

"Who even called it 'game night'?" Josh wondered, looking around.

"That's what *Alex* told me it was," Sidra told.

Alex rubbed her hands down her pants. "Well…okay maybe I misheard." She tossed her arms up in the air. "Let's just play something *anyway*."

"Hide-and-seek in the dark?" Mark suggested.

"Fuck no, y'all are not playing hide-n-seek in my damn

house," Chasity barked. "Alex falls too damn much."

Malajia snickered as Alex made a face at Chasity.

"Let's play a couple's game," Will suggested.

"Umm, not *all* of us are couples," David chortled, typing on his phone.

Mark looked at him. "Bro, you've been on that goddamn phone all night, who you texting?"

David looked up at him, frowning. "I'm texting *my business*," he spat.

"Wack," Mark hurled, earning an eye roll from David, who went right back to texting. "Anyway, the only ones not in a couple are *David*, Josh and—"

Malajia put her hand over Mark's mouth to stop his rambling. "Shhhh, stop talking baby."

"Thanks," Sidra muttered, folding her arms. It was bad enough that she was uncertain of where she and Josh stood on not only a relationship, but also on their friendship. She didn't need to be reminded of that.

"Shit I can't believe *Alex* is finally *in* a damn 'couple,'" Mark joked. "She was a *bitter* ass back in college. And a dumbass *out* of college. The last dude she dated was stupid."

Malajia glared at him. "I thought I said stop talking," she hissed.

"Funny Mark," Alex bristled. "And technically I'm *still* not in a 'couple', so you have no idea what you're talking about."

Eric looked at her. "You're not?" he asked her.

Alex met his stern gaze with one of her own. "Did we confirm something that I know nothing about?" she sneered.

"I thought we *did*," Eric contradicted.

Alex rolled her eyes. "Well, *clearly* there's a disconnect somewhere," she grunted.

Eric held his gaze. "Since *when*?"

"Eric, this is not something that I want to discuss in front of my friends, so just drop it all right," Alex huffed, agitated. The room fell silent. Alex looked around. "What is everybody looking at? Never seen people have a disagreement before?"

Eric cleared his throat, then looked at Jason. "Can I use your bathroom?" he asked. He needed to step away from Alex for a moment.

"Sure man, upstairs, first door to the left," Jason directed, gesturing to the staircase.

"Thanks," Eric said and made his way upstairs.

Chasity stood from her seat and signaled for Alex. "Alexandra, come holla at me outside," she said.

"Chasity, I'm not—"

"*Now*," Chasity demanded, eyeing her sternly.

Alex let out a huff, but didn't argue. As she followed Chasity to the door, she noticed that the other girls had all stood up and proceeded to follow. "Really? Do *all* of you need to come?"

"You already know the answer to that question," Malajia ground out, pointing to the door. "Now get your ass outside."

Alex let out a quick sigh. "Can I get my coat?"

"No, it's not that cold out, get to going," Malajia countered, nudging Alex.

Alex sucked her teeth but complied. Once outside, they moved to the middle of the yard. Alex folded her arms. "Why am I out here?" she spat.

"Because your attitude has been stank all night," Chasity charged, folding her arms.

"*Stank*," Malajia emphasized. Alex rolled her eyes. "And it got even *stanker* when *Eric* showed up."

"That's not even true," Alex defended.

"It *is*, Alex," Emily cosigned.

"I know that I just got here not too long ago, but I noticed a difference in you too, Alex," Sidra jumped in. "What's going on with you?"

Alex let out a huff. "Nothing."

"Bullshit," Chasity threw back.

"Right, *clearly* you have some sort of issue with Eric," Malajia stated. "And what's up with that shit you said to him? And in front of everybody. That was rude."

"Malajia, you act like you've never had disagreements with your man in front of us," Alex threw back.

"Oh, so he's your *man* now?" Chasity taunted. "'Cause according to what I just heard, y'all aren't a couple."

Alex rolled her eyes. "Oh whatever."

"Alex, last time we talked about Eric, you guys were going

to give a relationship a try," Sidra softly put in.

"Yeah, what the hell changed?" Malajia pressed. "I know it's not another prospect, 'cause your pickens have been slim for a while now."

Remembering her conversation with Alex on the subject, Emily pushed her hair behind her ears, looking away.

"Yeah, keep picking on me, that's nice," Alex grunted, putting her hands on her hips.

Sidra touched Alex's arm. "Come on Alex, talk to us," she pleaded.

Alex ran a hand over her hair. "Look I... I just think that maybe a relationship isn't really in the cards for us anymore," she explained. Her revelation was met with stunned looks.

"Alex, cut the vague shit, what *happened*?" Chasity cut in, annoyed. "Just a few weeks ago you were *literally* tripping over this man, and now you're not interested in *being* with him?"

"It's other factors involved that I didn't *know* about at first," Alex replied.

"Like *what*?" Malajia asked, flustered. "Why are you being so secretive?"

Alex hesitated, and Emily couldn't take it anymore.

"Eric has a child," Emily blurted out.

"Emily!" Alex exclaimed.

"*What*?" Emily countered. "*That's* the factor in which you're speaking of, right?"

Alex rolled her eyes.

"He has a child?" Sidra asked.

"Yeah," Alex muttered. "She's two."

Chasity looked confused. "Is that *all*?"

Alex glared at her. "What do you mean, is that *all*?"

Chasity was taken aback, and it showed on her face by way of a frown.

"That's a *lot*," Alex fussed.

"Why are you so *mad*?" Malajia questioned.

"I'm not *mad*—" Alex put her hands up. "Look, when I imagined my relationship with Eric, it did *not* include him having a child with someone *else*."

"You act like he had a baby on *you*," Malajia argued. "It's been five years and life *happens*."

"Yes, I *know* that Malajia," Alex bit out.

"Eww," Malajia threw back of Alex's attitude.

"Look, I expected him to have other relationships, *I* did *too*, but I didn't get *pregnant*. That's something that I made sure I was careful enough not to let happen *before marriage*," Alex argued.

Chasity and Malajia briefly glanced at each other, then looked back at Alex, raising their hands. "I mean, the *twins* were conceived after Mark and I got married but umm... Yeeeeaaah," Malajia reminded.

"Twice," Chasity added, fixing Alex with a glare. "Lost one, was holding the other in my wedding pictures."

Alex lowered her eyes to the ground. "Shit," she mumbled. The last thing that she had meant to do was trigger the bad memories of Chasity and Malajia's first pregnancies.

Sidra looked at Alex. She folded her arms, frowning slightly. "Alex, really?"

Alex let out a sigh. "I didn't mean to make it sound—"

"Yes, you did," Chasity cut in, putting her hand down.

"I *told* you how that came off, Alex," Emily muttered.

Alex shook her head as she glanced away.

"I mean...does he take care of his child?" Sidra slowly drew out.

"Well, *damn* Sidra," Malajia scoffed, folding her arms.

Sidra put her hands up. "What? It's a valid question," she defended.

"*Yes* Sidra, Eric takes care of his child. There is no question about that," Alex ground out. "And I can't believe you're not on my side about this."

"*Clearly* I have my own issues, so I am the *last* person to judge someone's life decisions," Sidra replied. "Sorry, you're on your own here, Alex."

Alex let out a deep sigh. "So, *nobody* understands where I'm coming from?"

"You act like that man was busted offering two-dollar hand jobs at a bus stop," Malajia hissed.

"What the hell?" Sidra asked, confused.

Malajia waved her hand. "Just making a point," she clarified. "He had a baby, so the hell *what*? It's not a *bad thing*.

And he's handling his business as a man and a father. Why are you *judging* him for it?"

"I'm *not!*" Alex belted out. "And I never said that having a baby is a *bad* thing. But I have a right to not want to insert myself in a situation that is not ideal and being in a relationship with someone who already has a child with someone *else*, is *not* ideal for *me*."

"Is that *so?*" a deep voice asked before any of the girls could respond.

The girls stood in stunned silence for a moment.

"Ooooohhhh," Sidra muttered finally.

Alex's back was to the door; she looked nervous. "Shit," she winced. "He heard that?"

"Yeah, yeah sounds like he did," Chasity confirmed, running a hand through her hair.

"How mad does he look?" Alex whispered.

Emily peered over Alex's shoulder. "Pretty mad."

"Yeah, he looks like he wants to throw a drink in your face right about now," Malajia mocked.

Alex frowned. "Well, will y'all at least jump him if he *does?*" she ground out.

"I'm not allowed to fight anymore, and you would deserve it anyway," Chasity joked.

Alex glowered at Chasity. "You're still evil, you know that?" she snarled.

"Yes," Chasity taunted, turning to walk away. "I'm going inside. Good luck with that."

"We should *all* probably go back inside," Sidra suggested.

"Not *you* Alex," Malajia chuckled.

"No, *clearly* not me," Alex bit out, annoyed.

Malajia looked over at the door. "Baby! We about to play some spades," she hollered, walking away.

"Yeeeaaaahhhh!" Mark bellowed from inside.

Emily put her hand on Alex's shoulder. "Umm, are you okay—" Alex snapped her head towards Emily, glaring at her. "Okay then," Emily relented, quickly removing her hand.

Sidra grabbed Emily's hand and pulled her away.

The girls disappeared inside. Alex, unable to face Eric, put her hand over her face. "Umm...how much of that did you hear exactly?" she asked.

Eric walked over and stood in front of her. His arms were folded, a scowl frozen on his face. "Enough," he spat out.

Alex was speechless.

"You wanna fill me in on what I *did* miss though?" he questioned, agitated.

Alex put her hand up. "Eric, look—"

"Is this gonna be the truth, or bullshit?" he cut in.

Alex closed her eyes. "I—"

"Because *clearly* you were bullshitting when you told me that you didn't have an issue the night I told you that I was a father," Eric barked. Alex shut her mouth. "*Clearly* you have an issue with my daughter."

"I don't have an issue with your *daughter*," Alex defended.

"Then it's the fact that I *have* her, that's the issue," Eric clarified.

Alex put her hands together in an effort to keep calm and gather her thoughts. "Listen... It's not that having a child is a bad thing... I love children and I want to have some of my own one day," she began. "But...I never saw myself being with someone who has one with someone else."

"You're naïve to think that things work out exactly how we envisioned," he returned.

Alex sighed. "Yes, I know that," she countered. "But let's be fair, you sprung this on me *after* I told you how I felt about you. You didn't give me the chance to decide beforehand."

Eric thought for a moment. "You know what...you're right. I *should* have told you about my daughter before that night," he agreed. "That was a misjudgment on my part."

Alex just folded her arms and was silent as he spoke.

"But I'll say this, my daughter and I are a packaged deal, there is no if ands or but's about that," he stated matter-of-factly.

"I get that Eric," Alex mumbled.

"Good," he bit out. "And despite how you're acting at the moment, I still care about you."

Alex stared at him. "I still care about you too," she said.

"And I understand that you need time to decide if being with me is right for you or not." he added.

Alex let out a sigh.

"So, when you get your shit together, give me a call." Eric punctuated his response by turning and walking to his car.

Alex's mouth fell open as she watched him get into his car and speed off. Hearing someone clear their throat, she slowly turned around to see all of her friends huddled in the doorway. Alex stared at them, annoyed.

They shot each other awkward glances.

Mark abruptly snapped his fingers. "Damn it Sidra, why you tell us the leftover mac and cheese was out here?" he belted out, earning laughter from the group.

Sidra's eyes widened. "What?!" she exclaimed, perplexed.

"Always lying and shit," Mark replied, going back into the house.

"Mark, you're stupid," Jason laughed, going back inside.

"Eric checked the *shit* out of her," Malajia commented, causing Chasity to snicker.

"Malajia, be nice," Emily urged.

"Fuck no, she deserved it," Malajia laughed.

Alex just stood there fuming as she watched her friends disappear inside. Alone, she ran her hands over her hair, letting out another sigh in the process.

Chapter 33

Walking down the hall of Josh's apartment complex, Sidra rubbed her trembling hands together. Her stomach was in knots, had been ever since she received a text message from Josh earlier that morning, confirming their meet up time.

Sidra was dreading the conversation. While she wanted to get clarity on where they stood, she was afraid of what that meant. Hesitating for only a moment, Sidra knocked on the door. The doorknob turned; it took everything in her to not turn and run away.

Josh pulled open the door and looked at her. "Hi," he greeted, tone even.

She fought to keep eye contact with him. "Hi."

"Come in." He moved aside to let her pass.

Sidra nodded, then entered the apartment. She looked around; this was the first time that she'd been in Josh's apartment. It was nice. Neat, which wasn't a surprise. Josh was neater than most guys that she knew.

"Thanks for coming," Josh said, cutting through her thoughts. He walked into the kitchen and grabbed two chairs from the table.

"Sure," Sidra mumbled, removing her coat. She watched him bring the chairs in and arranged them in the living room; facing each other. "Umm, where do you want me to hang this?" she asked, gesturing to the coat in her arms.

"Just set it on the couch," he answered. "Are you hungry? Thirsty?"

Sidra did as she was told, then took a step forward. "No thank you, I'm okay."

Josh gave a slight nod. "Come sit down."

Sidra slowly walked over and sat in one of the chairs. "Why are we sitting on—"

"I want to make sure that we're facing each other," he cut in. "I need you to look me in my face."

Sidra glanced down at her hands, rubbing one with the other. Josh wasn't beating round the bush. Clearly, he wasn't for any games. "Josh, are we about to have an argument?"

"That's not my intention," he answered, sitting down. "If I seem to be on the defense, it's just because I'm confused."

Sidra looked at him. "I understand," she replied.

"*Do* you?" he challenged.

Sidra nodded. "Yes." She pushed some hair over her shoulder. "I know that I...me holding that from you all this time, I know that it wasn't right."

"Then why did you *do* it?" Josh asked her point-blank.

Sidra shrugged. "I don't know."

Josh rolled his eyes. "If you're not going to be honest with me Sidra, you might as well leave," he spat.

Sidra ran her hands over her face, her anxiety intensifying. "Okay Josh, I—" She took a deep breath. "At the time I...I thought that it would be best for you if you just moved on with your life."

"Without *you in* it?" Josh questioned, frustrated. "Why would you think that I *ever* wanted to do that?"

Sidra looked down at her hands again.

"Sidra, look at me," he demanded.

Sidra reluctantly met his gaze.

"Why would you think that after everything that I went through trying to handle you *not* having feelings for me, that keeping the fact that you *did*, was a good idea?"

"*Because* of what you went through," Sidra threw back, upset.

"What are you talking about?" Josh asked, confused.

"I've hurt you, or contributed to you *being* hurt, on *more* than one occasion," Sidra tried to explain. "I *hurt* you by being with James, I *hurt* you by telling you that I didn't love you the way you loved me, then *I* was the reason that December broke up with you."

"Sid, I've told you before, my breakup with December was *not* your fault," Josh argued.

"In a way it *was*," Sidra contradicted, feeling tears well up in her eyes. "If I hadn't told my brother about how you felt, it never would've gotten out—" she wiped her eyes.

"You want some tissues?" Josh asked her, sincere.

"No," she answered, briefly eyeing the wetness on her hands. "You may not blame me, but *I* do."

"You *shouldn't*," he insisted.

Sidra just shook her head as she pushed her hair behind her ears. It didn't matter what he said; she would always blame herself for that.

Josh leaned forward as he pondered his next question. "I have to ask you," he began after a moment. "When I told you how I felt...did you really *not* feel the same way about me then?"

Sidra looked at him; she squinted through her tears. "*No*," she answered, offended.

"You really think that question was out of line?" he ground out, picking up on her attitude.

"*Yes*," she threw back. "What kind of person would I be if I let you pour your heart out to me, just to *lie* to you?"

"The same person who would get on that plane five years ago *knowing* that you were lying to me," he countered.

Sidra's words got caught in her throat. She wiped her face again as she glanced off to the side, gathering her thoughts. "I *promise* you...when you told me...I didn't feel how I feel now," she answered. "At that time, I really *did* just see you as my friend and I'm sorry if you don't believe me, but it's the truth."

Josh let out a deep sigh. "Okay."

Sidra looked back at him.

"When *did* your feelings change?" he asked.

Sidra took a deep breath. "Before...before James and I broke up."

Josh looked shocked. "Are you *serious*?"

"Yes," she confirmed. "I just started feeling like something was different in my relationship with him...and then I realized that that something different was *me*." She fiddled with her hands again. "He broke up with me because he felt that we weren't right for each other anymore...and he was right. My feelings for him had changed...and so did my feelings for *you*."

"Did you ever tell him?" Josh wondered.

Sidra shook her head. "There was no point," she replied, somber.

Josh looked away for a brief moment, before looking back at her. "You still haven't told me your reason for not telling *me* the truth."

Tears filled Sidra's eyes. She hated being vulnerable, but she had to be if she had any hope of Josh ever trusting her again. "Honestly," she choked out. "…I didn't feel like I deserved—" she put her hands over her face.

Josh sat there, seemingly unfazed by her tears. But what Sidra didn't know was that he desperately wanted to comfort her. Josh hated seeing her cry, always did. But he also knew that if he did what he wanted to do in that moment, that he wouldn't get the truth out of her. And he wanted it; he *needed* it. "Sidra," he softly called.

She wiped her eyes once again. "I'm sorry." She sniffled. "I just…I didn't feel like I deserved you," she admitted.

Josh looked confused. "What?"

"After *everything*. After everything that I *put* you through why should I, after I *finally* get my shit together, get to come out and say 'hey, I'm *finally* in love with you too Josh, disrupt your life, drop whoever you're seeing and come be with *me*'?" Sidra ranted. "That wasn't fair to you."

"No, you hiding the *truth* from me wasn't fair to me," he argued.

Sidra couldn't hold it in anymore, she busted out crying. "I'm so sorry."

Josh rubbed his face. "You didn't want to disrupt my life, when you *are* my life." He clenched both his jaw and his fist, eyeing Sidra with pain in his eyes "You didn't even give us a *chance*. And on *top* of that, you cut me out of your life as a *friend*."

"I didn't want to cut you off," she sobbed.

"Yeah but you *did*." he maintained. "What was your reason for *that*, huh?"

Sidra sniffled. "I just thought it would be easier for me to let you go if I wasn't around you."

Josh shook his head. "Unbelievable," he muttered.

Sidra leaned forward and put her head in her hands as she sobbed. "I know I messed up," she admitted, lifting her head. With a tear-streaked face, she stared into his eyes. "I know that I handled everything wrong. I'm *so* sorry."

Josh just stared at her.

"Whether I leave here today as just your friend, or someone you never want to see again, I just need you to know that I love you *so* much," she poured out. "...I'm *in* love with you Josh and I know that I should have told you that a long time ago, but I *didn't* and..." she let out a sigh. "I ruined possibly the best thing that could happen to me, and that's something that I'm prepared to live with... Just like I'm prepared to live with the fact that you might just hate me."

Josh closed his eyes as he processed everything that had been said. At last, he fixed his gaze on her. "I don't hate you," he said after a moment.

Sidra looked at him in astonishment. "You don't have to say that just to make me feel better."

"I'm not," he promised. "I may be upset with you, but I could never *hate* you...just like I can't stop *loving* you... No matter how hard I've tried to over the years."

Sidra got up from her seat and sat on Josh's lap. She wrapped her arms around him, not knowing if he'd hug her back. But lucky for her, he did. "I'm sorry," she sobbed on his shoulder. "I'm sorry."

Josh didn't respond, he just held on to her.

Sidra didn't know exactly what Josh's silence meant. She moved her face from his shoulder and looked at him. She wanted to ask him what he was thinking, what he was feeling. Did he want her to leave? Did he forgive her? Could he ever trust her again? Though the questions raced in Sidra's mind, she was within inches of his face, staring into his eyes with his arms wrapped around her waist—she wasn't focused on any of them.

She gently touched his face, mentally outlining every detail of it.

Josh avoided Sidra's gaze. Though he hugged her out of instinct, he was still frustrated with her. Sidra's actions robbed him of time with her, made him question his feelings, at times even his life choices. But as Sidra's hand moved along his face,

Josh found it hard to maintain his frustration. Finally, he met her gaze. The moment that he locked eyes with Sidra, the sternness in his face faded, along with the anger that he'd been holding on to. The only thing that ran through his mind was how much he loved her. Putting his hand on Sidra's face, gently wiping the tears from her cheeks, Josh eyed her with longing.

Sidra closed her eyes. Leaning her face into one of his hands, she grabbed hold of the other. Feeling one of his hands move down her back, Sidra opened her eyes. Throwing caution to the wind, she leaned in and kissed him.

Josh sensually kissed her back. He had no more questions; he didn't want to talk anymore. The woman who he had loved most of his life was in his arms; in that moment, that was all Josh cared about. He maneuvered Sidra's slender frame in his arms and then stood, picking her up.

He carried her to his bedroom and laid Sidra on his bed. Their hormones were sent into overdrive as their make out session intensified. Neither Sidra nor Josh ever thought that this would happen. Now that it was happening, neither wanted it to stop.

Josh removed his shirt and helped Sidra remove hers. Feeling his hands work over her, she knew what was about to happen. And as much as she wanted it, she needed to tell him one more thing. "Josh wait," she breathed, stopping him.

He looked at her. "What's wrong?"

"Umm, I just wanted to tell you before we…" she hesitated.

"Sidra, what's wrong?" he asked her, concerned. "You want to stop?"

She shook her head. "No," she breathed. "But I think you should know that…I haven't done this before."

Josh held a quizzical gaze on her. "You're kidding."

Sidra once again shook her head. "I'm not… I'm still a virgin."

Josh was practically speechless. He could have sworn that she had lost her virginity to James the weekend of her twenty-second birthday. "Wait, I thought—"

"I didn't," she cut in, eyeing him intently. "I *couldn't*…not with him."

Josh held his gaze. His lips curled into a slight smile. "Okay," he crooned, before kissing her again.

Undressing each other fully, Sidra returned his kiss passionately. Heat radiated through her body as Josh's hands roamed over her, working his kisses down her body. Clawing at the sheets beneath her, soft moans escaped Sidra as Josh pleased her. Not having a moment to come down after her release, Josh moved up her body. As he planted kisses on her neck, Sidra's anticipation was at an all-time high. She wanted *all* of him. She wanted to give him what she had held onto her entire life; what she'd saved *for* him. As he slowly and gently received it, Sidra, high on pleasure and emptions, let tears fill her eyes, holding on to him as if she'd never let go.

Chasity sat in her bathroom on the edge of her bathtub, looking through her phone. She needed the quiet as she counted the minutes. Hearing a small knock on the door, she looked up. "Yes?"

"Mommy?" Kayla called.

"Yes?" Chasity repeated.

"What are you doing?"

"Just...waiting on something," Chasity answered. "Did you need something?"

"Yes."

Chasity ran her hands through her hair, taking a deep breath. "What is it, baby?"

"Can you and Daddy take me to the park today?" Kayla asked.

Chasity felt like smiling at the sound of her child's little innocent voice. But she was tired and didn't feel well. "Mommy is tired today... You can go with Daddy when he gets back from Grandmom and Granddad's house."

"But...I want you *both* to go," Kayla whined.

"Don't whine Kay," Chasity said, stern. "We can go tomorrow, okay? I promise."

"Okay."

Thinking that Kayla had walked off, Chasity went back to looking at her phone.

"Mommy?"

Chasity lifted her head up again, letting out a deep sigh. "*Yes*, Kayla?"

"You want to play kitty tea party with me?" Kayla asked.

Chasity couldn't help but chuckle slightly. "This child and these cats," she muttered to herself. Shaking her head, she pinched the bridge of her nose. "I'll play a little later. I just said that I was tired."

"Aww, why are you always tired?" Kayla complained.

"I think I have a pretty good idea," Chasity mumbled. "Go play in your room."

"Okay."

She heard Kayla walk off, singing in the process, just as Chasity's alarm went off on her phone. Setting the phone down, she reached over and grabbed a pregnancy test from the sink. Chasity stared at it, smirking a little.

"Yeah…*this* is why," she spoke, staring at the pink plus sign on the stick. She set it back down and ran her hands through her hair again, letting out a deep sigh. She was pregnant with her and Jason's second child, out of a job, and Jason had yet to find another one, while waiting for the axe to drop at his current one.

"Nice timing," she huffed.

Malajia cradled her cell phone between her ear and her neck as she shoveled a piece of apple pie into her mouth. "I can't believe Dad's still mad about that apple pie going missing," she said between bites. She snickered as her mother ranted. "Why doesn't he just buy another one? …Oh, Aunt Mary made it…with *love*, huh?" Malajia cut another piece with her fork. "*That's* why it's so damn good," she muttered. "Huh? …Nothing," she quickly corrected. "Look, tell Dad to stop girlin'. That serves him right for trying to hide a whole pie. That was just selfish."

Hearing a knock on her door, Malajia craned her neck to peer in the living room. "Mom, I gotta go," she said, setting her pie on the counter. "Love you, bye."

Malajia hung up the phone and walked to the door. Peering

out of the peephole, she smiled as she opened the door. "Hey you," she said to Sidra. Malajia gave her a hug and invited her in.

"Hey Mel," Sidra replied, as Malajia shut the door behind her.

"What a nice surprise," Malajia beamed.

Sidra raised an eyebrow. "I told you *earlier* that I was stopping over."

Malajia laughed, "I know," she admitted, gesturing to the couch. "Come on, sit."

Sidra walked over and slowly sat down on the couch as Malajia sat down next to her.

"You cool?" Malajia asked, seeing Sidra adjust her position.

"Yeah." Sidra took a deep breath and looked around. "It's quiet," she observed. "Where are the boys?"

"Mark took them to his parents' house for a visit," Malajia answered.

"Aww," Sidra pouted. "I was hoping to see them before I left."

"Shhh," Malajia hissed, shaking her hand in Sidra's direction.

Sidra looked confused. "What?"

"Girl, don't talk them up," Malajia joked. "I got the house to myself for a few hours."

Sidra giggled, but the humor left her face as she just sat quietly.

Malajia stared at her. "What time does your plane leave tonight?"

"Seven," Sidra answered, monotone.

Malajia nodded. "You all packed?"

"No," she answered, tone not changing.

Malajia looked down at her freshly done nails. "So...what happened with Josh yesterday?" she asked. She knew that Sidra was going to meet up with Josh to talk the day before; Sidra had told her after she'd received Josh's invitation.

Sidra looked at her own nails. "We umm...we talked."

"Yeah?"

"Yeah," Sidra answered. "I told him the truth about why I

did what I did..." She held her gaze down at her hands. "I told him how sorry I was about everything."

"How mad was he?" Malajia wondered.

Sidra shrugged slightly. "Well, he didn't *yell* at me this time," she alluded.

Malajia tilted her head. "Hell, that's an improvement," she commented. "Josh can be an emotional ass."

Sidra looked at her, stern.

Malajia caught her stare. "What? *You know* it's true," she maintained. Sidra just turned away. "So? ...What happened? What did he say?"

Sidra was silent, and it made Malajia worry. She didn't know how Sidra would handle Josh rejecting her again. But Malajia was prepared to be there for her, if that was the case.

"Is he still mad?" Malajia pressed. "Did he accept your apology?"

"Umm...I don't know exactly," Sidra said finally.

Malajia made a face. "What do you *mean*, you don't know?" she scoffed.

"I mean, I don't *know*," Sidra stressed.

Malajia ran a hand over her forehead. "So...you went over there to have this heart to heart and straighten things out, and you mean to tell me that you left him not knowing how he *felt*?" Malajia questioned. "Not knowing if he forgives you, or hell if he even still *likes* your ass?"

Sidra gave a nod. "Pretty much," she muttered.

Malajia scrunched her face up. "So, you didn't even *ask* him?"

"I didn't get a *chance* to," Sidra explained. "I got...distracted."

"With *what*? Dirty dishes?" Malajia admonished. "You didn't stop the conversation to clean his apartment, did you? 'Cause that's such a *you* thing to do."

Sidra looked at her, face void of any humor. "No, I didn't get distracted by *dirty dishes*," she ground out. "I got distracted by...sex."

Malajia's eyes nearly bulged out of her head. "Whoa what?!" she exclaimed.

"Josh and I ended up...sleeping together last night," Sidra

clarified.

Malajia's mouth was open. "Wait, wait…" she put her hands up. "No bullshit? You lost your twenty-seven-year-old virginity to Josh, last night?"

Sidra stared at her. "You're making jokes," she bit out.

Malajia grabbed Sidra's hand. "No, no sweetie, I *promise* I'm not," she assured. "I'm just shocked, that's all."

"Yeah, me too," Sidra admitted, looking away.

"Well…are you *okay*?"

"Yes," Sidra replied. "I'm a little *sore*, but I guess that's to be expected."

"Yeah, it is," Malajia confirmed. She studied Sidra. "You wanna tell me about how it…was?"

Sidra rolled her eyes. "Malajia, I'm not you. I'm not gonna sit here and give you the details about everything that we did—"

"Wait hold up, what all did y'all *do*?" Malajia cut in, intrigued.

"Stop it," Sidra urged.

"Let me find out Joshua put it down like that," Malajia teased.

"Malajia, stop it," Sidra pleaded, embarrassed.

"Nope, you gotta give me *something*," Malajia pressed. "I will hold you hostage until you do."

Sidra let out a huff. "Fine Malajia," she reluctantly agreed. "He was really, *really* attentive… and that's all I'm giving you right now."

Malajia did a dance in her seat. "Heyyyy, get it Josh, get it Josh," she teased. Sidra put her hand over her face. Malajia laughed as she pulled Sidra into an embrace. "I'm just messing with you. I'm sure you'll tell me later how he made you sing soprano."

Sidra jerked out of Malajia's grasp. "I hate you."

Malajia giggled, then got serious. "Sid, all teasing aside. I know it wasn't planned but… You don't regret it, do you?"

"No, of *course* not," Sidra assured. "I *wanted* to do it. I wanted to do it with *him*, I just… I don't know what it means."

"You two didn't talk afterwards?"

"No, we fell asleep, and when I woke up earlier, he was

gone," Sidra explained.

"He didn't say anything?" Malajia asked.

Sidra shrugged slightly. "He left a note that said that he had to run out and to make myself comfortable."

Malajia squinted. "Who the hell still leaves *notes*?" she chortled.

"Josh," Sidra answered. "And *me*, so keep your judgment."

Malajia shook her head emphatically. "God, if you two aren't perfect for each other, I don't know who is," she muttered then looked back at Sidra. "So…you left that bed and drove your ass up *here,* instead of waiting on him to get back, butt naked?"

Sidra looked at her. "Is that what *you* do for—"

"Yup," Malajia answered, cutting off her question. Sidra shook her head. "Girl, *why* did you *leave*?"

"I don't know," Sidra replied, somber. "…I guess I was afraid of what he might say when he got back."

"Sidra, you can't think that him sleeping with you meant nothing," Malajia stated. "He's not that type of guy, *especially* not when it comes to *you*." She gave Sidra a slight nudge with her hand. "Princess, you gotta stop this."

Sidra ran a hand through her hair, letting out a heavy sigh. "I'm just scared Malajia," she confessed. "I haven't been this scared in a long time."

Malajia held a sympathetic gaze. "I know sweetie," she consoled, giving Sidra's back a light rub. "But you have to face this. You have to go get things clear with him…and you need to do it before you get your ass back on that plane later."

Sidra sighed again and gave a slight nod. "You're right," she agreed. "I will, I just need to decompress for a few minutes."

"Hell, you just drove almost an hour to see me, you *earned* a few moments of decompression," she teased.

Sidra chuckled. "Drove up here like a fool," she joked.

"A *damn* fool," Malajia teased, earning a laugh from Sidra. "But that's okay. We've all be fools at some point. And I promise you, everything will work out how it's supposed to."

Sidra smiled at her. "I know…thank you."

Malajia smiled back. "Anytime." She pushed her hair over

her shoulder. "You know me and the other girls are conference calling your ass about this later, right?"

"Yes, I know," Sidra said, shaking her head. "Not gonna give me a few days to absorb it huh?"

"You've absorbed *enough*," Malajia joked.

Sidra playfully poked Malajia in the arm.

Josh removed a bottle of juice from the refrigerator and proceeded to pour himself a glass, when a knock at his door stopped him. Setting both the juice and glass on the table, he headed for the door and opened it.

Seeing Sidra standing there, he smiled at her.

She stared at him. "Hi." Josh gently took her hand and pulled her inside. "It smells good in here," she commented as he shut the door.

"Thanks," he replied, leading the way to the kitchen. "I know you have a long flight ahead of you tonight, so I figured I'd send you off with some dinner."

Sidra glanced at the plates of salmon, rice, and string beans sitting on the table. She smiled slightly. This was a different Josh than had greeted her yesterday; it seemed like his frustration with her had vanished. "That's sweet, thank you."

"Sure." He stood in front of her, studying her. She could barely look at him. He grabbed her hand and held it. "You okay?"

She nodded.

"Why did you leave earlier?" he asked. The last thing Josh had wanted to do when he awoke that morning with Sidra resting soundly in his arms after their night of passion, was to leave her. But the things that he needed to take care of, he wanted to take care of early in order to get back and spend as much time with her as possible before she got on the plane back to California. But when he'd returned, she was gone.

"I had to go back to my parents' house to get changed and stuff," she answered. "Then I took Mom's car and went to see Malajia for a bit."

Josh nodded. "Oh okay." He stared at her; she looked nervous, antsy. "Sidra, I can tell that something is on your mind."

"There is," she confirmed.

"Well…what is it?"

Sidra looked up at him. "Josh…what did last night mean? ' she asked, point-blank.

Josh smiled a bit, then without warning, he lifted Sidra up and sat her on the counter, bringing her face to face with him. "Don't worry, I cleaned it," he said.

She shook her head. "I didn't say anything."

"I know, was just saying," he returned, putting his arms around her waist. "What do you *want* last night to mean?"

Sidra let out a quick sigh. "Josh, I'm serious."

"So am *I*," he promised.

Sidra tossed her arms in the air, slightly. "I know what I *want* it to mean…what I *hope* it means," she began. "But…I just don't know. I never got an answer from you as far as where we stood after everything. Do you forgive me? Am I going back to California *single*? Are we back to just being friends? …I don't know."

Josh tightened his grip around her waist. "I do forgive you," he said.

She held a hopeful gaze on Josh. "Yeah?"

He nodded. "Yeah," he affirmed. "Was I upset? Yes. Did I wish that things were handled differently? Yes."

Sidra glanced down as she played with the fabric on his t-shirt.

"But…I'm old enough to know that things don't always go as we hope," he added. "We both could stand to handle things better. So, we need to make sure we do that going forward."

Sidra's gaze was still focused on the red fabric, but she nodded.

"I said all that to say…" he put his finger under her chin and lifted it up, making her look at him. "You are going back to California…mine," he said.

Sidra smiled, "Yeah?"

Josh nodded, "Yeah."

Sidra wrapped her arms around him and squeezed him tight. He hugged her back. "Really?" she asked again, pulling back. "So like…we're actually in a *relationship*?"

Josh nodded. "Yes." He touched her hair. "If that's what you still want."

"Yes, it's what I want," she confirmed. "I mean, I'll admit that I'm a little nervous because of the fact that we live so far apart... Long distance relationships—"

"Work when people *make* it work," Josh cut in.

"I know Josh, but this isn't a four-hour drive... This is a six-hour *flight*," Sidra pointed out.

"So? We both can afford to fly." Josh smiled. "Listen, I know you've done the long-distance thing before but, this is different... I'm not him."

Sidra grabbed his face with her hands. "I know that," she said. "You're right. We'll be okay."

"Yeah, we'll make time to see each other... We'll talk all the time," Josh put out. "So, when you call, I'll be sure to *answer*," he joked. Sidra giggled. "You make sure you do the same."

Sidra put a hand up. "I promise."

Josh let out a sigh. "Okay well...we should probably eat dinner now," he suggested. "Your flight will be leaving before you know it."

"I don't want to go," she whined.

"I know," Josh consoled, hugging her. "I don't *want* you to leave but you *have* to."

"I know," she sulked.

He gave her a quick kiss on her lips. "So, when we're done, we should get going."

"Okay," she said, tracing his features with her finger.

"I'll follow you to your parents' house so you can drop the car off and get your stuff," he added. "That way I can take you to the airport."

Sidra stared at him longingly. "Okay."

Josh opened his mouth to say something else, but was too focused on her face to say it. All he wanted to do was relive last night. He gave her another kiss, this time deepening it. "Take a later flight," he breathed against her lips.

"Okay," she breathed in return.

Josh picked her up in his arms and carried her back to his bedroom.

Chapter 34

"Alex, this looks amazing," Marlene gushed, peering over Alex's shoulder at her laptop screen.

"Yeah, I know," Alex agreed, reaching for her cup of coffee. "I even had IT run it live and there was not *one* glitch, non-working link, button...*nothing.*"

Marlene smiled. "*This* is the kind of work that we need for this company's site," she praised.

"I agree," Alex smiled back.

"Do you think the person who did this would be interested in having a meeting with us?"

Alex looked confused. "You mean like an interview?" she asked.

"I guess you can say that."

"A meeting I get, but why would they even *have* to interview?" Alex wondered. "You've already seen the work."

"Protocol Alex," Marlene chuckled. "*Everyone* has to go through the interview process. Especially for a position like this."

Alex nodded in agreement. "Makes sense," she said. "I'll see if I can get it set up."

"Yes, please," Marlene approved, heading for the door. "Good work as usual."

"Thanks." Alex smiled as Marlene walked out of the door. But as soon as the door shut, her smile faded. While she was happy about the praise from her boss, the fall out with Eric had Alex in a funk. She grabbed her cell phone from her desk, pulled up Eric's number, and stared at it. She held her finger over the call button, but hesitated. It had been a few days since they'd last spoke, when he'd basically given her an ultimatum. And she'd been pondering it ever since. Letting out a sigh, Alex put the phone back on her desk face down, and put her head in her hands. She let out a sigh. "Why is this so damn difficult?" she muttered to herself.

The phone rang, and she quickly snatched it up, putting it to her ear. "Hello?"

"Did you call Eric yet?" the voice on the other end asked.

Alex put her hand over her face. "No Em, not yet," she sighed. "I know, I'm being stupid."

"I didn't say that," Emily said.

"Yeah, but *I'm thinking* it," Alex replied.

"Alex, it's not stupid to want what you want," Emily consoled. "But...you might be a bit *crazy* to throw away your potential dream man because his life isn't wrapped in a perfect bow."

Alex's mouth dropped open. "Well...shit," she chuckled. "You've gotten skilled at telling me about myself."

"If only I could perfect that when it comes to others," Emily joked, then coughed.

"You okay?" Alex asked, concerned.

"I'm okay," Emily assured. "I'm just coming down with a little cold...*again.*"

"Aww, poor baby," Alex sympathized. "You're not at work, are you?"

"No," Emily answered. "I took the day, and now instead of resting, I'm working on a few things."

"Like what?"

"Sand jars," Emily smiled. "I got this idea to do them as table décor and it'll double as a wedding favor." When silence fell on the line, she let out a sigh. "You think it's stupid, don't you?"

"No, of course not," Alex soothed.

"I mean, I know it's a bit off for a winter wedding that's nowhere near the *beach*, I just—"

"You don't owe anybody any explanation for what you want to do regarding your wedding Em," Alex stated. "And I mean *anybody.*"

"You're right, thanks," Emily returned.

"Anytime, and if you need *anything*, please let me know," Alex pleaded. "Hell, now that Sidra and Josh finally hooked up, I'm the only single one out of us girls, so I have *plenty* of free time."

Emily managed a giggle. "I'll keep that in mind," she promised. "But I have to go, we'll talk later."

"Later," Alex said, ending the call. She took a sip of her coffee and got back to work.

Jason's eyes were fixed in a stern stare as he typed on his work laptop. With a new software to develop, Jason had been tasked with going over the details and prepping the project, so it could be handed over to the Phoenix team. Only a call to his work phone snapped him out of his trance. He picked it up. "This is Jason."

"Hey Jason, how's the prep going?" Patrick asked.

Jason paused his typing. "It's fine, just testing a few things before I pass it off."

"Great..." Patrick's voice trailed off.

"Is something wrong?"

"No," he replied. "But when you finish, I'd like to see you in my office... I need to talk to you about something."

Jason's mental red flag went up. "Uh, okay," he hesitantly put out. "Is umm...is it important?"

"It is."

Jason pinched the bridge of his nose. *Fuck.* "Okay. I'll let you know when I'm finished."

"Great," Patrick said, before hanging up.

Jason slowly put the receiver back in its cradle. He almost contemplated stalling his work longer than normal, just to avoid going to this meeting at all. As far as Jason knew, his boss was getting ready to tell him that he had to let him go. He'd been dreading this for weeks, and still, he was panicking. Jason grabbed his phone, sent a quick text message, then let out a long sigh, going right back to work.

"So look, I was thinking about planning a family vacation next summer," Trisha mentioned to Chasity as she unpacked groceries in her kitchen.

Chasity ran a hand over her face as she leaned against the

counter. "Okay," she replied.

Trisha placed some items into a cabinet. "I was also thinking that I would extend the invite to Jason's family too."

Chasity raised an eyebrow. "O-kay," she repeated, this time slowly.

Trisha chuckled. "What? You don't think it's a good idea?"

"Didn't say that, they're cool people," Chasity replied, tired.

Trisha looked at her. "You all right? You're looking a little queasy in the face."

Chasity squinted her eyes, perplexed. "What does that even look like?" she jeered.

Trisha let out a little laugh. "You're such a smart ass," she commented, going back to unpacking her items.

"I know," Chasity threw back, folding her arms.

As Trisha put more things away, Chasity felt her phone vibrate in her jeans pocket; she grabbed it and read the message from Jason. *'Chaz, I think they're going to lay me off today. My boss is acting weird, and I got called into a meeting. Try not to worry, we'll be okay. Love you.'*

"Shit," she mumbled, shoving the phone back into her pocket. This was not how Chasity saw her day going when she woke up that morning.

"You say something?" Trisha asked.

"No," Chasity lied.

"Okay." Trisha looked at her again, letting out a breath. "Putting stuff away in this damn kitchen is always a task."

"I still don't know why you *buy* all that shit; it's just *you* in here," Chasity jeered. "'Cause God forbid you rent this house out and get a place with your boyfriend."

"When I see a diamond, I'll consider it," Trisha sneered.

"Stop *breaking up* with him every five minutes, and I'm sure he'll *get* you one," Chasity countered.

Trisha rolled her eyes.

"You're evil, you *know* that. Where do you think *I* get it from?" Chasity asked.

Trisha flagged Chasity with her hand. "Mind your goddamn business," she ground out.

"When you stay out of *mine*, I'll stay out of *yours*," Chasity shot back, defiant.

Trisha made a face in retaliation. "*Anyway*, you're right about one thing. I *do* buy too much food," she admitted. "I'll take some of this stuff to Mom's house. Do you want some of it too?"

"No, I'm cool," Chasity declined.

Trisha shrugged. "Okay, well help me pare down," she requested, opening some of the cabinets.

Chasity rolled her eyes, then proceeded to help. "Why do you even *have* this?" she asked, pulling a container of baking powder from the cabinet.

Trisha looked at her. "In case I bake something."

Chasity made a face. "You don't *bake*," she pointed out, slamming it on the counter. "Don't make me mad today."

Trisha giggled. The humor left her face when she saw Chasity stop what she was doing to put her hand over her face again. Concern filled her face. "Seriously, are you all right?" Trisha wondered, rubbing Chasity's arm.

Chasity nodded. "Yeah," she answered, going back to looking through the cabinet.

Trisha's gaze lingered on Chasity for a moment, but she refrained from saying anything else. Hearing a knock on the door, she headed for it. A moment later, she walked back into the kitchen with a guest.

"Look who's here," Trisha smiled.

Chasity looked over, but didn't say anything.

"Hey there cousin," Aja smiled.

Chasity just stared at her. She knew that she was coming off as rude for not speaking, but she feared that if she did, she'd throw up.

"I stopped by to say hi on my way to hang out with some friends, but since *you're* here, maybe you can join us," Aja proposed, still smiling.

Chasity held an uninterested gaze on Aja.

Trisha put her hand over her face and turned away, trying not to laugh in Aja's face.

Chasity opened her mouth to respond. Then, just as she thought, the urge to vomit came. She covered her mouth and ran past them to the bathroom.

Aja shot Trisha a questionable look.

Trisha put her hand on Aja's shoulder. "She's…not feeling well," she explained.

"Oh, sorry to hear that," Aja sympathized. "I'll just get going then."

"Okay," Trisha said as she walked Aja to the door.

"Should I call her later?" Aja asked, looking at her.

"Yeah, no," Trisha advised. "She'll call you when she's better." Trisha knew that was a lie, but that seemed to satisfy Aja, who just smiled and walked out the door.

Trisha shut the door, then made a beeline for the half bathroom. She stood by the door and listened as Chasity continued to throw up. "I guess you *lied* when you said that you were okay," she calmly said through the closed door.

"I *am*," Chasity insisted.

Trisha folded her arms. "You want me to make you some tea?"

"No," Chasity answered, traces of frustration in her voice. "Give me a minute, Mom."

"Okay," Trisha agreed. "I'll be in the den, come talk to me when you come out." She walked to the den and sat in one of the accent chairs. She glanced out of the window, staring at the tree out front… The branches were nearly bare, a sure sign that winter was arriving.

After a few moments, Chasity walked in and sat down across from her. Trisha stared at her, then slightly tilted her head.

Chasity stared back, confused.

Trisha smiled after a moment. "You're pregnant, aren't you?" she asked.

Chasity sighed, a look of relief fell upon her face. "Yes."

Trisha clasped her hands together. "I had a feeling," she beamed.

Chasity squinted at Trisha. "Did you *really*?"

Trisha chuckled. "Well…I had *hoped*," she confessed. "You haven't been feeling well lately, and you weren't fooling me with that 'I'm fine' mess."

"Nope, never *could*," Chasity admitted, leaning back in her seat.

"When did you find out?"

"A few days ago," Chasity answered.

"You tell Jason yet?" Trisha asked.

Chasity shook her head. "I planned on telling him later tonight," she revealed. "I was just waiting on my doctor to confirm, which she did earlier... Now I don't know if tonight is the right time to say anything."

Trisha frowned. "What do you mean, you don't know if it's the right time?"

Chasity shrugged. "It just might *not* be."

Trisha leaned forward. "You *make* it the right time," she said. "Now that you know for certain, don't keep it from him."

"I mean of course I'm going to *tell* him," Chasity assured. "It's just that... I think he's having a bad day at work and... I don't know."

"Knowing how Jason is, him finding out that you two have another baby on the way will erase his bad day in a heartbeat," Trisha assured.

Not in this case, Chasity thought.

"So, you follow through with your plans to tell him tonight, okay?" Trisha insisted.

Chasity nodded, but didn't say anything.

Trisha smiled bright. "I'm so excited— Oh my God, Kayla is going to make such a *wonderful* big sister," she squealed.

Chasity chuckled at Trisha's excitement. "You're so dramatic."

"So what?" Trisha returned with a wave of her hand. "Ooh, can I tell your grandmother?"

Chasity put a hand up. "Mom, you can't tell *anybody* until I tell *Jason,*" she demanded. "I *mean* it."

Trisha put her hands up. "Okay, you have my word." She leaned back in her seat. "Chaz...did you *have* to throw up when Aja was talking to you?"

Chasity laughed. "I didn't plan that, but it was *so* worth it."

Trisha shook her head in amusement. "You're horrible."

Leftover grilled chicken salad and to-go cup of fresh

lemonade in hand, Sidra sauntered into her office building. She had spent her lunch hour at the local bistro, talking with Josh on the phone; Sidra was beaming.

Robin smiled as Sidra approached her desk. "Look at you grinning all hard," she observed, leaning forward.

Sidra shook her head in amusement. "Stop it," she chortled.

"Uh huh, came back from Thanksgiving break with an extra pep in your step," Robin dug in.

"Thanksgiving was weeks ago," Sidra pointed out, adjusting the items in her hand.

"And you've been peppin' and steppin' ever since," Robin insisted.

Sidra chuckled a bit, "Funny."

Robin tapped her fingernails on the desk. "So, do you want to share what or who has you so happy?"

"No ma'am. Now answer these phones before you get into trouble," Sidra threw back.

Robin giggled, "Very well." Hearing the phone ring, she pointed to it. "Right on time."

Sidra chuckled as she walked by. Once inside her office, she closed the door behind her. Setting her leftovers on her desk, she sat down. Piles of file-filled folders waited for her on her desk.

Ever since returning from the holiday break, Sidra had been working nonstop. She'd been doing everything to help prepare her colleagues for their upcoming cases, but even though she'd done the work, she had yet to see the inside of a courtroom.

Leaning back in her seat, she let out a sigh. After a moment, she got up and headed out of the office.

On her way to her destination, she was stopped by Carlie walking out of her own office. "Hi," Carlie greeted.

Sidra pushed some of her hair behind her ear, successfully concealing her urge to roll her eyes at the woman. Carlie had been on vacation, followed by an out of state business trip; Sidra hadn't seen her since before Thanksgiving, which was no complaint for Sidra. "Hi Carlie, I'm sort of in a hurry, so excuse me."

Carlie put a hand out as Sidra went to walk away. "Okay,

but can I just have a quick moment?"

Sidra let out a quick huff. "Yes, what's up?"

Carlie fiddled with her hands. "I just want to make sure that we're cool."

Sidra looked confused. *Were we ever?* "Why are you asking me that, Carlie?"

"I know you were kind of offended by the comments that I made about your friend while we were in Arizona, then I had lunch with your other friend—"

"Josh? You're talking about Josh? The friend who came to see *me* and somehow ended up making plans with *you*," Sidra cut in, tilting her head.

Carlie cleared her throat. "Well…yes," she confirmed. "Nothing ever came of that, but I just want you to know that there was no motive or anything—"

Sidra put a hand up. "Carlie, we don't have to speak on this anymore," she interrupted. "Both situations are irrelevant now, so let's just keep our working relationship as it was, okay?" She wasn't lying; Carlie was irrelevant to Sidra, and that's how she intended to keep it. There was no point in dwelling on the situation.

Carlie nodded. "Okay, that's fair," she said. "Curious though…do you know why Josh broke our dinner date?"

Sidra smiled slightly. "Yes," she answered. Carlie stared at her with anticipation. "He has a girlfriend."

Carlie frowned. "Wait, he did?"

"Didn't *then*, but does *now*," Sidra clarified. "And before you decide to say anything remotely inappropriate or disrespectful about him, please be advised that the girlfriend is me."

Carlie's mouth fell open in shock. "Oh! …Wow, I, umm. . . I—"

"You don't have to say anything. Now if you'll excuse me," Sidra said, before walking away, leaving a stunned Carlie standing there. *That was so satisfying*, she thought.

Approaching an office, Sidra delivered a light tap to the door. Upon getting the okay to enter, she opened it. "Hi Mr. Shaw," she greeted.

"Sidra, what can I do for you?" he asked, looking up at her.

"Oh, good work on reviewing those forms. Perfect as usual."

Sidra smiled slightly. "Thank you," she replied. "I uh, I have a question."

"Fire away," he prompted.

Sidra took a step closer to his desk, fiddling with her hands in the process. "I wanted to ask...if there are opportunities for growth within this firm."

Mr. Shaw tilted his head. "As in?"

"As in...possibly moving on from being a paralegal, to a junior attorney," Sidra clarified.

Mr. Shaw adjusted some pens on his desk. "Now Sidra, when we hired you, you were well informed that there wasn't an opportunity for growth here," he replied. "We're fully staffed with attorneys."

Sidra let out a sigh. "Yes...I remember," she muttered. "Okay, then... Even if I can't grow here, is there an opportunity for me to at least accompany one of the attorney's in the courtroom? I can assist with—"

"Sidra," Mr. Shaw interrupted. "While other firms do things differently, here, paralegals do not enter the court room. It's just our policy."

While Sidra stared at him stone faced, on the inside she was kicking herself. The job choice that she had made two years ago out of fear was now biting her in the behind. As long as she stayed there, she'd be stifled. Sidra gave a nod. "Okay," she said finally.

Mr. Shaw smiled. "Now, you're great at what you do. Keep up the good work."

Sidra squinted slightly. "Thank you for your time," she replied, walking out of the office.

Chasity sat at the kitchen table, staring at the flame flickering on the counter, bouncing her leg up and down in a nervous rhythm. Chasity had returned home from her mother's house, then prepared dinner. Now she was patiently waiting for Jason to get home. She hadn't heard from him since he'd texted her earlier about his meeting, and she couldn't decide if that was a good or a bad thing. But she *did* know that whenever he walked through the door, she was prepared to hear what happened. Or at least, she was *trying* to prepare herself.

Hearing the key jingle in the door, Chasity took a deep breath. She glanced over as the door opened, offering a slight smile when Jason walked in. "Hey."

"Hey," he returned, closing the door behind him. He set his briefcase and coat on the couch, and walked into the kitchen. Jason gave Chasity a kiss on her cheek, before sitting at the table across from her.

Chasity stared at him. "You okay?"

Jason nodded. "Yeah," he drew out.

"Did you have your meeting?" she asked.

Jason nodded again. "I did."

So? ...How did it go?" she pressed. "What happened?"

Jason stared at her. "Umm...I think I'm gonna make a drink, you want one?" he asked as he went to stand up.

"I don't, sit down," Chasity commanded.

Jason complied, then ran a hand over his face.

"Babe...what happened?" she pressed, concerned.

Jason let out a sigh. "Well, like I said, I got called into a meeting today and umm..." he tapped his knuckles on the table a few times. "They umm..."

Chasity's heart sank. "Shit," she said. "They really did it? They really laid you off? After *everything* you've done for that company?" she was furious.

Jason put a hand up. "Chaz—"

"No fuck that, I don't care *what* you say. They are *fucked* up for that and I'm gonna send a virus though their shit," she fussed, standing from her seat.

"Baby, just calm down—"

Chasity pointed at him. "*You* might've been joking about that shit, but *I* wasn't."

"Chasity stop," he urged, calm.

Chasity stood there and held a questionable gaze on him. "What?" she asked. "And why are *you* so calm?"

Jason took a deep breath. "The meeting didn't exactly go how I *thought* it would," he alluded.

Chasity folded her arms. "What do you mean?" she questioned, frustrated. "Did they not lay you off?"

"No, they didn't," Jason replied, lightly tapping his fist on the table. "They umm… They offered me another job."

Shock appeared on Chasity's face. "Wait what?" she asked. "Are you serious?"

Jason nodded, smiling briefly. "Yeah," he confirmed. "A manager position. Overseeing a new development team."

Chasity went over and gave him a hug. "That's great baby," she gushed. "I'm excited for you."

Jason hugged her back, squeezing her tight. "Thank you." Parting from her, he stood from his seat.

Chasity folded her arms again, studying his demeanor. He didn't seem excited like he should be. "This is *good* news, right?" she said.

"It is," Jason replied, looking at her. "It's what I've been wanting. I was told that in a few years I can become a director."

"Then why do you look so sick in the face about it?" she observed.

Jason took a deep breath. "Chaz…the job isn't exactly…*here*."

She looked bewildered. "What do you mean?"

Jason once again hesitated.

"Jason, just spit it out. What's the problem?" she huffed.

"The job…is in Phoenix," he revealed.

Chasity frowned. "Phoenix as in *Arizona*?"

Jason nodded. "Yes."

She let out a sigh. "Damn…sorry that they couldn't offer you something *here*," she sympathized.

"Yeah," Jason muttered.

She shook her head. "It's fucked up that they would dangle that job in your face like that," she vented. "What did they say when you turned it down?"

Jason stared at her. "I *didn't* turn it down," he slowly drew out.

Chasity held a fiery gaze on him. "The fuck you *mean* you didn't turn it down?" she barked.

"I accepted the job."

She stared at him. "*Did* you?"

He nodded. "Yes."

"Well…that sucks for you because now you have to tell

them that you lied," she demanded.

"I'm not going to do that," he refused, voice calm.

"Are you out of your goddamn mind?!" she exploded. "How the fuck could you accept that job?!"

Jason pinched the bridge of his nose and let out a sigh. He wasn't at all surprised by her reaction; he'd been dreading it ever since he made the decision to accept. "Let me explain—"

"The *only* thing that you're allowed to explain to me is how you thought it was okay for you to make that fuckin' decision without *talking* to me first," she ranted.

"Babe, can you not scream curse words at me? Kay might hear you," Jason calmly requested.

"She's at my mother's. Stay your ass on the goddamn subject," she barked back.

Jason rubbed his face with his hand. "Right," he mumbled. His mind was so consumed with the conversation that he knew he had to have with Chasity, that he'd forgotten that she'd told him earlier that their daughter would be spending the night with his mother-in-law.

"Jason, you *know* that you can't take that job," she harped.

"Chasity I *can*, and I *did*," he argued.

Chasity jerked her head back at his response. *This boy can't be this goddamn stupid.* "And just *how* do you think you can do it, huh genius?" she challenged. "You can't travel back and forth every damn week."

"I wouldn't travel back and forth," he said.

Chasity ran her hand through her hair. "Then how the hell do you think you're gonna be able to do that damn job?" she drew her words out slowly, angry.

Jason held his gaze. "I'd relocate…" he paused for a moment. "*We'd* relocate."

Chasity's eyes widened. *Yeah, he's that goddamn stupid.* She could have thrown the whole table at him, food and all. "You must—I'm not moving to Arizona! Have you lost your mind?!"

Jason put his hands up. "Chasity come *on*, this is a great opportunity."

"For *you*!"

"For *us*!" he stressed. "They are giving me a *huge* pay

increase. I'll be making *six figures*. They're paying our relocation costs and even giving us a housing and car allowance."

"You think I give a shit about some damn allowance?" Chasity spat.

Jason rolled his eyes.

"No fuck that, you're gonna have to find something else."

"There is *nothing else* right now Chasity," he argued. "This job is what I've been working for. And I know that I shouldn't have said yes without talking to you first, but I just got so excited, and I thought that if I didn't grab the opportunity when they presented it to me, that it might go to someone else, and I couldn't let that happen."

"But you'd let your wife be pissed at you?"

"You being pissed at me won't result in us *both* being out of work and going broke," he stressed.

"If I divorce you and take all your *shit*, you'd be broke," she sniped.

Jason narrowed his eyes at her. "Yeah a'ight," he challenged. "You're not going anywhere, just stop it."

She rolled her eyes at him.

Jason shook his head. "Can you *please* just trust me on this?" he begged. "This will be good for our family."

"Picking up and moving our entire life across the goddamn country, leaving our family and friends behind is *not* great for us," Chasity flashed back, angry.

"If you would stop fighting me for *one* second, you'd see that I'm making the right decision," he barked. "We can be *secure*. I can help you start your business—"

"Don't make this shit about me," Chasity spat.

"It *is* about you," Jason threw back. "Everything I *do* is for you and Kay, for our *family*. Yes, *I want* this job, but it's *not* just for *me*. Kay's college fund can be taken care of. I can help my parents. *You* wouldn't have to be forced to sell the properties that your mother and your aunt gave you… We wouldn't need to worry about *anything*." He let out a huff when she didn't budge. "Look, be mad all you want but the decision has been made," he stood firm.

Chasity held a fiery gaze on him. She was so angry, she

didn't know what to do. "You know what," she began, backing towards the steps. "You wanna move? Then move," she hissed. "Enjoy hot ass Arizona by yourself."

"If you think I'm moving there without you and Kayla, you're crazy," he threw back, stern.

"And if *you* think that your children and I are moving, then *you're* crazy."

Jason slammed his hand on the table. "Damn it, Chasity—" he paused as a thought popped in his head. "Hold up," he said. "You said children, we have *one* child."

Chasity stopped on her way up the steps and looked at him. "Oh yeah, I'm pregnant," she barked.

His eyes widened. "*What*?"

"Yeah, I was gonna tell you in a better way, but you fucked that up. Goodnight," she sneered.

Jason made a move towards her. "Wait a minute. You can't just tell me that you're pregnant and dismiss me like that."

"Really?" she fumed. "You seem to be doing whatever the fuck *you* want, so why can't *I*?"

Jason was taken aback as she started stomping up the steps. "Chasity—"

"Leave me alone Jason!" she hollered down the steps.

Letting out a deep sigh, Jason sat down at the table. He put his head in his hands, trying to wrap his mind around the day's events. He'd gone from thinking that he was about to be fired, to being offered his dream job, to pissing off his wife by making a life changing decision without consulting her, to finding out that he was going to be a father again. It was a lot to handle at once, and Jason needed to keep it altogether if he had any hope of getting Chasity to see things his way.

Chapter 35

Malajia sat at her kitchen table, typing on her laptop, trying to enjoy a cup of coffee. She went to take a sip, but a loud screech from the other room startled her. She flinched, spilling coffee on her shirt.

"What the f—damn it!" she erupted, slamming the cup down. The remaining drops splashed onto the table; Malajia sucked her teeth. "Great Malajia, just add to the fuckin' mess."

She jumped from her seat, snatched a few sheets of paper towel off the roll, and wiped her hands and the table. Forgetting about her wet shirt, she stormed into the living room to see one of the twins dancing around in front of the TV.

"Marvin, can you please chill out for *five minutes*?" she barked at the animated little boy.

"Mommy look at the cartoon."

"I don't *need* to look at the cartoon, I've *seen* it like *ten thousand times* already," she ground out, pinching her fingers together. She glanced over at Marlon, who was sitting on the couch rubbing his ear, whining. "What is *your* problem?" she spat out.

Marlon didn't answer; he just laid his head on a pillow.

Malajia rolled her eyes, then pointed at Marvin. "Why don't *you* sit down like your brother?"

Marvin stared at her.

"Yeah that wasn't a *request*, go sit *down* little boy," she commanded, pointing to the couch. Marvin pouted as he slowly walked over. "I care nothing about that attitude," she grunted, following him with her eyes. When he flopped on the couch, Malajia shook her head. "In here making all that damn noise." She paused on her way back to the kitchen. "As a matter of fact, go upstairs."

Marvin began crying which made Malajia snap. "Shut up!" she hollered. "Just go."

Marvin shut his mouth as he headed up the steps. Marlon stood and as he went to walk, he stumbled and fell.

"What the—what did you even trip over?" Malajia fussed. Marlon picked himself up and slowly headed up the steps.

Malajia followed his progress up the steps, before letting out a huff and walking to the kitchen. She grabbed her phone from the table and dialed a number.

"Hey babe," Mark answered from his desk.

"Mark, I'm tired," Malajia barked into the line.

Mark stopped typing on his laptop and frowned in confusion. "Well take a nap Mel," he suggested, calm.

Malajia rolled her eyes. "I'm not referring to *sleep*," she bit out, pacing back and forth. "And even if I *was,* I doubt I'd get *any* with these damn kids and their nonsense."

Mark cradled the phone between his ear and his shoulder as he listened to Malajia rant.

"One of them has been whining *all* goddamn day and the other has been bouncing around like a freakin maniac," she fussed. "I'm sick of dealing with this all day, *every* day."

"Malajia, you need to calm down."

"Don't tell me to calm down," she argued. "You get to be kid free eight hours a damn day, watching videos on your phone, telling your dry ass jokes to your ugly ass coworkers and shit and *I* can't even enjoy a cup of coffee in peace."

Mark pinched the bridge of his nose. He was already having a rough day at work, trying to close out a troublesome audit that he'd been working on for weeks. The last thing he needed was Malajia yelling at him. "Look, can you not do this right now? I'm already stressed out," he pleaded, trying not to raise his voice.

Malajia stopped pacing; her eyes widened. "*You're* stressed out?!"

"Woman—" Mark paused when his work phone began to ring. "I don't have time for this, my boss is calling me."

"Great," she hissed.

"Yeah, great," Mark bit out, hanging up.

Malajia eyed the phone in disgust before putting it back on the table.

"When is the final payment due for the venue?" Will asked, carefully placing a small sand and seashell filled jar into a cardboard box.

Emily glanced over at him from where she sat on the floor of the living room, wrapping her handmade bouquets in tissue paper. "Will, please be careful," she pleaded, eyeing the box. "I'd hate for any of them to break. It took me forever to finish those."

Will smiled at her. "I promise, I'm being careful," he assured. "All seventy-five jars will make it to the venue in one piece."

Emily ran a hand over her hair. "Yeah, just bubble wrap them first to be sure."

Will shrugged, then walked over to a box of craft items and peered inside. "Um babe...I don't see any bubble wrap in here."

Emily put a hand over her face. "Crap, I didn't pick any up," she realized, irritated. She stood up from the floor. "I'll go get some."

Will stood in front of her as she let out a cough. "Hey, hey, slow down a bit," he urged, putting his hands on her shoulders. "You're still sick, you don't need to go out in the cold. *I'll* go get it."

Emily ran a hand over her face; she was drained. She'd been up all night finishing the last of her projects, while still battling her cold. "Okay," she sighed.

"Do you want me to make you some tea first?" Will asked, concerned.

"No, thanks, but can you grab me some water?"

Nodding, Will headed for the kitchen. "Oh, I still need to know when the final payment for the venue is needed."

Emily grabbed her wedding folder from the coffee table then slowly sat on the couch. Thumbing through it, she landed on an RSVP card. "Damn it," she huffed, frowning.

Will glanced over at her. "What's wrong?" he asked. "Is it late?"

"No, it's not that," Emily clarified. "The final payment isn't due until two weeks before the wedding."

"Then what's the matter?"

Emily rubbed her eyes. "I just noticed that one of my aunts added three extra people to her RSVP card," she told. "This invite was only for her and my uncle."

Will frowned. "She can't *do* that. We're not paying for extra plates."

Emily tossed the folder down. "God knows how many *others* did this crap," she vented. "I haven't had time to go through them all." She sat back in her seat. "I'm so over...*all* of this." She looked over at Will. "I had to cover Jazmine's part of the bills *again* this month—"

"Are you serious?" he snapped. He handed Emily a bottle of water. "Emily, I'm tired of her shit. She has to go."

"I know—" Emily's words were interrupted by a coughing spell.

Will sat down next to her, softly patting her back. "Did you take any medicine today?"

Emily nodded as the coughing subsided. "Earlier," she answered. "I ran out."

"I have some upstairs," he said, standing up. "I'll go grab it."

"Okay," Emily replied as Will hurried out of the apartment. Once the door closed, she leaned her head back against the cushion and tried to close her eyes. However, her cell phone made a noise, making her sit up. Reaching for it, she eyed a text message from her mother.

You left your scarf here, do you want me to put it up for you?

Emily rolled her eyes and tossed the phone down on the cushion next to her. "She can't be serious," she muttered in anger. Hearing the door open, she breathed a sigh of relief. "The cold medicine you have, is it the kind to put me to sleep?"

"I can think of *another* way to put you to sleep," Jazmine grunted, stepping inside.

Emily glanced over, rolling her eyes. Refusing to speak, Emily just leaned back against the couch pillows.

Jazmine stomped over and stood in front of Emily.

Emily eyed her skeptically. "I'm really sick right now, so whatever it is—"

Jazmine reached inside her jeans pocket and pulled out some money. "Here's your stupid bill money," she hissed. "And I don't want to hear any shit about it being late."

Emily frowned. "*Okay*, do you have to be so *mean* about it?" she threw back. "And I *do* have a right to be upset that you were late with it. I really didn't have money to cover your part this month."

Jazmine rolled her eyes. "Whatever Emily, it's here *now* isn't it?"

Emily held her frown. "Wow," she ground out.

Jazmine rolled her eyes. "Look, I may have this money in my *hand*, but I really can't spare it right now," she bit out. "I borrowed this from a friend because you kept bitching about it, but I'd like to not have to pay this back."

Emily pinched the bridge of her nose. "I'm sorry, but that's really not my problem Jaz," she said.

Jazmine just fixed an angry gaze.

"What?" Emily threw back. "You're not okay with borrowing from other people, but you're perfectly fine with living off of *me*? As long as you *have*?"

Jazmine held her gaze, but didn't say anything.

Emily sighed. "I really don't have the energy for this right now." She held her hand out for the money.

Jazmine tossed the cash on the floor at Emily's feet. "Whatever, just take it."

Emily looked down at the scattered bills in disbelief. She put her hand down, then looked at Jazmine, who was making her way towards the kitchen.

"I know you didn't just throw money at me," Emily said, tone eerily calm.

Jazmine turned around. "Girl, you got your money, leave me alone."

Emily stood up, facing Jazmine. "I *know* you didn't just throw *money* at me," she repeated, voice rising.

"I *did*, what are you gonna do about it?" Jazmine challenged, folding her arms.

Emily's eyes widened in anger. "Pick it up!" she screamed.

"You pick it up and *hand* it to me like you have some sense!" Jazmine just stood there while Emily continued to go off. "You are *unbelievable*!"

"Emily, we *both* know you can't *make* me hand you that money," Jazmine taunted. "So you might as well stop whining about it and pick it up."

Emily gasped; she was furious. "I swear to *God*, you are the most disrespectful, *ungrateful* person I've met in my *entire life*," she fumed. "After *everything* you've put me through, I *still* let you live with me! Even after you walk around here giving me your ass to kiss, disrespecting me, and refusing to contribute *anything*, I *still* helped you... You never even said *thank you*!"

"Now you're throwing the fact that you *help* me in my damn face?!" Jazmine yelled back.

"Are you *kidding* me?!" Emily screamed. As Emily went to yell more, coughs came out. She patted her chest, trying to get her coughing spell to pass.

The door opened and Will bolted in, cough medicine in hand. Seeing Emily distressed, he tossed the bottle on the couch and rushed over to her, patting her back. "You okay?" he asked.

"No, I'm not," Emily grunted, jerking Will's hand off of her. "Jazmine, I'm not playing with you. Pick it up."

Jazmine took a step toward Emily. "I *said* I'm not—"

Will instinctively stood in front of Emily, blocking Jazmine from getting to her.

"What are *you* gonna do?" Jazmine challenged, sizing Will up. "Put your hands on me, and my brothers will tear you apart."

Will shook his head. "For you to think that I'd actually *hit* you just goes to show how delusional you are," he sneered.

Jazmine smirked. "No *you're* the delusional one, marrying this waste of air," she snarled, pointing to Emily.

Emily eyed Jazmine with fire in her eyes. "I'm sick and tired of you!" she belted out, trying to move around Will to lunge at Jazmine.

Will quickly backed Emily against a wall. "No, no, no, she's not worth it Emily."

Jazmine laughed. "Oh let her go. She can't beat me, and

she *knows* it."

"Jazmine, just leave," Will urged, trying to calm Emily down.

Jazmine shook her head and headed for the door. "If that money is still on the floor when I get back, I'm keeping it," she warned, walking out.

As soon as the door slammed shut, Will let Emily free. "I can't *take* her anymore," Emily ranted, tearing up.

"Emily, just move in with me *now*," Will insisted. "We'll be married in less than two months—"

"No, I shouldn't *have* to do that," she fumed. "This is *my* place. I'm *tired* of her."

Will let out a sigh. As happy as he was that Emily was finally at her wits end with her sister, he didn't know if Emily would actually make her leave. And even if she *did*, Jazmine never took Emily seriously. He walked over and grabbed the money from the floor, then went to hand it to Emily.

She just stared at it as tears flowed. "She just—*threw* it at me," Emily explained. "She has *no* respect for me. I don't even care that she doesn't *like* me, she doesn't even *respect* me."

Will held a sympathetic gaze as Emily wiped her tears.

"I need a minute," she said, walking into her bedroom and shutting the door.

Malajia sat on the couch, flipping through the channels. It had been a few hours since she'd spoken to Mark, and she had yet to calm down. *Why didn't his stupid ass call me back yet?*

Hearing one of her twins call her name from upstairs, Malajia rolled her eyes. "God," she huffed to herself.

"Mommy, I'm hot," Marlon complained.

"If you'd stop jumping around, you wouldn't *be* hot," Malajia snarled.

"I wasn't jumping," he whined.

Malajia vigorously rubbed her face with her hand. "Boy— go lay down and take a nap," she demanded. Not hearing another word, Malajia rose from the couch and walked to the thermostat. *It's not even hot in here, that damn boy has too much energy,* she thought, eyeing the seventy-five-degree reading. Hearing the door open, she turned around to see Mark walking in.

She glanced at her watch. "Hmm, a quarter after three," she mentioned. "*You're* home early."

Mark tossed his coat on the loveseat. "I know," he said, tone low.

"It's not hot in here is it?" she asked.

Mark shook his head. "No."

"Okay, I didn't think so," Malajia mumbled, folding her arms. "So…about earlier today—"

Mark put his hands up. "Malajia if you plan on yelling at me again, I suggest that you save it," he warned.

Malajia frowned. "First of all, I wasn't *going* to yell at you."

He shot her a knowing look. "You sure about that?"

She hesitated. "Well no. But *you obviously* have an attitude now, so I guess we *both* can't be up in here mad."

Mark didn't respond; he just rubbed his face with his hands and sighed.

Malajia walked back over to the couch. "So why *did* you leave work early? I thought you were working on a big audit."

Mark stared out in front of him. "I was," he muttered. "I didn't *want* to leave early but I didn't have a choice."

Malajia looked at him, confused. "Why?"

"Because they let me go."

Malajia's face hadn't changed. "Let you go *where*?"

Mark stared at her. "Malajia, I got laid off today," he revealed.

Malajia's mouth dropped open; she frowned. "Wait…are you *serious* right now?"

"You think I would *play* about something like this?" he ground out, scowling.

Malajia put her hands up. "No, baby that's not what I was saying— " She put her hands over her mouth; she was in complete shock. "What exactly happened?"

Mark leaned over the back of the chair. "They decided to downsize our entire department," he informed, sullen. "They said with the main office in New York having enough auditors, there was no longer a need for them in the PA office."

Malajia slowly walked over to him and rubbed his back. She felt terrible; she'd called him to yell at him earlier, then he had to turn around and deal with this. "I'm sorry," she said, sincere.

"This is completely fucked up," he fussed. "They do this shit around the *holidays*?"

"I know," Malajia consoled, wrapping her arms around his waist. She leaned her head on his back.

"What the fuck am I gonna do?" he huffed.

"We'll be okay," Malajia assured.

"*How* Mel?" Mark asked, flustered. "We have a house, two cars and two *kids*."

Malajia lifted her head up and went to speak, but Mark stood up straight, halting her words.

"You know what, I'm sorry," he said, removing her hands from his waist.

"What are *you* sorry for?" she asked. "This wasn't your fault."

"I know, but I shouldn't be bothering you with this shit," he reasoned.

Malajia moved around, standing face to face with him. "What do you mean you shouldn't be bothering me?" she wondered, perplexed.

"I mean what I said," he replied, stern. "I'll handle it, don't worry about it. We don't need to talk about it anymore."

"Stop treating me like I'm gonna break or something," Malajia argued. "We can't *not* talk about it."

"Mel, I *said* I'll handle it," Mark stressed.

"But you don't have to *handle* this by your*self*. I'm trying to tell—"

"Malajia, just please let me have a few hours without you arguing with me, okay?" he snapped. "Just give me that."

Malajia put her hands up. "Okay, fine," she relented, watching him walk upstairs. "Mark," she softly called.

He stopped and turned around, looking at her.

"You want something to eat or…*anything*?" She didn't know what to say. She knew that he was stressed out and worried about their finances; she was too.

"Nah, I'm good. Thanks though," he solemnly uttered.

Mark went to continue his journey up the steps, but paused. "Do me a favor?"

She glanced back up at him. "Sure."

"Don't tell anybody about this," he requested. "Not even Chasity."

Malajia nodded. "Okay." She ran her hands through her hair and let out a long sigh once he disappeared upstairs.

Chapter 36

Malajia's thoughts were racing as she poked at her lemon bar. It had been nearly a week since Mark had been laid off, and both she and Mark were stressed. In an effort to get her mind off of it for a moment, she had called Chasity to meet her at one of their favorite spots: a quiet coffee shop along a small street, fifteen minutes from their homes.

"You gonna keep stabbing it or are you gonna eat it?" Chasity asked, eyeing the hole filled treat.

Malajia looked up. "I think stabbing it is working for me right now," she joked in return. She picked it up and took a bite. "This shit is dry," she complained, mid-chew.

Chasity wanted to laugh, but didn't. A lot was on her mind as well. She and Jason were still at odds over his job acceptance. He had refused to turn down the promotion, and she had refused to move. The tension was so bad that Jason had resorted to sleeping on the couch the past few nights.

Malajia sipped her coffee, then grimaced. "Ugh, why does everything here suck today?" she griped, wiping her mouth.

"My *tea* doesn't suck, so maybe it's just you," Chasity uttered.

"Yeah, maybe," Malajia shrugged. "I'm surprised you didn't order that damn white chocolate latte that you always get when you come here."

"Yeah well, I'm cutting down on caffeine," Chasity replied, tapping her nails against her tea mug.

"Why? Too jittery?"

"No, too pregnant," Chasity revealed.

Malajia's mouth dropped open. She certainly wasn't expecting to hear that; she put her hands up. "Whoa, hold up," she began. "You serious?"

Chasity nodded.

Malajia smiled. "Aww, congratulations," she gushed, reaching over and tapping Chasity's hand.

Chasity smiled slightly. "Thanks."

Malajia picked her lemon bar back up. "Can't say that I'm surprised though," she added, taking a bite.

Chasity looked perplexed, but didn't say anything.

Malajia swallowed her food, then chuckled. "The cantaloupe gave it away," she explained. "You ate that shit all the time when you were pregnant with Kayla."

Chasity nodded slowly. "Yeah, and it pissed me off every single time."

Malajia laughed. "Remember after you had her, Mark tried to give you a piece and you threw it at him?"

Chasity let out a laugh. "I didn't throw it *at* him."

"Fine, you threw it past his face, but still," Malajia amended.

Chasity shook her head. "Yeah, I remember," she said, laughter subsiding.

"I better be the first one you told," Malajia bit out.

"If you're talking about after *Jason*, and my *mother*, then yeah you are," Chasity ground out.

Malajia put a hand up. "I should've been told *before* Ms. Trisha," she jeered.

Chasity rolled her eyes. "Not in the mood for your shit right now."

"Understood." Malajia nodded. "Are you happy about it? 'Cause you don't seem like you are."

Chasity sighed. "I am," she assured. "The timing is just...*off*."

"Your lack of job?"

"Among other things," Chasity muttered. She hadn't told anybody about Jason's job offer. "We haven't told anybody else yet... Jason and I are kind of fighting right now."

"Fighting about *what*?" Malajia questioned.

"Stuff," Chasity alluded. "Anyway..." she rubbed her face with her hands and let out a huff. "Let's talk about something else."

"You gonna make me the Godmother of this baby too?" Malajia beamed.

"Something other than *me*," Chasity stressed.

Malajia gave a nod. "Fine," she agreed. She watched as Chasity sipped on her tea. She wanted desperately to tell her about what was going on in her *own* household, regarding the layoff, but she'd promised Mark that she wouldn't. "So umm…you remember when I told you that I was going on job interviews?" she asked.

Chasity nodded, reaching for her lemon square.

Malajia watched her take a bite and chew it. "You don't think it's dry?" she asked.

"I'm too hungry to care."

Malajia snickered. "Anyway, I ended up interviewing with my old company for a marketing specialist position," she said, rubbing the back of her neck. "And well, they seemed to have forgotten about all those videos I used to watch on my down time there, because they offered me the job."

"Really?" Chasity reacted, excited. Malajia nodded. "Are you gonna take it?"

Malajia sighed. "I *want* to," she admitted. "And to be honest, I *need* to right now," she carefully added.

"You *should*," Chasity advised. "You talk to Mark about it?"

Malajia shook her head. "Not yet. Just got the offer yesterday."

"Are you *going* to talk to Mark about it?"

Malajia sighed. "I *have* to. I have to let them know soon either way."

"Well, at least you're *going* to talk to him about it and not just accept the fuckin' shit without *telling* him," Chasity griped. "Like *some* dumbass people do."

Malajia raised an eyebrow. "Uh…you cool over there sis?" she wondered of Chasity's words. "Them hormones aren't kicking in yet, are they?"

"I'm good," Chasity deflected, taking another bite of her food. She coughed and Malajia laughed.

"*Told* you that shit was dry."

After leaving the café with Malajia, Chasity picked up her

daughter and made her way back home. Jason wasn't due home from work for a couple of hours, so she figured she'd try to relax. She sat on the couch, and not a moment later, her cell phone rang. Letting out a sigh, she retrieved it from her jeans pocket and looked at the ID.

Seeing who it was, she answered. "What's up Alex?"

"Heeeeey Chaz, how's it going sweetie?" Alex sang.

Chasity narrowed her eyes; she recognized Alex's tone of choice. "What do you want?"

Alex sucked her teeth. "Can I just call to check in on my friend? *Damn*," she griped.

Chasity felt a little bad. "Sorry, what's up?"

"Okay so, I *do* want something, actually," Alex admitted; this time Chasity sucked *her* teeth. "But I *did* want to check on you too, I just—"

"My patience, Alex."

"What are you doing next weekend?" Alex blurted out.

Chasity leaned back on the couch. "Nothing. Same shit, different day, why?"

"Well...I would like for you to come up to New York." Alex paused when she didn't get a response. "Chasity?"

Chasity just shook her head and pinched the bridge of her nose. "For *what*?"

"I want to see you," Alex sputtered. "I figured we could hang out. I could show you around—"

"I've been there plenty of times Alex, not a fan of the crowds," Chasity bit out.

"Come on Chasity, I really think this will be a good time," Alex pleaded. "We haven't spent any one on one time together in a while... I know you're stressed about being out of a job, *I'm* stressed with the stuff *I* have going on," she let out a sigh. "I just want to hang with my girl."

Chasity let out a loud huff.

"Please?" Alex smiled. "Come up? ...Stay till Monday?"

"*Monday*?" Chasity barked. "You said the week*end*?"

"What's an extra day?"

"A *lot* when you have to make arrangements for a child."

"*Bring* her," Alex proposed.

"*Hell* no," Chasity refused.

Alex sighed again. "Fine sis I get it, but I still think it'll be fun if you *do* come, though." She paused. "It'll be like—"

Chasity rolled her eyes. "If you say it'll be like college, I'm gonna choke you through this phone," she warned. "Not *everything* needs to be a reminder that I lived with your heavy-footed ass back in college."

Alex gasped. "Well now that you've gone out of your way to insult me, you evil heffa, you *owe* me this visit now," she ground out. Hearing a noise, Alex sucked her teeth. "Are you laughing?"

Chasity had her hand over her mouth, a failed attempt to keep her laughter in. "Fine," she relented, laughter subsiding. "I'll come."

"Well, I *would* let out a yelp of excitement, but you just pissed me off," Alex grunted.

Chasity chuckled, "I'm not sorry."

"Whatever," Alex huffed. "Anyway, I *am* excited," she admitted finally. "I'll make sure my guest room is all clean and pristine for your bougie self."

"That would be nice," Chasity chortled.

"You need me to send you money for the train?" Alex offered. "I know with you not working and all, money is probably tight."

Chasity frowned slightly. "I'm driving, and you don't have to keep bringing up the fact that I'm not working," she bit out.

Alex was taken aback. "Geez, defensive much?"

Chasity rubbed her face in aggravation. "Whatever. Like I said, I'm driving," she spat.

"Okay…it's settled then," Alex replied. "See you Friday."

"Yeah," Chasity muttered.

"Oh and um…bring a dressy outfit…like *business* dressy."

"Huh?!" Chasity exclaimed. "For *what*?"

"For umm…look, I gotta get to a meeting, I'll call you later."

Chasity didn't get a chance to respond; Alex had abruptly hung up the phone. Deciding not to dwell on it, Chasity tossed her phone aside and laid down on the couch.

Alex walked down the hall to her boss's office and stuck her head inside. "Marlene, we're good to go for the interview," she said.

"Perfect," Marlene beamed. "If her personality is as good as her work, the job is hers without a doubt."

Alex winced; she wasn't exactly sure how good Chasity's personality would be once Alex revealed the real reason why she wanted her to come to New York. "Umm…does she have to actually be *nice* or just professional?" she slowly drew out. "*Professional*, she's got down to a T."

Marlene, taking the question as a joke, laughed slightly. "If *you're* vouching for her, I'm sure she'll be everything we need."

Alex smiled. "I do vouch for her," she assured. She glanced at her watch. "I'm going to head out now, see you tomorrow."

Alex headed back to her office to retrieve her belongings. As she walked out of the building, she received a phone call on her cell. She smiled when she looked at the caller ID. "Hey Ma," she answered, excited. She hadn't spoken to her mother in a little over a week; that was the longest she'd ever gone without speaking to her.

"Alex, did you leave money here when you were visiting for Thanksgiving?" Mrs. Chisolm spat into the line.

Alex stopped walking, moving to the side to allow people to pass by her. "Ma—what are you talking about?" she asked.

"Alexandra Danielle Chisolm—"

"Damn it," Alex whispered, pinching the bridge of her nose. It was rare, but when her mother was truly annoyed with Alex, she called her by her full name. "Okay listen…I *did* but it wasn't that much."

"Since when is *five hundred dollars* not much?" Mrs. Chisolm argued.

Alex cursed to herself. "Umm, where did you find it?"

"In the cookie jar on top of the fridge."

Alex rolled her eyes. "I'm gonna kill her," she muttered low. "Ma, listen, I know you said to stop giving you money and

I *have*," she half-told. "I just figured with Christmas coming up, you'd need a few extra bucks to do more around the house and for the family—"

"I know we didn't have much when you were growing up, but we have managed to do just *fine* for Christmas over the years without any added help," her mother ground out.

Alex's eyes widened. She felt like she'd just taken a dig at her mother for her upbringing, which was not her intention. "Wait Ma, I didn't mean it like that," she assured. "I honestly was trying—"

"You know, you are one hard-headed child, Alexandra," she cut in, angry.

Alex rubbed her face and let out a sigh.

"I'm sending this back to you," Mrs. Chisolm stated.

"Just give it to Semaj Ma, I know he could use it," Alex pushed back.

"It's not your job to take care of your brother *either*. I've told you that before."

Alex tossed her free arm up in the air. "Okay fine, do what you want to do," she relented.

"It'll be in the mail tomorrow."

Alex went to say something, but her mother abruptly hung up. "Great, what a way to end the damn work day," she griped to herself. Walking at a hurried pace down the block, she decided to make another call. "Sahara, I thought I told you to hide the money little by little," she barked into the voicemail. "Ma found the *whole* five hundred in the cookie jar. You *suck* at being discrete. Call me back so I can yell at you some more...bye."

Hanging up, she clutched the phone in her hand and continued her hurried pace. Despite the cold wind whipping past her, Alex slowed down. She'd walked the path from her office building through the city countless times, but she had yet to notice that the holiday lights and decorations had been put up. Though it was freezing, the sights made her feel warm inside. Seeing a couple standing a few feet from her, huddled up together and looking at the decorations, made her smile slightly.

God, I want that, she thought. Then her smile faded—she could have *had* it. Taking a deep breath, Alex looked at her phone. Pulling up Eric's number, she texted him one word; '*Hi*'. She'd hoped it would be enough to get a response from him, if he hadn't deleted her number already. Before she was able to put it back in her bag, her phone rang. Hoping that it was Eric, she checked the ID. She sucked her teeth. "Hello?" she barked.

"*First* of all—" Sahara began.

"No, no first of all," Alex interrupted, speeding her pace back up as she continued arguing with her sister.

"How long are you on break for?" Josh asked David before taking a bite of his burger.

David picked up a few fries from his plate. "Until after Christmas," he answered, putting them in his mouth.

Josh had closed the shop for the day, deciding to grab a bite to eat with David, who'd returned home to Delaware for winter break.

"Nice," Josh commented. "That's one of the things I miss about college; the breaks."

David chuckled. "Yeah, well at least you're out here working, being a productive member of society."

"*You* work *too*," Josh pointed out.

"In the same lab that I study in," David returned. "I'm there all day and night."

"Having second thoughts about getting your PhD?" Josh wondered.

David thought for a moment as he reached for his cup of soda. "No, it's what I've always wanted," he said. "I know that it'll be worth it once I'm finished."

Josh smiled. "This is true."

David ate some more of his food. "So…you and Sidra, huh?"

Josh nodded. "Yeah, weird right?" he chuckled. "After all these years, who would've thought that this would actually happen?"

"*You* did," David laughed.

"No, I *hoped* it would," Josh corrected. "But after junior year, that hope fizzled, you know?"

"Well, it just goes to show how many surprises life has," David stated, grabbing his burger. "How is the long-distance thing going?"

Josh let out a sigh. "Of course we're not *fans* of it, but we're making it work," he answered. "We talk every day, sometimes three or four times a day, and we're going to just make it a point to visit each other when we can." He took a sip of his drink. "As a matter of fact, I plan on going out there soon."

"Well, I commend you two for being committed to making it work," David praised. "Being that far away from each other can't be easy, but I'm confident that everything will work out how it should."

"Yeah," Josh sighed.

"It'll be cool if she came *back* though," David chortled.

"Nah, she's already settled there," Josh said. "*I'd* actually have more freedom to—"

David looked concerned when Josh paused. "You cool?"

Josh nodded. "Yeah, something just crossed my mind, that's all." He took another bite of his food. "Everything is good," he said between chews.

"Okay." David ate some more of his food. "So umm…guess who I heard from recently," he added after a few moments.

Josh looked at him. "Who?"

"Nicole," he answered.

Josh's eyes widened. "Really?"

David nodded. "She texted me while I was at Jason and Chasity's house after Thanksgiving," he revealed. "Said 'hope you had a great Thanksgiving. Been thinking about you.'"

Josh slowly nodded. "Oh, so *that's* why you were glued to your phone most of the night," he realized, amusement in his voice.

David nodded back. "Yeah, I kinda got excited about it," he admitted. "Haven't seen her since we ran into each other at homecoming."

"So…what does that mean?" Josh wondered.

David sipped his drink and shrugged. "Nothing really, I guess," he answered. "We've just been casually texting. Talking about day to day stuff."

"You haven't called her?"

David shook his head. "With texting, I can gather my thoughts first," he explained. "With *talking*, I'll sound like an awkward, thirsty idiot."

Josh laughed a bit. "Come on man, give yourself more credit than that."

"I don't *deserve* more than that," David laughed off. He then sighed. "To be honest, I'm scared to hear her voice because I'll just become a mess all over again."

"It's okay that you miss your relationship with her," Josh consoled.

"Yeah well, *missing* her won't make us *be* together, so it's a waste of mental energy," he concluded. "I mean we ended because of distance… That hasn't changed, so I doubt that she'll want to start over."

"You never know," Josh placated, shrugging. "I'm sure she didn't just text you out the blue for no reason. Sounds like she may be having a change of heart."

"Yeah right," David sulked. "I don't know, maybe I should just start dating again."

"David man, take it from me, you can't go into a new relationship until you get over your last one," Josh advised. "That wouldn't be fair to you *or* the person you're dating."

David let out a sigh. "Right."

Josh stared at David for a moment. "You should call her."

David shook his head. "I *can't*," he sighed. "At least not now."

Josh gave a nod. "I understand…take all the time that you need."

Malajia drummed her nails on the arm of the couch. She was in deep thought, but Marlon walking up to her, coughing, snapped her out of those thoughts. "Cover your mouth," she calmly said. "What's up?"

"I'm tired," he pouted.

Malajia looked confused. "There's a very simple solution to that problem my dude, take a nap," she bit out.

"I don't wanna take a nap," he whined.

"Boy—go lay down, *please*," she huffed. "Your brother has been bouncing all day, Mommy needs a minute to herself."

Marlon turned away and slowly walked upstairs, just as Marvin let out a scream.

"What are you *doing* Marv?!" Malajia bellowed up the steps.

"Playing with cars."

Malajia smacked her hand against her forehead. "Cars are *not* that loud in real life!" she hollered. "Chill out."

"Okay," Marvin replied.

Malajia tossed her hands up as she rose from the couch. "Mom said I'd get all the shit I did as a child, back, and her ass wasn't lying," she muttered to herself. The front door opened, and she looked at Mark as he walked in. "Hey," she muttered.

Mark tossed his coat on the arm of the chair. "Hey." He flopped down on the couch and pinched the bridge of his nose, sighing in the process.

"You feel any better after visiting your parents?" she asked him.

Mark looked up at her. "Sure."

She tilted her head. "You sure?"

"Um hmm," he muttered. "I told Dad about the job."

Malajia's eyes widened, slightly. He was adamant on people not knowing that he had lost his job. She was surprised that he told his father. "Oh yeah? What did he say?"

"He offered to make a call at the firm that he works at to get me an interview," Mark answered, unenthused.

"Well...that's good," she beamed, hopeful.

"I told him no."

Malajia frowned. "Why would you do that?"

"I don't need handouts," Mark bit out. "I can provide for my family just fine without them."

"Mark, it's not a handout," Malajia argued. "It's not like your father is *giving* you the job, he's just putting in a good word for you. You used to *be* an accountant. Hell, you were *good* at it—"

"And I *hated* it, you remember that?" Mark spat.

"I *do* remember that, which is why I was happy when you

changed careers," Malajia replied, trying to keep calm. "But our hands are tied right now."

Mark stood up from his seat. "Malajia, we'll be fine," he hissed.

"Mark, stop trying to pacify me," she snapped. "I *know* you're feeling uncertain, I *know* you're frustrated, I *see* it. *I* am too."

"Look, if you want to get yourself worked up over this, then do you, but I told you I'll handle it," he ground out, heading for the door.

"Oh, and *now* you're being a dismissive asshole," she threw back. "Way to handle it *husband*."

Mark rolled his eyes. "Whatever yo."

"Yeah, whatever," she flashed back. "Look, before this turns into a full-blown argument—"

"I don't even *want* to argue."

Malajia made a face. "Well, it's *happening*," she spat.

Mark pulled his hands down his face.

"I need to tell you something."

Mark looked at her. "Malajia—unless you're about to tell me you're pregnant again, can it *please* wait?"

"No—" Malajia was about to say something else, when they heard noise come from upstairs. "God," she huffed. It was clear that her sons had yet to take their naps.

Mark grabbed his coat. "I'm going for a walk."

Malajia stormed over and snatched the coat from his hand. "Bullshit, you stay your ass in here and deal with your fuckin' sons. *I'm* going for a walk," she demanded.

"Fine, you ain't said nothing," Mark boasted.

"*Good*," Malajia flashed back. "And make dinner, while you're at it."

"Frozen pizza it is." he barked, heading for the kitchen.

"Make a damn vegetable too!" she yelled after him.

Mark stalked back into the living room. "We don't *want* no goddamn vegetables!" he yelled back.

Malajia was about to unleash a profane ridden rant, but loud crying from upstairs caught both of their attention. "What is it *now*?!" she erupted.

Malajia and Mark bolted up the steps. Malajia busted through the children's door, ready to scold them for being rowdy, only to find Marlon throwing up and Marvin crying next to him.

"Oh my God," Malajia panicked, running over to Marlon.

"The hell?" Mark reacted, grabbing the first cloth he saw to wipe his son off. As he wiped Marlon's face, Malajia felt his forehead.

"Mark, he's burning up," she sputtered, picking him up in her arms. When he started shivering, Malajia broke down. "What's wrong baby?" she cried.

Mark picked Marvin up and tried to calm him down, while trying to soothe Malajia in the process. "Come on, let's take him to the hospital," he urged.

Tears spilled down Malajia's face; she couldn't hear what Mark was saying, all she could see was her sick child in her arms. "What happened? What's wrong?" she sobbed.

Mark touched her arm. "Mel, come on, we have to go," he said.

Malajia grabbed a throw blanket, putting it over Marlon, and hurried out of the room behind Mark.

Chapter 37

"How long are you going to be gone?" Jason asked as Chasity headed for the door, overnight bag in hand.

"I'll be back Monday," she ground out, walking out the door.

"Chasity," he called, voice stern.

She spun around. "What?" she barked, walking back in, shutting the door in the process.

"We need to talk," he said.

She put her hand up. "Jason, unless the next words out of your mouth are 'I turned that job down', we have *nothing* to talk about."

Jason ran his hands down his face in agitation. "Look, I'm sorry okay," he belted out. "I *told* you that I know what I did was wrong."

"And yet you *still* haven't done what I *told* you to do to make it *right*," Chasity argued.

Jason let out a loud sigh.

"I can't believe you're making *me* out to be the unreasonable one—" Chasity continued.

"That's *not* what I'm doing," Jason argued. "I know why you're mad, I *get* it. But this is the only option that we *have*."

"Whatever yo," she fussed, turning to walk out.

Jason took a step forward. "You think I *want* to pick up and move across the goddamn country?" he asked; she stopped and rolled her eyes. "You think I *want* us to be fighting? You think I *want* to sleep on the couch *alone* when I could be sleeping next to my pregnant *wife*?"

Chasity turned around and looked at him, a frown on her face. "You think *I* want to be fighting? *Especially now*?"

Jason shook his head. "No, I *don't* but that seems to be all that we're doing." He ran a hand over his head. "How do we fix this?"

"You *know* how," she ground out.

Jason looked defeated. "I *can't*," he said. "I'm sorry but…I can't do that. As a man, I have to do what's best for my family and *this* is it."

Chasity shook her head. "Then as of right now, we're still fuckin' fighting."

Jason watched her storm out of the house. "I love you Chasity," he called after her.

"Save it, Jason," she hurled back, slamming the door in the process. Chasity stormed to her car, popped the trunk, and tossed her bag in, getting in the driver's seat. Snatching the seatbelt across her chest, she fastened it. She went to push the start button, but stopped when she felt tears fill her eyes. She hated fighting with Jason more than anyone; it was taking its toll on her. Unable to hold her tears in, she put her hands over her face and cried.

Malajia paced the small hospital room floor, holding a fussy Marlon in her arms. She'd been pacing ever since the doctors had left the room to get Marlon's test results nearly twenty minutes ago. The Johnson's had rushed the three-year-old to the emergency room nearly two hours ago, and had yet to find out exactly what was wrong with him.

"Babe, you need to sit down," Mark urged, cradling Marvin in his arms.

"No, I need for these slow ass doctors to hurry the fuck up," Malajia fussed, angry. "Like how long is this gonna *take*?"

Mark sat Marvin down on the chair, then walked over to Malajia and gently grabbed her shoulders, bringing her pacing to a halt. Mark ran a hand over Marlon's warm head before wrapping his arms around both of them. He didn't say anything, he just hugged them. Tears began to flow from Malajia as she buried her face into Mark's chest. She and Mark might have been at odds, but in this moment, none of that mattered.

Mark guided Malajia over to the bed and prompted her to sit down. She shifted Marlon in her arms and began rocking him.

"I can't believe this is happening," she vented.

Mark grabbed her hand and held it. "I know," he agreed. "We just have to pray that it's nothing too serious."

Malajia shook her head, but didn't say anything. She felt guilty, remembering the times that Marlon had let it be known that something was wrong with him, but she didn't pay attention. *I'm such a shitty mother*, she thought.

Mark ran a hand over his head. "Should we call anybody?" he asked her.

Malajia was too deep in thought to respond.

Mark shook her hand. "Babe," he called.

She glanced up at him, eyes red. "Huh?"

"Do you think we should call anybody? Our parents?" Mark asked.

Malajia shook her head. "Not yet," she muttered. She was too distraught to deal with a bunch of phone calls. With them would come questions, and bombarding of more people at the hospital; Malajia wasn't prepared to deal with. Not until she knew for sure what was going on with their son.

"Daddy," Marvin softly called.

Mark and Malajia both looked over at him. "You okay little man?" Mark asked.

"Is Marlon okay?" the little boy asked.

Malajia couldn't bring herself to answer; she just turned away in an attempt to hide the fact that she had begun to cry.

Mark rubbed Malajia's shoulder as he focused on his other son. "He'll be okay," he replied. His tone was confident, even though on the inside Mark was just as terrified as his wife.

Not more than a minute later, the door opened. Both Mark and Malajia perked up, focusing on the pediatrician as he walked in.

"What did the results say?" Mark charged.

"What's wrong with him? Is he going to be okay?" Malajia followed up, not bothering to mask the panic in her voice.

The doctor studied the papers in his hand for a moment, before glancing up at them. "Based on what I'm seeing, Marlon has an ear infection," he stated.

"Ear infection?" Malajia repeated.

"How serious is it?" Mark followed up.

"It's pretty common in children," the doctor answered. "I'm going to give him some ear drops that will help break the fever and ease the pain, and we'll treat the infection with antibiotics. If the fever breaks in the next hour, you can take him home. If not, we'll just keep him overnight."

"Okay, just do whatever you need to, to make him better," Mark said, grabbing Malajia's hand again and holding it.

"Absolutely, I'll be right back with the drops and we can get started."

Mark nodded as the doctor walked out the room. He looked down at Malajia, who let out a long sigh. "He'll be okay," he promised.

Alex darted for the door when she heard a knock. Squealing with delight when she saw Chasity through the peep hole, she quickly pulled the door open. "Hey sweetie," she gushed, enveloping Chasity in a strong hug.

"Alex, I can't breathe," Chasity grunted after a moment.

Alex giggled as she pulled back. "Sorry." She grabbed Chasity's hand and pulled her into her apartment. "Come in, come in," she beamed, closing the door behind them.

Chasity looked around. "You changed some stuff around," she observed, voice dry.

Alex grabbed the overnight bag from Chasity's hand. "Oh yeah, I forgot you haven't been here in a while," she recalled. "Yeah, I did some redecorating, added a few things here and there."

Chasity looked at her. "It looks nice," she complimented, even toned.

"Yeah? Not too bohemian?"

Chasity stared at her for a moment. "I wouldn't even know what that looks like," she replied, earning another giggle from Alex.

Studying Chasity, Alex's smile faded, her brow furrowed with concern.

"What?" Chasity wondered, catching the look.

"Your eyes are red, you okay?"

Chasity nodded. "Yeah, just allergies," she deflected. She

didn't want to admit that she had cried most of the two-and-a-half-hour drive to New York.

"Oh," Alex said. "Well, have a seat," She directed Chasity to the couch, then sat down next to her. "I know that drive was crazy."

"Yeah, I made a bad choice by driving," Chasity admitted, running a hand through her hair.

Alex waved a hand. "I hear you. I *refuse* to buy a car while living out here." She glanced towards the kitchen. "You want something to relax you? I have some wine—"

"No, I'm good on the wine," Chasity declined. "Water or juice is fine."

"Okay." Alex jumped up and headed for the kitchen.

Grabbing her phone from her purse, Chasity let out a sigh. She typed up a message to Jason, letting him know that she had made it safely, then erased it. She was too mad at him to even text. She tossed the phone on the cushion next to her. After a moment, she placed a hand on her stomach and gave it a rub; she felt bad. With her first pregnancy, although nervous, she had been excited and in a good headspace. But with this one, there was tension, so much so that Chasity hadn't told anyone outside of Jason, her mother, and Malajia. She felt like she couldn't even celebrate this baby; Chasity didn't feel bad for herself, she felt bad for her child. "I'm sorry," she whispered.

When Alex emerged from the kitchen, holding a glass of apple juice and a plate of food, Chasity quickly removed her hand from her stomach. "Thanks," she said, when Alex handed her the glass.

"Of course." Alex smiled, flopping down on the couch. She held the plate out in front of Chasity. "You want some?"

Chasity took a sip of her juice, then glanced at the crackers topped with a brown substance. "What the fuck *is* it?" she grimaced.

"It's crackers with hummus," Alex explained.

Chasity looked at her. "Why would you ever offer me that?" she grunted; Alex busted out laughing. "It looks like baby shit."

Alex's laughter intensified. "Oh come on!"

"Get that away from me," Chasity demanded.

Alex sat the plate on the coffee table in front of her. "You are so *rude*," she chortled. "How are you gonna come up in here, insulting my snacks."

"You insulted *me* by bringing that bullshit *out* here," Chasity flashed back.

Alex wrapped her arms around Chasity's shoulders. "I'm glad you're here," she gushed, pulling her close.

"Yeah, yeah," Chasity muttered, letting a smile come through. "Thanks for inviting me. Now get off."

Alex gave her a playful nudge, then stood up from the couch. "Come on, let me show you to your room."

"You sending me to bed already?"

"No, but I'm sure you want to put your stuff up," Alex reasoned. "Come on and stop being difficult."

Chasity stood from the couch and followed Alex into the guest bedroom. "Thank God, you don't have that brown ass décor in *here*," Chasity jeered.

Alex's mouth fell open. "Wait, I thought you said that my décor in the living room was nice."

"It *is*, but that doesn't mean I want to *look* at it while I'm trying to sleep," Chasity threw back.

Alex narrowed her eyes at her. "Whatever," she bit out, tapping Chasity's arm. "Put your stuff away, because we're going out. I have plans for us to go to Christmas town today."

Chasity raised an eyebrow. "*Christmas* town?"

"Yeah," Alex beamed. "They have some cool shops where you can buy handmade items. And we can drink hot cocoa, while we walk around looking at all the Christmas lights."

Chasity stared at her.

"Doesn't that sound cool?" Alex grinned. "After that, we can go to dinner, then go to this art show where they let you paint your own picture."

Chasity pushed some of her hair over her shoulder. "Alex, do me a favor and step back a little bit," she requested.

"Sure," Alex complied, backing towards the hall.

"Just a little more," Chasity prompted, giving Alex a nudge.

Alex backed out of the room. "Okay, but *why*?" she asked, skeptical.

Chasity put her hand on the door. "I just want to see if this works," she said, moving the door back and forth.

Perplexity masked Alex's face. "What, you mean the *door*?"

"Yeah, yeah, perfect," Chasity said, before shutting the door in Alex's stunned face.

"Seriously?" Alex ground out. She went to twist the doorknob, but heard the lock twist first. "Did you really lock me out of my own room?!"

"It's mine until Monday," Chasity hurled through the closed door.

Alex banged on the door. "Chasity, I'm not playing with you girl, open up!" she ranted.

"Nah, you can go the fuck to Christmas town by your-goddamn-self."

"You are so damn *ignorant*!" Alex exclaimed, banging on the door some more.

Mark jogged to the door when he heard a knock. "Hi," he said to Mrs. Simmons.

"Hi Mark," she replied, giving him a long hug. "You look tired," she commented once they parted.

Mark rubbed his face. "Yeah," he agreed.

"Understandable," Mrs. Simmons sympathized, walking in the house. "It's good that you were able to take off of work so you could be here."

Mark's eyes shifted. "Yeah," he sputtered, grabbing his coat. "Hey, would you mind staying here with Malajia while I go pick up Marlon's medicine?"

"That's what I'm here for," Mrs. Simmons smiled. "Go on, I got it."

"Thanks," he breathed, heading out the door.

Mrs. Simmons set her purse and coat on the couch, then made her way upstairs. Walking into the twins' room, she saw Malajia sitting in a rocking chair, rocking Marlon in her arms while Marvin sat on his bed, whimpering. Malajia, eyes red and face streaked with tears, glanced up and saw her mother looking at her.

"I hate when they get sick," Malajia sniffled.

"Awww, I know sweetie," Mrs. Simmons consoled. She walked over and gave Malajia a kiss on her forehead, before pulling up a chair and sitting next to her. "No parent likes to watch their child suffer."

Malajia wiped her face with the sleeve of her shirt. "Yeah," she muttered.

Mrs. Simmons looked at Marvin. "What's wrong Marvin?"

"He's upset because his brother's not feeling well," Malajia answered.

Mrs. Simmons held her arms out for him. "Come here buddy, come to Grandmom." The little boy slid off the bed, wiping his eyes with the back of his hand. He walked over and jumped into his grandmother's outstretched arms.

Malajia sighed. "I just want him to get better."

"I know, but it's only been a day. It's going to take time honey," Mrs. Simmons soothed. "I remember when Melissa had an ear infection, those first few days seemed like an eternity."

"Yeah," Malajia agreed.

"But soon enough that girl was back to running around, screaming at people," Mrs. Simmons chuckled.

Malajia was too exhausted to laugh. She had stayed up the entire overnight stay in the hospital, not even taking so much as a nap when they'd gotten home that morning.

"I just... I just feel..." Malajia felt herself tear up again as she looked down at her child. "He was acting— I should've noticed that something was wrong with him," she sniffled.

Mrs. Simmons touched Malajia's hand. "Malajia, don't do that to yourself," she pleaded.

"No Mom, for *days* he was showing signs," Malajia argued. "He was hot, he kept holding his ear, he was off balance—I just kept getting frustrated—I failed him. I am *failing* as a mother."

Mrs. Simmons shifted her position to face Malajia. "Now you stop that," she urged, stern. "You are a *great* mother Malajia, I will *not* have you thinking otherwise."

"Then *why* am I always so damn *agitated*?" Malajia vented.

"You are a mother of twin toddlers. You are overwhelmed

and exhausted and that is *normal*," Mrs. Simmons stressed.

Malajia just shook her head in denial as she continued to rock her son.

"Children get sick honey. And they get hurt sometimes, it *happens*," Mrs. Simmons said. "Do you know how many trips to the hospital that I've taken over the years with you girls?"

Malajia just looked at her mother.

"Girl, *you* shoved peas up your nose when you were four years old because you didn't want to eat them," Mrs. Simmons revealed; Malajia couldn't help but snicker through her tears. "Little sneaky ass almost gave me a damn heart attack."

"Why do all of the horror stories of us growing up always include *me*?" Malajia wondered, somewhat amused.

"Because you were my most *special* child," Mrs. Simmons joked, rubbing Malajia's arm. Malajia let out a little laugh. "And probably my favorite."

Malajia looked at her. "That's so sweet of you to lie like that."

This time Mrs. Simmons laughed. "No, it's true," she promised. "You definitely *challenged* me the most, but I also learned the most *from* you."

Malajia gave a small smile.

"Seriously, stop beating yourself up, okay?" Mrs. Simmons urged.

Malajia just sighed.

"You should've let me come spend the night at the hospital with you."

"Please, the room was crowded enough with me, Mark's extra tall self, and Marv," Malajia said.

Mrs. Simmons chuckled a bit.

"Just hearing your prayers were good enough," Malajia added. After Marlon had settled the previous evening, Mark and Malajia had made calls to their family and friends to let them know what was going on. Not surprisingly, they'd received an outpouring of love and support.

Mrs. Simmons watched Malajia as she yawned. "You and Mark need to take a vacation," she suggested. "Just the *two* of you. For at *least* a week."

"Yeah well, we might not be able to afford one," Malajia

muttered.

"I mean not at this very *moment*, I know you have Christmas coming up and you're already going away for your friend's wedding—"

"No, it's not that…" Malajia hesitated. She had kept her promise to Mark and hadn't said anything about him losing his job to anyone. But not being able to talk to anybody about what she was feeling, was just one more thing keeping Malajia on edge. Nevertheless, in that moment, she just wanted to focus on her child's recovery. "Nothing," Malajia deflected. "You're right, we need a vacation."

Mrs. Simmons rubbed Malajia's arm again, and both women continued to rock the boys in silence.

"I don't know *why* you didn't get the people at the hardware store to come out and do this," Jason said, removing an electric drill from a toolbox.

"Because I know what I'm doing *myself*," Mr. Adams answered, laying out instructions. "You think this is the first door that I've put on this house?"

Jason shook his head. "No, but—"

"If you mention my heart, I'm going to kick this toolbox across the yard," Mr. Adams spat.

Jason shot him a side-glance. "Yeah, *that'll* be good for it," he sneered.

"Funny." Mr. Adams began to peel the packaging from his new storm door.

With Chasity out of town, and needing to get his mind off of their fight, Jason had gone over to his parents' house to help his father install the new door that Jason had bought for them.

"I need for you all to stop worrying about my heart. It's been years since my heart attack. It's *fine*."

"You can say whatever you want, but it won't stop us from worrying," Jason threw back, helping his father remove the wrapping.

Mr. Adams chuckled. "You sound like a parent."

"I *am* a parent," Jason chortled in return.

"Ahh yes," he agreed. "How can I forget that little

bouncing angel in the house?"

Jason shrugged.

Kyle walked up to the house. Seeing the materials spread out, he quickly turned back around. "Oops, forgot something from the store—"

"You get your ass back here," Mr. Adams barked, stopping Kyle in his tracks. Jason snickered. "You're going to help put this door up. This is *your* fault anyway."

Kyle tossed his head back. "I'm not good with this handy man stuff," he groaned.

Mr. Adams shot him a stern glare. "You want me to call your mother out here?"

Kyle darted for the toolbox. "*God* no, she'll just yell at me," he complained, reaching inside for a tool.

"Here, first take this packaging stuff to the curb," Mr. Adams commanded, pointing to the spot.

Kyle let out a huff as he grabbed the packaging.

Jason shook his head at him. "He never wants to do anything," he said in an aside to his father.

"Yeah, well he better do *something*," Mr. Adams grumbled. He stood up, dusting his jeans off. "Let's get this door up; I want to make sure it's a fit before I start drilling holes."

Jason grabbed one side of the heavy door and helped his father lift it. He held it in place while his father marked spots with a marker from his shirt pocket. Even if it was considered work, Jason enjoyed this time spent with his father. He hadn't spent much one on one time with him lately, and he realized that with his new job offer, he wouldn't get a chance to for a long time.

"So...I have to tell you something," Jason began.

"Kyle, it doesn't take that long to drag boxes to the curb," Mr. Adams barked at his younger son, then turned his attention to Jason. "What's up?"

"I got offered a new job," he answered.

Mr. Adams smiled bright. "Really?" he asked. Jason nodded. "Is it what you want to do?" Jason again nodded. "Congratulations, I know you—"

"I'll have to relocate," Jason cut in. "...to Arizona."

Mr. Adams's face fell. "Oh…"

"Yeah," Jason confirmed.

Kyle walked up and helped Jason steady the door. "Why do you both look so sad?" he chuckled. "Ooh, are we not doing this right now?"

"Your brother is moving to Arizona," Mr. Adams informed.

Kyle looked at Jason. "Word?"

"Phoenix to be exact," Jason clarified. "And yeah."

"How does Chasity feel about that?" Mr. Adams questioned.

"She is *not* happy," Jason told. "And I know that had a lot to do with the fact that I kind of sprung it on her… I accepted the position without talking to her first."

Both Kyle and Mr. Adams winced.

"Trust me, I already know," Jason assured. "I've been trying to convince her that it's a good move for us but…she's not having it." He sighed. "I don't know, it's to the point where I'm thinking of just turning it down."

"I don't think that you *should*," Kyle suggested.

"I can't *drag* my family somewhere they don't *want* to go," Jason sulked.

"I think that she'll go," Kyle predicted. "She's just mad right now. She loves the hell out of you man, I know she'll be supportive."

Jason shot Kyle a glance. "Look at you giving advice," he joked.

"I mean, I know a *little* something," Kyle boasted, rubbing his chin.

Jason laughed a little. He then looked at his father. "What are you thinking, Dad?" he asked.

"That I'll miss you," Mr. Adams admitted. "But I also think that you're doing the right thing for you and your family and…that I'm proud of you."

Jason smiled. "Yeah?"

Mr. Adams nodded. "Always *have* been," he assured. "You've always had a vision for your life and you never let anyone deter you. Not even *me* with the whole pro football thing… You graduated college and finished grad school, even while having a baby and getting married…and now you have the opportunity to have the career and life that you always wanted…so yeah."

Kyle patted Jason on his arm. "Dad's right," he said to him. "I admire you man."

"Thanks guys," Jason, replied, grateful.

"You're a tough act to follow," Kyle added.

"I never wanted you to follow me. I want you to follow your *own* path," Jason advised, stern. "Wherever that takes you."

"Even if it's to Arizona with *you*?" Kyle asked, hopeful.

Jason raised an eyebrow. "No," he shot down.

Kyle laughed. "Worth a shot," he shrugged. "No, I'll figure out what I want to do... I promise."

"Thank God," Mr. Adams commented.

Kyle chuckled. "Hey look, I say we put this door down and go get some drinks," he proposed.

"You're not getting out of this," Mr. Adams grunted.

Kyle lowered his head and let out a sigh.

Chapter 38

"Chaz, I said that *I* would make the chicken parmesan," Alex insisted from her kitchen table, watching Chasity stir sauce in a pot. "You were supposed to *relax* this weekend."

Chasity put a hand up. "No, you just tried to put cashews on the chicken. You're not allowed anywhere near the food I'm eating," she griped.

Alex laughed. "Oh stop it, I was going to grind them up and use them to make the crust," she defended. "They're really good."

"Damn it, I said no," Chasity barked, much to Alex's amusement.

Chasity had been in New York with Alex for two days, and Alex had laughed more than she had in weeks. It felt good to hang with Chasity one on one. But she felt a knot in her stomach when she thought about what she had to tell her: her ulterior motive.

"Well...it smells good," Alex praised. She grabbed a head of lettuce from the table. "Will you at *least* let me make the salad?"

Chasity looked over at her, eyes narrowed for a moment. "Fine. I guess you can't fuck *that* up."

Alex shook her head. "Cool...I can toss some of these cashews in—" Alex busted out laughing yet again when an oven mitt came flying at her. "I'm *kidding*."

"You're lucky this isn't nine years ago, or I would've thrown this *pot* at you," Chasity spat.

"Ugh, thank *God* you're not that evil anymore," Alex chortled. She then looked up at Chasity. "Well—"

"Shut up."

Alex snickered as she began to prepare the salad. After Chasity put her sauce on simmer and checked her breaded chicken in the oven, she went over and sat down at the table next to Alex. Chasity reached for a tomato, but Alex smacked her hand.

"Ow!" Chasity shrieked in shock.

"Salad is *my* job," Alex reminded, pointing a piece of lettuce at her.

Chasity rubbed her hand. "Childish," she muttered.

Alex laughed a bit. "So…are you having a good time?" she wondered, finishing her prep.

"I *am*, actually," Chasity answered, folding her arms on the table. "I needed the break. When I went to California, I spent most of the time trying to talk Sidra's ass off the ledge."

"Yeah, *I've* just been downing red wine to deal with *my* messed up decisions," Alex joked.

"This is true," Chasity commented.

"*Speaking* of wine, you've been letting me sip *alone* this entire time," Alex mentioned.

"Not a big fan of wine, you know that," Chasity deflected.

Alex shrugged. "Fair enough," she relented. She let out a deep sigh. *Girl, you might as well get what you need to say out while she's relaxed.* "What time are you leaving tomorrow?"

Chasity shrugged slightly. "Early probably," she answered.

"*How* early?" Alex pressed.

Chasity shot Alex a skeptical look. "Trying to kick me out Alex?" she jeered. "I can leave *now*, you know."

Alex put a hand up. "No sweetie, that's not it," she assured. "I love having you, seriously. I wish you could stay longer… I just was wondering because…"

"Because what?"

"Because um…" Alex ran a hand over her hair.

Chasity watched her. "Just gonna do that with salad residue all on your hand, huh?"

Alex quickly looked at her hand. "Jesus," she uttered, wiping the tomato remnants from her hand with a paper towel. "Guess I have no choice but to wash this mess now," she griped, examining a few strands of her hair. "Why didn't you stop me?"

"It was much funnier this way," Chasity laughed.

Alex made a face. "Well go ahead and laugh," she sneered,

folding her arms on the table. "Okay, so I have something to tell you and I don't know how you're gonna take it."

The humor left Chasity's face. "Alex, come on, not now," she pleaded. She had enough going on; she didn't need another thing upsetting her.

"Just hear me out, Chasity," Alex insisted. Chasity rolled her eyes. "It's not bad."

"Just say it." Chasity demanded.

Alex took a deep breath. "Okay...you remember when I asked you to create the website for me?" she began. Chasity nodded. "Well...I wasn't exactly honest about what I needed it for."

Chasity stared at Alex, waiting for her to get to the point.

"I didn't need it for a side project... I needed it so that I could show my boss."

Chasity looked confused. "Why?"

"Because I wanted to show her how good you are at building websites."

Chasity held the same confused look. "*Why?*" she repeated.

Alex cleared her throat. "Because...I kind of told her about you and what you do and—"

"If I have to ask 'why' one more goddamn time, I really *am* gonna throw that pot at you," Chasity cut in, annoyed.

"My job is looking for a new head of the web development department and I told her that you would be perfect for it and she wants to meet you...tomorrow...for an interview," Alex quickly blurted out. "There, I said it."

Chasity sat there, dumbfounded and annoyed. "You—" She pinched the bridge of her nose in an effort to gather her thoughts. She glanced up at Alex, glaring. "So, you lied to me."

"No, that's not—"

"You told me you wanted to hang out with me, and this whole time you got me to come up here just so I can go to some interview for a job that I did *not* apply for. Hell didn't even *know about*," Chasity ranted.

"Sweetie, I *did* want to hang out with you, that wasn't a lie," Alex promised. "But yes...I did withhold *that* part of it."

"You can't drop shit like that on me—on *anybody*," Chasity argued.

"I know, and I'm sorry," Alex replied, sincere.

Chasity tossed her hands up in frustration. "Your dumbass sorry don't mean shit, and even if I *did* agree to this shit, I'm not *prepared* for a fuckin' interview."

"Look, I'll admit that I didn't really think this through," Alex quickly put out. "But you're here now so… Can you just…go?"

"*No*," Chasity refused, eyeing Alex as if she were crazy. "I'm not interested."

"Chasity, it's a great position—"

"*Not interested*," Chasity barked, standing from the table.

Alex jumped up in front of her, preventing Chasity from walking out of the kitchen. "Okay listen, can you at *least* just go and hear them out?" she begged. "For *me*, please?"

"Why would I do that, you fuckin' liar?" Chasity hissed.

"Because I told my boss that I would get you in front of her and she's *expecting* me to do so," Alex explained. "I know that I put you in an awkward position and again, I'm sorry. I promise you can cuss me out four ways from Sunday afterwards, just *please* go meet with her… As a favor to me so I don't lose my job… Please?"

Chasity let out a loud, frustrated sigh. She was angry, but as angry as she was, she didn't want her friend to lose her job, even if it was because of Alex's own stupidity. "Fine, Alex," Chasity huffed.

Alex squealed with delight and went to hug Chasity.

"Don't," Chasity barked.

Alex immediately put her arms down. "Sorry," she muttered. "Thank you, I appreciate you so much."

"Whatever. Check the food, I need to lay down," Chasity sneered, moving around Alex. "You gave me a goddamn headache."

"I love you," Alex called after her. Chasity ignored her as she walked out of the kitchen. Alex smiled to herself in satisfaction. *She's pissed now, but just wait until she hears how much the jobs pays. There's no way she's gonna turn it down.*

Sidra tossed her phone in her bag. "What part of I'll be

right back don't these people understand?" she griped to James as they stood in line at a local pastry shop.

"Work on your nerves, huh?" James joked, eyeing several donuts and pastries through a glass covered shelf.

"Unfortunately," Sidra muttered, looking up at a menu. "Ooh, they finally have the peppermint swirl," she beamed. "I'm gonna have that in my latte."

James made a face. "Ugh, what is it with you and my wife and that damn peppermint mess?"

Sidra giggled. "Don't be a hater sir," she teased.

James laughed in return. With James's building not too far from where Sidra worked, often times they'd run into each other at the shop during their morning coffee run before James had taken leave to look after his wife and child. Now that he was back to work, the run-ins resumed.

Her phone made a sound, and Sidra grabbed it from her purse. Eyeing a message from Josh, she smiled.

James studied her as she responded. "I take it that message wasn't from work," he joked. She chuckled. "Whoever sent that has you showing every tooth."

"Hush," Sidra chortled. She placed her latte and pastry order with the barista; James did the same.

Once they received their food and drinks, they sat at a small table. "Might as well stall as long as possible," James said, blowing his coffee. "It's too nice to be stuck in the office."

Sidra's fingers moved across her phone screen. "Tell me about it," she agreed. She set her phone down, then reached for her peppermint latte. Blowing on it for a few seconds, she took a careful sip. Her eyes nearly rolled in the back of her head.

"*That* good huh?" James chortled, reaching for his donut.

"It's perfect," Sidra confirmed, breaking off a piece of her chocolate danish. "How is it being back at work?"

James took a few bites of his food. "Like I never left," he chuckled.

"That much work, huh?" Sidra wondered.

James shrugged. "Eh, nothing I'm not used to," he answered. "We're getting an influx of new clients. More clients equal more work." He took a careful sip of his hot coffee. "Can't say that I'm complaining."

Sidra looked at him. "How do you plan on spacing all of that work out?"

"By hiring a few more attorneys," James answered.

Sidra took a bite of her pastry. "Oh," she said once she swallowed it. "So...you put the position out there already?"

James looked at her. "We will soon," he replied. "Would you like for me to let you know when I do?"

Sidra took a deep breath. "I umm...maybe," she alluded.

James sat back in his seat. "Okay," he said. "Sidra...we're not looking for another paralegal. I want that to be clear."

"I understand," she replied.

James smiled. "In that case, when we post the position, I will let you know so that you can submit your resume," he said. "If you want, I can—"

"No, no favors, no strings pulled... *If* I decide to apply, I want to go through the process like everyone else."

James put a hand up in surrender. "Fair enough," he agreed. Sidra just nodded. He took a few more sips of his beverage. "So...work talk to the side, are you going to tell me what has you smiling hard?"

Sidra broke into a smile. "Someone I'm seeing," she answered.

James looked surprised. "What? You're actually dating again?"

"Well..." she scratched her head. "It's more than dating... He's my boyfriend."

Excited, James extended his hand for her to shake. "Congratulations, I'm happy for you."

Sidra shook his hand, grinning. "Thank you."

"Found someone here who won't make you yank the necklace from your neck, huh?" he teased.

Sidra laughed a little. "Ugh, I was so mad about my chain," she remembered. "But that guy was just the worst."

"Yeah," James agreed. "Well that's great. Whenever you're both free, we'd love to have you both at the house for dinner," he offered, then chuckled. "I swear Joyce has been dying for some adult company. Other than me, that is."

"Oh, I'm sure," Sidra replied. Her eyes shifted. "Thank you for the offer, but that might not be possible right now, since he doesn't live here."

"Oh? He's outside of the city?"

"State," Sidra clarified. "He lives on the East coast."

James gave a slow nod. "Trying the long-distance thing again, huh?"

Sidra studied him. "Yeah," she uttered. Sidra was hesitant to reveal too much of her relationship with Josh to James. Not only because she and James had already tried the long-distance thing and failed at it, but because it was Josh—the man who James had warned Sidra about developing feelings for her, before Sidra even knew how Josh really felt. She didn't know how happy James would be if he knew.

"Well, whenever he's in town, feel free to take us up on our offer," James insisted.

Sidra just offered a small smile and nodded.

Malajia peered in the boys' room at her children. She'd been standing at the door for the past fifteen minutes, just watching them. Marlon was sitting on the floor, stacking the colored blocks that Marvin was handing him. She smiled when they broke into laughter after their block tower tumbled.

Malajia wanted to go in and play with them, but she felt like she'd smothered them enough over the past two days. Hearing her name being called, she turned around to see Mark walk out of their bedroom.

"You still stalking them, babe?" he chortled.

"Yeah," Malajia answered, glancing at him. "They're so cute."

He walked up to her. "Yeah, I know," he agreed, holding his hand out. "Come on."

She placed her hand in his.

He led her downstairs. "You want something to eat?" he asked her, walking into the kitchen.

Malajia leaned over the counter. "No, I'm fine, thanks."

Mark nodded as he grabbed a few items from the refrigerator. "Little man seems to be feeling better," he mentioned.

Malajia let out a sigh of relief. "Yeah, that medicine is

kicking in really good." she agreed. "Thank God he was able to sleep most of the night."

"*You* didn't sleep *enough*," Mark recalled.

Malajia looked at him. "Neither did *you*," she threw back. Both Mark and Malajia had spent most of the night in their children's room, keeping a close watch on Marlon while he slept. They were happy that the children were rested, even if they weren't.

"I know right," Mark chuckled. "I'll probably fall asleep in the middle of eating and shit."

Malajia chuckled, then let out a yawn. "I think it's cute that Marv calmed his little hyper self down to play with his brother while he's recovering," she said after a moment.

"I know, normally they'd *both* be swinging from the damn curtains," Mark replied.

Malajia laughed. "Where did they get *that* from?"

"*Me* most likely," Mark joked; Malajia laughed again. "I got my ass tore up a *lot* as a child. I was always doing some stupid shit."

"As did I," Malajia added, raising a hand. She tapped her fingernails on the counter.

With Mark's job loss, followed by their son being sick, Malajia and Mark hadn't laughed together in a while. It felt good to do so. But her smile faded; she was sort of dreading what she was about to bring up.

She stood there, watching Mark prepare himself an omelet, made with peppers, onions, spinach, tomatoes and shredded cheddar cheese. Suddenly, her appetite came back.

"Ooh, can you make me one?" she asked.

Mark stopped in the middle of putting the ingredients away. He tossed his head back in aggravation. "Come *on* Mel, I *just* asked you if you wanted something," he complained.

"*First* of all, it was like ten minutes ago," she argued. "Second, yours looks good so it made me hungry."

Mark grumbled a few words, yet began prepping another omelet.

Malajia shook her head. "Anyway…I have something that I want to talk to you about," she began.

Mark looked up at her. "Are you pregnant?"

Malajia frowned. "Why do you keep assuming that I'm pregnant, every time I say that I want to talk to you?"

Mark shrugged.

Malajia rolled her eyes. "*Anyway*," she ground out. "*No,* I'm not pregnant… It's about a job."

Mark rolled his eyes. "Malajia, I'm *looking* okay," he said, defensive. "I don't plan on being a damn bum, I applied for—"

She put a hand up. "Whoa, chill out, I wasn't talking about you," she cut in.

Mark let out a sigh, pinching the bridge of his nose in the process. "I'm sorry, I don't mean to be an ass— It's just frustrating," he admitted, apologetic. He removed the finished food from the nonstick pan and set it on a plate. "I hate not working, you know."

"I *know* that, which is why I don't want you to feel like I'm putting pressure on you," Malajia reasoned.

Mark looked at her. "Okay," he uttered.

"Look Mark, we're in this *together*," she added, pushing her hair over her shoulder. "Which is why…"

Mark frowned in concern when Malajia's voice trailed off. "Which is why, what?"

"Which is why…I'm thinking about getting—" she let out a quick sigh. "No, I *got* a job," Malajia revealed.

Mark held his gaze on her. "Oh?"

Malajia nodded. "Yeah…my old company. I applied for an open position there and they offered me the job."

"Really?"

"Yeah," Malajia studied his face; it was blank, she couldn't read him. "They're just waiting on me to accept." When he didn't say anything, Malajia let out a sigh. "Can you say something?"

"You gonna accept?" her husband ground out.

Malajia studied her nails. "I *want* to," she admitted. "I think I *am*, actually."

"Congratulations," Mark dryly threw out.

Malajia rolled her eyes. "Thanks for that sarcastic ass well wish," she spat.

"What do you *want* me to say?" Mark threw back.

"How about tell me what you're *feeling*," Malajia argued.

Mark grabbed his plate from the counter and made his way out of the kitchen. "I don't feel like this right now," he grunted.

Malajia spun around to face his departing back. "Mark," she barked at him. He stopped walking, but didn't turn around. "Don't do that shit to me. Don't just walk the hell off."

Mark turned around, stepping back inside the kitchen. "You really want to do this right now, Malajia?"

She was taken aback, and it showed on her face.

"How long were you job searching?" he hurled. "Was it just after I lost my job, or was it back when I saw you updating your resume on your tablet a while ago?"

Malajia frowned. "Hold up," she barked, putting a hand up "So, you can't remember to throw your drawls in the goddamn hamper, but you can remember a resume on a damn screen from like *two months* ago?"

"That's really funny," he spat.

Malajia rolled her eyes.

"Come on Mel, it's only been a week since I got laid off," Mark pointed out. "So, for you to look, apply, interview and be *offered* a position in that short amount of time is a little unheard of."

"It is *not* unheard of, it *happened*," she argued.

"Just be honest woman, *damn*," Mark demanded, upset.

Malajia folded her arms in a huff. "Fine," she relented. "I've been looking for a job for a while now. There, I said it."

Mark stared at her, disappointed. He shook his head. "Like I said, congratulations."

Malajia watched him walk out of the kitchen, following him into the living room. "So, you're really mad at the fact that I'm getting a damn job?" she hissed.

"No, I'm mad at the fact that you've been *lying*," Mark argued.

Malajia tossed her hands up in frustration. "You act like I fuckin' *cheated* on you or something!" she wailed. "No, I wasn't exactly honest about me wanting to go back to work. Yes, I went on interviews when you thought I was going to appointments. But, I'm telling you *now*."

Mark's eyes widened. "You're the *same* person who cussed me out because I watched a *show* without you!" he hurled back, sitting his plate on the coffee table. "But you expect *me* to be okay with the fact that you did that shit behind my back."

"It's a fuckin' *job*!"

"I *asked* you if you wanted to go back to work," Mark argued, pointing. "I asked you and you said 'no'."

"I *know* I did," she admitted.

"So why did you do that?"

Malajia rubbed her face with her hand. "I just felt—"

"You know what, it doesn't even matter, I don't care," Mark bit out, grabbing his plate and moving towards the steps.

"No the fuck you *didn't* just cut me off," Malajia snapped. "*Now* you're being an asshole."

"What else is new?" Mark grunted, walking up the steps.

Malajia watched him head up the steps, her mouth hanging open. "What the *fuck* just happened?" she said to herself. She couldn't believe they were fighting yet again. Over it, she stormed out of the house.

Chapter 39

Alex paced the floor of her apartment in anticipation. Chasity had been gone for over two hours, and she was dying to know what was going on.

Alex had woken up that morning hoping that Chasity had not gone back on her word to interview at her company; she was relieved when she hadn't. Having the day off, Alex resisted the urge to call in to her job to find out how things were going. Instead, she paced. Hearing a knock, she darted for the door, yanking it open.

Chasity stared at her as if she'd lost her mind. "What, were you *standing* by it?" she wondered.

"No," Alex made a face. "I was over there," she said, pointing to the spot where she'd been pacing not even two feet away.

Chasity walked in and Alex shut the door. "I was gonna leave straight from your job, but figured I'd stop back to say bye."

Alex looked disappointed. "Oh…didn't think you were going to leave right away."

"I have to get back home, Alex," Chasity stressed. "I miss my child." She missed her husband too, but Chasity was still too mad at him to admit it aloud.

Alex smiled. "I understand," she replied. "Don't know why I'm surprised; I saw you put all your stuff in the car before you left for the interview."

"Um hmm," Chasity muttered.

Alex rubbed her hands in anticipation. "So?" she pressed. "How did it go?"

Chasity took a deep breath. "It went okay," she answered. "I met your manager, and the director of the IT department, and they had me write some stupid program. I guess to see if it was really me who created that webpage that you sneakily gave them."

Alex closed her eyes as Chasity's burrowed through her. "I said that I was sorry about that."

"It's whatever at this point," Chasity dismissed, putting a hand up.

"Well...what happened?" Alex asked. "I mean, did they like you?"

"I *guess* so," Chasity answered, nonchalant. "They offered me that job."

Alex's mouth fell open in excitement. "Oh my God, I *knew* they would," she beamed, clapping her hands together. "I'm so happy for you. You're gonna *love* it there."

Chasity wasn't smiling. In fact, she looked confused. "Alex—"

"This is gonna be so much fun, we can have lunch together every day," Alex rambled, excited. "You'll get used to the commute, trust me. Oh, do you think Jason would mind if I steal you away for a few nights so we can have girls' night out? Oh, the job has an excellent day care—"

"Alex," Chasity called, ceasing Alex's words.

"What's up?" Alex smiled.

"I'm not going to be working with you."

Alex looked confused. "I mean, I know you won't be in my *department,* but you'll be in the same *building.*"

"No, I *won't,* because I didn't accept the job," Chasity spat.

Alex frowned. "What do you *mean,* you didn't accept it?"

"I mean, I didn't accept it," Chasity hissed.

Alex's mouth fell open. "Why *not*?"

Chasity frowned. "Because I didn't *want* it," she threw back. "Never *did.*"

Alex was in complete disbelief. "Chasity—how could you just turn down a job like that?" she harped, upset. "It's the perfect job."

"Perfect for *who*?" Chasity argued.

"For *you,*" Alex stressed.

"No, it's *not,*" Chasity explained. She was trying her best not to get upset, but her temper was rising. She had already done Alex a favor when she really didn't want to, and now Alex was badgering her about it.

Alex was dumbfounded. "Chasity, this is a great job—"

"Have you *done* the job? Do you actually *know* what a position like that entails?" Chasity sniped. "*I* do."

"You've never had a *manager* position though," Alex argued.

"Considering the fact that I did more work than my *actual* manager, I'd beg to differ," Chasity threw back. "Now get off my damn back."

Alex sucked her teeth; she was livid that Chasity could make this choice and be so nonchalant about it. "You *do* realize that you're passing up a job, right?" she questioned.

Chasity shot her a challenging look.

"A *job*," Alex emphasized. "Lest you forget it's something that you don't *have* right now."

Chasity frowned at her. "How many times are you going to mention the fact that I'm not working like I don't fuckin' *know* that?" she snarled.

"So you're actually *okay* with not working right now?" Alex spat. "I mean, does bringing in *no* income *really* sit well with you?"

Chasity took a step forward. "You might want to stop. I'm *so* serious," she warned.

Alex ignored her. "Look, I didn't set that interview up for you to just turn down their offer. You're throwing away a great opportunity and a *lot* of money," she ranted. "I stuck my neck out for you, and you just made me look bad."

"Bitch I did not, nor have I *ever asked* you to do *shit* for me," Chasity snapped, pointing at her. "*You* tricked *me*, *you* lied to *me*. *You* begged *me* to do this."

Alex let out a huff.

"And for the record, your company needs to get their weight up salary wise, because I made that pathetic amount they tried to offer me when I was *junior* developer at my *old* company."

Alex made a face at the insult. "Whatever, at least it would've been more than you have *now*," she bit back.

"What, you think I'm *broke*?" Chasity scoffed.

"I didn't say that," Alex amended. "I'm *just* saying—"

"You know what, it doesn't even matter what you think, just shut your ass up," Chasity barked.

"Seriously?!" Alex exclaimed.

"Yes, *shut up*," Chasity fumed. "You keep harping on the fact that I'm out of a job, a job that I *willingly* walked *away* from by the way," she stressed. "I walked away because I didn't want to work for anybody anymore. So why would you think that I would want to go *back* to doing it?"

"Chasity come on, I get the whole 'I want to work for myself thing' but face it, trying to start a business isn't easy. In fact, it takes *money* to start a business," Alex sneered. "What? You're gonna rely on *Jason's* paycheck alone to take care of all your bills *and* start your business? That's a little selfish don't you think?"

Chasity stared Alex down, fire in her eyes. She wasn't sure how this argument started or why Alex was acting so self-righteous, but she knew that she needed to end it before she hurt the girl. Chasity took another step in Alex's direction. "Don't project your bitter, broke ass childhood household memories on to me," she bit out.

Alex's eyes widened. "*Excuse* me?!" she wailed.

"Yeah, you heard what the fuck I said," Chasity maintained. "You still feel some kind of way because you had to work in school? You feel bad 'cause Mommy and Daddy couldn't send you money while you were in college? Poor baby," she mocked.

"That was *so* uncalled for!" Alex yelled, stomping her foot on the floor. "And I am *not* bitter about my upbringing Chasity, that would be *you*."

"Wrong and stupid as always," Chasity hurled back.

"You are freakin' unbelievable," Alex hurled as Chasity turned to leave. "And for the *record*, 'know it all' I'm *happy* that I grew up the way that I did."

Chasity paused, but didn't turn around.

"Growing up what *your* spoiled ass considered *poor*, made me work harder so that I could get to where I am right now," Alex preached. "It made me make smart decisions such as *not* turning down a job for foolish reasons such as *pride*," she shook her head. "You want to penalize me because I saw an opportunity to help you and took it, then *fine*, but I won't let you make me feel bad about it."

Chasity slowly turned around. She folded her arms and glared. "You think you're better than me," she concluded.

Alex tossed her hands in the air in frustration. "Oh my G— are you *kidding* me?" she fumed. "*That's* what you got from what I just said?"

"You *like* throwing up the fact that I'm out of work," Chasity argued. "It's not because you're *concerned*, it's because you think that you *finally* have something over me. That you can look down on me, like you think *I* did to *you* in college."

Alex's eyes widened in disbelief. "What?"

"You think I didn't notice how jealous you looked every time I bought something, or every time you came to my house?" Chasity snarled.

"I wasn't *jealous* of you, girl," Alex hissed.

"Of what I *had*, you *were*," Chasity threw back.

Alex rolled her eyes. Chasity had a point; Alex did feel jealous at times when it came to Chasity and her wealth. Up until now, she thought that she'd hid it well. "Well now that you brought this shit up, *did* you look down on me?" Alex grunted.

"*No*, and fuck you for thinking that I did," Chasity spat back.

Alex put a hand up. "Listen, contrary to what you think, I am *not* looking down on *you*," she insisted, angry.

"Good, because you *can't*," Chasity retorted. "There is *nothing* that you have right now, that I don't or haven't *already* had."

"You know what, screw you, Chasity," Alex spat. "Do what you want, but don't come crawling back to me and my little company when you deplete whatever savings you have, trying to start a business that you *won't* be able to maintain with that nasty attitude of yours," she fumed. "And for the record, you have *no* paycheck coming in while *I* have a *steady* one, so I'd say that right now, I have more than *you*."

"Once again, you think money is everything," Chasity mocked. "You're a lonely, bitter bitch and that's all you'll *ever* be."

"I'll be sure to cry lonely tears into my wallet," Alex threw back, smug.

Chasity clenched her jaw; she was over this argument. "You know what," she began, putting a hand up. "Since you got it like that, pay me for that project I did for you."

Alex was taken aback. "What?"

"Yeah, since my savings account is being depleted, I need all the money I can get," she mocked. "My freelance charge for what I did for you is fifteen hundred, run me my shit."

"You are being really petty right now," Alex ground out. "I'm not paying you fifteen hundred dollars for something that probably took you an *hour* to do."

"No?" Chasity challenged. She eyed a large glass vase on a nearby stand. "That's fine," she said, pushing the vase to the floor; it shattered, sending glass everywhere.

Alex flinched. "You're gonna pay me for that!" she screamed.

Chasity grabbed the doorknob. "Take it out of the fuckin' money you owe me!" she yelled back, snatching the door open.

Alex was furious. "God, you want to talk about what *I'll* always be?!" she yelled. "After *all* this damn time, you're *still* overly aggressive, rude, hurtful and *violent!*"

"Cry about it in your *wallet*, bitch," Chasity hurled.

Alex gasped. "I sincerely hope you're not being that way to your child," she hurled.

Chasity stopped dead in her tracks and spun around; her eyes widened in fury. "The fuck did you just say?" she challenged, taking several steps in Alex's direction.

"One thing I know you *aren't* is hard of hearing," Alex sniped, moving to meet Chasity face to face. "What I said is true and *sad*. You know what *you* went through growing up with an angry mother figure, I would *hate* for you to repeat that cycle with Kayla."

Chasity felt her blood run cold; that Alex would even insinuate that she treated her child how Brenda had treated her, made her see red. Fire in her eyes, Chasity balled her fists at her sides.

Alex stared her down. "You want to hit me, don't you?" she taunted.

"I do," Chasity fumed.

"Go ahead," Alex provoked. "Prove me right."

Chasity's jaw clenched; her fists were so tight that she felt her nails digging into her own skin. Chasity was practically shaking; the only thing stopping her from punching Alex in the face was the fact that she was pregnant. She backed up. "Fuck you, Alex," she hurled.

Alex watched as Chasity stormed out of the apartment, slamming the door in the process. The force of it knocked a picture from the wall.

Alex exhaled deeply. Shaking, she ran her hands over her hair. "What just happened? What just happened?" she repeated. She couldn't believe that a fun weekend had just ended on such a sour note.

Alex had made a conscious effort not to fight with her friends; she felt that at their age, it was beneath them. She was devastated. Sitting on her couch, she put her face in her hands as tears filled her eyes. Her cell phone rang; she grabbed it from her coffee table "Hello?" she answered, voice trembling.

"Alex, Mom and Dad found out that you were paying their bills online," Sahara spoke into the phone. "Mom is pissed at you. I think you need to talk to her."

"Shit," Alex sighed. *Great, just what I need, another fight.* "I can't do this right now."

Chasity pushed the glass doors to the apartment building open and stormed out. She was on her way to the building parking lot, when she felt her head pound. She stopped and placed a hand on her forehead and took a few deep breaths. The argument with Alex was just the icing on the cake of a bad week; she just wanted to get in her car and go.

As she stood off to the side, waiting for the pounding in her head to pass, she heard a man's voice call her name. She ignored it.

"Chasity?" he called again.

Both confused and angry, she turned around. *God, not now,* she thought seeing the man approach. "Dad," she grunted.

Derrick stood in front of her. "What are you doing here?"

Chasity wasn't in the mood to have a conversation. "It

doesn't matter, I have to go," she quickly put out, trying to move around him.

He stepped in her way, stopping her departure. "Hold on, can you at least say hi to me?" he asked.

"Hi," Chasity huffed, trying to move around him again. He stepped in her way once more, making her even angrier. "Dad, I don't have time for this, I have to go," she snapped.

Derrick held a concerned gaze on Chasity; clearly she was upset. "What's the matter?"

"Nothing," she insisted. *God, will you just move!* Her head hurt and her emotions were on high. If she didn't get away from him, she was afraid that she would bust out crying on the spot.

"Clearly that's not true," Derrick maintained, stern. He put a hand on her arm. "Look, I won't get into the fact that you're here in New York and didn't drop a line to tell me you were in town—"

"I don't owe you—" She put a hand over her face as she tried to calm herself down. "I just— I can't do this right now Dad. I have to go."

Derrick stared at her. Something was wrong with his daughter, and no matter how much she didn't want him badgering her, he wasn't about to let her leave without at least finding out what had her so upset. "Chasity...what's wrong?" he pressed, tone soothing.

Chasity looked at him. In her head, she put together what she wanted to say to get him out of her face. But when she tried to speak, she couldn't get the words out. Tears spilled down her cheeks instead as she continued to stare at him.

Derrick felt his heart sink at the sight of his daughter crying. He would've hugged her, but he didn't know if she would pull away or not. Instead, he gently took hold of her hand. "Come with me," he urged, pulling her along as he walked down the block.

"Where's Jazmine's slacking behind?" Dru asked into the line.

Emily cradled the phone between her ear and her shoulder as she looked over papers. "I don't know and don't care," she sneered. "I haven't seen her since our last argument."

While her students were having lunch that Monday afternoon, Emily was sitting in her classroom going over homework assignments. She was being honest with her brother. Ever since she and Jazmine had gotten into it a few days ago, Emily hadn't seen her. Whether the girl had moved out without taking her things, or whether she just went into the apartment while Emily was at work, she didn't care. As long as Emily didn't have to lay eyes on her ungrateful sister, she couldn't care less where Jazmine was or what she was doing.

"Well, she left me a message asking to borrow money and I've been trying to call her back to cuss her out and tell her 'no' to her damn ear," he vented.

Emily rolled her eyes. "I was hoping that she called to ask you to move in," she grunted.

Dru let out a sigh. "Look Em, you know I'd let her move in just to take her off your hands, but we both know she won't stay with me because I refuse to let her sit around and be lazy," he said. "She'd be working *and* taking classes."

"I just don't know *why* she refuses to grow up." Emily vented. "She's *thirty*, it's ridiculous and *sad*."

"It is, but it's not your problem," Dru consoled. "Anyway, sorry for ruining your day."

"My day is never ruined when you call me," Emily assured, smiling slightly.

Dru let out a chuckle. "Same here," he said. "Talk to you later."

"Bye." Emily hung up the phone. Setting it on her desk, she leaned back in her seat. Emily let out a long sigh, rubbing her eyes with her hands.

A tap on the classroom door made her look up. "It's open," she called. She smiled slightly when she saw who'd peered their head in. "Hi Ms. Breanne," she greeted the elementary school principal.

Breanne returned a warm smile. "Emily, I've told you so many times, just call me Breanne."

Emily looked embarrassed. "Sorry."

Breanne waved a dismissive hand. "No need to apologize." She walked in. "Working through your lunch again?"

Emily glanced down at the papers on her desk. "I don't really call it work," she said. "It's actually relaxing me a bit."

Breanne gave a nod. "You're one of my best teachers, you know that?" she praised.

Emily smiled bright. "I didn't, but thank you."

"You are," Breanne affirmed. "You genuinely love your students, and go above and beyond for them. You are a valued asset here at this school."

As flattered as Emily was by the words coming out of her boss's mouth, she couldn't help but feel like there was something Breanne *wasn't* saying. "Thank you, umm…am I being transferred or something?" she asked.

"No, why would you think that?"

Emily shrugged. "I don't know, it's just a feeling."

Breanne put a hand on Emily's desk. "Trust me, you'd be the *last* person that I would transfer if it came to that," she assured. "No, I just wanted to give you your praises. Especially since I've been noticing that you've been a little down lately."

Emily let out a sigh. *God, I wish I was good at hiding my feelings like some of my friends.* "I'm sorry, it's not because of work."

"Emily, stop apologizing," Breanne consoled. "It's okay, I just wanted to make sure *you're* okay."

Emily gave a little nod. "I'm fine."

"Good," Breanne smiled. "Well, I also wanted to let you know that after school lets out Thursday, we're having a brief staff meeting."

Emily successfully hid her annoyance. She hated staff meetings; she'd much rather be working on her projects. "Okay, I'll be there."

Chasity laid on the pink comforter covered twin bed, clutching a pillow to her chest. It'd been nearly two hours since she'd ran into her father while leaving Alex's apartment. Derrick had taken Chasity to his condo so she could calm down. While he refused to let her leave until she felt better, he did give her space and allowed her to seclude herself in one of his three bedrooms.

Her eyes roamed the space as she laid there in silence. Hearing a knock on the door, she slowly sat up. Chasity took a deep breath. "Yes?" she called.

"Can I come in?" Derrick asked through the door.

"It's your place," she replied, tone even.

Derrick opened the door and stuck his head inside. "You okay in here?" he cautiously asked.

Chasity shrugged slightly.

Derrick walked in, holding a mug in his hand. "Figured you could use some tea," he offered. "I mean, if you don't want this, I could get you something else," he sputtered when she didn't answer right away.

Chasity held her hand out when he made a move to leave. "No, tea is fine," she said.

He walked over and handed it to her.

"Thanks," she said.

Derrick stood there for a moment as Chasity took a few careful sips of her tea, almost as if he was unsure of what to do next. After another moment, he sat down on the edge of the bed. "Is it okay?" he asked of the tea.

Chasity nodded as she set the mug on the nightstand. She glanced around the room.

"How do you like it?" Derrick asked. "I figured since this is where Kayla sleeps when she spends the weekend with me, I'd decorate it how she likes it."

"It looks like a pink crayon threw up in here," Chasity commented.

Derrick let out a deep laugh. "Well, it's what she wanted," he explained. "The last time she was here, she picked out all of those stuffed animals over there." He pointed to an array of stuffed toy cats sitting on a white cushioned bench near the window.

Chasity glanced over and shook her head. "You've *got* to stop spoiling her," she said.

"Can't," Derrick admitted. "She's a good kid, she deserves it."

Chasity sighed. "Yeah, she is."

"You know…she reminds me of *you* at that age," he said. "You were just as determined, animated, expressive, and sweet.

You even loved pink as much, if not more than *she* did."

Chasity ran a hand through her hair. "Yeah well, *clearly* things have changed," she muttered.

Derrick's smile faded. "Listen, I know—"

"Don't," she requested.

Derrick put a hand up. "Okay," he relented. He knew how much Chasity hated when he brought up their past. She might've wanted to forget it, but it was still with him every day. "So…you want to tell me why you were in New York this weekend? I thought you hated it here."

"I do," Chasity confirmed. "I should've just stayed my ass home." She shook her head. "I came up here to visit a bitch."

Derrick was taken aback. "Oh—okay."

"A friend of mine," Chasity clarified. "I thought she wanted to spend some time with me, and it turned out she wanted something *from* me… We got into a pretty bad argument."

Derrick listened intently. "Well, I'm sure whatever was said, she didn't mean it."

"She meant it," Chasity sneered.

"Even still, I'm sure she's sorry for what she said," he added, trying his best to ease her mind.

"Don't care," Chasity threw back.

Derrick had to admit, he didn't know what to say to Chasity to make her feel better. He couldn't remember a time where he was able to comfort her about much of anything; it was one of many things he regretted.

He opened his mouth to speak, but Chasity's phone beeped, halting his words.

She grabbed her phone from the nightstand and looked at it. It was a text message from Jason.

What time do you think you'll be home?

She rolled her eyes. "Never, so fuck you," she mumbled, low, texting back. *Later*, she sent. Tossing the phone down on the bed, she put a hand over her face and sighed again. Running the same hand over her hair, she sat back and tried to take a breath.

"Everything okay?" Derrick asked.

Chasity sucked her teeth. "No, everything is *not* okay," she snapped, feeling her temper rise. "Why are people so damn stupid? No, why are *men* so damn stupid?"

Derrick sat there stunned. Chasity had gone from barely engaging to a full-on rant. "Maybe if I had some specifics, I could answer that for you," he cautiously put out.

Chasity debated on whether she wanted to share them or not. But she needed a man's point of view, and he was the only one there. Chasity took a deep breath and adjusted her position on the small bed. "How did I sleep on a bed this size in college?" she complained.

Derrick went to get up. "We can move—"

"I'm fine," she cut in, putting a hand up.

Derrick sat back down and stared at her in anticipation. "So…what man is stupid? Besides *me* that is."

"My husband," Chasity spat.

Derrick looked confused. "Jason?"

Chasity clenched her jaw and gestured towards his neck as if she was about to choke him. "*Focus* Dad," she ground out.

Derrick gestured toward her. "I'm sorry. Please continue."

"Anyway, he accepted a job without talking to me first," she vented. "He just told them yes, like an idiot. And it's an *out of state* job. Out of state as in *Phoenix, Arizona* and he *refuses* to back out of it. He just expects us to pick up and move across the goddamn country like it's nothing." She folded her arms and sat back against the padded headboard. "I'm…pissed off. Like, I really want to punch him in the neck."

Derrick took a deep breath as he absorbed what he'd just heard. "Wow," he muttered.

"Yeah, wow," she grunted, looking at her nails.

Derrick adjusted his position on the bed. "Okay, can I ask you something?"

"Sure," she replied, unenthused.

"How good is the job?"

She rolled her eyes. "That doesn't matter."

"It *does*, actually," Derrick insisted. "Jason is a smart, reasonable, and responsible man. I'd like to believe that he wouldn't accept a job that would change your situation *that* drastically if he didn't honestly believe that it was in the best interest of you all." He put a hand up when Chasity went to protest. "Granted, he *should* have discussed it with you first," he agreed, sensing what she was getting ready to argue about. "But...even if he *did* talk to you first...would your displeasure at the situation still be the same?"

Chasity held a frown on her face as she pondered this. "I don't want to *move*," she slowly drew out.

"I know...and in all honesty, I don't *want* you to either," Derrick returned sincere. "But you have to think about what is in the best interest of your family. And if this job is as big as I imagine it to be, then this move is it. So just consider it..." he let out a sigh. "But this is just the opinion of someone who never did what was in the best interest of *his* family, so you can take it for what it's worth."

Chasity let out a deep sigh of her own. "Don't know *why* I thought that life would be simpler after college," she grunted.

Derrick chuckled. "Welcome to adulthood," he said. "*Real* adulthood."

Chasity just shook her head and rubbed her stomach. "Some bullshit."

Derrick let out a laugh. His smile faded. "Have you told your mother about the offer?"

Chasity shook her head no.

"So, I'm the first to know?" he smiled.

"Yes," Chasity answered, almost amused by his reaction. "You're smiling like a creep."

Derrick laughed again. "Damn, you're blunt," he said, amused. "One of the many things I appreciate about you... Your child takes after you in that aspect too. When I spoke to her the other day and asked her what her favorite thing for me to cook was, so that I can make it the next time she comes, she told me that she prefers pizza over anything."

"She played you— She just likes pizza and will try to eat it every chance she gets," Chasity replied.

Derrick's laughter subsided. "What am I going to do if you decide to actually move?" he asked, tone somber. He let out a deep sigh.

Chasity held her gaze on him. "Well...*if* I decide to move...you'd just have to come visit," she offered.

Derrick's eyes lit up. "Yeah?"

She nodded. "I meant what I said, I want you to be a part of your grandchildren's lives," she said.

"What about being a part of *your* life?" he wondered.

Chasity pondered her thoughts. "Dad, I don't hate you, but I—" she tried to figure out what to say to him. It was true, she didn't hate him, but she realized that she had yet to forgive him. She wondered if it was worth her energy to still hold on to her resentment. "We'll see," she said after a moment. She glanced at her watch. "I should get going." She stood up.

Derrick stood up as well. "You sure you can't stay a little longer?" he asked. "It's nice having you here."

"I have to go, I'm sorry," she maintained.

Derrick nodded. "I understand. Are you okay with driving? Do you want me to send you home in a car?"

"No, I can drive," Chasity assured, grabbing her phone and shoving it into her pocket.

"At *least* let me drive you back to your car," he insisted.

"Okay Dad," she accepted. The distance wasn't that far; she could've walked it. But she figured she'd allow him to see her back to her vehicle, if it would make him feel better. As she went to walk out of the door with Derrick following, she stopped and turned around. "Oh yeah, I'm pregnant again," she nonchalantly threw out, walking out of the room.

Pleasantly surprised, Derrick stood there. "Really?" he beamed.

"Yes," Chasity threw over her shoulder.

"Does your mother know?"

"Yes."

"Damn it," Derrick grimaced, making Chasity snicker.

Chapter 40

Malajia took a sip of her cocoa and picked up a chocolate chip cookie. "Did you bake these or buy them?" she asked Geri, who was busy cleaning the kitchen. Malajia took a bite and chewed. "Never mind, they actually taste good—you bought them."

Geri glared at her from the sink. "If you're going to be a bitch, you can get out."

"Nah, I think I'll stay a while," Malajia threw back, taking another bite of her cookie.

Geri sucked her teeth as she went back to cleaning. "I swear, I should have never told you that I was home," she grunted.

"You forget, I have a key," Malajia chuckled. "I would've just let my fine ass right on in here."

Malajia took another sip of her cocoa. Her car had to go to the shop for an inspection, and it wasn't too far from her sister's place in Philadelphia. Malajia had decided that instead of waiting at the shop, she'd just kill time with Geri. "You have any Kahlua or something?"

"Nope," Geri answered.

Malajia scrunched her face up. "Why *not*?"

Geri stomped her foot on the floor. "Because my first priority after waking up this morning was not buying liquor for *your* drunk ass," she huffed.

Malajia rolled her eyes. "But your greedy ass bought *cookies* and shit," she threw back. Catching Geri's death stare, Malajia put a hand up. "I'll shut up."

Geri shook her head and sat down on a bar stool next to Malajia. "How long until your car is finished?" she asked.

Malajia took another sip of her drink. "It's already finished," she nonchalantly replied.

"How do you know?"

"They called me like a half hour ago," Malajia revealed. "I just don't feel like taking that twenty-minute walk to the shop to go get it."

"Ask Dad to drop you off when he gets back from the hardware store," Geri suggested.

Malajia nearly choked on her drink. "*Dad?*"

Geri nodded.

"The hell is he doing in a hardware store in *Philly*? His ass needs to be back in Baltimore getting on Mom's nerves," Malajia griped.

"Well, I finally decided to change the color of these white ass walls, so Dad said he would paint for me," Geri explained.

Malajia rolled her eyes. "Whatever, I would rather *walk* than ask that man for a ride," she grunted, texting on her phone. "I just asked Mark to pick me up."

Geri laughed. "Lazy ass."

"*Tired* is more like it," Malajia replied.

Geri grabbed a cookie and took a bite of it. "Tell Mark that he doesn't have to knock, he can just come in," she said mid-chew. Malajia gave a nod as she texted the information. "How is everything going by the way?" Geri asked.

Malajia shrugged slightly. Hearing a sound from her phone, she glanced at it. *Be there in twenty,* it read. She sent one more text then looked back at Geri. "Things are fine."

Geri set her bitten cookie down and looked at Malajia. "So, when were you gonna tell me that Mark lost his job?" she asked, catching Malajia off guard.

"The fuck?" Malajia blurted out, shocked. "How do *you* know that Mark lost his job?"

Geri let out a sigh. "Okay, I'm sure I'm violating some law here, but my insurance company handles COBRA for Mark's company," she explained. "I was working on a few cases and saw his name come up on one of them. You only qualify for COBRA when—"

"I know what the hell COBRA is and what the qualifications are, and you damn right you're violating confidentiality laws," Malajia grunted. "I should snitch... Unless you can help us erase that hospital bill for Marlon."

"Can't and won't happen," Geri denied.

Malajia sucked her teeth. "Your ass is going to jail then. You're of no use to me anyway."

Geri flagged her with her hand. "Whatever, back to my question...are you guys okay?"

Malajia panicked. She had kept her promise thus far, not telling anybody about Mark losing his job. Now Geri knew, and all she could think about was that Mark would blame her for it. "Geri *please* tell me that you didn't tell anybody about this."

"No, I wouldn't do that," Geri promised.

Malajia put her hand on her chest and let out a sigh of relief. "Thank God," she breathed. "I could only imagine what Dad would say if he found out."

Geri sighed. "Yeah, Dad be trippin' with the way he treats Mark," she agreed.

Malajia tapped her hand on the table, eyeing Geri with wide eyes. "*You* see that shit *too*?"

"Of course," Geri confirmed. "We *all* know how ignorant Dad can be."

Malajia shook her head. In a way, she was glad that Geri knew; now she could vent to someone. "But to answer your question *truthfully*... Mark is stressed even though he pretends *not* to be and that's stressing *me* out."

"Well are you *surprised*?" Geri asked. "He's the *sole* provider for your family."

Malajia frowned at Geri. "You ain't gotta stress that shit, I *know* he was the only one working," she sneered, much to Geri's shock. "What, am I not supposed to be stressed too?"

"Whoa, what are you so mad for?"

"Because everybody acts like it's nineteen fifty-eight and shit," she fussed. "Like he's supposed to just take on everything by himself."

Geri looked confused. "I never *said* that, sis."

Malajia flagged Geri with her hand. She might have overreacted, but she wasn't about to apologize for it. "Whatever," she grunted. "Well, it doesn't even matter, because it won't be that way anymore." She folded her arms on the table. "I was offered a job."

"I didn't know you were *interviewing*," Geri replied.

"Didn't think it needed *broadcasting*," Malajia sneered.

"Well, are you going to take it?" Geri asked, ignoring Malajia's attitude.

"More than likely." Malajia took another bite of her cookie.

"I have to ask, are you going back to work because you *want* to, or because you feel like you *have* to?" Geri probed.

Malajia let out a quick sigh. "Does it matter?" she huffed.

"*Yes*, if it's not something that you want right now."

"It *is* what I want," Malajia admitted, playing with a piece of napkin. "This stay-at-home mom thing isn't for me anymore. Don't get me wrong, I *love* my babies more than anything, but me not doing what I really want to do is frustrating me. All I'm doing is taking it out on them, and I feel like shit because of it."

Geri ran a hand over her hair as she listened. "Wow, I had no idea that you were feeling this way," she commented.

"I guess I don't run my mouth as much as everyone *thinks,* huh?" Malajia bit out.

"No, you do," Geri stated, blunt.

Malajia sucked her teeth, taking another sip of her cocoa.

"Well...how does Mark feel about you going back to work after all this time?"

Malajia rolled her eyes, letting out a heavy sigh. She didn't want to vent *too* much about Mark. Although she was upset with him, she didn't want to badmouth him to anybody in her family.

Sensing Malajia's hesitation, Geri reached over and tapped Malajia's hand. "Come on Malajia," she urged. "You can talk to me. It'll stay between us."

Malajia sighed again, "Fine...he has an attitude about it," she revealed.

"Why?" Geri wondered.

"Because...I kinda didn't tell him that I was actually *looking* for a job," Malajia carefully said. "He had no idea that I wanted to go back to work... I just sprung it on him after he lost *his* job."

Geri squinted at Malajia. "Sis, you know you're wrong for that right?"

"For *what*? Wanting to go back to work?" she asked, offended.

Geri quickly shook her head. "No, for not being honest with him," she clarified.

"You know what, I'm really not tryna hear that shit, Geri," Malajia fussed. "It's not that serious."

"*You* might not think so. To *you* it's just a job," Geri explained. "But to him, you kept something from him. Something was important to you, but instead of talking to him and sharing your feelings, you snuck around."

"Oh my God, why do *both* of you act like I was having a damn affair?" Malajia blurted out.

Geri rolled her eyes. "I get what you're saying, but you didn't trust him enough to tell him the truth."

"That is such bullshit." Malajia was annoyed. She didn't understand why her sister refused to be on her side. "So, *I'm* the bad guy because I kept one little secret to avoid hurting his feelings."

"Malajia, you're not listening—"

Malajia folded her arms in a huff. "No, I'm *not* because you're not making any damn sense."

"I don't know why you're shocked, she never *did* listen," Mr. Simmons cut in, startling both girls. Geri and Malajia turned around in their seats to see him standing in the living room, holding two cans of paint.

"Could've *sworn* his knees would crack to let us know he was coming," Malajia grunted.

Geri stifled a laugh as she reached out and smacked Malajia's hand.

Mr. Simmons ignored the comment; he just held a stern gaze.

"Dad, you nearly gave us a heart attack," Geri mentioned.

Malajia stared at her father, who hadn't yet said another word. "How much of our conversation were you eavesdropping on, Dad?" she asked him. She had a feeling that he'd entered the house prior to the moment when he spoke.

Mr. Simmons walked into the kitchen, setting the paint cans by the pantry door. "Enough to know that Mark was fired from his job."

Malajia frowned. *Shit!*

"I always *knew* he'd get fired one day," Mr. Simmons mocked.

Malajia held a fiery gaze on her father. "Dad, what you *won't* do—"

"Malajia, ignore him," Geri muttered.

Malajia put a hand up. "No," she hissed to Geri, still eyeing her father. "*First* of all Dad, neither *one* of us said that he was *fired*," she spat. "You drew that conclusion on your own because you just want to find something to say about him. Second, he was *laid off*, not fired."

"Either way you slice it, he's not working," Mr. Simmons threw back.

Malajia looked confused. "What does slicing have to—" She flagged him with her hand. "Doesn't even matter."

Geri shook her head at the bickering. "Come on you two, stop it or I'm calling Mom," she warned.

Malajia looked at her watch as she stood up from her seat. "*He* needs to stop it," she argued.

"I'm *not* going to stop worrying about my girls," her father argued back.

Malajia tossed her arms up. "Dad cut it *out* already. I'm perfectly fine," she barked. "Worry about Dana and her hoeing."

"Ooh girl, *you* noticed that *too*?!" Geri exclaimed. "She *swears* she's slick with it."

Malajia shot Geri a side-glance, but declined to respond.

"Say what you want, I'll always worry about your well-being," Mr. Simmons pressed, walking towards her. "Your husband is out of work, that means your bills aren't getting paid, your rent isn't getting paid—"

"Since it's clear that you've been listening for a while now, I'm *sure* you overheard that I'm going back to work," Malajia fumed, putting a hand up. "And you act like Mark won't find another damn job."

"And how long do you think *that's* gonna take?" He scoffed, "Knowing how lazy he can be, I'm sure he's in no rush to find one."

Malajia was at her wits end with her father and his treatment of Mark. "Will you *stop* it!" she yelled.

"No, *you* stop being naïve when it comes to that—that *fool*," Mr. Simmons barked back.

Geri stood up. "Seriously, cut it out," she snapped.

Malajia was furious. "I'm tired of you being a damn jerk to Mark," she fussed at her father. "Why can't you see that he is *not* that same teenager? It's been *years* and he has changed *so* much."

"It doesn't matter *how* much time goes by, he'll always be a fool to me," her father grunted. "You should've listened to me when I told you to call off that wedding." He folded his arms, smug. "I *told* you that you were making a big mistake by marrying him. *Now* look what you've gotten yourself into."

Malajia opened her mouth to retaliate, but was drowned out by Mark's voice. "You told her *what*?" he asked, voice dangerously calm.

Startled, Malajia spun around to find Mark walking into the kitchen. "Geri, you need a goddamn bell on that door or something," she hurled at her stunned sister.

Geri winced. "Noted."

Malajia looked back at Mark. "Babe—"

"You told her that marrying me was a mistake?" Mark asked Mr. Simmons, cutting Malajia off. His expression was furious.

Mr. Simmons looked Mark up and down "Yes, I did," he admitted.

"Why would you do that?" Mark fumed.

"I didn't think you were a good choice for her," he answered. "I *still* don't."

Mark shook his head. He already knew that Malajia's father didn't care for him, but he had no idea the extent of it until now. "Wow," he ground out.

"Mark, forget him," Malajia pleaded, reaching for his arm.

Mark moved his arm out of the way. "What exactly is your problem with me, Richard?" he barked.

"Mr. Simmons to *you*, boy."

"I don't owe you *any*more respect," Mark threw back. "And I think you might wanna refrain from calling me *boy*, old man."

Mr. Simmons' eyes widened. "I outta—

"Ooh, everybody chill out please?" Geri begged. The last thing she wanted was a fight between her father and brother-in-law in her house, or at all. "Dad, can you stop?"

"Babe, he's not worth it," Malajia insisted.

Mark had no intention of leaving without saying exactly what was on his mind. "For years I've shown you the upmost respect. I've let all of your little slick comments against me slide," Mark fumed. "I just took it because you're Malajia's father."

"That's right, I'm her father and I know what's best for her, and that isn't *you*," Mr. Simmons spat.

Mark stared him down. "Yeah? Well I'm her *husband* and *I* know what's best for her and my children, and it's not being around *you*." He looked at Malajia. "Let's go."

Malajia looked at him, then at her father. She was so angry at her father for putting her in this position. "Dad, you need to apologize," she fumed.

"Nah Malajia, I don't need a damn apology from him. I *need* you to come get in this car so we can leave," Mark hissed at her. "*Now*."

Malajia looked back at Mark; her husband looked like he was ready to explode. "Okay," she relented. She grabbed his hand and allowed him to lead her out of the house.

Geri looked at her father and folded her arms, shaking her head in disappointment. "I'm telling Mom," she fumed, heading to get her phone.

Mr. Simmons put his hand over his face. He could only imagine the tongue lashing that he was about to endure from his wife once he got home.

Malajia put her seatbelt on as Mark put the car in gear. She looked over at him; his face was masked with anger. "Mark—"

"Just don't," he muttered.

Malajia looked confused. "Wait, you're not mad at *me*, are you?"

Mark looked at her, but didn't say anything.

Malajia's eyes widened in shock. "Mark, you think I was *condoning* that shit?" she charged.

"I didn't say that," Mark replied. "I'm sure you gave him an ear full as only you can."

Malajia jerked her head back at his nasty tone. "Then why do you sound so spiteful?"

"I wish you would've told me what he said."

"Why?" Malajia asked, confused. "It's not like I was ever going to *listen* to him."

"Doesn't *matter*," he argued. "You should've told me. You stay keeping shit to yourself and that's not cool Malajia."

Malajia put her hand up. "Okay look," she began, trying to keep her temper in check. "Telling you wasn't going to do anything but piss you off. And like I said, my father's opinion of you doesn't mean *shit* to me. *Clearly*, 'cause I *still* married you."

Mark rubbed his face. "I've been smiling in that man's face, walking on eggshells *hoping* that he would like me," he ranted. "*Hoping* that he didn't still see me as that same idiot that I was back then. *Hoping* that he would respect me as a man."

Malajia felt her heart sink as she held a sympathetic gaze on him. Mark was already dealing with feeling inadequate, and now his feelings were hurt. He felt disrespected and she couldn't help but feel responsible, since she was the one who had asked him to come pick her up.

He grabbed the steering wheel. "If I would've known the extent of his hatred for me, I wouldn't have wasted my goddamn time."

Malajia opened her mouth to speak as he pulled out of the driveway, but didn't exactly know what to say. She wanted to hold his hand to offer some silent comfort, but figured that he would just pull it away. Staring straight ahead, she just let out a sigh as they rode in silence.

Chasity sat on the chaise lounge in her bedroom, reading a book. She was hoping that the words on the page would offer an escape from her reality. But as good as the book was, her mind wasn't focused on it. She'd been back from New York for two days and had yet to speak to Alex. Despite the conversation with her father, she had yet to lose her attitude with Jason either. It was eating at her more than her rift with her friend.

Jason walked into the room. "Hey."

Chasity looked over at him, but declined to say anything.

"I'm about to go to the store, you need anything?" he asked.

She shook her head.

He ran a hand over the top of his head. "You sure?"

She nodded.

Jason let out a sigh. He hated when Chasity gave him the silent treatment; he almost preferred her yelling at him, than not speaking to him at all. "Okay," he muttered, then turned to walk out of the room. He stopped and turned around. "Okay, I can't do this with you anymore."

Chasity rolled her eyes and put the book back up to her face.

Frustrated, Jason, walked over and went to reach for the book.

She moved it out of his reach, frowning up at him. "You *better* not snatch it from me," she warned.

"I *wasn't*," he flashed back. "But give it to me, we need to talk." He held his hand out. Chasity was an expert at tuning him out; a book would just take her focus even more.

Not feeling like putting up a fight, she pushed the book into his hand. Jason tossed the book on the bed, then took a seat on it across from her. He fixed his gaze on her. "I'm *tired* of fighting with you Chasity."

She felt the same, but she didn't say anything. She just folded her arms and let him speak.

"Look, I know you hate the fact that I accepted the job without talking to you first, and for the *hundredth* time, I'm *sorry* for doing that," he began, sincere. "I know that you're mad that the job is in Arizona, but I can't *change* that. I wish I could, but I can't." He took a deep breath. "And I know you want me to not take this job but…I *can't*." He put his hand on his chest. "I *want* this job babe. I *need* this job and I *know* I'll be good at it."

Chasity just stared at him, silent.

Jason searched her face for any sign of emotion, but all he

got was an indifferent stare. He exhaled deeply as he stood from the bed. "Baby...I know how much you've already done for me," he said. "When I was going through grad school, working that crappy tech support job, you took on most of our financial responsibility. There were nights that you stayed up to help me study for finals, even though you were exhausted. You balanced your career, being a wife and mother, while supporting me in my dreams, and I love and appreciate you for that, more than you'll probably ever know... I just want to give you and our children everything—" he took a deep breath. "I *know* it's a lot to ask of you, but I'm just asking you to support me one more time." His eyes were pleading. "I...I need you to trust me." When she didn't respond, he rubbed his hands over his face and began to walk away.

Chasity watched as he headed for the door. "Jason," she called.

He turned around and looked at her.

She signaled him with her hand. "Come here," she softly said.

Jason walked over and stood in front of her. She moved her legs from the cushioned ottoman, giving him the opportunity to sit down. "Listen to me," she began, grabbing his hand and holding it. "I don't want you to feel like you owe me for supporting you while you were in grad school, because you don't."

"I just—"

"You *don't*," she stressed, cutting him off. "I'll *always* support you, you gotta know that."

Jason nodded. "I know."

She let out a deep sigh. "Jase my apprehension has nothing to do with your abilities. I know you'll be great at that job, I just—I really *don't* want to move."

Jason glanced down at her hand in his. "I know you don't." He glanced back up at her, squeezing her hand. "I understand how you feel," he sighed. "I don't want to pick up and leave either when our whole life is here. I *wish* the situation was different, but it *isn't*."

Chasity looked off to the side as she pondered. Taking a deep breath after a moment, she looked back at him. "You *really* feel that this is the right thing for us?" she asked him.

Jason nodded. "I *really* do."

Chasity ran her hand over her face for a long moment. She wasn't lying, she didn't want to move. However, she also knew that the days of thinking only of herself were far behind her. "Okay," she said finally.

Jason held his gaze on her. He wasn't sure exactly what that meant. "Okay?" he questioned.

She gave a slight nod. "Okay," she repeated.

Jason's eyes widened slightly. "Yeah?" he asked.

She nodded.

Jason's smile could have lit the entire block. He leaned over and wrapped his arms around Chasity, squeezing her. "Thank you," he breathed against her hair. "I love you so much."

"I love you too," she replied, hugging him back.

Jason parted from their embrace, touching her face with his hand. "I promise you, I'll make this up to you."

"Yeah, you just had better. Arizona is fuckin' hot," Chasity jeered.

Jason chuckled a bit. "I'll make sure our house is fully air conditioned."

Chasity offered a slight smile, then took a deep breath. "We're moving," she resolved. "Okay... *When* exactly?"

Jason grabbed her hand again. "We have to be there by the first week of February."

Chasity's eyes widened slightly. "So, we have less than two months to find a place to *live* in Phoenix, pack up an *entire* house, and make moving arrangements *with* the entire house full of shit to get it across the country."

Jason winced; hearing it out loud was overwhelming. "I'll take care of every arrangement; I don't want you to stress."

"I'm gonna be stressed *regardless*, so we'll handle this together," she replied. "We'll be fine."

Jason smiled once again. "We will be," he agreed. Both elated and grateful, Jason gave Chasity's hand a kiss, moving in for a kiss on her lips. He put his hand on her stomach and leaned his face close to it. "Hi little one," he said to their baby.

"Your mommy finally allowed me close enough to speak to you."

Chasity couldn't help but laugh.

Chapter 41

Cradling her phone to her ear, Emily took a sip of her bottled water as she gathered some folders from her desk.

"You want to talk about last night?" Will asked on the other end.

"Not really, you already made your point," Emily griped into the line.

"Emily, I know you don't like my suggestion, but I really think it's best," Will said.

"I don't want to talk about this anymore," she huffed. "Especially since I have to sit through this stupid meeting today— Damn it!" she snapped when papers slid from her folder to the floor. She flopped down on the chair and pinched the bridge of her nose.

There was a pause on the line. "Are you okay?" Will asked finally.

Emily squeezed her eyes shut as a few tears formed. Her bad day had started the night before when Jazmine had showed back up at her apartment after crashing with a friend of hers for days. If her just being there wasn't bad enough, she'd snapped at Emily for moving her belongings, which turned into an argument. When Will had to intervene, he scolded Emily for allowing Jazmine to even set foot back in her apartment, resulting in the two of *them* arguing.

Emily and Will rarely argued. The fact that they had, and over her sister, had kept Emily up all night. She was tired in more ways than one.

Emily yanked a tissue from a box on her desk, wiping her eyes with it. "I have to go," she said, hanging up. Emily dabbed her eyes once more, then tossed the wet tissue in the wastebasket next to her desk.

She glanced over at her classroom door as it opened.

"Hey Emily," a fellow teacher smiled.

Emily forced a smile. "Hi Norma."

"You ready to head over to the meeting together?" Norma asked.

Emily just offered an unenthused nod as she stood from her desk. She gathered her papers from the floor and placed them back into her folder.

"You can leave the papers."

Emily looked confused. "Um…why?"

"It's a pretty informal meeting, just going over a few things. Nothing that would require papers," Norma informed.

Emily was still confused, but decided to not question it. She left her folder on the desk, and followed Norma out of her classroom. Emily was silent as they walked in stride. She glanced over at her smiling coworker and fought the urge to roll her eyes. Everyone was much too chipper for her today.

Approaching the teachers' lounge, Norma paused short of opening the door and looked at Emily. "Smile," she encouraged.

For the love of God! Emily just stared at Norma. "Can you open the door?" she asked, gesturing to the knob.

Unfazed by Emily's sour mood, Norma shrugged, "Don't say I didn't warn you," she chuckled, opening the door.

Emily didn't respond as she watched Norma walk inside. Letting out a sigh, she walked in after her. Emily flinched and let out a loud gasp when "Surprise!" was belted out by the room full of people.

Once Emily had composed herself, she glanced around the room to see the smiling faces of her fellow teachers and the principal. The lounge was decorated with white and light pink wedding themed décor. From the crape paper wedding bells, to the streamers, to the balloons, small pink bubble filled favors, paper plates and eatery, to the table full of gifts—it was clear the group had put in time and effort for her.

"Congratulations on your upcoming wedding Emily," Breanne beamed.

"Yeah, we know we're like a month early, but we wanted to do this shower for you before winter break," Norma chimed in, grabbing a white "Bride-to-be sash" from a small table.

Emily was so overwhelmed with their kindness that tears began to well up in her eyes. She put her hands over her face. "Thank you," she sputtered between sobs.

Breanne walked over and put her arms around Emily. "You're welcome," she gushed. She pulled away, as another teacher handed Emily a tissue. "I told you, you're appreciated, and we want you to know how excited we are for you."

Emily smiled, wiping her eyes in the process. "You guys just made my day, you have *no* idea."

"Emily, I call dibs on the rest of this cake if it's not gone when we leave," someone bellowed from across the room.

Breanne turned toward the voice. "Marcia, we already denied that request earlier," she hurled. "The cake goes with Emily."

Emily laughed.

"Thanks for the ride home," Emily said to Norma as she stepped out of the car, juggling two large gift bags and her purse in her hands.

"Anytime," Norma smiled. "Do you need any help?"

Emily shook her head. "Nope, I can manage. See you tomorrow." Emily made her way into the building as her coworker pulled off. She smiled to herself as she entered the elevator. Pushing the button to her floor, she reminisced about her shower; she had enjoyed herself. It was the first time in a long time that she had enjoyed something wedding related.

Stepping off the elevator, Emily adjusted the bags as she headed for her door. Retrieving the keys from her purse, she adjusted her bags once more and unlocked it. Pushing the door open, she rolled her eyes at the unwanted guest in her living room. "Jaz," she spat out, shutting the door behind her.

Jazmine turned around, glaring at her. "You broke my shit," she charged, angry.

Emily set her bags on the floor, shooting her perplexed glance Jazmine's way. "Excuse me?"

Jazmine held up a clock radio. "You broke my shit," she repeated. "I took it out of the box that you *threw* my stuff in—"

Emily rolled her eyes.

"I turned it on and it's not *working*," Jazmine harped.

"I didn't break *anything* of yours," Emily flashed back.

Jazmine stormed to the kitchen and tossed the radio into the trash. "Who told you to touch my stuff, Emily?" she fumed.

Emily rubbed her face with her hands. Another argument with Jazmine was the last thing that she wanted to deal with after having a nice afternoon with her coworkers. "God Jaz, like I told you *last night*, you were gone for *days*. I thought that you found someplace else to stay, so I packed up your things so everything would be in one place when you came to get it," she explained. "Like always, I was trying to *help* you."

"So, you think just because I spent a few days out that I wouldn't be coming *back*?" Jazmine questioned.

Emily stared at her for a moment. A million thoughts were running through Emily's head, a million things that she wanted to say to Jazmine. And any other time, those thoughts would have remained inside of her head. But at this point, she was tired of not speaking her mind; she was tired of just putting up with her sister's crap. "I *hoped* you wouldn't," Emily admitted at last.

Jazmine was taken aback. "Seriously?"

Emily looked confused. "What do you want from me Jazmine?" she hurled. "You want me to keep letting you stay here, while you *refuse* to respect me?" She pointed to herself. "No, I'm *tired*. I want my space back, I want my *peace of mind* back… You have to go."

Jazmine flagged Emily with her hand dismissively as she headed into the bathroom. "Whatever, I better not find any more of my stuff broken."

Emily walked to the bathroom and stood in the doorway, watching Jazmine place her toiletry items on a shelf near the sink. "Did you not hear what I said?" Emily asked.

"Girl, I don't have time for your empty threats," Jazmine spat. "I'll give you your little bill money in two weeks."

"Why? So you can throw it at me again?" Emily threw back, folding her arms. "No, I've been managing just find without it. I want you out."

Jazmine stopped stacking her items and glared at Emily, but didn't say anything.

Emily was furious. "I'm not *playing* with you, Jazmine," she stressed.

Jazmine sucked her teeth, spinning around to face Emily. "What are you gonna do? You gonna *make* me leave?" she taunted. Emily's eyes widened in anger. "Didn't think so, now get out of my damn face, so I can finish putting my shit back up." She then grabbed one of Emily's items from the shelf and tossed it in the sink.

Enraged, Emily smacked Jazmine's things from the shelf to the floor.

Jazmine pushed Emily's hand away from the shelf, then she shoved her. "Bitch, don't touch my stuff!" she wailed.

Emily shoved her back, causing Jazmine to stumble so hard that she nearly fell into the tub. "*You're* a bitch and keep your goddamn hands off me!" Emily yelled back.

Stunned, Jazmine tried to maintain her balance.

"I mean it, get the hell out, *now*," Emily stood firm. She was so angry that she was panting. Emily stormed out of the bathroom, grabbed her purse from the living room, then went into her bedroom. She slammed her room door shut, and began pacing the carpeted floor. She tried to calm herself down, but couldn't. She grabbed her phone and dialed Will's number.

"Are you on your way home?" she blurted out as soon as he picked up.

Recognizing distress in her voice, Will instantly became concerned. "Yes, I'll be there in about fifteen minutes. What's wrong?"

"I'm done, Will," she vented, still pacing. "I told Jazmine that she has to leave. I can't take—" She paused when she heard the sound of something shattering. "Hold on," she said to him. She moved closer to the door, then heard the noise again. "I think she's breaking stuff."

"What?!" Will exclaimed. "I'm on my way baby."

"Okay," Emily said, before abruptly ending the call. She snatched open her bedroom door, scanning the living room with her eyes. Not seeing anything out of order, Emily squinted in confusion.

Hearing the shattering sound again, she glanced over towards the kitchen. Jazmine was bent over a large box—the box that she'd stored her finished wedding projects in. Emily's eyes widened.

"What the hell are you doing?!" Emily yelled. Her mouth dropped open when she saw Jazmine raise a hammer and smash it in the box, creating that same sound. That's when it hit her: Jazmine was breaking Emily's favors and decorations with that hammer.

Emily darted over, grabbed the back of Jazmine's shirt, and pulled her away from the box. Jazmine stood back amused as Emily glanced down into the box. It was full of broken glass, sand, seashells, crystals and flowers. The girl had even pulled her handmade bouquets apart; the strewn flowers were littered across the kitchen floor. Not thinking, Emily reached inside the box to grab one of the flowers, cutting her hand on a piece of glass.

Yanking her hand back, Emily winced in pain. Blood gathered and spilled from her wound. Emily began hyperventilating; all of her hard work, all of that time, destroyed. Furious, Emily slowly looked up at Jazmine. Her older sister was standing there, proud of herself.

"Now how do *you* feel about *your* shit being broken?" Jazmine mocked, tossing the hammer down at Emily's feet.

Angry tears filled Emily's eyes as she held her injured hand in the other. "Why did you do that?" she panted.

Jazmine folded her arms and smirked.

"*Why* did you do that?" Emily repeated louder, voice pained.

Jazmine shrugged. "Why *not*?" she boasted.

Emily couldn't pinpoint what was worse: the fact that her wedding items were destroyed, or the fact that they were destroyed by her sister. Someone who, despite her treatment of Emily, Emily still loved and looked out for. Her family. Her blood. She couldn't believe that Jazmine was that evil and hateful.

Without warning, Emily grabbed the hammer from the floor, stood up and hurled it in Jazmine's direction.

Shocked, Jazmine darted out of the way. The hammer flew into a vase on a nearby table, breaking it and sending glass shards to the floor. "Are you out of your fuckin' mind?!"

Jazmine yelled.

Emily grabbed a glass that Jazmine had left on the counter and hurled it. While Jazmine was ducking the object, Emily charged at her.

"Emily, what the fuck? Are you crazy?!" Jazmine screamed, stumbling back onto the couch.
Emily jumped on top of her. She tried to stop Emily at the wrists, as Emily wrapped her bloodied hands around Jazmine's neck.

Jazmine gasped as she pried her sister's hands away. "Emily, stop it!" she screamed, struggling to push Emily off. For the first time in her life, Jazmine was the one afraid.

Jazmine managed to push Emily off her, and delivered a kick to her stomach, knocking the wind out of Emily. It sent Emily falling onto an accent chair, grabbing her stomach in pain.

Jazmine jumped off the couch. "You're out of your goddamn mind," she raged. "I should beat your ass just like I did when we were kids."

"We're not kids anymore you stupid bitch!" Emily erupted. Jumping up and lunging at Jazmine again, Emily knocked her to the floor. Seizing the opportunity, Emily jumped on her and started wailing on her sister with her fists.

Though Jazmine fought back, she took several punches in return. She had no idea how strong Emily was, or how hard her younger sister could hit. Tears filled Jazmine's eyes as she took another punch to her face. The girls tussled and fought, until Jazmine pushed Emily off her yet again. As Emily fought for her balance, Jazmine jumped up and charged at her. Emily moved out of Jazmine's range, and tripped over a throw pillow that had been knocked to the floor during their fight.

Jazmine watched as Emily fell backwards, hitting her head on the coffee table and falling to the floor. Trying to catch her breath, Jazmine stood there looking down at Emily, who was sprawled out on her back. Emily's eyes were closed. Jazmine nudged Emily's leg with her foot; there was no movement.

"Emily," Jazmine called; there was no answer. "Emily," she tried again.

Worry finally started to register on Jazmine's face. She slowly moved closer, kneeling next to Emily. She gave her arm a shake. "Emily." When Emily still didn't budge, Jazmine's eyes widened; her breathing became shallow. "Shit," she panicked. As she jumped up in search of a phone, Will barged through the unlocked door.

Will's eyes darted to Emily lying motionless on the floor. "Oh my God." Rushing to her side, he kneeled and began shaking her. "Em, baby wake up," he pleaded, voice trembling. "Wake up." He snapped his head toward Jazmine, who was standing there with her hands over her face. "What the fuck did you do?!" he hollered at her.

Chapter 42

"Ma, can you *please* stop yelling at me for *one* second?" Alex pleaded into the line. She sat at her kitchen table with her head resting in one hand, her phone in the other. Four days after receiving the phone call from Sahara, Alex had finally gathered the courage to call her parents back. Alex was now taking the verbal lashing that she'd expected.

"How many times have I told you that we don't need your help, Alexandra?" her mother barked.

Alex pinched the bridge of her nose. "God," she mumbled. This wasn't what she needed after the day that she'd had. After Marlene had expressed her disappointment over Chasity turning down the job, Alex had no choice but to come clean to her boss about how she had manipulated Chasity into interviewing for the position. Having already been chastised by her boss for her deception, Alex's mood was low as it was. Being reprimanded yet again wasn't helping.

"Listen, I'm sorry that I went behind your back, but I honestly don't get what the big deal is," Alex bit out.

"The big *deal* is that your father and I *told* you to stop giving us money!"

"But I didn't *give* you money in your *hand*. I just paid a few bills so it's not really the same thing," Alex threw back as a poor excuse to defend herself.

"You're joking right?" her mother hissed.

Alex put her head on the table, letting out a loud sigh in the process.

"You don't *listen*, that's your problem!"

Alex let out another sigh. "One of *many* apparently," she bit out. Hearing a beep on her phone, she pulled it from her ear and looked at it. She breathed a sigh of relief seeing

Emily's number. *Yes! An excuse to end this call with Ma.* She put the phone back to her ear. "Ma, can I call you back in a few minutes?" When she didn't hear anything after a second, she looked back down at the phone. "She really just hung up on me," Alex muttered, clicking over. "Em, girl, I'm *so* happy to hear from you right—wait, *Will?*" her brow furrowed in confusion. Will had never called her, let alone from Emily's number. Alex heard the panic in his voice. "What's the matter? ...*What?!*"

"Where the hell are *you* going?" Malajia asked, pointing to an open suitcase on the floor next to Chasity's king-sized bed.

Chasity ignored her as she placed several items inside it.

Malajia sucked her teeth. "You realize that I won't stop talking until I get my answer, right?"

Chasity let out a huff. "God, will you *please* go home?" she asked, exasperated. Malajia had been over her house since earlier that morning, and Chasity was tired of her.

"I told you when you asked me that *earlier* that Mark is being an *ass* right now, so I don't wanna be there," Malajia threw back.

"*I've* been a *bitch* to you since you *got* here, and yet you're still in *my* face," Chasity sniped, folding a shirt.

Malajia made a face at her. "Look, I need a distraction right now, so just tell me where you're going."

Chasity let out a sigh. "Fine Malajia, I'm going to Phoenix with Jason for a few days," she answered.

"Oh," Malajia replied. "He's going out there for work again?"

"Um hmm," Chasity muttered.

"Well...that's nice that you're going to chill with him while he's there," Malajia shrugged.

"Um hmm," Chasity repeated. She and Jason had yet to tell anyone outside of their parents about their upcoming move across the country. Chasity wasn't sure how her best friend would take the news, and she didn't feel like dealing with one of Malajia's dramatic tantrums.

"When are you leaving?" Malajia probed.

"Sunday."

Malajia played with some fabric from a throw pillow. "A trip sounds nice," she said. "I need a break."

Chasity glanced over at Malajia; she looked tired. "How's Marlon feeling?" she asked. Chasity felt bad that she hadn't been in town when Malajia's son fell sick. But once she'd returned from New York, she had made sure to stop by and spend time with her.

Malajia ran a hand through her hair. "He's *much* better," she replied, relieved. "Back to his terrorizing self."

Chasity chuckled.

"Thanks again for coming over and helping me out that day…*especially* after all that bullshit you went through with Alex."

"Please, you don't have to thank me for that," Chasity dismissed, waving her hand.

Malajia gave a nod, then paused for a moment. "*Speaking of Alex*—"

"I'd prefer if you *didn't*," Chasity sneered, going back to her packing.

Malajia put a hand up. "Look, you know I agree with you that she was totally out of line for what she did *and* said," she began. "But we agreed a long time ago that we'd do better with resolving arguments than we did back in school."

"The bitch compared my mothering to Brenda, so fuck a resolution," Chasity fussed.

Malajia winced. "Yeah, I've got nothing to defend that part," she admitted. She let out a sigh. "I'll change the subject."

"Perfect," Chasity jeered.

"Mark lost his job," Malajia blurted out.

Chasity spun around. "Say what?"

Malajia looked at her, nodding. She couldn't take it anymore; she needed to talk to Chasity about *everything*. Malajia figured since both of their parents and her sister already knew about it, there was no harm in telling Chasity "Yeah, like two weeks—" Her phone rang, cutting her off. She grabbed it from the bed and checked the ID. "It's Alex," she announced.

Chasity rolled her eyes and walked into her private bathroom. "You could've kept that announcement to yourself."

Malajia shook her head as she answered. "What's up Alex?" Malajia put a hand up at the sound of Alex's hysterical yelling. "Girl, calm your ass down, what's wrong with you? Did they run out of bagels at the store or something?" Malajia's face went from confused to shocked as Alex yelled into the phone. "Wait *what*?!" Malajia pulled the phone from her ear. "Chasity, Emily is in the hospital!" she belted out.

Chasity, who was fussing with items under her bathroom sink, stood up and poked her head out. "What did you say?"

Malajia stood up and walked over to her. "Emily is in the hospital," she repeated. She put the phone on speaker. "Alex, you're on speaker, I'm here with Chaz."

"Emily is in the hospital," Alex blurted out. From the trembling in her voice, it was clear that Alex had been crying. "Will called me and said that she got in a fight with Jazmine and hit her head."

Chasity's eyes widened. She and Malajia looked at each other, shocked.

"What the fuck?" Chasity snapped, angry.

Malajia put her hand on Chasity's arm to try to calm her.

"He said that she's still unconscious... I'm going down there," Alex sputtered.

"Where are you now?" Malajia asked her. She might have been calm on the outside, but on the inside, Malajia was panicking.

"On the train," Alex told. "I talked to Sidra, she's trying to get a flight out." She sniffled. "I can't believe this. I'm so pissed, I'm freaking shaking right now."

Malajia let out a huff. "We jumping that bitch when we see her," she fumed. Chasity walked back into the bathroom as Malajia continued talking.

"Are you two coming down?" Alex asked.

"Absolutely," Malajia confirmed. She glanced in the bathroom; Chasity was standing at the sink with her hands over her face. "Chaz, you wanna head down there tonight?"

Chasity just nodded, but didn't say anything.

"We're gonna get ourselves together and we'll be on our way," Malajia said to Alex.

"Okay, see y'all in a few hours," Alex replied. "Love you

both."

"Love you too, but stop that crying all on the train and shit," Malajia jeered. "People gonna think you soft."

"Bye Malajia," Alex bristled.

Malajia hung up the phone, running her hands through her hair as she walked into the bathroom. Chasity had yet to remove her hands from her face; Malajia gave her arm a gentle shake. "Hey, you okay?" she asked.

Chasity removed her hands from her face. Her red eyes and the tears streaking down her face revealed that she had been crying. She neglected to speak, opting instead to just shake her head.

Malajia tilted her head as Chasity wiped her eyes with her hand. "Hormones?" she assumed.

Chasity once again shook her head. She was worried about Emily; she hurt for Emily. Emily had gone out of her way to be a good sister to Jazmine, despite how badly Jazmine treated her, and all it got her was hurt. Although Chasity's family issues differed from Emily's, she knew how it felt to be hurt by those who were supposed to love you.

Malajia let out a sigh, fanning her face in an effort to keep her own tears from surfacing. She reached out and hugged Chasity tight.

Sidra grabbed her jacket from the back of her chair, then darted for her office door. Forgetting her purse on her desk, she rolled her eyes, then ran back for it. When her phone rang, she picked it up. "Hey Josh," she said into the line.

"Hey, you're not still in the office, are you?" Josh asked.

"I'm trying to get out of here now," Sidra huffed. "Luckily I was able to get a last-minute flight out. I can't believe this shit happened, I'm ready to snatch Jazmine bald."

"I know, but try to stay calm," Josh placated. He was aware of what had happened; news traveled quickly through their group.

Feeling like she needed to catch her breath, Sidra leaned against her desk and placed two fingers on the bridge of her nose. From the time that she had received the panicked phone call from Alex about what happened to Emily, Sidra had been on edge.

All afternoon, Sidra had been trying to get updates on Emily's condition, having conference calls with the other girls on their plans to get to Emily right away. On top of trying to push through important meetings at work, and trying to find a last minute flight to Virginia, Sidra was stressed to say the least.

Josh heard her let out a long sigh. "You *have* to keep calm baby," he insisted, concerned. "I know how stressed you get."

Sidra closed her eyes, trying to hold the few tears that were forming at bay. "I know, I know," she repeated. "My being a ball of crazy mess won't be good for Em." She took a deep breath. "I'm okay."

"You *sure* you don't want me to go down there?"

"No, we girls got her," she said. "Just keep her in your prayers."

"You know I will."

Sidra stood up right, then headed for the door. Upon opening it, she saw Mr. Shaw approaching.

"Sidra, I need those updates for the Warner case."

Sidra placed her purse strap on her shoulder as she adjusted the phone in her hand. "Hold on a second, Josh," she said into the line. She looked at her boss. "I just finished emailing everything to you," she informed.

He glanced at his phone once a notification came in. "Ah, I see," he chuckled.

Sidra was in no mood for work related chatter. "Right, so you have everything. I have a flight to catch."

He looked perplexed. "You're going out of town?"

"Yes, I have a family emergency, so I need to leave like *right now*," Sidra stated, anxious. She glanced at her watch.

"This is a big case Sidra, how long are you going to be gone—"

"Mr. Shaw with all due respect, I've done everything that I was supposed to do," Sidra cut in, trying her best to remain calm. "Anything further can be handled by the actual attorney. I'm *not* one and you've made it clear that I'll never *be* one while working at this firm, so *please* excuse me, my family needs me."

Mr. Shaw folded his lips inward for a moment, before stepping aside to let her past. "Your family will be in my prayers. I'll see you when you get back."

"Thank you," Sidra ground out, walking off. She placed her phone back to her ear. "Hello."

"He had some nerve," Josh ranted of her boss.

Sidra shook her head as she maintained her hurried pace. "Yeah," she agreed.

Alex paced the waiting room floor, arms folded across her chest. She'd been at Paradise Valley Memorial Hospital for over three hours. She'd taken a cab directly from the train station, overnight bag and all. Looking up, she saw Will walking down the hall towards her. "Will, is she awake yet?"

Will stopped in front of her, shaking his head. "Not yet," he answered.

Alex let out a long sigh. "Well, what are they saying? Is she in a coma or something?"

Will rubbed his hands over his head. "No, she's not in a coma, she's just…unconscious." He rubbed his face. "Doctors are monitoring her brain and everything. They're not saying anything about brain damage, she…she just has to wake up."

Alex, seeing how much Will was trying to hold it together, reached out and hugged him. "Everything's gonna be okay," she consoled.

"Yeah," he said. They parted from their hug. "Her father is here."

Alex folded her arms again. "And her mother?"

Will sighed. "On her way. She's riding with her brothers… To be honest Alex, I don't even *want* Ms. Harris in that room with Emily," he sneered. "I'm tired of people treating my fiancé like shit."

Alex didn't blame him. "Just focus on Em right now. We'll deal with everything else as it comes," she tried to console him.

Will nodded. He let out a deep sigh, pinching the bridge of his nose in the process. "I wish we hadn't argued before—"

Alex put a hand up. "No, don't do that to yourself," she said. "*Please* Will, Emily will be okay. She's stronger than she thinks she is."

Will rubbed his face with his hand. "Yeah," he agreed. "I gotta get back to her."

"Of course," Alex approved. "I'll be here. The other girls are on their way so if you guys need *anything*, let us know."

Will looked at her. "She'll be happy to know that."

"We wouldn't be anywhere else," Alex replied, giving Will a pat on his arm. "Now go ahead, I'll hold down the fort out here."

Will gave a nod before heading back down the hall.

Alex went back to her pacing. After a few moments, she grabbed her phone from her jeans pocket. As she went to check it, she heard her name being called. Glancing up, she saw Malajia walking down the hall next to Chasity. Alex smiled with relief.

"That traffic was a hot ass mess," Malajia commented, giving Alex a hug.

"I know it was," Alex replied, patting Malajia's back. Alex parted from their embrace, then looked at Chasity, a hopeful look on her face. "Hi Chasity."

Chasity just looked Alex up and down, but didn't respond.

Malajia looked at Chasity. "Chaz, we have to put it aside for right now, okay?" she urged. "For Em."

Annoyed, Chasity closed her eyes then let out a long, deep sigh that sounded more like an angry hiss. After a moment, she opened her eyes, but still didn't say anything.

Alex shot Malajia a confused look.

Malajia put her hands up. "She didn't slap you, so take it for what it's worth right now," she advised.

Alex opened her mouth to speak to Chasity again, then closed it. She did want to talk to Chasity to clear the air, but decided to hold off for now.

"What are they saying?" Malajia asked, folding her arms across her chest.

"She's still out," Alex informed. "But the good news is that they don't see any brain damage."

"Thank God," Malajia breathed, putting a hand on her chest. "So, what exactly *happened*?" she probed. "I mean, did Jazmine attack her?"

Alex shrugged slightly. "All I know is what I told you on the phone earlier," she answered. "Will just said that she and Jazmine got into a fight and Emily fell—at least that's what Jazmine told him while he was calling the ambulance."

Malajia clenched her fist. "And where is that raggedy bitch *now*?"

"Apparently she ran off before the ambulance got there," Alex filled in, angry. She put her hands up. "Let's not talk about her anymore please, we don't need to be angry when Em wakes up…agreed?"

"Yeah," Malajia agreed as Chasity walked away to go sit down.

Alex followed Chasity's progress with her eyes. "Mel, she *has* to talk to me at some point," she said.

"You and I *both* know that Chasity doesn't *have* to do anything she doesn't feel like doing," Malajia pointed out. "You're talking about the queen of grudges here."

"Come on, she's being ridiculous," Alex vented. "This situation with Emily is *far* more important than our silly argument."

Malajia shot Alex a curious look. "Alex, you *do* realize I know everything you said to her, right?" she asked.

Alex rolled her eyes as she looked away.

"So, you *might* want to chill on calling her feelings about what you said, ridiculous," Malajia warned. She knew that Alex had the tendency to brush over how people felt when it came to things that she did and said. "You fucked up and what you're *not* gonna do is use this horrible thing that happened to Em as a way to brush that shit under the rug."

Alex's mouth fell open as her head snapped back in Malajia's direction. "Malajia, I'm not—"

Malajia jerked her hand up. "Alex, I'm pissed, exhausted, and hungry, you *don't* want to get on my nerves right now," she warned.

Alex closed her mouth.

Malajia put her hand down. "I love you, but I *will* slap you tonight."

Alex narrowed her eyes at Malajia. "*Emily* is the focus right now," she reiterated. "Have you heard from Sidra?"

"I talked to her a few hours ago; she was boarding her flight," Malajia informed.

Alex nodded. "Okay…thanks."

"For checking your ass, no problem," Malajia mocked before walking away, leaving Alex standing there.

Alex stood up from her seat and stretched. Another two hours had passed, and Emily's condition still hadn't changed, yet the girls were still hanging at the hospital waiting room. "I need coffee or something," Alex spoke. "I'm going to go get some." She looked at Malajia, who was sitting next to her, stretching her neck. "You want some coffee?"

"No, I want some damn *food*," Malajia griped. "Is the hospital cafeteria open?"

"I don't think so and even if it *was*, I don't think you'd want that food," Alex said.

"Anything is better than *air*," Malajia grunted.

Alex yawned, then put a hand on her hip. "You want a snack out of the vending machine?"

Malajia rolled her eyes. "I *guess* that'll do for now," she muttered.

Alex craned her neck to see if Chasity had emerged from the bathroom where she'd gone, ten minutes ago. "You think Chaz would want a coffee?" she asked Malajia.

"No coffee," Malajia said. "If you want to get her something, get her a ginger ale and a snack," Malajia advised. "As a matter of fact, get her ass *two* snacks. You know she's a bitch when she's hungry."

"Okay," Alex said, then headed off for the vending area.

Malajia leaned back in her seat and let out a sigh. She looked over as Chasity approached. "You okay?" she asked.

"No. Apparently my morning sickness isn't sticking to the *mornings* this time around," Chasity complained, sitting down next to Malajia. She leaned her head back against the wall and rubbed her stomach. "I literally have nothing left in my stomach."

"Poor baby," Malajia sympathized. "I *definitely* don't miss that shit."

"Neither did *I*," Chasity muttered.

"When are you gonna tell the others?" Malajia wondered.

"I don't know. Soon I guess," Chasity answered.

"Fair enough." Malajia pulled her phone out; she sucked her teeth. "Damn it, Mark called like four times," she huffed. "This reception in here sucks."

"You didn't call him when you got here?" Chasity asked.

"I *texted* him," Malajia grunted. She stood up from her seat. "Let me go call his ornery ass back."

Chasity chuckled as Malajia walked off. She grabbed her own phone and proceeded to send a text message. Alex appeared after a moment and sat down next to her, setting food and beverage items in the empty seat on the other side of her.

"Where did Malajia go?" Alex wondered, looking around.

Chasity ignored her as she continued to text on her phone.

Alex let out a sigh, then turned to face Chasity. "Look, can we just talk this out please?"

"I do not want to do this shit with you right now, Alex," Chasity ground out, still eyeing her phone.

"I know you don't, but I think that we *should*," Alex insisted. "You think Em wants us fighting right now? When she wakes up all she needs is positivity."

Chasity shot Alex a stern look. "Don't do that," she warned. "I can be positive for Em and ignore *your* stupid ass at the same time."

Alex put her hands up in surrender. "Fine." She turned around in her seat. Grabbing a soda and two snacks, Alex held them out in Chasity's direction. "I grabbed these for you," she informed.

"You wasted your money," Chasity sneered.

Alex sat the items back down, letting out a huff in the process. It was awkward silence for a while as Alex sipped her coffee and Chasity texted on her phone. "I'm sorry okay," Alex blurted out. "I really am."

"Wasting your breath like you wasted your money," Chasity sniped.

Alex shook her head as she took another sip of her coffee. She didn't care if Chasity didn't want to hear it; she was going to say what she needed to say. "I admit that I was wrong. From lying to you, to asking you to do something that you didn't want to do, to reacting how I did and to saying what I said...*all* of it." She looked back at Chasity who was ignoring her. "Are you listening to me?"

"No."

"God I am *apologizing* to you, doesn't that mean *anything*?" Alex stressed.

"No, it *doesn't*," Chasity hissed, glaring at her. "You apologizing to me for some shit that you obviously meant, is pointless."

"You really think I feel that way about you?" Alex asked, upset. "I was *angry* Chasity, we *all* say shit when we're angry. You called *me* a lonely bitter bitch."

"And I fuckin' *meant* it," Chasity argued.

Alex set her coffee on a stand next to her chair, adjusting her position in her seat. "Look, I know that my comment about your mothering is what really pissed you off—"

"Leave me *alone* Alex," Chasity warned.

Alex went to say something else, but Malajia walked up, interrupting them. "What did I miss?" Malajia asked, sitting in between the two of them.

"Chasity refused to accept my apology," Alex grunted.

"So what? It was probably half-assed anyway. Did you get the snacks?" Malajia dismissed, looking at Alex.

Alex frowned at Malajia, then handed her a pack of pretzels. "You're lucky I don't want to waste my money."

Ignoring Alex, Malajia opened the pack and took a pretzel out. She took a bite, looking at Chasity. "Did Alex get you snacks?"

"Yes, but her stubborn ass won't *take* them," Alex ground out before Chasity could answer.

"Chasity, you better *feed* that baby," Malajia said, immediately covering her mouth as both Chasity and Alex looked at her. There was a shocked look from Alex on one side, and an angered stare from Chasity on the other. "I *so* didn't mean to say that out loud."

"Chasity, you're pregnant?" Alex charged.

"Never, *never* will I tell you anything else," Chasity hissed at Malajia as she turned herself around in her seat.

"I'm *sorry*," Malajia insisted, taking another pretzel out of the bag. "Here, a peace offering. I know you're hungry."

Chasity smacked the pretzel from her hand. Malajia's mouth dropped open in shock as Chasity stood from her seat and walked off.

"*Ooh* you rude," Malajia said, as she went back to eating her pretzels.

Hearing muffled voices, Emily's eyes fluttered open. Her sight was blurry; she blinked a few times to focus. She tried to move, but the pain in her head and neck made her stop. Using only her eyes, she scanned the room. *Where am I?* she thought, not recognizing her surroundings. Confused and in pain, her eyes began filling with tears. Hearing a familiar voice in the distance, she called out.

"Will," she croaked.

Will, who was talking to a nurse, looked over. Seeing Emily's eyes open, he rushed over to her bedside. Grabbing her hand, he sat down next to her bed. "Hey you," he smiled down.

As the nurse walked over and checked her vitals, Emily panicked. "Where am I?" she asked.

Will grabbed a tissue from the box on the stand next to him and gently wiped the tears from her face. "You're in the hospital," he answered.

"How are you feeling Emily?" the nurse asked, shining a small light in her face. Emily squinted from the brightness. "I'm sorry, I was just checking your pupils."

"My head hurts," Emily whined.

"I can imagine, you banged your head pretty hard," the nurse informed.

Emily frowned slightly.

"How does your hand feel?" the nurse asked.

Emily looked at her bandaged hand. "It hurts."

"You cut your hand pretty badly, you needed stitches," she said, finishing up her check. "Your vitals look good Emily, I'm going to go grab the doctor so he can do a second check," she announced.

Will nodded at the nurse, before turning his attention back to Emily. He held her hand secure in his. "Your dad went—"

"I hit my head?" Emily asked.

Will nodded. "Yeah babe, you did," he answered. "How much do you remember?"

Emily glanced up at the ceiling for a moment as she tried to recall anything. "Right now, not much," she admitted.

"They said that you might be a little hazy at first but...I'm sure you'll remember soon." Will wanted her to remember; he *needed* her to. He hated what her sister had done and wanted Emily to just be done with Jazmine altogether.

Emily just nodded, then winced. "Ow," she whined.

"I know, try not to move too much, okay?" Will soothed. Emily just let out a sigh. "Your dad is here... Your brothers are on their way here with your mom."

"I don't want her coming in here," Emily ground out.

Will held his gaze on her. "Em, are you *sure*?" he asked.

"Yes," Emily confirmed. "I may not remember how I hit my head, but I *do* remember how my mother has been acting towards me, and I just don't want her around me right now."

Will nodded. "Whatever you want," he said. "I'll text your brothers and tell them."

Emily managed a slight nod.

"Your girls are here," Will informed.

Emily's eyes widened slightly. "Really?"

Will nodded. "Yep, as soon as I told them what happened, they made their way here." He smiled. With Emily's blood sister behaving the way that she was, Will was truly happy for the friendship that Emily shared with them.

Emily let out a sigh as the doctor walked back into the room.

Chapter 43

"I just got a text from Sidra, her plane landed," Malajia tiredly announced, rubbing her eyes with her hand.

"We know, we *all* got the same text in group chat," Chasity bristled, leaning her head back against the wall.

Alex sat up and stretched; she glanced at her watch. "It's after midnight," she announced.

"We *know*, we *all* see the clock on the goddamn wall in front of us," Chasity griped.

Alex leaned over and glanced at Malajia. "Should we attribute her nastiness to hormones?" she jeered.

Malajia leaned forward. "No, this is *normal* cranky her," she replied.

Chasity rolled her eyes.

"We haven't been given an update in over two hours," Alex complained. "I'm trying not to worry too much, but—" She looked up and saw Will approaching.

"Ladies, she's awake," he announced, happy.

The girls instantly jumped up. "Can we see her?" Alex asked.

"Is she okay?" Chasity followed up.

"Does she remember anything?" Malajia added.

"She's still a little foggy and she has some pain, but the doctors said that she'll be okay," Will informed. "They are going to keep her for another day or two, just to be on the safe side."

"Makes sense," Alex agreed, rubbing the back of her neck. "Can we see her?"

Will let out a long sigh. "Sorry…not tonight. They want her to rest and visiting hours were over at nine," he regretfully informed.

"Damn," Malajia muttered. "At least they didn't kick us out of the waiting room."

"Yeah," Will agreed. "She knows that you're here though… She wanted to see you but—"

"No, we understand," Alex jumped in. "We'll be back in the morning."

"Visiting hours start at seven," Will said.

Chasity rubbed the back of her neck "I'm gonna go find a hotel," she tiredly said.

"Shit, we better hope there's rooms available," Malajia pointed out, grabbing her purse. "We might be sleeping in the damn car."

"I'm sure that won't be necessary," Chasity put out, even toned.

"Can I bunk with you Malajia?" Alex asked, hopeful.

Malajia snickered. "I'm going where *she* goes," she teased, pointing to Chasity. "So you might be in the car alone sis…that's if you're allowed *in* it, 'cause she drove hers."

"Can I offer a suggestion?" Will interjected, grabbing their attention. They looked at him. He reached into his jeans pocket and pulled out a set of keys. "It's kind of a mess at the moment but…you can stay at Emily's place. I know she wouldn't mind."

Alex grabbed the keys from him. "We'll clean it up for her," she promised. "Thank you."

"Yeah, thanks," Malajia called after him as he walked away. "How many bedrooms does Emily have again?"

"One," Alex answered.

"Oh…Alex you on that floor bee," Malajia said. She snickered as Alex narrowed her eyes.

Alex, Chasity, and Malajia rounded the corner to approach Emily's apartment door and found Sidra standing there. Sidra looked over at them, smiling. She darted over, arms outstretched. The girls embraced in a group hug.

"You said she woke up?" Sidra asked once they parted.

Alex nodded. "Yeah," she answered. "They said that she's going to be okay."

Sidra placed a hand over her chest and let out a long sigh of relief. "You have *no* idea how my anxiety was on that flight."

"Oh, we can imagine," Malajia said as they made their way to Emily's door.

"That was nice of Will to give us the keys," Sidra commented, as Alex stuck the key in the door. When Sidra had landed, she'd turned her phone back on and received several messages, one being that they were staying at Emily's for the night.

"I hope Em got some food in here." Malajia yawned.

"You breathed all on my neck," Chasity complained, putting her hand on her neck.

"God, Alex hurry up so we can put her ass to sleep," Malajia griped, giving Chasity a nudge.

"I'm going as fast as I can," Alex assured, turning the key. She pushed the door open.

"Oh, Sidra, Chasity is pregnant," Malajia announced.

Sidra looked over at Chasity wide-eyed, as Chasity just shook her head. "Oh my God, really?" Sidra beamed as they walked into the dark apartment.

Alex felt around and flipped the light switch. They looked around; the couch and love seat had clearly been moved from their normal spot, judging by the grooves in the carpet, and some throw pillows were on the floor. Scanning the area further, they saw glass on the floor.

"Watch that glass ladies," Sidra warned, pointing.

Malajia shook her head at the shards, then focused her attention back on the couch. "Help me with this couch, somebody," she said.

Chasity walked over and put her hands on the other side.

"Wait, I don't think you should—"

"Alex, I'm not fuckin' handicapped, okay and I told you to stop talking to me." Chasity spat, helping Malajia move the couch back in place.

Alex put her hands up. "Sorry, God," she huffed, moving over to the love seat.

Sidra glanced at Malajia. "These two still fighting I see," she commented of Chasity and Alex.

"You think?" Malajia replied, sarcastic.

As Alex nudged the love seat back in place, Sidra moved over to where the glass was. Noticing the small dark stains on the floor, she frowned. "Is that blood?" she asked, horrified.

The girls walked over and looked down at the stain. "*Looks like it.*" Malajia sighed. "I swear to God, we need to find out *exactly* what the fuck happened up in here."

Even though they knew that Emily was going to recover from her injuries, it didn't make seeing the signs of her struggle any easier.

Sidra choked back tears. "I gotta try to get that out," she said, heading for the bathroom in search of cleaning supplies.

"I don't think blood can come out of the carpet Sid," Alex pointed out.

"I don't *care* Alex, I'm at least going to make it as light as possible," Sidra fussed. "She doesn't need to come back and see that."

"You're right," Alex agreed.

Sidra stepped into the bathroom and flicked the light switch. Seeing several toiletry items in the sink and on the floor, she shook her head. Grabbing several bottles of cleaning items and a sponge from under the sink, she returned to the living room. "I want to pick up that stuff in the bathroom, but I don't know if it's Emily's or Jazmine's."

Malajia looked at her. "If it's *Jazmine's* it's going in the fuckin' trash," she grunted.

"I know, that's why I want to be sure," Sidra replied, making her way over to the stain.

As Sidra started spraying a mixture of different cleaners on the spot, Alex carefully grabbed a few glass shards.

"Can someone please get me a trash bag to put this glass in?" Alex asked, glancing back at the girls.

Chasity paused from arranging throw pillows on the couch. "Yeah," she quietly said. After searching Emily's linen closet and the bathroom, Chasity made her way to the kitchen in search of the trash bags; she paused short of entering. Eyeing a cardboard box, and the glass and flowers strewn across the floor, Chasity frowned. "Come over here," she called to the other girls.

They immediately complied. "What's wrong?" Malajia

asked.

Chasity pointed to the mess.

Sidra walked over and peered inside the damaged box. "Oh my God!" she belted out.

"Are these Emily's wedding favors and bouquets that she made?" Malajia asked, looking for herself.

Sidra bent down and picked a discarded pink rose off the floor. "Yes," she confirmed, angry. "She was so happy when she finished them, she sent me a picture."

"What *happened* to them?" Alex charged.

Chasity folded her arms in frustration. "I'll give you *one* fuckin' guess," she fumed.

Alex's mouth dropped open. "Whoa, you think Jazmine destroyed this stuff?"

"You *don't* think Jazmine destroyed this shit?" Malajia questioned, gesturing to the mess with her hand.

Sidra tossed the flower on the nearby table. "I'm pissed the fuck off," she snapped. She put her face in her hands, feeling herself tear up again. "How can somebody be that goddamn evil towards their own *sister*?"

Alex reached out and put her hand on Sidra's arm, giving it a rub. "I know sweetie," she consoled, letting out a sigh. "Let's just finish cleaning up and get some rest."

Emily laid in her hospital bed, eyes closed. She tried desperately to sleep, but sleep wasn't happening. What *was* happening was Emily's recollection of the events that had landed her in the hospital the day before.

As both the conversation and fight with her sister filled her memories, Emily's eyes filled with tears. The feeling of them rolling down her cheeks forced her eyes open. She wiped her eyes with the back of her hand and slowly, painstakingly sat up in bed. Having hardly moved the night before, she was now feeling every bit of soreness in her body.

Emily carefully sat back against the pillows, then put her hands over her face as tears continued to spill. Alone in the room, she let herself cry out her frustrations, hurt, and pain.

Hearing a quick knock on the door and seeing it open, Emily sucked up her cries and wiped her face.

"Hey baby girl, I brought you some food," Mr. Harris smiled, holding up a fast-food bag.

Emily laid her head back as she tried to keep herself from tearing up again. "Thank you, but I'm not hungry," she muttered.

Mr. Harris sat down at her bedside, setting the bag on a small table. "I understand, but you should eat soon."

Emily looked at her hands. "I will," she mumbled.

Her father sat and looked at her. "How are you feeling this morning?" he wondered. Although he was calm now, the worry, panic, and anger that he had felt after receiving the phone call from Will was insurmountable.

Emily shook her head. "I'm okay," she downplayed.

Mr. Harris just sighed; he knew that wasn't true. "Your mother—"

"Daddy, with all due respect, I'm not changing my mind. I *don't* want to see her," Emily cut in.

"I wasn't going to persuade you otherwise," he assured, grabbing her un-bandaged hand. "You have every right to be upset after everything that she's putting you through." He let out a sigh. "Though she refuses to leave this state until you leave this hospital, she is honoring your wishes."

Emily shot him a questionable look.

"Yeah, she didn't take it well when I initially told her," Mr. Harris admitted. "But after a good hour of arguing with her, she relented."

Emily shook her head. Although it hurt not to have the comfort of her mother in her time of need, she was too angry to put her mother's behavior aside. As her father began taking the food out of the bag and setting it on the table, Emily let out a long sigh. "I remember what happened," she announced.

Mr. Harris looked at her, but didn't say anything.

Emily pushed herself back further in her bed. "I told her that she had to move out and—" she felt herself getting emotional again. "She'd been gone for days and I packed her stuff up because I was hoping that she had found somewhere else to stay. She was there when I got in from work and she

accused me of breaking something of hers which I *didn't*."
Tears spilled from her eyes. "We argued, and I told her that she
had to leave. She dismissed me as usual and I told her that I was
serious… Things got a little physical at first, then I went into
my room to call Will… I heard something breaking—" Emily
sniffled. "She took a hammer and broke all of my wedding
stuff… I mean, she was standing over my box, just smashing—
she was *breaking* my stuff, right in *front* of me."

Mr. Harris rubbed his face with his hand as he listened to
Emily's recount of events. Anger didn't even begin to describe
how he felt about his eldest daughter.

"I asked her why she did that and she looked at me and said
'why not?'" Emily recalled, bitter. "I just…I lost it and I threw
the hammer at her—I attacked her." She rubbed her injured
hand. "I wanted to hurt her as bad as she hurt me," she said,
voice cracking. "Last thing I remember is her pushing me and I
fell, then blacked out."

Mr. Harris rubbed Emily's arm as she started crying again.
"I hate her," Emily cried. "I *hate* her."
Her father pulled her into a hug and held her as she cried.

Jason poured milk into a small bowl of marshmallow
cereal, setting it on the kitchen table in front of Kayla. "Here
you go," he smiled.

Kayla picked up her spoon. "Thank you," she smiled back.
"Daddy, when is Mommy coming back?"

"Soon Cupcake," he replied. "She's visiting Aunt
Emily…You miss her?"

Kayla nodded as she began eating her cereal.

"Yeah, me too," Jason said, sitting down to his own bowl
of cereal. He took a bite and grimaced at the overly sweet taste.
"God, how did I ever eat this crap as a kid?" he commented.
Kayla laughed at him; he too chuckled after a moment. He
glanced at his daughter while she ate. He and Chasity had yet to
tell her that they were moving, or that she was going to be a big
sister. He wondered how she'd take the news. "You looking
forward to staying with Grandmom and Grandpop for a few
days while Mommy and I go out of town?"

Kayla smiled and nodded.

A knock on the door interrupted their conversation. Jason got up from the table and made his way over to answer it. He opened it; Mark was standing there with his children. "Hey man, what's up?"

Mark rubbed the back of his neck as he hesitated. "Umm…"

Jason frowned in concern. "Everything okay with you, bro?"

Mark let out a sigh and shook his head. "Not really," he admitted. "Can I talk to you?"

Jason moved aside to let them in. "Of course," he said as they stepped in.

Mark waved to Kayla. "Hey little mama," he smiled.

Kayla eagerly waved back. "Hi Uncle Mark." She then waved to the boys, who were all too happy to see her.

Mark looked at Jason. "My bad Jase, I wasn't trying to interrupt y'all time."

"Sit down man, it's fine," he assured. "Kay, you can go eat in your room okay."

"Really?" she beamed.

"Yeah…just don't tell Mommy," Jason joked.

Kayla grabbed her bowl and headed for the steps. "Mommy said it's bad to keep secrets."

Jason chuckled at her little voice. "She's right, you can tell her." He looked at the boys. "Boys, do you want a snack?"

Mark put a hand up as the boys went to accept. "No, they just had like *five* snacks. They're good." He looked at them. "Go take that game and go up with your cousin."

The boys, handheld game in hand, scurried up the steps after Kayla.

"Kayla, if they get out of line and start pulling out all your cat stuff, feel free to rough them up," Mark joked.

Jason chuckled again. "You might regret that. She may be sweet, but she is still her mother's child."

"Good, they *need* it," Mark replied. "They spilled cereal all over the damn couch earlier playing 'jump around hippos.'"

Jason looked confused. "What the hell—"

"Man I don't *know*, they just keep making up shit," Mark interrupted, rubbing his face.

Jason laughed as he headed for the kitchen. "You want anything to eat or drink?"

"Got any liquor?" Mark asked.

Jason looked at him, perplexed. "You want liquor at ten in the morning?"

"Don't ask me stupid questions dawg, just pour," Mark threw back, shaking his hand in Jason's direction.

Jason chuckled as he pulled a bottle of liquor from a cabinet and a glass. He set them both on the table as Mark sat down. "What's up?"

Mark poured himself a drink and took a sip. "I just feel like shit," he answered, letting out a sigh. "I'm not in a good headspace right now."

"Why?"

Mark hesitated for a moment. "I lost my job," he revealed.

Jason's eyes widened. "Are you serious?"

"Unfortunately," Mark confirmed. "Laid off man. Like two weeks ago... Feels like two *years*."

"Wow...I'm sorry to hear that," Jason sympathized. He remembered what it felt like when he'd thought he was going to lose his job. He couldn't imagine actually losing it. He felt terrible for Mark.

"Thanks," Mark sulked. "I've been applying for other auditing positions, but I haven't gotten any interviews yet."

"Don't beat yourself up, it's only been two weeks," Jason consoled.

"It's two weeks too *long* when you have a family," Mark pointed out, taking another sip of his drink.

"I get it, but finding a new job takes time."

Mark sighed. "Time, I don't have," he said. "We have bills... Oh and Malajia is going back to work."

"Yeah?" Jason asked.

Mark nodded. "Yep."

"You don't seem too happy about it," Jason observed, picking up on Mark's tone.

Mark rubbed his face with his hand. "It's not that I'm not happy about it," he clarified. "I know that's what she wants…apparently that's what she *been* wanting. She stayed home all that time because of me."

"I'm sure she understands why you wanted her to."

Mark shrugged slightly. "I just wanted to be the one to take care of my family like *my* father did and *her* father did."

"After my mom had Kyle, my father took care of the household too," Jason stated, folding his arms on the table. "But that's because that's what they agreed on as a couple. That doesn't mean that that's the way it's supposed to be nowadays. Especially if that's not what you *both* want."

Mark sighed again. "Look, I get it," he said. "I wasn't doing it to make it seem like I run anything—"

"You don't run that household," Jason joked.

Mark laughed. "Not even a *little* bit," he agreed, amused. The humor left his face. "I don't know… It doesn't help that now *she* has a job and I *don't*… Makes me feel like shit."

"Mark, you'll get *another* one."

Mark spun his glass around on the table. He shook his head. "Maybe," he sulked. "It also doesn't help that Mel's dad thinks I'm a goddamn loser."

Jason frowned. "Still?"

"*Still*," Mark vented. "You know he told Malajia that she was making a mistake by marrying me?"

Jason leaned back in his seat. "That's fucked up."

"Yeah, and she didn't even *tell* me that shit," Mark fussed. "I overheard it when I went to pick her up the other day. Had me smiling all in his old ass face and shit."

"You really expected her to tell you that?" Jason questioned.

"*Yeah*," Mark answered, annoyed. "Wouldn't *you* want to know?"

"I wouldn't *care*," Jason threw back. "You weren't marrying her *father*."

"You get what I'm saying, stop being a jackass," Mark fumed.

Jason put a hand up. "As someone who dealt with parent issues when it came to not liking who I was with, let me tell you, that you need to put your energy into your marriage," he advised. "Blaming Mel for her father's views isn't gonna help anything."

"I'm not *blaming* her," Mark argued.

"Okay fine, you have an *attitude* with her about it," Jason amended. "Lie and say you don't."

Mark rolled his eyes.

"Her father being an ass is not *her* fault," Jason pressed.

Mark sighed. "Yeah, I know… It just sucks."

"Sucked for Chaz too," Jason admitted. "My mom was on some bullshit while we were in college, but she eventually realized that in order to continue to have a good relationship with *me*, my mother needed to get over her issue with *Chasity*.. She *did* and all is well now."

"I don't see things being *all well* between me and her dad," Mark denied. "I'm a grown man and he *keeps* disrespecting me. I just wonder if my boys ever heard him talking shit about me. Would they believe it if they did?"

"To *hell* with him," Jason ground out. "To hell with what he *thinks*. His opinion doesn't matter. The *fact* is that you're not a loser. You are a good man, father, husband, son, and friend. He just needs to deal with the fact that you aren't going anywhere."

Mark nodded, but didn't say anything.

Jason gave Mark a quick pat on his arm. "Seriously bro, stop being so hard on yourself."

Mark took a deep breath. "I'll try," he replied. He took another sip of his drink. "Thanks for the talk Jase."

"Anytime."

"I know that we can get on y'all nerves sometimes, but I'm happy to be living around the corner from you two," Mark mentioned.

"Nah, y'all don't get on our nerves," Jason denied.

Mark shot Jason a knowing look.

Jason chuckled. "Okay when you knock on our door for breakfast at seven in the damn morning on a Sunday, it *does* get on our nerves," he admitted.

Mark laughed.

"No but…we're happy to be living around the corner from you guys too," Jason admitted. "It's a shame that that won't be the case soon."

Mark frowned. "What do you mean?"

Jason's eyes widened; he hadn't meant to say that last part out loud. "What?" he said.

"You said that you living around the corner from us won't be the case soon," Mark reminded. "You moving or something?"

Jason scratched his head, hesitating. "Umm...yeah."

Mark looked disappointed. "Really? Where?"

"Phoenix," Jason revealed. "...Arizona."

Mark's head jerked back. "Well shit," he said. "Why all the way out *there*?"

Jason rubbed his face. He wasn't sure if he wanted to share his new job news with Mark, who was clearly upset over losing *his*.

Mark, sensing his hesitation, fixed a stern gaze. "Jase, come on man," he pressed. "Why are y'all moving all the way out there?"

"I got a new job offer...and it's out there," Jason revealed finally. "We have to leave in February."

Mark stared at him. "Management position?"

"Yeah."

"Good salary?"

"*Hell* yeah," Jason confirmed.

"Moving allowance?" Mark asked.

"Yup."

"Chaz fighting you on it?"

"Not anymore," Jason replied.

Mark nodded slowly, then after a moment, extended his hand out. "Congratulations," he sincerely said, a warm smile. "I'm happy for you."

Jason shook his hand, smiling back. "Thank you."

Mark nodded. "Hell, we'll have a new place to visit," he said, leaning back in his seat. "*That* and California... Sidra is gonna kick our asses if we come see y'all and not her...and I'm pretty sure that Josh's happy ass will be running out there before we know it."

"Yeah, I can see that." Jason chuckled. "Listen, Mel doesn't know yet. Chaz is gonna tell her, just not sure when."

"I won't say anything," Mark promised. "Hell, she didn't tell *me* that y'all are about to have another kid."

"What the hell?" Jason frowned.

"Yeah, I overheard her talking to Chaz a few days ago," Mark admitted. "Congrats on that too."

Jason shook his head in amusement. "Thank you."

Mark took another sip of his drink and made a face. "Okay I can't take this liquor anymore, you got any food?" he asked, rubbing his stomach.

Jason chuckled. "You want some marshmallow cereal?"

"Hell yeah, that shit be hittin'," Mark replied, earning a laugh from Jason as he pushed the box of cereal in front of him.

Chapter 44

"Em, can't you ask them to give you something other than that nasty gelatin crap?" Sidra scoffed, picking up a container of the red jiggly food.

Emily chuckled a bit. "It can't be all *that* nasty, Chasity is tearing it up," she said, pointing to Chasity, who was eating another container of it.

"Mind your business Emily," Chasity sneered, taking another spoonful. After a long night, the girls were finally able to visit Emily in her hospital room that following morning.

"Her pregnant ass eats everything," Malajia said, peering in a cabinet.

Chasity rolled her eyes at Malajia as she continued eating.

Emily smiled at Chasity. "Aww, congratulations," she gushed.

"Thank you." Chasity made a face as she looked at the half empty gelatin cup. "This shit *is* nasty foreal."

Emily giggled.

Alex shook her head at Chasity, then glanced at Emily. "How long do you have to stay in here?" she asked.

Emily sighed as she leaned back against her pillows. "I'm being released tomorrow morning."

"Then we'll be in town until you get home," Sidra chimed in, adjusting her position in a chair.

"You girls don't have to do that," Emily said, playing with the fabric of her cover. "I know you have lives to get back to—"

"*You're* a *part* of our life, so we're staying," Alex insisted, grabbing Emily's hand.

"Ain't nobody tryna rush back to no damn Mark," Malajia griped. "Trust me, I don't mind being here."

Emily looked around at her friends. "Thank you, I really do appreciate you being here for me."

Sidra opened her mouth to speak, but was drowned out by the sound of rustling. She glanced over to Malajia, and saw her removing items from the cabinet. "What are you doing?" she frowned.

"Getting first aid shit," Malajia answered, without a qualm.

Sidra sucked her teeth as she watched Malajia pocket a handful of items. "Mel—girl put those back!"

"Yeah, don't be disrespectful," Alex jumped in, annoyed.

Malajia put her hand up. "Fuck that, I can take them," she argued back. "They wouldn't leave 'em in here if they didn't expect us to take them… I got two karate chopping boys, I need all the free medical shit I can get."

Sidra shook her head, then looked at Chasity. "Chasity, get your girl, please."

Chasity shook her head. "I agree with her. Mel, hand me some of those," she said, holding her hand out.

"*Really* Chasity?" Sidra sneered.

"Leave me alone," Chasity grunted as Malajia handed her several items. She put them in her purse. "When you have kids, you'll understand."

Sidra flagged her with her hand, then ran a hand over her hair.

Malajia walked over and sat down on the bed. She looked over at Emily's tray of food and reached for her juice. "Ooh, apple juice," she beamed.

Emily grabbed it and held it out of reach. "No, I *want* this."

Malajia slammed her hand on the bed. "Gimme the goddamn juice Emily!" she belted out.

"No, and stop yelling it's making my head hurt," Emily threw back.

Malajia put a hand up. "You're right, my bad," she apologized.

Alex shook her head. "So Em…what exactly happened? Based on how your place looked when we got there last night…it looked like a major struggle took place," she asked after a long moment. "I mean do you remember *anything*?"

"I remember *everything*," Emily cut in, somber. Emily watched her friends' expressive faces as she told them all that had happened, just as she had for both her father and Will. Their angered reactions were not a surprise.

"You should've stabbed that bitch," Chasity grunted.

"You ain't lyin'," Malajia chimed in, angry. "After all that her raggedy, broke, jealous ass put you through, she deserved *everything* that you did."

Sidra was so annoyed that she could hardly speak. "I swear—I can't even—"

"Okay everybody, calm down. We don't need anybody else ending up in here due to aneurysms," Alex calmly put in.

Emily slowly shook her head. "I mean she *stood* there, smirking at me like it was *fun* for her to see me so upset. Like it was *fun* for her to just destroy my stuff like that…after I tried to help her—" Emily pinched the bridge of her nose. "I am *so done* with her."

"Just know that I can get you legal representation if you need it," Sidra offered. "I know several great lawyers, I can have her crap put out ASAP."

"We didn't want to touch her shit, but we'll happily toss that garbage on the curb *today*," Malajia boasted.

"No, don't even worry about that. My father said he'll remove it," Emily informed.

"Is she going to be staying with your father?" Alex asked.

"No. He refuses to allow that," Emily answered. "I think he's done with her also." She folded her arms. "That's on her… She can suck an egg."

Malajia busted out laughing, as Chasity looked at Emily.

"I'm sorry, you said she can suck a *what?*" Chasity teased, putting a hand to her ear.

"She said an egg," Malajia howled. Even Sidra and Alex couldn't help but to laugh.

Emily winced as she tried not to laugh herself. "Please don't make me laugh, my head," she begged, putting a hand on her head.

"My bad Em," Malajia managed to get out as her laughter subsided.

"Of all things to suck…an egg," Chasity commented, earning a loud snicker from Malajia.

Sidra pointed at Chasity as she tried to keep from laughing again. "Chasity, stop it," she demanded.

"Sorry," Chasity chortled, putting a hand up.

Sidra looked at Emily. "You okay?" she asked, seeing Emily rub her temples.

Emily nodded.

Sidra let out a sigh. "So... What does your *mother* say about all this?" she asked, tone spiteful.

Emily looked at her. "I don't really care," she answered, honest. "I'm just tired." Tears began to well up again. "I'm supposed to be getting *married*. This is supposed to be the best time of my life, and my family is making it the *worst*... I keep thinking that I should just cancel everything, and Will and I should just go away."

"Is that what you really want?" Alex asked her.

Emily shook her head as tears flowed. "But what choice do I *have* when—"

The girls gathered around her. "You have a choice and your choice should be to keep your plans," Alex consoled, rubbing Emily's arm. "Those who *really* want to see you happy, will be at your wedding celebrating with you."

"Yeah, you know it's always a party with just *us*," Malajia jumped in.

Emily wiped her eyes again.

"Sweetie, the time of you handling everything on your own is over," Sidra said. "You have *us*, and you know that anything you need, we'll do... You don't have to worry about *anything*."

"I will cuss everybody the fuck out," Chasity said. "I don't even *need* a reason."

Emily managed a chuckle through her tears.

"Yeah, we got you sis," Malajia chimed in. "Now let's stop fussy bussin' around and get some *real* food in here," she proposed. "Anybody want pizza or burgers?"

Alex glanced around the room. "Pizza Shack anyone?"

"Girl if you don't—just *no*," Malajia scoffed.

"Yeah, I'll pass," Sidra added, examining her nails.

Alex looked at Emily. "Em?" she smiled.

"Alex, *two* people just said no," Malajia spat, annoyed.

Emily shook her head. "Honestly, I eat *enough* of it," she admitted.

Alex then looked at Chasity. "What about *you* Chaz?"

"Why do you insist on talking to me?" Chasity ground out. "I should *actually* hit you this time."

Malajia busted out laughing at the salty look on Alex's face. "You salty with that wack ass attempt to get her to talk to you," she goaded.

"Chasity, you're being ridiculous," Alex huffed.

Chasity didn't bother looking in Alex's direction, or saying another word. She just flipped her the finger.

Sidra shook her head.

Emily glanced back and forth between Chasity and Alex, surprised. "Wait, are you two fighting?"

"Yes Em, we *are* and *one* of us refuses to forgive the *other* one," Alex sneered, pushing her hair out of her face.

Chasity flipped her off again, this time pushing her hand closer in Alex's direction.

"What happened?" Emily wondered.

"*I'll* tell you later Em," Malajia said.

"How are *you* gonna tell her and it has nothing to *do* with you?" Alex hurled, pointing at Malajia.

"All right enough," Sidra cut in before Malajia could respond. "We're not here to upset Emily any more than she already is."

"Exactly *Alex*," Malajia emphasized.

Alex sucked her teeth as she flagged Malajia with her hand.

"So, what are we going to eat?" Malajia asked the girls as they moseyed down the hospital hall. After spending most of the day visiting with Emily, the girls were finally leaving the hospital.

"It doesn't matter as long as it's tacos," Chasity said.

Malajia looked at her. "So, it *has* to be tacos?" she jeered. "*We* don't get a choice?"

"*You* can go where you *want*, but I'm taking *my* car to get *tacos* so back the fuck off, bitch," Chasity snarled.

Malajia shook her head as Sidra laughed.

"Can I make a suggestion?" Alex chimed in.

"No, apparently we all have to eat tacos because of prego and her stupid cravings," Malajia sneered.

"No, I wasn't talking about food," Alex clarified. "We should do something nice for Em when she comes home."

"Way ahead of you Alex," Sidra said. "Chasity, do you mind if we make a stop on the way back to Emily's?"

"As long as I get food first, I don't care," Chasity agreed, folding her arms.

Alex opened her mouth to comment, but halted when she saw Jazmine standing by the information desk, speaking with someone.

"You've got to be kidding me," Sidra fussed.

"No, the hell she *didn't*," Malajia followed up.

Jazmine turned to head down the hallway only to be startled by the girls, mere feet away from her. They had halted their pace and if looks could kill, she'd be dead by now.

Jazmine had every intention of trying to avoid them, but she had no choice but to pass them in order to get to her destination. Slowly walking up to them, she couldn't help but feel on edge. The girls whom she deemed her baby sister's bodyguards were standing in front of her. She could only imagine what they were thinking, or what they would do.

The girls sized Jazmine up. Although they'd heard the details from Emily, Jazmine's black eye and bruised cheek confirmed that Emily had put up a good fight.

"Looks like *somebody* got tore the fuck up," Malajia taunted, glaring at Jazmine.

Jazmine rolled her eyes. "Look—"

"Shut up bitch, what the *fuck* are you doing here?!" Chasity snapped. The sudden burst of rage caused not only Jazmine to flinch, but the other girls as well.

"Well damn," Malajia muttered, amused as she placed her hand on her chest.

"I don't owe you—"

"She said shut the fuck up," Malajia barked, cutting Jazmine off. "I *know* you don't think you're going to see Emily. You got us *all* the way chopped."

Jazmine folded her arms and took a deep breath. "I don't

owe you any explanations, and you can't *stop* me from seeing her," she replied, calm.

The girls stared at her.

"See, she got me fucked up," Chasity said.

Malajia knew what was about to happen next; she put her arm out to stop Chasity, who was making a move in Jazmine's direction. "Baby, baby, baby," she quickly reminded.

"Malajia, take her outside," Alex urged, giving Malajia a nudge.

"I will," Malajia agreed. "After I snatch her ass."

Alex grabbed Malajia as she too went to lunge at Jazmine, though Jazmine was backing up. "No, no! You can't fight in the damn hospital are you crazy?"

"Alex, bushy brows got it coming," Malajia argued, smacking Alex's hand off of her.

"Sidra, will you help me talk some sense into them, please?" Alex begged, glancing at Sidra.

"Nope," Sidra refused, holding her glare on Jazmine as she stood with her arms folded.

Alex sucked her teeth as she looked back at Malajia and Chasity. "Go to the car, *both* of you," she commanded.

Both Chasity and Malajia shot Alex challenging looks.

"I'm serious, this is *not* how we're going to handle this. This is *not* what Emily needs from us," Alex argued.

Malajia sucked her teeth. She hated to admit it, but Alex had a valid point. "Damn it, I *hate* when she makes sense," she grumbled. She grabbed Chasity's arm. "Come on."

"I'm not fuckin' *moving* until she leaves this goddamn hospital," Chasity refused.

"Yes, you *are,* or I'm calling Jason to tell him that you're trying to fight," Malajia warned.

Chasity gritted her teeth, but knew it was in her baby's best interest to comply. The longer she stood there, the more she was inclined to attack. Chasity looked at Alex and Sidra. "Don't let her—"

Alex looked back at her. "We *won't,*" she promised.

"Come on," Malajia urged, giving Chasity's arm a tug.

Alex watched as Malajia and Chasity walked off.

"Are you done?" Jazmine sneered. "Or are you going to

continue to threaten me in the middle of the hospital?"

Alex turned to Sidra, then glanced down at Sidra's fist; it was balled up tight. "You wanna fight too?" she asked Sidra.

"Yup," Sidra confirmed, tone eerily calm.

Alex gave her a gentle nudge. "Okay, you go to the car too," she ordered.

"No, I can control myself for *now*," Sidra refused. She took a deep breath. "Jazmine, let us make this clear to you. You're *not* going into that room. Emily doesn't want to see you and frankly, we feel that you're a threat to her."

Jazmine sucked her teeth as she made a move to go around them. "Please," she grumbled.

"Jazmine, we're serious," Alex fumed, as she and Sidra blocked her path. "Please don't force our hand."

"You bitches want me to cause a scene? Is that what you want?" Jazmine ranted, frustrated. "Just let me the fuck pass."

"The only *bitch* here is *your* bum ass," Sidra threw back, taking out her cell phone. "And since you want to cause a scene, let me grant your wish by calling the police."

"And say what?" Jazmine challenged. "You're the ones who are harassing *me*."

Sidra smirked. "Well, we're within good reason. You see the person that you viciously assaulted and left critically injured is lying in a hospital bed, and has expressed fear that you'd come to cause her more harm, and here you are."

Jazmine's eyes widened. "I *just* want to see her to see if she's okay."

Sidra shook her head. "No, I like *my* explanation better," she taunted, signaling for a security guard who was standing off to the side observing.

"Jazmine, Emily's well-being is no longer your concern. Not that it ever *was*," Alex chimed in, folding her arms. "You stay away from her."

Jazmine glanced over at the guard and proceeded to back away, as he began to walk over.

"Leave willingly or be arrested," Sidra spat.

Jazmine shook her head. "Fuck you both," she seethed, turning and hurrying off.

Alex followed her progress down the hall and on to the

elevator. She looked at Sidra, who was signaling to the guard that everything was okay. "Sid, you are vicious," Alex commented, impressed. "Honey, you are *definitely* meant to be a lawyer."

"Yeah…I know," Sidra agreed.

Josh removed several bags of frozen items from a plastic grocery bag. "I keep telling Mom that she doesn't have to send food over here," he said to Sarah. She was sitting at his kitchen table, sipping on a cup of tea.

"You know how she is. She always over shops for herself, so she gives us the extras," Sarah explained.

Josh held up a bag of frozen vegetables. "Does it always have to be extra *peas*?" he wondered.

Sarah nearly choked on her tea as she laughed. "Yeah, I don't know what's up with all those bags of peas."

Josh shook his head as he put the items in the freezer.

As Josh moved around the kitchen, putting items away, Sarah watched him. "So how is everything going?" she asked. "And before you start talking about how good the shop is doing, keep in mind that I work there so I already know."

Josh chuckled a bit.

"You know I'm referring to your relationship with my favorite soon-to-be sister-in-law," Sarah clarified.

Josh laughed a little. "We're not engaged yet."

"I know, but don't act like you haven't been thinking about it," she threw back, removing the tea bag from her cup.

"Of *course* I've been, but that doesn't count 'cause I wanted to marry her since high school," he pointed out.

Sarah shot him a knowing look.

"We *just* became a couple," he explained. "I think we need to be *that* for a minute before you start planning a wedding."

Sarah put her hands up. "Fair enough," she relented. "So…how is everything *going*?"

"So far so good," Josh replied, sitting down at the table. "We talk every day, video chat…you know, doing what we *can* do while living so far apart."

Sarah gave a nod as she took another sip of her tea. "Yeah,

I know the distance thing is going to be tough," she sympathized. "Especially since, like you said, you *just* became a couple." She set her cup down. "I don't mean to sound like a downer, because you know that I'm rooting for this wedding and my future nieces and nephews—"

Josh chuckled.

"But how are you going to spend any real time together?" she wondered. "You both have careers, so it's not like you can travel that often."

"I know…but we'll make it work," Josh insisted. "I plan on going out there in the next week or so to see her."

Sarah smiled. "That's good," she approved.

Josh let out a sigh as Sarah continued to sip her tea. He didn't want to admit it, but despite what he'd said, and what he'd told Sidra when they first became official, Josh wasn't okay with the long-distance thing. It wasn't that he felt like their relationship wouldn't last; he just hated being that far apart from Sidra. Not seeing her every day was eating at him.

He looked up at Sarah. "I think it's time that I start giving you more responsibility at the shop."

Sarah was taken aback. "How did we go from talking about your relationship to the shop?" she asked, confused.

"The thought just popped in my head," Josh explained.

Sarah gave him a confused look. "I don't mind taking on new stuff," she said. "But can I ask why? I mean, am I not doing enough *now*?"

Josh's eyes widened. "No, that's not what I'm saying," he assured. "You're doing plenty, trust me I couldn't run it *without* you… I just feel like it's time that I started passing more on to you because I know you can handle it."

Sarah shrugged. "Okay then," she relented.

Josh ran a hand over his head. "Damn, I'm sorry," he said after a moment.

"For what?"

"For making you think you were slacking at work." After all the work that Sarah had done over the years, including maintaining her sobriety, he didn't want to make her feel bad.

Sarah reached over and put her hand on Josh's arm, giggling in the process. "It's okay JJ," she assured. "You never made me feel that way, I appreciate everything you've done for me."

Josh smiled as he patted her hand. "Come on, you don't have to do that," he said. "You've earned it."

Sarah smiled; she couldn't have been happier. After everything that she had put her brother through growing up, she was happy that she had not only earned back his love, and trust, but she'd earned the respect. "See, you're gonna make me sit up in here and make you dinner."

"As long as it doesn't include peas, I'm cool with it," Josh joked.

Sarah busted out laughing.

Chapter 45

Will jumped out of the car and hurried over to the passenger side. He pulled open the door and gently took hold of Emily's arm, helping her out of the car. "You okay?" he asked.

Emily stood against the car, looking at him. "Yes." She smiled slightly. "You didn't have to help me out of the car. I'm perfectly mobile."

"Sure, I did." Will countered, grabbing her overnight bag from the back seat. "Be prepared to be waited on hand and foot." He stood in front of her. "You might have been able to convince your family to head back now that you're out of the hospital, but you can't get rid of *me* that easily."

Emily grabbed his chin with her hand. "No, I suppose I *can't*," she agreed.

He leaned in and gave her a quick kiss on the lips, before taking her hand and leading her into the apartment complex.

Once they stepped out of the elevator, they headed for Emily's door. "You sure you don't want to stay up at my place?" Will asked her.

Emily shook her head. "No, I'm fine being here for tonight," she answered. "The girls are here until tomorrow. I just want to spend time with them *outside* of the hospital."

Will gave a slight nod as he reached into his pocket for her spare key. "Whatever you want babe."

Approaching Emily's apartment door, they heard muffled sounds coming from inside.

Will frowned in concern. "Are they arguing?" he asked, sticking the key in the door.

"Wouldn't be the first time," Emily said both unfazed and amused. Once the door opened, both she and Will stepped in.

Alex, Chasity, and Malajia were sitting in the middle of the living room floor, doing something that Emily couldn't make out.

"Chasity, I'm sick of your shit," Malajia wailed. "You're done! Give it here."

"Leave me *alone*, Malajia," Chasity hurled back.

"What's going on?" Emily managed to ask over the noise. She was careful not to raise her voice too much for her head was still sore.

The girls stopped bickering and looked at her. "Hey Em, you're home," Alex beamed.

Malajia made a face at Alex. "Way to state the obvious," she sneered.

Alex sucked her teeth as she flagged Malajia.

Emily shook her head, then turned to Will. "You can go ahead, I'm fine."

Will set her bag on the couch. "Okay, I'm heading to the store, you need anything?"

"We went food shopping for her Will, so save your money." Alex smiled. "I mean, unless you still *want* to get her more stuff."

Emily shot Alex a wide-eyed glance. "Really?"

"Of course," Alex confirmed with a nod.

Will softly tapped Emily's arm, giving her a kiss on the cheek. "I'll check on you a little later," he said.

Emily nodded as she headed over to the couch.

"Thank you for everything, ladies," Will said to the girls.

"No thanks needed homie," Malajia replied, waving at him.

Emily carefully sat down on the couch, as Will walked out of the apartment, shutting the door behind him. She glanced around the apartment. "Thank you for cleaning," she said, solemn. "Not going to lie, I was afraid to see what this place looked like after everything."

"It looked like a crime scene, but with less blood," Chasity muttered, fussing with something in her hand.

Emily sighed. "Yeah." Zoning her focus on the living room, Emily saw a large white sheet in the middle of the floor, covered with bags of colored sand, small mason jars, glue guns, flowers, ribbon, containers of glitter and jewels. Emily held a quizzical look on her face. "You girls decided to do arts and crafts or something?"

"*Some* of us are doing arts and crafts, and *others* are

fucking shit up," Malajia jeered.

Chasity cut her eye at Malajia, but didn't say anything as Alex once again sucked her teeth.

"Sweetie, we're redoing your wedding favors," Alex corrected, a smile on her face.

Emily sat there with her mouth open. "You what?" she put a hand on her chest, feeling herself well up with emotion. "Oh my God."

Malajia glanced over, seeing tears fill Emily's eyes. "Come on with all that mushy shit," she joked.

"I appreciate you girls so much," Emily sniffled, wiping her eyes.

"We told you that we got you," Malajia said, leaning over and giving Emily's leg a pat. "We were *hoping* to have this done by the time you got home, but *Chasity's* non-artistic ass is prolonging shit," she griped.

"Fuck off Malajia, I'm doing the best I can," Chasity argued.

Malajia snapped her head towards Chasity and pointed at her. "You're supposed to swirl the goddamn sand to make a design. Not just dump it in there," she barked. "You saw the picture of the one that Emily did. The white sand is *swirled* in the tan sand. Get your shit together."

Chasity felt her temper rise each time Malajia snapped at her. "Leave me *alone*, I said."

Alex shot a glance Emily's way, shaking her head in the process. "*Now* I can see why you didn't ask us to help you before," she joked.

"Shut up Alex, 'cause the bouquet you got over there looks sorry. Nobody's carrying that, bullshit." Malajia charged.

Emily looked around. "Where's Sidra?" she asked.

"In your room on the phone," Alex answered. "Malajia's mouth was disturbing her call."

Malajia sucked her teeth, "I wasn't even that loud," she bit out. Seeing Chasity pour more sand into her jar, Malajia slammed her hand on the floor. "Bitch—I said pour and swirl!"

Fed up with Malajia's nit-picking and yelling, Chasity quickly picked up one of the unopened bags of sand and was getting ready to throw it at Malajia. But Alex lunged forward first, practically rolling over the supplies to grab Chasity's hand.

"No, that's the last bag of white sand. Can't risk it breaking," Alex said, taking the bag from Chasity's grip.

Chasity nudged Alex's hand away from her.

"Fuck the sand, what about my *eyes* had it bust on my face?" Malajia fussed, pointing to herself.

"You would've *deserved* that, leave her alone," Alex dismissed, moving back to her space. "You've been picking on her all day."

"I do *not* need you to defend me," Chasity snapped at Alex.

Alex tossed her hands up in the air in frustration. "I can't talk to you, and I can't stick up for you, got it," she huffed.

Emily adjusted her position on the couch. "Please don't argue over favors," she softly said. "Here, let me help—"

"No, you sit there and relax," Alex ordered.

"Okay," Emily relented, sitting back against the couch cushions. "Can I make a suggestion though?"

"Of course," Alex answered.

"To make the designs in the sand, use a popsicle stick to swirl it," Emily advised.

Chasity looked over at Malajia, who was staring back at her with a silly expression. "Bitch, now say sorry," she demanded.

"For *what*?!" Malajia exclaimed.

"For getting on my goddamn nerves about my sand art," Chasity fussed, pointing at her. "You kept criticizing me, making me feel like I was messing shit up, when I really *wasn't*."

Malajia sat there dumbfounded as Chasity continued to air out her frustration. What confused her even more was the fact that Chasity's eyes started filling with tears. "Are you kidding me right now?!" Malajia belted out.

Emily's mouth opened. "Chasity, are you crying?" she asked, full of sympathy.

"I can't *do* this art shit," Chasity ranted, slamming her sand filled jar on the floor. She wiped her eyes with the sleeve of her shirt. "I was just trying to help, and she keeps fuckin' yelling at me."

Emily reached out and touched Chasity's shoulder. "Aww. Malajia that's terrible," she scolded.

Malajia sat there with her mouth open, as Chastity stood up from the floor.

"I don't wanna do anymore," Chasity sniffled, heading for the bathroom.

Upon the door shutting, Malajia looked around. "Y'all *know* I didn't hurt that girl's feelings," she said. "Those are hormone tears."

"Pregnant or not, you *were* being hard on her," Alex chided, reaching for the glue gun. "She said when we started that she wasn't good at stuff like this."

Malajia tossed her hands in the air. "Oh come on, I—" Her words were cut off when Sidra walked out of the bedroom.

Emily looked over and went to stand up.

"No, no, sit," Sidra said, hurrying over and giving Emily a long hug. "Glad to see you out of that hospital bed, sweetie."

"Glad to be *out* of it," Emily agreed.

Sidra looked over at the craft process on the floor. "How's it going in here?"

Alex pointed to Malajia. "Malajia made Chasity cry," she told.

"Oh my God," Malajia huffed, putting her hand over her face, as Sidra shot Malajia a glare. "Y'all *know* she's not that sensitive, it was the *hormones*," she defended.

Sidra shook her head at Malajia; there was no point arguing with her. She looked at Emily and smiled. "We'll have these all finished tonight," Sidra promised, moving some of Emily's hair behind her shoulder.

Emily smiled a grateful smile.

Sidra looked down at her phone. "Oh and I took care of the RSVP's that you were still waiting on," she said.

Emily looked surprised. "Are you serious?"

Sidra nodded. "I've been calling people all day," she revealed, showing Emily the call log in her phone.

Emily gave Sidra a hug. "Thank you."

"No thanks needed sweetie," Sidra said. "My planner hat is on and I'm whipping everybody and everything into shape."

"Code for irking the shit out of people," Malajia grunted, carefully placing seashells in her sand-filled jar. "You should've seen how she was acting in the craft store yesterday."

Sidra just shrugged as Chasity walked out of the bathroom.

"You all done, crybaby?" Malajia mocked.

Chasity flipped Malajia off as she went back and sat down in her spot on the floor. Emily leaned over and hugged her from behind. "I appreciate your help," she consoled.

Chasity patted Emily's hand. "I know," she replied, tone low.

Sidra sat on the floor and reached for a few faux flowers. She paused when she saw Alex wrapping ribbon around a bouquet. "Alex, whose bouquet is that?"

Alex looked up, perplexed. "Umm, a bridesmaid's...*mine*, I guess."

Sidra pinched the bridge of her nose and sighed. "Bridesmaid bouquets have white roses in the middle with a few pink roses on the sides," she said. "What *you* have there is all white and they're not even bunched together right."

Alex looked down at the bouquet. "It's not that bad," she argued. She glanced up at Emily. "Em, what do *you* think?"

"Umm..." Emily's eyes shifted. "Good effort," she pacified.

Malajia busted out laughing at the salty look on Alex's face. "She spent all that time on that one silly ass bouquet," she teased. "Ol' scarce ass, leaning bouquet and shit."

Sidra, Chasity, and Emily couldn't help but snicker. Alex, not the least bit amused, made a face and snatched the ribbon off to start again.

Emily reached for a slice of pizza and took a bite. "I swear, as many times as I've eaten this, I can honestly say it's good pizza," she said between chews. "Or is it just me?"

"It's just you," Malajia jeered, taking a bite of her pizza. "This Shack pizza still taste like grease."

Alex narrowed her eyes as she paused mid-bite. "And yet your greedy butt is on your third slice," she observed.

With the wedding projects finished up, the girls were now

relaxing in Emily's living room, eating take-out food and talking.

Malajia let out a laugh. "I'm hungry," she admitted. "Hell, you *kept* bringing it the hell up, so we let you get it to shut you up."

Alex looked shocked as she chewed her pizza. "*You* mentioned it," she corrected, earning a snicker from Emily and Sidra. "*You're* the one who said, 'we might as well go ahead and get that Shack pizza'."

Malajia had a silly look on her face. "Why you always gotta bring up shit that's irrelevant?" she spat. "That's why you and Chaz are beefing *now*."

"Leave me out of this please," Chasity calmly said from the love seat.

Alex slammed her hand on the floor. "How is it irrelevant?" she fussed.

"Hey okay, stop it you two," Sidra cut in, bringing her glass of wine to her lips. "Malajia, stop being an ass."

"She *can't*, it's the one thing that she's *good* at," Alex ground out; Sidra nearly choked on the liquid in her mouth as she tried not to laugh.

"Boooo, with that weak ass comeback," Malajia jeered, unfazed.

Sidra shook her head at the banter, then grabbed a bag from the coffee table. "Where are the chocolate chip cookies?" she wondered.

"Chasity ate them," Malajia told.

Chasity looked up from her food and sucked her teeth. "Why do y'all keep treating me like some greedy bitch that eats up all the goddamn food?" she griped, annoyed. Her reaction earned laughter from the girls.

"So, did you eat them or not?" Sidra teased.

Chasity glared at Sidra. "Make me slap those buttons off that blouse," she reacted. Sidra shook her head in amusement. "No, I *didn't* eat them."

"Yeah, she's right," Malajia admitted, adjusting her position on the floor. "I fucked them things up when y'all were getting plates and shit."

Annoyed, Alex tossed her arms in the air. "Damn it

Malajia, you ate the *entire* bag?" she huffed.

"Do you *see* anymore?" Malajia mocked.

Alex sucked her teeth. "You sure *you're* not pregnant?" she asked Malajia.

"Hell *yeah* I'm sure," Malajia replied, confident. "My birth control is on point."

Sidra balled up the empty bag and set it on the coffee table. "Speaking of birth control," she began. "I've been thinking and I don't see myself taking any."

"Shit, whether it's a pill, a shot, an IUD, I don't give a good goddamn. As long as it prevents Mark's twin holding sperms from attacking my goddamn egg," Malajia jeered.

Sidra let out a laugh. "No *seriously*, I've been researching side effects and I'd just rather not," she said. "I guess it's the nitpicker in me."

"Sticking with only condoms, huh?" Malajia teased. She chuckled. "Yeah, you'll see how long that lasts… One good drunk night and it's *oops*."

Sidra made a face at Malajia. "I don't even *get* drunk," she countered.

"Okay, we'll revisit this in a year," Malajia predicted, pointing a piece of crust Sidra's way.

Sidra waved a dismissive hand Malajia's way, taking another sip of her wine.

Alex put her hand up. "Sidra, I still…*still* can't believe that you and Josh are actually together," she said.

"Me *either* sometimes," Sidra admitted, amused. "But we are… I mean, the distance is hard but we're making it work the best we can." She ran a hand over her hair, moving it over her shoulder. "To be honest though… This is one of many times that I regret moving."

"Sidra, you shouldn't do that to yourself," Chasity said. "You know that you can't go back and change anything. You can only go forward."

"Yeah Sid, and think about it. Everything that happened, brought you two where you guys are now," Emily added, giving Sidra's arm a rub.

Sidra shook her head. "I hear you ladies, I do but…" she sighed.

"I may bitch about not seeing you often, but ain't shit for you in Delaware." Malajia jumped in, adjusting her position on the floor. "I might not have agreed with you going to California at *first* because of your cowardly ass reasons and all, but I'm proud of you for taking a leap and building your life out there."

Sidra side-eyed Malajia. "Thank you...despite that unnecessary comment."

"Nothing unnecessary about stating facts," Malajia maintained, unfazed.

Sidra rolled her eyes.

Alex took a few sips of her drink, then cleared her throat. "Sid, I agree with Mel, you should definitely stay out there," she said. "Think of all of the career opportunities out there. I'm sure the demand for lawyers are—"

"Sidra has made it perfectly clear that she isn't a lawyer and ain't trying to be, so I don't even know why you're using that argument to keep her ass there," Malajia jeered.

Chasity flashed a scowl Malajia's way. She already knew about Sidra's insecurities when it came to moving forward in her career, and Malajia's criticisms would only make Sidra feel worse. "Malajia—I should've glued your damn mouth shut when I had that glue gun earlier," she spat.

Malajia snickered.

Sidra narrowed her eyes at Malajia. "You're just determined to keep up with your rude commentary, huh?" she bit out. When Malajia shrugged yet again, Sidra sucked her teeth. "Anyway, I never said that I was *never* going to be a lawyer... As a matter of fact, after some reflecting..." she glanced at Chasity, winking at her. "And talking with someone whose opinion and perspective I value."

Chasity smiled slightly.

Sidra took a deep breath as she turned her attention back to the whole group. "...I think I'm ready to advance in my career," she revealed.

Malajia smiled, putting a hand over her chest. "Awww, you value my opinion?" she gushed.

"No," Sidra jeered.

Alex giggled at the salty look on Malajia's face. "Sidra, I'm so happy to hear that," she praised. "I told you, you were meant to do this."

"Thanks," Sidra replied. She swirled the remaining liquid around in her glass. "Which brings me to a bit of a dilemma... If I decide to stay in California, there are a few firms that I have my eyes on, and one of them is James's firm."

"Really?" Alex asked.

Sidra nodded. "James's firm is one of the top firms in the city." she replied. "When I interned there, I was amazed at how much clientele they had. Excellent reputation, great benefits, growth opportunities, they're willing to mentor and—in all honesty I regret not taking that position they offered." She tossed a hand up in the air. "Hindsight, right?"

"It sounds like a great choice, and you seem to have your mind made up about applying," Alex mentioned. "What exactly is the dilemma?"

Sidra looked down at the contents in her glass, but hesitated to speak.

Malajia raised a hand. "I think I know," she said. "It's Josh, isn't it?" Sidra looked at her, nodding.

Alex frowned at Malajia. "What does Josh have to do with where she works?" she sneered.

"Because James is Sidra's ex," Malajia pointed out.

Alex jerked her head back. "*And?*" she scoffed. "What? Is she supposed to base her decisions around what *Josh* feels? He doesn't control what she does, or who she works for."

Malajia rolled her eyes. "Alex, nobody said that shit—" She then flagged Alex with her hand. "Sid, ignore Captain 'No Man's' judgmental ass questions."

"Please, me not having a man has nothing to do with anything," Alex snarled. "I have a right to question why my friend is apprehensive about working where she wants."

Sidra put a hand up. "I get what you're saying Alex, I do, and I can appreciate your point of view," she said. "You're right, I shouldn't worry about what Josh thinks about where I work, but because of who I'd be working *with*, I *do*."

"Sidra, you haven't been with James since *college*," Alex pointed out. "The man is married with a child now."

"As if being married and having a child stops some dudes from hitting on you," Malajia chortled. "Or are you *that* naïve?"

Alex pointed a warning finger at Malajia. "You know what—"

"Malajia, you may be right about *some* guys, but I honestly don't have anything to worry about with James. He's *been* over me for a long time, and is madly in love with his wife who has become a friend of mine," Sidra cut in. "I just wonder if Josh still feels some kind of way towards James."

Chasity squinted her eyes at Sidra. "You really think Josh is *that* immature?"

"No Chasity, I *don't*," Sidra answered. "But…I don't know, do you think it would be disrespectful if I *did*?"

Chasity let out a sigh. "*I* don't think so. If you had taken the job initially, then you'd already be working there and Josh would just have to deal with it, even if he did have an issue."

Sidra nodded slowly. "This is true."

Chasity adjusted her position in her seat. "Besides, like someone just said, you and James *been* over," she followed up. "But, given that you and Josh are in a relationship and because you're even *questioning* it, I think that you should just talk to Josh about it. Even if it's only to give him a heads up."

Alex sucked her teeth. "Now I'm *someone*?" she directly at Chasity.

Chasity let out a huff. "Sorry Sidra, I meant like an *asshole* said," she amended, looking at Sidra.

Sidra put her hand over her face to conceal her chuckle, as Malajia busted out laughing.

Alex just rolled her eyes.

"No, but you're right, I'll have a conversation with him about it," Sidra promised.

"*Still* think it doesn't matter either way," Alex stood firm. "Would *you* be jealous if he worked with *December*?"

"Yeah, probably," Sidra admitted.

"Well damn," Alex reacted. "At least you're honest."

Sidra shrugged, nonchalant as she sipped the rest of her drink.

Alex took a deep breath after a moment of silence. "So…" she began, hesitant. "I reached out to Eric." She pushed some of her hair from her face. "A few times actually and…he has yet to respond."

Chasity rolled her eyes. "Serves your ass right," she muttered under her breath.

"You said it serves her right Chasity? I know that's right," Malajia blurted out.

Chasity sat up in her seat, shocked. "How in the entire *hell* did you hear that?" she barked. "I'm not even sitting next to you."

"I have a nosey person's hearing," Malajia laughed. "Like Alex didn't think I heard her bust her ass earlier while she was in the kitchen, but I heard it."

Alex let out a gasp as laughter resonated around her.

"Yeah, we *all* kinda heard it," Emily hesitantly put out.

"That's not— I moved a chair while I was looking—"

"Alex, stop lying. It *happens*, just own your fart!" Malajia interrupted, loud.

Annoyed, Alex grabbed a throw pillow that she was leaning on and threw it in Malajia's direction. Laughing, Malajia ducked, letting the pillow hit the wall behind her.

"Anyway," Alex began, still irritated. "Yes, I didn't exactly handle things well with Eric I know, but *he's* the one who said that when I get my shit together that I should reach out to him, and now he's not responding."

"And you're *shocked* by that shit?" Chasity snapped.

Alex looked at her. "Oh *now* you're talking to me?" she spat.

"You're an idiot," Chasity hissed, ignoring Alex's question. "You really think that after you practically spat on that man for having a child, that you can contact him just because you're feeling lonely or *horny* and expect him to answer?" She gave Alex a look of disgust. "You're full of shit."

Alex narrowed her eyes at her. "Do you get satisfaction from being such a bitch?" she fumed.

"Ouch," Chasity mocked. "Fuck you."

"No, thank you," Alex threw back.

"*Somebody* needs to," Malajia muttered, amused, earning a glare from Alex.

"Please you two, stop arguing," Emily cut in, putting her hands up. "It's giving me anxiety."

"Sorry Em," Alex replied the same time that Chasity said,

"Fine."

"I know you two are mad at each other right now, but I just want my last night with my *real* sisters to be fight free," Emily stressed.

"We understand," Sidra said, rubbing Emily's arm.

Emily offered a slight smile.

Malajia sat up and put her arms around her knees. "*Speaking* of sisters…*your fake ass* one showed up at the hospital yesterday," she said.

Emily's eyes widened in shock. "She *what*?"

"Malajia, I thought we said we weren't going to tell her just yet?" Alex directed at Malajia.

"Please, nobody agreed to that. Emily had a right to know," Malajia threw back. Alex threw her hands up in surrender.

Sidra looked at Emily. "It's true, she was coming in as we were leaving," she filled in. "She didn't tell anybody?"

"Nobody is dealing with Jazmine right now, including my *mother* so I've heard," Emily spat, bitter. "What could she *possibly* want?"

"She was talking some mess about coming to check on you," Malajia said. "And she almost got her ass beat."

Emily let out a loud sigh. "Well, she never made it to my room obviously."

"Because I threatened to call the police on her if she went near you," Sidra informed.

Emily looked at her. "Good," she approved, angry. "If I never see her again, it'll be just fine with me."

"You want to file a restraining order?" Sidra asked. "Press charges?"

Emily shook her head. "She's not even worth the time and energy it'll take to do that," she said. "Her stuff is out of my apartment and she is out of my life so… I'm fine now."

"After I drop this kid, you want me to beat her ass?" Chasity offered.

Emily couldn't help but chuckle. "*Maybe*, I'll let you know," she replied.

"Shiiiiit, from the looks of her face, Emily did a good job her *damn* self," Malajia praised.

Emily shook her head. "I'm far from a fighter," she sulked.

"You don't have to be a *fighter* to whoop somebody's ass," Malajia pointed out.

"All facts," Chasity agreed, amusement in her voice. "Y'all remember how hard *Sidra* fought freshman year."

"And I'd do it *again*," Sidra chuckled, grabbing the wine bottle from the coffee table and filling her glass halfway. "Nobody jumps me and gets away with it." She tilted her glass at the girls. "Still love y'all for having my back." She took a sip from her glass. "I mean, getting arrested and nearly getting kicked out of school, because you all cared enough about me to actually get revenge...that's real friendship."

"And I'd do it again," Chasity said.

"In a goddamn heartbeat," Malajia followed up.

Alex nodded in agreement.

Chapter 46

Chasity unlocked her front door and pushed it open.

"Mommy!" Kayla exclaimed, running towards her.

Dropping her overnight bag to the floor, Chasity smiled as she bent down and welcomed her daughter's hug. "Hi, baby." Lifting her daughter in her arms, Chasity stood up as Jason approached. She smiled at him. "Hey."

Jason grinned, "Hi." He leaned in and gave her a kiss on the lips, wrapping his strong arms around his family. "How's Emily feeling?" he asked, parting from the embrace.

Chasity sat Kayla down on the loveseat. "She's feeling better," she answered, stretching. With Emily settled in at home, the girls had made their way back home early Sunday afternoon.

"Good…that was scary," he commented, rubbing the back of his neck.

"Tell me about it," Chasity agreed, walking to the kitchen table. As she went to sit down, Kayla ran over to her.

"You wanna hear about me and Daddy's trip to the zoo yesterday?" she asked.

"Sure," Chasity replied, tired. She sat and listened as an animated Kayla told every single detail of her zoo adventure.

Once she ran upstairs to retrieve a drawing that she had made, Chasity looked over at Jason; he had his hand over his face, laughing. "How much sugar did you give her?" she jeered.

"A *lot* of it," Jason joked in return.

"Nice," Chasity returned, sarcastic.

Jason walked over and sat down across from her. "You still feel up to taking this flight?"

"You mean this five-hour flight that we have to leave for in like three hours?" Chasity sneered, rubbing her face before running a hand through her hair. "Not really, but I'm still going." She let out a sigh. "Sorry, I don't mean to give you attitude. I'm just tired." After the events of the past few days, Chasity was exhausted.

Jason reached out and grabbed her hand, giving it a kiss. "I know," he soothed. "At least you'll get to sleep on the plane and all day while I'm at work tomorrow."

She rubbed the back of her neck. "I guess."

"I took off on Tuesday, so we can use that time to go check out some houses," Jason proposed. "If we can't find our dream home right away, we can just move into something close enough and move again after the baby comes."

"I'll be damn near in my second trimester by the time we move there," she pointed out. "I don't want to settle in somewhere, then have to move again in a few months," Chasity shot down.

Jason nodded. "Okay."

"You want me to call my mom and ask her to send us some listings out there?" Chasity asked, playing with a napkin on the table.

"Of course," Jason replied.

Chasity nodded. "Okay."

Jason caressed her hand in his. "So, when do you think we should tell Kayla about us having to move and about the baby?"

"Soon," Chasity answered. "I just hope the fact that we have to move doesn't upset her too much. After all, she'll have to be away from her grandparents, and you *know* she loves them more than us."

Jason let out a laugh. "A damn shame that's true," he joked. Chasity softly laughed too. "She'll be okay," he assured, laughter subsiding.

"Yeah," Chasity sighed.

Jason paused for a minute. "Mark knows about the move."

Chasity's eyes widened. "Shit."

"He said he's not gonna tell Malajia," Jason said, knowing her reason for panicking. "He's letting *you* do it."

"Can I wait until we're already out there, to tell her?" Chasity whined.

Jason chuckled, "No." He gave her hand a gentle squeeze. "If *I* can deal with my mother's dramatic meltdown at the news, *you* can deal with your best friend's response."

"Your mom *did* show her ass when you told her," Chasity chuckled. "Like slid down the wall and *everything*."

Jason put his hand over his face, shaking his head in amusement. "That was so goddamn dramatic," he recalled. "Dad had to actually pick her up and put her on the couch. Then she slid her ass back down to the floor."

Chasity laughed as she remembered the scene.

Jason chuckled a bit. "*Your* mom was so chill when we told her."

Chasity vigorously shook her head. "That was a whole ass *front* because she called me and cried on the phone later that night," she revealed, annoyed. "Wouldn't be surprised if she was sliding down a wall her-*damn*-self while she was snottin' all over the phone."

Jason busted out laughing.

"I had to talk her *out* of moving to Phoenix *with* us," she added.

"Our parents sure mean well, but their actions…" Jason joked.

Chasity shook her head as she stood up from the table. "Let me go chill with my baby before I have to leave her again," she said, making her way towards the stairs.

"She drew like five kitty pictures for you," Jason chortled.

Chasity giggled as she headed up the stairs.

Malajia cradled her cell phone to her ear as she slowly walked towards her house. "Mom, I already told you that you and I are good, it's *Dad* that I have the problem with," she said. "…Well, I appreciate you cussing him out, but that still doesn't make it better…" she approached her door and let out a quick huff. "Please, we *both* know he'd only be apologizing to keep from having to still sleep on that couch," she sneered. "It won't be sincere." Malajia retrieved her keys from her purse. "I hear you, but listen, I have to go… Love you too, bye."

Malajia ended her call, then stuck her key in the door. *God, I don't feel like dealing with this man's attitude right now.* The only times that she'd spoken to Mark over the past few days was when she'd given updates on Emily's condition. Now that she was back home, a conversation needed to be had; she just wasn't ready for it.

Opening the door, Malajia took a deep breath. Walking into her house, she dropped her overnight bag on the floor.

"Mommy's home!" Marlon exclaimed as he and his brother darted off the couch and ran for Malajia.

Smiling, Malajia bent down and held her arms out. They jumped into her arms; she closed her eyes and squeezed them. Taking a deep breath, Malajia kissed both of their little cheeks.

"Did you have fun with Dad?" she asked, parting from their embrace.

The boys nodded. "We got to play karate chop man," Marvin beamed.

Malajia looked confused. "What in the—" she quickly shook her head. "Never mind. None of your bones are broken and you have all of your teeth, so…"

She stood up as the boys ran back for the couch and jumped on it. "Did you miss us Mommy?" Marvin asked.

"Of *course* I missed my boys," she answered.

"We missed you too," Mark said.

Hearing his voice, Malajia glanced over and saw him standing in the entry way. She folded her arms as he approached. "You sure about that?" she questioned, voice dripping with disdain.

Mark nodded. "Yes," he answered, sincere. Mark crossed the room and wrapped his arms around her tight. She hugged him back, but didn't say anything.

After his talk with Jason, Mark had done a lot of reflecting; he knew that he hadn't been handling his feelings in the best way. He felt responsible for the rift with his wife, and it was eating at him. Once they parted, he looked at the boys. "Boys, go play in your room," he ordered. "Mommy and Daddy need to talk."

Malajia watched the boys run upstairs without a word. She looked at Mark. "No whining? No falling out? …Whose kids *are* these?"

Mark chuckled as he pointed to the couch. "How was your trip back?" he asked her.

"Fine," she said, sitting down. "I had Chaz drop me off at

Geri's. I just chilled with her for a bit."

"I *figured* you stopped somewhere," he said. "Jason said that Chaz got home like two hours ago."

Malajia shook her head. "I swear, y'all some snitchin' ass dudes," she jeered.

Mark couldn't help but chuckle. "Well, you didn't answer my text when I asked when you'd be home, so I called Jason and asked if he'd heard from Chaz."

"Very well," Malajia muttered after a moment. She glanced around the living room. "The house doesn't look like a tornado hit... I'm impressed," she mentioned, even toned.

Mark too looked around. "I refused to have this house be a mess when you got back," he said. "I can honestly say that being with the boys alone for just these past few days, I have a whole new appreciation for all that you do for them *and* me."

Malajia looked at him, but didn't say anything.

He grabbed her hand and held it. "Look Mel, I'm sorry for acting like a jerk...shit not acting, for *being* a jerk."

Malajia took a deep breath, almost like a sigh of relief. "It's okay," she said.

"No, it's *not*," Mark insisted. "Yeah, I'm dealing with shit, but I shouldn't take it out on *you*."

Malajia patted his hand. "Well, it's not like I haven't done it to *you* before, so we're even," she attempted to joke.

Mark tilted his head, eyeing her intently. "I'm being serious, babe."

She gave a half smile. "I know."

"And...I didn't mean to make you feel bad about going back to work." He shook his head in shame. "I didn't mean to make you feel like I don't support you or your decisions... You know I'll support you in *anything* you want to do, I just— I was just blindsided, that's all."

"Look, I know that I should've been honest about wanting to go back to work," Malajia admitted.

"Why *weren't* you?"

Malajia shrugged slightly. "I just... I didn't want you to think that you weren't doing a good job at providing," she explained. "I know that you had this whole plan of taking care of everything—"

"I just didn't want you to have to *worry* about anything," Mark cut in.

"Mark, I *know* that, and I do appreciate you for wanting that, but—" She sighed. "A lot of women would *love* to be a stay-at-home mother…that's just not what *I* want. It's *never* been what I wanted," she calmly explained. "I mean… It was fine when I first had the boys but, after a while I just felt like my *entire* life was all about them and you and—I *missed* getting up and going to work every day. I *missed* contributing to this household, I missed my drive, I missed…*me*."

Mark let out a sigh. "Damn… I wish you would've just *told* me that, babe."

"I know," she agreed.

"Malajia, I don't want you to ever feel like you have to hold back who you are or what you want for me," he said. "I'm not that dude… I love you, and I just want you to be happy."

Malajia tilted her head, eyeing him adoringly. "I love you too," she replied. "And you and the boys *do* make me happy…my crazy boys."

Mark laughed slightly; he gave her hand a kiss. "If you haven't already …please accept the job."

Malajia smiled back. "I will."

Mark gave an approving nod. "Good." He took a deep breath.

Malajia touched his face. "Mark…I know that you've been stressing about being out of work. I get that you feel useless right now," she began.

Mark glanced away.

"I want you to understand that you're not," Malajia stressed. "There is nothing useless, lazy or inadequate about you. You are the best husband to me and the best father to those boys. So don't forget that, okay?"

Mark sighed heavily. "Okay."

"And please, *please* don't let my narrow-minded father make you forget that," Malajia pleaded. "I wish you didn't even have to be *subjected* to his bullshit."

"It just is what it is at this point," Mark resolved. "He's your father. I'll never tell you to stay away from him, but *I* just can't be around him right now."

"Shit, neither can *I*," Malajia agreed. "I mean I love him, always *will*, but until he acts right, I'll just keep my distance."

Mark leaned over and gave her a kiss on the lips. "I know you don't really want to do that, but I appreciate you saying it anyway."

Malajia gave his face a pat. Leaning in, she gave him another kiss. "So, did you take care of dinner?" she asked after a moment.

Mark hopped up from the couch with excitement. "Sure did. I mean I didn't *make* it yet, but I got all the stuff for it," he beamed. "I'm about to shock the shit outta you with what I have planned."

Malajia followed him to the kitchen with curiosity. "Mark, what are you planning on making?" she asked, skeptical. "And don't be a smart ass and say pizza."

Mark chuckled as he removed the lid from a large pot. "Nah, it's not pizza," he promised.

Malajia leaned over the counter. "So, are you gonna keep me in suspense or tell me what it is?"

Mark looked at her, grinning from ear to ear. "Okay so you know how much you like crabs right?" he began.

Malajia nodded. "*Love* them, why?" She gasped. "Ooh, did you get me a platter?"

Mark pointed at her. "Even *better*." He pointed to a large paper bag that sat near the stove. "I'm gonna *make* you some, myself."

Malajia's smile faded. "Um…yeah babe, you don't have to do that—"

"Nah, listen. I got a perfect seasoning mix, some butter— they gonna be on point."

Malajia opened her mouth to object; she was picky about her crab legs. But seeing how excited Mark was to make them for her, she gave a nod instead. "Okay," she said. "You bought the frozen ones?"

Mark shook his head. "Nope. *Fresh*."

Hearing noise from the counter, Malajia slowly looked over. The brown paper bag *moved*; she stood up straight. Her eyes widened; breath caught in her throat. "*How* fresh?"

"Live baby, live," Mark boasted, reaching for the bag.

"Mark no!" she exclaimed as he went to open the bag. He looked at her. "You've never handled live crabs before. Those things are *no* joke unless you know what you're doing."

Mark looked offended. "Malajia *chill*. Don't you have any faith in your man?"

"You *know* I do, but not when it comes to *this*," she explained.

Mark flagged her with his hand. "You trippin'." Mark picked up the bag and opened it. As he went to dump the live blue crabs into the pot of boiling, seasoned water, a crab claw shot out of the bag, startling him. "Oh shit!" he belted out, dropping the entire bag to the floor.

Malajia let out a scream as seven crabs scurried out of the bag and began darting around the kitchen.

"Shit!" Mark yelled, running around the kitchen with the pot top trying to catch them. "Babe, save yourself!"

"Don't let them out the kitchen!" Malajia screamed, bolting out of the kitchen into the dining room.

"Goddamn it, these things are fast!" Mark belted out. When one snapped at him, he dropped the top and ran out of the kitchen. He grabbed chairs from the dining room table and lined them against the entry way—a sad attempt to keep the crabs from migrating elsewhere. "Fuck y'all," he hissed at the creatures.

Mark, panting, looked at Malajia; she was standing in a corner doubled over with laughter. "You're—you're gonna tell the others about this, aren't you?" he assumed.

"Hell yeah," Malajia managed between laughs. Tears were running down her face.

Mark nodded his head, giving his wife a salty look. "Thought so."

Alex sat near a window overlooking the crowded New York street as she slowly ate her taco salad. Having returned to work after being off the past few days, Alex felt sluggish. She couldn't figure out if it was because she was physically tired (even though all she did after she returned home from her seven-hour train ride the day before, was sleep), or if she was just mentally tired. Between Emily's situation, the rift with her parents whom she had yet to call back, Eric not returning her texts, and her beef with Chasity; Alex felt like she could break at any moment.

Reaching for her glass of iced lemon water, she took a long sip then sat the glass down. Her cell phone rang, and Alex quickly checked the ID. Her eyes widened; it was her parent's home number. Taking a deep breath, she answered. "Hey Ma…" Alex frowned at the rants coming through the line. "Are you serious?" she asked, upset. "…No disrespect Ma, but you're being ridiculous… You're really about to send me the bill money *back*? *All* of it?" Alex rolled her eyes and leaned back in her seat. "Okay, I can't do this with you. I'll call you back when you aren't yelling." Alex abruptly ended the call, then quickly jerked her coat on, gathered her things, and stormed out of the restaurant.

Alex navigated the sidewalk with haste, making it back to her office building in less than ten minutes.

Safely at her desk again, she opened her laptop to begin working. But a notification from her phone interrupted her before she could get started. It was a text from Sidra; she let a smile come through.

Opening it, Alex found several pictures of herself and the girls from college and recent years. '*Aww, look at us'*, the message read. Fond memories filled Alex as she scrolled through the shots of them hanging on campus, of graduation, Chasity's and Malajia's weddings, baby showers, and holidays. One final picture popped up as she was scrolling. It was a picture of just her and Chasity, with the message "*fix it."*

Alex rolled her eyes, then dialed Sidra's number. The line picked up immediately.

"Did you like the pictures?" Sidra asked innocently.

Alex shook her head. "You know, it's really low to send all these happy memories with an ulterior motive," she sneered.

"I sent the pictures to *everybody*," Sidra explained.

"What about the *last* picture?"

"I sent it to Chasity too," Sidra confirmed.

"Did you send that '*fix it'* message to her too?" Alex bit out.

"*No*, because she doesn't need to fix it, *you* do," Sidra threw back. "And before you argue with me, keep in mind that I know what was said."

Alex sucked her teeth.

"Come on Alex. Next month we'll all be together again for Emily's bridal functions, so I need—no I *demand* that you and Chasity get back on good terms before then," Sidra stressed. "Your tension will *not* ruin Em's weekend."

"Look, Chasity and I are mature adults, we can coexist without causing tension," Alex argued.

"No, you *can't*," Sidra contradicted. "And you're only acting like you don't care because she won't talk to you."

"Which is all the more reason why that message needs to go to *her* and not me. I've apologized multiple times and she won't accept it," Alex replied, upset. "I'm out of options."

"Alex—you know what, I'll yell at you later. I have to go now," Sidra dismissed.

"Bye." Alex hung up, then leaned back in her seat. Sucking her teeth yet again, she sent a text message to Eric. *'Hi...just checking on you.'* She stared at the phone for several moments. When she didn't get a response, she sighed and tossed it on her desk. She pinched the bridge of her nose when someone knocked on her door. "Come in." Alex perked up when Marlene walked in.

"Alex, do you have those updated edits on those articles that I asked for?" Marlene asked. "The copyeditor needs them by close of business today."

Alex looked confused and glanced at her laptop. "I'm sorry, I'm not finished just yet, but I thought the deadline was close of business *tomorrow*."

"No Alex, it's *today*," Marlene stressed, stern.

Alex looked at her email, then closed her eyes. *Shit!* She'd been so preoccupied that she had misread her assignment's due date. "Oh my God," she said, horrified. "Marlene I'm so sorry, I—"

"Alex, I already gave you an extension because of your family emergency last week, but this needs to be done today," Marlene chastised.

"I know. This is totally unprofessional, and I'll rectify it," Alex promised. "It'll be done before I leave tonight, you have my word."

Marlene let out a sigh. Alex was a favorite employee of hers; the girl's work was always impeccable. "Alex…is everything okay? Mixing up deadlines is not like you."

Alex took a deep breath. "It doesn't matter what's going on in my personal life, it shouldn't affect my work," she admitted.

"Listen, having happy employees are important to me; you know how big I am on taking care of your personal *and* mental health," Marlene said. "So, if you need to take some personal time, you *can* and you *should*."

Alex looked up at Marlene, concerned. "I'm sorry, am I being suspended?" she asked. "I'll get this finished and I'm sorry about the whole IT job thing—"

Marlene put a hand up, silencing Alex's rambling. "No, that is not what I meant," she assured, sincere. "While the job situation was *disappointing,* it was no harm done. We'll find a candidate, and I know you'll get this assignment done, you always do."

Alex let out a sigh of relief.

"Just remember that not only is it important to have a thriving professional life, but in order to be happy and fulfilled, your *personal* life needs to thrive as well," Marlene advised. She walked to the door. "Let me know if you need anything."

Alex gave a nod. "Okay, I will," she said. "And your advice is noted. Thank you."

"Sure," Marlene smiled. "Now get to work."

Alex managed a chuckle. "Yes ma'am." Once Marlene walked out and shut the door, Alex let out a long sigh and started scanning the articles on her laptop screen, determined to make them perfect.

Chapter 47

Sidra craned her neck as she peered through the airport crowd. Not seeing who she was looking for, she glanced at her watch. She'd been standing in the airport baggage claim area for nearly twenty minutes. "Come on, where are you?" she whispered to herself. Glancing out of the window, she let out a sigh.

"Looking for something?"

Startled by the male voice close to her, Sidra let out a scream as she spun around. Josh was standing there, carry-on bag in hand; she smiled and jumped into his arms. Josh let the bag fall to the floor as he lifted her up, giving Sidra a long embrace. Placing her back to her feet, he planted a loving kiss on her lips.

"What took you so long?" Sidra asked, delivering a light tap to Josh's chest.

Josh chuckled as he reached down and retrieved his bag. "Well, I had to wait until the other fifty passengers ahead of me got off the plane before *I* could," he answered. "You know, I'll never understand why those in the back of the plane stand up when it lands. They still have to wait."

Sidra giggled. She was excited. After returning to California earlier that week, she was pleasantly surprised when Josh had announced that he would be flying down to visit her that weekend. After everything that happened with Emily, then coming back to a ton of work, Sidra was looking forward to a relaxing weekend with Josh.

She grabbed his hand. "Come on, let's get out of here and get you some food," she beamed. "I know those pretzels that they gave you were salty."

Josh chuckled. "As all hell." He adjusted his bag in his hand as they headed for the exit. "Where did you park?"

Sidra pointed to the parking lot across the street.

"Do you want me to drive back?" he offered as they made their way across the street. "I know how much you hate highways."

Approaching the car, Sidra let out a sigh of relief. "Yes, I appreciate you," she replied, digging into her purse and retrieving her keys. "The traffic coming down here had me ready to pull my hair out."

Josh shrugged. "It *is* rush hour."

"Whether it's rush hour or early morning, I *still* hate the highway," Sidra ground out.

Josh chuckled a bit. He waited for Sidra to hit the automatic lock key, before opening her car door to allow her to get in. He then jogged around to the trunk, placed his bag inside, and climbed into the driver's seat.

Sidra watched as Josh adjusted the mirrors and the seat. "Seat too close to the wheel, huh?" she teased.

Josh let out a laugh. "Need the leg room." He pushed the start button, then looked over at Sidra, who was putting her seatbelt on. Josh stared at her while she fixed her hair in the visor mirror. He tilted his head, gazing at her in longing. He'd left California just a friend, and had returned as her boyfriend; Josh still found it all hard to believe.

"Okay, let's get out of this parking lot and find somewhere to eat," Sidra beamed, looking at him.

Josh smiled back and gave a nod as he pulled off.

Chasity stood on the porch overlooking the backyard. Her eyes roamed over the grass and palm trees, zoning in on the silhouette of mountains in the distance. She was so mesmerized by the scenery, that she barely heard Malajia's voice.

Chasity glanced at her phone; Malajia's frowning face was staring back at her through the screen. "Huh?"

"You're really gonna make me repeat all of that?!" Malajia belted out, annoyed.

"I didn't hear you," Chasity replied, even toned.

Malajia narrowed her eyes, staring intensely. "I swear to God, you're lying."

Chasity chuckled a bit.

"Anyway," Malajia ground out. "When are you flying back? I accepted that job and I start work in two weeks, so I need to go through your closet. I need your work clothes."

"Fuck off Malajia," Chasity spat. "And I come back tomorrow."

Malajia sucked her teeth. "Come on bitch, I ain't got no extra *money*," she barked. "Christmas is coming up and shit." Malajia flagged the air with her hand. "You know what, fuck them kids."

Chasity just barely suppressed a chuckle. "What happened to all that shit you had when you *were* working?"

"I want *new* shit," Malajia barked.

Chasity let out a huff as she pinched the bridge of her nose. "God," she muttered. "Whatever. You can borrow some of my work clothes for now," she offered. "And I mean *borrow*. I want my shit *back*."

Malajia let out a squeal of delight. "You know I love you right? With every fiber of my being," she gushed.

"Eww," Chasity grimaced, earning a laugh from Malajia. "I gotta go."

"Oh hold up, we need to go over the details for Em's bridal weekend," Malajia cut in just as Chasity was about to hang up.

"I *can't* right now. Call Sidra," Chasity proposed.

"Girl, Sidra is busy getting dicked down by Josh all weekend. Ain't heard from her prissy ass since his plane landed yesterday," Malajia sneered.

Chasity laughed. "Well, good for her," she approved. "We'll deal with it when I get back."

"Very well," Malajia sighed. "Bye."

"Bye." Chasity ended the call just as Jason walked out of the house. She looked at him.

"You okay out here?" he asked.

"Yes, and I would've been okay *in there*." She bit out, gesturing to the inside of the house.

"Too much damn dust," Jason scoffed. "You don't need to be breathing that mess in."

Chasity shook her head. "They're still working on the house Jase, what did you expect?"

"For you not to be breathing in all that dust," Jason threw back, eyeing her. "What do you think so far?"

"You mean of what you let me *see*?" she ground out; Jason smirked. "I like it." She folded her arms. "It's bigger than the house we have now."

Jason nodded. "Four bedrooms, two and a half bathrooms, brand new—" He glanced around the backyard, then sighed. "I wonder if they're going to try to sell it right out instead of renting it." He ran a hand along the back of his neck. "If they sell, the down payment *alone* would be more than our savings… I won't be making the new salary until we move down here and we need to have a place to live *beforehand*."

"Mom said we can rent to own," Chasity revealed, nonchalant.

Jason's eyes widened slightly. "When did she say that?"

"Oh, I was talking to her after you made me leave," Chasity informed, holding her phone up. "She'll get us all the details, along with a set completion date. She said she'll fly down here and sit in their face to make sure it's done if she has to."

Jason laughed. "I love her."

"Yeah," Chasity agreed.

Jason smiled. "Well, then I guess I should say, welcome to our future home Mrs. Adams."

"Don't be corny," she jeered, earning a playful tap to her behind from Jason. "I'm ready to go."

With a nod, Jason took Chasity's hand and led her to their rental car. Once situated, Jason started the car and adjusted the air. "You hungry?" he asked.

"No, I'm fine," she answered, adjusting her seatbelt.

Jason glanced at her after a moment. "In all honesty babe…how does it feel to be back in Arizona after all this time?"

Chasity stared out of the window. "It's actually not as bad as I *thought* it would be," she admitted. "…Honestly, I never had a problem with *Arizona*. It was just who I lived with while I was here."

Jason nodded slightly; the fact that Chasity didn't seem miserable being out there reassured him that this move would be a good thing. "How far is Tucson from here, by the way?" he asked after a moment.

"Like two hours. Maybe less."

Jason gripped the steering wheel. "Don't kill me but...you want to take a ride out there?"

Chasity shot him a skeptical glance. "Why?"

"Well, you still own that house, and you haven't been there since you left for college," he pointed out. "You don't think you should at least go *check* on it?"

Chasity pushed her hair behind her ear, sighing in the process.

Jason reached out and touched her arm, giving it a rub. "Nothing is going to hurt you in there," he consoled.

"I know," Chasity replied. "I just— I've put a lot of shit behind me, and I'm afraid that if I step foot back in there that I might get angry all over again, and I don't want to do that."

"I understand that," Jason said, sincere. "Tell you what. We'll drive out there and when we pull up, if you start to feel weird or angry, you won't have to get out. I'll turn right back around."

She raised an eyebrow. "You'll really turn right around after driving damn near two hours?"

Jason put his right hand up. "I promise."

Chasity turned around in her seat as she thought for a moment. She had to admit, she was curious to see what the house looked like now. She wasn't sure if Trisha had it completely cleaned out, or if she'd left everything there while keeping up with the maintenance. "Okay...let's go," she said finally.

The two-hour ride from Phoenix to Tucson was quiet. An hour into the drive, while Chasity silently stared out of the window, Jason wondered if asking her to go out there was a good idea. Her silence made her hard to read.

Pulling up in front of the house, Jason peered out the window. "Is that it?" he asked, despite the GPS letting him know that they had arrived.

Chasity stared at the house. "Yeah," she answered, even

toned.

Jason turned the car off. He glanced over at Chasity as she slowly removed her seatbelt. "You okay?" he asked.

"I'm good," she answered.

Jason gave a nod and opened his door. He walked around to the passenger's side and opened Chasity's door. "I don't know why I imagined this house being a two-story," he commented as she got out.

"No, and I hated the fact that everything was on one floor." Chasity griped of the single story, three-bedroom home. "I could always hear everything." She reached into her purse and grabbed the keys. "Good thing I always keep the key with me. Otherwise it would've been a salty ass drive."

Jason chuckled. He took her hand as they walked up the concrete path.

Chasity looked around. "The outside looks the same," she commented of the tan and cream exterior. The yard was void of grass; instead it was landscaped with a few bushes, mulch and pebbles. The one car garage was located on the side of the house. An iron gate lead to the back yard on the opposite side.

Standing in front of the door, Jason held his hand out for the key. Once Chasity handed it to him, he unlocked the screen door, followed by the main door. He glanced at her. "Wait out here, while I check it out first."

Chasity sucked her teeth. "Boy, ain't nobody standing out here," she griped.

"Look, your mom might be maintaining the house, but the fact is that nobody *lives* here," he stressed. "So, I need to make sure that there isn't some squatter roaming around, stubborn ass."

Chasity rolled her eyes. "Fine Mr. Over-protector," she mocked. "Go in there and get your ass beat by a goddamn bug."

"Yeah a'ight." Jason scoffed, walking inside.

Chasity folded her arms, letting out a sigh as she waited for Jason to complete his inspection. She closed her eyes as a cool breeze brushed by her. December in Arizona wasn't cold; it felt more like springtime on the East coast. Glancing over at the yard, she remembered how she used to play with the small rocks as a child. Arranging them in different shapes on the sidewalk, stacking them as high as she could, then knocking them down. She'd even snuck some in the house on occasion. Chasity was almost in a haze until something flying by her face interrupted her trip down memory lane. She let out a scream and bolted into the house.

"Baby, you all right?!" Jason yelled, darting from the hallway.

"No, I'm *not* all right! A fuckin' big ass bug just flew past my goddamn face," Chasity spat, both startled and annoyed.

Jason pinched the bridge of his nose. "Chaz, you were supposed to wait until I gave the all clear."

Chasity frowned at him. "Did you *not* hear what I just said?"

Jason just shook his head, letting out a sigh.

"I'm not standing out there anymore, so your inspection is over." Chasity looked around the living area as her breathing returned to normal. "Damn, *everything* is different," she commented of the décor, furniture, and electronics.

"Really?" Jason wondered.

"Yeah," Chasity confirmed, walking into the dining room. "Brenda must've gotten rid of everything after Dad and I moved out," she assumed. She glanced into the kitchen, but did not go in.

"You want to check out the bedrooms?" Jason folded his arms. "I didn't get a chance to look in before you ran in here because of a flying ladybug," he teased.

Chasity glared at him; she did not appreciate the teasing. "It was a fuckin' flying *cockroach*, you ass."

Jason laughed. "Shit."

"Yeah, exactly," Chasity bit out. "Get ready for *those*, and scorpions. Welcome to the fuckin' dessert."

Jason winced, traces of humor now gone. "Sounds like we'll be having a high exterminator bill."

"Yup," she agreed. She glanced around the living room once more. "I'm ready to go; your kid is getting hungry."

Jason ran a hand over his head. "You don't want to check out the rest of the house first?"

"For what?" Chasity huffed. "It'll be weird being in Brenda's old room, knowing that she's dead and *my* old room is probably gutted." She ran a hand through her hair. "Doubt she wanted any reminder of my presence once I left."

"We came all this way and probably won't be back any time soon," he pressed. "Might as well take a look."

Chasity let out a long sigh. "*Fine* Jason," she relented, walking down the hallway with him in tow. Standing outside of Brenda's closed door, she reached for the doorknob, then stopped. "I just don't wanna go in there."

"Okay," Jason replied, tone caring. "You don't have to; I'm just gonna open the door to make sure it's clear."

Chasity nodded. "Okay." She moved away from the door as Jason slowly opened it and peered inside. He stepped in and after a minute or so, came back out.

"It's clear," he informed, shutting the door. "There's bedroom furniture in there, but nothing on the dressers or anything."

"That's not surprising—she brought everything with her when she moved back East," Chasity explained, moving over to her own room door. She looked at Jason. "You really wanna see an empty ass room?"

"You used to live in it, so yes," he assured, offering a smile.

Chasity rolled her eyes. "Fine," she muttered, gesturing to him. "After you."

Jason chuckled slightly. "Hold on a sec," he said, opening the door. He walked inside and peered around while Chasity stood, examining her manicured nails.

"All clear babe," Jason called from inside.

Letting out a sigh, Chasity hesitated for a moment before walking inside. Stopping in her tracks, her eyes widened as she looked around. "The hell?"

Jason frowned in concern. "What's wrong?"

"It's…my room looks *just* how it did when I left," she revealed, slowly walking around. Everything was exactly as Chasity remembered; from the paint on the walls, to the bedroom furniture, to the decorations—even the items on her dresser, just as she had put them so long ago. Chasity approached an accent chair that sat near a window. A pink throw blanket was draped across the back; she tilted her head.

"This isn't mine," she mentioned. "I think this was *hers*." Chasity glanced out the window, focusing on the mountains in the distance.

"Maybe Brenda sat in here often," Jason thought. "Maybe...maybe it was her way of being close to you, even though you were gone."

"Maybe," Chasity muttered, still staring out the window. "When she would lock me in here, I used to spend hours looking out this window," she said, pointing outside.

Jason walked over and looked.

"I used to imagine myself packing my shit, jumping out of this window, and running in that direction."

Jason wrapped his arms around her from behind, then planted a loving kiss to her cheek.

"I'm fine," Chasity assured, picking up on his thoughts. She moved from his embrace, and proceeded to walk around, touching various items in the room. Walking over to her closet, she opened it and looked inside. The hangers that she had snatched her clothes from when she was packing to leave for college were still there. Some hung on the bar, while others laid on the floor. Chasity looked at the top shelf. Seeing a black shoe box, she grabbed it.

Jason watched Chasity, box in hand, sit on the edge of her bed. "What's that?" he asked, sitting down next to her.

"Stuff," she answered.

"Are you gonna open it?"

Chasity shrugged. "Sure," she answered, tone dry. She pulled the top off, setting it behind her on the bed. Reaching inside, she pulled something out.

Jason stared at the formation of painted rocks on a piece of wood. "What is that?"

Chasity smirked as she stared at the formation. "It's umm...it's a rock band."

Jason slowly looked up at her; his lips curled in a grin. "You said it's a what?"

Chasity narrowed her eyes at him as he fought to contain a laugh. "Look, damn it—"

Jason busted out laughing.

"Shut the hell up, I was like nine when I did this shit." she barked, successfully containing her own urge to laugh. "Brenda took my toys, all I had was those stupid ass yard rocks."

Jason kissed her on the cheek. "Aww, I'm sorry baby. It's cute," he placated.

"Yeah, whatever," she ground out, setting the art piece off to the side. "It's stupid." She reached back into the box and pulled a paper from it. She and Jason both looked at it.

He pointed to the abstract drawing on the paper. A smile crossed his face. "You drew that?"

Chasity handed it to him, then removed another drawing. "Yeah," she admitted, solemn. "I used to draw a lot when I was young." She pulled another paper out. "I knew I wasn't good at it; but it passed the time…that and *rock people*." Chasity had blocked a lot of her childhood out, but her love of drawing back then, she hadn't. It was something that she had kept to herself; something that calmed her while she was going through hard times at home. When she left Tucson for college nine years ago, she'd left her need to draw behind.

Jason removed more of her drawings. "You never thought that you were good?" he asked.

She shook her head.

Jason held a picture up to her face. "Babe, *look* at this," he prompted. "This is *really* good."

Chasity shot him a skeptical look. "Are you just saying that because you're afraid I'll cry if you tell the truth?"

"No," he chuckled, setting the picture on his lap. "I *mean* it; these drawings are amazing."

Chasity smiled slightly. "Thanks."

"At least we know where our daughter gets her creativity," Jason mused. "The girl loves to draw, paint—"

"Put pink glitter on *everything*," Chasity finished.

Jason laughed, "*That too*."

Chasity put her pictures back in the box. "You know, people would say that Kayla is nothing like me," she began, reflecting. "In a way I was glad, because I didn't *want* her to be like me… I want her to be *better* than me."

Jason held an attentive gaze on Chasity as she spoke.

"But I'm starting to realize that she's more like me than I thought," she concluded. "In fact, she's *just* like I was at her age. She's sweet, she's trusting, she's creative, and *happy*." She looked at Jason, worry in her eyes. "I get scared sometimes that she'll also inherit the *worst* part of me."

Jason took her hand and held it. "Chasity, trust me when I say that Kay is lucky to have *every* part of you," he said.

Chasity hesitated to speak for a moment; she couldn't believe that she was going to say what she was about to. "You know what else scares me?"

"What's that?"

"That somewhere inside of me is the worst part of my *aunt*."

Jason's brow furrowed in confusion. "What?" he replied. "Chaz, you are nothing like your aunt. *Nothing*. I don't care *how* frustrated you get… Hell, *I* get frustrated sometimes too, it's *okay*."

"Jase, I just— I don't want to ruin her," Chasity confessed. "She's such a good child and sometimes I feel like I don't deserve to be her mom."

Jason had never heard Chasity express these fears. He was stunned. Clearly he saw her mothering totally differently than what she saw in herself. He adjusted his position on the bed so that he was facing her. "Listen to me. You could *never* ruin her," Jason stressed, serious. "You are an *amazing, loving* mother. I *see* that, I *know* that and *she* knows it. She loves and *adores* you. I don't want you to ever think or feel otherwise. You hear me?"

Chasity looked at him, uncertainty in her eyes. After a moment, she nodded. "I hear you."

"I *mean* it, baby."

"I know," she replied. "Thank you."

"You don't need to thank me for telling the truth," Jason soothed. He gave her a kiss on the lips.

Chasity glanced around the room once more, letting out a deep sigh. Almost as if she was releasing a burden that she had been holding inside. "I'm ready to go."

"You got it," he said. As they walked out of the room, Jason looked back at the box that she'd left on the bed. "I think you should give your art to Kayla," he suggested. "She'd love it."

 Chasity looked back at the box. "Yeah?"

 "Absolutely." Jason walked over and grabbed it. "She'll love this rock band too."

 Chasity put a hand up. "Jase—don't bring that bullshit."

 Jason laughed. "It's coming with us," he insisted.

 Chasity chuckled. "*Fine*, just don't show it to anybody."

 Jason followed her out of the room. "Deal," he promised.

Chapter 48

Emily cradled her cell phone to her ear, eyeing a hairclip on a shelf. Picking up the pink crystal clip, she examined it. "How is your research going?" she asked into the line.

"You know I did not call to talk about my *research*," David replied. "How are you feeling?"

Emily set the item back on the shelf and walked over to a chair. Sitting down, she let out a sigh, pushing some of her hair behind her ear. "I'm okay."

"Are you sure?" he pressed.

"Yeah," she answered. "Headaches come and go, but the doctors say that that's to be expected." Emily appreciated the fact that David—although swamped with his work—had taken the time to call and check on her. "My job gave me the week off to recuperate, and Will's been taking good care of me so yeah... I'm okay."

"I hate that the whole thing even *happened*," David sympathized.

"Yeah," she muttered, somber. Emily glanced around the bridal shop. Thanks to Sidra's reminder of all things wedding related, Emily had made her way to Jersey that Saturday for another dress fitting. The last time she had been there, her mother was with her. It made this visit a somber one. "Can we talk about something else?"

"Sure," David obliged. "Like what?"

"Do you plan on bringing a date to my wedding?" she asked.

"Huh? —Umm..."

Emily managed a chuckle. "You're probably the smartest man I know, surely that question shouldn't stump you."

"Ha ha," David jeered. "But to *answer* your question…I don't know yet… Maybe. I sorta started talking to someone recently, so…"

Emily was intrigued. The topic of David's mystery woman was a welcomed distraction from the stuff going on in her head. "Oh really?"

"Yeah…like I said, it's recent," he explained, then paused.

"That's great David," Emily smiled. "Who is she? You might as well bring her. Tell me her name so I can let Sidra know… She's doing the place cards for me."

David laughed. "Nice try to get information."

Emily giggled. "I promise I wasn't trying to be sneaky," she assured. She paused for a moment. "Now that you're talking to someone new…I guess that means you've finally moved past Nicole, huh?"

"Umm…" David sputtered. "Listen, I promise that I will personally let Sidra know should I decide to bring a date."

Emily shrugged; clearly David didn't want to delve further, and she respected that. "Okay, fair enough," she replied. She glanced up when she saw a bridal shop worker head up to her. "David, I have to go, I'll call you later."

"Okay, take care Em."

"You too." Emily ended the call and placed the phone into her purse. She stood up. "Hi," she greeted.

"Hi Emily, I'm Amanda, I'm sorry to keep you waiting," the polite young woman said.

Emily adjusted her purse strap on her shoulder and shifted her coat from one arm to the other. "It's okay."

Amanda gestured to the altering room. "The tailor is ready for you," she informed.

Emily nodded as she allowed Amanda to lead the way.

Amanda glanced back at her. "Your gown is beautiful by the way," she gushed.

Emily smiled. "Thank you."

"So is the other dress."

Emily looked confused. "*What* other dress?" she asked.

"Oh, not yours," Amanda chuckled, approaching a door. "A member of your bridal party is here getting her dress altered as well."

Emily stopped short of entering the room. She looked at Amanda. "I'm sorry, there must be some mistake," she said. "*I'm* the only one with an appointment today."

"Really? That's weird," Amanda replied, perplexed. "The woman came in about twenty minutes before *you* did... She's back there now."

Confusion didn't leave Emily's face as Amanda opened the door. Emily stepped in the room, stopping when she saw someone sitting in a chair. Emily frowned at the women staring back at her. "You've got to be kidding me," she snapped, before storming out.

Ms. Harris jumped from her seat and darted out of the room. "Emily," she called as her daughter continued her quick departure out of the bridal shop. She followed her to the sidewalk. "Emily!"

Emily spun around. "What?! What do you want? Why are you here?!" she snapped.

Ms. Harris put her hands up, stopping a few feet away. She let out a deep breath and tried not to focus on the freezing weather. "Emily," she began. "I had this appointment for a while now." She took a step forward. "Remember? I made it last time I was here with you."

Emily jerked her coat on and yanked it shut. She was livid. "And you really thought that it was a good idea for you to keep it, knowing that I would be here too?" she spat, folding her arms across her chest. "I can't even get fitted for my damn *dress* without stress."

"My intention wasn't to stress you, I just wanted to see you." Ms. Harris's tone was almost pleading. She folded her arms. "I—I didn't get to see you while you were in the hospital and I just wanted to make sure that you were okay."

Emily stared at her, disgusted. She shook her head and started to walk away.

"Emily, please!" Ms. Harris belted out, stopping Emily in her tracks. "I don't want to— I miss you, and I'm over— I just want to get past this."

Emily turned around, eyeing her mother as if she had lost her mind. "We *can't* get *past* this," she threw back.

"Yes, we *can*," Ms. Harris insisted. "I'm not mad anymore—"

"You really think I *care* if *you're* still mad?!" Emily yelled. Ms. Harris flinched at the bass in Emily's voice.

Emily took a step towards her. "*I'm* mad, *I'm* mad!" she fumed, patting her chest. "I'm mad that I broke the promise that I made to myself after I moved out of your damn house to never let *anyone* manipulate me ever again. I'm mad that I ignored my intuition and allowed Jazmine to move in with me. I'm mad that I actually trusted *you* and thought that you had truly changed—'

Ms. Harris stood there speechless as Emily continued.

"I'm mad that I've allowed you *both* to ruin this time for me. I'm not even *excited* about my wedding anymore," Emily fumed, tearing up. "After everything that I've endured, I can't even enjoy *this*." She shook her head. "I hope you're happy."

Ms. Harris sniffled as tears fell from her eyes. "Baby, I never wanted—"

"Mom, I just can't," Emily cut in, voice trembling. "I'd tell you to not come to my wedding, but we both know you'd never honor my wishes."

"Emily...I don't want to cause you any more stress and pain than I already have," Ms. Harris replied, somber. "So, if me not being at your wedding will make that happen, then as much as it would kill me, I'll honor that."

Emily couldn't stop the tears from flowing, but refused to sob out loud. Yes, she was angry with her mother. But unlike Jazmine, deep down Emily knew that she wanted her mother at her wedding. After all, she still loved the woman.

"Fine," Emily agreed after a moment. Not having anything else to say, she turned and walked off, leaving her crushed mother to put her hands over her face and sob out loud.

Sidra walked into her bedroom, holding a tray with two plates of food and two glasses of orange juice. "Hungry?" she grinned.

Josh glanced up at her, pleasantly surprised. "I thought we were gonna go *out* to breakfast," he recalled, sitting up in bed.

Sidra walked over and set the tray on the bed, then

carefully took a seat next to it. "I'd rather stay in."

Josh surveyed the plates of pancakes, cheese eggs, turkey bacon, and fruit. He grabbed a plate and fork. "You know we've barely left this apartment," he crooned, reaching for the syrup.

Sidra blushed as she picked up the glass bottle of maple syrup and handed it to him. "I know."

Sidra and Josh had spent the weekend making up for lost time—not leaving the house and barely leaving the bed. It was the most relaxed that Sidra had been in months.

Josh ate some of his food, then glanced at Sidra, who was sipping her juice. "My shirt looks good on you," he mentioned, smirking.

Sidra looked down at the baggy grey t-shirt of Josh's that she had on. She pushed some of her disheveled hair from her face, then grabbed a piece of bacon. "Thank you, just know that you won't be getting it back."

He chuckled as he ate more of his food.

Sidra took a bite of bacon, then let out a sigh as she chewed. "I'm sad that it's Sunday already," she moped. "I wish you didn't have to leave tomorrow."

"I know," Josh agreed. "Next time I'll stay longer."

"Next time I'll come to see *you*," Sidra proposed. "I don't want you to think that you're the one who has to travel."

"I don't mind," Josh assured.

"But it's not fair to you," Sidra insisted. She took another sip of juice, then let out another sigh.

"It's fine," Josh insisted. "We're making the best of the situation."

Sidra looked at him. "Yeah, the best of the situation means resorting to seeing each other once a month, *if* that?"

Josh frowned slightly at her somber tone. "Sid...are you starting to have doubts?" He wondered how the conversation shifted so quickly.

She touched his arm. "No, of *course* not," she assured. "I just... I guess I'm in my feelings because you're leaving tomorrow, that's all."

Josh leaned over and gave her a comforting kiss on her cheek.

A notification chimed on her phone; Sidra grabbed it from

the nightstand. Reading the email from work, she rolled her eyes.

"Great," she muttered.

"What's wrong?" Josh wondered.

"Nothing, just work stuff," she grunted. "I'm getting frustrated with that too... Ready for a change."

"I think that change will be good," Josh approved. "Especially since you aren't able to advance where you *are*."

"Yeah," Sidra muttered, looking away. She was quiet for a moment, pondering. While she had already made up her mind to leave her current position and company, she had yet to apply to James's firm. She wanted to talk to Josh first. But in talking about their distance, her mind was brought back to something else. She glanced over at him. "What if I found a job back in Delaware?" she proposed.

Josh stared at her but didn't say anything.

"I mean, it's a win win," Sidra explained. "I get a new job and we won't have to do the long-distance thing anymore."

Josh shook his head as he stood from the bed. "Sidra no, you've built your life out here."

"So?" Sidra shrugged, following his movement with her eyes.

"*So*, I'm not gonna let you give it up to move back to Delaware, for what? Me?" he argued, grabbing his sweatpants from a nearby accent chair.

Sidra watched him put his pants on, a frown forming on her face. "Josh, why *wouldn't* I?"

"Because that's crazy," Josh insisted, facing her. "You have a better chance to advance your career out *here*."

"That's not necessarily true," Sidra threw back, traces of agitation in her voice. "Law firms are *everywhere*."

Josh ran a hand over his face, sighing in the process. "Come on Sid, you know what I mean."

Sidra stood up from the bed. "I don't get it. Do you *not* want me to be close to you?" she fussed. "I would think you'd be excited that I'm even *considering* it."

Josh shot her a stern gaze. "Are you really picking a fight with me my last day here?" he questioned. She rolled her eyes and folded her arms. "And why am I being penalized for keeping you from making a decision that you *know* you'll regret later on?"

"The only thing I regret right now is *starting* this conversation," Sidra spat.

Josh ran a hand over his head. "Look, the calls every day, the trips...they'll work for however long they need to," he assured.

"Right," Sidra grunted, examining her nails.

"I have some things that I'm working on. So just be patient okay," he added, calm.

"Sure," Sidra spat. She regretted bringing the topic up; now, she was irritated. It was clear to her that Josh was perfectly fine with their distance. She however, wasn't.

Josh tilted his head as he stared at Sidra. Her tone had gotten short and she looked tense. "You're mad."

"No Josh, everything is fine," Sidra ground out, turning away from him. "I'll stay all the way out *here* and find a new job... I'll just go ahead with my plan to apply to James's firm," she muttered.

Josh frowned slightly. "What did you say?"

She glanced at him. "James's firm is hiring for a junior attorney and I'm considering applying," she confessed. Josh folded his arms; the frown had yet to leave his face. "Do you have an *issue* with that?" Her tone was almost taunting.

"Do I have an issue with you working with *James*?" Josh ground out. "No, I *don't*."

"Then what is the attitude for?" Sidra goaded.

"The fact that you said it like it was a threat," Josh pointed out. "Like some ol' 'you don't want me to move, so I'll go to James,' shit."

Sidra rolled her eyes. "Joshua don't do that, you know that's not even what I meant."

Josh snatched his sweatshirt from the chair. "Yes, you did," he insisted, upset. "You forget I know you and how spiteful you can be when you don't get your way." He jerked the shirt on. "You thought you could play on an insecurity that I *used* to have to get *back* at me."

Sidra's eyes widened. "Josh—"

"Save it," Josh spat, cutting her off. He headed for the

door. "I'm going for a walk."

Sidra watched in shock as Josh stormed out of the room, slamming the door behind him. The loud smack made her flinch. Sitting back on her bed after a moment, Sidra put her face in her hands and let out a deep sigh.

Chasity grabbed her cup of hot white chocolate and took a sip. "Oh my God, this is *so* good," she rejoiced, taking another sip.

Malajia side-eyed her. "You extra as shit over some hot chocolate," she teased. She held her hand out. "Let me get some."

Chasity moved her cup out of Malajia's reach. "Fuck outta here," she spat. "No, you drink that peppermint ass latte you got."

"This shit is nasty. I don't see how Sidra likes this," Malajia griped, adjusting the purse strap on her shoulder. The week before Christmas was upon them, sending Chasity and Malajia to the mall to do some last-minute shopping. Stopping for hot drinks, they made their way to the toy store.

"I can't believe my dumb ass messed around and waited to do this damn shopping," Malajia complained, eyeing toys on a shelf. "This is some bullshit."

"Well, you had a lot going on," Chasity consoled. "Don't be so hard on yourself."

Malajia looked at her, a hopeful expression on her face. "Did *you* wait till the last minute too?"

Chasity quickly shook her head. "No, I got all of my shopping done after Thanksgiving. You're on your own, procrastinator," she jeered.

Malajia sucked her teeth. "Well fuck you and your one kid having ass bank account," she sneered. Chasity snickered. "Yeah kee kee *now*, just wait till that second one is born."

"Yeah yeah," Chasity dismissed, waving a hand.

"You might get a boy this time," Malajia predicted.

Chasity looked at her, eyes narrowed. "You just want me to go through all that boy shit *you* go through."

"God, *please*. I just need *someone* who understands my

pain," Malajia whined.

"Doesn't one of your sisters' have a son?" Chasity asked.

"Fuck her, I don't talk to Tanya like that," Malajia scoffed, flagging the air with her hand.

Chasity laughed. "Will you stop it?"

Malajia tossed her head back and let out a groan. "Fine," she said. "My babies are amazing little boys and I love their little bad asses. Which is *why* I'm in this crowded ass store looking for toys and shit."

Chasity chuckled as they navigated an aisle. She took a deep breath as she eyed the shelves. She didn't know why, but she felt that this was a good time to tell Malajia about her plans to move. Looking at Malajia, Chasity opened her mouth to speak.

"Can you believe Sidra's ass is in trouble with Josh *again*?" Malajia began, amused.

Chasity shook her head. "That girl still hasn't learned to hone her petty skills yet," she joked. "Just firing shit off unnecessarily, and it accomplished nothing."

Malajia laughed. "I know right? She tried to be a smart-ass, throwing James's name up and shit and it backfired; now Josh is pissed at her." The girls had gotten the scoop about the argument firsthand from Sidra after Josh had left California a week ago. "Talking about she didn't mean it like that."

"Yes, she did," Chasity contradicted. "She'll be all right though. She has officially been reintroduced to the wonderful world of relationships."

Malajia snickered. "Yup, where you love them, but want to smack em' in the back of the head with a frying pan from time to time."

Chasity chuckled. "I can't find one lie there." Stopping in another aisle, Malajia began eyeing the toys. Chasity looked at her. "Okay so...I have to tell you something."

"Tell me what?" Malajia wondered, picking up a toy.

"Something that I'm pretty sure you're not going to like," Chasity vaguely replied.

Malajia set the toy back down and glanced at her. "You ain't getting your work clothes back, I already told you, you burnt."

Chasity frowned at her, then quickly shook her head. "Whatever yo," she dismissed.

"That wasn't it, I assume," Malajia concluded, putting her finger on her chin.

"No," Chasity sneered. She leaned against a shelf. "So...Jason got promoted at his job."

Malajia's eyes widened with glee. "Really?" she beamed. Chasity nodded. "About damn *time*. I know he's excited."

"Yeah, he is," Chasity answered, nonchalant. "We *both* are. It's...it's a really good opportunity."

Malajia smiled. "I *know* that money must be right."

Chasity nodded slowly. "It is."

Malajia studied Chasity's face; she didn't seem excited. "You don't look happy about it. Is there a catch or something?"

Chasity hesitated for a moment. "The thing is...the job is in Phoenix... And we have to move there."

Malajia's easy expression gave way to a concerned frown. "You mean Phoenixville, Pennsylvania, right?" she asked.

Chasity shook her head, "No."

"Phoenixapolis, New Jersey?"

Chasity frowned. "The fuck is Phoenixapolis—"

"I don't *know* okay, I just didn't want to say—" Malajia let out a huff. "I didn't want to say Phoenix, *Arizona*."

Chasity held a sympathetic gaze on the visibly upset Malajia.

"That's what you mean, right?" Malajia pressed, sadness filling her voice. "You guys are moving to Arizona?"

Chasity nodded after a moment. "Yeah," she confirmed, somber. "February."

Malajia opened her mouth to speak, but closed it as she tried to process what she had just heard. Her best friend, her confidant, someone she thought of as a sister, was moving across the country in a little over a month. Malajia pouted. "But...I can't follow you to Arizona."

"I know," Chasity sympathized. When Malajia poked her lip out, Chasity stomped her foot on the floor. "Come on Malajia, don't do this to me, you know I'm hormonal."

Malajia put her hand over her face. "You can't leave me here with all these damn Mark's," she whined. "I'm gonna lose my damn mind."

Chasity tried to stifle a laugh as she reached out and hugged Malajia. "You'll be fine," she soothed.

Malajia wrapped her arms around her, hugging her tightly. "What am I gonna do if I can't come bother you every day?"

"You can always bother me over the phone."

Malajia playfully nudged Chasity off her. "Bitch, I told you before, that ain't the same and you *know* it," she fussed.

Chasity folded her arms as Malajia wiped a tear from her eye. "Are you okay?" she asked.

"*No*," Malajia grunted. She let out a sigh after a moment, then looked back at Chasity. "Is this really what's best for you guys?"

"Yeah," Chasity nodded. "We really think it is."

Malajia finally let a small smile come through. "Then I'm happy for you," she said. "I hate that you're *leaving* but…"

"I know, me too," Chasity agreed. "Look on the bright side, you have somewhere else to visit."

"Just know that when I come down there, I'm staying at *least* three weeks…at *your* house," Malajia threw out.

Chasity pushed her hair over her shoulders. "You better get your PTO weight up before you talk about going *anywhere* for three weeks."

Malajia made a face. "You petty."

Chasity laughed a little.

Malajia thought for a moment. "It's no possibility I can leave the boys with Mark and move down there with you, is it?" she joked.

"No, you fuckin' dead beat," Chasity threw back.

Malajia busted out laughing. "Very well." She let out a deep sigh as her laughter subsided. "You know you're my best friend… I love you and I'll miss you."

Chasity narrowed her eyes. "I'm not *dying* Malajia."

"Bitch—I just wanted you to know," Malajia ground out, flinging her hand in Chasity's direction.

Chasity snickered. "I know," she nodded. "Same…my forever pain in the ass."

Malajia smiled and gave a slight nod. Running her hands over her hair, she let out a huff. "Well, I might as well get these damn toys and go have like five drinks... You done made me depressed."

"Sorry," Chasity replied.

"Yeah, you just had *better* be," Malajia joked, giving Chasity a playful tap on her arm.

Malajia glanced around the shelves. "What the hell am I gonna get these kids?" she wondered, unenthused.

Chasity eyed a package on a shelf; she pointed to it. "Aren't those the toys from that cartoon the boys like?"

Malajia snapped her head in the direction. "Oooooh!" she belted out, darting over. She snatched the package from the shelf. "Yeeeeesss, they *love* these damn Rescue Barks. They be hype as shit when the theme song comes on."

"I bet," Chasity chortled.

Malajia looked at the price; a frown formed on her face. "The *fuck*?" she snapped. "Yo, *why* is it thirty dollars for a box of *dogs*?!"

Chasity busted out laughing.

"Like seriously?" Malajia ranted, slamming the package back on the shelf. "Five little ass dogs for thirty fuckin' dollars! I ain't got it."

"Will you *stop* it?" Chasity laughed.

"Man *fuck* them dogs," Malajia complained. "They getting books and socks for Christmas."

Chasity grabbed her stomach as tears spilled down her cheeks. "I swear to God, I'm about to pee on myself."

Malajia vigorously scratched her head. "And I gotta buy *two* of 'em," she ranted. "'Cause God forbid they *share*." She stomped her foot on the floor. "That's *sixty dollars* on *ten* dumbass dogs, that'll end up behind the oven next week... The fuck is a Rescue Bark anyway? They don't rescue *shit* but little ass squirrels and mice and the occasional cat, then they start dancing at the end of the show for no fuckin' reason. Nobody asked for that bullshit."

Chasity wiped her eyes as her laughter subsided. "Mel, just get the goddamn toys so we can *go*. I'm hungry."

Malajia sucked her teeth and snatched a pack from the shelf, walking away.

"Malajia," Chasity called after her, stern.

Malajia stopped. Sucking her teeth again, she snatched a second pack from the shelf. "Happy now?" she hissed. "I'm fuckin' broke, so guess who's buying lunch?"

Chasity followed Malajia's progress in amusement as the girl stomped out of the aisle. "That's all you're getting them?"

"Yep! Now bring your ass on!" Malajia threw over her shoulder.

Chapter 49

Alex stepped out of the cab and headed to her parents' front door. Letting out a deep sigh, she gave the door a knock. Taking her boss' advice, Alex had finally decided to fix her personal life. Through the work week, she'd taken a trip to Philadelphia to visit with her parents. She wasn't sure if they were ready to see her, but *she* was ready to put this issue with them to rest. Having them upset with her was eating at her.

Alex eyed her brother once he opened the door.

Semaj smiled a taunting smile. "You are in *so* much trouble."

Alex made a face at him. "Yeah, yeah, go ahead and rub it in," she jeered as he stepped aside to let her in the house.

"Oh, I *will*," he assured. "For once, it's not *me*."

Alex flagged him with her hand, then set her bag down. "Can you just tell Ma that I'm here please?" she asked, removing her coat.

"Ma! Sneaky bill paying Alex is here!" Semaj yelled at the top of his lungs.

Alex stared at him. "You *sure* you're about to be eighteen?" she jeered.

Chuckling, Semaj took off upstairs.

Alex shook her head, then made her way over to the couch and sat down. She ran her hands down her jeans as she waited. Hearing someone walk down the steps, she glanced up and saw her mother. Alex offered a half smile; it slowly faded under her mother's stern gaze.

Alex let out a quick sigh. "Ma, come on," she pleaded. "You know I can't take it when you're mad at me."

"Well, you shouldn't do things that make me mad," Mrs. Chisolm countered. "Did you get the money that I sent?"

"Yes," Alex answered. "Got it yesterday…" Alex lowered

her head momentarily and shook it, before lifting it back up. She let out a sigh. "How did you find out?"

Mrs. Chisolm sat on the love seat across from her. "When you neglected to help me set up an account on the bill pay sites like I *asked* you too, your *brother* helped me," she explained. "Imagine my surprise when we already had accounts set up that were being paid by *you*."

Alex looked down at her hands.

"You *do* know that you used a card with your name on it right?" Mrs. Chisolm spat.

Alex resisted the urge to roll her eyes at her mother's snarky tone. "Yes, I know," she calmly replied. "I honestly didn't think that you'd ever go online to pay your bills."

Her mother fixed an angry gaze. "Of *course* not," she mocked. "You just think that your parents are two stupid, old people who wouldn't catch on."

"Come on now Ma, don't do that," Alex cut in, stern. "I don't think you're stupid, *far from* it," she assured. "And I didn't mean any harm by doing what I did... I honestly, *honestly* just wanted to help."

"Did we *ask* you for it?" Mrs. Chisolm barked.

"No, you didn't ask me for it," Alex admitted. "But...I just wanted to do what I could to help alleviate some of the financial stress that you guys go through...that you've *always* gone through." She ran her hands over her hair. "Is helping my family out *really* that *bad*?"

Mrs. Chisolm relaxed her frown. She knew that Alex was just doing what she felt was right, but she needed to make Alex understand that what she felt was right, wasn't exactly right for other people. Mrs. Chisolm leaned forward, eyeing Alex intently. "Alexandra, I know your heart...it's big and you've always wanted to help people," she began, sincere.

"Not just people, *you* guys," Alex maintained. "I watched you struggle—"

"And I watched *you* struggle," Mrs. Chisolm threw back. "Do you know how hard it was to not be able to put you through college? To watch you work *and* go to school? To watch you work on your breaks to give yourself the things that financially we weren't *able* to?"

Alex sat back in her seat. She hated that her mother still felt bad about that. "I'm not ashamed of what I had to do," she said. "Hell, considering some of the things that my friends went through with *their* families, us not having money was a walk in the park."

"I hear what you're saying, Alex," Mrs. Chisolm said. "I get it. But it still doesn't take away the fact."

Alex sighed.

"You really think that after all that, that we'd want you to take care of *us*?" Mrs. Chisolm shook her head. "No, we want you to take care of *yourself*."

Alex felt herself becoming overwhelmed with emotion. "I just—I didn't mean to insult or upset you guys. I love you more than anything, and I just wanted to do what I thought was right," she explained, wiping the tears from her eyes.

Mrs. Chisolm rose from her seat and sat next to Alex on the couch. She wrapped her arms around her child and hugged her. "I know sweetie," she consoled. "You've always been a good daughter. You've always done more than you *should*." She patted her back. "But we aren't your responsibility, okay?"

Alex nodded as she held on tight.

"Your father and I are *fine*; your brother is *fine*," she assured, calm.

Alex pulled back and wiped her eyes. "I know, and I get it," she said, pushing her hair from her face.

"And I'm not saying that you can't do nice things— especially for your brother—but that does *not* include paying bills," Mrs. Chisolm clarified. "You understand?"

Alex nodded.

Mrs. Chisolm put her hands on Alex's face, then gave her a kiss on her cheek. "You okay?" she smiled.

"That depends, is Dad still mad?"

Mrs. Chisolm waved a dismissive hand. "Child, you know your father can't stay mad for anything," she said. "He was over it after a day."

Alex laughed a little. She was relieved that the relationship with her parents was back on track, yet her spirit was still disturbed; she had two more relationships in need of repair. "Do you mind if I sleep in my old room for the night?"

"Of *course* not; you are *always* welcome," Mrs. Chisolm assured.

Alex smiled.

Mrs. Chisolm stood up. "Do you want me to fix you something to eat?"

Alex let out a sigh. "Thanks, but not yet," she declined. "I have to go out for a few."

Chasity focused on her laptop screen while her fingers moved across the keyboard. She took a quick sip of her tea, then went back to typing.

Trisha walked downstairs with Kayla in tow. "Do you want anything while we're out?" Trisha asked Chasity.

Chasity looked up from her laptop. "No, and I feel some kind of way that you didn't invite me to go see Christmas lights with you two," she jeered.

Trisha shot Chasity a knowing look. "Do you *really* care about Christmas lights?" she questioned, amusement filling her voice.

Chasity chuckled a bit. "No, not really."

Trisha laughed, adjusting the pink scarf on Kayla's neck. "Besides, this is Mom-Mom and Cupcake time," she cooed, lightly tapping Kayla's nose with her finger. "I'm getting as much time in as I can..." she then looked at Chasity, "antes de mudarte," she spoke.

Chasity shot Trisha a wide-eyed look, as Kayla looked at her. "Before *who* moves?" Kayla asked.

Trisha's eyes widened in shock as she looked down at her inquisitive granddaughter.

"She understands *Spanish*, mother," Chasity hissed, annoyed.

Trisha put her hand over her mouth. "I am *so* sorry," she sputtered.

Chasity narrowed her eyes at her mother; she and Jason had agreed not to tell Kayla about their move until after Christmas.

"Mommy?" Kayla called.

"Daddy and I will tell you later, baby," Chasity promised,

still holding her gaze on her own mother. Chasity's words seemed to satisfy Kayla, who took off for her shoes.

Trisha smiled nervously at Chasity. "You want me to bring you back some ice cream?" she asked, an attempt at a peace offering.

"*No*, big mouth," Chasity spat.

Trisha snickered. "Tacos?"

Chasity squinted. "Yes," she spat out, earning a laugh from Trisha. "Anyway," Chasity dismissed, looking back at her laptop. "Just so you know, your web programmer should be fired."

Trisha put her hand over her face and shook her head. "See, I *told* you that my site was messed up again," she complained. "Did you fix whatever the issue was?"

"Almost," Chasity answered. "Should be done soon."

"You are my angel," Trisha praised, clasping her hands together. "You know, I'm in contact with plenty of business owners, big *and* small, who could use someone with your skillset to handle their websites."

"Thanks, but I have a few clients that I'm working with now," Chasity replied, typing. "Just a few freelance jobs here and there until I'm settled and able to take more on."

Trisha nodded in approval. "You know I approve of you starting your own design company, and I'll support you with whatever you need."

"I know and thank you," Chasity replied. She smiled at her excited, bouncing daughter who was waiting by the door. "You two have fun."

Trisha blew a kiss to Chasity, then headed for the door. "We will," she assured as she and Kayla waved, heading out the door.

Chasity used the rare quiet to finish her web task; luckily for her, it took less than a half hour. She closed her laptop, and pushed herself back from the table, intent on making herself another cup of tea.

Her plan was derailed by a knock on the door. Chasity frowned as she headed for it; she wasn't expecting company.

Peering out of the peep hole, her frown turned into a full snarl. "The fuck?" she muttered to herself. Opening the door, she met her unexpected guest with an icy gaze.

Alex stood there, almost as if she was unsure of what to say. "Hey," she said after a moment.

"*Hey*?" Chasity questioned, annoyed.

Alex looked down at her tan and cream furry, calf length winter boots.

"What are you *doing* here?" Chasity wondered.

Alex met her gaze. "I came to umm…" she shivered. "Can I come in? I swear I can't feel my fingers."

Chasity rolled her eyes, but stepped aside to let Alex in.

"Thank you," Alex replied, grateful. She rubbed her hands together as she tried to warm up. "It's freezing out there."

"It's *winter*," Chasity sneered, closing the door.

"Right," Alex muttered.

Chasity folded her arms. "What are you doing here?" she repeated.

Alex let out a sigh. "I'm in town visiting my parents, and I figured that since I wasn't far from you that I'd come see you…to talk to you in person," Alex explained; she put a hand up when Chasity went to speak. "And before you yell at me for not calling first, you don't *answer* my phone calls."

Chasity rolled her eyes, but didn't say anything. Alex had a valid point.

"And Malajia said that you were home so, here I am," Alex further explained.

Chasity glared at Alex for a moment, then rolled her eyes again. "Whatever. Sit your frozen ass down," she grunted, pointing to the couch.

Alex let out a sigh of relief; she would've hated to have made the trip just to be put right out. She was appreciative. She removed her coat and set it on the love seat as she sat down on the couch. Chasity sat down next to her.

Alex adjusted her position to face Chasity, rubbing her shoulders in the process.

Chasity grabbed a decorative throw blanket from the accent chair and tossed it at Alex. "Here, your shivering is annoying me."

Alex chuckled a bit. "Thank you," she replied, wrapping the cozy blanket around her shoulders. "It's nice to know that you care."

"Um hmm," Chasity grunted, fixing Alex with an intense stare. "You came here to say *what* exactly?"

"That I'm sorry."

"You said that already," Chasity spat back.

"But I need you to know how much I *mean* it," Alex countered. When Chasity sucked her teeth, Alex took a deep breath. "Listen, I know that how I went about the whole job thing—"

"Alex, I don't give a shit about that damn interview," Chasity cut in, annoyed. "Did you put me in an awkward position? Yes. Did it piss me off? Yes. But I'm not upset with you about *that*. It's how you reacted when I turned it down and the shit that you *said*."

Alex took a deep breath. "I know," she agreed, sincerely. "I didn't have a right to be upset with you because you turned it down, and I *especially* didn't have a right to come at you the way that I did." She put a hand on her chest. "The stuff that I said—Chasity, I... I can't justify it. It was wrong and unnecessary... *Especially* my comments about how you are as a mother."

Chasity shook her head. "You know...I question myself *a lot* when it comes to being a mom," she admitted, frustrated. "I have *no* idea what I'm doing—and I make mistakes, but the *one* thing that I *do* know is that I'm determined to raise my daughter the complete opposite of how *I* was raised, and for you to even *insinuate* that I would be violent with her..." she took a deep breath. "You thinking that about me is *fucked* up."

Alex put a hand over her face and shook her head, ashamed of herself. She began to tear up. "I know."

"It was fucked up and it hurt me," Chasity confessed. She shrugged slightly. "Maybe I'm just being sensitive, but I just thought that you thought better of me."

Alex removed her hand from her face, and put it on Chasity's arm. "Of course I do. I didn't mean to hurt you Chasity, I swear to God," Alex pleaded, tears spilling. "I *know* that you're a great mom. And I *don't* look down on you, in fact I respect and *admire* you, always *have*."

Chasity looked at Alex as she spoke.

"I was being a *terrible* friend, and I know that," Alex added, sincere. "I love you and I am *so* sorry." She wiped her face with her hand. "...I hope that you can forgive me one of these days."

Chasity held her gaze on Alex. It was true, Alex had hurt her feelings, but she was coming to her with sincerity and remorse. The girl worked her nerves at times, but Chasity still loved her and deep down, she knew Alex's heart. "Okay Alex it's fine... We're fine."

Alex sniffled as she wiped her eyes. "You don't have to say that just because I'm sitting here crying," she said.

"You *are* an ugly crier and all, but that's not why I said it," Chasity jeered.

Alex chuckled.

"We're good, let's just move past it," Chasity proposed.

Alex reached out and gave Chasity a hug. "Thank you. Love you."

"Love you too," Chasity replied, then parted from the embrace. "Listen, I know I made the comment about you being lonely—"

Alex waved a dismissive hand. "Don't worry about that, I deserved it," she cut in.

Chasity put a hand up, silencing her. "I'm sorry for that," she said. Alex offered a slight smile. "I know that jokes are made because we're an ignorant, disrespectful group of friends—"

Alex laughed a little.

"*But*," Chasity continued. "I want you to know that there's nothing wrong with being by yourself," Chasity's tone was sincere. "It doesn't mean that you're lonely. You don't *have* to be in a relationship; it's a not mandatory life goal."

"I know that sis, and I *was* perfectly fine being single for the time that I was," Alex confessed. "It allowed me the time that I needed to get to know myself on another level, but at this point in my life I actually *want* one." She removed the blanket from her shoulders. The chill was gone. "And I want that with *Eric*."

Chasity tilted her head. "You sure?"

Alex moved some of her hair from her face. "Yeah. I mean,

I at least want to give us a *shot*," she amended. "If it doesn't work out, then it's not meant to be, but I think I owe it to myself…to *both* of us to *try*."

"Kid and all?" Chasity asked.

Alex nodded. "It's worth a try," she stood firm. Sighing, she glanced off to the side. "But of course, I went and messed shit up with my…*ways* and now he's not talking to me… Yet again." Alex pulled her phone from her purse. "He hasn't responded to any of my texts."

Chasity frowned. "You've only been texting him?"

Alex nodded. "Like I told you girls back at Emily's, I texted him a few times… Nothing."

Chasity pinched the bridge of her nose. "God, you are so dense— Alex, *call* that man."

"Call him and say *what* exactly?" Alex questioned, holding her arms up.

"The same shit you just said to *me*," Chasity countered. "Don't nobody want no goddamn 'what are you doing?' texts after you acted like a *jackass*."

"Well damn, Chasity!" Alex exclaimed. "I *do* say more than 'what are you doing?'. God girl, give me more credit than that."

"Nah, I won't because I know you too well," Chasity threw back. Alex rolled her eyes, but didn't say anything. "Call him or take your ass to go see him face-to-face."

Alex vigorously shook her head. "He'd probably slam the damn door in my face."

"Maybe, maybe *not*," Chasity said. "You told me a long time ago that it's easy to ignore someone when they're not standing in front of you. It's time for you to take your *own* advice, sis."

Alex turned her lip up. "The *one* time I give good advice, it comes back to haunt me," she jeered.

Chasity chuckled.

Alex let out a sigh. "Chaz, I can't just go see him. He lives in Connecticut—that'll be a long trip just to be turned away."

"Yet you brought your ass here to see *me*, not knowing if *I'd* slam the door in your face," Chasity threw back.

Alex sighed yet again. "I mean…it's not the same

situation," she muttered, a sad attempt at an excuse.

Chasity stared at her for a long moment before shaking her head. "A goddamn shame," she grunted.

Alex couldn't help but laugh a little. "I know, I know." She put her hand over her face.

Chasity let out a quick sigh, then held her hand out. "Let me see your phone," she demanded.

Alex handed it over without question. She watched as Chasity's fingers moved around her screen. "What are you looking for?"

"Huh?" Chasity muttered, tapping the screen. She then put the phone on speaker.

Alex, hearing the line dialing, looked confused. "Who did you just call?" she asked, amused.

"Eric."

Alex's eyes widened. "What the hell?!" She moved to grab the phone, but Chasity held it out of her reach. "Are you out of your damn mind? Hang up!"

"Stop bitchin'," Chasity snapped through clenched teeth, smacking Alex's hand away from her.

Alex began to sweat as the phone kept ringing. "Oh my God, hang up!" She snatched the phone just as the line picked up.

"Hello?" Eric answered.

Alex's mouth gaped open; she was scared and didn't know what to say. Instead of gathering her words, she hung up.

Chasity frowned as Alex slammed her phone on the couch, then hid her face behind her hands.

"What did you do that for?!" Chasity exclaimed.

Alex jerked her head up and pointed in Chasity's face. "I *hate* you! Why did you call him?!" she erupted.

"Because *you wouldn't*," Chasity flashed back.

Alex's mouth opened; she was furious. "You—what is *with* you doing this sneaky shit lately?" she hurled.

Chasity's response was halted when Alex's phone rang. They both looked down; it was Eric calling back.

"Shiiiiit," Alex panicked, pulling her hands down her face.

"You gonna answer that?" Chasity taunted.

Alex frowned at her. Chasity went to grab the phone, but

Alex put her hand up. "You touch it and I *will* smack you," she warned.

Chasity looked at her. "Why would you do that?" she asked, feigning hurt. "I'm pregnant."

Alex narrowed her eyes as the call dropped. She looked at the missed call message and sighed. "Great," she huffed, picking the phone back up. She took a deep breath and dialed back.

The line immediately picked up. "Hello?" Eric answered.

Alex pinched the bridge of her nose. "Hi Eric…it's Alex."

"I know, I still have your number saved," Eric replied.

"Right," Alex replied, waving her hand in Chasity's direction when the woman snickered. Though the phone wasn't on speaker, the volume was up high; Chasity could hear everything. "Um…my phone call…it was an accident." She closed her eyes tight; she instantly regretted her words.

Chasity rolled her eyes, then stood up from the couch. She could no longer be a witness to Alex's foolishness. "I'm gonna go find a damn snack," she muttered, heading for the kitchen.

"Oh," Eric replied, not hiding his disappointment. "Okay then."

"No I— It's just that I'm visiting a friend—"

"Don't blame that shit on me!" Chasity belted out from the kitchen.

Alex pulled the phone from her ear. "Shut *up* Chasity," she hurled back.

"Listen Alex, if we're not going to talk, I have to go."

"Eric, I may not have meant to dial you *now*, but that doesn't mean that I *don't* want to talk to you," Alex quickly cut in, sensing Eric's frustration with her. She knew how immature this call was. She could've sought privacy in Chasity's house to talk to Eric, but she needed time to get her thoughts in order. "That being said…can I call you back another time?"

"Sure Alex," Eric replied after a moment. The frustration in his voice had not waned. "Later."

Alex let out a sigh. "Later," she muttered once he'd hung up. She tossed her phone back on the couch, and hid behind her hands again.

Chapter 50

Malajia speared a piece of pumpkin pie with her fork and placed it into her mouth as she sat at her desk. She closed her eyes as she chewed. "Babe, you gotta tell your mom that she makes the best pumpkin pie," she said into the phone.

Mark chuckled. "You still eating that damn pie?" he asked. "Christmas was like two weeks ago."

"So? You act like *you* wasn't just eating them Christmas greens last night," she threw back. Mark laughed; she too broke into laughter.

"How's work?" he asked, laughter subsiding.

Setting her fork down, Malajia let out a happy sigh. With the holidays finally over, Malajia was back to work and she couldn't be happier. "It's good," she beamed. "Getting back into the swing of things."

"Good, I'm glad you're happy," Mark said, sincere.

"Thanks," she smiled. "How are you holding up still being at home with the boys?"

"Oh, we chillin'" Mark assured.

"Still haven't heard anything from any perspective jobs?"

Mark sighed. "Nope... I swear it was so damn easy getting a job right out of college," he recalled. "And that was with *no* goddamn experience. *Now*, it's like I can't get an interview for *shit.*"

"I know baby, but something will come along," Malajia consoled, playing with the ink pen on her desk.

"Yeah," Mark sighed. "Anyway, your mom came over for a little bit, earlier today. She said she was visiting Geri and decided to stop over."

"She lying like shit, she ain't visit no damn Geri. Geri ass been at work all day," Malajia contradicted. "She just didn't want to make it seem like she drove all the way up here just to see the boys, since we didn't go to Baltimore for Christmas."

"Yeah, she's still pretty salty about that," Mark told.

"So?" Malajia spat. "I told her that Dad needs to apologize first."

"You really think that's gonna happen?" Mark asked, unconvinced.

Malajia sighed. "If he's the man that I *hope* he is, he *will*..." she shook the somber thoughts from her head. "Whatever, I'm not tryna talk about that old ass man anymore."

"If you say so," Mark replied. Deep down, he knew how much Malajia hated not talking to her father.

Malajia sighed again as she looked at her watch. "I gotta go. I'm meeting up with Chasity after work for a bit, we're going to be going over some bridesmaid shit," she said. "You want me to pick up dinner?"

"Nah, I'll handle it," Mark assured.

Malajia smiled. "Oh, I can get used to this," she cooed. "What is my sexy husband gonna make for dinner?"

"Frozen pizza."

Malajia put her hand over her face and let out a sigh. "Good Lord," she mumbled.

Mark laughed. "Sike naw, I'll think of something," he promised. "Don't worry about it."

Malajia just shook her head in amusement.

Sitting at her kitchen table, Emily wrapped a glass plate in newspaper, carefully placing it into a box. She sighed as she repeated the process. After a moment, she stopped and looked around.

Her apartment was a cluttered mess. With her wedding merely weeks away, and her lease almost up, Emily was finally packing up her apartment and getting things ready to move in with Will. She let out another sigh and rested her face in her hands; she just couldn't shake her somber mood.

God Emily, get it together. Lifting her head, she went to grab another dish, but was interrupted by her phone ringing. She grabbed it from the table and looked at the caller ID. "Hey

Will," she answered.

"Hey, how's the packing going?" he asked.

Emily shrugged. "It's going," she answered, unenthused. "I'm making progress, I guess."

"I don't even know why you're actually *packing,* when we can just grab stuff little by little and walk it upstairs," he chuckled.

"I don't know," she replied, tone dry. "If nothing else, it's keeping me occupied." She ran a hand through her hair. "Are we putting my furniture in storage?"

"No, yours is much nicer than mine," he replied. "We can move it up here and mine can go in storage...or the trash."

Emily wanted to crack a smile, but couldn't. "Okay, sounds like a plan."

Her tone was not missed on Will. "You okay babe?" he asked after a moment.

"Sure," Emily replied, tone not changing. Her mood was so bad, even talking to her husband-to-be couldn't even cheer her up.

"So how does it feel not having to deal with all of the wedding stuff, now that you've finally relinquished your wedding planning duties to your girls?" Will began, at an attempt to cheer her up.

Emily managed a small smile. "It's nice... I don't know what I'd do without them." Though Emily had been reluctant to ask the girls for help—afraid that she would put too much on them—she was happy that they had taken the task from her. At least *that* part of her stress was gone.

"Yeah, they have everybody whipped into shape," Will chortled. "My Mom said that Sidra was a life saver when the shop that my parents are using to get their dress and tux, tried to act like they weren't going to have their alterations done in time."

"Yeah, she probably threatened to sue them," Emily joked of Sidra.

Will laughed a little. He sucked his teeth after a moment. "Crap, I have to get back to work, I'll see you later."

"Okay," Emily replied, hanging up.

Sighing again, Emily stood up. Her eyes roamed around the

space once more; it was her first apartment. A place that she was once happy in. Thanks to her sister, she no longer had fond memories here. It was just a reminder of another good moment that she was robbed of.

As Emily went to grab more dishes from her cabinet, she heard a knock on her door.

She frowned slightly. "Wonder who that is?" she muttered to herself. Will was still at work, and Anthony was at his grandparent's house; she wasn't expecting any company. She walked to the door "Who is it?" she softly called.

"Delivery for Emily Harris," a female voice answered.

Emily frowned slightly. She wasn't expecting a package either. However, she had started to receive some wedding gifts from guests who weren't going to be able to make the wedding. Shrugging, she opened the door.

Her curiosity gave way to pure disgust when Emily saw who was standing there. "Seriously?" she hissed at Jazmine.

"I figured that if I said it was me, you wouldn't have answered," Jazmine explained.

Emily held her icy gaze, but didn't say anything. She couldn't believe that Jazmine had the audacity to show up at her door after everything that she'd done. Emily hadn't heard from the girl since their fight, and she was hoping that Jazmine would've stayed gone.

Jazmine folded her arms. "Emily…I think we need to—"

"No," Emily spat as she went to slam the door in her face. Jazmine put her hand out to stop her.

"Get the hell away from my door!" Emily yelled.

Jazmine put her hands up cautiously and stepped back slightly. "I didn't come here to fight with you—"

"What are you *doing* here?" Emily cut in, upset.

"I just want to talk."

Emily held her hand on the door and eyed Jazmine with confusion and anger. "*Talk*?" she sneered. "Talk?!"

Jazmine flinched at the bass in Emily's voice.

"That *last* thing that I want to do is *talk* to *you*," Emily fumed.

Jazmine ran a hand over her forehead. "Look Emily, I'm sorry okay," she said. Her words didn't sound sympathetic, it was like Jazmine barked them at her.

Emily tilted her head. Her interaction with Jazmine this time was different. Emily was no longer intimidated by her, and she no longer cared *about* her. "You can't even lie right," she sneered. "What? You need a place to stay again?" she taunted. "I heard that you tried to stay with Brad... How did that go?"

Jazmine rolled her eyes. "I think you know that our brothers and parents have practically disowned me," she bit out.

"Oh? How does that feel?" Emily sniped.

Jazmine ran her hands over her hair and let out a quick sigh. "Not that you *care*, but I'm staying with a friend in Jersey right now," she informed. "She's letting me crash there while—"

"You're right, I *don't* care," Emily hurled. "Stay away from me."

As Emily went to close the door once more, Jazmine took a step forward. "Emily, despite what happened—" she took a deep breath as Emily paused once more. "Despite how I acted, how I felt about you...I never wanted to see you hurt like that."

Emily looked off to the side as she shook her head.

"I admit, you hitting your head like that scared me," she said. "I never wanted our feud to go that far."

Emily snapped her head in Jazmine's direction. "It was a one-sided feud that *you* created, Jazmine," she raged, tears representing years of hurt and anger in her eyes. "I never did *anything* to you. But you've done *nothing* but treat me like *shit* my *entire* life."

"Emily—"

"No," Emily cut in, voice cracking. She wanted Jazmine gone from her life, but she wanted to tell her how she felt first. "There's nothing that you can say to me to make me forget or forgive everything that you've done," she vented. "You've disrespected me, and I put up with it time after time, because I hoped that *one* day you would stop and realize what you were doing. I hoped that one day you would give a *fuck* about me, but it's clear that you never did and you never *will*."

Jazmine stood there listening. For the first time, she looked as if she had remorse.

"You don't love me and that's fine," Emily concluded,

tears falling. "And if me getting hurt had to happen for me to *finally* get it and cut you out of my life for good…*that's* fine too."

Jazmine looked down at her sneakers. "I guess…I guess I have no choice but to live with that," she muttered after a moment. "I don't know what else I can say besides that I'm sorry that I hurt you."

"I don't want your apology…I want you to stay away from me," Emily countered.

Jazmine looked at Emily for a long moment, before nodding slowly. "Okay," she agreed, somber.

Emily stared at her older sister, fighting the urge to bust out into a full-on cry. She meant it; she wanted nothing to do with Jazmine, but it didn't mean that her heart wasn't heavy. It was her sister after all, and Emily had no choice but to love her. But she also knew that it was in her best interest to cut ties with Jazmine. "Okay," Emily said, and punctuated her response by slamming the door in Jazmine's face.

Jazmine stared at the door for a long moment. The reality of what had just taken place had hit her; because of her unnecessary jealousy; her disregard, her bitterness, she'd just lost her little sister forever. Taking a deep breath, she turned and walked away.

"You *still* haven't spoken to Josh?" Chasity barked into her laptop video camera.

Sidra put her hand over her face and let out a sigh. "I mean we talk briefly here and there…like a 'hey, I'm still alive' check in. But no, we haven't actually *talked*," she admitted. "He's still upset with me."

Chasity shook her head. "You're a fool, you know that?" she goaded.

Sidra rolled her eyes. With Emily's wedding closing in, the girls were getting together more often to plan her bridal parties and go over wedding details. With Sidra being out of the area, video calls were the norm. "Look, I *want* to apologize, but he doesn't stay on the phone long enough for me to do that."

Alex, taking advantage of a day off, had made the trip

down from New York. She was at Chasity's house, waiting for
Malajia to arrive. She glanced over at the screen from the
counter. "It's been like three weeks, he's *still* mad?" she
condemned. "I'm sorry, but that's ridiculous."

Chasity snapped her head towards Alex from where she sat
at the dining room table. "Hey, you shut up and get back to
wrapping those glasses," she ordered, pointing at her.

Alex rolled her eyes as she reached for one of the glasses
on the counter and wrapped it in bubble wrap. While the girls
were waiting, Chasity decided to take advantage of the extra
hands and enlist Alex's help with her packing.

"I mean she *does* have a point—" Sidra began.

Chasity looked back at her screen. "*You* shut up too, she
doesn't have a point, which is why her scared ass can't get shit
right with Eric *now*," she cut in, ceasing Sidra's excuses. "Go
ahead and lose *your* man listening to *Alex.*"

"Point taken," Sidra muttered after a moment.

Alex sucked her teeth. Chasity had a point; she had yet to
call Eric back. "You know what, I don't have to sit here and be
insulted," she ground out.

"You *do* if you don't want to sit out on that cold ass
porch," Chasity goaded.

Sidra shook her head. "What time is Malajia coming
over?" she asked, changing the subject.

Chasity stretched her neck from side to side. "She should
be on her way, she got off work not too long ago."

"Okay well, I have a meeting to go to before I get out of
here for the day, so just text me when Mel gets there. Hopefully
I'm not in there too long," Sidra said.

"Okay Sid, talk to you later," Alex said, wrapping an item.

Sidra blew a kiss into the screen. "Love you both."

"Love you too," Alex replied, the same time that Chasity
grunted. "Ugh."

Sidra giggled. "So rude," she said to Chasity before ending
the call.

Chasity ran her hands through her hair and let out a groan.

"You okay over there, Miss Bossy?" Alex mocked.

Chasity made a face at her. "No," she spat, standing up.
"I'm *sick* of being in this cluttered ass house."

Alex placed a wrapped glass in a nearby box. Chasity's normally neat and pristine home had become a mess of boxes, bubble wrap, and suitcases. "Well sweetie, you're packing up a whole *house*. You *have* to expect clutter."

"I'm about to hit everything with a fuckin' blow torch and just start from scratch when we get there," she griped, grabbing a bottle of juice from the refrigerator. With their move to Arizona less than a month away, Chasity was stressed.

Alex chuckled a bit, before a somber look fell upon her face. "I can't believe you're actually moving that far away," she moped. "First Sid and now *you*."

"Yeah, I know," Chasity agreed.

Alex let out a sigh. "Can...can you take Malajia *with* you?"

Chasity chuckled.

"*Please*?" Alex begged. "Because with *you* gone, she's gonna bug the hell outta *me*."

Chasity opened her juice. "I don't think you'll have that problem," she said. "She don't half like your ass anyway."

Alex's mouth fell open in shock. "You lie! She *loves* me."

"Okay," Chasity chuckled, sipping her juice.

Alex went to say something, when the front door opened.

"Hey," Malajia greeted, walking in. She removed her coat and tossed it, along with her purse, on the couch. She held up a bottle. "I brought wine."

"I can't *drink* it," Chasity grunted, setting the rest of her juice on the counter.

Malajia shrugged as she moved a box aside with her foot. "I wasn't sharing *anyway*."

Chasity rolled her eyes. "Oh, Alex said that she wants me to take you with me to Phoenix because you're gonna start bugging her once I'm gone," she told, much to Alex's shock.

"Oh my God! *Really* Chasity?" Alex exclaimed.

Malajia shot Alex a narrowed eyed glare, before looking back at Chasity. "She ain't gotta worry about that, 'cause I don't half like her ass no way, no how," she shot back.

Chasity busted out laughing, as Alex gasped. "Disrespectful," Alex ground out.

Malajia sat down at the table, unfazed by Alex's reaction. "You got any food cooked?" she asked Chasity.

"Fuck no, I don't even wanna *be* in here right now,"
Chasity said, folding her arms. "Let's go out to eat."

"We're gonna video chat Sidra at a noisy restaurant?" Alex
pointed out.

Chasity thought for a moment, then grabbed her phone
from the table. "Good point, let's go to my mom's. She got all
that space and she'll make me tacos."

"Ooh, I'm down," Malajia approved. "You think she'll let
me spend the night?"

Alex squinted. "Girl, stop trying to run from your family,"
she ground out.

Malajia flipped Alex the finger.

Chasity placed a call and put the phone to her ear. "Mom
are you home? ...Okay, I'm coming over with Mel and Alex, we
need your den... Make me tacos... I don't *wanna* say please, I
want you to make me tacos... I'm carrying your grandchild,
make me tacos!"

Malajia laughed as Chasity hung up her phone. "She hung
up on you, didn't she?"

"Yeah, after she cussed at me and called me a disrespectful
brat," Chasity confirmed, amusement in her voice.

"Bet money your spoiled ass gets those tacos though,"
Malajia predicted.

"I will," Chasity boasted. "She might *throw* them at me,
but I'll get 'em."

Alex shook her head as she giggled.

Sidra let out a sigh as she walked out of her meeting. After
an hour of listening to the people in her firm drone on, she was
mentally drained. Shifting the files in her hand, she made her
way to her office and shut the door. She set her work down and
glanced at her watch. "Good, it's time to get out of here," she
said aloud, eager to get home and video chat with her girls.

As Sidra grabbed her purse and slung it over her shoulder,
her cell phone rang. She grabbed it and looked at the caller ID.
Her eyes widened a bit at the sight of Josh's name; the tension
between them had her on edge every time he called.

"Hey," she answered.

"Hey," Josh replied. "You still at work?"

"Leaving now. Why, is everything okay?"

"Yes, things are fine," he answered. "Listen, I'll be down there in a few days."

Sidra ignored his curt tone; she just focused on what he'd said. "Really? I thought that you weren't planning on coming until after Em's wedding, since we'll see each other in a few weeks anyway."

"I thought it would be better if I come down there sooner," he alluded. "Will that be a problem?"

Sidra raised an eyebrow. "No, it's no problem," she answered, nonchalant. Though she was feeling a bit anxious, her voice hid it well.

"Okay cool, I'll talk to you—"

"Josh wait," Sidra interrupted. "Before you come down, I really want to say that—"

"We'll talk when I get there," he cut in.

Sidra was silent for a moment. The fact that he didn't seem angry worried her; Josh seemed indifferent, something that reminded her of a past situation with James. Before he'd broke up with her during senior year, James had sounded the same way. She let out a deep sigh. *Damn, I messed up yet again.* "Okay Josh... See you in a few days," she said finally, resolved.

"See you."

"Bye," she sulked. She hung up the phone and took a deep breath, before heading out of her office.

Alex looked over at Chasity, who was concentrating on eating her food. "You really got your tacos," she chuckled.

Malajia snickered as she grabbed her glass of margarita. "*Told* you," she said. She took a long sip, relishing the taste. "Yaaaasss, Ms. Trisha, these margaritas are hittin'!" she bellowed into the living room from the den.

"Thank you, sweetie," Trisha replied, poking her head in to check on them. She looked at Chasity. "How's your virgin margarita?" she asked her.

Chasity rolled her eyes. "It's missing liquor," she jeered.

Trisha shook her head in amusement. "As sad as I am that

you're moving, I kinda like the idea of not being subjected to your hormonal attitude," she threw back.

"Oh, this isn't hormonal," Chasity countered, setting her empty plate on a nearby end table.

Trisha flagged her dismissively. "I'm heading out, you ladies stay as long as you need to."

"Oh, I will," Malajia called after her. "Hell, don't be surprised if I move in."

Alex ran her hands over her hair as she leaned back in her cushy accent chair. "Malajia—"

"Mind your business," Malajia spat, taking another sip of her drink.

Chasity, hearing a text come through on her phone, glanced at it. "Sidra said she's ready to video chat," she announced. Alex and Malajia moved their seats closer to Chasity as she prepared to make the call on her laptop.

"Somebody's breath is really hot on my goddamn neck," Chasity bristled.

"It's *mine*, now shut the hell up and make the call," Malajia bit out, causing Alex to snicker hard. "Sick of your shit."

"Whatever," Chasity grunted, pushing a few keys.

The girls waved once Sidra's face popped up. "Hey girls," Sidra greeted, a glass of white wine in hand.

"Hey Sid, rough day at work, huh?" Alex questioned. "I see the wine."

Sidra took a sip and set the glass down. Finally home, Sidra had hoped to unwind a bit. But with Josh's phone call heavy on her mind, relaxation wasn't happening. "Work was work. Nothing I'm not used to handling," Sidra replied, pushing her hair behind her ear. "Hey, before we talk about Em, can I mention something to you ladies?"

"Of course," Alex replied.

Sidra took a deep breath, almost as if she didn't want to say the next words. "I… I think Josh is going to break up with me," she revealed, finally.

The three girls stared at the screen, silent. Their facial expressions varied from Chasity's annoyance, to Malajia's confusion, to Alex's shock. Malajia pinched the bridge of her nose and let out a deep sigh.

"Sidra—shut up," Chasity spat.

"*Thank* you," Malajia chimed in, tossing a hand up. "Dramatic ass."

Sidra's mouth fell open. "Well *damn* heffas!" she belted out.

Alex put a hand up. "What I think they *meant* to say, was that there is no way that Josh would break up with you," she placated.

"No, I *meant* shut up," Chasity reiterated. "Nobody has time for Sidra's bullshit today."

"Yeah girl, I love you and all and you know I'm all for offering a listening ear, but like Chaz said, we don't have time for this," Malajia added, shaking her hand at the screen. "Josh ain't breaking up with you, so stop it. You can cut that man's dick off, grind it up and serve it as a hamburger to him, and his whipped ass would say, 'but she fed me though.'"

Chasity stared blankly out in front of her. "Wow," was all that she could say regarding Malajia's extreme scenario.

"How does your mind come *up* with mess like that?" Alex bristled.

"She's crazy and disgusting, *that's* how," Sidra sneered.

Malajia tossed her arms up in frustration. "What? Am I *lying*?" Chasity just shook her head, as Alex flagged Malajia with her hand.

Sidra rolled her eyes. "Rude, just rude," she bit out. She decided not to harp on it for the time being. "Let's get on to this wedding topic."

"We were *about* to before you started with that nonsense," Chasity pointed out.

"Bridal shower please!" Sidra snapped, trying desperately to change the subject.

"Okay so…I know that I should've mentioned this sooner, but I wanted to wait until we were all together," Alex began serious.

"What are you talking about?" Sidra asked. "Mention what?"

"Well… Emily told me that with everything going on with her family… She doesn't *want* a bridal shower and bachelorette party," Alex informed.

Chasity looked at her, frowning. "When did she tell you *that*?"

Alex sighed. "She told me when I talked to her about a week ago," she revealed. "I was asking if she was excited about everything, and that I was looking forward to seeing her for the upcoming shower, and that's when she told me."

"Ain't nobody thinkin' about Emily. We're *doing* something for her," Malajia dismissed with a wave of her hand. "Besides, we already started buying decorations and shit."

"I agree with you Malajia, she deserves it," Sidra agreed. "*Especially* after everything that she's been through... Do you know that because of all the tension with Emily's mom, her two cousins stepped down from being bridesmaids?"

"Man fuck those dry ass bitches. They never mattered anyway," Malajia spat.

"Emily's family is *really* pissing me the fuck off," Chasity vented.

"I know," Sidra sympathized. "Emily is the sweetest person that I know; she doesn't deserve this nonsense."

"She's been so depressed lately, I feel so bad," Alex put in, somber.

"Which is all the more reason why we need to do something nice for her," Malajia pointed out. "That's not only our duty as her bridesmaids, but as her *friends*."

Chasity thought for a moment. "Okay so, we won't do a *traditional* shower and bachelorette party," she began.

"What are you thinking?" Sidra wondered, intrigued.

"How about we just do a girls weekend," Chasity suggested. "Just us five in a nice hotel or something."

Alex was grinning from ear to ear. "I *love* it," she approved, excited. "There won't be a bunch of people that she isn't comfortable with, yet we can still *shower* her with a good time."

"That was fuckin' corny, but yeah," Chasity threw back, pointing at Alex who in turn sucked her teeth.

"Okay, so are we going to do it up here, or in Virginia where *she* is?" Malajia asked.

"I say we go to *her*," Sidra chimed in.

"I'll start looking at hotels," Alex piped up. "Are we still

J.B. Vample

doing it the same weekend that we were planning her shower?"

"Don't see why *not*," Sidra replied. "I already have my flight booked for that date anyway."

Alex clasped her hands together. "I'm so excited, I think that a weekend with us is *just* what Em needs to lift her spirits," she beamed. "And we can *still* use the decorations—"

"Wait, instead of a hotel, let's find a lodge," Chasity suggested.

"You think we can find one *available* on such short notice?" Malajia wondered. "I mean, we're only like three weeks away from when we want to do this."

"I'm sure we can find something," Chasity answered, confident. "My dad actually owns one down there in Virginia," she continued after a moment. Her revelation was met with stares. "And the looks are *for*?"

"Damn bitch, you was holding out?" Malajia blurted out. "When did *that* happen?"

"Does it really *matter*?" Chasity huffed. "I'll talk to him, and as long as nobody is scheduled to be there that weekend, it shouldn't be an issue."

"Shit, it doesn't matter if someone *is* scheduled, they'll just have to bounce," Malajia boasted, folding her arms.

"Well perfect. Chaz, let us know when everything is definite, and we can go from there," Sidra said. "I have some ideas of activities we can do."

"Ooh, ooh, can we get a stripper?" Malajia eagerly requested, raising her hand.

"Yes," Chasity and Alex answered, the same time that Sidra said, "No."

Malajia busted out laughing. "Ahhh, your uptight ass is outnumbered," she hurled at Sidra. "Stripper it is."

Sidra's mouth fell open. "Chasity, Malajia, you two are *married*."

"So?" Chasity scoffed the same time that Malajia said "*And*?"

"We're not gonna *screw* them, we're just gonna *look* at 'em," Malajia added.

Sidra shook her head. "I don't know why I'm surprised," she ground out. "But Alex, you too? Really?"

"Girl, I'm horny and *alone*. I need someone to look at and possibly touch me," Alex threw back, unfazed.

"I know *that's* right, Alex," Malajia praised, giving Alex a high five. Malajia chuckled when Sidra sucked her teeth. "Sid, you act like we didn't already agree to this. We mentioned swinging dicks during homecoming."

Alex put her hand over her face, trying to suppress her building laughter.

Sidra stared at the camera, unamused. "I'm just going to ignore that," she muttered. "But look, Emily is not the 'stripper' type, you *know* that."

"*She* ain't gotta look at him, she'll be all right," Malajia threw back.

As much as Sidra wanted to battle over this issue, she knew that there was no point. She was outnumbered, and even if she weren't, she knew the girls well enough to know that they were going to go through with their plans anyway. "Fine, get your little nasty stripper," she scoffed.

"Oh, he won't be *little*," Chasity muttered, earning laughter from Malajia and Alex.

"Fine," Sidra sneered.

Alex let out a sigh of delight. "I'm liking the lodge idea better than the hotel anyway," she said. "I mean, let's face it, we're owed a lodge do-over because the *last* time we were there, it wasn't necessarily a good time."

Chasity and Malajia both simultaneously shot Alex lethal glares.

Alex, catching their glares, wiped the humor from her face. Given everything that had transpired at Lunar Lodge their junior year of college, her joke wasn't appropriate. No matter *how* much time had passed. "Yeah, that umm, that situation will never be funny," she admitted, apologetic.

"Wow Alex," Sidra commented. "That was in poor taste."

"Hush Sidra, isn't Josh supposed to be breaking up with you?" Alex threw back, earning a loud gasp from Sidra.

Chapter 51

Sidra sat at her kitchen table, slowly sipping her cup of coffee. She let out a sigh, staring at the breakfast ingredients strewn across the counter. She had every intention of making her and Josh breakfast, but didn't have the mental energy; she had just elected to make coffee. Besides, Josh had yet to wake, or so she thought.

"Morning," Josh greeted, stepping into the kitchen.

Sidra turned around and faced him. He was shirtless; she liked him shirtless, but she couldn't focus on that right now. "Morning," she replied.

He eyed the mug in her hand. "Any more coffee made?"

"Of course." Sidra gestured to the half-filled coffee maker on the counter. She went to stand. "I'll make you a cup."

Josh put his hand out as he made his way to the counter. "No need, I can get it myself."

Sidra sat back down. "Okay," she quietly said. She watched in silence as Josh prepared himself a cup of coffee. *He seems like his normal self,* she thought. It didn't feel that way when Josh had arrived at her apartment from the airport the night before and gone straight to sleep. She didn't get a chance to talk to him like she had hoped.

Sidra looked at him as he sat down at the table across from her. "How did you sleep?" she asked.

Josh took a sip of his coffee. "Good…I was tired last night."

Sidra nodded slightly. "I could tell."

"Long day, long flight," he added.

"Yeah," Sidra muttered. She wrapped her hands around the warm mug and studied the liquid still lingering inside. "Josh," she called after a moment.

"Yeah?"

She looked up at him. "I know that we've been talking and everything since your last visit, but things still seem off," she began. Josh just stared at her. "And I know that it's because of how I acted... I'm sorry if you felt—" She paused and took a deep breath as Josh held his gaze on her. "No...I'm sorry *that* I tried to hurt your feelings because I was upset with you," she admitted. "It was petty and immature."

"Yes, it *was*," Josh confirmed, stern.

"And if you would've done the same to me, I would've been angry too," she added.

"Yes, you would've," Josh replied.

Sidra sighed. "I'm sorry... I'm still a work in progress, but I know how to acknowledge my faults now and the only thing I can do is learn from them and do better."

Josh let out a sigh as he moved his coffee cup aside. "Look, neither one of us are perfect," he admitted. "And to be honest, it's been a little hard for me transitioning from being just your friend, to being your boyfriend."

Sidra's heart sank as she looked down at the table. *I knew it...shit.* "I didn't know you felt that way."

Her sullen tone wasn't missed by him. "I don't think you understand what I mean," Josh said.

She shot him a quizzical look. "Then what *do* you mean?"

"How I used to react to things for one, I know that I can't react that way anymore," he tried to explain. "When I'm annoyed with you, I can't just not talk to you. I know that I have to do a better job at communicating because we're in an actual relationship now."

Sidra nodded. "I understand what you're saying," she replied. "I know that I need to work on the communication thing on *my* end too... And my...*immaturity* when it comes to some things as well."

Josh too nodded. "We're getting to know each other on a different level now," he pointed out.

"Yeah, I know...and the distance isn't making it any easier," she admitted. "Which is why I got so upset when you shot down my idea about me moving back East."

"Sidra, I only did that because I know that moving back there isn't what you really want," he explained. "Which brings me to *another* point, we can't go back to just thinking of ourselves. We have to consider what's also best for the other person."

Sidra reached over and took hold of his hand. "You're right," she agreed, she exhaled deeply. "Staying here, *is* better for my career."

Josh gave her hand a light squeeze. "I *know* it is."

She glanced off to the side. "But…what about *us*, Josh?" she asked; then looked back at him. "I can't lie, I don't like the long-distance thing… It's killing me."

Josh took a deep breath. "I know," he agreed. "You remember when I told you that I was working on some things?"

Sidra nodded.

"Well…I think I'm getting closer to fulfilling my plan," he alluded.

Sidra tilted her head. "*What* plan?"

Josh smiled after a moment. "My plan to eventually move *here*."

Sidra's eyes nearly popped out of her head. "Wait, what?" she leaned forward. "Joshua, are you serious?"

Josh nodded. "Yeah," he confirmed.

Sidra could've jumped out of her seat with excitement. "Wait, what about the shop? You can't just abandon it."

"It wouldn't be abandoned. I'd still own it. The workers that I have are excellent at their jobs, the clientele is solid, and Sarah would run the place for me," he informed. "Besides, I've been wanting to expand to a different area, and I figured that I could open a new shop *here*."

Sidra put her hands over her mouth. "Did you *just* think of this?"

Josh shook his head. "You mean opening a new shop? No. Moving here to California? …Well, if you want to call me deciding this after we got together as me *just* thinking of it, then sure."

Sidra couldn't help it anymore; she darted from her seat and wrapped her arms around him. "Oh my God, I love you," she gushed.

"I love you too," he crooned, holding onto her. "But Sid, it won't happen overnight. I still have to find a—"

She parted from her embrace and looked at him. "No, I don't care how long. Just the fact that you are even *planning* this is enough to make me happy right now." Sidra had been worrying all this time over nothing. She sat on his lap and wrapped her arms around his neck. "And here I thought that you came down here to break up with me."

Josh rolled his eyes. "Yeah, you might have made me angry, but I'm not stupid."

"I know," she chortled. She leaned her head on his shoulder. "Sorry for our fight."

He rubbed her back. "It's okay," Josh consoled. "It's not the first argument we've had, and it won't be the last."

Sidra sighed, "Yeah, I know." She lifted her head up. "But let's just make a pact not to have as many arguments as Mark and Malajia."

Josh laughed.

"Those two will argue and damn near get a divorce over who can do the robot the best," Sidra added.

Josh laughed some more. "Fact. And the truth is, it's neither *one* of them."

Sidra giggled, but after a moment she grew serious. "Well, I guess I should tell you that I've decided to go ahead and apply for the position at James's firm," she revealed.

Josh looked at her. "Good. You deserve to work where you'll be valued. I'm sure you'll get the job," he replied, sincere. Sidra smiled at him. "Sidra, I don't have *any* issue with James. My animosity towards him in the past was a mixture of my feelings for you, jealousy, and frankly, my immaturity," he admitted. "We're all adults, and I only want what's best for you and for you to be happy."

Sidra touched his face, eyeing him adoringly. "Just another case of me worrying over nothing."

"That won't stop. You're high-strung, but I love you," Josh joked, earning a playful poke to his arm from Sidra. Josh tapped her thigh with his hand. "You want me to make us some breakfast?"

"Now that I know that you can actually *cook*, yes," Sidra

agreed.

Josh gently moved Sidra from his lap and stood up. "If you liked my stuffed shells, wait till you try my spinach omelet," he boasted, moving towards the refrigerator.

Sidra sat back down and sipped her coffee in anticipation as Josh maneuvered around the kitchen.

Alex grabbed a bag of celery sticks from the refrigerator. She removed the stalks from the plastic, rinsed them in the sink and proceeded to cut them into halves. Her cell phone was cradled in her shoulder as she worked. "I spoke to Will today and he's on board with Emily coming to the lodge," she spoke. "He agrees with us, she *needs* this."

"You wanna tell her, or should we just kidnap her?" Chasity asked.

Alex laughed a little. "I think we can get her to come with us without having to kidnap her," she said. "But I *do* think it should be a surprise."

Chasity sucked her teeth. "Damn it, and I went and bought handcuffs and a blindfold for nothing."

Alex paused short of grabbing a bottle of ranch dressing from the refrigerator. "Your nasty self already had those things, *didn't* you?"

Chasity busted out laughing. "Mind your business."

Alex shook her head in amusement as she sat down at her table, pouring dressing into a small dish. "Anyway, this is off topic but...I'm about to call Eric...on *purpose* this time."

There was a pause on the line. "You should've *been* done that," Chasity ground out.

"I know, I know, call me an idiot later but right now, talk my nerves down," Alex pleaded, dipping a stalk in the dressing. "My stomach is in knots."

Chasity let out a sigh. "I'm not good at giving pep talks Alex, you *know* this."

"Yes, I do, but can you just *try*?" Alex insisted.

"Fine," Chasity agreed. "Um...everything is gonna be— I can't do this with you. Suck that shit up, get off my damn phone and just call him," she snapped.

Alex put her head on the tabletop and laughed. She didn't know why she expected anything different to come out of Chasity's mouth. "Leave it to you to tell me what I *need* to hear," she resolved, amusement in her voice. "I'm getting off. Love you."

"Gross," Chasity returned, earning another laugh from Alex. "Call me later and tell me the stupid shit you said."

"I will," Alex chortled. "Later."

Alex ended the call, then ate a few more ranch covered celery stalks. Getting her fill, she washed her hands in the sink, sat back at the table, and picked her phone up. Taking a deep breath, she dialed Eric's number and put the phone to her ear. She closed her eyes, expecting to get his voicemail; she was surprised when he answered. "Hi Eric."

"Did you mean to call me this time?" Eric asked.

Alex let out a deep sigh. "Yes, I did," she promised, tapping her fingernails on the tabletop. She had practiced what she wanted to say to him in her head all day, but now that he was on the line, her speech flew out of the window. "How are you?" she asked after a moment.

"I'm fine," he replied. "You?"

"I'm…I'm okay," she said, hesitant. "To be honest, I'm better now that I'm talking to you… Listen, I know it's been a while, but I—"

"Are you home?" he cut in.

Alex looked bewildered. "Yes."

"I'm actually in New York now, do you want to meet me?"

Confusion left her face, replaced by surprise. "Uh—*sure.* Yeah, I can do that," she sputtered. "You want to meet at the place we went to the last time you were here?"

"Yeah, that'll be fine," Eric answered. "Let's say an hour and a half? I have to finish up some work first."

"An hour and a half sounds good." Alex grinned. "See you then."

"See you," Eric confirmed, then ended the call.

Alex set her phone down and her grin turned into a full smile. She wasn't sure what to expect when she called him, but she was pleasantly surprised that he wanted to see her. She looked at her watch. "I guess it's time to get cute," she mused to herself, standing up.

Alex took a long sip of her water as she glanced at her watch. Noticing the time, she let out a sigh. *Where is he?* she wondered, setting her glass back down.

Alex had been sitting at the restaurant bar waiting on Eric for the past forty-five minutes. After the first half hour had passed, she went ahead and ordered herself an appetizer. The celery that she had eaten earlier did nothing for her hunger.

Another five minutes passed, frustrating Alex. Shaking her head, she grabbed a piece of coconut shrimp and took a bite. As the minutes continued to pass and she continued to munch away on her food, her frustration gave way to anger. *He stood me up,* she concluded. *This bastard stood me up as payback.*

Alex stuffed another piece of shrimp into her mouth, then reached into her purse, intent on grabbing her phone. "He got some goddamn nerve," she grunted between chews, grabbing hold of it.

"Still talking to yourself, I see," a male voice said, as a hand gently touched her shoulder.

Alex startled, so much so that with a mouth full of food, she let out a scream and nearly fell out of her seat.

"Whoa!" Eric reacted, grabbing her arm to steady her.

Alex quickly swallowed her food and tried her best to regain her composure.

"Are you okay?" he asked, concerned.

Angry and embarrassed, Alex's head snapped in his direction. "Announce yourself next time," she bit out.

Eric chuckled a bit as he held on to her. "I apologize, I didn't mean to scare you," he said. "But seriously, are you okay?"

"No, I'm *not* okay," she ground out, wiping the crumbs from her shirt. "I almost fell my big ass out of my seat." She sucked her teeth when the grease from her fingers stained the tan fabric. "Perfect," she hissed, snatching a napkin from the counter. "I'm surprised you showed up."

Eric took a seat next to her at the bar. "Why are you

surprised?" he asked, confused. "*I* asked *you* to meet me."

Alex let out a quick huff as she looked at him. "Maybe because you're an *hour late*," she ground out.

Eric returned her gaze and opened his mouth to respond, but just stared at her instead.

Alex frowned. "What? Why are you looking at me like that?"

Eric slowly picked up another napkin. "You umm…you might want to wipe that piece of coconut from your chin," he offered, holding the napkin up for her to take.

Alex sucked her teeth, snatching it from him. "Of *course* there's food on my damn face," she griped, wiping it off.

Eric dissolved into laugher.

Alex squinted at him. "I'm glad you find this funny," she spat, tossing the soiled napkin on the counter.

Eric put a hand up. "I'm sorry, but the way you flung yourself in your seat earlier," he recalled, laughing.

Alex narrowed her eyes at him as his laughter subsided.

"Listen, I'm sorry that I'm late," he apologized, sincere. "The meeting that I had ran a bit longer than scheduled. Then… Well, you know how bad New York traffic is."

"You couldn't call me to say that you were running late?" Alex questioned.

Eric looked bewildered. "I *did* call you. It went right to voicemail."

Alex rolled her eyes as she snatched the phone from her purse. "Eric, I didn't get *one* missed call from you," she fussed, pushing buttons on her phone; nothing happened. She lowered her head and shook it. "Looks like my phone is dead."

"Oh, *is* it?" Eric challenged.

Alex let out a nervous chuckle. "That would um…explain the lack of notifications." *Nice going, Alex.* Alex took a deep breath; she'd gotten angry with him over nothing. "I'm sorry for snapping," she apologized.

Eric ran a hand over his hair. "It's fine," he assured. He looked around. "You want to get a table?"

Alex nodded.

The pair were seated at a corner table in mere minutes. "You want to order dinner?" Eric asked, picking up a menu.

"Yes," Alex replied, looking at her menu. "Like the celery I had earlier, that shrimp did nothing for me."

Eric chuckled as he glanced over the items on the page.

After placing their orders, Alex and Eric sat there, waiting on the other to begin the conversation. "So…I'm happy to see you," Alex began.

"Same here," Eric replied. "What made you actually call me foreal this time?"

Alex ran a hand over her hair. "Damn, just straight for it, huh?"

"No time like the present," he pointed out.

"Right," Alex mumbled; she took a deep breath. "Figured it was time that I talked to you. You know, since my *texts* weren't working."

"No, they *weren't*," Eric admitted, stern.

Alex folded her arms and sat back in her seat. "Is there a reason why you never responded to them?" she asked, point-blank. "I mean, you *did* say for me to contact you when I quote unquote, 'get my shit together'."

Eric held a stern gaze on her. "For one, I knew when you sent those texts that you still weren't ready for a real conversation," he countered. "They were amateur at best."

Alex's mouth fell open. "Oh *really*?" she sneered.

"Wouldn't *you* think that of a 'hey' text after where we left off?" he threw back.

Alex rolled her eyes and looked off to the side.

"Second…I said for you to *call* me," he pointed out.

Alex looked back at him. "Woooow," she drew out, resentful. "Well, aren't you *literal*?"

Eric let out a sigh. "Listen Alex…to be honest, after that last conversation, I didn't expect to hear from you *at all*," he admitted. "So, when you first texted me, I didn't know what to make of it."

"Why would you think that I wouldn't ever contact you again?" she wondered, confused. "I mean, after everything, I thought that we were friends."

Eric narrowed his eyes, "Let's not do this again," he replied, stern. "This is taking me right back to that mess from college."

Alex put her hands up in surrender; he had a point. "Fine, I get it," she said, resolved. "And you're right, I *wasn't* ready to talk then…but I still don't understand why you thought you'd never hear from me again."

"Alex, you in so many words said that you couldn't date me because I have a child," he reminded.

Alex frowned. "Eric, that's *not* what I said."

"What *did* you say?" he threw back.

Alex took a moment as she tried to remember. "I *said* that… I never saw myself being with someone who has a child with someone else."

Eric raised an eyebrow. "Tell me how that's different," he countered.

Alex let out a huff.

"Look, I'm not mad at you," he promised. "You have every right not to put yourself in a situation that isn't ideal for you. Which is the reason why I expected you to stay away. To be honest, until you *accidentally* called me, I was trying to let you go…*again.*"

Alex sighed. "Damn," she muttered. "I didn't know you felt that way."

"Yeah," he confirmed. "Because after I thought about it, I realized that I wouldn't have blamed you if you decided to let me go."

"If you didn't blame me for how I felt, why did you get upset when I *told* you how I felt?" Alex wondered.

Eric rubbed his chin with his hand as their food arrived. Once the server left the table, he looked at her. "Two reasons," he began, putting up two fingers. "The way I found out how you felt, would make anybody upset."

"How so?"

"You stood out there with your friends and talked about—"

"Eric, my friends are my confidants, I tell them everything. I'm not even about to lie to you about that," she cut in.

"I know how close you are with your friends," Eric assured. "I'm not mad that you talked to them, I was upset because you talked to *them* before you talked to *me* about how you felt."

Alex glanced off to the side again, silent.

"Not only *that*, but you came off like a jackass when I confronted you about what you said," he added. "*And* you judged me."

"I *didn't* judge you." she argued, glaring at him.

"You *did*," Eric insisted. "I didn't sleep with some random girl and get her pregnant. My ex and I were in a relationship for a few years. It didn't work and we split, but we successfully co-parent like adults. So, it might not be *your* ideal situation, but it is *my reality*."

"I get that Eric, I do," Alex said, calm. "Trust me, I'm aware of how I am sometimes, and you're right. I *was* judging you and I'm sorry about that. I really am."

"I appreciate that," Eric nodded. "And *I'm* sorry for not being upfront with you about everything in the beginning."

"I appreciate that as well." Alex let out a deep breath. "So…where do we go from here?"

Eric stared at her. "That depends on *you*," he answered. "Not going to lie, I miss you. But as much as I was ready to see where a relationship with you could go, I would never want you to do something that you're not comfortable with."

Eric—"

"That being said," he maintained, cutting her words off. "That doesn't mean that I don't *want* us to be friends. Despite my comment earlier, I'm mature enough to handle just being that to you if that's what you want."

"It *isn't*," Alex replied. "I don't want to be *just friends*, I want to be *with* you."

Eric tilted his head as she spoke.

"It's what I wanted then *and* now. I'm just nervous because I've never dealt with anything like this before," she stressed. "I mean, I know that not all situations like yours are attached to drama, and I know that you say that the co-parenting relationship with you and your daughters' mother is amicable, I just…" she sighed. "I don't know."

Eric leaned forward. "Okay listen… If this is really what you want, then how about we just take things slowly," he proposed.

"You think that we *can*?" she chuckled.

"That again, depends on you," Eric joked in return. "You know how you get."

Alex blushed as she scratched her head. "Uh yeah...especially when it's been a minute," she agreed.

Eric let out a laugh, then took a deep breath. "I just want you to be comfortable."

"Thank you," Alex smiled. "And I just want you to know that my apprehension has *nothing* to do with your baby girl. It's just the *situation*."

"I know," he said. "I get it."

Alex nodded. "Okay." She couldn't believe that her day was ending with the beginning of a new relationship, with someone who had been on her mind since she'd graduated college. "Now that I actually think about it," she began, leaning forward. "Given the crap that I've been through with men in the *past*, I'm sure being with you even with all of this, will be cake."

Eric laughed as he lifted his drink. "Here's to cake," he said as Alex raised her glass to his. "That I will eat off of you when we decide to stop taking things slowly."

Alex busted out laughing. "See? Don't start nothing you can't handle," she challenged.

"We *both* know that I can *handle anything*," he threw back.

Alex began to feel hot. She quickly tapped her glass to his. *You damn sure can.* She took a quick sip of her drink, then set it down. Picking up a napkin, Alex quickly fanned herself. "All right, topic change," she proposed as Eric began eating his food. If she didn't get the topic off of sex, she knew that she would propose skipping the meal entirely and heading back to her apartment. "So...is being my date for my friend's wedding part of the 'starting slowly' category?" she asked.

"If that's what you want," Eric smiled.

She smiled back. "It is."

"Then, you have yourself a date."

Chapter 52

Shifting her book bag from one arm to the other, Emily walked into her apartment complex. Though work wasn't necessarily hard that week, Emily felt like she'd run a nonstop marathon. She was drained mentally and physically, and she attributed it to her mood—still in the dumps. She just wanted to lock herself in her apartment and be left alone.

"Thank God it's Friday," she muttered to herself as she stepped into the elevator.

The phone in her hand rang. Emily checked the caller ID— it was the hotel where her wedding was being held. Emily stared at the screen, allowing the call to go to voicemail. Once it was clear that a message had been left, she listened to it. "I don't even care," she grunted; it was just some bubbly woman. checking in to confirm last minute guest head counts.

At last, the elevator stopped on her floor; she stepped off and made her way to her door. She shoved the phone into her purse and retrieved her keys. Unlocking her door, she pushed it open. Once inside, she screamed. "Oh my God! What the hell?!"

Malajia and Chasity were sitting on Emily's couch, staring up at her.

"Damn Em, wake the whole complex, why don't you?" Chasity jeered.

"I know right?" Malajia cosigned. "Rude."

Emily slammed her door shut and dropped her book bag to the floor with a thud. Shocked didn't even begin to describe how she felt. "What the *hell* are you two doing in here?" she ranted, still trying to calm herself. "You nearly gave me a damn heart attack. How did you get into my apartment?!"

Malajia put a finger up. "Oh yeah, the last time we were down here, and Will gave us your key, I went and had a copy made. Because like, why *wouldn't* I have a key to your place?" she explained.

Chasity let out a deep sigh as she tried to refrain from commenting on Malajia's ramble.

Emily stood there confused. She put her hand on her head. "Malajia—*what*?" she bit out.

"*Exactly*, Emily," Chasity commented.

"Shut up Chasity," Malajia threw back.

Emily took a step forward, hands up. "Okay you two, I *need* to know what you're *doing* here," she stressed. "And *why* you decided to scare me half to death, rather than *call* me."

Chasity opened her mouth to respond, but Malajia quickly jumped in.

"We were in the neighborhood and we wanted to see you," Malajia stated, confident. "Figured we could take you to dinner."

Chasity folded her arms. She smirked, but didn't say anything.

Emily frowned. "Why would you two just *be in the neighborhood*?" she asked, folding her arms. "What reason do you have to be down here when you both live up near *Philadelphia*?"

"Yup, *thought* so," Chasity muttered. She knew that Malajia's hasty explanation would draw questions from Emily. Amused, she was wondering how Malajia was going to explain herself out of this.

Malajia's eyes shifted. She looked at Chasity. "You wanna jump in here?" she asked.

"Nope, you got it," Chasity quickly threw back.

Malajia sucked her teeth. "Bitch," she hissed. She looked at Emily and took a deep breath. "Umm—*what* was your question?"

Chasity tapped Malajia's shoulder. "She wanted to know why—"

"Shut the hell—" Malajia put a hand up to calm herself down. Chasity's mocking wasn't helping. "I heard the damn question." She wrung her hands as she tried to think. *Come on girl, you lie like a pro. Think of something*, she coaxed herself. She snapped her fingers. "Okay ooh, so we came here because

Chasity's dad—"

"Dad lives in New York, try again," Chasity cut in.

"Chasity had to—"

"Nope," Chasity cut in once again.

Malajia rolled her eyes. *Fuck!* "Umm, Paradise Valley University had—"

"You two are the *last* people who would drive all the way down here for anything PVU related," Emily cut in, annoyed.

"She's got a point, Malajia," Chasity teased.

"You know what, fuck you Chasity, I'm done. It's on you now," Malajia huffed, turning away from both of them.

Emily shook her head at Malajia, then looked at Chasity. "Chaz, what's going on?"

Chasity sighed. "Okay, look Em, we came down here because we wanted to check up on you," she explained. "We both had some time so, we just decided to make this drive."

While Emily's defenses lowered at bit at Chasity's confession, Malajia's attitude increased. She snapped her head in Chasity's direction.

"Are you kidding me?!" Malajia ranted, tossing her arms up. "You made me go through all that bullshit when I could've just said *that*?"

"Malajia, stop fuckin' breathing on me before I throw up on you," Chasity huffed.

"Malajia, you can't blame Chaz for that. It's not *her* fault that *you* always have to add some sort of lie to a story," Emily threw in.

Malajia made a face at Emily. "Shut up Emily, you don't know my life," she snarled.

Emily rubbed her face with her hands and let out a sigh. "Look, as much as I appreciate you two making the four-hour drive down here to check on me, I had a really long week," she said. "I'm tired and I just want to unwind by myself."

Malajia's mouth fell open. "You're kicking us out?"

"I love you, but yes," Emily confirmed.

Malajia jerked her head back. "Well…shit," she muttered. "Okay whatever, but before we leave town, we just want to take you to dinner."

"Malajia, I'm not hungry," Emily argued.

"But *we* are," Malajia threw back. "Come on, just get in the car, and let us take you someplace nice."

Emily was trying to remain calm, but Malajia's pushing was irritating her. "What part of *no*, don't you get?" she snapped.

"Ooh," Chasity chuckled, amused.

"*First* of all, you didn't say '*no*'. You said you weren't *hungry*," Malajia argued.

"It's the same thing!" Emily hurled back.

"It's *not*, you baby bitch," Malajia spat, earning a snicker from Chasity. "And you call yourself a teacher."

Emily put her hand up. "Malajia, go home."

"Emily, don't *make* me spend the night *just* to piss you off," Malajia sneered. "I brought my overnight bag and *everything*."

Emily glanced over at the overnight bag that Malajia had gestured to. "That's *mine*."

"Well it's *mine now*," Malajia taunted. She looked to Chasity, who was just staring out in front of her, amusement gone from her face. "I don't like the cut of her jib, *you* do something," she demanded.

Emily rolled her eyes.

Chasity sat quietly for a moment, then she pinched the bridge of her nose.

Emily took a step forward. "Chasity, are you okay?" she asked, tone caring.

Malajia put a hand up at Emily. "No don't come over here *now*, your arguing done gave her a headache," she spat. "You *know* she's pregnant, you ignoramus."

Emily ignored Malajia and focused her attention on Chasity, who began breathing heavily. "Seriously, Chaz are you okay?"

Malajia looked at Chasity; she was getting concerned herself. "Hey, hey, stop that shit," she said, giving Chasity a nudge. "You cool?"

Chasity busted out crying.

"What's the matter?" Emily panicked.

"We came all the way down here because we were worried about you, and you're just yelling at us, and kicking us out,"

Chasity cried, hand on her face.

"Oh my God," Malajia reacted, stunned.

Emily looked and felt guilty.

"We don't deserve it," Chasity sobbed. "We're just trying to be good friends, we don't deserve to be treated like this."

Malajia rubbed Chasity's back. "See what you did Emily?" she barked.

Emily put her hands on her chest. "I'm sorry," she sputtered. "I didn't mean to come off like— I'm sorry, what can I do?"

"Let us take you out for a little bit," Malajia answered as Chasity's cries became louder.

"Okay, okay…just let me freshen up," Emily relented. She moved in to give Chasity a hug.

Malajia's hand jerked up, halting her. "Don't touch her, you've done enough," she barked to a stunned Emily. "Just hurry up."

Emily nodded, then scurried for her room.

Malajia followed Emily's progress with narrowed eyes. Once the room door shut, Chasity removed her hand from her face; all crying abruptly ceased.

Malajia squinted at her. "Hold up…you *faked* that shit?" Malajia whispered.

Chasity wiped her eyes with her hand. "Uh huh," she revealed.

"Then where did those damn tears come from?" Malajia asked, bewildered.

"If I don't blink for a long period of time, my eyes start to water," Chasity admitted, nonchalant.

Malajia pointed at her. "You—you always find a way to impress me," she said, proud.

Chasity chuckled.

Sidra untied a balloon from a balloon weight, adjusted the height, then retied it.

Alex watched her, amused. "Sid, it was already even," Alex observed.

"It *wasn't*," Sidra denied, adjusting the balloon bouquet.

Alex shook her head as she concentrated on her task of arranging trays of snacks and wine glasses on the glass coffee table. "I hope Em likes what we're doing for her," she mentioned. She looked up at Sidra, who was concentrating on fixing more decorations. "You don't think she'll be upset with us, do you?"

Sidra looked at her. "Well, she said that she didn't want any bridal parties, and this *technically* isn't a party," she reasoned.

Alex bit her bottom lip; she couldn't help it, she was worried. With Chasity and Malajia charged with the task of picking up Emily, Sidra and Alex had spent the time decorating at the rented lodge. While Alex was on board for the surprise get together in the beginning, now that the weekend had arrived, she was having second thoughts. "I know, I just— I don't want to upset her." She sighed. "I hate that she's not enjoying herself."

"Me too," Sidra agreed. "Which is why it's up to us to make sure that she *does*." She pushed some of her hair behind her ears. A knock sounded on the door, sending her darting for it. "It's Chaz," she announced to Alex, peering through the peep hole. She pulled the door open. "Hey."

"Where's Mel and Em?" Alex charged as Chasity walked in.

"I left their asses in the car," Chasity bristled, removing her coat. "Em has an attitude and Malajia keeps bothering her. I almost threw *both* of them out."

Sidra chuckled. "Malajia better leave her alone."

"Does Em have any idea what's going on?" Alex wondered.

"No. She thinks we're just taking her someplace to eat," Chasity answered.

Hearing Emily's elevated voice, Sidra glanced outside through the open door. "What is Malajia *doing* to her?"

"I don't even care anymore," Chasity grunted.

Alex walked over to the door; the three girls watched Malajia try to guide a blindfolded Emily from the car to the lodge.

"Malajia, can I *please* take this stupid blindfold off?"

Emily snapped, stomping her foot on the ground as Malajia grabbed hold of her arm. "Why do I even *need* this just to go to *dinner*?"

"We already *told* your ass that the place is a surprise, so shut the hell up," Malajia hurled back. "Now don't get on my nerves with your million damn questions."

Emily stood still as Malajia tugged on her arm. "Get on *your* nerves?!" she erupted. "You've *been* on *my* nerves."

Malajia gasped. "Why do *I* always get your damn attitude?"

"Because you keep doing the most," Emily grunted, snatching her arm from Malajia.

"Fine, walk your blindfolded ass to the entrance by yourself," Malajia huffed, folding her arms.

"Malajia, help that girl to the damn door!" Chasity yelled at her.

Malajia sucked her teeth. "How the hell did I get stuck with this shit?" she vented, stomping her foot on the ground.

"Chasity, can you get her away from me please?" Emily barked.

Malajia grabbed hold of Emily's arm yet again. "Nope, she *can't*. I'm all you got, now come the hell on," she sneered, giving Emily a yank.

As Emily went to take a step, she stubbed her toe on a stone, taking a spill to the ground. "Ouch!"

"Malajia!" Alex yelled as she and the others rushed outside.

"Wait, is that Alex?" Emily asked, sitting on the cold ground. Irritated with the entire situation, Emily removed the fabric from her face. Alex and Sidra were in front of her, trying to help her up; Emily squinted in confusion. "What's going on?"

Chasity walked over to Malajia. "You can't do *shit* right," she snapped, poking her in the forehead.

"Ow!" Malajia shrieked, grabbing her forehead. "That was uncalled for."

"So is your nonsense," Chasity threw back, walking inside.

Emily was still perplexed as Sidra and Alex guided her to the front steps of the lodge. "Wait, I don't understand. What's going on?"

Once all were inside, Alex closed the door behind her. "Em, are you okay?"

"I fell on my butt on below freezing concrete, but I'm sure I'll live. What's going *on*?" Emily pressed, tossing her arms in the air. She watched as her four friends stood in front of her.

"Well, we hoped to unveil this a *better* way, but of *course Malajia* ruined it," Sidra sniped. Malajia rolled her eyes.

"Em...welcome to your bridal weekend," Alex added, hesitant. She raised her arms. "Ta-da."

Malajia rubbed her face. "She really said ta-da," she muttered, agitated.

Emily looked at them, eyes wide. She opened her mouth to speak, but shocked everyone by busting out crying instead. "I'm sorry," she sobbed, and made a dash for the stairs.

"Bathroom is upstairs to the left sweetie," Alex called after her. Hearing the door shut, she let out a sigh.

"*That* was not my doing," Malajia charged, pointing to the staircase.

"Wow," Alex sulked. "I hope we didn't make her feel worse."

"She'll be fine, just give her a minute," Chasity assured, heading for the kitchen.

Sidra sighed as she, Alex, and Malajia followed. "Are you sure about that?" she asked.

"Not really. Just felt like the right thing to say," Chasity replied, grabbing a chocolate covered strawberry from a tray on the counter.

"That's what we get for trying to be sneaky," Sidra commented. "She already told us that she didn't want to do anything... We should've listened to her."

"*Whose* idea was this anyway?" Malajia wondered, slightly amused.

"Chasity's," Alex blamed.

"Fuck you Alex, it was *all* of ours," Chasity threw back, earning a snicker from Alex. "I'll shove this strawberry right up your goddamn nose."

"Fine we're *all* to blame," Alex resolved, tapping her hand on the countertop.

Malajia grabbed a brownie from a tray. She chuckled. "We suck as bridesmaids, yo," she said. "Can't even cheer the bride up."

Alex shook her head. "A damn shame," she agreed. "Crack open that wine."

Emily ran her hands under the cool water and splashed some on her face. Grabbing one of the folded towels from a glass shelf, she dabbed her face dry, looking at herself in the mirror. Her eyes were red, and her face was puffy. *What is wrong with me?* She felt terrible over how she'd reacted.

Letting out a long sigh, Emily dried her hands on a fluffy white towel and sat on the edge of the massive whirlpool tub. She ran her hand through her hair and scratched her scalp. "Get yourself together Emily," she said to herself.

Taking one last moment to breathe, Emily rose to her feet and made her way down the stairs. The living room now empty, she had a chance to take in the beautiful space. The lodge that they had gone to their Junior year of college was nothing compared to this fully furnished, five-bedroom, two-story space. Emily set her eyes on the pink and white bridal decorations that were expertly placed around the living room. She smiled. Hearing voices coming from the kitchen, Emily slowly headed for the entrance. The girls were gathered around the kitchen counter island talking; she walked in.

"Hey," Emily said softly.

They turned around and looked at her.

Sidra tilted her head slightly. "Are you okay?" she asked, tone full of concern.

Emily nodded as she fiddled with her fingers. "I'm sorry for reacting like that."

"It's okay," Alex placated. "We just wanted to do something special for you. We didn't mean to upset you."

Emily walked over to the counter. "I'm not upset. I appreciate this, I really do," she promised.

"You don't have to stay if you don't want to," Chasity said.

"I want to," Emily assured. "Is it overnight?"

"Nope, the whole weekend," Malajia informed. "Will knows; we talked to him about it."

Emily managed a smile. "Okay." No matter how down she was, Emily was going to force herself to have a good time. "You have any wine over there?"

"Sure do, and the hard stuff too," Malajia chuckled.

"Wine will do for now," Emily chortled, as Sidra handed her a glass.

Chapter 53

Taking a bite out of a chocolate drizzled pretzel, Emily chewed and took a sip of her wine spritzer. "How many of those pretzels did I eat?" she asked.

"Shit, *all* of them," Chasity grunted, earning a snicker from Emily.

"They were so good though," Emily laughed, setting her glass down on the coffee table.

Later that evening, after eating dinner, the girls were settled in the living room in front of the lit fireplace, eating treats and conversing.

Sidra ran a hand through her hair as she leaned back against the couch cushions. "Does Will have any plans this weekend, with you being away?" she asked.

Emily shook her head. "No," she answered. "I told him that he should go hang out or something. He deserves to have a good time."

"*You* deserve to have a good time *too*, Em," Alex pointed out.

"I am," Emily assured.

"You *deserved* a huge shower and bachelorette party," Sidra added.

Emily tapped her fingernails to her wine glass. "I just… I don't want to be around my family right now…my aunts and cousins," she said. "They would just be asking me why my mom wasn't there and why she's not coming to the wedding—"

"Wait, your mom really isn't coming to your wedding?" Malajia charged, putting a hand up.

Emily looked at Malajia, shaking her head.

"That's fucked up," Malajia fumed. "My dad hated that I was marrying Mark, but at least his ignorant ass was *there…and* walked me down the aisle. Attitude and *all*."

"I—I told her not to come when I was arguing with her and she agreed," Emily informed, somber; she shrugged. "It's fine. It's for the best, I guess... It's fine."

The girls shot each other glances, while Emily focused her attention on the flickering flames in the fireplace. They knew all too well that Emily wasn't being honest with herself.

"Okay, let's change the subject," Alex proposed, adjusting her position on the carpeted floor.

"Here's a good subject," Sidra said, reaching for her glass of wine. "Chasity, I am *so* happy that you are moving to Arizona," she began, her tone excited.

"I don't know *why*, I'm still not coming to visit you," Chasity jeered, earning laughter from everyone but Sidra, who just made a face.

"You're lying and you know it," Sidra shot back. She flagged Chasity with her hand when Chasity turned away from her. "*I'll* come visit *you*, and I'll make sure to do it often, *just* to get on your nerves."

"Sidra, annoying Chasity with frequent unannounced visits is *my* job," Malajia hurled, pointing at Sidra.

Chasity pinched the bridge of her nose and let out a sigh. "God," she muttered.

"And here she goes with that territorial mess again," Alex chuckled.

Sidra shot a confused look Malajia's way. "What *are* you twelve? Is this middle school?" she sneered. "Chasity is *our* friend too, you know."

Malajia fixed Sidra with a stern stare. "Don't test me Sidra," she warned.

"Oh shut up," Sidra threw back, dismissive. "As always you're blowing a bunch of hot air and it's all for nothing."

Emily giggled as Malajia rolled her eyes. "Malajia, don't be sour. You still have me and Alex on this end."

"Emily shut up, nobody wants y'all and you *know* it," Malajia grunted.

Emily gasped as Alex sucked her teeth. "Em, don't pay that mess any mind. When she gets tired of dealing with Mark, she'll come calling us to hang out," Alex sneered.

"At least *I have* a man to be tired of," Malajia threw back.

"And who says that *I don't*?" Alex returned, folding her arms.

"Wait, *do* you?" Sidra asked curious. "*This* is new."

"Well—" Alex began then paused. "…I started seeing Eric again." Her revelation was met with shock.

"Wait, when did this happen?" Malajia asked. "Last time I checked, you acted like a damn fool when Chasity called him for you and you hadn't called him since."

Alex narrowed her eyes at Malajia. "Nope, not gonna smack you right now," she refused. "Anyway, I *did* end up calling him finally and we met up. We started talking, cleared the air and…we're going to give it a shot. Start slow."

"So, does this mean that you're finally okay with the fact that he has a child?" Emily wondered.

Alex thought for a moment. "My issue was never with his daughter, it was the *situation*." she explained. "He understands where I was coming from, and I understand that he and his child are a package deal, so…I'm willing to try and see where it goes." She rubbed her arm with her hand. "He says that there is no drama with the mother, and until I see otherwise, I'm good."

"Y'all bang again yet?" Malajia asked.

"No, but *God* I *want* to," Alex huffed, earning laughter from the girls. "It was easy to refrain from sex when I wasn't dating, but having someone who I know for a *fact* can—" She fanned herself with her hand. "Y'all pray for me."

Malajia laughed. "She gonna jump on Eric while he asleep and shit," she teased.

Alex laughed. "I so *would*, which is why he can't spend the night yet."

Malajia looked at Emily. "Em, it won't be long before *you* jump on *Will*," she teased.

Emily looked embarrassed as Sidra rolled her eyes.

"God Mel," Sidra scoffed.

"What?!" Malajia snapped. "Is she *not* about to get it in after she's married?"

"Oh wow," Emily commented, amused.

"We *get* that, but the first time with your husband should be treated as more than just a roll in the hay," Sidra sneered.

Chasity looked at Sidra and slowly shook her head. "You

would be the only one who still uses the term 'roll in the hay'," she jeered.

Alex laughed. "Who came up with that anyway?"

"Right? Like who wants to roll around butt naked getting banged on some hard ass hay?" Malajia commented.

Sidra let out a loud huff. "Whatever, tease my verbiage all you want, but you know I'm right."

"You the *only* one complaining about what I just said, which makes it all the more apparent that you are *wrong*," Malajia threw back. She turned her attention back to Emily. "Are you excited about your wedding night, Em?"

The embarrassment on Emily's face intensified. "Oh come on, Malajia," she pleaded, putting her hands over her face.

"Leave her alone," Alex jumped in.

"Oh my God— You know what, if I would've known that girl talk was gonna be ruined by prudes, I—"

"Your ass would *still* be here, so shut up," Chasity cut in.

Malajia snickered. "Yeah, who am I kidding?" Malajia agreed. "No but all jokes aside, Em we're your girls, and we know you've been going through a lot and holding a lot in," she said, sincere. "So now is the perfect time to share how you're feeling."

Emily shifted in her seat. "Okay," she relented, putting her hand up. "I *will* admit that I am…looking forward to my wedding night but I'm really…like, *really* nervous."

"Why are you nervous?" Alex asked.

"Because—" Emily felt frazzled as she tried to express how she was feeling. The topic of sex wasn't something that Emily discussed frequently. "I mean—I have no idea what I'm supposed to *do*. When I lost my virginity, I just *laid* there."

"We *all* did," Malajia chortled.

Emily rolled her eyes. "You're teasing me," she pouted.

Malajia, amusement still on her face reached over and patted Emily's leg. "No, I'm *serious*."

"Sweetie, you don't have to be nervous, trust us," Alex assured, rubbing Emily's arm. "*Nobody* knows what they're doing when they start having sex. But the beautiful thing is that this time around, you'll be with someone you love and who loves you, and I'm sure he'll be patient with you and you'll both learn what each other likes."

"That is such a *mom* response," Chasity sneered, rolling her eyes.

"What? Am I *lying*?" Alex asked, shocked as laughter erupted around her.

"No, but ugh," Chasity scoffed, flicking her hand in Alex s direction.

Alex flagged Chasity with her hand.

Emily opened her mouth to ask a question, but closed it. "Never mind," she said. putting a hand up.

"Come on Em, what were you going to say?" Sidra asked as Malajia grabbed the half empty bottle of wine and poured some in Emily's empty glass.

"Sounds like this calls for some more liquid courage," Malajia chuckled, handing the glass to Emily.

Emily giggled, then took a sip.

Malajia held the bottle up. "Anybody else want more?" Alex held her glass out, allowing Malajia to pour some. She then pointed the bottle at Chasity. "Chaz you want some— oops," she teased, setting the bottle on the table.

Chasity narrowed her eyes at Malajia.

"You salty you gotta sip on ginger ale all weekend," Malajia dug in, relishing her annoyance.

Chasity snatched a white chocolate covered strawberry from a tray on the coffee table. "Fuck you, I'm not pressed over some dry ass wine," she grunted, taking a bite.

Alex giggled as she went to touch Chasity's stomach. "Aww—"

"Don't touch me, Alex," Chasity spat.

Alex quickly moved her hand. "You were so much nicer the *last* time you were pregnant," she ground out.

"To *who*?" Malajia blurted out, while Sidra and Emily looked confused. "Shit definitely not to *us*. Not to her *man*, not to her *momma*, the *doctors*, the *mailman*, *nobody*," Malajia added, counting on her fingers. "In fact, her bitchiness *intensified.*"

Chasity glared as her friends laughed at her expense. Yet she elected not to respond, concentrating on her strawberry.

Malajia let out a little laugh as she picked up a plain

strawberry from a tray. "Here Chaz, put this strawberry in your ginger ale to add a little razzle dazzle, you salty, sober bitch," she teased.

Chasity smacked the strawberry from the laughing Malajia's hand, sending it tumbling to the floor. "Emily say what you were about to say before I beat Malajia's ass," Chasity demanded.

"Your threats mean nothing," Malajia taunted, doing a dance in her seat. She grabbed her own glass of vodka and cranberry and took a long, drawn out sip, staring at Chasity in the process.

Sidra chuckled. "Malajia, will you stop it?"

Malajia put a finger up as she continued to drink her beverage.

Chasity looked at Sidra. "Sid, you wanna be the Godmother to my baby?" she asked.

Malajia choked on her drink. Coughing hysterically, she set the glass down on the floor. "Sidra, I will cut you," Malajia gasped in between coughs.

Sidra rolled her eyes. "I'd make a *great* Godmother, just so you know Chaz," she assured.

"So *what*? Be one to Alex or Emily's future kids," Malajia threw back before Chasity had a chance to respond.

"Anyway, Emily, what were you going to say, sweetie?" Sidra directed, flinging a dismissive hand Malajia's way. "We've wasted enough time on her."

Emily adjusted her position once again. "So...what kind of stuff do guys *like*?" she sheepishly put out.

"To stick their dick in something," Chasity grunted, causing Malajia to snicker.

"Chasity, retract your horns," Sidra warned.

"I'm *sorry* okay," Chasity belted out, tossing her arms in the air in exasperation. "I'm still hungry, I taste metal, my fuckin' chest is sore, I want a damn drink, and I'm horny."

"We understand sweetie," Alex placated, rubbing Chasity's shoulder.

"I said don't touch me," Chasity snapped.

Annoyed, Alex gave Chasity's arm a nudge, before grabbing the tray of remaining chocolate covered strawberries.

"*Here* girl," she grunted, shoving the tray in Chasity's hands. "God, Jason is a *Saint* for putting up with all of that."

"What I *mean* is," Emily cut in, bringing the subject back. "…should I get something special to wear to bed?"

"You mean like lingerie?" Malajia asked. Emily nodded. "Girl, just sleep butt naked."

Emily put her hand over her face and shook her head.

Sidra giggled. "I don't think Will would care *what* you sleep in," she assured.

Alex put a finger up. "*But* we *do* have some things that he might like to see you in," she said, getting up from her seat. Emily watched in curiosity as Alex headed upstairs. It took less than a minute for her to return, several gift bags in hand. Alex smiled as she set the bags in front of Emily. "These are for you."

"Awww, you didn't have to get me anything," Emily gushed.

"Of *course* we did, it's your shower…*kind* of," Sidra added. She clapped her hands together. "You have a gift bag from each of us."

Smiling from ear to ear, Emily sat up and set her drink down.

"Just so you know Em, we didn't get you that mess from your registry," Malajia began. "Let them old people get you coffee makers and shit."

Emily giggled as she looked at the tag on one of the bags. "Ooh, this one is from Sidra," she beamed, removing the tissue paper.

"Sidra, how much paper did you put *in* there?" Alex teased, watching Emily pull out several sheets of the sparkly white paper.

"I wanted it to look pretty," Sidra defended, humor in her voice.

Emily reached inside and pulled a basket out of the large bag. She read the little pink card. "Bridal stress relief kit," she read aloud.

Malajia watched with annoyance as Emily removed and examined, a lavender eye pillow, jar of calming bath salts, bath bombs, candles, expensive wine, crystal glasses, and a two-hundred-dollar gift card for a spa.

"Oh wow, thank you Sidra," Emily beamed, hugging her.

"You're welcome," Sidra smiled. "There's one more thing in the bag."

Emily quickly looked inside, then pulled out a folded item. She unfolded the long satin white robe and glanced at the large "Bride" written in crystals on the back. "Aww, I love this," she gushed, giving Sidra another hug.

Malajia's face was still masked with annoyance as the two parted from their embrace. "I swear, you always gotta be the bougie one," she sneered.

"Malajia, back off all right," Sidra threw back.

"Ol' snotty ass bridal gifts," Malajia muttered. "I wouldn't use that bath bomb Em, unless you want a goddamn yeast infection."

Sidra frowned at Malajia as snickers resonated. "Don't blame bath bombs on your wacky PH balance," she threw back.

"Boooo, you just found out how your dusty old vag *works*, so shut up," Malajia threw back, making a face.

Sidra put her hand up. "Whatever Malajia—"

"Em, why don't you open mine next?" Alex cut in, trying to diffuse the impending argument. She reached over and grabbed her bag, handing it to Emily.

Emily set Sidra's gifts aside, then began digging in the new bag. She blushed as she pulled out several revealing night gowns. "Oh wow—um, these are interesting," Emily chuckled. She held one up. "Does this even cover *anything*?"

"Nope, that's the point," Alex laughed. She directed Emily to reach back in the bag.

Emily pulled out a small box. Her eyes widened when she saw the picture on the box. "A *bullet*?"

Sidra covered her face in embarrassment, as Malajia and Chasity erupted with approval.

"Yessss Alex!" Malajia wailed, giving Alex a high five.

Emily stared at Alex wide-eyed. "Wow," she reacted, amused. "I'll need this even though I'll be married?"

"Hell *yeah*!" Chasity and Malajia bellowed in unison.

"Girl, you better get with the program," Malajia added.

"What you gonna do when that man isn't home and the moment hits you?"

"Or when he's on your goddamn nerves in general and you don't want him touching you," Chasity chimed in.

Malajia pointed at her. "There you go," she chuckled.

Alex laughed. "They're right," she agreed. "Sometimes you just need to take care of *yourself.*"

"And the finger gets tired, *don't* it Sidra?" Malajia teased.

Sidra narrowed her eyes at Malajia. "*My* way works just fine, I have no need for additions," she scoffed.

Chasity sat up in her seat, staring at Sidra. "So, you've *never* used a vibrator of *any* kind?" she asked.

Sidra shook her head. "Never had a reason to."

"Girl, do you know how much easier using a vibrator is?" Malajia jumped in.

Sidra rolled her eyes; this conversation was making her uncomfortable. "Look, you do you how you want and I'll do—never mind," she grunted, earning snickers from the girls. "This isn't about me, this is about Em."

Emily set her gifts aside, smiling. "Thank you, Alex."

Malajia adjusted her position and clapped. "Okay so Chaz and I went in on—"

"Do *not* put my name on that bullshit in that bag of yours," Chasity interrupted.

Malajia's mouth fell open. "Whatchu mean? I picked out good gifts," she argued.

Chasity flagged Malajia with her hand as she reached down and grabbed a small bag. "Emily, Malajia is on her own with that bullshit that she got you," she ground out. She handed her own gift to Emily.

Emily eagerly withdrew a small box and card. Opening the box, her eyes nearly jumped out of her head. "Oh my God, is this real?!" Emily squealed, holding up the diamond and light blue topaz tennis bracelet to the light.

"It is," Chasity confirmed.

The other girls groaned and sucked their teeth.

"And *once again,* she has to outdo everyone else," Alex sneered, tossing a hand up.

"Yeah, that's *exactly* what I was thinking when I bought

this over a year ago," Chasity spat, voice dripping with sarcasm.

"Fuck you Chasity, we were supposed to go in on a gift *together*," Malajia snarled. "You left me hanging."

Chasity snapped her head in Malajia's direction. "Malajia I swear to God— I fuckin' *told* you that I wanted to get her a gift to cover her 'something new' and 'something blue'. I *told* you when I found it and I *told* you how much it was, and *you* said you didn't want to spend that much money, even if it was half, you fuckin' cheap ass bitch," Chasity hurled back, annoyed.

Malajia gasped. "Well damn, that's how you *really* feel?!" she exclaimed. "You don't even *care* about that traditional bridal shit."

"*She does*, now leave me the fuck alone!" Chasity yelled.

"That's a really beautiful, thoughtful gift Chaz, and I'm mad that I didn't think of that," Sidra muttered, folding her arms.

"I bet you *are*, bath salts," Malajia taunted, watching Emily try to place the bracelet on her wrist.

Malajia reached up and smacked Emily's hand. "It ain't your wedding day yet, open mine," she demanded.

Emily rubbed her hand and fixed Malajia with a frown. "That was unnecessary."

"Hush and open my gift," Malajia threw back, unfazed. "The best was saved for last anyway."

"Trust me, it wasn't," Chasity sneered.

"Shut up," Malajia ground out. She watched with eagerness as Emily dug her hand into the large bag that Malajia handed to her.

Emily looked utterly confused as she pulled several packages from the bag.

Sidra glared at Malajia. "Malajia, did you buy the entire sex store inventory?" she spat, eyeing the items, which included furry handcuffs, edible underwear, various sex toys and sex games.

"Emily, don't be a prude like Sidra, get your freak on with your man," Malajia said, ignoring Sidra.

Sidra sucked her teeth as she grabbed something that had fallen out of Emily's bag. "Hold up. You're talking about *my* gifts and you turn around and get her *pearls*?"

"You might wanna put those down Sidra," Chasity warned as Alex nodded in agreement.

Sidra looked confused. "What? It's a *necklace*."

Malajia put her hand over her face and shook her head. "First of all, that is not a *necklace*, those are *beads*," she clarified.

Sidra's confusion didn't leave her face. "What's the damn difference?"

"A necklace goes on your neck and those beads go up your ass," Malajia threw back.

Sidra immediately tossed the string of beads at Malajia. "Eww!" Sidra bellowed in disgust.

"What? It's not like they're *used*," Malajia shrugged.

Sidra's face was masked with disgust. "You are such a *freak*," she condemned, exasperated.

Malajia shrugged, unfazed. "I can teach you a few things."

"No, thank you," Sidra scoffed.

Malajia ran a hand through her hair. "You know what, I forgot—those beads can't fit up your ass anyway with that stick still up there," she mocked, earning a snicker from Chasity.

Alex pinched the bridge of her nose and shook her head. "Jesus," she muttered.

Annoyed, Sidra grabbed a throw pillow and tossed it at Malajia.

A knock on the door interrupted Malajia's loud laughter. Malajia glanced at her watch.

"I wonder who that is," Sidra asked curious.

Malajia, not saying a word, jumped up and headed for the door. She peered out the peep hole and let out a happy gasp.

"Malajia, who's at the door?" Alex wondered.

Chasity looked over at Malajia, noticing the sneaky look on her face. "Yeah Malajia, who's at the door?" she repeated, suspicious.

Big smile on her face, Malajia grabbed her purse from the chair then grabbed a "bride-to-be" sash and tiara from a bag on the floor. With curious eyes on her, she set the tiara on top of Emily's head and tried to put the sash on too.

"Malajia—"

"Shut up and put this on," Malajia ordered Emily, cutting

her words off. She removed a folded wad of money from her purse and slapped it into Emily's hand, before darting back for the door.

"Malajia, will you stop acting weird and just tell us who is at the damn door?" Alex hurled, annoyed.

"You'll see," Malajia alluded.

Emily looked confused as she unfolded the wad of bills; it consisted of one-dollar bills. "What's with all of these ones?" she wondered aloud.

Chasity pinched the bridge of her nose. "Oh God," she huffed.

"Oh God what?" Sidra wondered.

"You'll see," Chasity alluded as Malajia opened the door.

All eyes fixed on the door as a tall, dark skinned, muscular police officer walked inside. "Excuse me ladies, but I received a—"

"We ain't got time for no speeches," Malajia dismissed, waving her hand. "Now strip."

"Yes ma'am," the man smiled as Malajia began playing music on the speaker in the living room.

Sidra looked horrified as the man began removing his uniform. "You *seriously* went through with this nonsense?" she scoffed.

"Good, God almighty," Alex muttered of the man's buff physique, fanning herself with her hand.

Chasity chuckled at Alex, then turned to Malajia. "This was supposed to be planned for *tomorrow* Malajia," Chasity stated, shaking her head.

Malajia was dancing to the music as the stripper made his way over to a shocked Emily.

"I know, but I just felt the need to change the day," Malajia beamed.

"You're the bride-to-be, I take it," he smiled at Emily. Emily was so busy staring at him that she didn't answer. She eventually nodded.

Sidra jumped up as the stripper went to reach for Emily's hand. "Em, you don't have to let him dance on you if you're not comfortable," she jumped in.

"Girl, sitcho uptight ass *down* and let that man rub on

Emily, please," Malajia snapped at Sidra.

Emily, snapping out of her trance, put a hand up. "Umm, I don't know if being rubbed up on is a good idea," she protested as the man gyrated in front of her. "I'm kinda a 'born again virgin'."

Malajia rolled her eyes as Sidra folded her arms smugly. "Exactly," Sidra directed to Malajia.

Alex stood up and walked over to Emily. "Well, *I'm* not. Give me those damn ones," Alex demanded, holding her hand out.

"Yes Alex!" Malajia celebrated as Emily handed over the wad of bills, and her bride-to-be tiara. "Get him girl!"

"Alex—"

"Shut up Sidra," Alex cut in as the stripper began gyrating and dancing on Alex.

Chasity laughed at the salty look on Sidra's face.

Alex was busy dancing with the stripper as she shoved some ones in his G-string. Without warning, he grabbed her thighs, lifting her up; she wrapped her legs around his hips as he continued dancing.

Alex let out a scream of delight as she held her arms in the air, letting the rest of the bills fall over their heads.

"*Damn* he strong," Malajia blurted out, hand over her chest. She fanned herself with her other hand.

Chasity busted out laughing again as she grabbed another strawberry from the nearby tray. "Emily, I think Alex is gonna steal your vibrator tonight," she joked, earning a snicker from Emily.

"Fuck that, *I* might steal it," Malajia chimed in, dancing her way over to the stripper.

"God," Sidra huffed in disgust, as Chasity howled with laughter.

Chapter 54

Mark sat at a bar, devouring his plate of hot wings and sipping his drink. "This place just needs to give me the damn recipe for these hot wings," he commented in between chews.

Jason, who was eating his burger sliders and French fries next to him, shook his head as he chuckled.

"Nah, I'm trippin'. Mel's wings taste better anyway," Mark amended, wiping his hands on a napkin.

Jason took a sip of his drink. "You miss her, don't you?" he asked, amusement in his voice.

Mark made a face. "Naw, me and the boys chillin'," he denied. "...I miss her *cooking* though."

Jason shook his head. "Always lying," he condemned.

"Whatever," Mark grunted, grabbing his phone. "But I'mma call her anyway and see what she doin'."

Jason busted out laughing. "She's gonna cuss you out."

"Nah, she wants to hear my voice, I know it," Mark boasted, putting the phone to his ear. He smiled when the line picked up. "Hey babe— Damn, I can't call you?— I just wanted to say hi—hello?" Glancing down at his phone, Mark sucked his teeth. "Yo, she is so goddamn disrespectful."

Jason laughed once again. "I *told* you."

Mark sucked his teeth again as he put his phone back into his pocket.

Jason glanced up at the entrance. "Here comes Josh," he announced.

"About time," Mark spat, grabbing another wing.

Josh removed his coat and pulled out a chair. "What's up fellas?"

"Keep your pleasantries, you buying a round of drinks, garage man," Mark spat.

Josh shot a confused look Jason's way.

Jason put a hand up. "He has an attitude, ignore him," he dismissed.

Josh chuckled. "That should be easy."

Mark shot him a glare. As he went to open his mouth to fire back a retort, the words got caught in his throat, as someone else approached. "Where the hell did *you* come from?" he belted out, seeing David standing there.

David looked confused as he sat down. "The car."

"Shut up, you know what I mean," Mark threw back as Jason greeted David with a handshake. "We weren't expecting to see you until Em's wedding."

David sat down in another empty chair, scooting himself up to the bar. "Well, I'm actually on another small break right now, so I decided to just come down as opposed to staying up in Ohio," he answered.

"You staying with your dad?" Jason asked, signaling for the bartender.

"Nah, I'm staying with Josh," David answered. Josh nodded in confirmation.

"Y'all gonna be rooming together just like old times and shit," Mark teased.

David fixed him with a stare. "Your jokes are getting cornier and cornier man," he ground out, to which Mark laughed.

"Shit, I was hoping nobody would notice," Mark replied, sipping his drink.

Once David and Josh received their order, the four guys spent time in silence, enjoying their food and drinks.

"Guys," Mark prompted after a moment, grabbing the guys' attention. "Do y'all miss college?"

"You mean the *work*?" David asked.

Mark shook his head. "No, I mean just…the *experience*?" he clarified. "I mean, I know we all went through some shit then, but *overall*—"

"Overall, it was a great experience," Jason finished. "Even though I feel like I left there with the best part, the *entire* experience I do miss sometimes."

Mark shot Jason a glare. "Man, we *know* you bagged Chasity from college. You ain't gotta throw that in there," he mocked.

Jason laughed. "What? I love my wife," he threw back.

"I love *mine too*, but you don't see me throwing her up every five minutes," Mark argued.

Jason looked confused; the humor had left his face. "Did you *not* bring up Malajia when we were talking about wings earlier?"

Mark opened his mouth to retort, but realized that he had no argument. "Whatever yo, that's why I was gonna ask Chaz out freshman year," he taunted. "That is until she punched me in the stomach during our football game... I realized then that she was too evil for me."

"That's a lie, but Malajia liking *me* first, is a *fact*," Jason threw back.

Mark slammed his glass down. "Fuck you, ain't nobody need a reminder of that shit," he barked.

"Yeah? Leave me alone then," Jason tossed back, unfazed.

"Okay, you two chill," Josh interjected, amusement in his voice. "You two ended up with who you were meant to be with."

"*We know*," Mark spat a Josh.

"As did *I*," Josh proudly boasted, ignoring Mark's attitude.

"That shit don't count. Sidra played your lovesick ass in college," Mark bit out, grabbing his drink again.

Josh narrowed his eyes at Mark, then looked at Jason. "Jase, tell us again how Malajia wanted you freshman year."

Mark slammed his glass down and covered his ears. Loud noises erupted from him, an effort to drown out the words.

David and Jason busted out laughing.

Josh shook his head at Mark, letting out a sigh. "But back to your original question Mark, I *do* miss college," he agreed. "Don't get me wrong, I'm glad that I'm no longer working part-time at the Pizza Shack anymore—"

Mark chuckled, "Old ass pizza and shit."

"That you kept eating like it was going out of style," Josh countered.

"You damn right, it was free," Mark threw back, tipping his drink at Josh.

"*But*...I do miss how carefree some of the times were,"

Josh added, folding his arms on the counter.

David smiled. "Yeah," he agreed, reflecting. "I can't believe some of the stuff that you guys got me to do." He chuckled. "*Including* dragging me on a road trip to Miami for spring break. A trip that we were *not* invited to."

"The girls were *pissed*, but we had fun didn't we?" Jason recalled, amused.

"Yeah, once we got past Mark's driving," Josh added. "Lost hours in that car with his silly ass."

Mark made a face in retaliation. Then had a thought. "We *did* have fun, *didn't* we?" he asked.

Jason looked confused. "I *just* said that."

Mark put his hand up. "Shut up, what would you guys think of reliving one of our college memories?"

The guys stared at Mark, confused, yet intrigued.

Emily reached for a glass pitcher of orange juice. "You girls really outdid yourselves with this breakfast spread," she gushed, looking at the plates of food spread out on the large cream marble dining room table.

The plates of fresh fruit, French toast, waffles, pastries, bacon, sausage, eggs, grits, bagels, spreads and an assortment of juices, looked like it could have been placed in a hotel buffet. After a long night of bridal games, talking, reminiscing, and laughs, the girls' moods and appetites had lifted.

"I think we might've gone a little overboard," Sidra chuckled, grabbing a bowl of whipped cream from the counter. "Even *Malajia* doesn't eat this much."

Malajia paused in mid-grab of a piece of bacon, and looked at Sidra. "I tell you what I definitely *won't* be eating, that nasty ass whipped cream you called yourself making," she mocked.

Sidra sucked her teeth as she sat the glass bowl on the table. "This is *far* from nasty," she threw back. "I get no complaints."

"From who, *Josh*?" Malajia ground out. "Of *course* he'll eat that watery bullshit."

Sidra gave the side of Malajia's head a poke. "Hush," she spat.

Alex sat down at the table and handed Emily a china plate. "You want me to fix your plate?" she asked her.

Emily chuckled. "No, thank you." She took the plate from Alex. "I told you, you don't have to dote over me."

"I *told* Alex to stop breathing on you and shit," Malajia teased, earning an eye roll from Alex. Malajia scanned the table, then frowned. "Chasity, hurry up with those damn pancakes," she barked, looking back at her. Chasity was at the stove, finishing up with a stack of pancakes. "Cupcake ain't here, you don't need to make smiley faces on them. Just bring them over here."

Chasity looked at Malajia, narrowing her eyes at her. "I wouldn't put a smiley face on *yours anyway,* you raggedy bitch."

Malajia snickered hard as Sidra shook her head.

Alex laughed a little as Chasity walked over with the plate of pancakes. "Aww, Chaz, you make smiling faces on pancakes for your baby?" she gushed.

"Shut up," Chasity huffed, setting the plate on the table.

Emily giggled at Alex's salty face. "They smell good… Everything smells and looks so good," she beamed.

As the girls began to fix their plates, Sidra looked at Emily. "Em, on behalf of Malajia's crazy self, we apologize for the stripper last night," she said.

"You damn sure ain't gotta apologize for me, 'cause I'm nowhere *near* sorry," Malajia threw back.

Sidra cut her eye at her.

"Besides, *Chasity* was in on that too," Malajia told. "Alex punked out at the last minute, and shit."

Chasity just shrugged as she ate some of her food, while Alex let out a little laugh.

Sidra flung her hair over her shoulder, then shook her head.

"Listen, there's nothing to apologize for." Emily giggled. "I mean, strippers aren't *my* thing but at least you got your money worth with Alex."

Alex snapped her fingers, "Yup," she boasted recalling the intense dance session that she had with the stripper.

Malajia laughed. "At least I know I won't have any issues with *Alex's* bachelorette party."

"Nope, not a one," Alex assured, doing a dance in her seat. "Did you see the way he picked my ass up?" Alex grabbed a napkin and fanned herself. "That cold shower after that dance was *needed*."

"Girl, call Eric when you get back and give him some," Malajia joked, earning a snicker from Alex.

Alex chuckled as she had a thought. "Malajia, *speaking* of calling people, who were you yelling at on the phone last night?" she asked.

Malajia sucked her teeth as she poured syrup on her food. "Mark's ass," she answered. "I told him not to call me this weekend."

Alex laughed.

"The *entire* weekend?" Sidra asked, appalled. "He's your *husband*."

Malajia shot Sidra a confused look. "*So*?"

"*So*, what if he just wanted to say that he loves you? What if something was *wrong*?" Sidra wondered.

"*First* off, I already know his black ass loves me—I can wait until I get home to hear that shit," Malajia scoffed, waving her hand in Sidra's direction. "Second, I already told him, anything that happens while I'm gone, his ass is on his own."

Emily laughed a little. "That's terrible Malajia."

Malajia tossed her arms in the air. "He didn't *want* shit," she argued. "He *never* does. When me and Chaz were on the road to you Em, he called me talking about 'babe, we're out of toilet paper'," she mocked. "Like boy—take your stupid ass to the store and *get* some. What the hell am I gonna do from the car and shit."

Chasity laughed as she recalled that moment of their car trip.

Malajia shook her head. "I'm glad you find that shit funny, Chasity," she fussed. "You *know* he's irkin'."

Emily looked at Chasity. "Did you tell Jason the same thing?" she asked.

Chasity shook her head as she cut a piece of her pancake. "No, I actually like when he calls."

Malajia rolled her eyes. "God, you two are so fussy bus."

"No, that's just *normal*," Sidra jumped in, in defense of

Chasity. "It's *you and Mark's* relationship that is weird."

Malajia flagged Sidra with her hand. "Wait until Josh moves in with you. You'll get sick of his ass too."

Sidra smiled at the thought of her and Josh living together.

Malajia glanced over at the big smile on Sidra's face and rolled her eyes. "Never mind," she grumbled. "Y'all are gonna be sickening like Chasity and Jason..." She tapped her finger to her chin. "On second thought, nah, you're on some *other* shit. At least Chasity cusses Jason out."

Sidra busted out laughing; Chasity shook her head as she concentrated on eating her food.

"I *do* cuss Josh out," Sidra argued, laughter still in her voice.

"No, he cusses *you* out after you do dumb shit, trying to be petty," Malajia threw back, pointing her fork in Sidra's direction.

Resolved, Sidra put her hand over her face and shook her head.

"Well Em, we have more games and stuff for later, but do you want to do anything special today?" Alex asked in between chews of her food.

"Ooh, lets hit a club," Malajia suggested, dancing in her seat.

Chasity looked at her. "At eleven in the morning?" she asked, sarcastic.

Malajia pointed at Chasity and winked at her. "It's never too early to party, always remember that."

Emily set her fork down. "I really just want to relax like we've been doing," she said. "With everything that's been going on, relaxation and time with you girls is just what I need."

Sidra placed a hand on her chest. "That's so sweet Em," she gushed.

"Sooo, we're staying *in* tonight is what you're saying?" Malajia concluded, tone unenthused. Chasity backhanded her on the arm.

"That's perfectly fine Em, whatever you want," Alex agreed, rubbing Emily's arm.

Emily just smiled.

Until a knock on the door caused her and the other girls to

look in the direction of the living room.

Sidra looked at Malajia.

"What?" Malajia asked, confused.

"That's not another *stripper* is it?" Sidra sneered.

"Shit, not that I know of," Malajia shrugged.

When another knock sounded, the girls stood up and headed for the window in the dining room. "Anybody see a car?" Alex asked, craning her neck.

"We are *all* looking out the same window, Alex," Chasity sneered, rolling her eyes. "Can't see shit from this angle."

"I don't even know why you acknowledged that, Chaz," Malajia chuckled.

Alex let out a huff as she made her way towards the living room, tightening the belt on her long robe in the process. "I'm gonna see who it is," she ground out.

"You wanna take this spatula in case you need to smack whoever it is, in the face?" Malajia asked, grabbing a spatula from a plate.

Alex rolled her eyes. "This is a five-star cabin, I doubt I'll have anything to worry about," she assured.

"Tell your dad we said thanks again for letting us use the place," Sidra whispered to Chasity.

"I said it once, he gets it," Chasity whispered back, smartly.

Sidra sucked her teeth,

The four girls stood in the dining room entry way as Alex walked up to the front door. Alex glanced back at them. "So, y'all are *really* gonna let me open the door alone?"

Malajia shrugged. "I offered you a spatula, you didn't want it."

"I'm not allowed to hit anybody," Chasity chimed in.

"It's my bridal weekend," Emily added.

"I…I just redid my nails," Sidra joined in.

Alex narrowed her eyes in agitation at her friends, before shaking her head. She slowly moved the covering to the peephole, then glanced out. "Are you kidding me?!" she erupted.

"What's wrong?" Sidra charged, hurrying into the living

room.

"On second thought, Malajia give me the damn spatula," Alex fussed, holding her hand out in Malajia's direction.

"I gotchu' girl, let me get some knives too," Malajia charged, running back for the table to gather more utensils.

"Alex, who's at the door?" Chasity frowned.

Alex glanced back at the girls, then let out a long sigh as she grabbed for the doorknob.

"Wait, why are you opening the door?!" Malajia exclaimed, darting from the kitchen, utensils in hand.

"You'll see," Alex grunted, pulling the door open. Stepping back, she lowered her head and made her way back to the girls.

Confusion gave way to shock when Jason, Mark, Josh, and David walked in, smiles on their faces.

"What the fuck?" Chasity snapped.

"Oh *hell* no!" Malajia chimed in, annoyed.

"What are you guys *doing* here?" Sidra added, folding her arms.

"You guys seriously had nothing better to do than drive all the way down here to bother *us*?" Alex harped.

The smiles faded from the guys' faces. They figured that the girls would be shocked, but they weren't expecting this level of anger. The guys stood there with overnight bags in hand, looking nervous.

"Um—surprise!" Mark blurted out, tossing his arms in the air.

Everyone shot Mark a confused look.

"What?" Jason questioned.

Mark looked at him. "I literally had nothing else to say," he defended. He then snapped his fingers. "Oh no, I got it." He looked back to the girls. "We wanted to surprise y'all just like we did in Miami freshman year."

"You mean when you *crashed* our spring break trip, *uninvited*?" Chasity spat.

Mark's eyes shifted. "But...we had fun though," he stammered.

Chasity rolled her eyes at Mark, then looked at Jason. "Jason," she called, stern.

Jason looked at her, wide-eyed. "Huh?"

"Did that really sound like a good idea?" she slowly drew out.

Jason rubbed the back of his head nervously. "Um… I mean—" He gave a nervous chuckle when Chasity fixed him with a piecing gaze. "You look so beaut—"

"Shut up," she spat.

"Okay," Jason muttered.

Malajia eyed Mark with disdain. "I should throw these fuckin' knives at your damn face," she hurled.

"Damn babe, all that?!" Mark exclaimed, holding his arms up.

"And David, where the hell did *you* come from?" Malajia hurled, pointing at him.

David's eyes shifted nervously. "Umm…I'm on a break," he cautiously put out.

Malajia sucked her teeth, then turned to Sidra for assistance. Instead, she and Josh were staring at one another longingly. Malajia sucked her teeth. "Sidra, no," Malajia barked, backhanding Sidra.

Startled, Sidra grabbed her arm and let out a yelp. "Ouch! What the hell Malajia?!"

"You do *not* get to make googly eyes at Josh's blockheaded ass right now," Malajia argued, inciting snickers from everyone but Josh and Sidra. "No, cuss his ass *out*."

"But…I missed him," Sidra pouted.

Chasity rolled her eyes as Malajia waved her hand at Sidra dismissively. "Sidra, you are such a disappointment," Chasity commented.

Sidra gasped.

"Listen in our defense…it was Mark's idea," Josh told, pointing. Jason and David nodded in agreement.

Mark looked at the guys in shock. "Damn, what happened to 'we're in this together'?" he argued.

"*Nobody* said that shit and you know it," Jason argued.

"It doesn't even matter," Alex interjected, stopping the pending argument between the guys. "If we would've crashed *your* bachelor weekend, you'd be mad."

"Y'all *did*!" Mark belted out, tossing his arms in the air.

"Hey! That don't count, we had a joint party," Malajia

threw back of her and Mark's pre-wedding parties.

"No—No we *didn't!*" Mark barked back, exasperated, then pointed to Malajia. "You were mad 'cause I was at the strip club, so you brought your drunk ass there and stole all my ones."

Malajia tried to conceal her chuckle, but was unsuccessful.

"That stripper was mad as shit at them quarters I tossed," Mark grunted.

This time Malajia did laugh. "She was ugly anyway."

Alex waved her hands. "Not the point, this weekend is about Emily," she cut in, annoyed. "So, you guys need to go."

"Well, why don't you let *Emily* decide?" Jason taunted, folding his arms.

"No, we're deciding *for* her, so get the fuck out," Chasity spat.

"Emily has her own voice, *Chasity*," Mark taunted.

"Oh shut up," Chasity bit back.

The guys looked at Emily. "Em, do you want us to leave?" Josh asked.

Emily looked around as all eyes were now on her. "Well—"

"Em, it's 'sister' time this weekend," Alex prompted. "Don't let it be ruined by these fools."

Emily shrugged. "Well...I mean they drove all this way—" The girls let out a collective groan, while the guys cheered.

"Em, you've always been my favorite," Mark smiled, pointing at Emily.

"Well, she can *have* you, 'cause I'm sick of your ass," Malajia grunted, walking back to the kitchen.

Mark held his arms out as he followed. "Mel, I can't get a hug?"

"Hug *Emily!*" Malajia yelled from the kitchen.

Emily giggled as Mark gave her a hug. "Good to see you," she said.

"You too," Mark returned.

Alex let out a long sigh as Sidra and Josh embraced one another. "Y'all might as well come get some breakfast," she said resolved, walking back to the kitchen.

"Great, I'm starving," David rejoiced, heading for the kitchen.

Mark pushed by David and rushed for the kitchen, nearly knocking him over in the process.

"Damn it Mark!" David bellowed, regaining his balance.

"My bad, I was tryna get to the bacon," Mark said.

Jason smiled as he walked up to Chasity; he was met with a death stare. "I can't get a kiss?" he asked, hopeful.

"*Kiss* my ass," Chasity spat, walking away from him. Jason just chuckled; he expected nothing less.

Josh shook his head as the rest of the group headed for the kitchen, leaving him and Sidra standing there. He looked at her, then let out a chuckle when she delivered a light slap to his chest. "Ow," he laughed. "What was *that* for?"

"For crashing," she threw back, pointing at him.

"I'm sorry, it was my own fault for listening to Mark," Josh replied.

"You know nothing good ever comes from listening to Mark," Sidra joked.

Josh shrugged. "Well…I got to see you sooner than I expected, so something good *did* come from listening this time."

Sidra blushed as she looked away. Her smile turned to confusion when she looked out the window. "Umm guys, it's starting to snow," she announced loud enough for everyone to hear.

"Of *course* it is," Malajia fussed from the kitchen. "Bullshit always follows Mark, so I'm not even surprised."

"Hey!" Mark bellowed.

Chapter 55

Alex shook her head and sighed as she stared out of the bay window in the living room, a cup of tea in hand. "Even if we *wanted* to go out, that snow isn't letting up at all," she commented, taking a sip.

Sidra ran a hand through her hair as she sat on the couch. "At least it's supposed to stop soon," she mentioned. "I'm sure the roads will be clear by tomorrow afternoon."

Hours had passed since the snow began, and it had yet to cease. It had certainly put a damper on the girls' moods. The guys were getting on their nerves, which didn't help the situation either.

Malajia looked over at Chasity, who was sitting in an accent chair. "Chaz, what time do we have to check out tomorrow?" she asked.

Chasity looked confused. "I'll leave when the hell I *want*," she said, then ran a hand over her stomach. "But y'all asses are getting out by tomorrow afternoon," she added.

Alex's mouth fell open. "You're not leaving *with* us?" she eyed Chasity with confusion. "I thought we were all supposed to leave *together*."

"My man is here, and my in-laws want Kayla for an extra day, so fuck y'all," Chasity jeered, earning a snicker from Malajia. Sidra shook her head in amusement.

Alex successfully concealed her laugher. "You're triflin'," she hurled, inciting a laugh from Chasity.

Emily walked down the steps, cell phone in hand.

"Everything good with Will?" Malajia asked, looking at her.

Emily nodded as she flopped down on the couch. "Yeah, it's not snowing too bad where we live," she answered.

"What a difference two hours make," Malajia commented. She stretched and looked at her watch. "I'm hungry." she glanced back at the kitchen. "Aye! What's taking y'all so damn long with dinner?!" she yelled into the kitchen.

"Right, how long does it take to make hotdogs?" Alex grunted, sipping her tea.

"Shut up, ain't nobody making hotdogs!" Mark yelled back.

Malajia snickered. "Come on, we hungry."

"It's almost done, hush," Jason hurled.

Malajia's mouth fell open. "Mark, are you gonna let—"

"The man said hush!" Mark interrupted.

Chasity's laughing caused Malajia to glare at her. "Really? We let our men check each other now?" she hissed.

"Not each other. just *you*," Chasity teased.

Malajia narrowed her eyes at her. "I hope you got twins in that demon womb of yours," she ground out. Chasity sucked her teeth in return.

"Oh wow," Emily commented, amused.

David walked out of the kitchen. "Ladies, dinner is ready," he announced.

Within moments, the group was gathered around the dining room table.

Malajia pinched the bridge of her nose. "Y'all spent all this time in here only to make some damn spaghetti?" she ground out.

"*First* of all, it's baked ziti," Mark threw back.

"*First* of all, I know *you* had no parts in making that, 'cause it actually *looks* good," Malajia countered.

Mark sucked his teeth.

Josh rubbed his hands together. "We have baked ziti, homemade garlic bread, and César salad," he informed, proud.

"Good job on making all of this," Alex beamed, sitting down.

"Y'all *made* us," Mark grunted, sitting down.

"Oh you're absolutely right. You actually thought that *we* were going to cook?" Sidra boasted, reaching for a piece of garlic bread from a tray.

"They sure *did* and was salty as hell about it," Malajia

laughed. "All stupid, talking about 'what's for dinner'?"

Mark stared at her annoyed. "*I'm* the only one who asked that," he pointed out.

Malajia grabbed a spoon and scooped some ziti from the pan. "I know," she taunted, unfazed.

Over the next hour, the group enjoyed their meal while they talked.

"So Em, how excited are you for the wedding?" Josh asked.

Emily looked down at her plate as she ate some more of her food.

Sidra loudly cleared her throat, prompting Josh to glance at her. "You okay?" he asked, concerned.

Sidra took a sip of water as she nodded. All of the girls knew how Emily was feeling about all things wedding. "Let's change the subject," she suggested.

Josh looked confused. "Did I say something wrong?"

Emily gave a half smile. "No, you didn't say anything wrong Josh," she clarified. "Um, if you mean am I excited about marrying Will? Yes, absolutely."

The confusion was still prominent on Josh's face. "I don't understand. You're not looking forward to your wedd—"

"*God* Josh," Chasity blurted out, tossing her hands in the air.

Sidra pinched the bridge of her nose and let out a sigh.

"Sidra, shut him up *please*," Malajia spat, reaching for her drink.

"I know, I know," Sidra agreed, sighing.

Emily pushed herself back from the table. "Excuse me," she said, leaving the kitchen.

"*What* am I saying *wrong*?" Josh wondered, holding his hands up.

"Josh, just close your mouth bro," Jason muttered, eating his food.

"Josh, Em isn't exactly excited about her wedding. Family issues and such," Alex calmly explained. "She's been going through a lot over these past few months and she's just over all of it."

Josh looked apologetic. "Damn, sorry I didn't mean to

damper the mood."

"Oh it's not *your* fault," Malajia assured, then turned to Sidra. "It's *yours*."

Sidra tossed her arms in the air in frustration, then put her head in her hands.

"You should've gave his ass a pep talk when he got here,'" Malajia pointed out. "Even *David* knew not to ask anything."

"That's not a valid argument. David's ass never asks *anything*," Mark jeered.

David made a face at Mark. "I *do*, which is why I already know about what's going on because I *call* Em," he threw back.

"Oops, he shut *your* wrong ass up," Chasity sneered.

Mark looked at Malajia. "You gonna let—"

"Yup," Malajia cut in, nonchalant.

Emily returned to the table a few moments later and sat down. All eyes were on her. "What?" she asked, looking around.

"Are you okay?" Alex asked, sympathetic.

Emily chuckled a bit. "I'm fine, I just had to use the bathroom," she said, pushing herself up to the table.

After a few moments of silence, Mark took a sip of his drink. "Okay so what are we gonna do tonight?" he began. "Any games to play?"

"Well, we have a bunch of bachelorette party games that we were *gonna* play, but we doubt that you'll wanna play pin the dick on the muscle man," Malajia nonchalantly replied.

Alex couldn't help but laugh at the look on the guys' faces.

"Nah, we good on that," Mark threw back. "But seriously, we gotta come up with something to do."

"Karaoke?" Sidra suggested.

"Something *fun*," Mark stressed, earning an eye roll from Sidra. "Come on, we used to make up some cool shit back in school."

"Did we *really*?" Alex chortled, peering out of the window. "Thank God, it stopped snowing."

"Alex—you announcing the wrong shit. We ain't going nowhere tonight *anyway*," Mark argued, shaking his hand in her direction.

"We could build snowmen," Emily suggested, breaking a

piece of garlic bread. Her suggestion was met with blank stares. "What?" she meekly asked.

"Emily, don't get put out," Mark grunted.

Emily busted out laughing.

Malajia shook her head. "Girl, ain't nobody tryna play in no snow," she sneered. "We're like thirty."

"Speak for yourself," Sidra threw back. "I still have three years until I turn thirty. Don't age me up."

"I don't *have* to age you up, them smile lines already *are*," Malajia mocked.

Sidra threw a balled-up napkin at her. "I do *not* have smile lines, you hag," she barked at the laughing Malajia.

Mark slammed his hand on the table, startling everyone and grabbing their attention. "Come on y'all," he barked.

"Did you *have* to bang on the damn table?" Alex asked, angry.

Mark slammed his hand on it again, annoying Alex even more. "If we don't come up with *something* it's gonna be a dry ass night."

"*You* can go the fuck *home*," Chasity sneered.

"*Exactly*," Alex cosigned, eyeing Mark with disgust. "Lest you forget, we never invited you to come here in the *first place*. We would be having a good time with*out* you."

"Alex, I stopped listening to you once you said 'exactly'," Mark mocked, pointing at her.

Alex sucked her teeth as Malajia snickered.

Jason reached for his drink. "Y'all already know that if we don't think of something, Mark will bitch the entire night," he chortled.

"Shoot, after a while he'll be Malajia's problem," Josh laughed.

"No, he'll be *your* problem, 'cause he ain't sleeping in *my* room," Malajia jeered, sipping her wine.

Mark flagged Malajia with his hand.

"You know, there's nothing wrong with just catching up," David proposed, folding his arms on the table. "I mean, how often are we all together anymore?"

"Nah, not good enough," Mark dismissed. His complaining was met with groans.

Malajia slapped her hand against her face. "God," she grunted. "Look, since it's apparent that he won't shut the fuck up, let's just play truth or dare. We can't go wrong with that."

Mark once again slammed his hand on the table, startling them.

"Will you *stop* that shit?!" Chasity snapped.

"Mark, relax bro, *damn*!" Jason barked, fed up with Mark's antics.

"My bad," Mark laughed. "But good plan Mel," he praised.

"I don't think I've ever played truth or dare before," Emily chuckled.

"You're not missing anything," Sidra muttered. "It's so stupid."

"Nah, it's fun and I have a way to make it more interesting," Mark replied, excited. "Let's hurry up and finish this wack ass food, so we can go play in the living room."

Everyone watched as Mark began scarfing down his food.

"Everybody eat slowly so it'll piss him off," Jason ground out, earning laughs from everyone but Mark, who flipped him the finger.

Chapter 56

An hour later, dinner finished and kitchen cleaned, the group sat in front of the fireplace, enjoying their dessert.

Alex cut a piece of her chocolate cheesecake, and placed the forkful into her mouth. "Oh my God, Chasity *where* did you get this cheesecake from?" she asked, mouth full. "This is so good."

Malajia eyed her in disgust. She placed her arms around Mark's neck, who was sitting on the floor in front of her. "You all spitting on the carpet," she scoffed.

"Shut up, girl," Alex barked back, rolling her eyes. "Anyway, Chaz?"

"Ask Jase, he picked it up for me," Chasity answered, adjusting her position on the couch.

"I'll give you the info," Jason promised.

Alex smiled. As she went to cut another piece, Mark, who was sitting on the floor near her, jerked his arm out, accidentally knocking the small plate from Alex's hand.

"Damn it Mark!" Alex screeched, watching her precious cheesecake fall to the floor.

"Oh shit," Mark reacted, laughing.

Chasity flashed a fiery gaze Mark's way. "Clean it the fuck up," she demanded.

Mark put his hands up. "My bad."

"That was the last piece!" Alex harped, grabbing the plate and slamming it on the nearby end table.

"What were you even *doing*?" Malajia asked him, annoyed.

"I was about to say something," Mark chuckled, making a move to get up from the floor. As he tried to stand, he grabbed hold of Alex's shoulder and pressed on it. "My bad, I need help getting up," he said, staring at Alex intensely.

"Get the hell off me!" Alex erupted, jerking away from him.

Malajia reached over and slapped Mark's leg as he stood all the way up. "Stop playing and clean that mess up," she demanded.

Mark laughed and headed for the kitchen.

"The cleaning stuff is under the kitchen sink," Sidra called after him.

Jason rubbed his face. "It's always *him*," he jeered.

"*Always*," David agreed as Josh nodded in agreement.

Malajia shook her head, sighing in the process. "I have no argument."

Within moments, Mark was back in the living room, paper towels, carpet cleaner spray and rag in hand. He kneeled in front of the stain and began his task of cleaning. "Okay, so about this truth or dare game," he began.

Sidra let out a loud sigh as she folded her arms. "Ugh," she scoffed.

"Just let it happen, Sid," Malajia advised, rubbing Sidra's shoulder.

"I was thinking, why not do a little twist on it," Mark suggested, still cleaning.

"And what twist would *that* be?" Josh asked.

"We all write down a bunch of questions and dares, then put them in a hat," Mark answered. "Each person picks from the hat and can make whoever they want, answer the question or do the dare."

Alex looked confused. "Wouldn't it just be simpler to play the *normal* way?"

"Alex, you lost me after you said 'wouldn't,'" Mark mocked.

Malajia busted out laughing at the angered look on Alex's face.

"I can't stand you," Alex hissed at Mark.

As Mark went to throw the soiled paper towels and rag away, Malajia piped up. "I actually like Mark's idea," she said. "It'll go faster because the questions will already be on the paper. We won't have to wait for people's slow ass thoughts."

"Down for the cause, I love it," Mark praised from the

kitchen. "I'mma bring this bottle of tequila in here, 'cause we gonna need it for my dares."

"Oh God, it's not that nasty shit you bought, *is* it?" Josh complained.

"It is," Mark confirmed, proud.

Malajia stood up. "Ooh, I have the perfect hat and shot glasses," she beamed, running for the steps.

Sidra sighed. "I have a notepad in my purse." She stood up and made a beeline for her pocketbook.

"You *would* have a notepad in your purse," Mark mocked, returning to the living room.

Malajia headed back down the steps, plastic bag in hand. She stood in front of the group as she dug into it. "Here's the hat we can use," she announced, pulling a black baseball cap with a foam penis sitting a top of it.

"What the fuck?" Mark blurted out as laughter erupted from Chasity and Alex.

"What?" Malajia asked, feigning innocence. "It's a *hat*."

"Why is there a *dick* on it?" Mark asked her, pointing to it.

Malajia rolled her eyes. "It was *supposed* to be a bachelorette hat for Em to wear, but she was being corny."

"Malajia, I just don't want to wear penises," Emily meekly put out.

Malajia looked at her, stunned. "Wait, Em, you actually said the *word?*" She looked at Sidra and laughed. "Sidra, *she* said 'penis' and *you* still *can't.*"

"Back off, Malajia," Sidra spat. "It would be *you* to buy that ridiculous hat."

"Actually, *Chasity* bought this penis hat," Malajia told, pointing to Chasity.

"I *did* buy the penis hat," Chasity confirmed, nonchalant.

Jason put his hand over his face and shook his head.

Sidra tossed her arms in the air. "Can you stop saying pe— *stop* it," she fussed.

Malajia snickered. "Well...we're using the penis hat—" She snickered again when Sidra sucked her teeth. "So grow up and get the hell over it."

Mark sucked his teeth too. "At least take the damn thing *off* of it," he suggested exasperated.

"No! It stays on," Malajia barked back.

"Can we just write down our questions so we can get this over with please?" Sidra huffed.

Ten minutes later, all questions and dares were in the hat, which sat in the middle of the coffee table.

Mark rubbed his hands together. "All right, let's get this started," he said. "Let me get a shot first. Mel, where are the shot glasses that you said you had?"

Malajia reached over and grabbed something from the bag. "Oh, here you go," she said, setting a small shot glass with a plastic penis inside in the middle of the table. The item was met with silence. The girls were desperately trying to hold in their laughter, while the guys looked annoyed.

"I will throw that shit in the goddamn fireplace," Mark threatened, causing the girls to break into laughter.

"There are *real* shot glasses in the kitchen," Sidra said, pointing to the kitchen. "Guys, I apologize on the behalf of these two," she added, gesturing to Chasity and Malajia, who were still laughing.

"I'll get them," David volunteered, getting up.

Malajia put her novelty glass back in her gift bag and moved the bag aside.

"Mel, what all do you have in that bag anyway?" Alex wondered.

"You'll see soon enough," Malajia vaguely replied as David returned to the living room, shot glasses in hand. He handed one to Mark.

Mark poured himself a shot and quickly downed it. "I'll go first," he said, reaching into the hat. He pulled out a piece of paper and read it. "Okay...David, how many chicks have you banged?" he asked.

David looked confused. "Is that the actual question?"

Mark chuckled. "Nah, it said, 'how many sexual partners have you had?'" he replied, showing the paper. "But my way sounds better."

"Mark, that was a stupid question to ask David. You know he's only been with *Nicole*," Alex condemned, "And there's nothing wrong with that, so leave him alone."

Mark shot Alex a side-glance as he pointed at David.

"David, answer the question."

David rubbed the back of his neck; he hesitated. "Two," he slowly put out.

"What?!" Alex exclaimed. "I thought Nicole was the only one."

"Ha! Wrong as always!" Mark hurled at Alex, pointing at her.

David shrugged slightly. "I hooked up with my lab partner once, over a year ago," he answered.

"Okay David," Malajia praised. "Done got himself a fuck buddy."

David looked embarrassed. "Stop it, it was *one* time, we both understood it to be just that. She's not interested in me romantically and vice versa. We're friends." He then glared at Mark. "Wasn't gonna let me divulge that information on my own terms, huh?"

"Do I *ever*?" Mark dismissed, placing the paper on the table.

Alex leaned over and reached for the hat. "My turn." She pulled a paper from the hat. She read it then busted out laughing. "Malajia."

Malajia looked at her. "Bring it on," she challenged.

"You have to do the worm for one minute," Alex revealed, laughter filling her voice.

Malajia snatched the paper from Alex's hand as everyone busted out laughing. "No the fuck it *doesn't* say that!" she barked.

Alex put her hand up. "I swear to God, it does."

Malajia read the paper. "*Who* the fuck wrote this?" she snapped, looking around at the group. "Y'all petty."

"Malajia, stop whining and do it," Mark egged on. He pointed to the space in front of the coffee table. "Go."

Malajia sucked her teeth as she stood up and made her way to the space. She kneeled on the floor and let out a loud, angered sigh. "I don't even know how to *do* this shit," she complained.

Chasity reached over on the end table and grabbed her phone. "Hold up, I gotta record this," she laughed.

"Fuck you Chasity," Malajia barked.

"Malajia, do it, so we can move on," Sidra goaded as she adjusted her position on the couch.

Malajia looked at the floor and sucked her teeth. "Can I just take a shot or something?" she begged.

"Do it!" they yelled at her.

"Fine!" Malajia snapped, flopping down on the floor. She let out a groan as she began her attempt at the worm. If her flopping her body repeatedly on the floor wasn't annoying her enough, the amount of hysterical laughter erupting from her friends certainly was.

"My ankles!" Malajia screamed, still flopping.

"Yoooo, babe, you look stupid as shit," Mark laughed.

Chasity cracked up laughing as she kept her phone steady on Malajia.

"You look like a fish out of water," Alex laughed.

Malajia screamed when her foot hit a table. "Damn it!"

"She's gonna break something, watch," Sidra predicted, amused.

Emily was laughing so hard that tears were spilling down her face.

"Has it been a minute yet?!" Malajia yelped, still flopping

"Almost," Alex laughed.

Malajia looked over at her. "You're not even looking at your watch you big bitch!"

David looked at his watch. "Time is up Mel," he said, wiping a tear from his eye.

Malajia laid sprawled out on the floor, trying to catch her breath. Rolling over, she laid on her back. "I fuckin' hate y'all," she grunted.

"Chaz, did you get it all?" Jason asked, still laughing.

"Yup," Chasity replied, putting her phone down. "I'll play it back on the TV later."

Malajia stood up from the floor and angrily made her way to the couch.

Mark reached out for her hand. "How ya ankles feel?" he teased.

Angry, Malajia punched him on the arm. "Fuck you."

"Ouch!" Mark bellowed mid-laugh, grabbing his arm.

Malajia flopped down on the couch and folded her arms in

a huff. "Somebody else go before I quit," she huffed.

Emily leaned forward and drew a paper. She read it, then giggled. "I guess this question is for anybody," she said. "Who in here had a crush on Chasity freshman year?"

Chasity looked confused. "What the hell—" Before she could finish her rant, all of the guys' hands shot up in the air.

"Of *course* you all did," Alex chuckled as Sidra shook her head.

Chasity rolled her eyes, then glanced over and saw that Malajia had her hand up as well. "Put your fuckin' hand down, Malajia," she spat.

Malajia laughed "*What*? I'm allowed to have a girl crush," she defended. "With your sexy self."

Chasity turned her face up in disgust, "Ugh."

Sidra folded her arms. "I'm not surprised," she said. "*Everybody* crushed on her."

"Don't hate on my sis 'cause y'all were busted freshman year and nobody liked y'all," Malajia joked to Alex and Sidra. Alex flagged Malajia with her hand. Malajia then pointed to Emily. "And Em *you better* not say anything with them floral sheets your ass used to wear."

Emily snickered. "I didn't even *say* anything," she threw back, pointing to herself.

Sidra narrowed her eyes at Malajia. "I *wasn't* hating, and I was *never* busted," she scoffed. "*Everybody* knows I dressed better than you. Hell, half the time, you didn't even *wear* clothes."

"Aht, aht, keep your wack ass comeback over there," Malajia dismissed, flinging her hand in Sidra's face.

"Okay, my turn," Josh jumped in, grabbing a paper from the hat. "Okay, it says… 'pass-a-sounds'," he drew out slowly. He scratched his head.

"Pass a *what*?" Alex wondered, bewildered.

"What is that?" David chimed in.

Sidra put her hands up. "Malajia," she griped. "That made up word has *Malajia* written *all* over it. This is the same person who made up 'fussy bus'."

Malajia was unfazed by the confusion. "It means that you can pass your turn to someone else," she answered. The room fell quiet.

Jason pinched the bridge of his nose and let out a long sigh as Mark fought the urge to laugh.

Chasity shook her head, annoyed. "She's fuckin' irkin," she said of Malajia.

Malajia tossed her arms in the air. "Oh my God, sue me for trying to be innovative and create a new word," she huffed. "Just pass your damn turn Josh, you were about to be corny anyway."

"That was such a waste of time," Sidra spat, pushing her hair behind her ear.

"*You're* a waste of time," Malajia shot back.

Sidra just made a face at her in retaliation.

Josh shook his head as he set the paper on the table. "Anybody is welcome to take it."

Mark jumped up. As David went to raise his hand, Mark slapped it. "Put your goddamn hand down," he barked.

Annoyed, David backhanded him in retaliation. "Ow!"

Unfazed, Mark cleared his throat. "*I* got a question," he began, then pointed to Jason. "Jase," he called.

Jason looked at him as he took a sip of his drink.

"You ever tell Chaz how you cried like a bitch when she went into labor?" Mark blurted out.

Jason choked on his drink. Chasity patted his back as he began coughing.

"No, he did *not*, will you stop lying?" Alex spat. "I was at the hospital, remember?"

Mark shook his hand in Alex's direction. "Nah, this was *before* he got to the hospital," he told. Jason stared daggers at Mark as he spoke. "Remember Jase? You were helping me put together some shit that Malajia decided to buy for our apartment, and you got the call from Chasity's mom telling you that she was in labor." He was amused as he continued his story. "Yo, he damn near tripped and fell as he ran out the door. I ended up driving 'cause his ass was too damn paranoid to drive. He called his mom to tell her that the baby was coming, and he went from talking normal to busting out crying and shit." Mark laughed, "Talking about, 'Mom, I heard her in the background, she sounded like she was dying, is that normal

Mom? Is she gonna die? I don't want her to die Mom.'"

Jason narrowed his eyes as Mark laughed hysterically. "You big, dumb goofy bastard," Jason grunted.

Chasity snickered as she rubbed Jason's back in an effort to calm him down. She had heard the story, because Jason had eventually told her, but she knew that Jason didn't want everyone else to know.

"Mark, that's horrible," Sidra condemned. "Making fun of him for being nervous."

"*Exactly*," Alex jumped in. "*Any* man would be nervous about their woman giving birth. *Especially* hearing how much pain she was in."

"Oh please," Mark shot back. "I was cool as shit when Mel went into labor."

Jason jumped up and pointed to Mark. "He's fuckin' lying yo!" he snapped.

"I believe it," Malajia muttered, in agreement with Jason.

Mark shot a shocked look Jason's way. "Whatchu mean?!"

"Bro, we were at the grocery store when you got the call about Malajia," Jason recalled. "All he heard was 'emergency' and he flipped the entire cart, filled up to the damn *brim* with food over, and ran down the damn aisle screaming like a maniac."

Malajia busted out laughing. "Are you serious?" she asked, looking at Mark.

"Yes, *dead* serious," Jason confirmed.

Mark sucked his teeth. "That is *not* the same thing," he argued. "Malajia's pressure went up and they had to do emergency surgery. I had to get out of there, so I did what I had to do."

Jason's eyes were wide. "Are you fu— Mark, you could've just left the cart standing where it *was*! There was *no* need whatsoever to flip the cart *over*. You left all that shit in the middle of the aisle for no reason," he hurled back. "You were being an idiot as *usual*."

"Yo, he is so *dramatic*," Malajia belted out, laughter subsiding. "The whole cart though?"

Mark rolled his eyes at her. Then looked at Jason. "You happy you got that off your chest?" he sneered.

Jason gritted his teeth and snatched a paper from the hat. He read it. "Nah, not yet. Get your dumb ass outside and make a snow angel."

"What? Hell no," Mark refused.

Jason turned the paper around for Mark to see. "It says it on here, and I choose *you* to do it, so shut the fuck up and do it."

Mark clapped his hands as he stormed towards the door. "Fine, you ain't said shit," he boasted. He went to grab his coat.

"Nope, no coat," Jason barked.

Mark looked at him. "Come on man, I'mma catch pneumonia," he begged.

"You gonna cry about it?" Jason taunted.

"No, I'll leave that to *you*, you little bitch," Mark threw back. Jason grabbed a pillow and threw it at Mark, hitting him in the face with it.

"Uncalled for!" Mark bellowed, rubbing his eyes. Letting out a sigh, he snatched open the door. As soon as he stepped out, he turned around to see everyone huddled behind him. "What? Y'all don't trust me to do it?"

"Nope," Josh confirmed, holding his phone up. "Hold on, let me hit record really quick."

Mark sucked his teeth. "Y'all petty."

"Babe, say something to the boys, 'cause I'mma show them this when we get home," Malajia teased, holding her phone in his face.

Mark put his middle finger close to the screen.

"That's fine, they don't know what that means, I'll show 'em anyway," Malajia threw back.

Mark rolled his eyes as he hopped off the step. "Come on man, it's brick."

"We *know*, so hurry up so we can go back inside," David quipped, holding his phone up to record.

Mark let out a loud groan as he sat down in the snow and laid back. He tried to drown out the sound of laughter as he began making his snow angel.

"Bigger wings Johnson, we need bigger wings," Alex egged on, clapping her hands.

"Shut the hell up!" Mark yelled. Waving his arms a few

more times, he hopped up from the ground and began shaking the snow off him. "This is some bullshit," he grunted, storming towards the house.

"Smile for the camera," David laughed, putting the phone close to Mark's face.

"Get that camera outta my face," Mark barked, smacking the phone from David's hand.

"Are you serious?!" David wailed as his phone fell into the snow. He quickly retrieved it and wiped it clean.

"He salty," Malajia chuckled as she walked back in the house behind the others.

Alex laughed as she sat down in her chair. "Mark, go dry off before you sit on the furniture."

Mark paused in the midst of wiping the snow from the back of his head. He glared at Alex, walked over, and proceeded to sit on her lap, wet clothes and all.

"No! Get off me," Alex shrieked, trying to push Mark off of her. "You play too much!"

Mark stood up. "Now *your* ass is damp too," he mocked.

Alex was annoyed. "You are so damn *childish*," she griped, holding the wet shirt away from her body.

Mark ignored her as he sat on the floor by the fireplace, grunting incoherently.

Sidra shook her head and pulled a note from the hat. "Okay...Emily," she began. "Tell us something that we don't know."

Emily took a long sip of her juice as she thought. There wasn't much that her friends didn't already know about her. "Umm..." she tapped her finger on her chin. "Oh! Alex, while we were roommates freshman year, Malajia used to use your body wash," she told.

Malajia's eyes widened as Alex's head jerked in Malajia's direction. "Malajia," Alex charged, annoyed.

"Emily, I never told you that," Malajia threw at Emily.

Emily laughed. "You didn't *have* to, I *saw* you take it from her shower caddy every morning after she left for class."

Malajia put her hand over her face, as Alex's eyes burrowed through her like a laser.

"Then when Alex was out of *hers*, you started using your

own," Emily added.

"Malajia—I was *wondering* why it was going so fast," Alex snapped.

Malajia's mouth fell open. "So, you were just sitting there *watching* me, you creep?" she hurled at Emily, ignoring Alex's question.

"Mel, did you *really* expect me to say anything back then?" Emily defended, pointing to herself. "You wouldn't have stopped doing it *anyway*."

"Malajia?!" Alex belted out, clapping her hands to get Malajia's attention.

"*What?*" Malajia snapped back. "Don't blame *me* for that cheap ass body wash going fast. It was watery as shit," Malajia defended. "It took *twice* as much to get clean."

"And yet, you never *were*," Chasity muttered.

"Shut up Chasity, I heard you bitch," Malajia bit out, causing Chasity to snicker.

"You were complaining about it and yet you still *used* it," Alex threw back, angry. "And caused me to spend what little money I *didn't have*, replacing it."

"Look, I needed to preserve *mine* longer. I did a smart thing, and you just mad *you* ain't think of it," Malajia taunted.

Sidra rubbed her forehead. "Wow," she commented. She could just imagine how annoyed Alex was. *She* would be *too*.

"Shit ain't have no scent *either*. Poor ass body wash," Malajia scoffed.

"*Again*, you still *used* it," Alex harped.

"And I'd do it again," Malajia spat back.

Alex folded her arms in a huff and sat back in her seat.

Sidra put her hands up. "Chasity, it's your turn," she prompted, gesturing to Chasity. "We'll be doing this all night, messing around with Malajia."

Malajia shot Sidra a side-glance, but didn't say anything.

Chasity grabbed a paper and read the words. "Y'all stupid," she chuckled.

"Well, what does it *say*?" Alex pressed, impatient.

Chasity glared at her. "It says that *your* hype ass has to growl every time somebody talks until it's your turn again," she spat.

Alex's mouth fell open as her friends busted out laughing. "Why did you direct that to *me*?"

"Because, you don't rush me," Chasity sneered, balling up the paper and tossing it on the table.

Mark looked at Alex. "You salty as shit," he teased.

Alex glared daggers at him.

"Um, we don't hear growling Alex," Malajia taunted. "Does anybody hear growling?"

"Nope," the group answered in unison.

Alex rolled her eyes before letting out a deep sigh.

Malajia leaned forward and held an intense gaze on Alex. "Now Alex—" Before she could finish her sentence, Alex started growling.

"Yo, how long does she have to do this?" Josh asked, laughing as Alex continued to growl.

"Until it's her turn again," Mark answered. His laughs grew louder when Alex continued growling. "Her throat gonna be sore like shit tomorrow."

Alex stomped her foot on the floor in agitation. "Somebody go, please," she begged.

"Somebody get a dictionary so we can read every word in it," Mark commented, amused. Hearing Alex's growls grow closer, he turned around. Alex was inching closer in his face. "Why you all in my goddamn face?" he belted out. "Breath hot as shit."

"Please, *please* somebody go so I can be *done* with this mess," Alex pleaded.

Josh grabbed a paper. "*I'll* go—" he shook his head as Alex growled again. "That's a shame," he chortled, reading. The humor left his face as he focused on the word on the paper. "*Swap-de-whop*?" he read aloud.

Malajia busted out laughing.

Sidra smacked her face with her hand as snickers and laughter sounded around the room. "God, next time we do this, don't let Malajia write anything," she griped.

Malajia was nearly in tears. "My word is *killin'* it," she managed to get out through her laughter.

"Can y'all say fewer words?!" Alex yelped, smacking her hand on the arm of the chair.

"Shut up and growl," Malajia threw back.

Emily spat out her juice as she laughed.

Josh rolled his eyes. "I don't even wanna— Mark, just take my turn, I don't even know what that word is supposed to mean," he grunted.

"Why did you choose *him*? You *know* he's gonna make somebody do something stupid," Sidra ground out.

"Sid, I just don't know. That's the second card I pulled with a made-up word, I'm not thinking straight," Josh answered, flustered.

"You mad, he did that swap-de-whop," Malajia put in, causing Mark to laugh.

"Just zip it Malajia." Sidra sneered.

Mark tapped his finger to his chin as he looked around the room. His eyes focused on one person. "Chasity," he called.

"What?" Chasity answered, voice dripping with disdain.

Mark thought for a moment, then a sly smile crept across his face. "Do you think I'm ugly?" he asked.

"The fuck?" Jason reacted as Chasity made a face in disgust.

Mark immediately put his hands out. "No disrespect homie," he said to Jason. "None to *you or* my wife."

Malajia waved a dismissive hand. "Hell, ain't shit to *me*, it ain't like she *want* your ass," she dismissed. "Hell, she don't half *like* you."

Mark shot her a side-glance. "Thanks babe," he spat, sarcastic. Malajia giggled.

Mark turned his attention back to Chasity. "Now look, whenever the opportunity presents itself, Chasity fixes her lips to say *all types* of shit about me," Mark began. "Whether it's calling me stupid, crazy, an idiot—"

"All of which are *true*," Alex muttered.

Mark pointed at Alex, keeping his attention on Chasity. "I don't hear growling."

Alex sucked her teeth.

"Anyway, while I know that I *can* be those things, one thing I know that I'm *not*, is ugly." Mark smiled. "*She* knows it too and I want her to admit it."

Chasity sucked her teeth. "Boy, leave me alone," she spat.

Mark folded his arms in determination. "Chasity, do you think I'm ugly?" he pressed. "Do *not* lie."

Chasity just stared at him, annoyed, but didn't say anything.

Mark put a finger up. "Hold that thought," he said, standing up. "I feel like I need to be close to you to get the full effect of your answer."

Chasity let out a huff as Mark headed over in her direction. "Get the fuck away from me," she barked.

Mark stood next to her. "Move over," he demanded, gently nudging her arm.

Chasity smacked him on the arm. "Don't fuckin' touch me," she snapped.

"I know, but move over," he insisted, tapping her shoulder.

She jerked her arm away from him, then tapped Jason's leg, prompting him to move over. Reluctantly, Chasity made room on the couch for Mark to squeeze right next to her.

Mark stared right in her face, smiling. He ran his hand over his head. "Hold up, gotta fix the waves," he muttered.

Jason pinched the bridge of his nose and shook his head. "Mark, just know if she kills you, I will testify on her behalf."

Mark chuckled a bit as he focused on Chasity. "So…do you think I'm ugly?"

Chasity stared at him, eyes narrowed. Then suddenly she put her hand over her mouth and began dry heaving.

"No, no!" Mark yelped, as everyone made a move to jump to her aid.

"Mark, don't be a jerk, you *know* she's pregnant," Sidra jumped in.

"No, shut up, she's full of shit," Mark fussed. He fixed a stern gaze on Chasity. "Chasity, that baby ain't cause you to throw up all this time. Ain't nothing wrong with your lying ass *now*. Stop tryna get out of it."

Chasity removed her hand and rolled her eyes. "*Fine*," she grunted.

Mark moved closer to her face. "Answer the question," he taunted. "Do you think I'm ugly?"

Chasity stared back at him. If looks could kill, Mark would be dead.

Josh leaned forward. "Damn, look at the vein in her neck," he observed, amused.

"Girl, you're gonna give yourself an aneurysm," Malajia chimed in. "Just tell my baby he's fine, it's okay."

Jason rolled his eyes in disgust. "Shouldn't Alex be growling right now?" he grunted.

"Damn it, Jason!" Alex exclaimed.

Mark held his position and his taunting gaze. "I will sit in your face all night," he taunted. "Now Chasity. My friend, my sister, and one of the best cooks I know—no offense Mel."

"Shit, none taken. Why do you think *I'm* always tryna get a plate?" Malajia threw back, unfazed.

Emily giggled. She admired how Mark and Malajia could take jabs at each other, and not take them seriously.

Mark held his gaze. "Do you...think...I'm ugly?"

Chasity felt her lip begin to twitch; she could've slapped him clean across the face. Clenching her jaw tight, she finally answered, "No."

"No *what*?" Mark taunted.

Her eyes became slits. "No. I don't think you're ugly," she managed to get out, teeth still clenched.

"So, what *am* I?" Mark dug in.

"Come on Mark, stop it," Sidra charged.

"Hush Princess," Mark demanded; Sidra rolled her eyes. "Chasity, if I'm not ugly, what *am* I?"

If Chasity was faking her urge to vomit before, she certainly wasn't now. She dreaded even the thought of saying what she knew she had to. She balled her fists up at her sides. "You...are...handsome... You fuckin' dick," she angrily got out, through her still clenched jaws.

"Yes! I knew it," Mark rejoiced, facing the rest of the group and tossing his arms up in victory.

In the middle of Mark's celebration, Chasity raised her hand to smack Mark in the back of the head.

Jason grabbed her hand before she could. "Whoa, whoa," Jason reacted, laughter in his voice. "Let's not cause any brain damage tonight, okay."

"You better move boy," Malajia joked, looking at her nails.

"Yeah, good idea," Mark agreed, quickly getting up and

moving away from Chasity. "Totally worth it though."

Rubbing Chasity's back with one hand, Jason looked at Mark and drew his hand across his neck, a gesture for Mark to cut it out with the taunting. "Enough," he demanded.

Amused, Mark put his hands up in surrender.

"Can I go now?" Alex pleaded, leaning her head on her hand. The growling had grown tiring.

"Nope, my turn." Malajia grabbed a paper, read it, then jumped up in delight, "Yes, yes!" she erupted, excited.

Sidra was confused. "Whatever is on that paper can't be *that* exciting," she sneered. Everyone snickered; Alex's growling could be heard in the background.

Malajia grabbed the bag that she'd brought downstairs earlier and pointed at Sidra. "Sidra," she called, ecstatic.

Sidra's face held a worried look. "Huh?"

"You have to get up in front of everyone and dance," Malajia said.

Sidra made a face. "Is *that* all?" she replied, confident. She stood up. "That's nothing."

"*While wearing* all of this bachelorette party stuff that we bought for Emily," Malajia threw in.

Sidra paused mid-step. "*Excuse* me!"

"Oooh," Emily reacted, laughter in her voice.

"Yup, you about to be covered in dicks and shot glasses," Malajia taunted.

Sidra was mortified. "I am *not* wearing those nasty, gaudy things," she refused, looking to her boyfriend for aid. "Josh, *say* something."

Malajia put her hand out as Josh put his hands up in surrender. "Nah, Josh can't save you. Get your bougie ass over here and put these penises on," she demanded.

Sidra folded her arms like a child as the room filled with laughter. "I'm not playing *shit else* with you guys," she huffed, stomping over to Malajia.

"My damn throat hurts," Alex complained, smacking her forehead with her hand.

Sidra stood in seething silence, while Malajia placed all of the items on her. There were colorful beads with shot glasses around her neck, glow in the dark plastic glasses with penises on the corner over her face, a sash over her outfit, penis shaped lollipops in her pants pockets, plastic flashing rings were placed on her fingers, and a tiara with penis antennas atop her head. Malajia ran to the closet and grabbed something else.

"Yo, y'all trippin," Mark reacted when his wife returned with a large penis shaped balloon.

"Come on Malajia, she's suffering enough," Josh chimed in, sympathetic.

"Don't care, hold this," Malajia demanded.

Sidra held a fiery gaze on Malajia as she snatched the balloon from her grasp. "I will kill you in your sleep tonight," she warned through clenched teeth.

Malajia smiled at her. "Now…*dance* heffa," she ordered.

Sidra stood there, defiant for a moment. Realizing that she had no choice, she let out a long sigh, clenched her teeth, and began to dance.

"Harder, shake it!" Malajia demanded. She nearly fell out, howling at the sight of Sidra doing a variety of dances with all the items on her person.

It only intensified Sidra's anger.

"Poor baby," Josh commented, trying desperately to hold his own laughter in.

Chapter 57

Sitting on a couch, Alex exhaled deeply as she played with strands of her hair. Staring out in front of her, her mind was consumed by her thoughts.

"I'm out of whipped cream."

Eric's voice snapped her back to reality. She glanced up and saw him standing over her, holding two large mugs. She smiled at him. "It's fine, I really didn't need the whipped cream in my hot chocolate anyway," she replied, taking the mug from him.

Eric sat down next to her on the love seat, then took a careful sip of his hot chocolate. He pulled the cup back and looked at it approvingly. "You were right, those chocolate bombs make a great cup of this stuff."

Alex gave a nod. "I know right?" she agreed, leaning back into the couch. She glanced over at Eric while he sipped on his drink, smiling to herself.

The night that Alex had returned to New York from Emily's bridal weekend, she and Eric had met up for a date. A week had passed since. She was sitting out on Eric's glass enclosed balcony at his apartment in Connecticut, and she couldn't be happier.

"Thanks for inviting me up here for the weekend," she said. He looked at her. "After the week I've had at work, I needed the change of atmosphere." She smiled at him. "*And* for earlier. I *really* needed *that.*"

Eric tipped his mug to her; he grinned. "Of course."

Alex sipped her drink. As much as she had tried to hold off from sleeping with Eric, when she arrived at his apartment earlier, she couldn't resist it any longer. While it wasn't planned, she certainly didn't regret it. Eric was even better than she remembered. "Are you sure you're okay with your daughter being with her mom all weekend?" she asked. "I hope I didn't inconvenience you or your baby."

Eric laughed a bit. "Alex, I told you, this is our routine," he reminded. "Zoe's mother and I rotate weeks. It's her week."

Alex pushed some of her hair out of her face. "I know you told me, I just—"

Eric touched her chin with his hand. "Relax okay." He soothed. "She's good."

Alex nodded. "Okay."

They sat in comfortable silence for a few moments. "So," he began. "Are you excited about next week? I'm sure you're ready to party."

Alex took a deep breath as she thought of Emily's upcoming wedding. As much as she was looking forward to celebrating her friends' new chapter in her life, she knew that Emily wasn't happy and because of that, *she* couldn't feel happy.

Picking up on the silence, Eric looked at her. "You okay?"

Alex sighed. "Yeah, sorry...I just— I'm worried about Em."

"What's going on with her?" Eric wondered, adjusting his position in the chair.

"She's depressed... Some of her family have really hurt her and it's taking its toll," Alex explained. "I feel so bad, she doesn't deserve this. She deserves to have her wedding be the best day of her life and—certain people are ruining it and it makes me mad... It makes me want to *do* something about it."

"What do you think you can do?"

Alex looked out in front of her. *Something that I'll surely get cussed out for.* "Umm...I have an idea," she alluded. She then waved a hand. "But enough of that for now. Let's talk about something else."

"Whatever you want," Eric agreed, leaning back.

Alex leaned her head on Eric's shoulder as she stared out at the night sky. She'd deal with her plan later. For now, she was determined to enjoy her weekend.

Sidra rubbed her face with her hands before going back to

working on her laptop. A notification chimed on her phone; she grabbed it and read the text message.

'Sid, I have an idea of how to help Em, but I need your help convincing Chasity and Malajia.' It read. *'We'll talk when I see you in a few days.'*

Confused, Sidra went to dial Alex, but her office phone rang before she could. Sidra answered. "Yes?"

"Sidra, Josh is here to see you," Robin informed.

Sidra smiled. She was happy that Josh had decided to fly down a few days ago. She was looking forward to spending some more one on one time with him, before traveling back East for the wedding.

Sidra checked her appearance in the mirror as a knock sounded on the door. "Come in," she called. She stood up from her seat when Josh entered. "Hey you."

"Hey yourself," he replied. "You ready to go to lunch?"

Sidra nodded as she gathered her purse and phone from her desk.

Josh tilted his head, studying her; she looked drained. "You all right?"

"Just tired," she muttered. "It's crazy. Now that I've interviewed for that position, just *being* here is sucking the life out of me."

"Have you heard back from them?" Josh asked, folding his arms. "Have they made a decision yet?"

Sidra shook her head as she closed the distance between them. "Not yet," she moped. James's firm had responded to her application only a few weeks ago in record time. They'd even managed to squeeze her interview into the schedule right before Emily's bridal weekend. But as Sidra waited to hear back on their decision, her nerves and self-doubt were at an all-time high. "I'm nervous babe," she confessed. "What if I missed my opportunity?"

Josh held a sympathetic gaze.

"What if... What if by me turning them down back then— putting off being a lawyer..." she shrugged. "What if they realize after talking to me, that what they *thought* was great then, isn't so great now?"

Josh moved towards her. "Sidra, you're doing it again," he

said. "You're doubting yourself. You have to stop." He put his hands on her shoulders. "You have to realize how brilliant you are." She offered a slight smile. "Don't worry, I'm sure you'll get a call."

"Okay…thank you."

Josh smiled back, planting a kiss on her lips. "Anytime." He took her hand. "Now, let's go eat."

"You want to eat here?" Josh asked Sidra as they stood in front of glass encased pastry trays.

Sidra shook her head. "No, I just wanted to stop in and see what kind of pastries they have," she answered. Though she was hungry and looking forward to a savory meal, Sidra couldn't pass by her favorite café without stopping in to see what sweet treats they had for the day. "I love this place."

Josh chuckled. "I know. Every time we've been in this area, you stop here," he commented.

Sidra giggled in return. "Right."

Josh wrapped his arms around her waist, a gesture that Sidra welcomed. She put her hands on his and leaned her head back against his chest.

"You should try the new chocolate cream puffs," a man said.

Recognizing the voice, Sidra's eyes widened. She and Josh both turned to see James standing there. *Shit, I would pick the one place that James frequents, too!* Though Josh had made it clear to Sidra that he had no issues with James, she couldn't help but feel a bit nervous. Talking about it was one thing; seeing the man face-to-face was another.

"Hi James," Sidra greeted, successfully masking her uneasiness.

James smiled back.

While Sidra was thinking of something else to say, Josh extended his hand in James's direction. "Good to see you again, James," he greeted.

James eagerly shook Josh's hand. "You too Josh."

Sidra breathed a sigh of relief as the two men exchanged pleasantries.

"Sidra tells me that you're a father," Josh mentioned. "Congratulations."

James nodded with enthusiasm as he reached into his pocket for his wallet. "Thanks man." He opened it and showed Josh a picture of his son.

Josh smiled. "He's adorable," he complimented.

"Thanks," James repeated, then let out a chuckle. "He has both my wife and I wrapped around his little finger."

"I can imagine," Josh said.

James looked at his watch. "I have to go, but congratulations to you both," he said.

Josh and Sidra both looked confused. "What are you congratulating us for?" Sidra asked.

"On your relationship," James answered, shocking Sidra. "You've been in here a million times, and no one has *ever* had their arms wrapped around you like that, so I just figured."

"Oh," Sidra breathed, amused. "You're right."

James nodded at her. "Good to see you happy," he said. It was the truth; James had made it a point to look out for Sidra over the past years. After all, she was still his friend. Knowing that she was with Josh made him happy. James knew that with Josh, Sidra was in good hands.

"I am," Sidra assured, grinning.

James grabbed his to-go order from the counter. "Oh Sidra, I probably shouldn't be telling you this...but I'm one of the bosses, so I will," he mentioned.

Sidra stared at him with anticipation.

"You'll be receiving a call from the recruiter at my firm, tomorrow," James informed.

Sidra's eyes widened. "Really?" She then raised an eyebrow. "Wait, is it good news or bad news?"

James smiled. "I wouldn't have mentioned it, if it was bad," he alluded.

Sidra's smile was bright as she glanced up at Josh, who rubbed her shoulder.

"Oh," James began, looking at his watch yet again. "Josh, whenever you'd like, I'd like to invite you both to dinner at our house," James brought up. "Joyce and I could use the double date. We're up to our eyeballs in diapers right now."

"Appreciate the offer man, we'll keep you posted," Josh replied.

"Okay great," James nodded. "See you around, and Sidra…congratulations."

"Thank you *so* much," Sidra replied, grateful.

"No thanks needed, you're brilliant," James complimented. Giving a wave, he walked out of the café, leaving Sidra both stunned and excited.

She jumped up and down, clapping in the process.

"You did it, babe," Josh praised, excited.

"I'm going to be a lawyer," Sidra gushed.

"You're going to be a lawyer," he confirmed, hugging her.

Sidra pulled away, glancing at him. "Can I go put my two weeks in now?"

Josh chucked. "Wait for your phone call first," he suggested.

Sidra laughed. "Right."

Trisha spoke on the phone as she paced the living room floor. Hearing the keys turn in the door, she glanced up and smiled when she saw Chasity walk in. Trisha waved; Chasity gave a slight head nod in return.

"Okay perfect, thank you so much," Trisha said into the line before hanging up. She set her phone on the coffee table, then put her hands up. "Great news baby," she beamed.

Removing her coat, Chasity looked at her. "What's that?" she asked, tone unenthused.

"Your house is ready," Trisha replied, excited. "Just got off the phone with the contractors. Everything is all set for your move next weekend."

Chasity nodded slightly. "That's great." Her tone hadn't changed; she walked over to the couch and sat down.

Trisha took a seat next to her. She looked at her. "It's a beautiful house," she praised. "I've been getting pictures from the team."

"It is," Chasity agreed. "Thanks for all of your help with it."

"No need to thank me, you know that," Trisha said,

touching Chasity's arm. She studied her for a moment; Chasity seemed down. "You okay?"

Chasity once again nodded slightly.

"Okay good." Trisha adjusted her position on the couch. "You excited for Emily's wedding this weekend?" she asked.

"Sure," Chasity answered.

Trisha frowned slightly, beginning to worry. "Chasity, are you *sure* everything is okay?" she pressed. "I know you had a doctor's appointment yesterday, is the baby all right?"

"Baby is fine Mom, I'm fine," Chasity bit out.

Trisha put her hands up in surrender. "Okay, okay," she placated, letting out a sigh after a moment. "So…you guys all packed?" she began. "When is the moving truck coming?"

Chasity took a long breath as she ran a hand over her stomach. "Yeah, the house is all packed," she answered, tone dry. "We're pretty much living out of our suitcases… The movers will be down next Wednesday, Jason is flying down on Thursday, and Kayla and I will be flying down on Saturday."

"You taking the cars?" Trisha asked.

"Jason gave his car to his brother and he's gonna get a new one when he gets there… My car is being transported there," Chasity answered.

Trisha nodded. "Makes sense," she commented, playing with the bracelet on her wrist. "It's weird," she said after a moment. "In a little over a week, you'll be—"

"Gone," Chasity finished, somber.

Sadness fell over Trisha. She knew that the time was approaching, but she in no way was ready to say goodbye to her daughter. As much as she wanted to break down, Trisha knew that she had to maintain a level head. "Yeah," she muttered. She looked at Chasity, who was staring out ahead of her. "How is Kayla taking everything? I know you and Jason told her a few weeks ago."

"She's actually okay with it," Chasity answered, tone low. "Not sure if it's because she doesn't really understand what that fully means or not."

Trisha tilted her head. "I'm sure she does," she replied, sincere. "She's a smart girl."

"Yeah," Chasity agreed.

Trisha held her gaze on Chasity. "So…how do *you* feel now that it's so close?" she carefully asked. "Are you scared?"

Chasity shook her head slightly.

"That's good to know," Trisha said. She didn't know why she felt the need to ask her next question, yet she did. "Are—are you sad?"

Chasity hesitated for a moment. Then, with glistening eyes, she looked back at her mother. She nodded as tears began to spill.

Trisha's heart broke. "Oh sweetie," she soothed, rubbing Chasity's shoulder.

"I'm sorry," Chasity sniffled, wiping her eyes with her hand.

"Don't be sorry," Trisha replied, caring. "You have every right to feel that way. You're uprooting your whole life."

"I know and I'm okay with my decision to move. I know that it's a good opportunity for us, I just—" Chasity paused as she tried to calm herself down. She knew that their move date would eventually be upon them. But as the date grew closer, Chasity was having a hard time keeping herself together.

"You just *what*, baby?" Trisha pressed, tone comforting.

"I just… I keep trying to convince myself that I don't need to be here," Chasity answered, tears falling. "That I don't need to be near *you*, but I *do*. I need you and I don't know what I'm gonna do without you."

Chasity's confession had tears flowing from Trisha's eyes; she fanned her face with her hands. "God, I promised myself I wouldn't break down in front of you," Trisha sniffled. "I know how you feel because I need you *too*. You're my best friend, and I'm going to miss you being so close."

Chasity wiped her eyes again.

"I mean, who am I going to go to lunch and vent with when that man of mine gets on my nerves?" Trisha wondered.

Chasity chuckled through her tears. "Your sister-in-law."

"I don't like your Uncle John's wife, and you *know* that," Trisha sneered, wiping her eyes. She then chuckled. "No but…this is hard for me too," she said, grabbing Chasity's hand. "But what gives me comfort is knowing that you're going to be just fine. You always *are*. You've always been stronger than I ever have been."

Chasity just looked at her.

"You don't need me... Trust me, you've got this," Trisha consoled.

Chasity took a deep breath. "You sure?"

Trisha touched Chasity's face with her hand. "Absolutely," she promised. She pulled Chasity into a loving embrace, holding her longer than she should. Finally pulling away, she wiped the tears from her face. "But don't get it twisted, I *will* be visiting often. And when it's time for you to have that baby, I'm coming down and staying at *least* three weeks."

Chasity laughed a bit. "Okay."

"And I'm not staying in a hotel," Trisha added. "So have my bedroom ready."

The humor left Chasity's face. "What?"

Trisha busted out laughing at her reaction.

Malajia turned her car off. "Has Alex lost her goddamn mind?" Malajia barked into the phone, grabbing her purse from the passenger's seat. "Sidra—you *do* know this is crazy right? ... Does Chaz know about this?..." Malajia stepped out of the car. "Well, call me after y'all talk to her... Hell *no* I'm not gonna be on that call. Y'all can take that cuss out on y'all own, hit me up when it's over." She chuckled at Sidra's response. "I'm home now, I'll talk to you later... Bye."

Tossing her phone into her purse, Malajia made her way towards her front door. After the long day of work she had just endured, she was glad to be home. Even though she knew the rest of her day would be filled with packing for the upcoming weekend.

As she grabbed her keys from her purse, she heard someone call her name. Startled, she spun around, dropping her keys in the process. She quickly retrieving them from the cold ground, snapping upright in a flash.

Her father was sitting in his car, parked on the street in front of her house, the window rolled down.

"What the hell?!" Malajia snapped.

Mr. Simmons offered a small smile. "Hi Malajia."

Malajia's face was masked with confusion. "Dad—you *do* remember that I was stalked at one point, right?" she fussed. "You can't be sneaking up on me like that."

Mr. Simmons looked apologetic. "Oh— I'm so sorry— I—"

"What the hell are you *doing*?" she cut in, angry.

"I'm umm…sitting in the car," he replied, gripping the steering wheel.

Malajia rolled her eyes. "I can *see* that, old man."

Mr. Simmons couldn't help but chuckle. "I've been sitting here for about an hour now," he revealed. "I was waiting on you to get home."

Malajia rubbed her forehead. She was cold, tired, and hungry; she wasn't in the mood for her father's nonsense. She hadn't seen or spoken to the man in over a month. "Dad—"

"Get in the car, Malajia," Mr. Simmons ordered.

Malajia jerked her head back. "No," she refused.

Mr. Simmons let out a deep sigh. A tired look was on his face. "Please?" he begged.

Malajia was conflicted. She was standing in front of the home that she shared with her husband, who her father had disrespected too many times. She felt that she should just walk away, but she just couldn't. He was still her father.

Sucking her teeth, Malajia walked to the door, then yanked the handle. The door didn't budge; she stomped her foot on the ground in agitation. "Un*lock* it Dad, *God*," she huffed.

"Ooh, sorry, sorry," Mr. Simmons quickly put out, pushing the unlock button.

Malajia let out a huff as she got into the car, then slammed the door shut, bundling her coat to her neck. "Dad—turn the *heat* on," she fussed, gesturing her hand towards the vent. "What is *wrong* with you?"

Mr. Simmons turned the car on, adjusting the heat. "Better?" he asked her.

"Not *yet*, you *know* how long it takes this car to warm up," Malajia sneered, rolling her eyes. "Dad…why have you been sitting outside my house in the cold like a creep for the last hour?"

Mr. Simmons tapped the steering wheel. He knew why; it

was the same reason why he drove past his daughter's house every time he was in the area, unbeknownst to Malajia. "Malajia—" he took a deep breath. Mr. Simmons was never one to bare his feelings; he was a hard man at times, and stubborn. In the past, he could get away with it. But now, he couldn't. And Malajia was just as stubborn as he was. He locked eyes with her as she stared back at him with anger and questioning on her face. "I'm here because...I miss my grandsons," he said.

Malajia scoffed. "Oh, is *that* all?"

Her father shook his head. "No...I miss *you* too."

Malajia looked away. "Dad—" She took a deep breath. "Did Mom send you here?"

"No, I came here on my own," he replied. "Don't get me wrong, she's been cussing me out damn near every day, but coming here was solely *my* decision."

"Hmm. How's that couch feel?" Malajia ground out.

"Like a damn brick."

Malajia wanted to laugh, but she couldn't. She wasn't in the mood. "Look I'm not gonna lie, I miss you too but I—I can't—" She let out a quick breath. "Mark is my *husband* dad," she stressed, looking at him. "Those grandsons that you *miss* so much? He is their *father*."

"I know," Mr. Simmons acknowledged.

"*Do* you?" Malajia bit out. She was trying her best not to yell at him, but all of the anger and disappointment she felt for her father had surfaced.

"Yes," he replied, holding his gaze on her.

"Then *why* do you *keep* being an *ass* to him?" Malajia barked. "After *all* this time, you *refuse* to change your behavior and it has put me in a— I'm sorry for what I'm about to say, but it has put me in a *fucked* up position Dad."

Mr. Simmons let out a sigh. "I know," was all that he could say.

"Then *stop* it!" Malajia yelled. Before she knew it, tears were spilling down her cheeks. "You think I *like* cutting you out? Do you have *any* idea what this is *doing* to me?" He opened his mouth to speak, and she put her finger up. "Don't," she barked. "Mark didn't *tell* me to cut you off, I did that on my own. Contrary to what you *think*, I have my *own* damn mind."

"I know you do Malajia, always did," Mr. Simmons placated.

Malajia shook her head as she wiped the tears from her face. "I have watched my husband try his *hardest* for *years* just to get you to like him, and you continue to just spit in his damn face."

Mr. Simmons could do nothing but lower his head as his daughter ranted. He knew that he deserved it.

"You think you were just hurting him, but you hurt *me too*," she added, disappointed. "And the sad part is, you don't even *care*."

"You think I don't care about you?" Mr. Simmons began, looking at her. "I *love* you."

"Then *act* like it," Malajia threw back. "And while you're at it, *act* like you trust me to make the right decisions for *my* life."

Mr. Simmons rubbed his hands over his face and clasped his hands together, trying to keep himself composed. "Malajia…listen. You have to understand," he began. "When I first met Mark…I thought he was just…a *fool*."

"Yes, I *know* that Dad, we *all* know that," Malajia hissed.

"And I thought that you dating him was just your way of rebounding after dealing with that…that—"

"Don't even say his name," Malajia demanded. The entire Tyrone ordeal was far behind her, but she still didn't want to hear it.

"I just felt that you could do better Malajia," Mr. Simmons finished. "As your father, I just wanted better for you. You deserve to have the best of *everything,* and I just didn't think that Mark was it." He let out a sigh. "—I guess I was wrong."

"You *are* wrong," Malajia confirmed. "You have *no* idea how good Mark is for me. How good he is *to* me. He's been there for me and supported me through the darkest times in my life. You just don't even know."

"Malajia—"

"No, like you *really* don't even know," Malajia cut in. She hesitated for a moment, then took a deep breath. "Dad…when I was a Junior is college, I had an abortion," she told.

Mr. Simmons's eyes looked like they could've popped out

of his head. "What?"

Malajia nodded. She had promised her mother during her senior year of college that she would eventually tell her father about it, but she never felt that it was the right time. Until now. "Yeah," she confirmed. "It wasn't Mark's, I'll leave it at that."

Mr. Simmons put his face in his hands as he tried to process it.

"For a while, Mark was the only person who knew," Malajia revealed. "I thought he would hate me, or look at me differently but...he *didn't*. He was so supportive and caring and—I would've never gotten through that time in my life *without* him." She looked at her father. "You have *no* idea how much he *loves* me. You might not *like* it Dad, but he *is* the best for *me*. I love him and if it comes down between you and him, I'm choosing *him*."

Mr. Simmons took a deep breath as he closed his eyes. Finding out that Malajia had gotten an abortion was the last thing that he expected. His little girl had been through so much pain, and here he was contributing to it. He looked at her, eyes filled with emotion. "I'm sorry," he said, remorseful. "I know that I've been a complete asshole and I—I want to make it right. I *will* make it right."

Malajia hoped that he was telling the truth; she was tired of the resentment. "How do you plan on doing that?" she asked, voice tired.

"My first step...apologizing to Mark. Face to face," he proposed.

Malajia looked out the window towards her front door, uncertain.

"Can you call him and ask him to come to the door please?" Mr. Simmons requested.

Malajia let out a sigh. "I—I'll go ask him... Wait here," she said, getting out of the car.

"Okay."

Malajia slowly walked to her house. Her mind was racing as she opened her front door. She appreciated her father's effort, but wasn't sure if Mark would at this point. "Babe," she called once she entered the house.

Mark emerged from the kitchen. "Hey," he beamed. "How

was work?"

"It was...work," she answered, setting her purse down. She looked up as Mark walked over to her.

"Guess what?" he said.

"What?"

"I have an interview," he revealed.

Malajia clasped her hands together. "Really?" she squealed.

Mark nodded. "Yeah, it's next week." Malajia wrapped her arms around him, pulling her husband in for a big hug. He chuckled a bit as he hugged her back. "It's for an Internal Audit position. I haven't interviewed in a minute but—"

"Babe, you're gonna kill it, don't worry," Malajia soothed, rubbing his back. She knew how much Mark wanted to get back to work; she was excited for him. So much so that, for a moment, she'd forgotten that her father was still outside. She parted from Mark. "Umm—"

"What's up?" Mark wondered, seeing the change in Malajia's mood. She almost looked worried.

"Mark...my dad is outside."

Mark frowned. "Excuse me?"

"Yeah," she confirmed. "He was— We talked and... He would like to talk to you."

Mark rubbed his face. "Mel, I just got some good news for the first time in over a month, I'm really not trying to have your dad ruin that."

She reached out and grabbed his arm. "I know, and I'm sorry to spring this on you right now, but I didn't know he was coming and—" Malajia let out a sigh. "I know after everything that he's put you through, it's not fair for me to ask you to talk to him, but...I *am*, so just... Please, even if it's only for a minute."

Mark stared at Malajia. He knew that the deterioration in the relationship with her father was affecting her, even though she tried to hide it. He let out a sigh, running a hand over his head after a moment. "Okay, fine," he reluctantly agreed, "Tell him I'll come out to the porch."

Malajia nodded as she sent a text to her father. She watched as Mark put on his coat and sneakers. "Do you want me to come out with you?" she asked him.

He looked at her and shook his head. "I'm a grown ass man, dawg," he threw back.

She giggled as her husband walked out the door. Her humor gave way to worry as Mark shut it behind him. *God, please fix this.*

Mark, stood on the porch, arms folded. He held a stern gaze as he watched Malajia's father approach.

"Hello Mark," Mr. Simmons greeted, stepping up on the porch.

Mark gave a nod. "Malajia said you wanted to talk to me?" he asked, holding his gaze.

"Yes," Mr. Simmons answered, shoving his hands into his coat pockets. He sighed. "Listen, I'm not a man of many words—"

"Tuh," Mark reacted, interrupting Mr. Simmons's speech. He scratched his head, then gestured for him to continue.

"Look, I know that I haven't been the best father-in-law—"

"Not true, you've actually been the *worst*," Mark sneered.

Mr. Simmons sighed. "I deserved that," he admitted. "Listen, Malajia means the world to me and I just want to make things right for her."

Mark put his hand on his chest. "Richard, she means the world to *me too*," he professed, stern. "I mean, I'm not *perfect*, but I do the best that I can for her and our children."

"I know you do, Mark," Mr. Simmons assured sincere.

Mark shook his head. "Then why do you keep treating me like I'm an *enemy*?" he asked, flustered. "I'm not who I used to be… I don't know what else I can do to get you to understand that."

Mr. Simmons took a step forward. "You don't have to do anything son, *I'm* the one who needs to change," he said. "I'm an old, stubborn fool, who's set in his ways… I was so focused on who you *were*, I wasn't seeing who you *are*."

Mark just stood there, listening.

"I've been wrong…and I'm sorry," Mr. Simmons apologized.

Mark nodded slightly after a moment. "I umm…I appreciate that." He let out a sigh. "You know, I never expected you to like me, but…I just wanted your respect."

"You have it," Mr. Simmons promised. He extended his hand. "You have my word."

Mark hesitated for a moment. He was tired of the drama, and he knew that Malajia was too. He would do anything to make his wife happy, and if it meant giving her father a chance, then he would do it. Mark shook the man's hand in a firm grip.

Mr. Simmons smiled. "Well, I won't keep you any longer," he said. "Have a good evening son."

"Thank you, sir," Mark replied. "You too."

Mr. Simmons went to walk away, but paused. "What do you say when the weather breaks, we go fishing?" he proposed.

Mark smiled briefly, "Sure."

"Great."

Mark watched as Mr. Simmons stepped into his car, before opening the door to go back inside the house.

"Shit!" Malajia yelped as the door hit her in the face.

"Yo, what the hell?" Mark panicked as Malajia grabbed her face. "Babe, why the hell were you by the door?"

"I was listening! You *know* I'm nosey," Malajia barked, rubbing her face. Luckily Mark didn't push the door hard, or she would've suffered more than a light smack to the face.

Mark had to fight to hold in his laugh; it came out as a muffled snicker. "You okay?" he asked, touching her face with both hands.

She narrowed her eyes at him. "I'm glad you find this funny." Her annoyance with him lasted only a moment; she had heard the conversation word for word. "But I'm good now…thank you." She meant that in more ways than one.

Mark smiled at her. "You're welcome," he replied, leaning in to give her a kiss.

Chapter 58

Sidra glanced over at Alex, who was nervously tapping her hand on the table. "You all right over there?" Sidra wondered.

"Sure," Alex answered, unconvincingly. "I'm good."

"Well, *I'm* not," Chasity sneered, folding her arms. "I do *not* want to be here."

"Shit who you tellin'?" Malajia chimed in, pushing her hair over her shoulders.

Alex let out a long sigh as she ran her hands over her hair. After spending the past few days begging and pleading with the girls, Alex had finally managed to get them to agree to a lunch meeting.

"Look, I share your apprehension," Sidra placated to Chasity and Malajia. "When Alex told me her plan, I fought her on it too…but, this isn't about *us* right now."

"That girl is gonna be *pissed* when she finds out what we're doing," Chasity ground out, looking at Sidra.

"Maybe…maybe *not*," Sidra argued. She looked at Alex. "You want to jump in here Alex?"

"Yes, sorry. My stomach hurts," Alex groaned.

Malajia eyed her in disgust. "Eww, take your gassy ass on the other side of the table."

"Shut up girl," Alex sniped, making a face. "It's not *gas*, it's nerves." She ran her hands over her hair again. "Look, like Sidra said, I understand, I really do… We're not exactly this person's favorite people—"

"She *hates* us," Malajia muttered.

"You're probably right, but like *us*, it's not about *her*," Alex pointed out. "Hopefully she can see that. After all, she *did* agree to this lunch."

"That don't mean shit—she probably called ahead to have our food poisoned," Chasity hissed.

Alex shook her head.

Malajia played with a napkin. "I don't know. I mean, as annoyed as I am to be here, I get what you're trying to do Alex but… What if this backfires?" she asked Alex. "What if we make shit worse?"

"We can't make things any worse than they already *are*," Alex pointed out. "We just have to trust that things will work out for the better."

Sidra was about to say something, but the patron entering the restaurant made the words get caught in her throat. "Here goes nothing," she muttered to the girls.

Alex let out a whine. "Ugh," she grimaced, nervous.

"Alex, you *better* not fart, I swear to God," Malajia ground out, earning a snicker from Chasity.

Alex backhanded her on the arm. "I said, shut up. I'm *not*."

The four girls went quiet as their invited guest took a seat across from them. "Hello girls," she greeted.

"Hi Ms. Harris," Alex greeted on behalf of the other girls. "Thank you for meeting with us."

Ms. Harris looked at the four girls seated in front of her. The last thing she expected was a call from Alex two days ago, inviting her to meet for lunch in a small restaurant in New Jersey. "I'm surprised you all have time for this. Nothing better to do?"

The bite in her voice was immediately picked up.

"Oh, I can think of a *million* better things I could be doing right now," Chasity bit back, eyeing Emily's mother intensely.

Sidra put a hand up to her face. "Chasity, curb it," she muttered.

"Fine," Chasity grunted, rolling her eyes.

Ms. Harris let out a sigh. "Does Emily know you're here?" she questioned.

"No ma'am, she doesn't," Alex answered, respectfully.

"Can you explain to me why you are doing this behind her back?" Ms. Harris spat.

Chasity clenched her jaw, but refrained from speaking. She knew her attitude would only intensify the situation.

"As a matter of fact, shouldn't you be getting ready to head down for her wedding?" Ms. Harris harped. "Aren't you supposed to be her *bridesmaids*?"

"You know what—" Malajia began, putting a hand up.

Sidra grabbed Malajia's hand and put it down. "Ms. Harris, we are coming to you respectfully, so we are asking that you not snipe at us," Sidra said, stern. "We're all adults here."

Ms. Harris squinted her eyes in agitation, then after a moment gave a nod. "Okay."

Alex flashed a grateful smile Sidra's way, before turning back to Ms. Harris. "Look…the reason why we're here is *because* of Emily's wedding," she began. "We know…we know that you're not going."

Ms. Harris folded her arms. "Yes, *and*?" she grunted.

"*And*, we think that you should reconsider," Alex suggested, calm.

Ms. Harris shook her head. "Emily doesn't want me there."

"Ms. Harris, do you *really* believe that?" Sidra jumped in.

"She *said* it."

"Because she was *angry* with you," Sidra threw back. "I mean, we *all* say things when we're angry, but she didn't *mean* it."

Malajia sighed. "You are her mother and no matter *how* mad she might be at you, if you missed her wedding she would be *devastated*," she added.

Ms. Harris glanced off to the side, shaking her head in denial. "Listen, on some level, I can respect what you're trying to do here, but Emily said what she said. So, I'll respect her wishes."

Chasity sucked her teeth. "I'm leaving," she ground out, making a move to get up.

"Chaz, don't leave," Alex pleaded. "We agreed to do this *together*."

"I don't care anymore," Chasity snarled.

Sidra rubbed her temples with her fingertips as she let out a sigh. It hadn't even been fifteen minutes, and this conversation was already going left.

Ms. Harris frowned. "Look, you can make any case that you want, but I know Emily—"

"No, you *don't*," Chasity snapped, angry. "You *don't* and *that's* the goddamn problem."

"Oh God," Alex muttered to herself.

Ms. Harris folded her arms in a huff again, but didn't say anything.

"You know who *knows* her? *We* do," Chasity fussed, gesturing to herself and the other girls.

"Yup," Malajia cosigned.

"And we are *telling* you that you missing her wedding is *not* what she wants," Chasity argued. "But you're too damn *selfish* to see it."

"I'm *not* selfish," Ms. Harris barked back, slamming her hand on the table.

Malajia put her hands up. "Okay I can't— You really don't think so?" she hurled, upset. "Aside from *Jazmine*, *you* have ruined this experience for Emily."

Sidra shook her head in disgust at Ms. Harris.

"*Ruined* it," Malajia stressed. "All because you couldn't get what you wanted on *her* day and you don't think you're selfish?"

"You have *no* idea how hurt your daughter is right now," Chasity added. "You probably don't even *care* and that's fucked up." She stood from the table. "How can you live with yourself as a mother?" she spat, before walking out.

Malajia sucked her teeth at Ms. Harris's lack of response. "This was a waste of time," she muttered, getting up to follow.

Sidra watched both girls walk out of the restaurant. She looked back at Ms. Harris, who was staring out of the window. "I can't believe you're really acting like this," she hissed, standing from her seat. "It's a shame because Emily thought that you had changed... After everything that she went through with you during college— She deserves better."

Alex put her hands over her face and sighed as Sidra walked out of the restaurant. This was not how she saw this meeting going, but sadly, she wasn't surprised. She lifted her head and gazed at Ms. Harris. "I would apologize for how my friends came off, but I *can't*, because I understand their frustrations," Alex began. "And I agree with them."

"I see now. Your intention was to bring me here, and attack me," Ms. Harris sneered.

Alex shook her head. She was seeing firsthand how right

Emily was about her mother playing victim. "Ms. Harris, that was *not* our intention, and you know that," she calmly contradicted. "Maybe I should've met you alone," she muttered to herself. "We had the right intentions, but used them on the wrong person... You clearly aren't interested in hearing anything that we have to say because you just don't like us. You never *have*, and that's okay. You don't *have* to, but Emily loves us and whether you like it or not, *we* love her *too* and that is the *only* reason why we did this."

"I know you're not insinuating that *I* don't love my daughter," Ms. Harris snapped.

"I never said that," Alex calmly threw back. "I know you do."

"You're damn *right* I do," Ms. Harris hurled in anger as she slapped her hand on the table. "I *love* my baby. More than myself."

Alex stared at Ms. Harris as emotion filled the woman's eyes. "You know...you can love someone and *still* hurt them," Alex pointed out. She grabbed her purse. "I should go."

"Yes, you should," Ms. Harris sneered, wiping a tear from her eye with a napkin.

Alex paused mid-step, turning around. "You know, we did lie about *one* thing," she alluded.

Ms. Harris looked at her with disdain. "And what lie is *that*?"

"With or without you, Emily will enjoy her wedding," Alex bit back. "Because *we'll* be there to make sure she does." Alex punctuated her response by walking away, leaving Ms. Harris sitting there alone, full of tears.

Alex made her way outside to the parking lot. She walked over to Chasity's car and peered inside at the girls. Then she tapped on the driver side window.

Chasity pushed the automatic button to roll it down. "Can I help you, Captain Save-a-bitch?" she jeered.

Malajia and Sidra snickered.

Alex sucked her teeth. "Come on now, the three of you had already walked out, I couldn't leave right away. I had to try to talk to her again," she reasoned.

"And how did that go?" Chasity asked, sarcastic as she looked at Alex.

Alex sighed. "No change."

"No *shit*," Chasity threw back, then rolled the window back up.

Alex gasped. "Seriously?"

"You shoulda rolled out with *us*; we were supposed to leave as a unit," Malajia spat from the passenger seat. "You fucked up."

Alex sucked her teeth, then pulled the handle to the back door. It was locked. She smacked the window with her palm. "Stop being childish, Chasity!"

"Stop smacking my goddamn window, Alexandra," Chasity threw back, eating a French fry.

"It's freezing out here!" Alex complained of the late January weather.

"You shoulda thought about that before you decided to sit there and kiss her manipulative ass," Malajia mocked.

Sidra leaned forward from the back seat. "Come on, let her in," she urged. "It *is* cold out there." She reached for one of Malajia's fries.

"Sidra don't touch my food," Malajia barked.

"Girl, shut up. You act like you didn't just steal some of my mozzarella sticks a few minutes ago," Sidra threw back.

"Them things was dry anyway," Malajia scoffed. "Wasn't even no cheese in one of 'em."

"Oh whatever," Sidra drawled, rolling her eyes.

"Let me the hell in!" Alex demanded, angry.

Chasity looked over at her. "Calm your ass down," she sneered, hitting the unlock button on her door.

As soon as Alex heard the lock click, she opened the door and jumped in the car. Shivering, she tried to focus on the heat coming from the vents. "I don't care *what* y'all say—" She paused when she saw the fast-food bags. "Where did this food come from?"

"The fast-food place next door," Sidra replied, sipping her drink. "We grabbed it before we got to the car."

"Damn, that was quick," Alex commented.

"Well, we were *starving*," Malajia huffed, grabbing her burger from her bag. "We never got to order anything from the restaurant."

"Makes sense I guess." Alex looked around. "Did y'all get *me* anything?" she asked, hopeful.

"We did, but Chasity ate it," Malajia told.

Chasity shook her head and grabbed some more fries from her bag. "No, I didn't, she's lying."

"So, you *didn't* eat my food?" Alex smiled.

"No, we just didn't get you any," Chasity bluntly answered, much to Alex's disappointment and Malajia's humor.

"She salty," Malajia laughed.

Alex folded her arms like a child. "Every last one of you makes me sick," she huffed.

Emily laid in the bed, wide awake. She glanced at the clock on the nightstand: eight forty-five AM. Emily was exhausted; she'd barely gotten any sleep the night before and she didn't know if it was due to excitement or dread. Either way, it was only minutes before she had to be up.

Before Emily could push the covers off her, her room door opened. She watched as her pajama clad friends busted into her room.

Malajia ran and went to hop on Emily's bed. "It's your wedding day!" she belted out. Missing her landing, her feet slipped from the bed, causing her to take a spill on the floor.

Sidra and Alex busted out laughing.

"It's always *you*," Chasity bit out, annoyed as Malajia laid out on the floor, making pained noises.

"I just fucked my back up," Malajia groaned from the floor.

"*And* you just made all this noise. We are in a damn hotel," Sidra scolded, mid-laugh.

Emily sat up in her bed; she didn't have it in her to laugh. She scratched her head, noticing that her satin scarf had slipped; she pulled it the rest of the way off. Alex walked over to her, a glass of orange juice in hand. "Happy wedding day sweetie," she gushed, giving Emily a hug and her juice.

"Thank you," Emily murmured, taking a sip. Emily had hoped that when she'd arrived at her bridal suite two days ago, her mood would pick up. She even tried to enjoy herself when the girls showed up the day before. Despite manicures, pedicures, lunch, and the sleepover in her two-bedroom hotel suit, she just couldn't.

Sidra sat at the foot of the king-sized bed.

Chasity went to step over Malajia, but Malajia grabbed her leg. "Help me up," she demanded.

"Get off me," Chasity snapped, slapping Malajia's hand off her.

Sidra looked down at Malajia and shook her head, before looking back at Emily. "Breakfast is here. We have about two hours to eat and get ourselves together. The hair stylists and makeup artists will be here at eleven, the photographer will be here at three-thirty and we have to be down at the venue by four-thirty, but I'll be going down there after I get dressed to make sure that everything is set up," Sidra laid out.

"Well…damn," Malajia commented, finally picking herself up from the floor. "Your anal, stuffy, overly organized nonsense finally came in handy," she jeered, smoothing hair from her face.

Sidra cut her eye at Malajia, but refused to respond to her.

Alex sat on the bed, next to Emily. "Come on, let's get you up and get you fed," she suggested, tone soothing.

Emily sighed. "I'm not really hungry."

"Sweetie, you should try to eat something *anyway*," Sidra insisted.

Emily nodded after a moment. "Okay." She pushed the covers off of her. *I've gotta shake this bad mood*, she thought. Standing up, she stretched.

"Don't even ask about that champagne from last night," Malajia said. "I polished that off before I went to sleep."

Emily shook her head. "I *wasn't*. It's nine in the morning," she mumbled.

"Never too early for sex or drinks," Malajia reasoned, examining the pale pink polish on her manicured nails.

"Girl—" Alex flagged Malajia with her hand, then looked at Emily. "Ignore her sweetie," she said, walking over and giving Emily a gentle nudge out of her room door.

Emily stepped into the living room area and saw the glass trays of pastries, scrambled eggs, bacon, bagels, fruit, juices, cream cheese, coffee, tea, cereal, and yogurts. She immediately went for the coffee. Before she could grab the pot, Sidra took it.

"No, it's your day, you relax. I've got it," Sidra insisted, smiling.

Emily smiled back. "I appreciate it."

"Of course, just tell me what you want, and I'll plate it up and bring it over to you," Sidra added, moving around the space.

"A little bit of everything is fine." Emily went to the cushy couch and sat down. She looked around; she didn't know why she was just now taking in the extravagance of the hotel space, but she was impressed by it. "I hope the wedding is as beautiful as this room," she put out, tone low.

"It will be *perfect*, don't worry," Alex assured, pouring a glass of orange juice.

"Yeah well, it surely *costs* enough," Emily mentioned, examining the engagement ring on her hand. In looking at her ring, she thought of Will. She sighed; she was being selfish, letting her mood ruin their big day. *I just want to talk to him.* She glanced up and offered a smile as Sidra handed Emily her plate of food. "Thanks Sid."

Sidra gave a nod, then went back to the kitchenette counter with the other girls.

As Emily began taking small bites of a jelly covered croissant, she let her mind continue to wander. She was silent as the girls ate and conversed. Until Malajia's ear piercing scream snapped her out of her thoughts. "What happened?" Emily asked, startled.

"Are you *kidding* me?!" Sidra yelled, slamming her hand on the counter. "That was *right* by my damn ear."

"That scream was *completely* unnecessary," Alex scolded.

"Malajia what *happened*?" Emily asked, setting her plate on an end table next to her.

Malajia pinched her fingers together and closed her eyes as she tried to calm herself down. "Chasity took the last cheese danish," she slowly put out. She opened her eyes to see everyone staring at her. Malajia looked at Chasity, who was too busy laughing while eating said danish to even bother responding.

Sidra pinched the bridge of her nose. "So…you screamed like a freakin' maniac near my ear because of a *danish*?" she slowly said.

"Not *just* a danish, a *cheese* danish. The *best ones*," Malajia argued. "She saw me reaching for it, and she just snatched it right from me."

Emily put her hand over her face and began laughing. It was the first time she'd laughed in days.

Sidra held her fiery gaze on Malajia. She couldn't believe how dramatic she was.

Malajia caught her stare, "*What*?!" she wailed, holding her arms up. She then looked at Chasity, who was still eating the pasty. "Bitch, you gonna *give* me the rest of that goddamn danish," she demanded through clenched teeth.

Chasity moved back as Malajia reached out and tried to grab her hand. Frustrated, Malajia moved around the counter to get to Chasity.

"Leave me *alone* Malajia," Chasity barked.

"Malajia, will you *relax*?" Alex added, hands on her hips.

As Malajia took a step towards Chasity, she tripped over the belt of her pink satin bridesmaid robe. She tried to grab for the counter to steady herself, but only ended up grabbing hold of a tray of bagels, pulling the entire tray on top of her as she fell to the floor.

"Of course! *Of course* this would happen," Sidra erupted, agitated.

Malajia laid there covered in bagels, salty, as Chasity, Alex, and Emily erupted with laughter.

Chasity grabbed her stomach and sat down on a chair. Tears were spilling down her face. "You see her face? She was scared as shit!"

"Always the dumb one," Sidra spat, folding her arms in a huff. "Now the stylist is going to be wasting time, combing bagel crumbs from your damn hair."

Emily was laughing so hard that she slid off the couch.

Malajia just laid there, shaking her head.

Chapter 59

Jason rubbed his eyes, then went back to adjusting his tie.

"Still hungover?" Mark teased, putting his tie around his neck.

Jason looked at him, then let out a laugh. "A little," he admitted. "I don't know what the hell I was drinking last night, but that shit was on another level."

Mark laughed. Like the girls, the guys had arrived in Virginia the day before. That evening they, along with Will's best man and other groomsmen, had taken him out for a bachelor night.

After eating and getting dressed in their rooms, the guys made their way to Will's suite to await the photographer.

"I still can't believe my alcohol tolerance is higher than all of yours," David chortled, adjusting the collar on his tux jacket.

"Couldn't tell, the way your drunk ass was laid out in the limo last night," Mark threw back.

David narrowed his eyes at him. "I wasn't drunk, I was *tired*," he told. "I didn't get to take a nap when I got in yesterday."

"Oh yeah, you were chillin' with your *friend* before you met up with us," Josh teased.

David smirked, but didn't say anything.

Mark looked over at Will, who was brushing his hair in the mirror. "How you feelin' man? You nervous?"

Will smiled. "Not at all," he assured. "I'm excited, actually."

"Yeah, you just *better* say that," Dru joked.

Will laughed. "I hear you. Don't worry, Emily is in good hands."

"I know," Dru approved, giving Will a strong handshake. "You're a good man. You make her happy."

Will just smiled. Though deep down, he only hoped that were true. He knew better than anybody that Emily hadn't been her normal self lately. He'd tried to cheer her up, but nothing helped. He just hoped that she felt better now that the wedding day was finally here.

"Anybody want to do a shot?" Brad interjected, holding up a bottle of dark liquor.

"God no," Jason grunted, rubbing his face.

"Hell *yeah*!" Mark belted out, excited.

Emily, clad in her white satin 'bride' robe, sat at her vanity mirror in her bridal suite. Hours had passed; makeup and hair were completed for all the girls. Emily had yet to put her gown on, though the girls were all in their bridesmaids' gowns. Emily just played with the rose gold pendant necklace in her hand as she stared at it.

"See Em, I *told* you I'd get into my dress." Alex chuckled, running a hand down her figure in her pale pink A-line, sleeveless, floor length gown. "No alterations needed. I *just* got this thing zipped."

"You look great, Alex," Sidra complimented, adjusting the sparkly pins in her updo.

Malajia played with the split in her gown. "Em, despite the shit I gave you, these gowns are sexy as hell," she grinned. "Who would've thought that pale pink would look good on me... Then again, *everything* looks good on me."

"Not about *you* today, Malajia," Alex scolded.

"I'm glad you like the dress Malajia," Emily replied, tone low as she continued to stare at the necklace in her hand.

Malajia glanced over at Chasity, who was putting on her crystal drop earrings. "Chaz, how far along are you?"

Chasity looked at her, confused. "Almost thirteen weeks, why?" she asked; her eyes widened slightly. "Shit, am I showing that much?"

"Girl, *where*?" Sidra chortled. "You look perfect."

Malajia laughed. "No, I was just wondering because your baby boobs are looking pretty damn great," she teased.

Chasity narrowed her eyes at her. "Keep your eyes on your

own tits, you freak," she scoffed, flinging her curled hair over her shoulder.

Malajia snickered.

Sidra glanced at the time on her phone. "Em, it's time to get you into your dress," she announced.

Emily set her necklace on the dresser. "Okay," she muttered. She removed her robe as Alex brought her dress to her. She was silent as the girls helped her step into and tied her into her sleeveless A-line, princess gown.

"Is the corset too tight, sweetie?" Sidra asked, moving some of Emily's curled, flowing hair over her shoulder. She'd elected to wear her hair in a half pinned back, half down curled style. The part that was pinned back was secured with a rhinestone comb.

"No, it's fine," Emily replied. She smoothed her hands down her torso, looking at herself in the mirror.

"You look absolutely beautiful," Sidra gushed, clasping her hands together. "Like a princess." The other girls commented in agreement.

Malajia glanced over at Chasity. "God, don't start that crying shit," she barked at her.

"Leave me alone," Chasity whined, dabbing her eyes with a napkin.

Emily managed a chuckle. "Thank you," she said. "And...thank you for always being here for me. I don't know how I'd get through this day without you."

The girls smiled at her. "We're family," Alex reminded, touching Emily's arm. "We'll always be here."

Emily held her arms out, and the girls moved in for a group hug. Hearing a tap on the door, Sidra darted over to it. "Who is it?"

"Emily's father," the man answered.

"Ooh yes, let his fine ass in," Malajia crooned, waving her hand.

Emily shot Malajia a stern look as she carefully sat back on her stool. "Malajia," she warned.

Malajia laughed. "Sorry, couldn't resist."

Emily gestured to the door. "You can let him in."

Sidra opened the door and as soon as Mr. Harris, clad in his tux walked in, he immediately smiled bright. "You look absolutely perfect," he beamed.

Emily smiled back. "Thank you, Daddy."

He pulled up another stool and took a seat in front of her, then grabbed her hands and held them. "I'm so happy for you and so proud of you," he gushed. Emily just held her smile. "Will is going to fall over when he sees you."

Emily giggled. "I *hope* not," she joked.

Mr. Harris chuckled in return. He took a deep breath. "Your brothers are ready and excited..." he looked down at her hand. "I umm...I haven't heard from your m—"

"It's fine Daddy, I don't expect you to," Emily cut in, somber. "Mommy isn't coming... It is what it is."

Mr. Harris shook his head. "You know, I can't believe she's—"

"Really, it's fine. I told her not to come so she's honoring my wish, it's fine," Emily quickly cut in.

Mr. Harris looked into Emily's eyes. Judging by the quickness in her voice and by the sadness in her eyes...he knew that she was lying. He wished there was something that he could do to make all of Emily's pain and troubles go away. But he knew that he couldn't. All that he could do was support her and be there for her, and walk her down the aisle. He patted her hand. "Okay," he said. He then touched her chin and smiled. "I'm ready whenever you are."

Emily just smiled back.

"Em, the photographer is outside," Sidra announced, looking at her phone.

"That's my cue to get out, I guess," Mr. Harris chortled, standing up.

"Yes, you go to the guys' suite. Your photographer is there as well," Sidra ordered, guiding him out the door. She then signaled for the photographer to come in. "We're just about ready," Sidra told the smiling woman.

"Yeah, let me just put my necklace on," Emily said.

"You want some help?" Alex asked.

"No, I got it Alex," Emily assured, picking the piece of jewelry up. She went to open the clasp. Noticing that it was stuck, she frowned. She tugged on it, only for the clasp to snap off. She gasped out loud.

The girls turned around. "What happened?" Malajia wondered, concerned.

Emily stared down at the broken necklace. She opened her mouth to try to get the words "my necklace broke" out, but all that came out were cries. The girls stood there shocked and confused as Emily broke down, crying hysterically. Emily slammed her necklace on the dresser and put her hands over her face as she wailed.

The girls rushed to her aid.

Alex kneeled in front of Emily, trying to remove her hands from her face. "Emily, what happened?" she panicked.

Emily was crying so badly that she started heaving.

Chasity looked at the photographer, who was standing in stunned silence. "You, out," she commanded, gesturing to the door.

The woman quickly obliged, running out and shutting the door behind her.

"Emily, talk to us sweetie," Malajia pleaded, rubbing Emily's back. "You're gonna pass out if you don't calm down."

Sidra grabbed a box of tissues and a bottle of water from a stand and went over to Emily. She tried to hand them to her, but Emily just pushed Sidra's hands away from her as she continued to cry.

Alex stood up. She frantically put her hands on her head; her eyes were wide. "I—I don't know what to do."

"Then move," Chasity spat, taking Alex's place in front of Emily. She pulled Emily into a hug and let her cry on her shoulder.

Sidra went to the door.

Malajia looked at her. "Sidra, where are you going?" she asked.

"To get someone who can calm her down," Sidra replied, before darting out of the room.

Sidra ran all the way to the other side of the hotel floor. Arriving in front of the guys' door, she knocked.

"Who is it?" a male voice asked.

"It's Sidra," she answered. The door opened and she walked in. All of the guys looked at her.

"Okay Sid." Mark complimented of Sidra's look.

Josh was smiling from ear to ear. "You're beautiful," he gushed.

She smiled back. "Thank you." She quickly snapped out of her lover's daze and looked at Will. "Will, you need to come with me."

Will looked confused. "Is everything okay?"

Sidra didn't want to alarm the men, especially Will and Emily's brothers, but she knew that she had to say something. "It's Emily, she needs you," were her words of choice.

As Will made his way to the door to follow Sidra, Mark put his hand up. "Nah, tell Em, ain't no early nookie," he joked.

Sidra snapped her head at Mark. "It's serious," she alluded. The humor immediately left Mark's face.

Concerned, Dru and Brad stepped forward. "Sidra, what's wrong with her?" Dru asked.

"She just needs Will right now," Sidra threw out, walking out the door.

Will followed her out. "I got it," he assured her brothers, shutting the door behind them.

Sidra filled him in as they headed back to Emily's room.

"I think everything that she has been trying to suppress just came out," Sidra told him as they approached the door.

Will rubbed his face with his hand and sighed. He felt terrible for Emily.

Sidra looked at him. "You ready?"

"Always," he assured.

Sidra gave a nod, then knocked on the door. "It's me. I have Will."

Emily, whose crying had calmed just a bit, looked up at the door. "What? Why did you bring him? I can't see him now," she hurled at the door.

"Umm, sweetie, this is *not* the time for superstitions. You need your man," Malajia pointed out.

Emily stood up as Malajia went for the door. "No, I don't care about *superstitions*, I'm a fuckin' *mess*," she sniffled. "It's our wedding day and...I'm a mess... I don't want him to see me like this."

"Emily," Will softly called through the door. "You're not a mess. You're emotional and you have every *right* to be," he said, tone soothing. "I love you regardless, and I'm not leaving until I know you're okay."

Alex put her hand on her chest as she tried to keep her own tears from flowing. She looked at Emily. "Talk to him, Em," she urged.

Emily wiped her eyes with a tissue. She took a deep breath, and nodded.

With that silent gesture, Chasity, Malajia, and Alex made their way out the door, leaving Emily alone.

"Umm Will, she really wanted the first time that you saw her in her gown to be when she walked down the aisle," Sidra told.

Malajia sighed. "Sidra—"

"I know, but you can still talk to her," Sidra cut in, interrupting Malajia's protest. "Will stand out here, and Em can stand behind the door."

"I'm fine with it, whatever gets her to talk to me," Will agreed. Once the girls offered him encouragement, they walked off, leaving Will standing there. He leaned his back against the door, then opened it a crack. "Em," he softly called.

Emily took a deep breath. "Yes?"

"Can you come stand by the door please?" he asked.

Emily slowly walked to the door and leaned her back against it. Will reached one of his hands through the crack. Emily glanced down at it, then smiled a bit through her tear-streaked face. She put her hand in his and closed her eyes as she felt him squeeze it.

"Hi," he said.

She sighed. "Hi."

"Are you okay?"

Emily shook her head, "No," she answered honestly. "I broke my mother's necklace," she revealed. "It was the only thing that I had of her here, and I broke it."

Will was silent as she spoke.

"This…is *not* how this day was supposed to go," she vented. "We're supposed to be *happy*, and I feel like I'm ruining it for you."

"You're not ruining anything baby," Will placated.

"Yes, I *am*," Emily insisted, tearing up again. "It's *my* fault. I *let* this happen." She sighed. "I wish I could just— I wish my mom was here," she admitted. "I wish that she cared about me enough to be here for me."

Will closed his eyes and let out a sigh. "You deserve to have everything you want, and that includes having your mom here," he said. "I don't know why she's not here—"

"I told her not to come," Emily cut in.

"And she knew damn well, you didn't mean that," Will jumped in. "You were upset with her, another thing that you had a right to feel."

Emily sniffed.

"Listen, I don't know much, but I do know *this*," Will began. "The people who are here *right now*, love you. And *I* know that *I* love you and I want to marry you today, no matter what."

Emily smiled, but didn't say anything.

"So, let's do this. Let's get married… We'll deal with anything that comes after, together, I promise," Will added. "Everything will work out how it's meant to."

Emily took a deep breath; a calm came over her. "Okay," she said.

Will smiled. "Yeah?"

"Yes," Emily replied, squeezing his hand. "Can you tell my girls to come back, please?"

"Of course," Will beamed. "Oh, you want to hear something that'll make you laugh?"

"I could *use* a laugh," she answered.

"Last night while we were at the bar, Brad got so drunk that he thought his own reflection was trash talking and he tried to fight himself," Will told.

Emily busted out laughing. "What?"

"Yeah, it was hilarious. I have it on video," he added. "I'll show you later."

"Okay," Emily said, still laughing.

"Love you," Will said, letting go of her hand.

"Love you too."

Will made his way down the hall back to his suite. As he rounded the corner, he laid eyes on someone he hadn't expected to see. He frowned at the woman standing in front of him.

"Hello Will," Ms. Harris greeted. "You look handsome."

Will squinted his eyes at Emily's mother. "Thank you." The woman was certainly dressed for a wedding. "So, you actually came."

Ms. Harris nodded. "Yes."

"*After* you caused my fiancé unnecessary stress and pain," he bit out.

Ms. Harris looked down at her shoes. "I know... I've been terrible, and selfish, but I'm here and I— I just want to lay eyes on my baby right now...please."

Will struggled with whether he should allow Emily's mother to see her or not. He had just gotten Emily calm and he was afraid that if her mother went in, she would just rile Emily up again.

"Will I promise you, I'm not here to upset her," Ms. Harris cut in, sensing Will's hesitation. "You have my word."

Will took a deep breath. "Room 318," he told.

Ms. Harris gave him a grateful smile, before heading down the hall.

Emily was trying to touch up her makeup, then decided against it. "No, I need Malajia for this," she said to herself. Hearing a knock on the door, she smiled. "Come in, I'm fine now. *Foreal* this time."

Hearing the door open, but not the usual chatter, she looked over and her eyes nearly bulged out of her head.

The breath got caught in Ms. Harris's throat. She put her hand to her chest and gasped. "You look like an angel," she gushed.

Emily stood up from her seat, eyes fixed on the woman before her. "Thank you," she managed to get out. Emily couldn't help but be skeptical. As much as she wanted her mother to be a part of her wedding, now that she was there, Emily couldn't help but wonder if she had an ulterior motive.

Ms. Harris quickly made her way across the room and

enveloped Emily in an enormous hug. She squeezed her daughter tight as tears filled her eyes and spilled down her cheeks. "I love you so much," she sniffled. "I'm sorry, baby… I'm so sorry for everything."

Ms. Harris knew that she had to say more, she *wanted* to say more. She'd hurt Emily's feelings, had been a major contributing factor in ruining a time that was supposed to be happy for Emily with her selfish behavior. Her mother needed to admit this…and how she felt responsible for Jazmine's actions towards Emily. This was a conversation that she owed Emily, a conversation that she *would have* with Emily…just not at that moment, not on her wedding day.

Emily didn't say anything. She too knew they needed to talk. But she was just glad that her mother was there for her. Emily just wanted to get married to the love of her life and enjoy her day. Closing her eyes, and letting out a sigh of relief, Emily hugged her mother back.

Chapter 60

"Yo, I hope I don't bust my ass while walking down the aisle," Malajia whispered, clutching her bouquet to her chest. "I should've broken these heels in."

Alex chuckled. "You realized you just jinxed yourself, right?" she said, peering over Malajia's shoulder.

Malajia sucked her teeth. "You know what, I'll pass-a-sound that jinx to *you*," she spat. "*You're* the one always falling anyway."

Alex nudged Malajia lightly in the back of her head. After an eventful morning, it was finally time for Emily to walk down the aisle. The groom, groomsmen, and Anthony were already standing up front, waiting on the women and parents.

Malajia looked behind her at Emily. "Em, how come you didn't pick a maid-of-honor?" she wondered. "You're supposed to have one."

Emily smiled. "You *all* are, actually," she revealed. "You and Chasity are Matron's of honor because you're married, and Sidra and Alex are Maid's of honor."

Sidra put her hand on her chest. "Awww," she gushed. "That's so sweet."

Malajia twisted her lip. "Cop out," she jeered, earning a hard nudge from Chasity. "Ouch!" Malajia bellowed.

"Shut the *hell* up," Chasity demanded through clenched teeth. Malajia had been running her mouth since before they'd gotten in line to walk, and Chasity was tired of hearing the sound of her voice.

Emily shook her head in amusement. Now that it was time for her wedding ceremony, despite a few nervous butterflies, a sense of calm had fallen over her. She stood there smiling, clutching her father's arm.

As Will's parents started making their way down the aisle, Alex touched the flower clip in her wavy hair, and took a deep breath. "I don't know why I always get nervous before I get ready to walk down the aisle," she mentioned.

"*I* don't know why either," Malajia threw back. "Like the *last* two times, ain't nobody gonna be paying attention to your ass except for the photographer."

Alex made a face at her. "*Eric* will be."

Sidra snickered at the salty look on Malajia's face.

As Ms. Harris received her signal to walk down, she took a step forward.

"Mom, can you come back here for a minute please?" Emily asked.

Not hesitating, Ms. Harris did as she was asked.

The girls exchanged glances with one another, but didn't say anything. They were just as shocked as Emily when Ms. Harris showed up, but neglected to ask Emily what had happened when they were alone. They figured it wasn't the time.

As Emily watched her friends begin to make their way down the aisle, she looked over at her mother, who was standing there confused.

"Wasn't I supposed to walk down after Will's parents?" she wondered.

Mr. Harris smiled a bit. "No... You're supposed to walk down with *us*," he alluded.

Ms. Harris squinted in confusion. "I don't—"

"We're walking her down *together*," he revealed.

Ms. Harris stood there for a moment; she put her hand on her chest. While she was grateful, she also felt bad. She looked at Emily. "Babygirl...I appreciate this but—don't do it because of me. I don't deserve it because of how I acted."

Emily looked at her. "Mom, I didn't just decide this," she revealed. "This is how I always *planned* it... It was always supposed to be a surprise."

Ms. Harris's mouth fell open and she shot her ex-husband a glance. He nodded in confirmation.

Tears welled up in her eyes. Her daughter had planned to have her walk her down the aisle all along, and she'd acted out and gotten upset over nothing. "Emily, I—"

"I know," Emily cut in, looping her arm through her mother's. "I know you want to say a lot to me, but it can wait. I just want to get married," she tilted her head. "Okay?"

Ms. Harris smiled and nodded. "Okay."

Emily gave her mother's arm a slight shake. "I'm glad you're here."

"Me too… I wouldn't want to be anywhere else," Ms. Harris promised.

"Yoooo, these drinks are hittin'," Mark bellowed, dancing up to the group with a full glass in each hand.

Josh shook his head as he placed his arm around Sidra's shoulder. "It's a good thing we're all staying here at the hotel an extra night," he chortled. "This open bar will be taken full advantage of."

"Hell, as much as we *paid* for it, y'all better drink everything up," Will chuckled.

With the wedding ceremony, cocktail hour, and photos over with, Emily, Will and their guests were on to enjoying the reception.

"Everything turned out perfectly," Alex gushed as Eric approached her with a drink.

Will gestured his head to Emily, who was standing at his side. "It was all *her*," he praised.

Emily smiled up at him. "Aww, thanks babe," she beamed. "He picked out the appetizers though."

Jason held a small plate of finger food. "Who knew a little baked potato would be so good," he said, reaching for the item on his plate.

"Ooh, I was looking for another one," Chasity cut in, grabbing it before he laid his fingers on it.

Jason tossed his head back and let out a sigh as Chasity ate it. "Babe, that was the last one," he complained. "You've been taking my appetizers *all night*."

"The baby wants it," Chasity spat.

Jason looked at her, trying to keep a straight face. "Chasity, you *know* you can't keep using that ex—"

"The fuck I *can't*," Chasity cut in. Jason put a hand up in surrender as he laughed.

"You might as well get used to it," Alex joked at Jason.

"Already *am*," Jason returned, shaking his head.

Emily looked at Eric, who had his arm around Alex. "Thanks for coming," she said, smiling.

"Of course, thanks for the invite," Eric smiled back, then gestured to Alex. "An invite that *she* finally extended."

Alex rolled her eyes to the sky. "Ha ha," she mocked. "There's no need to remind everybody that I was being a—"

"Bitch?" Chasity finished.

"Damn, too slow," Malajia grunted as she snapped her fingers. "But yeah."

Alex made a face at them. "Whatever," she hissed through clenched teeth.

Eric just laughed.

Malajia looked at Mark as he took a sip from one of his glasses, then sipped the other. "So, you really strolled your tall ass over here with two glasses and didn't bring *me* one?" she ground out.

Mark frowned. "Man, you better walk your ass over to that bar and get you a drink," he threw back.

Annoyed, Malajia licked two of her fingers and stuck them in one of the glasses.

"Malajia, that's gross," Sidra scoffed.

"Mark, the glass is mine now, so give it to me," Malajia spat, ignoring Sidra.

Mark sucked his teeth and handed her the glass. "You always showing the fuck off," he grunted.

"Shut up, you already knew better," Malajia boasted, taking a sip. She coughed. "Ugh, this one is nasty, give me the other one."

"Fuck outta here, you drink that shit," Mark argued, moving his other arm away from her. Malajia couldn't help but laugh.

Sidra was about to say something, when someone caught her eyes. "Why *hello* David," she smiled; everyone greeted David in the same exaggerated enthusiasm as he walked up.

David shook his head.

"Where did your date disappear to?" Malajia asked. "You know, the date that you kept a *secret* until today."

David chuckled. "She's in the bathroom."

"You two looked all lovey dovey and shit," Chasity teased, earning snickers from the group.

David laughed. "I mean...we're good. One day at a time," he said. Before anyone could say anything else, David's date walked up.

"Why *hello* Nicole," they all greeted in unison.

David put his hand over his face and shook his head. Their silliness never ceased to amaze him.

"Hi guys," Nicole giggled. "Beautiful wedding Emily. I'm so happy for you."

"Thank you, Nicole," Emily replied, moving some hair over her shoulder. "It's good to see you two back together."

"Yeah, don't y'all break up again so we don't have to see David's ass crying over video call," Mark muttered. When he saw that all eyes were on him, he winced. "Shit, I said that out loud?"

"That's it, no more drinks," Josh said, taking the glass from Mark's hand.

"I never cried on video call," David argued, annoyed.

Mark tossed his head back. "Oh, my bad, it was over the *phone*," he amended, snarky. "*Either way* your bitch ass was *crying*."

Nicole shot David a sympathetic look. "Aww David—"

"Don't even feed into it," David cut in, shaking his head at her.

Emily turned around as the wedding coordinator tapped

her shoulder. "Are you ready for the bouquet toss?" she asked, holding Emily's bouquet in her hand.

Emily nodded as she retrieved it. "Come on ladies," she chortled, signaling for Alex, Sidra, and Nicole to follow her.

Mark pointed to Eric and laughed. "He nervous as shit right now," he joked, earning laughter from Eric and the other guys.

"You put him all on the spot," Malajia commented.

Emily stood in the middle of the floor as the DJ began her song choice for the bouquet toss. She held her bouquet high in the air.

"I hate these things," Sidra complained in an aside to Alex as she folded her arms.

Alex giggled. "Don't wanna be *that* girl running for the bouquet, huh?"

Sidra laughed a bit.

"Are you ladies ready?!" Emily bellowed, receiving enthusiastic confirmation from the ladies behind her, Emily began counting. "One…Two…" she then turned around and faced the confused group. Smiling, she walked over and tossed the bouquet directly at Sidra, who caught it in shock.

As cheers rang out around her, Sidra gazed at Emily with wide eyes. "Emily!" she exclaimed.

"You're next, I can see it," Emily replied, pointing at Sidra with glee.

Sidra put her hand over her face in embarrassment, as Alex put her arms around her neck. "See? And you didn't even have to run for it," Alex added, excited.

Mark looked at Josh. "Ahhhh!" he teased, pointing at him.

Josh looked at him and laughed as Will walked up to him.

"Here you go," Will laughed, tossing a garter at him, which Josh caught on instinct.

"What, did y'all *plan* this?" Josh asked, looking at the light pink garter belt.

"Duh," Chasity laughed.

"And don't be waiting all long to propose either—we need another party soon," Malajia added, shaking her hand in Josh's direction.

Josh shook his head at her, then caught a glimpse of Sidra holding her new bouquet close. Catching his stare, the two smiled at one another.

Sidra and Alex headed up to them.

"You gotta go put that garter on her Josh," Malajia prompted, gesturing to the dance floor. "Time to gyrate and feel her up in front of everybody."

Sidra vigorously shook her head, eyes wide. "No, no, not happening," she protested. If standing for the bouquet toss was embarrassing enough, sitting on a chair in the middle of the dance floor, with all eyes on her while Josh performed a seductive garter placement ritual on her, would be mortifying.

Will laughed. "Yeah, Emily cut that part out," he explained. "She already knew."

Sidra put a hand over her chest, breathing a sigh of relief. "My girl," she praised.

Malajia eyed Sidra with disdain. "You prudish hag," she grunted.

Chasity busted out laughing, while Sidra just made a face in retaliation.

Will grabbed the guys' attention. "Come on fellas let's do some shots," he suggested.

"Yesssss!" Mark bellowed as he and the other guys followed Will to the bar.

Chasity looked at Malajia; Malajia hung her head and shook it in embarrassment. "He's gonna piss you off *all night*," Chasity teased.

"I *know*!" Malajia yelped, holding her arms up. "I'm gonna hide in your suitcase when you leave next week. You can't leave me with this."

Chasity just shook her head.

Alex glanced over at Sidra and giggled. "Girls, she is holding onto this bouquet in a vice grip," she teased.

"Umm hmm, talked all that shit about bouquet tosses not meaning anything," Chasity commented. "*Now* look at you."

"Oh shut up," Sidra dismissed, flagging her.

Malajia looked at Alex. "*You* wanted that bouquet, huh?" she teased. "Wish that was you and shit."

"Not really," Alex chuckled. "Right now, I am perfectly happy just *dating* Eric," she assured. "We'll see where it goes."

"*That's* good to know," Chasity said.

Alex looked at her, raising an eyebrow.

"Because when Emily gave it to Sidra he was like 'thank God,'" Chasity added.

Alex frowned. "*Did* he?"

Malajia nodded in agreement. "He punched the air and everything."

Alex's jaw tightened. "Oh *really*?" she hissed.

"No," Chasity admitted, as Malajia quickly shook her head.

Alex sucked her teeth, while Sidra busted out laughing "That's not funny," Alex bit out.

"Stop lying then," Malajia chuckled.

Alex flagged them as she looked over at Emily; she sighed happily. "Look at her," Alex gushed as they watched Emily laugh and dance with her brothers. "She's so happy."

"Yeah," Sidra agreed. "I'm glad everything worked out."

They watched as Emily's mother approached her children and hugged them.

"I'm glad her mom showed up today," Alex added, watching the pleasant exchange. "She might be...a *handful* but we can all admit that she *does* love Emily."

"I *guess*," Malajia replied. She smirked when she saw Ms. Harris look in their direction. "She's looking over here. She's probably calling us a bunch of heathen bitches under her breath and shit," she jeered.

"You're probably right," Sidra chortled. She frowned when Ms. Harris began walking in their direction. "Hold up...is she coming over here?"

"*Can't* be," Alex denied. Her eyes widened when her approach continued.

"The hell?" Malajia spat.

"Nope," Chasity refused, turning to walk away.

"Nah, we in this together fam," Malajia demanded, grabbing hold of Chasity's arm.

Chasity yanked herself free from Malajia's grip in anger, folding her arms over her chest. "I hate you," she grunted.

"You lie," Malajia chortled.

"Shhh," Alex hissed as Ms. Harris stopped in front of them.

Ms. Harris offered them a warm smile. "I meant to tell you ladies earlier that you all look beautiful," she said.

The girls side-eyed each other; they were skeptical to say the least.

"Umm, thank you," Alex spoke.

"You're welcome," she replied. Ms. Harris hesitated for a moment. "I umm… I *also* meant to tell you earlier…thank you."

This time, the confusion was clear on the girls' faces.

"Umm…yooou're welcoooome?" Malajia drew out, perplexed.

Chasity successfully held in a snicker, though humor did seep through on her face. Sidra just shook her head at her.

"Why are you thanking us?" Alex wondered.

"For…" Ms. Harris placed her hand to her chest and let out a deep sigh. "For being the sisters that Emily needs…the ones that she *deserves*."

The girls were speechless; this was the last thing that they expected to hear from Emily's mother.

"I—I should've said that to you sooner… I should've *seen* it sooner," she admitted. "I misjudged you all and…I'm sorry."

"Wow," Sidra replied, unsure of what else to say.

"You don't have to thank us for that Ms. Harris," Alex replied. "But we appreciate it."

Ms. Harris gave a nod, before walking away.

The girls looked at each other.

"What the fuck just happened?" Chasity asked in disbelief.

"Right?" Malajia chimed in. "Shit, that was *totally* unexpected."

"Oh my God, did you see my face?" Sidra giggled. "It was nice to hear though."

"It was," Alex agreed, happy. "It really was." She looked at the girls. "Maybe we can have a do-over lunch with her and Emily," she proposed.

"No," Chasity answered, the same time that Malajia said, "Nah," and Sidra said. "Uh uh."

Alex busted out laughing.

"Guys, this might be the last time that we're all together in one room for a while," David sulked, swirling the last of his drink around in his glass.

Mark sucked his teeth. "Come on man, don't be bringing the vibe down with your sentimental bullshit," he grunted, head leaned over the balcony.

"Mark, your drunk ass can't even hold your head up, so shut up," David spat back.

Head still leaned down, Mark put a finger up. "As soon as the room stops spinning, I'mma think of a comeback," he said.

Malajia laughed as she rubbed Mark's back. "Poor drunk baby," she joked.

As the reception finally came to an end, the guests had migrated to the heated balcony at the instruction of the hotel wedding coordinator. The group stood off to the side, relishing each other's presence and reflecting.

"But David *does* have a point," Alex pouted, holding onto Eric's arms around her waist. "In another day, we'll be going our separate ways once again... I'm not going to lie, I'm a little sad you guys."

Mark lifted his head. "Damn, Jase is leaving and shit,"

he sulked, running his hand over the top of his head. "Where am I gonna get all my free liquor from?"

Jason laughed. "Yeah okay," he said, amused. "I'll miss your freeloading ass too."

Mark smiled as he held his fist out for Jason to bump.

"Mark, you can always come have a drink with *me*," Josh smiled.

Mark's eyes shifted as he turned away from Josh.

Josh's smile faded. "Forget you then," he huffed, sounding hurt.

Mark busted out laughing. "I'm just messing with you," he promised. "You already know I'll have drinks with you."

Josh flipped him the finger.

Malajia flung her hair over her shoulder, then moved over to Chasity and wrapped her arms around her neck. "I'm not gonna miss Chaz because I'm going *with* her—"

Chasity let out a loud, tired sigh. "Malajia—no you're *not*."

Malajia jerked her hand up and put it in Chasity's face. "Yes, the fuck I *am*!" she snapped.

Chasity shook her head and rolled her eyes.

Malajia fanned her face as tears started forming. "I *hate* you for leaving me, bitch."

"She's drunk," Chasity jeered, gesturing to her with her hand.

Mark chuckled, rubbing Malajia's shoulder. "Aww, it's okay you cry baby," he teased. "You still have *me*."

"Don't nobody want *you*," Malajia hissed at Mark, wiping tears from her face; Mark just shook his head in amusement.

Emily played with the diamond and topaz bracelet on her wrist. "You know what?" she began, reflective.

"What's on your mind Em?" Sidra wondered, gently swinging her bouquet.

Malajia glared at her. "Sidra, there is no engagement ring in that goddamn bouquet, put it the hell *down*," she barked, flinging her hand in Sidra's direction.

Josh put his hand over his face and shook his head.

Sidra smirked. "I'll be sure to send you plenty of pictures of me and Chasity when we hang out together out West," she mocked; she stuck her tongue out at Malajia as Malajia flipped her the finger.

Emily giggled. "Anyway," she continued. "No matter who moves where, or what changes happen in our lives, I'm never worried because I know that no matter what, we'll always remain close."

"Yeah," Alex agreed. She then chuckled. "Thank God for our phone plans 'cause we rack up a *lot* of minutes."

Emily put her hand over her face to hide her building laughter as Alex's comment was met with silence.

Chasity looked confused. "Who the fuck still uses *minutes*?" she scoffed.

"Yeah, you lost me there, Alex," Sidra laughed.

"Got a new phone and still putting minutes on it and shit," Malajia added.

Alex's jaw tightened. "You know what? Forget it, I'm turning my phone *off* so you heffas won't call me," she grunted.

"You damn sure don't need to turn your phone off for that to be accomplished," Chasity jeered, inciting snickers and laughter at Alex's expense.

Eric planted a kiss on Alex's cheek. "Aww," he sympathized, laughter in his voice.

"You see how rude they are?" Alex complained, letting out a huff. "Remind me to grab some more cake before it's gone," she said in an aside to Eric.

"You would—"

"Shut the *hell* up Malajia," Alex barked, cutting Malajia's would be dig off. "*You especially* don't call me."

Laughing, Malajia shrugged as if she didn't care.

Will looked at the coordinator, who was trying to get his attention. He gave her a nod, and she returned the thumbs up. Will leaned over to Emily. "Hey, I added one more thing to tonight's festivities," he said.

Emily looked up at him. "Really?" she asked, intrigued. "What?"

He grabbed her hand and directed her attention to the night sky in front of them.

Emily was confused when she didn't see anything. "Umm, what—"

"Just watch," Will beamed.

Not more than a few seconds later, Emily was startled by a loud pop. Her shock turned to delight when it was followed by the sparkle of pink fireworks. "Oh my God," she gushed, putting her hands on her chest. She and the guests watched the firework display in awe.

Will wrapped his arms around her. "I know that I didn't have much say so in the planning, but I wanted to surprise you with something," he crooned.

Emily looked up at him, giving him a kiss on his lips.

"This is so beautiful Will," Sidra beamed.

"Emily, you better wear his ass *out* tonight," Chasity commented.

"Damn it! Too slow *again*," Malajia reacted, snapping her fingers.

"I know *that's* right," Alex agreed with glee.

"Oh my God!" Emily belted out in embarrassment.

Epilogue

"Did you get the updates that I sent to you?" Chasity asked into her cell phone as she leaned over her kitchen counter.

"Yes, I got them this morning," Trisha said into the line. "Perfect as usual, but I told you that you didn't need to rush. This could've waited."

"Mom, I may be your daughter, but you also hired me to do a job," Chasity replied. "So, I will continue to handle you like I handle my *other* clients by honoring my deadlines."

"Okay, okay you're right," Trisha relented, humor in her voice. "Contracting you to handle my website is one of the best decisions that I've ever made."

"I already know I'm good, you don't have to remind me," Chasity joked, earning laughter from Trisha.

The past year had been good for Chasity business wise. Not long after settling down in Arizona, she'd begun taking the steps to start her own web design business. She had gained quite a bit of clientele, some who had taken her on after severing ties with the company that she had previously worked for. Though she had plans to eventually expand, Chasity was managing well on her own.

"Oh, and thank you for taking Aja on as your intern," Trisha said. "She's so grateful and she's learning a lot."

"Yeah well, she's a smart girl, and she's been really helpful. Who knows, I might hire her when she graduates," Chasity admitted.

"She'd *love* that," Trisha said. "She looks up to you."

Chasity smiled a bit. Even though she wasn't too eager to get to know her cousin in the beginning, after a while, she'd decided to give communication with her a shot. The girl had grown on her. So much so that Chasity had begun tutoring Aja on her computer assignments via video conference. Once Aja had shown improvement, Chasity took her on as a remote intern for her company.

"Anyway, have you set a wedding date yet?" Chasity asked.

"Nope and he keeps asking me," Trisha chuckled. "It's only been six months since he proposed. Not sure what the rush is."

"Y'all are old," Chasity jeered.

Trisha sucked her teeth. "Yeah, whatever. *He* is, I'm not," she grunted. "You remember he's ten years *older* than I am."

"Doesn't take away from the fact that you're still old."

"Anyway," Trisha dismissed. Chasity chuckled. "But seriously, I'm thinking within the next year or so. Don't worry, you'll have time to prepare. You'll be my maid of honor after all."

"I never expected *not* to be," Chasity chortled. She glanced over at something. "Mom, I have to go, somebody is cutting up."

Trisha giggled. "Awww...I want to come back."

"No."

"Chasity come *on*! It's been like four months," Trisha argued.

"It's been a *month*," Chasity contradicted. "No, keep your ass *there* for a while... Besides, Dad is supposed to be coming down to visit in a few weeks and I don't have the mental capacity to handle *both* of your smothering asses at the same time."

"Fine," Trisha huffed, loudly. "He already called bragging about his upcoming trip. He's excited, so I'll let him have this one."

"How generous of you," Chasity said, sarcastic.

There was a pause on the line. "You're so goddamn rude," Trisha ground out. "Love you though."

"Love you too," Chasity chortled.

"Happy birthday, once again."

"Thank you," Chasity replied. "I'll call you tomorrow."

"Okay."

Chasity ended her call. She walked out of the kitchen and made her way into the living room. Setting her phone on a nearby stand, she approached the bassinet and peered inside. Chasity smiled. "You are *not* hungry little boy," she said, reaching inside and grabbing her six-month-old sons' little hand. When the baby started whining, she scooped him into her arms.

The moment that her son was in her arms, his whining stopped. "Spoiled just like your sister," she chortled. As Chasity rocked him in her arms, she glanced around her home, letting out a happy sigh. She couldn't believe what her life had become.

Growing up in turmoil, Chasity often wondered how her life would turn out. She never imagined that she would have what she did now. For the first time, she knew that everything that she had gone through, every choice that she had made, had brought her to the place that she was at in this moment.

The feeling of something rubbing against her ankle snapped her out of her reflective thoughts. Chasity glanced down and chuckled. "*You're* not hungry *either*," she said to the small grey kitten, clad in a pink collar, currently wrapping her tiny tail around Chasity's ankle. The kitten looked up at her, meowing. "You're cute though."

Hearing the keys jiggle in the front door, Chasity looked over at it.

"Happy birthday Mommy!" Kayla bellowed.

"Cupcake let me get the door open first," Jason chortled, pushing the door open. Once open,
Kayla darted inside, carrying a large card.

"Happy birthday Mommy!" she repeated, excited.

"Thank you, baby," Chasity replied, adjusting the baby in her arms. She held her free arm out as Kayla darted over and gave her a hug.

Kayla reached up and rubbed her brother's sock covered foot. "Hi Corey," she beamed. She looked back at Chasity. "I made you this card at school."

"Oh really?" Chasity asked. "Can you open it for me?"

Jason walked over, a dozen flowers, balloons and gift bag in hand. He greeted Chasity with a kiss on her lips, before kissing the top of his son's dark haired head. "All she talked about ever since I picked her up from school was how she couldn't wait to give you that card," he laughed, placing the items on the coffee table.

Chasity smiled as Kayla showed off her handmade card; it demonstrated the little girl's growing artistic skills with drawings and glitter. "I love it," she said.

Proud, Kayla set her card on the table, along with the other gifts. She bent down and held her hands out. "Princess Kitty," she squealed, coercing the kitten to her. "Mommy, did you feed her?"

"Yes, I fed her," Chasity answered, placing Corey back into his bassinet.

"Kay, go take your book bag upstairs," Jason ordered. "And wash your hands so we can cut Mommy's birthday cake."

"Yaaayyy!" Kayla bellowed, scooping her kitten up, then grabbing her book bag.

Jason shook his head in amusement as Kayla bolted up the steps. "I hope she never loses that enthusiasm," he said.

"I know," Chasity agreed.

Jason retrieved his cell phone from his pocket. He sent a text message.

"You checking up on your employees?" Chasity asked, rubbing the back of her neck with her hand. "Did they set the office on fire while you were off today?"

Jason laughed a bit. "Nah, my team is on point; they work just fine without me," he replied, putting the phone back in his pocket. Jason couldn't have been happier with his dream job; he was managing his team and the Phoenix office like a pro, and gaining recognition from his higher ups. "So," he began, looking at his wife. "I have a little surprise for you later."

Chasity looked intrigued. "Oh really?" she wondered. "You wanna give me a hint?"

Jason thought for a moment. "Well...it's something that I know you'll love, and I know you miss."

Chasity looked confused. "You mean a cat free house?" she joked.

"Stop it, you know you love Princess Kitty," Jason chortled.

"Yeah, yeah, I love Princess Kitty," Chasity admitted, unenthused. "I'm surprised Kay hasn't put a damn tutu on it yet."

"She tried, it won't let her," Jason said, amused.

After spending a good part of the afternoon with her family, Chasity was relaxing in her den alone, reading. Hearing commotion from the kitchen, she got up and made her way there. Upon entering, she saw Jason arranging items on the counter island.

Chasity frowned. "What's up with all of these bottles of liquor?" she asked, pushing her hair behind her ears.

Jason looked up at her. "Huh?"

"You're not deaf," Chasity ground out. She narrowed her eyes. "Hold up," she began, putting a hand up. "I know *damn* well, your *surprise* isn't getting me drunk and pregnant again."

Jason busted out laughing, "What? *No*," he promised.

"Okay 'cause *that* one in there is our last," she said, pointing to the living room where Corey's bassinet was.

"Babe, I promise, these are not— Wait, you don't want one more?" he asked, curious.

Chasity looked like she wanted to slap him. "Boy—"

Jason immediately put his hands up. "Okay, okay, we'll table that discussion for another time," he joked. Chasity sucked her teeth. Hearing a notification on his phone, he glanced at it and smiled.

"When did you get all this shit anyway?" she asked, picking up one of the bottles and examining it.

Jason quickly grabbed some glasses from the cabinet and set them on the counter. "I got this stuff yesterday after work and just had it in the garage," he answered.

Chasity was about to say something, when she heard a knock at the door. She glanced at it. "Who the hell is that?"

Jason began making his way out the kitchen with Chasity following. He didn't say anything.

"Jason, who is that?" she repeated. "And why are you acting so damn weird?"

"Not acting weird baby," he denied, heading for the door. "It's just company."

Chasity stopped walking and folded her arms as Jason

reached the door. "*Company?*" she scoffed. "*What* company? You know I don't like people."

Jason chuckled. "Yes, I know," he agreed. Not saying another word, he opened the door and smiled a bright, warm smile. Seeing Malajia and Mark eagerly standing there, he held his arms out. "Hey Mel—"

Malajia quickly ducked under Jason's arm. "It's not about you, homie," she threw out, dashing, arms outstretched towards a shocked Chasity.

Jason and Mark both watched as the girls embraced in a big hug.

"Damn Malajia," Jason chuckled.

"Don't even trip, she said the same thing to *me* this morning when I asked her what was for breakfast," Mark informed.

Jason laughed.

"It's good to see you brother," Mark beamed as he and Jason embraced.

"You too," Jason replied.

Malajia was still holding on to Chasity. "I missed yoooooou," she pouted. "I missed your face."

Chasity laughed. "Missed you too," she tried to shake Malajia off of her. "I can't breathe," she laughed.

Malajia held on. "It's okay, I'll do CPR on you if you pass out," she said.

Chasity shook her head as she allowed Malajia to hug her a bit more. "What are y'all doing here?" she asked once they parted. She had to admit, she was pleasantly surprised. Chasity hadn't seen Malajia face-to-face in a year, though they talked via video calls almost every day.

"We're here for your birthday boo," Malajia revealed, excited. "Happy Valen-birthday."

Mark walked over arms outstretched. "Missed you sis," he said to Chasity as they hugged.

"I *actually* missed you too," she teased.

"I'll take that," Mark laughed. "Jason flew us down for your birthday," he revealed.

Chasity looked over at Jason, who was smiling at her. She put her hand on her chest. Chasity didn't say anything, but her eyes spoke volumes. He winked at her. Jason knew how much Chasity missed their friends; he did as well. She had agreed to uproot their life and move across the country so that he could live his dream, and Jason loved and appreciated her more than she knew.

"Thank God, 'cause I was tired of Malajia crying in my damn face every night, talking about 'I miss Chasity,'" Mark teased, mocking Malajia's voice and mannerisms.

Malajia looked at him, frowning, "I *know you* ain't talking the way *you* was bitchin' about Jason leaving," she threw back.

Mark's eyes widened as Jason laughed. Chasity shook her head in amusement.

"Talking about 'damn man, I just wanna have a drink with my brother man'—"

"Hey, hey, shut up," Mark barked at her. "Snitch ass."

Malajia flagged Mark with her hand. "Oh my Gooood!" she squealed, peering over Corey's bassinet.

"Damn babe, you all screaming in the man's face," Mark pointed out.

Malajia dashed to the kitchen and washed her hands before hopping back over. She then bent down and scooped Corey up in her arms. "You are soooo cute," she gushed. The little boy stared back at her with bright eyes. Malajia looked over at Mark. "Baby, I think I want one more," she said.

Mark's eyes lit up. "Really?"

"Sike," she scoffed. "You salty." Mark sucked his teeth as Malajia went back to cooing at her Godson.

Jason laughed as he patted Mark on the shoulder. "Yeah, I was told no to more too," he admitted.

"A damn shame," Mark chuckled as he followed Jason to the kitchen. "You got food and drinks?"

"Food is ordered, drinks are already here," Jason replied.

"Yeeeessss," Mark rejoiced.

Malajia lightly patted Corey on his back as she rocked him. She looked at Chasity, who was adjusting his little shirt. Malajia smiled at her. "You look happy," she observed.

Chasity looked back at her. "I *am*," she confirmed.

Malajia was genuinely happy *for* her. "You know what's funny though?"

"What's that?"

"You moved out here to the desert with all this sun, and you're still bright as a lightbulb," Malajia teased, causing Chasity to laugh. "Oh, I'm ruining the rest of the surprise, 'cause they asses is late, but the rest of the group is on their way here too."

Chasity stared at her, successfully containing her excitement. "I'm telling Jason you ruined it," she said, walking away.

"No! He's gonna make me pay him back for my plane ticket!" Malajia yelled after her.

"Stop hollering near my baby," Chasity threw over her shoulder.

"About *time* y'all got here," Mark commented, pouring himself a drink. His words were met with confusion.

"What are you talking about? Everybody's been here for like *two hours* already," Alex ground out.

Mark laughed as he finished his pour. Over the past few hours, the rest of the group had filtered into the Adams's home. They were now gathered around the dining room table eating, drinking, and enjoying each other's company.

"I will never understand why you don't just ignore Mark," Sidra said to Alex, amused. "You get so agitated."

"Because he's a freakin' nut," Alex bit out, reaching for some chips from a bowl.

"You missed me though," Mark threw at her.

"A little," Alex admitted, humor in her voice.

Josh reached over and gave Mark a pat on his arm. "Congrats again on the promotion, Mark," he praised.

Mark smiled. "Thanks man," he replied. "Who knew that after working at that place for only a year, that I'd be promoted to senior auditor."

"*I* did," Malajia crooned, running a hand over Mark's hair.

Mark smiled back at her. "You're so cute when you lie," he joked, earning laughter from her and the rest of the group. Mark had been ecstatic when he was offered the job that he had interviewed for after Emily's wedding. Turned out, his new company valued him more than his last one; they showed it by promoting him quickly.

"So Malajia, are you sick of work yet?" Sidra asked, reaching for her glass of water.

"*Fuck* no," Malajia blurted out, confident. "I enjoy every one of those eight hours out of the house," she joked. "And with two steady incomes, maybe we can actually *buy* a damn house soon."

Mark held his hand up. "Up top," he said to Malajia, prompting her to give him a high five. "Chasity you might as well let Ms. Trisha know now that she's gonna be our realtor."

Chasity chuckled. "I'll tell her."

Malajia looked at Mark. "Can we move out *here*?" she asked, hopeful.

"No," Mark immediately threw back.

"Damn it," Malajia huffed, folding her arms.

Josh grabbed some chips. "You know, I think you two would actually love living on the West Coast," he chimed in. "It didn't take *me* long to get used to it."

"Man, ain't nobody listening to you. If Sidra lived in a damn hut in *Alaska* your ass would get used to it," Mark bit out.

Josh looked confused. "I think you meant *igloo*, and yes I absolutely *would*," he said.

"You know what I meant," Mark uttered, taking a sip of his drink. "And an igloo is just an icy *hut*, so you ain't correct shit."

Josh rubbed his face with his hand. "It's *not* though, but— never mind."

Sidra blushed as she pushed some of her hair behind her ear. Making good on his promise, Josh had made the move to California eight months ago and she couldn't have been happier. "It's been great *having* you there," Sidra said to him.

Josh smiled back at her.

"How's your new shop doing out there?" David asked.

"It's doing well," Josh answered, excited. "It just opened two months ago, but I'm getting a lot of business… Sarah is doing an amazing job running the garage back in Delaware— Everything is good…*great* actually."

"I'm so proud of him," Sidra gushed.

"Yeah, until he get all that car grease in your shower and

shit," Mark joked.

Sidra squinted her eyes. "I don't have a problem with *anything* Josh does in the shower," she threw back.

"Ooh," Alex laughed. "She zapped *your* ass," she hurled at Mark.

Josh winked at Sidra, "Appreciate you baby." Having a thought, he pushed his chair back. "Chaz, can you show me where the bathroom is?" he asked.

Chasity pointed to a corner. "There's a bathroom right over there Josh."

Josh looked in that direction. "Umm…I can't see it," he said. "Can you come show me?"

Chasity frowned in confusion. "Okay weirdo," she ground out, standing from her seat.

Malajia followed Josh and Chasity's progress as they walked off. "Sidra, get Josh's ass some glasses," she chortled.

"His eyesight is fine," Sidra dismissed, grabbing her water again.

"Where's your damn drink, Sid?" Malajia scoffed. "Hell, even *Em* has one," she pointed out, gesturing to Emily's half empty wine glass.

"You know it pays to mind your own business," Sidra sneered.

"*Does* it? *Does* it *really*?" Malajia mocked. Sidra narrowed her eyes at her. Malajia chuckled. "I'm messing with you, don't sue me Ms. Lawyer."

Sidra grinned. "I'm still a *junior* attorney for now, but based on the positive feedback that I've been getting, that can change sooner than I expected." A year into her new position, and Sidra's only regret was not becoming a lawyer sooner. "I am so much more fulfilled at work now. I love my job. I even got to cross examine a client in a major case and I killed it."

Malajia put a hand up. "I'm proud of you, but your snooty voice saying 'killed it' doesn't work for me," she jeered.

Sidra flagged Malajia with her hand.

"We're *all* proud of you Sidra," Alex commented. Sidra flashed a grateful smile Alex's way.

Hearing a notification on his phone, David grabbed it from the table and checked. Reading a message, he smiled and typed back. Once he finished, he set his phone back down. When he looked up, all eyes were on him. "What?"

"You cheesin like shit over there," Mark teased.

David put his hand over his face and shook his head as laughter resonated from his friends.

"Was that Nicole?" Sidra grinned.

David nodded. "It was," he confirmed.

"Was she cussing your ass out for not bringing her on this trip?" Mark asked. "*Especially* on Valentine's Day."

Jason scratched his head. "Yeah, I doubt he would be *smiling* if she was cussing him out," he pointed out.

"Shit, *I* smile when Mel cusses *me* out," Mark chuckled. "Shit be hilarious."

Malajia side-eyed him, but didn't respond.

"She was just telling me that she missed me," David put in, folding his arms on the tabletop.

"When is the next time you're going to see her?" Emily asked.

"In two weeks," David answered. "She has a few days off from classes, so I'm gonna go down to South Carolina to go see her."

"Oh, she's back in school?" Alex asked, grabbing more chips.

David nodded. "Decided to go back for her masters," he revealed. "I'm proud of her."

Emily reached over and patted David's hand. "Glad that you two are still going strong," she praised, smiling.

David smiled back, "Thanks Em."

Mark looked back and forth between Emily and David. "Yo…anybody else thought that Em and David would end up together when we met freshman year?"

David and Emily looked around in shock when everyone's hands shot up. "*Really?*" Emily wondered.

"What made you think that?" David questioned.

"Don't know, we just *did*," Malajia answered, shrugging.

"No, David and I have always been just friends," Emily assured. David nodded in agreement.

Malajia looked up as Chasity and Josh approached the table. "Damn, did you show him *how* to use the bathroom too,

Chaz?" she joked.

Chasity narrowed her eyes, then lightly smacked the back of Malajia's head.

Malajia grabbed the back of her head in shock. "What the—"

"She did the right thing, that *was* corny babe," Mark chuckled, cutting Malajia off.

Malajia sucked her teeth.

"Everybody move to the living room," Chasity ordered.

"Can I bring the chips?" Alex asked.

"No," Chasity threw back.

Malajia laughed at the salty look on Alex's face.

As they made their way to the living room, Alex tapped Chasity's shoulder. Chasity looked at her. Alex stopped walking and smiled, causing Chasity to frown.

"Why are you looking like a crazy person?" Chasity wondered, halting her progress.

Alex twirled some of her hair around her finger. "So…remember when we talked the other day about how proud I am of you for starting your web design business?"

Chasity held a skeptical look on her face. "Yeah," she slowly drew out.

"Well…how would you feel about taking on a new client?"

"What exactly are you getting at, Alex?" Chasity asked.

Alex took a deep breath. "I want to contract you for the magazine," she put out.

"Alex—"

"*Please!*" Alex belted out, desperate. "The manager that we hired last year, moved on to another job, and we need somebody who knows what the hell they're doing."

Chasity shook her head. "Alex, your company hires *in-house* designers."

"No, my boss said that she doesn't care; she will outsource if she has to," Alex told. "She just wants the best and *you are*…" she put a hand up. "And we'll have our weight up pay wise, I promise," she chuckled.

Chasity ran a hand through her hair and sighed. "Let me go over my current clients to see if I have room for another one right now," she said. "If so, then we can set up a video call when you get back to New York."

Alex jumped up and down, then wrapped her arms around Chasity. "I love you."

"Ugh," Chasity scoffed.

At last, Chasity and Alex joined the others in the living room. Mark looked over at them.

"Why you make us leave the table? The drinks and food was there," Mark asked.

Chasity pointed to Josh, who was standing in the middle of the floor. "Ask *him*," she alluded.

Everybody turned and looked at Josh, who had his attention focused on Sidra.

"Josh, how you come over somebody else's house dictating the moves and shit?" Mark hurled at him.

Josh cut his eye at Mark. "For *once*, shut up," he demanded.

Malajia busted out laughing at the look on Mark's face. "Salty," she teased.

Josh shook his head, then looked back at Sidra, "Okay so… I had planned on doing this a different way, but now that we're all here together…it's Valentine's Day… It just seems right," he began.

Sidra looked around, a little perplexed. "Josh—what are you talking about sweetie?" she asked, amused.

Josh walked over to Sidra and gently took her hand. He took a deep breath and smiled at her. "Sidra," he began.

Sidra looked up at him. "Yes?"

Alex, having a thought, abruptly gasped out loud. "Oh my—"

"Shut up, shut up," Chasity demanded through clenched teeth. Emily quickly nudged Alex for good measure.

Alex covered her mouth with her hand as she tried to contain her excitement.

Malajia glanced over. "What's going on over there?" she asked. "Y'all better not be keeping secrets."

"Malajia, shush," Emily ordered.

Josh blocked out the chatter as he stared into Sidra's eyes. "Sid…I'm not good at big speeches, so I'm just going to keep it simple and from the heart," he said.

Sidra, with her hand secure in his, just held her gaze on him.

"I have been in love with you most of my life and it truly is a dream come true that we're together now," Josh continued, sincere.

Sidra felt a wave of emotion come over her as Josh spoke.

"He all sentimental on Chaz's birthday and shit," Mark muttered.

"Malajia, can I smack him, *please*?" Alex huffed.

Josh touched Sidra's face with his free hand. "You're my best friend...my lover...and now..."

Sidra gasped when Josh bent down on one knee in front of her. "Wait, what?" she breathed, tears filling her eyes. Their friends were standing there, silent but brimming with excitement.

Josh reached into his pocket and pulled out a small grey box. "Now, I'd love for you to be my *wife*," he said. He opened the box. "Sidra?"

"Yes?" Sidra sniffled.

"Will you marry me?"

"Yes," Sidra blurted out. Applause and cheers rang out as Josh placed the solitaire diamond on Sidra's ring finger. He then stood up and pulled her into a loving hug, followed by a kiss.

"Smooth as shit, Josh," Mark praised, pointing at him.

"Right?" Jason chimed in. "Well done bro."

Sidra whispered something in Josh's ear as they held onto each other; Josh just smiled brighter and squeezed her tighter.

"I *knew* it, I *knew* that's what he was about to do," Alex squealed, clasping her hands together.

Sidra pulled back, fanning the tears from her face with one hand, while examining the ring on her other hand. "It's a princess cut!" she cried.

Josh chuckled. "Of course," he said, touching her face. "I love you."

"I love you too," Sidra breathed. The newly engaged couple kissed before being surrounded by their friends.

"I'm so happy for you Sidra," Emily beamed, hugging Sidra.

"Thank you Em," Sidra smiled back.

Malajia rubbed her face with both hands. "Oh my *God*, she's about to be a damn *bride*," she groaned.

Realizing what that meant, Chasity and Alex joined in with the groans.

Sidra laughed. "Oh come on, I'm not going to be that bad," she assured.

"Lying like shit," Chasity said.

Emily nodded in agreement as she laughed.

Sidra folded her arms. "Oh whatever."

Alex glanced over and saw the guys talking amongst themselves. "Ladies," she said, grabbing their attention. "Why don't we go sit out on the deck."

The girls agreed and made their way outside.

"Congrats again Josh," Jason said, giving him a pat on his back. "I'm happy for you bro."

"Thanks man," Josh replied. "Not gonna lie, I asked Chaz if it was cool to do this on her birthday." He chuckled. "I didn't want to get cussed out… That's what we were talking about when we stepped away."

"And what did she say when you asked her?" Jason wondered.

"She told me not to ask her stupid ass questions and to propose to Sidra," Josh chortled.

Jason laughed. "Yeah, figured," he said. "She would never be upset over that."

"Yeah, I know," Josh agreed.

Mark grabbed Josh's shoulder and gave it a shake. "Josh is about to join the married club," he boasted. "A *challenging* club, but an *amazing* club nonetheless."

Josh smiled. "I can't wait," he said. "I mean, getting married, starting a family…I'm looking forward to *all* of it."

"It's beautiful man, trust me," Jason promised.

Mark looked at David. "Are *you* gonna be next?" he asked.

"Who knows," David shrugged. "But I'm going to finish school first…" he sighed. "God, I have like five more years," he groaned.

"You know what David," Mark began, serious. "I'm proud of you… You're going to change lives one day… Your mother would be proud."

David smiled. "Wow...thanks Mark," he replied, grateful.

"Damn Mark, how much did you drink?" Jason joked.

"Right!" Josh cosigned, laughing. "Getting all sentimental on Chaz's birthday and shit."

"You know what, fuck y'all," Mark ground out.

Chasity, Malajia, Alex, Sidra, and Emily all sat comfortably out on the lit deck. Between the sunset, the mountains in the background and the cool breeze, it was truly peaceful.

Emily stared out at the scenery. "I swear, I could sit out here and stare at that backdrop for hours," she breathed.

"I actually *do* sometimes," Chasity agreed, adjusting her position on her seat. "I like it here."

Emily smiled at her. "I'm glad," she said. "I'm just...I'm so happy that we're all in such a good place in our lives... I hope it only gets better from here."

"Yeah," Sidra agreed, putting a hand on her stomach. She stared at her ring.

Alex tapped Sidra's leg. "Honey, you're *engaged*," she beamed.

"I know, can you *believe* it?" Sidra raved. "God, I love him so much."

"We know you do," Malajia said. "Just like we know you're gonna get on our goddamn nerves when it's time for you to plan your wedding... I'm tired already."

Chasity laughed while Alex shook her head in amusement.

"I know it just happened, but do you have any idea how soon your wedding will be?" Alex asked.

Sidra thought for a moment. "Umm...maybe in a year and a half I'm thinking."

Malajia jerked her head back. "*That* far?" she questioned.

"That's not far in wedding planning time," Chasity said.

Emily shook her head vigorously. "Not at *all*," she consigned.

"Not for *you* maybe, but for this one over *here*," Malajia said, pointing at Sidra, "The one who has a whole 'dream wedding' *book*, it's far."

Sidra waved her hand at Malajia. "I just… I need the time, that's all," she alluded. "The time to *plan*."

"Well, *whenever* your wedding will be, just know that we'll be there ready and waiting for whatever you need," Alex smiled.

"I know, thank you," Sidra replied, grateful.

"*Speaking* of talking, Alex anything changed with Eric since I talked to you yesterday?" Malajia blurted out.

Alex busted out laughing. "What?"

Chasity shook her head. "I *told* you about working on your segues Malajia," she criticized.

Malajia looked around. "Was it *that* bad?" she chuckled.

"Yes," Sidra confirmed.

"Totally out of left field," Emily added.

"Well, fuck it, it still got the job done," Malajia boasted. "So, answer the question Alex."

"No nothing has changed. Eric and I are still doing well, crazy," Alex replied, humor in her voice. "We're actually making plans to go on vacation together in the summer."

"That's good," Emily praised.

Alex let out a happy sigh. "Yeah…things really *are* good. We're enjoying just dating."

"So, no cohabitation anytime soon huh?" Malajia asked.

Alex shook her head. "No, we also enjoy our own *apartments*," she chuckled. "We're not in any rush, we're just…enjoying each other."

"How was it when you met his daughter?" Chasity asked.

Alex smiled. "It was great," she said. "Zoe is so adorable and sweet, and smart...and she adores Eric and vice versa… It's beautiful to see."

Chasity nodded in approval. "Her mother is not an issue?"

Alex quickly shook her head. "Oh no, she's *actually* pretty cool," she admitted, "I met her the day that I met Zoe… She's engaged to be married."

"Hmm," Chasity commented. "Go figure."

Alex looked confused. "What's *that* mean?"

Malajia put her hand to her ear. "Wait, do y'all hear that?" she asked. The girls looked at her.

"Hear *what*?" Alex questioned, still confused.

"It sounds like…it sounds like we were right, Alex," Malajia replied.

Alex squinted her eyes at Malajia, while Sidra and Emily laughed. "Really?"

"Yes *really*," Chasity jumped in. "We *told* you that you were being dramatic over *nothing*."

Alex sucked her teeth.

"Right, putting that man through all that. Holding out on all that penis for all that time for *nothing*," Malajia added. "Just a fool."

"Oh hush," Alex threw back.

"Anybody wanna hear Alex tell us that we were right?" Malajia asked.

"*I* do," Chasity said.

"*I* kinda do *too*," Sidra agreed, holding a hand up along with Emily.

Alex shook her head at her friends. "Y'all make me sick."

"We know, but you still gotta say it," Malajia teased.

Alex let out a loud sigh. "Fine…you ladies were right," she reluctantly answered.

In the middle of their celebration, the back door opened. Mark stuck his head out. "Uh, Chaz?" he called.

Chasity looked over at him. "Yeah?"

"Your son is in here acting light skinned," he sputtered.

Malajia busted out laughing as Alex shook her head at him. "*Wow* Mark," Alex condemned of the comment.

"What did you do to him?" Chasity frowned.

Mark stepped outside, holding a fussy Corey in his arms. "I swear to God, I didn't do *anything*," he promised. "Jase handed me the little man while he went upstairs to help Kayla fix her movie, and the bul just started squirming and crying and shit."

Chasity couldn't help but laugh a little. She held her arms out. "Give him here," she demanded.

Mark walked over and carefully handed Chasity her baby. "I thought we was cool my dude," he pouted to the baby.

"Are you *really* surprised that he started crying when he saw you?" Alex mocked.

Mark stared at her before letting out a loud exaggerated,

phony laugh, then walked back inside and shut the door.

Alex looked at Malajia, who was still laughing. "Girl, how do you *deal* with that every day?" she wondered.

Malajia shrugged, comically over exaggerated.

Sidra stared as Chasity effortlessly calmed the fussy little boy. She smiled. "You're so good at that," she praised.

Chasity looked at her. "Not all the time," she denied.

"No really...you're a great mom," Sidra stressed. She looked at Malajia. "You too, Malajia. I'm so proud of both of you."

"Aww thanks, ponytail," Malajia replied. "Being a mom isn't easy, but my kids are my everything and I wouldn't trade them for the world." She leaned back in her seat. "But baby, now that those twins are in pre-k...I be dropping them off to school happy as shit."

Chasity laughed as she rocked her son. "Probably be skipping behind them while they're walking to class."

"*Do* I?" Malajia boasted. "I even do a dance sometimes."

Emily laughed. "I can see you now, Mel."

Malajia shrugged. "Em, are you and Will trying for a baby?" she asked.

"Not just yet," Emily replied, crossing her legs. "We agreed to wait a few years... Maybe when I'm thirty, I don't know," she confessed. "For now, we're perfectly happy with just Anthony."

"I hear that girl," Malajia approved. "No need to rush...enjoy all that baby free sex."

Emily put her hand over her face in embarrassment.

"You can cover your face all you want Em, I know you be getting it in," Malajia teased. "It be the quiet ones."

"Stop it," Emily laughed, playfully tossing a throw pillow at Malajia.

Alex rubbed the back of her neck. "I'm with you on waiting Em," she said. "Hell, if I can make it to thirty-five or later before having any babies, I'll be perfectly happy. I am loving my life and my career right now."

"Not a thing wrong with that," Chasity said.

Alex smiled, then looked at Emily. "So Em, how does your mom feel about having to wait for you to have a baby?" she asked.

"My mother is happy and accepting with whatever I do, so she's just fine," Emily replied.

"I'm glad that you two are still in a good place," Alex said.

"We are," Emily confirmed. After she had returned from her honeymoon, Emily and her mother sat down and had that long, overdue, much needed conversation. Her mother was apologetic and remorseful; Emily had left satisfied and eager to move forward in their relationship. "We talk all the time, and we make it a point to get together every so often… She's being good."

Sidra nodded. "Have you spoken to Jazmine at all?"

"Nope," Emily answered. "And I'm fine with that." She pushed her hair behind her ears. "According to my father, she's working now so…at least she *trying* to get herself together so good for her. But I'm good with the distance between us."

"You know, just because someone shares your blood, it doesn't mean that you have to be close," Chasity pointed out. "Sometimes it really *is* best to keep your distance for your own sanity."

"I hear you Chaz and I do agree," Emily replied. "I want *no* parts of any negativity."

"I don't blame you," Sidra approved. Hearing Corey make a noise, she looked over. "Awww."

"God Sidra, stop drooling over the baby," Malajia teased.

Chasity looked at Sidra as she rocked her son. "Do you want to hold him, Sidra?" she asked.

"Of *course*," Sidra replied, excited. "But when we go back inside, because I need to wash my hands first."

"Okay," Chasity said.

"Do you want to have another one?" Sidra probed.

"Ask me in like five years," Chasity chuckled. "I need to make sure the memory of labor and delivery is *all* the way gone."

"Shit, don't even swing that question my way Sid," Malajia jumped in. "I am *done* done. Not nare nother baby is coming out of me."

Alex laughed. "Oh come on Mel, you don't want a little girl?"

Malajia stared at her. "Not…nare…nother," she reiterated, stern.

Alex put her hand up in surrender. "Okay, okay," she relented.

Sidra fiddled with her ring. "So…you remember the labor?" she asked.

"Yes," Chasity and Malajia answered in unison.

"I mean, it's all worth it once you hold them but god*damn*," Chasity recalled. "I did that shit natural too…*both* times."

"Shit, *I* was drugged up because I had surgery, but that recovery time…*sheesh*," Malajia relived. "But like Chaz said, it's worth it in the end."

Sidra slowly nodded. "Oh…that's good to know," she muttered, rubbing her stomach.

Chasity caught the gesture. "Mel, you saw that?" she charged.

"Yup, on it," Malajia chimed in.

Sidra, along with Alex and Emily, looked confused. "What?" Sidra asked.

"You touched your stomach," Chasity said.

"*So?*" Sidra replied.

"So, why'd you do that?" Malajia jumped in.

Sidra tossed her hand up. "Is that an *issue*?"

"Not an issue, but given the conversation that we were just having, I think it warrants a question," Chasity threw back.

"Boom!" Malajia blurted out, slapping her hand on the arm of her seat.

"Okay you two…I'm really confused," Alex jumped in. "What does Sidra rubbing her stomach have to do with anything?"

Chasity ignored Alex as she fixed a piercing gaze on Sidra; she was staring at Chasity wide-eyed. "Sidra."

"*What* Chasity?" Sidra threw back, flustered.

Chasity squinted. "Are you pregnant?" she asked.

Emily gasped, looking at Sidra in shock.

Sidra stared back at Chasity defiantly. She held it as long as she could, before putting her hands over her face. "Yes," she answered. She covered her ears when cheers rang out. "I hate

you Chasity, I *swear* you can see into people's souls," she said
as Emily hugged her.

Chasity laughed. "I know," she boasted. "Congratulations
Princess."

"Thank you," Sidra smiled. "I'm *so* nervous."

"Girl, you'll be just fine," Malajia promised, excited.
"You're gonna make a great mother boo…with your bougie
self."

Sidra laughed as she rubbed her stomach again. "Thank
you Mel, I appreciate that."

"Does Josh know?" Alex wondered.

"Yeah," Sidra answered. "I whispered it to him after he
proposed to me," she revealed. "I actually just got confirmation
this morning before our flight… I was planning on telling him
when we got back to our hotel later tonight but…it just seemed
like the right moment, you know?"

"*That's* why his smile got even bigger," Malajia recalled,
pointing at Sidra. "Squeezed you so hard, looked like he was
about to break a rib."

Sidra laughed. "Hush, it wasn't even hard."

"Wow, not *only* are you getting married, but you're about
to have a *baby*," Alex squealed. She clapped her hands together.
"I'll be right back," she said, jumping up.

Malajia watched as Alex darted into the house. "She hype
as shit," she joked.

"Josh is going to make a great dad," Emily beamed.

"I know," Sidra agreed. "Not going to lie, the timing isn't
necessarily perfect. Both of our careers—"

"Girl please, Josh owns his own business and you work for
James. You already know you can take off as long as you need
to and will still come back to a job," Malajia jumped in.

Sidra chuckled a bit. "I will be nine months pregnant in a
court room, I'm not even playing."

"I know that's right," Malajia approved. "And have the
baby hanging from your boob in the courtroom *afterwards*."
Sidra busted out laughing as she leaned over and gave Malajia a
high five. "Look all jokes aside, timing doesn't matter. You and
Josh are building a life together so there's nothing to worry
about," Malajia added, sincere.

Sidra let out a happy sigh. "You're right."

Within a few moments, Alex returned, holding a tray of full wine glasses. She sat down and carefully set the tray on the table. "I figured we need to make a toast," she announced, grabbing a glass.

"Wine for you Em," she said, handing a glass to Emily.

"Ginger ale for *you*, mommy to be," Alex smiled, handing Sidra her glass.

Alex grabbed another glass. "Ginger ale for you, because you're still breast-feeding Chaz," she said, handing it to Chasity.

She then grabbed the last two glasses. "Wine for you Mel—wait."

Malajia frowned when Alex pulled her hand back.

"Maybe *you* should drink ginger ale *too*," Alex said. "You need to get your body ready for that baby girl."

Malajia held her hand out. "Give me my goddamn drink Alex," she spat, earning a chuckle from Alex. She took the glass. "You coulda put vodka in *mine*."

Alex held her own glass of wine up. "I want to make a toast to us," she began. The other girls held their glasses up along with her. "To happiness, to love, to life—"

"I'll drink to that," Malajia blurted out, moving the glass to her lips.

"I'm not finished!" Alex exclaimed, halting Malajia's sip.

"Sorry," Malajia chuckled.

Alex smiled, growing sentimental at the sight of them. "Ten years ago when I stepped onto Paradise Valley University's campus I didn't know *who* I'd meet," she reflected. "I hoped to gain at least *one* new friend… I never expected to gain *four sisters*." The girls stared at her silent. "I know the rocky start that we all got off to, but deep down, even in the beginning I knew that we would forever be a part of each other's lives… You girls impacted my life more than you'll ever know and I love you all *so* much…and I know that no matter what happens in our lives, we will *always* be a family."

Sidra wiped her tearing eyes with her hand. "Damn it Alex, you made me cry," she sniffled.

Malajia smacked her forehead with her hand. "God, she about to be another crybaby," she huffed, earning a snicker from Emily.

Chasity just shook her head in amusement.

Alex giggled, then with a bright smile, she tilted her glass forward. "To us, ladies... Cheers."

All smiling, the girls tapped their glasses. "Cheers!"

Thank you for reading.

www.ingramcontent.com/pod-product-compliance
Lightning Source LLC
Chambersburg PA
CBHW070703100726
47907CB00001B/28